Black Magic Sanction

Black Magic Sanction

KIM HARRISON

EOS

An Imprint of HarperCollins Publishers

BLACK MAGIC SANCTION. Copyright © 2010 by Kim Harrison. All rights reserved. Printed in the United States of America. No part of this book may be used or reproduced in any manner whatsoever without written permission except in the case of brief quotations embodied in critical articles and reviews. For information address HarperCollins Publishers, 10 East 53rd Street, New York, NY 10022.

HarperCollins books may be purchased for educational, business, or sales promotional use. For information please write: Special Markets Department, HarperCollins Publishers, 10 East 53rd Street, New York, NY 10022.

FIRST EDITION

Eos is a federally registered trademark of HarperCollins Publishers.

Library of Congress Cataloging-in-Publication Data has been applied for.

ISBN 978-0-06-113803-4

10 11 12 13 14 OV/RRD 10 9 8 7 6 5 4 3 2 1

To the guy in the leather jacket

Acknowledgments

I'd like to thank Richard Curtis, my agent, and Diana Gill, my editor. The more I know, the more I appreciate them and what they do.

One

Tucking my hair back, I squinted at the parchment, trying to form the strange angular letters as smoothly as I could. The ink glistened wetly, but it wasn't red ink, it was blood—my blood—which might account for the slight tremble as I copied the awkward-looking name scripted in characters that weren't English. Beside me was a pile of rejects. If I didn't get it perfect this time, I'd be bleeding yet again. God help me, I was doing a black curse. In a demon's kitchen. On the weekend. How in hell had I gotten here?

Algaliarept stood poised between the slate table and the smaller hearth, his white-gloved hands behind his back. He looked like a stuffy Brit in a murder mystery, and when he shifted impatiently, my tension spiked. "That isn't helping," I said dryly, and his red, goat-slitted eyes widened in mocking surprise, peering at me over his smoked spectacles. He didn't need them for reading. From his crushed green velvet frock to his lace cuffs and proper English accent, the demon was all about show.

"It has to be exact, Rachel, or it won't capture the aura," he said, his attention sliding to the small green bottle on the table. "Trust me, you don't want that floating around unbound."

I sat up and felt my back crack. As I touched the quill tip to my throbbing finger, my unease grew. I was a white witch, damn it, not black. But I wasn't going to write off demon magic just because of a label. I'd read the recipe; I'd interpreted the invocation. Nothing died to provide the ingredients, and the only person who'd suffer would be me. I'd come away from this with a new layer of demon smut on my soul, but I'd also have protection against banshees. After one had nearly killed me last New Year's Eve, I'd willingly entertain a little smut to be safe. Besides, this might lead to a way to save Ivy's soul when she died her first death. For that, I'd risk a lot.

Something, though, felt wrong. Al's squint at the aura bottle was worrisome, and his accent was too precise tonight. He was concerned and trying to hide it. It couldn't be the curse. It was just manipulating an aura, captured energy from a soul. At least . . . that's what he said.

Frowning, I glanced at Al's cramped handwritten instructions. I wanted to go over them again, but his peeved expression and his soft growl convinced me it could wait until the scripting was done. My "ink" was running thin, and I dabbed more blood from my finger to finish some poor slob's name, someone who trusted a demon . . . someone like me. *Not that I really trust Al*, I thought, glancing at the instructions once more.

Al's spelling kitchen was right out of a fantasy flick, one of four rooms he had recovered after selling almost everything to keep his demon ass out of demon-ass jail. The gray stone walls made a large circular space, most of which was covered in identical tall wooden cabinets with glass doors. Behind the rippled glass, Al kept his books and ley-line equipment. The biological ingredients were in a cellar to which access was through a rough hole in the floor. Smoky support beams a good forty feet up came to a point over a central fire pit. The pit itself was a round, raised affair, with vent holes to draw the cold floor air in by way of simple convection. When it got going, it made a comfortable spot for reading, and when fatigue brought me down, Al let me nap on the benches bracketing it. Mr. Fish, my beta, swam in his little bowl on the mantel of the smaller fire in the fireplace. I don't know why I'd brought him from home. It had been Ivy's idea, and when an anxious vampire tells you to take your fish, you take your fish.

Al cleared his throat, and I jumped, fortunately having pulled my quill from the parchment an instant before. Done, thank God. "Good?" I asked, holding it up for inspection, and his white-gloved, thick-fingered hand pinched it at the edge where it wouldn't smear.

He eyed it, my tension easing when he handed it back. "Passable. Now the bowl."

Passable. That was usually as good as it got, and I set the painstakingly scribed bit of paper beside the unlit candle and green bottle of aura, taking up Al's favorite scribing knife and the palm-size earthen bowl. The knife was ugly, the writhing woman on the handle looking like demon porn. Al knew I hated it, which was why he insisted I use it.

The gray bowl was rough in my hand, the inside inscribed with scratched-off words of power. Only the newly scribed name I was etching would react. The theory was to burn the paper and take in the man's name by way of air, then drink water from the bowl, taking in his name by water. This would hit all four elements, earth and water with the bowl, air and fire with the burning parchment. Heaven and earth, with me in the middle. Yippy skippy.

The foreign-looking characters were easier after having practiced with the parchment, and I had it scratched on a tiny open space before Al could sigh more than twice. He'd taken up the bottle of aura, frowning as he gazed into the swirling green.

"What?" I offered, trying to keep the annoyance from my voice. I was his student, sure, but he would still try to backhand me if I got uppity.

Al's brow furrowed, worrying me even more. "I don't like this aura's resonance," he said softly, red eyes probing the glass pinched in his white-clad fingers.

I shifted my weight on my padded chair, trying to stretch my legs. "And?"

Al's focus shifted over his glasses to me. "It's one of Newt's."

"Newt? Since when do you need to get an aura from Newt?" I asked. No one liked the insane demon, but she was the reigning queen of the lost boys, so to speak, and knew everything—when she could remember it.

"Not your concern," he said, and I winced, embarrassed. Al had lost almost everything in his effort to snag me as a familiar, ending up with something vastly more precious but broke just the same. I was a witch, but a common, usually lethal genetic fault had left me able to kindle their magic. Al's status was assured as long as I was his student, but his living was bleak.

"I'll just pop over and find out who it is before we finish this up," he said with forced lightness, setting the bottle down with a sharp tap.

I looked at the assembled pieces. "Now? Why didn't you ask her before?"

"It didn't seem important at the time," he said, looking mildly discomfited. "Pierce!" he shouted, the call for his familiar lost in the high ceilings coated in shadows and dust. Mood sour, he turned to me. "Don't touch *anything* while I'm gone."

"Sure," I said distantly, eying the green swirling in the bottle. He had to borrow an aura from Newt? Jeez, maybe things were worse off than I'd thought.

"The crazy bitch has a reason for everything, though she might not remember it," Al said as he tugged his sleeves over his lace cuffs. Glancing at the arranged spelling supplies, he hesitated. "Go ahead and fill the bowl. Make sure the water covers the name." He looked at the image of an angry, screaming face scribed into his black marble floor. It was his version of a door in the doorless room. "Gordian Nathaniel Pierce!"

I pushed back from the table as the witch popped into the kitchen atop the grotesque face, a dish towel over his shoulder and his sleeves rolled up. "I'd be of a mind to know what the almighty hurry is," the man from the early 1800s said as he tossed his hair from his eyes and unrolled his sleeves. "I swan, the moment I start something, you get in a pucker over nothing."

"Shut up, runt," Al muttered, knowing that to backhand him would start a contest that would end with Pierce unconscious and a big mess to clean up. It was easier to ignore him. Al had snared the clever witch within an hour of his first escape, the demon taking great pains to keep us apart during my weekly lessons until Al realized I was ticked with Pierce for having willingly gone into partnership with Al. Partnership? Hell, call it what it was. Slavery.

Oh, I was still impressed with Pierce's magic, which far outstripped mine. His quick one-liners, in his odd accent, aimed at Al when the demon wasn't listening still made me smirk. And I wasn't looking at his long, wavy hair, or his lanky build, much less his tight ass, damn it. But some time shortly after seeing him naked under Carew Tower's restaurant, I'd lost the teenage crush I'd had on him. It might have been his insufferable confidence, or the fact that he wouldn't admit how deep in the crapper he was, or that he was just a little too good at demon magic, but for whatever reason, that devilish smile that had once sparked through me now fell flat.

"I'm stepping out for a tick," Al said as he buttoned his coat. "Merely checking something. A tidy curse is a well-twisted one! Pierce, make yourself useful and help her with her Latin while I'm gone. Her syntax sucks."

"Gee, thanks." The modern phrases sounded odd with Al's accent.

"And don't let her do anything stupid," he added as he adjusted his glasses.

"Hey!" I exclaimed, but my eyes darted to the creepy tapestry whose figures seemed to move when I wasn't looking. There were things in Al's kitchen that it was best not to be alone with, and I appreciated the company. Even if it was Pierce.

"As the almighty Al wishes," Pierce said dryly, earning a raised eyebrow before Al vanished from where he stood, using a ley line to traverse the ever-after to get to Newt's rooms.

In an instant, the lights went out, but before I could move, they flashed back to life, markedly brighter as Pierce took over the charm, telling me it wasn't the demon-curse light charm I knew. *Alone. How . . . nice.* I watched him meticulously drape his damp dish towel to dry on the top of the cushioned bench that circled the central fire pit, and then, jaw clenched, I looked away. Standing, I moved to keep the slate table between us as Pierce crossed the room with the grace of another time.

"What is the invocation today?" he asked, and I pointed to it on the table, wanting to look at it again myself but willing to wait. His hair fell over his eyes as he studied it.

"*Sunt qui discessum animi a corpore putent esse mortem. Sunt erras,*" he said softly, his blue eyes shocking against his dark hair as he looked up. "You're working with souls?"

"Auras," I corrected him, but his expression was doubtful. *There are those who believe that the departure of the soul from the body is death. They are wrong*, I silently translated, then took it from him to set it with the bottle of aura, bowl, and the name scribed with my blood. "Hey, if you can't trust your demon, who can you trust?" I said sarcastically, gathering up the pile of discarded signature attempts and moving them out of the way to the mantel. But I didn't trust Al, and I itched to look at the curse again. Not with Pierce, though. He'd want to help me with my Latin.

The tension rose at my continued silence, and Pierce half-sat on the slate table, one long leg hanging down. He was watching me, making me nervous as I filled the inscribed bowl from a pitcher. It was just plain water, but it smelled faintly of burnt amber. *No wonder I go home with headaches*, I thought, grimacing as I overfilled the bowl and water dribbled out.

"I'll get that," Pierce said, jumping from the table and reaching for his dish towel.

"Thanks, I'm good," I snapped, snatching the cloth from him and doing it myself.

He drew back, looking hurt as he stood before the fire pit. "I'll allow I've gotten myself in a powerful fix, Rachel, but what have I done to turn you so cold?"

My motion to clean the slate slowed, and I turned with a sigh. The truth of it was, I wasn't sure. I only knew that the things that had attracted me once now looked childish and inane. He'd been a ghost, more or less, and had agreed to be Al's familiar if the demon could give him a body. Al had shoved his soul into a dead witch before the body even had the chance to skip a heartbeat. It didn't help that I'd known the guy Al had put his soul into. I didn't think I could take another person's body to save myself. But then, I'd never been dead before.

I looked at Pierce now, seeing the same reckless determination, the same disregard for the future that had gotten me shunned, rightfully, and all I knew was that I didn't want anything to do with it. I took a breath and let it out, not knowing where to start. But a shiver lifted through me at the memory of his touch, ages ago but still fresh in my mind. Al was right. I was an idiot.

"It's not going to work, Pierce," I said flatly, and I turned away.

My tone had been harsh, and Pierce's voice lost its sparkle. "Rachel. Truly. What's wrong? I took this job to be closer to you."

"That's just it!" I exclaimed, and he blinked, bewildered. "This is *not* a job!" I said, waving the dish towel. "It's slavery. You belong to him, body and soul. And you did it intentionally! We could have found another way to give you a body. Your own, maybe! But no. You just jumped right into a demon pact instead of asking for help!"

He came around the table, close but not quite touching me. "I swan, a demon curse is the only way to become living again," he said, touching his chest. "I know what I'm doing. This isn't forever. When I can, I'll kill the demon spawn, and then I'll be free."

"Kill Al?" I breathed, not believing he still thought he could.

"I'll be free of him and have a body, both." He took my hands, and I realized how cold I was. "Trust me, Rachel. I know what I'm doing."

Oh my God. He is as bad as I am. Was. "You're crazy!" I exclaimed, pulling out of his grip. "You think you're more powerful than you are, with your black magic and whatever! Al is a *demon*, and I don't think you grasp what he can do. He's *playing* with you!"

Pierce leaned against the table, arms crossed and the light catching the colorful pattern of his vest. "Do tell? You opine I don't know what I'm doing?"

"I opine you don't!" I mocked, using his own words. His attitude was infuriating, and I looked at the bowl behind him, the remnant of others who had thought they were smarter than a demon now just names on a bowl, bottles on a shelf.

"Fair enough." Pierce scratched his chin and stood. "I expect a body needs proof."

I stiffened. Shit. Proof? "Hey, wait a minute," I said, dropping the dish towel to the table. "What are you doing? Al brought you back, but he can take you out again, too."

Pierce impishly put a finger to his nose. "Mayhap. But he has to catch me first."

My eyes darted to the band of charmed silver around his wrist. Pierce could jump ley lines where I couldn't, but charmed silver cut off his access to them. He couldn't leave.

"What, this?" he said confidently, and my lips parted when he ran his finger around the inside of the silver band and the metal seemed to stretch, allowing him to slip it off.

"H-How," I stammered as he twirled it. Crap on toast. I'd be blamed for this. I knew it!

"It's been tampered with so I can move from room to room here. I tampered with it a little more is all," Pierce said, sticking the band of silver in his back pocket, his eyes gleaming. "I've not had a bite of food free of burnt amber in a coon's age. I'll fetch you something to warm your cold heart."

I stepped forward, panicking. "Put that back on! If Al knows you can escape, he'll—"

"Kill me. Yeah, yeah, yeah," he said, hitting the modern phrase perfectly. His hand dipped into another pocket, and he studied a handful of coins. "Al will tarry with Newt for at least fifteen minutes. I'll be right back."

His accent was thinning. Clearly he could turn it off and on at will—which worried me even more. What else was he hiding? "You're going to get me in trouble!" I said, but with a sly grin, he vanished. The lights he had been minding went out, and the ring of charmed silver he had stuck in his pocket made a ting as it hit the floor. My heart thumped in the sudden darkness lit only by the hearth fire and the dull glow of the banked fire pit. He was gone, and we were both going to be in deep shit if Al found out.

Heart pounding, I watched the creepy tapestry across the room. My mouth was dry, and the shadows shifted as the figures on it seemed to move in the firelight. *Son of a bitch!* I thought as I went to pick up the ring of charmed silver and tuck the incriminating thing in a pocket. Al was going to blame me. He'd think I took the charmed silver off Pierce.

Edging back to the small hearth fire, I fumbled for the candle on the mantel, scraping wax under my nail as a focusing object, pinching the wick, and tapping a ley line to work the charm. "*Consimilis calefacio,*" I said, voice quavering as a tiny slip of ley-line energy flowed through me, exciting the molecules until the wick burst into flame, but just as I did, the ley-line-powered lights flashed high, and I jumped, knocking the lit candle off the mantel.

"I can explain!" I exclaimed as I fumbled for the candle, now rolling down the mantel toward Mr. Fish. But it was Pierce, tossing his hair from his eyes and with two tall grandes in his hands. "You idiot!" I hissed as the candle hit the scraps of paper and in a flash, they went up.

"Across lots like lightning, mistress witch," Pierce said, laughing as he extended a coffee.

God, I wish he'd speak normal English. Frantic, I brushed the bits of paper off the mantel, stepping on them once they hit the black marble floor. The stink of burning plastic joined the mess, and I grabbed the bowl of water, dumping it. Black smoke wisped up, stinging my eyes. It helped mask the reek of burning shoe, so maybe it wasn't all bad.

"You ass!" I shouted. "Do you realize what would happen if Al came back and found you gone? Are you that inconsiderate, or just that stupid? Put this back on!"

Angry, I threw the ring of charmed metal at him. His hands were full, and he sidestepped it. With a thunk, the ring hit the tapestry and then the floor. Pierce's hand extending the coffee drooped, his enthusiasm fading. "I'd do naught to hurt you, mistress witch."

"I am *not* your mistress witch!" Ignoring the coffee, I looked at the bits of burnt paper in a soggy mess on the floor. Kneeling, I snatched the dish towel from the table to sop it up. I could smell raspberry-flavored Italian blend, and my stomach growled.

"Rachel," Pierce coaxed.

Pissed, I wouldn't look up at him as I wiped the floor. Standing, I tossed the towel to the table in disgust, then froze. The aura bottle wasn't green anymore.

"Rachel?"

It was questioning this time, and I held up a hand, tasting the air as my eyes stung. Shit, I'd burned the name and gotten the charged water all over me. "I think I'm in trouble," I whispered, then jerked, feeling as if my skin was on fire. Yelping, I slapped at my clothes. Panic rose as an alien aura slipped through mine, soaking in to find my soul—and squeezing.

Oh shit. Oh shit. Oh shit. I'd invoked the curse. I was in so-o-o-o much trouble. But this didn't feel right; the curse burned! Demons were wimps. They always made their magic painless unless you did it wrong. Oh God. I'd done it wrong!

"Rachel?" Pierce touched my shoulder. I met his eyes, and then I doubled over, gasping.

"Rachel!" he cried, but I was trying to breathe. It was the dead person, the one whose name I'd scribed in my own blood. It hadn't been his aura in the bottle, but his soul. And now his soul wanted a new body. Mine. Son of a bitch, Al had *lied* to me. I knew I should have trusted my gut and questioned him. He said it was an aura, but it was a soul, and the soul in the bottle was pissed!

Mine, echoed in our joined thoughts. Gritting my teeth, I bent double and tapped a ley line. Newt had once tried to possess me, and I had burned her out with a rush of energy. I gasped when a scintillating stream of it poured in with the taste of burning tinfoil, but the presence in me chortled, welcoming the flood. *Mine!* the soul insisted in delight, and I felt my link to the line being severed. I stumbled, falling to kneel on the cold marble. It had taken control, cutting me out!

No! I thought, scrambling for the line in my mind only to find nothing to grasp. My chest hurt when my heart started to beat to a new, faster rhythm. What in hell was this thing! What sort of mind could make a soul this determined? I couldn't . . . stop it!

"Rachel!"

Eyes tearing, I blinked at Pierce, struggling to focus. "Get. It. Out of me!"

He spun, motions fast as he found the unburnt signature still on the table. There was a swallow of water left in the bowl. It had to be enough.

I am Rachel Morgan, I thought, teeth gritted as the soul rifled through my memories like some people shake old books for money. *I live in a church with a vampire and a family of pixies. I fight the bad guys. And I will not let you have my body!*

You can't stop me.

The thought was oily, hysteria set to discordant music. It hadn't been my thought, and I panicked. It was right, though. I was powerless to stop it, and as soon as it looked at everything and claimed what it wanted, I was going to be discarded.

"Get out!" I screamed, but its fingers reached into my heart and brain for more, and I groaned, feeling control over my body start to slip away. "Pierce, get it out of me!" I begged, doubled over on the cold black floor, silver etchings like threads under my cheek. Everything I didn't concentrate on was gone. The moment I lapsed, I would be too.

I smelled the scent of burnt paper, and the soft murmur of Latin. "*Sunt qui discessum animi a corpore putent esse mortem,*" Pierce said, his hand shaking as he brushed the hair from my face. Beside him was the empty bowl. "*Sunt erras.*"

"This is mine!" I cried gleefully, but it wasn't me screaming. It was the soul, who had found the knowledge that my blood could invoke demon magic and held it aloft like a jewel. I got in one clean gasp of air as it was distracted, and I opened my eyes. "Pierce . . . ," I whispered desperately, for his attention, then choked when the soul realized I still had some control.

"Mine!" the soul snarled with my lips, and I backhanded Pierce across the cheek.

Oh God, I'd lost, and I felt myself pull my legs under me to crouch before the fire like an animal. I'd lost my body to a thousand-year-old soul! My lips curled back, and I grinned at Pierce's horror, even as I tried to claw my way back into control. But even my connection to the ley line belonged to it.

"Get away from her!" I heard Al exclaim, and with the sound of smacking flesh, Pierce slid backward against the tapestry. *Al.*

Hissing, I spun to him, crouched and hands turned to claws. *It is a demon,* echoed in my thoughts, and hatred bubbled up, a thousand years of hatred demanding revenge.

I jumped at him with a howl, and Al grabbed me by the neck. I clawed at him, and he casually thunked my head into the wall. Pain reverberated between my skull and reason, and in the haze, my reactions were faster than the alien soul's. I took control, grabbed the ley line, and threw a protection bubble about the soul within me. It was still dazed from the thunk on the head, and I had the upper hand. But for how long?

Eyes struggling to focus, I latched onto Al's hands around my throat. God, I was never so happy to see him. "Rachel?" he asked, an understandable question at this point.

"For a little bit longer, yeah, you son of a bitch," I panted, terrified as I felt the soul in me start to recover. "You told me it was an aura. It's a goddamned soul! You lied to me! You lied to me, Al! And it's . . . taking me over, you son of a bitch!"

His eyes narrowed as he looked across the room at Pierce. "I told you to watch her!"

"Accident," Pierce said as he untangled his legs. "She dropped a candle. The early scratchings burned, and she put it out with the water. The soul wasn't harnessed by invocation before escaping. I twisted the curse to get it out of her. I don't understand why it didn't work!"

Al let go of my neck and swung me into his arms, cradling me. "You're not a demon, runt," he said distantly, talking to Pierce as he peered into my eyes. "You can't hold a soul other than your own."

But Al thought I could? I took a breath as I stared at Al's red eyes, then another, feeling the soul in me begin to push against the protection circle, probing, looking for a way to regain control. I jerked when a slow flame started in my mind, burning, expanding. It howled against the inside of my skull, and my hands twitched. "Get it . . . out!" I forced past my clenched teeth. I couldn't fight forever.

Al's goat-slitted eyes showed a flash of panic, and I felt him sit down before the fire, right there on the floor. "Let me in, Rachel. Into your thoughts. You've got Krathion in there. I can separate him from you, but you have to let me in. Let go and stop fighting so I can come in!"

He wanted me to stop fighting? "He'll take over!" I panted, gripping his arm when a new wave of outrage spun through me. "He'll kill me! Al, this soul is crazy!"

Al shook his head. "I won't let you die. I've got too much invested in you." The look in his eyes scared me—it wasn't love, but it wasn't just the fear of losing an investment either. "Let me in!" he demanded as I clenched in pain. Shit, I was drooling. He didn't say trust me, but it was in his eyes.

Inside me, I felt the satisfaction of a steady progression of fire. I wasn't driven enough to survive this. Maybe after being imprisoned in limbo for a thousand years, but not right now. Either let Al in or the soul won. I had to trust him. "Okay," I breathed, and as Al's eyes widened, I stopped fighting.

The soul screamed in victory, and my body shuddered. And then . . . I was nowhere. I wasn't in the echoing blackness of the demon collective, and I wasn't in the spinning, humming strength of a ley line. I was . . . nowhere, and everywhere. Centered for the first time in my life, alone and utterly understanding it all. There was no hurry, no reason, and I hung in a blissful state of no questions. Until one stirred in me. *Was this where Kisten had gone?*

I wondered suddenly, was Kist here? My *dad*? Was that his aftershave I smelled?

"Rachel?" someone called, and I gathered myself, trying to focus.

"Dad?" I whispered, not believing it.

"Rachel!" The voice became louder, and I felt a sudden pain.

Coughing, I took a huge gasp of air, my hair in my mouth, my face. The world was upside down, but then I realized I was on my hands and knees, taking snatches of air between the dry heaves. The sour taste in my mouth fought with the stink of burnt amber pouring off me. My face hurt with each gut-wrenching clench, and I felt it carefully with shaky fingers. Someone had hit me. But I was here, alone in my body. The perverted soul was gone.

I looked up from Al's floor to see a pair of elegantly embroidered slippers. Sending my gaze higher, I found an androgynous robe with a martial arts look about it, and above that, Newt's mocking expression. The demon was bald again. Even her eyebrows were gone.

Her face wrinkled when she saw me looking at her. "Honestly, Al, you're going to have to do better," she said, her words long and drawn out. "You almost let her kill herself. Again."

Al? That must be whose hand is on my back.

"Rachel?" Al said again, close and intent. I recognized it from that in-between place I'd been in. His hand fell away, and I sat back to bring my legs to my chest. Forehead on my knees, I hid from everyone. "What's she doing here?" I muttered, meaning Newt. Cold, I shivered.

"It's her," he said, his relief clear as I heard him stand. "Thank you."

"Don't thank me. This wasn't free." The soft shush of her slippers was loud, but I didn't look. I was alive. I was alone in my mind. Al had been in there. No telling what he'd seen.

"I ought to file charges of uncommon stupidity against you for letting her try this alone," Newt said dryly, and I took a deep breath. *Not out of it yet, apparently.*

"She wouldn't have been alone if, to begin with, you'd given me a suit-able soul," Al said, and I jumped when a blanket smelling of burnt amber fell across my shoulders. "Krathion? Are you insane? He was a lunatic!"

"One man's opinion," Newt said smugly, and I pulled my head up. "And what a typical male response," she added, glancing at me. "Blame everyone but yourself. You left Rachel in the middle of a highly sensitive curse. You could have brought her with you. Brought the bottle with you. But you left her alone. Face it, Al. You don't have the smarts to raise a child."

"You did this on purpose!" Al raged, sounding like a little kid calling foul. Newt looked smug, and Al turned away, frustrated.

Shaking, I tugged the blanket higher. They were my hands. *My* hands. Tears prickled when I looked at the small bottle on the table, green and swirling again. I wanted to laugh. Cry. Puke. Scream. "What's she doing here?" I asked again, my voice stronger.

"Krathion is insane," Al said. "It took two of us to get him back in the bottle."

I fingered the wool blanket, worried. I had a bad feeling that Newt had tried to kill me. "You were in my mind?" I asked her, fearful now.

Newt made a small sound of regret, stepping silently across the room. "No," she said petulantly as she stopped beside Pierce, slumped beside the empty tapestry. Even the moving figures made of weft and weave were afraid of her and had hidden. Pierce was nursing a swollen lip, and was sullen, even scared maybe. I was surprised to see him here at all.

"Al took teacher's prerogative," she said as she ran her fingers through his hair. Pierce stiffened, the tightening of his lips giving away his anger. "I merely put the soul back in the bottle once Al got it out of you. Gally, if you can't demonstrate the ability to keep her alive, then I will take over her care and get you a dog instead."

My eyes widened. Fear got me to my feet, and I wobbled until I reached for the table for balance. "It was my fault, not Al's. I'm fine. Really. See? All better."

Al stiffened. "I didn't leave her alone. I left her in the care of my trusted familiar. The curse was invoked by accident. One you probably planned."

Trusted familiar? I looked at Pierce, knowing laughter would sound hysterical.

"Excuses, excuses," Newt drawled, clearly seeing through it. "He tried to save her life. I see it in his thoughts." She shifted a stray hair from Pierce to set it straight. "It was his skill that failed him, not his spirit. He was here. You were not." Smiling, she turned to Al. "Think on that before you kill him."

"Kill him?" Al blurted out. "Why would I kill him?"

Yeah, seeing as he was Al's *trusted* familiar, but when Newt looked at the to-go cups spilled on the black floor, Al stiffened. His gaze flicked to Pierce, then me, and there it stayed, scaring me. Al thought I had freed him. The coffee had come from somewhere, and I couldn't line jump.

"No more warnings, Al," Newt said, and both Al and I jerked our attention back to her. "Your mistakes are starting to have an impact on all of us. Another error, and I take her."

"You planned this. You gave me a bad soul. That curse couldn't contain Krathion, even if she had done it properly." Al seethed, but not a whisper of power edged his hands, telling me he knew better than to threaten Newt openly.

My skin prickled as the tension rose. Newt was crazy, but Al would lose. I didn't want to belong to her. Al and I had an agreement, but Newt would see only master and slave. "I'm fine. Really!" I insisted, swaying on my feet and feeling my elbow throb. I'd hit something. Hard. Al, maybe? I didn't remember it.

Lips curled up almost in a smile, Newt sniffed as if she smelled something rank. "I don't understand this loyalty. He's wasting your time, Rachel. You'll have precious little of it if you're not careful. You could be so much more, so much faster. Best hurry, before I remember something else and decide you're a threat."

With hardly a breath of air shifting the candle flames, she was gone. Al let out a huge sigh and turned to me. "You stupid bitch."

He moved, and I darted back, slipping on the black floor and going down. His hand swung where I had been, and I skittered back until I hit the hearth.

"You freed him! For a cup of coffee!" Al raged.

"I didn't!" I protested, tensing for the coming smack as he stood over me. Fight back? Yeah, there's a good idea. I'd take my licks. Then I'd take them out on Pierce later.

"Algaliarept!" Pierce shouted, and Al hesitated, the sound of his summoning name being enough to give him pause. But it was the pure ting of metal hitting the marble floor that made me jump, not the back of Al's hand, and I watched the band of charmed silver roll toward us, spinning in ever smaller circles at Al's feet.

"I don't need her to slip your leash, demon spawn," Pierce said darkly, and something in his voice twisted in me. It was threatening, decisive, and utterly unafraid. I went cold at the sight of Pierce, his feet spread wide, a flicker of black vanishing from his spread fingers as he made them into fists. His eyes promised violence.

"I've been free since the moment you caught me," he boasted, making it into a threat. "I'm here to keep her alive among the putrid stink of you all, not wash your dishes and twist your curses. A needed post, if you're passing off soul-stealing curses as an aura supplement."

God help me, I think I'm going to be sick. "I don't need a babysitter," I said.

Pierce looked at me, deadly serious. "I swan you do, Rachel," he said, and my eyes narrowed.

Al harrumphed. His hand, once poised to smack me, had turned and was now offered to help me up instead. "How long have you known he could slip his charmed silver?" he asked.

"Not until he just did it," I said truthfully as he yanked me up. He let me go, and I flicked my eyes to Pierce. "You need to stop underestimating him, Al," I said, not wanting to be caught between them again. "You're right. He's going to get me killed." My gaze went from Al to Pierce. "Through his own arrogance."

Pierce's eyebrows rose as he felt the sting of that, but I wouldn't drop his gaze, still angry. Al, though, couldn't have been happier. "Indeed," he almost growled, clearly hearing more in my words than what I had said. "I think we've made enough progress for today, Rachel. Go home. Get some rest."

My lips parted, and my fingers fell from the blanket over my shoulders. I could not seem to stop shivering. "Now? I just got here. Uh, not that I'm complaining."

Al glanced at Pierce, looking as if he was mentally cracking his knuckles. Pierce was glaring right back, grim faced and determined. Idiot. As soon as I left, they were going to have a "demon to familiar chat." *I* wasn't going to be the one to clean up after it, though.

"Come along," Al said, taking my elbow and letting go when I hissed in pain.

"You're coming with me?" I questioned, and Al took my other, undamaged arm instead.

"If you're not here when I get back," the demon said to Pierce, "I will kill you. I may not be able to restrain you, but I can find you easily enough. Yes?"

Pierce nodded, grim new lines showing on his face.

I opened my mouth to protest, but Al had reached out and tapped a line. In an instant, I dissolved to a thought and was pulled into the nearest ley line, ribbons of energy that strung like threads between reality and the ever-after. Instinctively I flung up a protective circle around my thoughts, but Al had beaten me to it.

Al? I questioned, surprised that he was with me since it more than doubled the cost.

I told you to do nothing. I come back and find you possessed? I had to ask Newt for help. Do you know how embarrassing that is? How long it will take me to pay that off?

Our minds were sharing space, and though I couldn't hear anything he didn't wanted me to, he couldn't hide his anger with me and his unexpected worry about Pierce. Al was getting a dose of my anger at the man, too. Maybe that was why Al was taking me home when he could just as easily have dumped me off in the church's graveyard. He wanted a peek at my emotions.

The memory of my lungs was aching, but I felt him twist something sideways, and I stumbled as we popped back into existence, the fog that had been here when I left even thicker now. The glow from the back porch was a hazy blob of yellow, and I pulled the damp, foggy spring night deep into me. Four hours, and I was home.

"Student?" Al questioned, somewhat softer now that he'd seen my anger at Pierce, and I turned to him, thinking he looked like he belonged in the fog, wearing his elegant coat, tidy boots, and smoked glasses. "Do you have any idea the pressure I'm under?" he added. "The accusations you never hear about, the threats? Why do you think I double-checked that bottle Newt gave me? She wants you, Rachel, and you are giving her excuses to take you in any form she can!"

"I lit the candle because I was *not* going to sit in the dark when your *familiar* left and the lights went out!" I said, not about to take this meekly. "I didn't mean to drop it. The paper caught fire, and I dumped the water on it to put it out. The soul was freed. The *soul,* Al, you bastard. You knew I wouldn't do it if it was a soul."

He dipped his head, the fog blurring his features. "That's why I didn't tell you."

"Don't lie to me anymore," I demanded, braver now that I was back in my own reality. "I mean it, Al. If I'm going to go bad, let me make my own grave, okay?"

I had meant it to be sarcastic, but it rang frighteningly true. Frowning, Al began to turn away, hesitated, and then . . . came back. "Rachel, you don't seem to understand. Newt doesn't care if it's you or someone else who is able to kindle demon magic and begin a new generation of demons. She just wants to control who can. If Krathion had gained your body, she would've taken custody of you to protect the rest of us, because I certainly can't control a lunatic with the ability to invoke demon magic and jump between the ever-after and reality at will." He hesitated, his eyes meeting mine. "She doesn't care about you, Rachel. She only cares about what your body can do, and she wants to control it. Don't let her."

Scared, I tugged the blanket tighter around me, my feet getting damp in the long grass. No wonder the coven of moral and ethical standards had shunned me and Trent had bashed my head into a tombstone. I wasn't being smart about this. A simple curse like possession could negate me completely—give someone with less moral standing everything I had the potential for. And I had been ignoring that.

I exhaled, finally getting it. Standing there in my familiar graveyard, I felt a new chill of mistrust seep into me. *Son-of-a-bitch demons.*

Seeing it, Al grunted, seeming pleased. "Until next week," he said, turning away.

"Al?" I called out after him, but he didn't stop. "Thank you," I blurted out, and he halted, his back to me. "For getting that thing out of me. And I'm sorry." My thoughts went to Pierce and I grimaced. "I'll be more careful."

The door to the church squeaked open, and the sound of shrill pixy children carried out into the damp air. Al turned, his gaze going past me to Ivy's black silhouette waiting in the threshold. I'd said thank you. And apologized. It was more than I thought I'd ever do. "You're welcome," he said, his expression lost in the shadows. "I'll see what I can do about the no lying . . . thing." And inclining his head, he vanished.

Two

"I'll be over there," Ivy said like I was a three-year-old as she looked across the produce section to the meat counter and pointed.

"Oh for the love of the Turn!" I protested, exasperated. "Al let me have the day off because he wanted to beat Pierce to a pulp, not because I damaged my aura. I'm fine! Just . . . go pick out something for the grill, okay?"

The tall woman raised an eyebrow and cocked her hip as if she didn't believe me. I could understand why. Al rarely let me have his night off, and I think my coming back early had interrupted her plans. Though I'd seen no evidence of it, I was sure the living vampire took my weekly twenty-four-hour absence as an opportunity to slake her "other" hunger—the one that we couldn't find a bottle of in the grocery store.

"I said I'm fine," I growled, tugging the eco-friendly sack she made me shop with higher up on my shoulder. "Will you let me breathe?"

Giving me a look, she turned on a booted heel and walked through the produce section, looking like a model in jeans and a short black-and-dark-green jacket. Spiked boots made her even taller. Her lightweight cloth coat was a step away from her usual leather, but the gold trim made it scrumptiously rich. She was growing her hair out again, and the straight black was almost down to her shoulders once more. Ivy could have been a model. Hell, Ivy could be anything she wanted. Except happy. Ivy had issues.

"Good God," I muttered. "What a pain in the ass."

Ivy didn't miss a step. "I heard that."

Alone for the first time in hours, my tension eased. Today had not been fun. I hadn't slept well after getting back to the church. The sliver of trust I'd put in Al was seriously in doubt. Not that I *ever* trusted him, but I'd thought our arrangement had bestowed a measure of honesty between us. Guess not. I wasn't happy with Pierce either. He was a teenage crush from a time when life spread long and wide, and consequences reached only to Friday, date night. I was done entertaining crushes, angry with Pierce for having risked everything to impress me. I wasn't impressed, and he could fall into a volcano for all I cared.

It had almost been a relief to be awakened from a restless sleep at an ungodly ten in the morning by the sound of Jenks's cat, Rex, crashing into walls while chasing pixy kids. Ivy had actually made me breakfast, then hung around in the kitchen messing with her computer while I'd whipped up a batch of sleepy-time charms. Then she made me lunch. I'd finally told her I was going grocery shopping just to have some time alone. I figured she'd stay home, but no-o-o-o. Jenks had all but laughed his wings off and said he'd watch the church. Smart man.

Apparently I'd told Ivy just enough about Al's trickery to worry her. She knew enough about witch magic to realize that messing with auras might give me insight into how to save her soul. Maybe that was her problem. I was sure that my "progress" would make it to Rynn Cormel's ears, her master vampire and the man we both looked to for protection from other vampires. I should be thankful, but I really detested the dead vamp.

A soft prickling of my skin came from nowhere, and I turned to find Ivy at the meat case, her back to me as she leaned on the counter flirting with the butcher. The only other person in sight was a petite woman in an uptight office dress, her head cocked as she studied the cracker labels. She looked bland enough, but something had tripped my warning flags.

Tucking my hair behind an ear, I glanced to the front of the store and into the parking lot past the big plate-glass windows. It was dusk—the time when humans started to shun mixed areas of the city and stick to their own streets as Inderlanders took over—but the sun was still up, which meant the woman wasn't a dead vamp. It was unlikely she was a living one on her own this deep into the human side of things. She probably wasn't a Were for the same reason. That left a human looking for some magical help—highly doubtful—or a witch looking for the same.

She couldn't be a witch. I was shunned, and Cincy's entire witch population knew it.

Drifting to a stand with early strawberries, I mentally went through my short list of who might have followed me this deep into traditionally human territory, then winced when I went through the even shorter list as to why.

I snuck a furtive glance at her, her sensible brown shoes, nylons, and blah brown skirt giving me the impression of sophistication coupled with an appalling lack of imagination. The woman was as thin as a mannequin, but not nearly as tall, and her blond hair was slicked back as if she thought she had to eliminate all softness to make it in a man's world.

She looked up and I froze when we accidentally made eye contact. *Damn,* I thought as the woman blinked, her blue eyes wide, and smiled slowly—shocking the hell out of me. *Double damn.* She'd seen me come in with Ivy and was checking me out!

My face warmed. Eyes averted, I angled to put the display of strawberries between us. I was straight, but after losing three boyfriends in two years—one to illegal activity; one to the grave; and a third, not really a boyfriend but gone all the same because I'd been shunned—I wasn't up to trying to explain things to a nice-looking woman who had misread the nonverbal communication between Ivy and myself.

Undeterred, the woman drifted closer. One hand was in the pocket of her skirt-length, white cashmere coat, the other was holding the latest gotta-have purse, one that probably wasn't a knockoff. She must go to a tanning salon, because her soft amber glow was impossible to get during early spring in Cincinnati. Her nails were short, professionally polished, with white tips gleaming. The woman's upscale mien was completely at odds with the instrumental eighties being piped in, the bleach-faded tile, and the occasional blaring loudspeaker.

My frown deepened when a faint whiff of redwood overtook the smell of chlorine and the tart scent of strawberries. *She's a witch?* Crap, if she was a witch, then she knew damn well who I was. And if she knew who I was, she wasn't trying to pick me up. At least, not for a date. It was a job—one that involved black magic.

Slow down, Rachel. Relax, I told myself, not even seeing the fruit as I picked up a carton of strawberries, fidgeting. *Maybe she needs help and is scared to ask.* Hell, I'd be. When I wasn't playing demon student in the ever-after, I was an odd mix of bounty hunter, escort-through-troubled-waters, and a magical jack-of-all-trades—able to rescue familiars from trees and bring in the big bad uglies that no one else wanted to touch. I'd been shunned, yes, but maybe the trouble she was in was greater than her fear of being shunned for asking for my help. But she didn't look scared; she looked confident and in control.

Setting the carton of strawberries down, I retreated, my thoughts spinning to the last time I'd been accosted by a black coven member on a recruitment drive. He'd taken offense when I'd told him to shove his dark coven somewhere even darker, and then they'd tried to kill me.

Adrenaline seeped into me, slow and sweet, making my heart pound and my senses come alive. It felt so good, it scared me. A quick look told me Ivy was gone. The butcher, too. My kick-butt boots scuffed, and I pulled out my phone as if checking the time, sending a 911 to Ivy before shoving my cell into a back pocket. Even if Ivy was checking out the meat behind the counter, she'd come.

My jaw tightened as I stood before a bank of green veggies against the wall. My back was to the woman in a show of nonchalance, but I stiffened as her sensible shoes tap-tap-tapped to a halt eight feet away. Before me was a display of carrots. *Back off, babe, or I'll kill you with this carrot.*

"Excuse me," the woman said, and damn it if I didn't jump. "Are you Rachel Morgan?"

Her voice was high, almost too childlike to take seriously, and I turned, my fingers sliding off the damp carrots. Her height came in a few inches shorter than mine, heels and all. That hand was still in her pocket, and her smile had a touch of mockery. I didn't want any trouble, but I'd finish it if she started some.

"I'm sorry, do I know you?" I said just as sweetly, putting a bunch of carrots in my canvas bag. *Not very heavy. Need more weight.*

My gaze flicked past her. *Damn it, Ivy, where are you?* There could be anything in that pocket of hers. The woman didn't look like much, but then I didn't either in my jeans, boots, short red leather jacket, and scarf.

"Are you Rachel Morgan of Vampiric Charms?" the woman asked again, and I shifted to a stand of organic potatoes, trying to put distance between us. "Cincinnati's famously shunned witch. Right?" she insisted, her hand still in her coat pocket as she followed me.

Famous and shunned didn't go together as much as one might think, and I sighed. My first thought that she was a black witch seemed to be correct. Hefting my bag, I dropped a potato into it and felt my arm stiffen against the extra weight. "Not interested," I said tightly, hoping she'd do the smart thing and go away.

But I was never that lucky, and she leaned over the potatoes, eyes mocking. "Black magic doesn't scare me, and neither do you. Come with me."

Like hell I will. Disgusted, I set another potato in my bag and opened my second sight to take a look at the more nebulous view of the situation, managing to keep my reaction to a mild "mmmm." The woman's aura was spotless. That didn't mean she wasn't a black witch. She could be sloughing her smut onto someone.

"According to the press," I said as I dropped my second sight, "Rachel Morgan dresses in skintight leather and has orgies with demons. Do I look to you like I'm wearing skintight leather?" A third potato went in with the rest. *Almost heavy enough to knock you on your ass.*

Angular face smug, the woman tucked her clutch bag under her arm. Her hands were free now, and my smile vanished. "It's the demon part I'm interested in," she said.

Damn it, she *was* a black witch. All I wanted to do now was leave before I got banned from another store. "Not interested," I said tersely. "I don't do black magic. I don't care what the papers print."

"Tell me your name," she insisted, fingers twitching in what I hoped wasn't a ley-line charm. "Maybe I'll go away."

She wanted a positive ID. Crap, was there a warrant out on me again? Maybe she wasn't from a black coven at all, but from the I.S., fishing for an excuse to bring me in. I took a quick breath, a new worry filling me. I didn't want to be tagged with resisting arrest. "Okay, that's me," I admitted. "Who are you? Inderland Security? Where's your ID? If you have a warrant, let me see it. Otherwise, we don't have anything to talk about."

"I.S.?" she said, the skin around her eyes tightening. "You should be so lucky."

Damn it, Ivy, get your ass out here! I backed up, and she moved with me. "I wouldn't," I threatened, stumbling to a halt when my butt hit the produce shelf. "I really wouldn't."

But she reached into her pocket, her free hand up in a laughable display of asking for trust, and came out with a zip strip. "Put this on and come with me. Everything will be fine."

Oh yeah. Like I believed that. I didn't even know who she was. Head hurting, I eyed the thin band of plastic-coated charmed silver, then flicked my attention to Ivy, who finally breezed back into the produce area, coming to a wide-footed stop beside the strawberries to take in the situation. The zip strip was basically a cheap but effective version of Pierce's leash that would prevent me from doing any ley-line magic.

My heart pounded. "Everyone see this?" I shouted, and the whispers at the front grew louder. "I don't want to go with this woman, and she's forcing me to!" It was a thin attempt at CYA for the crap that was about to hit the fan, but I had to try.

Sure enough, she smiled—and then she reached for me.

I jerked back, but her fingers brushed mine. A twinge of ley-line energy threatened to equalize between us, strong and tingly. Hand pressed to my chest, I stared, shocked. She had a whopping big chunk of ever-after energy in her chi. Tons more than the average person could hold. *Who in hell is this woman?*

"Ivy?" I called out. "She's hot! Watch it!"

Taking that as fear, the woman reached for me again. Bad idea. My breath came in smoothly. I jumped backward and up—which is a lot harder than it sounds—my heels landing on the low produce shelf. Lettuce squished under my boots.

Ivy grabbed the woman by the shoulder and spun her around.

"You first, vamp," the small woman snarled, her blue eyes squinting in threat.

Grunting, I swung my potato-heavy bag, aiming at the back of the woman's head. Shock reverberated up my arms when it hit and she stumbled, one hand reaching for the floor before she went down. Ivy danced back when the woman rolled, finding her feet and looking pissed as she brushed at the grime on her nice white coat. From the front a frantic high-pitched masculine voice called for security.

Damn it, I'm running out of places to shop, I thought as I dropped the bag and jumped to the floor. The woman had fallen into a defensive stance. Breathing fast, I looked at Ivy. "Mind if I finish this?" I asked.

Ivy shrugged. "Go for it."

I was sure I was already banned, so, smiling, I went for it. The woman's eyes widened, and she retreated. Crescent kick, side, side, side . . . I backed her up to the broccoli without ever touching her. I could use magic, sure, but this way when the I.S. showed up—and they would—I could stand under a truth amulet and say I hadn't used magic. Which was exactly why my splat gun was safely at home in my nested bowls. Prudence sucked dishwater.

Expression hard, the small woman fell back into a produce shelf, and I landed a side kick square in her middle to push the air from her and maybe bruise a rib. "I said I wasn't interested!" I shouted as she wheezed, and I grabbed her coat and hauled her up. "You shoulda just walked." I thumped her head gently into the broccoli, then let go, leaving her dazed but not incapacitated. I didn't want a lawsuit, just for her to go away.

Still muddled, the woman darted her hand out and gripped my wrist. Fearing an influx of raw power I yanked back, but the sound of plastic ratcheting closed accompanied the sudden wash of ever-after spilling out of me. Like squeezing a tube of toothpaste, I felt my untapped strength vanish as I fell back, dizzy with the sudden absence in my chi. Dazed, I looked to see a zip strip around my wrist. She'd let me hammer at her just so she could get it on me? *Ah, shit. Jenks is going to laugh his wings off.*

I stared at the woman as she reclined against the display, smiling grimly at me, though her chest had to hurt. "Got you, Morgan," she said breathily as she held her middle, bits of lettuce in her hair. "You're not such a badass. We got you."

And who is we? "I don't work for black-arts witches," I said, not liking the tight feel of the strip against my skin. "I don't care what you heard."

"Black witch?" she panted, shoving me back so she could get up. "That's a laugh. Let's go."

"You just don't get it," I said, disbelieving. "Zip strip or not, I'm not going!"

The woman's eyes darted behind me at Ivy's soft scuff. Fingers dipping into her pocket, she flung out her hand and threw what was probably a splat ball.

"Ivy, no!" I shouted, spinning, but I was too late. True to form, Ivy had caught it, breaking the thin skin and soaking her hand. For an instant I thought it might be okay, but then Ivy gasped. Fear slid through me on seeing her fist covered in a black goo that crawled up her arm, growing as it went. *What in hell?*

"Dunk it!" I shouted, pointing to the lobster tank. "Ivy, douse it in saltwater!"

The watching employees shouted their approval as the living vampire ran to the meat department. Ripping the top off the tank, she shoved her arm in up to her elbow. Water sloshed out, and the fear etched on her face eased. Turning, she looked at the small woman—and smiled to show her pointed teeth. It was about to get nasty.

Skirt swaying and hair mussed, the woman backed up, but the eager look on her face as she mumbled Latin told me she wasn't afraid. Her hands were moving in ancient ley-line gestures. I had seconds to keep her spell from completion.

"That was a mistake, bitch," I said softly. Scooping up a melon, I threw it at her, trying to break her charm before it was set. She ducked, flinging a glowing ball of reddish ever-after as she fumbled for her footing. I dove to escape her charm, spinning to see it hit the tile with a hissing sound. My eyes widened at the sight of a putrid-looking mass of seething bubbles growing larger by the second, bubbling evilly. *What is she throwing? That can't be legal!* But by the look of savage eagerness on her face, I didn't think she cared.

"Who the hell are you!" I shouted.

"*Dilatare!*" she shouted, invoking her next curse right before she slipped on the squished lettuce and went down with a pained-sounding grunt. Her magic, though, had been loosed.

"Fire in the hold, Ivy!" I shouted when the woman frantically scrabbled away from the glowing ball of unfocused magic, diving behind an apple display. Her magic drifted like a ball of lightning until it rolled under the strawberries, where it exploded.

Employees screamed. Red stuff went everywhere. I ducked as sodden splats and thumps of containers rained down.

"What is *wrong* with you!" I shouted as I got to my feet and flicked away the sticky goo. Not only was this woman better than me at magic, she didn't mind getting dirty. Though bruised and covered in grime and strawberries, she was still smiling. She had the look of someone who didn't care, someone who knew no one would make her accountable for what she did. The bitch was above the law, or thought she was.

I glanced at Ivy, standing nearby and casually going through the woman's bag. Finding her ID, she held it up between two fingers and nodded. Taking that as a good sign, I ran for the woman. Shunned or not, we were going to settle this now. Just because I couldn't do magic didn't mean I was helpless.

White coat furling, she ducked out of my swing and I shifted away from her kick. It was sloppy. *You know just enough to get yourself in trouble,* I thought, then whipped my scarf off, tangling her wrist as she punched again. She pulled away, and I yanked her forward and down into my raised knee. Her breath came out in a whoosh and she bent double.

I let go of the scarf and shifted behind her, jabbing my heel at the back of her knee. Her leg collapsed, and she went down, still trying to breathe. "Oooooh, sorry," I said, then untangled my scarf, wincing at the sticky strawberry mess it now was.

Energized, I gave the woman the once-over to see if she'd had enough. Her tailored coat was a mess, and her hair had lost its perfect symmetry, lying in lank blond strands where there had once been perfection. Seeing her stare up at me, finally able to take a breath, I fell into a ready stance with my hands in fists. "Still think you're tougher than me, Strawberry Shortcake?" I said, not moving as Ivy settled in beside me. Hands on her hips, she breathed deep—and smiled. I knew Ivy had too much control and class to go for her, but it was unnerving as she somehow grew sleeker and sexier, eyes dilating to a full, hungry black.

From nowhere, a quiver rose through me at the memory of her teeth sliding into my neck, and the exquisite feeling of rising pleasure mixed with the blood-boiling sensation of coming ecstasy. Closing my eyes briefly, I pushed the feeling away. Beside me, I felt Ivy quiver, scenting my reaction. *No, Rachel. Everlastingly no.*

The kneeling woman watched as Ivy flicked first her bag, then her ID at her, both sliding to a stop before her. Motions unsteady, she got to her feet. She wasn't afraid, she was angry.

"It would have been easier had you come with me," she said, and Ivy cleared her throat in challenge. Lips pressed, the woman brushed off her skirt, picked up her handbag, and, leaving her ID, walked to the door, her head high and looking tiny next to the overweight manager in a white shirt and blue tie yelling at her.

Ivy slid up to me, and I held my breath. "You want me to stop her?"

I shivered, remembering how much she had held in her chi. My gaze slid from the subsiding mass of toxic bubbles to Ivy's arm, damp from the lobster tank. "No. You okay?"

"Yeah. It went numb is all. Like zombie prickles. How about you?"

The automatic doors slid open and she was gone. "Okay," I said, then picked up her ID. Vivian Smith, from California. It had to be fake, and I shoved it in my pocket.

A nervous patter rose from the watching employees. It was all over but the lawsuits, and I edged away from Ivy, slipping on strawberries as I gave her some distance to allow her a chance to get a handle on her instincts. The manager was at the service counter, fuming. He was working up his courage, though, and it wouldn't be long before he'd bring his high-pitched voice to me, a convenient scapegoat in heels and stringy, strawberry hair. This wasn't my fault!

The goo covering the floor looked like a bloodbath. A glint of silver among the red caught my eye, and I searched the produce section until I found my bag. The manager's complaints grew louder as I dug out my lethal-spell detector and my heavy-magic ley-line charm. I wouldn't put it past *Vivian* to leave a booby trap, but both spells stayed a nice healthy green. The silver was just plain metal with no charms attached. At least, no lethal ones.

"What is it?" Ivy asked as I picked it up. Wiping the goo off, I felt myself go cold and my knees go wobbly.

It was an exquisitely tooled silver brooch in the shape of a Möbius strip, and I swallowed hard, my shaking fingers curving to hide it. My gaze went to the floor, seeing the tile unmarked as the bubbles subsided, then to Ivy's arm—numbed, she said—and then to the broken strawberry display, realizing that that, too, could have been white magic. Extremely strong, but technically white magic, not black. *I am such an idiot.*

Over the last year or so, I'd been attacked by militant Weres, run down by elves on horseback, smacked around by angry demons, bitten by political vampires, eluded assassin fairies, and fought off angry banshees, deluded humans, and black-arts witches. But never had I made an error of judgment this bad.

I'd just publicly embarrassed a member of the coven of moral and ethical standards, the same group that had legalized my shunning.

Holy freaking hallelujah.

Three

The stuffed rat was pointed at the wall, staring at nothing as it crouched atop an overfilled file on the five-foot-tall cabinet in Glenn's office. The FIB detective was currently downstairs. As I'd figured, the grocery store had called the human-run FIB, not Inderland Security. Lucky for me, the I.S. hadn't even shown up. Long story short, I'd been asked to accompany an FIB officer downtown to file a report. They'd even let me sit in the front, sticky as I was. Ivy had followed in my car and was waiting downstairs. It was good to have friends.

It had been a quiet ride through Cincy to the FIB building, my thoughts circling. Had the coven been trying to talk to me, and I'd just flushed my chance at getting my shunning removed? But why not just tell me what was going on? Those charms Vivian had been flinging around hadn't been peace offerings. Had it been a test? If so, had I failed or passed?

I'd worked myself up into a very bad mood by the time we'd gotten here, but it had eased once Glenn had pulled me aside and snipped my charmed silver off even before I'd crossed the FIB emblem downstairs. Glenn was a good guy, complex in his thoughts and smart. His office, though . . . I looked at the mess, trying not to grimace.

A new flat-screen monitor was perched on his desk, a stack of files piled high beside it. The in-box was full, and the out-box held a couple of books on nineteenth-century serial killers. We were too deep into the FIB building for a window, but a bulletin board across from the desk gave the illusion of one, the clippings and sticky notes so old they needed thumbtacks. A new pressboard bookcase held a few textbooks, but mostly it was stacks of files and photos. Glenn was meticulous in his dress, and that usually carried over to his car and office. This mess was scary and not like him at all.

The floor was cold tile; the walls were an ugly, scuffed white; and the keyboard was old and stained with dust and coffee. Glenn had been Cincinnati's FIB Inderland specialist for almost a year now, and I wondered if I was seeing him trying to do everything himself. Even the phone cord was still draped across the floor in what had to be an OSHA violation.

My roving gaze settled on a gleaming glass-and-gold clock serving as a bookend. It didn't match the rest of the no-frills office, and I got up to read the inscription, grimacing when my coat pulled from the metal chair with the sticky sound of strawberries. The marble was cold on my fingers as I read, MATHEW GLENN, OUTSTANDING SERVICE, 2005. The clock was stopped, stuck at three minutes to midnight.

I set it down and checked my phone. Nine thirty. The sun had been down for hours. I wanted to go home, get cleaned up, eat something. What was taking so long?

Impatient, I went to the rat and turned it to face the room. Glenn had bought it with me at a charm shop last year, and I frowned when I realized the file it was sitting on was Nick's. Nick as in my former boyfriend Nick. Ex-rat, ex-boyfriend, ex-alive if I ever got hold of him Nick.

My shoulders tensed and I forced my jaw to not clench. Nick had been a rat when I met him. A real rat, with whiskers and a tail, transformed with witch magic by a peeved vampire who'd caught Nick stealing from him. I couldn't say much about that, though, since I'd been a mink at the time, thrown into Cincinnati's illegal rat fights for having been caught trying to pilfer evidence of illegal bio-drug activity from beloved city son Trent Kalamack.

Nick and I had helped each other escape, which might sound romantic but should have been a warning. He turned out to be a real gem when all was said and done, selling information about me to demons to help his career as a thief. A not very lucrative but nevertheless busy one, according to the file Glenn had on him. The FIB detective was still trying to track him down, not believing that he'd died going off the Mackinac Bridge last summer. The case had gone cold if the dust was any indication—but the file was still out.

I took a deep breath to wash the reminder of Nick away, and the faint scent of vampire tickled my nose. "Huh," I whispered and, sniffing, I made a circuit of the cluttered office, ending at Glenn's short, fashionable coat hung up on a wooden hanger behind the door. Eyebrows raised, I fingered the supple leather. Had Glenn been investigating something that put him in contact with vampires? He knew how risky that was. Why hadn't he come to us? He knew I needed the work.

Curious, I brought the sleeve to my nose to get a better sniff. I loved leather, and it was a nice coat, cut to show off the man's small waist and wide shoulders. I pulled the air deep into me to find under the expected smell of masculine aftershave a mellow tang of honey and hot metal. Deeper was a familiar scent of vampiric incense. A *very* familiar scent. *Ivy?*

Blinking, I dropped the coat's sleeve as footsteps approached in the hall. *Why does Glenn's coat smell like Ivy?*

Glenn strode into his office, almost shoving me into the wall when he pushed the door open. He slowed, making a surprised sound when he found my chair empty, then started when he found me behind him, pressed into the wall. His brown eyes were wide, and I blinked at the tall, clean-shaven man. "What are you doing behind my door?" he asked, planting his feet. There was a red file under his arm and a ceramic mug with rainbows on it in his hand.

I gave myself a mental shake to get the thoughts moving. "Uh, admiring your coat," I said, giving the brown leather a last touch. I wanted to sit down, but he was standing next to my chair. "I, uh, like the no-hair thing."

"Thanks," he said suspiciously as he moved his compact frame behind his desk. When we'd first met, he had short hair and a goatee, but this smooth-shaven nothing was nice. The coffee went on the corner nearest me, and the file was dropped beside the keyboard. He saw me eye the clutter, and I think he blushed through his dark, beautifully mahogany complexion.

I went to ask him about Ivy, then reconsidered. He and Ivy? No way. Though if they were, they'd look great together. His height was just a shade more than hers, and with his trendy clothes and attention to detail, he could play the part of a living vampire's boyfriend without missing a beat. Glenn was ex-military and worked at keeping his trim look. Right now, he'd gone no hair, and it made his stud earring stand out all the more, the glint giving him a hint of bad boy. The story he gave his dad was that he'd gotten it pierced so he could blend into the darker elements of Cincinnati, but I think he liked the small bit of bling.

Glenn looked up at my silence, his eyebrows raised as he indicated the rainbow mug. "I thought you'd want some coffee. This might take a while."

"Okay . . ." *He brought me coffee and rainbows,* I thought as I reached for it and sat down, feeling the bump my phone made in my back pocket. "They're pressing charges? For what? Killing a strawberry display? That wasn't even my charm. I told you, I didn't use magic. I know better. Get an I.S. team in there. None of the magic will have my aura on it."

He chuckled, irritating me even more. The painfully slow sounds of him typing clicked key by key as he worked off the open file beside him. "The I.S. is ignoring the incident completely, so sending a team to ascertain it wasn't your magic? You're going to take the hit for this," he said, his resonant voice dark and sexy. "Nice bit of passive harassment."

My eyes flicked to my strawberry-covered bag and the little silver broach tucked inside. Passive harassment was a good story, but I think the reason the I.S. didn't show was because the coven told them to back off while they brought me in themselves. Guilt and fear kept my mouth shut. Crap on toast, what if I'd ruined my only chance to rescind my shunning?

"I got the store to agree to disorderly conduct if you pay for the damages," Glenn said, starting as he noticed the rat looking at him. "Unless you know who did it?" he added, gaze alternating between me and the critter.

I thought about the ID in my bag, and I shrugged. "Vivian Smith from California?" I volunteered. *God, I'd called her Strawberry Shortcake. Could I dig my grave, or what?*

Glenn made a sound of both amusement and sympathy, his eyes on the screen. "I hope you make more than I do. I had no idea strawberries were that expensive out of season."

"Swell," I said, then sipped my coffee. It wasn't bad, but nothing tasted good since having that raspberry-mocha-whatever-it-had-been Al had ordered me last winter. I set the coffee aside and leaned over to get a look at Glenn's neck. He might not know that he smelled like vampire, but any Inderlander could tell.

Glenn felt my gaze and looked up from his slow excuse for typing. "What?"

I pulled back, worried. "Nothing."

Clearly suspicious, he pulled a paper from under the stack in the red folder and handed it to me. "Damages."

Taking the paper, I sighed. *How come my file is red?* Everyone else had a normal-colored one. "Hey!" I exclaimed, seeing the total. "They're charging me retail. Glenn!" I complained. "They can't do that." I shook it at him. "I shouldn't have to pay retail!"

"What did you expect? You can keep that. It's your copy."

I sat back in a huff and shoved it in my bag with my sticky scarf as he typed his slow, painful way through my report. "Where's this human compassion I keep hearing about?"

"That's it, baby doll," he said, voice smoother than usual. He was laughing at me.

"Mmmm. Can I go now?" I said dryly, not liking the "baby doll" tag but letting it go.

Glenn searched out a key and hit it with a sound of finality. Leaning back, he laced his dark fingers over his middle like I'd seen his dad do. "Not until Jenks posts your bail."

I groaned. Damn it, Ivy must have stopped at home first. One more thing to owe the pixy.

"He seemed proud to do it," Glenn said. "You can wait here, or go to the basement with the rest of the felons." His smile widened. "I vouched for you," he added, then leaned forward to answer his phone, now humming on the interoffice line.

"Thanks," I said sourly, slouching down as he took the call. How was I going to pay Jenks back? My share of the sale of my mom's house had been keeping me afloat lately, but I didn't want to tap into that to post bail. Robbie's half had gone to his upcoming wedding, and I was living on mine. It was hardly the statement of independence I'd wanted, but things would pick up. They always did around spring.

"Who?" Glenn said into the phone, his voice rising in disbelief, and then both Glenn and I looked toward the attention-getting tap on his door frame.

"Trent Kalamack," the feminine voice on the phone said clearly over the faint office noise, naming the trim figure in his two-thousand-dollar suit now silhouetted in the doorway, his arm slowly slipping behind him from where he'd confidently tapped on the door. Suave and self-assured, the man smiled faintly at the woman's awe.

"Next time, call *before* you send someone up," Glenn said as he stood.

"But it's Trent Kalamack!" the voice said, and Glenn hung up on her.

My breath slipped from me, almost a groan. Trent Kalamack. The obscenely successful, smiling businessman, ruthless bio- and street-drug lord, elf in hiding, and pain-in-my-ass-extraordinaire Trent Kalamack. Right on schedule. "Why is it you show up only when I need money?" I sat straighter, but I wasn't going to get up unless it was to smack him.

Trent still smiled, but the faint worry pinching his eyes tickled the back of my brain. Trent wasn't especially tall, but his bearing made people take notice, as if his baby-fine, nearly white hair, devilishly confident smile, and drool-worthy, athletic physique gained from riding his prize-winning horses wouldn't. All that I could ignore—mostly—but his voice . . . his beautiful voice, rich in variance and resonant . . . That was harder—and I hated that I loved it.

Trent was Cincinnati's most eligible bachelor, still single because of me. He'd thanked me for that in a weird moment of honesty when he thought we might die in a demon's prison cell. I was still wondering why

I'd bothered to save his little elf butt. Misplaced responsibility, maybe? That I'd saved his life didn't seem to mean anything to him, since he had tried to make my skull one with a tombstone not three seconds after I got us safe.

Apparently my helping him get the ancient-elf DNA sample from the demons to repair his species genome had been enough to earn my right to live, but I was sure he was still mad at me for having messed up his city council seat reelection plans by trashing his wedding. Rumors in the Were community had it that he was going to make a bid for the mayoral position instead. My gut clenched, and I winced as I flicked a gaze at him.

Where there had once been only irritation, there was now satisfaction in Trent's green eyes as he took Glenn's offered hand extended across his cluttered desk. My pulse raced—he'd called me a demon and tried to kill me. I wasn't. I was a witch. But he had a point—my children would be demons.

"Mr. Kalamack," Glenn said, hiding his fluster. "It's a pleasure."

All trace of Trent's feelings for me were hidden but for the barest tightening of his eyes. "Good to see you again, Detective," he said. "I trust Ms. Morgan is behaving herself tonight?"

Clearly uncomfortable, Glenn stopped smiling. "What can I do for you, sir?"

Trent didn't miss a beat. "I simply have something for Ms. Morgan to sign. I heard she was here, and I was nearby."

He turned expectantly to me, and my bobbing foot stopped. I don't know what disturbed me more, that Trent wanted me to sign something, or that he had known where to find me. Had my grocery trip already made the news?

Tired, I shifted my hand to cover up a particularly big splotch of strawberry on my knee. "What do you want, Trent?" I asked bluntly.

Trent's gaze noted everything before returning to Glenn. "Coffee . . . perhaps?"

Glenn and I exchanged a knowing look. "Why not," the detective said blandly, maneuvering gracefully out from behind his desk. "How do you take it?"

"Black, no sugar," Trent said, and I thought longingly of the time when that would have been enough for me, but no, I was turning into a coffee snob despite my best efforts.

Glenn nodded before he shifted past Trent, the rims of his ears turning red when he rotated the rat back to the wall before he left. His footsteps sounded softly, and I held my breath and counted to five. "What are you doing slumming?" I said as I swiveled the chair, trying to look casual.

"I'm here to help you."

I didn't even try to stop my laughter, and in response, Trent moved and settled himself on Glenn's desk, one foot on the floor, the other pulled up slightly like a *GQ* model.

"I don't need money that badly," I lied, forcing my gaze from him. "The last time I worked for you, you screwed things up so much that I got shunned. Nice of you to tell the press why I was in the ever-after, by the way," I finished sarcastically, and his brow furrowed.

Guilt? I wondered, not able to tell right now. If he had told the press I'd been there working for him, things might have gone differently. I'd have told them myself, but I doubted that Trent would've backed me up, and then I'd have looked twice the fool. The public knowing he'd been caught by demons would have seriously jeopardized his political agenda. That I couldn't make a living anymore didn't seem to matter to him.

Yet I couldn't help but wonder. First the coven trying to talk to me, and now Trent? Fishing for more, I rolled my neck against the top of the chair and looked at the ceiling. "I'm not working for you, Trent. Forget it."

The soft sound of a linen envelope against silk caught my attention, and I sat up as he extended an envelope he'd taken from an inner pocket of his suit. I looked at it like the snake it was. I'd gotten envelopes from him before. Slowly I leaned forward. My fingers didn't shake at all as I pulled the unsealed flap open and removed a heavyweight trifolded paper. Silently I scanned it, finding a casually worded, but probably more-serious-than-a-heart-attack contract that said I would work for Kalamack Industries and only Kalamack Industries. *Forever.* God, what was wrong with the man? Did he think everyone put money before morals like he did?

I dropped my hand to dangle the paper inches from the dirty tile. "I just said I wasn't going to work a job for you," I said softly, too tired of his games to be mad. "What makes you think I'll sign this? Be your witch? What happened to Dr. Anders? I've seen your retirement plan, Trent. Is she pushing up rare orchids in your gardens?"

Irritation furrowed his brow as he stooped to take the paper. Immediately I let go of it, and the sheet slid under my chair and out of his easy reach. Trent pulled back, peeved. "Dr. Anders is busy in the labs," he said.

"You mean she's too old to kick ass."

A smile showed, real and unexpected. "I prefer to say she is sedentary."

My focus blurred, my expression slipping into disgust and anger, not at Trent, but at myself for having mishandled the last year or so to the point where I was shunned and broke, living through the grace of my friends. "Trent . . ."

He leaned back against the desk, but I couldn't tell if his worry was real or contrived. "You're in trouble, and you don't even know it."

My thoughts went to the pin in my bag. Uncomfortable, I glanced out the open door, not wanting the office to hear this, but not wanting to be shut in a room with him either. *If you only knew the half of it . . .* "I'm sitting in an FIB office while my partner posts my bail," I said tightly. "I think I know I'm in trouble."

"I'm talking about the coven of moral and ethical standards," he said, and I couldn't help my start. "We had lunch. Rachel, I swear I didn't tell them what you are. They already knew."

The fear turned into a solid lump and fell to my gut. *What I am?* "You slimy little toad!" I whispered as I stood. Trent was on his feet in an instant, but he didn't back up. "You told them!" I exclaimed softly, hands in fists. "You told the coven I could invoke demon magic!" No wonder they were trying to snag me! Snag me, hell, they were going to freaking *kill* me!

The noise from the nearby offices filtered in. His eyes fixed on mine, chilling me. "I wasn't about to lie to them," he said stiffly. "They already knew. And yes, I confirmed that you were a witch-born demon and that your children will be demons able to exist on this side of the ley lines. They knew my father made you, too. I don't understand it." He frowned, clearly more worried about himself than me.

"You little bastard," I growled. "I never told *anyone* what *you* are."

"Because if you do, you die," he said, his chin raised and his color high. I could smell the scent of cinnamon and wine as his temperature rose. It wasn't as if Trent's being an elf was that great a secret anyway, but still he clung to it. Sort of like I clung to being just a witch when logic told me I wasn't.

"They're going to take you, Rachel," Trent said. "Dissect you to find out what makes you different. Unless . . ."

His eyes flicked to the paper under my chair. "I become your slave?" I said bitterly.

"Sign the paper, Rachel," he said dryly. "I lied for you. I told them I could control you, destroy you if necessary. It's the only reason they didn't murder you outright."

Oh. My. God. "Excuse me?" I said, furious. "You told them you can control me?"

Trent shrugged. "They're understandably uncomfortable with a demon running around this side of the ley lines."

"I am *not* a demon, you little cookie maker," I nearly hissed. "I'm a *witch*. And your dad didn't create me. He only made it possible for me to survive what I'd been born with."

His eyes narrowed. "A mistake that I'm honor bound to do my utmost to contain."

"Oh really!" My boot heels clunked as I moved until only feet separated us, my hands on my hips. "You want to *contain* me? Is that a threat, Kalamack?"

Trent arched his eyebrows and backed up a step. "I'm *trying* to help you, though now I can't see why. You have a way out of this. Sign the paper. Become my legal responsibility. The coven will stop trying to give you a lobotomy. I might even get your shunning revoked."

I was shaking, overwhelmed. I didn't believe him—I couldn't. He had turned my own people on me because he knew they were the only ones who had the finesse to bring me down.

"You planned this, didn't you?" I accused softly, very aware that a room full of FIB officers was just out of earshot. "You told them what I'm capable of so they'd come after me; then you hold out your little safety net thinking I'd fall right into it. Playing both of us against each other so you can't lose. God, Trent, Ceri was right. You *are* a demon."

Jaw clenched, Trent went to push the door shut. I leapt into motion and got in front of it, and Trent pulled back, stymied. "I didn't tell them," he said, so close I could smell his aftershave. "But if you own me in the ever-after, I'm going to own you here."

My mouth dropped open. "Those are words on a paper! I made you my familiar to get your ass out of there, that's it! Have I ever once even hinted at using you? Have I done the charm to forge a link between us? No! And I'm not going to!"

"But you could," he said, and for an instant, I saw fear flicker under his anger.

Disgusted, I crossed my arms over my chest. "I should have let you rot there, that's what I should have done, you ungrateful snot. Do you have any idea what I put up with from Big Al every week so you can sit at home and watch TV instead of playing blow-up doll to a demon?"

Stone faced, Trent looked at me, his tan pale and the hem of his slacks shaking. "I will not be owned, Rachel," he said softly. "Not even on paper. And *never* by a *demon!*"

I took a breath, exhaling when the sound of pixy wings broke the tense silence. Trent retreated, his head down as he calmed himself. The familiar cadence of Ivy's boots sounded over the ringing of a single phone, and I retreated deeper into Glenn's office.

"Rache!" Jenks shouted, his high voice coming clearly as he rounded the door ahead of Ivy. The pixy stopped short, hovering at head height, his wings flashing red with anger as he saw Trent tugging his cuffs down. "Holy crap, Rache," he exclaimed, coming in to buzz irritating circles around me. "What did you get greenie weenie for this time? Bowling in black socks?"

Trent gave us a dry look, eyes going to Ivy when she halted in the doorway. Glenn was behind her, and the man had to push to get past her, anxious to be back in his office and head off the coming interspecies incident. His jaw was clenched, but what had he really expected? Trent and I didn't like each other and we argued. A lot.

Even as angry as I was, I watched the swift exchange between Ivy and Glenn, wondering if the tension in the room was solely because of me, or if there was an undercurrent of a secret not shared. Ivy's irritation could easily be a cloak to hide guilt, and Glenn was equally hard to read when he was in his hard-assed FIB detective mode.

I wouldn't hold out my hand for Jenks to land, so the pixy alighted on my shoulder instead, coating my sticky jacket in a fading glitter of dust. He was dressed for the chill spring weather, his wife, Matalina, finally having perfected pixy winter wear that gave him both freedom of movement and protection against the cold that might send him into hibernation and possible death. The tight black silk, red bandanna, and wooden-handled sword about his middle made the four-inch man look like a mix of theater and inner-city gang member.

In a smooth motion, Trent swooped forward to pick up the paper from under my chair. I stepped back out of his reach, my instinct to keep space between us kicking in. Refolding the contract, he tucked it away in his jacket. "Let my office know when you change your mind," he said, then headed for the door, jerking to a stop when Ivy didn't get out of his way.

"Let us know when cherry lollypops come out your ass," Jenks said, and I leaned back against the tall file cabinet, arms crossed over my middle.

Glenn cleared his throat, and Ivy slowly moved out of Trent's way.

"Your team is as professional as always, Morgan," Trent said lightly. Nodding at Glenn, he turned and walked out. A buzz of conversation rose behind him from the open offices.

I exhaled, shaking. "I hate him," I said, moving to my chair and plopping into it, making Jenks fly up. "I really do."

A glitter of silver sparkles hit my hand an instant before Jenks did. "Did he wave money at you again?" he asked, telling me he hadn't been eavesdropping. "I told you I've got this, Rache. I don't even want you to pay me back."

I winced. If only it were that simple.

Ivy turned from watching Trent make his way to the elevators. "How much was it?" she asked, staying where she was so the accumulated emotion of the room wouldn't hit her as hard. Her eyes were dilated more than the electric lights warranted, but she looked okay, especially if I'd interrupted her plans this weekend and she was hungry. Glenn, I noticed, wasn't fazed at all by her state, almost nonchalant as he moved behind his desk. Yeah, they had definitely been spending time together. His cologne smelled kind of citrusy, too.

"He tried to buy her," Glenn said for me. "In exchange for getting the coven of moral and ethical standards off her back."

"How did he know it was the coven?" Ivy wanted to know, and I stared at Glenn.

"How do you know what Trent wanted?" I asked him, my foot twitching.

Smiling grimly, Glenn punched a button on his phone and a light went out. "How else would I win the office pool?" he said, leaning back in his chair. "Rachel, you are in deep doo-doo."

"Yeah, tell me about it."

"Doo-doo? Call it what it is," Jenks smart-mouthed. "She's so far up shit creek, she could float down with the rest of the turds." I sighed my agreement as he settled himself on the warmth of my hand. "What does the coven want?" he asked. "They already shunned you."

"Someone—Trent probably—told them what I was," I said softly, depressed. Glenn already knew. He'd been there the day I'd figured it out. "They want to put me in a cage and dissect me."

Ivy stiffened, and Jenks's tiny features bunched up. "You're a witch," he said vehemently, and I felt a sense of peace at his loyalty.

"Thanks, Jenks," I said, though I didn't know if I believed it anymore. "Trent fed them some line about how his father made me so he can control me. Destroy me, even. They'll let me roam free and in the wild if he takes legal responsibility for me."

"That's a lie," Ivy said from the doorway. "He can't control you. And he didn't make you. His father simply found a way to keep you alive."

I lifted a shoulder and let it fall. "Looks to me like he's doing a damn fine job of controlling me right now." Stupid-ass businessman. I still didn't believe him. No one else knew what I was capable of except my friends—and Newt, on a good day. Sighing, I thought back to who'd been there the evening Trent told Minias what I was: Marshal, Ceri, and Keasley—but they wouldn't say anything; neither would Quen, but if Quen knew, then so did Jonathan, the prick who organized Trent's life. Lee seemed the most likely candidate for playing let's make a deal with the coven, trading information about me to erase his own questionable dealings in black magic—if he cared to risk their finding out he was just like me. It had to be Trent.

Ivy's expression became pensive. Having born the brunt of a master vampire's attentions, she knew how easy it was to control someone through their emotions. She was still trapped in her own personal hell even though the lock had been broken and the door was wide open.

Behind his desk, Glenn looked unsure. "They can't do this. Even the coven of moral and ethical standards has to work within the law. Can't you file an appeal or something?"

At that, I smiled and Ivy slumped against the door frame. "Sure, but if I disappear, who's to say different? Ever wonder why witches generally don't make much trouble? We police ourselves, just like Weres and vamps. We have a long history of hiding, Glenn. The I.S. just picks up the ones who are stupid enough to be caught." Caught committing benign crimes like theft, larceny, murder—stuff humans were conditioned to deal with. It seemed ironic that bringing in the stupid ones was what I used to do for a living.

I was totally depressed now, and Jenks rose, his dragonflylike wings clattering for attention. "Rache, we've done kidnap prevention before. The weather is warm enough to string pixy lines in the garden, and we've got Bis now. They want you alive, right?"

"To start with, yeah," I said, not feeling any better. Ever since quitting the I.S., it seemed as if all I'd done was run. I was tired of it. But Jenks was right. We'd find a way around this. We always did.

Looking up, I met Glenn's eyes, then Ivy's. Taking a slow breath, I stood. "I'll call David when I get home," I said, dropping another bit of strawberry off me and into Glenn's trash. "He's great with paperwork. If you can't overpower them, you drown them in red tape." I managed a smile. "Thanks, guys. I don't know what I'd do without you."

"Die, probably," Jenks said with a laugh as we headed out.

But the thing was, he was right.

Four

Traffic among Cincy's tight buildings was clogged, the night gloom making the oncoming car lights all the brighter. It was going to be stop-and-go all the way to the interstate, and I almost wished I'd taken the longer way through Old Newport, but the FIB building was right in downtown Cincy, and the Hollows were just over the bridge. Once I got on the expressway, I'd be home in ten minutes.

"Accident?" I guessed, glancing across the narrow front seat of my convertible to Ivy, chilling as she watched nothing, her expression blank as she dwelled on who knew what. Her long fingers spun a world-weary, holed coin laced on a faded purple ribbon around her neck like it was a rosary. She kept it as a reminder that she couldn't love without hurt, and it worried me.

Jenks buzzed his wings to warm himself as he sat on the rearview mirror and looked backward. "You want me to go look?"

I flicked my attention to the heater controls, cranked to warm the already hot car. If he'd offered, it wasn't too cold for him outside, but for him to risk his core temp dropping to satisfy my curiosity was not what our partnership was about. "Nahh. It's probably nightwalkers."

Jenks's heels drummed against the mirror. "Sun's been down for over two hours."

I nodded, inching forward another three car lengths and just missing the light. Sighing, I cracked the window. It smelled like hot strawberries in here.

It had been forty years since the Turn and all the various Inderland species had come out of hiding to save humanity from extinction. Night and graveyard shifts had taken on entirely new meanings. What I was stuck in now was the dark-loving parts of Inderland trying to get to work and the late-working humans trying to get home. Rush hour shifted with the sun, two hours before sunrise and two hours after sunset being the worst. We were at the tail end of it.

My elbow went onto the tiny lip of the closed window and my fist propped up my head. Between Trent's offer and the coven wanting my head, I wasn't in the best of moods. A sigh slipped from me as I counted the people passing with cell phones against their ears.

"I told you not to worry about it, Rache," Jenks said, mistaking my worry. "I owe you lots more than lousy bail money."

"Thanks, Jenks," I said, accelerating when the light changed. "I appreciate it. I'll pay you back when I can." *I'm so sick of not being able to make it on my own.*

Ivy reached for the chicken strap when I took the corner tight, only to stop short at another light. "It's a slump," she said, her gray voice seeming to ease out of the dark corner of my car. "We all have them. It's part of being an independent."

"Yeah." Jenks dropped to the steering wheel, grapevining on it as the light changed and I turned. "Did I ever tell you about the time I was working for the I.S. to help feed my family? Matalina had just had another set of quads and things were looking ugly. I had to take a job for hazard pay to babysit this witch no one else would touch."

I couldn't stop my smile. "Best backup I ever had, or ever will have."

The pixy's wings moved faster as I accelerated. "Thanks."

A soft, happy sound came from Ivy, and he turned at the unfamiliar noise. The living vamp wasn't always gloomy, but she was never obvious about her good moods. The pixy took flight, buzzing an irritating circle around her. "I love you, too, Ivy," he said with just the right amount of sarcasm to keep things light.

Her long fingers waved him away, slowly so there was no chance of hitting him. Two years ago, if anyone had told me that I'd abandon my I.S. job to go independent with a living vampire and a pixy, I would've said they were crazy. It wasn't that we didn't do well together. We did. We did fantastically together. But my decisions, which always seemed sound at the time, had a tendency to backfire—badly. And the coven trying to kidnap me was really bad. Signing that paper of Trent's to get out of it was even worse.

I inched forward, eyes on the red taillights of the cars stopped on the interstate/parking lot. I wasn't going to let Kalamack's offer get to me. "So, Ivy," I said, trying to shift my thoughts. "What's going on with you and Glenn?"

The living vampire's eyes glinted as she flicked her attention to Jenks. "You told her!" she exclaimed, and my lips parted. *Told me? Jenks knew? Knew what?*

Jenks's wings clattered, and he flitted to the far side of the car, well out of her reach. "I didn't tell her nothing!" he shouted, laughing. "Tink's contractual hell, Ivy, I didn't tell her! She must have figured it out. She's not stupid!"

The car jerked as I hit the brakes before I needed to, but I wanted to look at Jenks. "Something *is* going on. I knew it!"

"There's no anything," Ivy protested, her face red in the light from the oncoming traffic. "Nothing is going on. Nothing!"

"Nothing?" Jenks blurted out, unable to keep quiet anymore. "You think—"

"Shut up, Jenks," Ivy snarled.

His wings humming, he hung in the middle of the car as if nailed to the air. He was holding his breath, and silver sparkles were drifting from him to make a light bright enough to read by. The pitch from his wings was starting to make my eyeballs hurt. Grinning, I looked across to Ivy. "You'd better tell me or he's going to explode."

"They've been on three dates," Jenks said, and Ivy snatched for him.

My smile widened as Jenks frantically darted about the car. "I can't!" he shouted. "Ivy, I can't! I can't not say anything!"

Sullen, Ivy slumped in her seat, giving up. "I can't believe you told her. You promised."

The pixy landed on the wheel as I put the car in motion and merged into "traffic" when a big SUV made some space. "He didn't tell me," I said as I waved thanks to the guy. "Glenn's coat smells like you." I made a face. "And honey. I don't want to know why. Really."

Jenks's wings halted. "Honey? Honey and gold?" he asked, and Ivy seemed to cringe.

"Yes," I said, able to identify the hot-metal smell now. "Sun-warmed gold. And honey."

Hands on his hips, Jenks turned to Ivy. "You told me Daryl was leaving."

Daryl? Who in hell is Daryl?

Ivy's expression became bothered. "She is. Soon as she finds a place."

She?

"Like that's ever gonna happen!" Jenks exclaimed. "The woman is sex in sandals!"

"Glenn isn't going to kick her out!" Ivy said loudly. "She's not well."

"No wonder with Glenn keeping her up all night doing the nasty!"

"Hey!" Ivy exclaimed, eyes going black. "That's uncalled for! He hasn't touched her."

"Whoa, whoa, whoa!" I said, sneaking glances at them both. "Who is Daryl?" *And why haven't I heard about her before?*

Jenks's wings stopped moving, and I thought I saw a flash of panic in him as Ivy forced her expression to neutral. Both of them seemed to pull three steps back in their thinking, and after a moment, Ivy said, "Just a woman we met on a run when you were in the ever-after. She needed some help. A place to stay. Glenn is putting her up until she finds her feet."

Jenks was silent as he looked at the car's ceiling, so I turned to Ivy— waiting.

"It's not any different from you foisting Ceri off on Keasley," she muttered. "I couldn't bring her to the church. Glenn is helping her out is all."

"Helping her right out of her clothes, I bet," Jenks said loudly, then darted to my shoulder when Ivy flicked her finger at him.

"She is not having sex with Glenn," Ivy continued. "I'd know."

"Yeah, you'd know because you're dating him," Jenks said. "Did you give him the dating guide yet?"

"Jenks!" she said, dismayed now, and he darted away from her snatch for him.

"How about kissing him? Did you at least kiss him yet?" he asked, laughing.

A low noise came from Ivy, almost a growl, and she seemed to melt into the car's darkness. My breath slipped out, and I put my blinker on to get in the lane for the bridge traffic; someone would let me in. Yeah, she'd kissed him—within an inch of his life, I bet.

I curled in my lower lip and glanced at Jenks. The pixy gestured for me to go for it, and I did. "Have you bitten him?" I asked, needing to know. He was my friend, too.

Ivy said nothing, and Jenks hummed his wings. "Did'ja?" he needled. "Did he?"

Still she said nothing, telling me she had, and I wondered if this might be a big mistake or one of the best things in Ivy's life. Glenn was nothing if not solid. "He doesn't want to go vamp, does he?" I asked, half joking but afraid of her answer. I was the last person to advocate shunning vampires as friends, but if you didn't know what you were doing, or the vampire was a real predator, you were in trouble. Glenn and Ivy were all of the above.

"No."

She was down to one-word answers, but she was still talking. Jenks's relieved expression told me it was more than she'd told him—which made me feel good. "Good," I said, careful to keep my eyes on the passing traffic to give her some privacy. "I like him the way he is."

"You'd like him more as a vampire. I can tell. I've seen it before." She sounded wistful, and I looked across the dark car at her, trying to hide my alarm.

"Ivy . . ."

"He doesn't want to go vamp," she said, flicking her eyes at me and then away. "That's one of the things I like about him."

Jenks winced, wings flat against his back. He knew as well as I that what *you* wanted didn't mean crap if the vampire you were with wanted something else. She was alive, so she couldn't turn him—only dead vampires could do that—but she could bind him, make him a shadow. Not that she would mean to, but accidents happened in the throes of passion. Hell, I roomed with her, and that was hard enough. Adding sex or blood to the mix could be deadly, which was why I'd finally made our relationship strictly platonic—that it had taken almost two years of confusing emotions and two bites between us to do it was beside the point.

I darted a nervous look at Jenks. "And he's okay with you going somewhere else for blood?" I asked hesitantly. Ivy never talked to me about her boyfriends. Her girlfriends either.

Gazing out the window at the night, Ivy said softly, "Who said I was?"

"No fairy-assed way!" Jenks exclaimed, and I gave him a look telling him to shut up.

Turning to us, she shrugged in embarrassment. "I told you I didn't need much. It's the act, not the amount. I'm not going to make him a shadow. Piscary taught me to be careful, if nothing else." Her eyebrows were raised in challenge as a flush colored her usually pale face. "Jealous?" she asked as she took in my alarmed expression.

Oh. My. God. "No, I think it's great," I finally stammered. Ivy and I had a . . . balanced relationship. Adding blood to it, no matter how right it felt, would destroy exactly what we admired most in each other. Her dating Glenn was a very good thing. I think.

"Um, you won't say anything to his dad, will you?" she asked. "Glenn wants to tell him. He's not embarrassed as much as not wanting to—"

"To deal with Edden telling him it's a bad idea to date your coworkers," I finished for her before she could even think to bring up the dangers of dating a vampire, even a living one.

Ivy pointed to a break I could slip into, and I hit the gas, eager to be moving again. "I'm being smart about this," she said as the car swung and we shifted from the momentum.

"I won't say anything unless Edden asks me first." *Ivy and Glenn? Am I that blind, or was I just not looking for it?* The bridge was ahead, and beyond that, the lights of the Hollows.

"Thank you," she said, her entire posture easing as she settled into the seat. "Glenn . . . I wasn't expecting this. He's not after my blood, and we like the same stuff."

From the rearview mirror, Jenks snickered. "Guns, violence, crime scene photos, leather, sex, and women. Yeah, I can see that."

"I think it's good," I said again, hoping he'd shut up, but it was pretty nearly the same list that had brought Ivy and me together.

Jenks laughed. "Has he let you hold his gun yet?"

I smiled as Ivy stiffened.

"The man has a big gun," the pixy continued, his words innocent, but his tone full of innuendo. "It's got shiny bullets. You like shiny, don't you, Ivy? I bet Daryl has seen his gun."

"God, Jenks! Grow up!" she exclaimed, and the pixy snorted.

We inched forward another car length, and Ivy swung her hair away from her face, the oncoming traffic lighting it. "You're okay with this?" she asked, as if she needed my approval, not because we'd almost been more than roommates, but because we had both loved Kisten and he was dead. I nodded, and she relaxed. My shoulders slumped at the reminder of his bright blue eyes, his lips curving up in a smile I'd never see again.

"Nice," Jenks said from the mirror. "Now she's thinking about Kisten. Way to go, Ivy."

I shrugged, eyes on the road. "And that's okay," I said, comfortable with the ache.

Ivy was silent as we moved forward and stopped, moved forward and stopped, lost in her own thoughts, probably tinged with guilt. I'd already had my rebound relationship. Solid, dependable, fun Marshal, who could scuba dive and roller-skate. It could have been a really great friendship, seeing that he liked complex relationships and I was nothing if not that, but then I got shunned and he left. I didn't blame him. I'd actually seen him a few weeks ago at the Old Newport Theater with a woman who had red hair longer than mine. He hadn't even waved, just looked at me and walked away with his arm around her waist.

A space opened before me, and I hit the accelerator as my lane started to move. I picked up speed, turning onto the bridge and bumping over the bad pavement. As I had expected, traffic eased, and I let up on my death grip on the wheel. Ahead of us, the Hollows was beautiful with light, and I sneezed, jerking unexpectedly. "Bless you," Ivy said and Jenks chuckled.

"That's funny," he said. "A vampire blessing."

I would have agreed with him, but my gut cramped up, stopping my words. "Ow," I said, putting a hand to my middle.

Ivy turned to me. "You okay? You look green."

"I feel green." Twisting, I took a quick look behind me to see if I could shift into the exit lane. "My gut cramped up is all. I'm fine." But I wasn't. I was dizzy, too. It was almost like the time— Shocked, I looked at Jenks. He was looking at me with the same horrified expression. Crap. It was after sunset. Someone was summoning Al, and since I had his summoning name, they were going to get me instead.

"Rachel?" Ivy questioned, clueless.

No! I thought, scared. I wasn't a demon. I could *not* be summoned like this!

But I'd been summoned before by black-arts witches trying for Al, and this was exactly what it had felt like.

My breath hissed in as another wave of pain hit me. A horn blew behind us, and I yanked the car back into my lane. "No," I panted through my teeth. "I won't go. You can't make me."

"She's being summoned!" Jenks shrilled, and Ivy's face, now close to mine, became terrified. "Ivy, she's being summoned!"

"Pull over!" Ivy exclaimed. "Rachel, stop the car!"

I couldn't think, it hurt that bad. My hands gripped the wheel and I seized, the engine racing until I jerked my foot off the gas. The car lurched, and my head hit the wheel. Tears pricked, and I held my breath, trying to make the world stop spinning. Damn it, I should have insisted that Al give me *my* password back. But as long as I had his, he couldn't abduct anyone.

"Ivy! Do something!" Jenks yelled as another pain ripped through me. I let go of the wheel to clutch my middle. Ivy grabbed the wheel as the car swerved. Vampiric incense rolled over me, and the car jerked as it hit the curb and swung back.

My head hit the wheel again, and a horn blew. "Ow," I moaned, trying to open my eyes. I could smell ashes. I wouldn't go. I was *not* a demon!

Vertigo hit, and I reached out, grasping anything as the ground was jerked from me, hands digging into the door, the seat . . . anything.

"Get out, Jenks!" Ivy screamed. "We're going to hit!"

There was a quick hum of wings, and then a terrifying jerk. The sound of plastic splintering and the screaming of wheels was loud. My face hit something that felt like a wall and smelled like plastic. The hold on my will cracked, and with the suddenness of a drop of water leaving a faucet, I felt my body suck inward, pulling my soul and aura with it.

And I wasn't in the car anymore.

The sudden cessation of pain was a shock. I tried to take a breath, but I didn't have lungs. I was in the ley lines, the warmth and tingling sensation familiar as I was pulled who knew where. Somewhere between my car hitting something and now, I had accepted the smut of the demon curse and the pain had vanished. It hurt only when you resisted.

Oh my God, Ivy and Jenks. They had to be okay. I think the airbag had deployed. We'd hit something, and I was okay, but Ivy and Jenks . . .

Anger replaced my fear. Someone had pulled me out of existence, causing an accident that I'd live through but that my friends might not. *Jenks,* I thought, imagining his fragile body against the glass, slowly going cold in the night air as no one looked for him. Damn it, someone was going to pay for this!

I'd traveled ley lines enough to know how to keep my soul together, and once I relaxed, it was absurdly easy. Al refused to teach me how to jump the lines by myself, but I could ride them. A tingling whispering through my thoughts gave me warning, and I stiffened as my aura rose through my mind, tapping into the demon archive to find out what I looked like, then turning the energy of the ley line into a body. At least, that's what Al said that itchy feeling was.

I shuddered, tasting the disjointedness of what felt like a broken ley line slice raw across my awareness, tasting of salt and cracked stone. The uncomfortable feeling ran through me like water in a saltshaker, and I squirmed as I felt myself take shape with an unusual slowness, as if everything was being checked twice.

My lungs were filling with air that was just a shade more substantial than I was, and I stumbled, not quite solid yet. I was standing, though, which was a lot better than showing up facedown. Not yet visible to my summoner, I sniffed deeply. There was no scent of burnt amber—I was in reality, and that was a relief. I'd be dealing with people. A demon might be a problem, but I could convince people to let me out, and then I could do some damage. I knew how to play this game. When summoned, demons couldn't lie except by omission, but I wasn't a demon.

There was a faint hum of chanting. I was in a high-ceilinged, round room, dimly lit with a white floor etched in black to make circles intersecting circles. *Granite,* I thought, thinking it was almost the inverse of Al's kitchen floor. I was trapped in the center of a huge six-pointed star that took up most of the room. The protection circle holding me was actually a shallow ditch made to contain salt, blood . . . whatever. It glowed faintly, the thick haze fading to a soft shimmer a mere three inches above the floor. The sound of gulls turned my attention upward to the open round skylight high above. No clouds, but the clear transparency of dusk told me it was sunset.

Holy crap! Was I on the West Coast? How in hell was I supposed to get home?

With a soft shiver, my aura finished rising through me, carrying the thought of my body with it and coalescing around my mind to leave a nasty taste of ash on my tongue. I had arrived.

Squinting, I brought a hand up to shade my eyes to better see the five people standing at equal intervals around the six-pointed star. I didn't look like Al, but he could appear as anything he wanted. Any demon summoner worth his salt would know that.

Abruptly I realized where the soot taste was coming from, and horror filled me. I was covered in ash. The faint white haze on my clothes was some dead person's ashes!

"Oh my God!" I shouted, smacking at myself to get it off. The chanting abruptly stopped as I danced about the interior of the circle, beating the chunky dust off me. It only made things worse, and I began coughing on someone's dead grandmother. My eyes watered, and I finally gave up, glaring at them from around my hair, now all over the place. Damn it, I was covered in strawberries and human remains. This was really gross, but the more I brushed at it, the more it stuck to my leather coat, like pixy dust on wet leaves.

Disgusted, I slowly turned in a circle to look at them. Jaw clenched, I tapped the nearest ley line, feeling that same disjointed cracked sensation again, and I wondered if this was why the U.S.-wide coven meetings were held here. If you weren't born to it, trying to use the ley lines on the West Coast would be like Russian roulette. Earth magic wouldn't work at all within a hundred miles of the ocean, a fact that led ley-line witches to think that they were superior to earth witches, but earth magic functioned on fresh water, and put a ley-line witch on a boat—any boat—and they were in trouble without a familiar. *I was on the West Coast? Al would laugh his ass off.*

Between us, the opalescent sheet of the ever-after showed a hint of all their collective auras, not a shade of black among them. My pulse quickened. This might be harder than I thought. These people looked professional, not like the laughable excuse for black-arts witches dressed in hokey black robes who had once summoned me into a basement. The summoning pattern was odd, too. Not that I'd been in the middle of many, but usually it was a five-pointed star, not six-. This was an old configuration. If it had been a friendly spell, I'd be at the position of power where I could draw from the other six. Here, I was their prisoner.

Two women, three men, varying ages. They were dressed professionally in pastels and dark colors—all solid, with no patterns that could disguise a written charm or symbol of power. The tallest had a laptop open on the high stool next to her. Their manner was subdued and confident, not excited, as I'd imagined, seeing as they were summoning a demon. All were looking expectantly at me. And outside the formal circle, standing submissively, like a dog, behind the woman with a laptop, was Nick.

Five

Y ou *toad!*" I shrieked, striding forward only to stop short at the shimmering wall of ever-after rising up from the protection circle. It hummed aggressively, and I pulled back, stymied. Hands on my hips, I glared at Nick, heart pounding and pissed, growing hot in my strawberry-and-ash-covered coat.

"You summoned me, didn't you!" I accused him, and Nick hunched, brown eyes avoiding mine. "I was *driving*, Nick. Ivy and Jenks were with me. We hit something, you little prick. If they're dead, I swear I will hunt you down. There is nowhere you can hide from me. *Nowhere!*"

A clatter of pixy wings turned into Jax, and Jenks's eldest son, dressed in black and looking so much like his dad it hurt, darted erratically in front of Nick. "I gotta get to a phone!" the pixy exclaimed, and he vanished through the open skylight and into the early dusk.

The sight of Jax was a shock, and realizing what I must look like—practically foaming at the mouth and raging like . . . a demon—I forced myself back from the barrier, the warning buzz having escalated into cramping my toes. Most circles didn't burn, but this one had been drawn to hold demons. To hold me. *I am not a demon. I'm not!*

The surrounding witches held to their posts to keep the circle strong, but Nick, who had apparently done the actual summoning, seeing that he knew Al's name, was picking up his stuff and jamming it in a worn, army-green satchel. "It's cold in Cincy, Nick," I said, shaking. "You son of a bitch. Even if he survived the crash, he's going to have a hard time staying alive."

The witch with the laptop shifted to draw my attention from Nick's grim expression. She was the tallest one there, wearing a black business suit and gray hose. Her legs were too muscular to be called pretty, and her sandy blond hair was in a simple cut with gray highlights. She looked familiar, like from a news article, but it wasn't until I saw her Möbius-strip pin holding a sprig of heather that I finally got it. Crap, it was the coven.

Worry colored my anger, and I moved back to the center of the circle, looking over my summoners again to see the balances in play. Vivian was still in Cincinnati, but if she had been here, there'd be three men and three women, an equal number of earth and ley-line users, all carefully selected to supplement one another's skills. Remembering Vivian's strength, I knew I was in trouble. Yes, they had been voted into the position, but they'd been trained for it from early childhood like Olympian athletes, skills and traditions embedded into them until magic was like breathing—instinctive, fast, and powerful. This was going to be . . . tricky.

The woman with the laptop seemed to be the high witch, since she did a quick look around at the others before asking Nick in a pleasant voice, "Is this Morgan, or the demon?"

I wrapped my arms around myself, wanting to demand that they let me out, but I knew they wouldn't. They wanted me in a hole in the ground—quick and quiet. I was in so much trouble.

Nick obviously knew it was me, but he came close, as if unsure, faded satchel in hand, shoulders at an uneven slant and a tired look in his eyes. He appeared old and weary, and the sheet of ever-after between us hummed as I moved so close that my breath came back to me. His wrist was a mass of scar tissue where his hand had almost been chewed off during his stint as a rat, and his black hair was longer than I remembered. Slowly, my hands formed fists.

I'd slept with this man, thinking he loved me. Maybe he had. But he'd betrayed me, selling secrets about me to demons and then trying to double-cross me after I'd saved his life. My fist jammed out, hitting the barrier inches from Nick's stomach. Pain cramped my hand and clawed its way up my arm. There was a collective gasp as I danced back, shaking my fist. Rubbing my knuckles, I met Nick's sad expression with a heightened feeling of bitterness.

"I thought you were smarter than this," he said, a toss of his too-long hair the only clue that I'd startled him. The demon scar on his brow that he'd gotten from Al showed for an instant, then was hidden. "Are they right?" he asked. "Did you go into partnership with Al? Is that why you showed up instead of him? God, Rachel. You were supposed to be the smart one."

"I didn't have much choice, Nicky," I said sharply.

His eyes flicked away for an instant—his only sign of guilt. "Neither do I. Remember that when this is done. I'm settling a debt *you* foisted on me," he said loudly. "Did you think I wouldn't have to answer for you running off with the focus?"

My chin rose. "It showed up on my doorstep with my name on it. Tell me you weren't going to sell it to the highest bidder. Tell me that, Nick."

"I was," he said belligerently, his attention shifting to the witches around us. "Them."

Them again. The same them who now had me circled like an animal. "Looks like I made the right choice in giving it back to the Weres then, huh?" I was so ticked I could scream.

Nick looked me up and down, his gaze lingering on my strawberry-covered coat before he put a hand to the back of his neck and walked away. "It's her," he said to the tall witch with the laptop, and there was a soft exhalation as they all relaxed.

My tension, though, spiked as the witches left their posts to join the tall woman at her computer. The humming of the barrier eased as they lessened their collective attention holding it, but the circle was still strong enough to stand.

The oldest man was wearing a large amulet, probably defunct this close to the coast. Earth-magic user, obviously, which made the older woman with the laptop their ley-line master. His cuff links were Möbius strips, and my face warmed when he handed Nick a stack of bills.

Nick shoved the money in his bag with unusual haste and turned to me. "We're even now," he said, his brow furrowed, and I flipped him off. His lips tightened and he looked away. "Don't call me again," he said the man as he started for an elaborately tooled wooden door, but upon reaching it, he hesitated. "You either," he said to me, and then he . . . sort of . . . smiled?

Don't call him? I thought. Like I ever would? But I forced my breathing to remain slow as I glimpsed the hallway beyond the door, an idea trickling through me. Carpet and soft colors, pictures on the walls. I was in a private home, not an institution. As the witches watched the door shut behind him, my hand crept back to my jeans pocket to find the lump of my phone. Holy crap, Nick had reminded me of a way to get out of here. An active phone line could break a circle—if one was skilled enough in taking them down.

The door snicked shut, and I heard a sigh from one of the five witches. "I really dislike that man," one said.

"Me, too," I said loudly, then pulled my fingers back from the cramping sensation of the barrier. It was still too strong—they needed to lower their guard more.

Apparently they'd been waiting for Nick to leave, because they gathered behind the sandy-haired witch with the laptop to face me like a jury. The woman looked to be an athletic forty, but I was willing to bet that her surfer-toned body was actually closer to a hundred. You don't find that grace or confidence in a mere forty years, even if you can keep your balance in a tight curl. Her short hair was bleached by sun and salt, not chemicals in a salon, and her narrow, angular nose was peeling from sunburn.

Balancing her was the older witch with that nonfunctioning amulet. He appeared to be about forty as well, and his clothes were stodgy and expensive looking. They clung to him a little tightly, telling me he usually had a slimming charm. Settling in behind them was the middle male/female pair who both appeared to be a spelled thirty, and behind them, a young, gawky guy who was more than likely Vivian's counterpart, probably close to my age and still gaining his full, deadly potential. They all wore the coven's Möbius glyph, the chunky thirtyish woman using it to hold back her long blond hair.

"Rachel Morgan," laptop woman said, her voice taking on a formal cadence. "You have been brought here before the coven of moral and ethical standards to answer for several serious crimes."

I sighed, holding little hope of coming out ahead here. "Why didn't you come see me? We could've settled this over coffee. It would have been less dramatic than Vivian destroying some store's produce section. The FIB was there and everything." I mentioned it only because I wanted them to know there was a report filed. This wasn't going to simply go away.

Sure enough, the woman looked up, cool and unshakable, but her finger twitched.

"Brooke?" the older man said in sharp warning, eying my strawberry-tangled hair. "We agreed Vivian was there for reconnaissance only."

Oh! It really is her name then, I thought. Brooke barely shrugged, but I could tell she was pissed at me. *Yeah, this is all my fault.*

"The subject's pattern changed. I was afraid we'd lose her," Brooke said. "There wasn't time to ask everyone's opinion. It was a calculated risk, and Vivian was willing to take it."

The *subject's* pattern changed, eh? Al sending me home early, perhaps? Just how long had they been watching me? Angry, I rubbed an ash-coated chunk of strawberry off my sleeve. "I don't care what Kalamack told you, I'm not a threat," I said, and there was a nervous shifting among them. Clearly they were surprised I knew he was involved.

Brooke's lips tightened, and she glanced back at them, irate. "We think you are."

"I'm not," I shot back, glancing at the witch with the long blond hair listening to the oldest man whispering in her ear. "Trent's a big drama queen."

Damn it, I was going to smack Trent. I was going to smack him good. I was not a demon to be pulled around like a pull toy.

Peeved, Brooke turned to the whispering behind her. "Will you do that later?" she griped, and I tested the barrier to find it still strong. The line I was connected to surged, and I scrambled to handle it. Earthquake, maybe?

The oldest man, the one with the useless amulet, gestured mockingly to Brooke to get on with it, and she gave him an equally sour look. *Is there a schism? Can I use that?*

The sun-bleached tips of Brooke's short hair swung as she focused on me. "What an elf thinks is of no concern. Your actions are. You have undergone the sentence of shunning but have not changed your ways. You leave us little choice, Rachel Morgan, and are hereby formally charged with willfully allowing a witch to be taken by a demon."

This was so full of crap, I almost laughed. I'd been cleared of this by the I.S. months ago. "Which one?" I shot out. I was being railroaded. This was so unfair.

Brooke looked annoyed by the interruption, but it was the oldest man who said, "You call him Al, I believe."

I grimaced. "Not the demon. Which witch?"

The gawky young man with the off-the-rack suit stammered, "There's been more than one?"

There had, but if they didn't know about Tom's dying and Pierce's taking his body, then I wasn't going to tell them. I pressed into the barrier, finding it wasn't humming anymore, but I jerked back as if it was. "I don't want to be blamed for someone else's stupidity. If we're talking about Lee, then yes. He dragged me into the ever-after and tried to give me to Al. I fought Lee, and lost. Al took Lee instead."

Brooke's smile was a bare hint of one, but it was ugly and I felt a shiver. "The better witch," she said, and I nodded, realizing she was not an honest, upright woman. I didn't care if her aura was a clean, almost clear blue; her morals were gray.

"Bet that didn't end up in your report," I said bitterly. "I *saved* the witch who tried to give me to a demon. Is that why you're doing this without a jury?"

The witches behind Brooke looked discomfited, but she simply glanced at the screen. "You are accused of calling a demon into a court of human law," she continued.

"To put a murdering vampire behind bars, yup. I did." No jury on earth would convict me for that. "What else you got?" My foot was shaking, and I pressed down on it to get it to stop. Brooke was starting to sweat, but it wasn't fear. It was excitement. She liked something.

"You are accused of giving a rare artifact to a Were to further your position in his pack instead of turning it over to us for proper reinterment," she said.

"You never told me you wanted it," I said, hand on my hip. Hey, if I was going down, I was going down bitching. "And I was David's alpha before I had the focus, so you can cut the crap about using it to better my position in a group that no witch cares about anyway." Worry for David rose up, and I felt my back pocket, ready to change my plan. "If you touch him . . ."

Brooke's eyes fixed on mine. "You are in no position to make threats, Morgan."

Not yet anyway. I exhaled, pretending to be subdued. *Just relax a bit more, and maybe I will be.* "Look," I said, feeling sticky, "the I.S. cleared me, and you shunned me. Case closed. You can't shove me in a hole to be forgotten." *I hope.*

The head earth witch with his salt-stymied amulet smiled, and the lonely sound of gulls crying came faintly as they settled on cliffs for the night. "Yes, we can," he said. "All of the listed crimes could be dismissed as the youthful exuberance of a young, talented witch. With the right conditioning, you might even be a candidate for my job when I step down. But with certain incidents coming to light, it becomes increasingly clear what you are."

Damn you, Trent. If I get out of here, I'm going to smack you so hard you won't be able to find your ass using both hands. "And that is?" I asked, knowing what he was going to say.

Facing me squarely, Brooke said, "You are demon spawn, Rachel Morgan. Survivor of the Rosewood syndrome, demon in all but birth."

Shit. Hearing her say it hit me hard, and I shouted, "I am not a threat to you!" I almost followed that with "and Trent can't control me," but I was scared. I wasn't ready to burn that safety net just yet, and I hated myself for it.

Brooke snapped her laptop shut with a sound of finality. "You *are* a threat, Morgan," she said loudly. "Your very existence is a threat to the entire witch society, and sometimes we are constrained to act on our society's behalf without them knowing. That's why you're here and why we are going to stick you in a little . . . tiny . . . hole."

Oh, ma-a-a-an, this is so full of crap! "You're afraid of me, isn't that it? Well, you should be if this is how you treat people!" I was shaking, but they weren't impressed, chagrined, or otherwise moved. Stymied, I crossed my arms over my middle and exhaled loudly, helpless.

"So all that is left is your sentencing," Brooke said, sounding happy about it.

Sentencing? Fear slid through me, and at my alarmed expression, Brooke smiled. They were railroading me into custody because a trial would bring it out into the open that witches were an offshoot of demons. Humans would massacre us in our sleep like they once had vampires.

This was so stupid. I was a *good* person. Shaking, my hand went back to my phone and pulled it out. I wasn't sure what to think of Nick right now. What was going to follow next was his idea. *Did he stick around to help me?* "Mind if I make my call now rather than later?" I asked, and the heavy man with the amulet paled. "You get a lot of bars out here, right?"

"Sweet Jesus, she has a phone!" he shouted.

Yes, I had a phone, something demons didn't. I wasn't a demon, and to treat me as such was going to be their undoing. Pulse racing and angry with all of them, I hit Ivy's number.

"Rachel?" Ivy immediately answered, and a knot of worry eased. Finally something was going my way. She was alive and sounded fine.

"Strengthen the circle!" the older man shouted, and they all moved, scrambling to get back to their spots. But it was too late. I had a real, irrefutable connection with someone past the bubble, and the damage had been done.

"Ivy, listen," I said, pressing my hand against the bubble to feel my skin warm but not burn. It was a very good sign. "Are you okay? Is Jenks?"

"Yes." Her voice came back, tiny and small. "He's pissed. Where are you?"

"I'm on the West Coast. Keep the line open, all right?"

As Ivy exclaimed her disbelief, I shoved the open phone in my back pocket. My two palms went to the bubble, and I pushed. I'd once taken a circle. I'd thought it had been an act of serendipitous timing, but now I wondered if it had been because I could hold the stuff of demons.

This circle is mine, I thought, filling my mind with the scintillating, broken energy, filling my chi and spindling the excess in my thoughts to dilute the entirety so the weak spots would show. Before me, I fixed on Brooke's eyes, smiling when the energy spilling into me scraped along my thoughts, the shattered West Coast line filling me as it burned through existing channels to my mind. The weak spot in the bubble glowed, and with a surge of hope, I concentrated, pulling more until I could see the lines of energy I was drawing off the bubble.

I squinted at my success, and Brooke's expression became worried. I widened the imperfection. The more I took, the bigger the instability got. It was working!

My thoughts burned, and I began to sweat. The five witches tried to shore up the barrier, but with a ping, the circle became mine. I gasped as the entire line suddenly spilled into me. A lesser witch would have fried her chi, but the jangling discordance flowed to my mind where I spindled it like mad until I managed to break from the ley line. *God, how could they stand manipulating this day after day?*

I fell forward, landing half out of the circle on my hands and knees. "Ow," I gasped, not from the bump, but from the force in my head. The circle had fallen, and I stared at Brooke, nothing between us but air.

"She's out!" the old man shouted, and I moved.

My boots slipped, and I scrambled on all fours to plow into the weakest member, the youngest, gawky male witch. He shouted in fear and fell back, his training forgotten. His head hit the tile and his eyes rolled back. I waited an instant to be sure he was breathing.

One down, I thought, then rolled and kept rolling. A yellow ball of force hit the wall, sending goo splattering. It was the oldest man, his head high and his jaw clenched. I yelped and dove for the cover of the middle-aged woman coming for me. Her eyes widened, and together we fell.

"Sweet mother of God!" someone screamed, and I thought I saw pixy dust.

Shaking the stars from my vision, I pushed the woman away and punched to knock her out. She blocked it—badly—and I grabbed her, swinging her around to take the next yellow ball from hell that the head guy had thrown. The goo hit her full on, and I gasped when the ugly yellow splotches grew on my coat. Panicking, I let go, scrambling out of my coat and dropping it as the woman who had taken most of the spell fell to her knees and began vomiting, yellow foam coming out of her mouth and ears. It might be a white spell, but it was still nasty.

"Oliver, stop throwing that shit!" Brooke shouted, and I looked up. The thought to call Al for help pinged through me and vanished. If I did, not only would I owe Al, but they'd be right in calling me a black witch. I was on my own. And not doing too badly.

Breathless, I ran at the middle-aged man holding a ley-line charm, grabbing his wrist and spinning around to stand facing his back and jam his own charm into his side. With a groan, he went down, taken by his own spell. I eased him to the floor, narrowly escaping being hit by that foaming-ball-of-vomit spell again.

"Oliver," Brooke shouted. "Knock it off! I want her conscious, not puking on my floor!"

Ignoring Brooke, Oliver pulled his arm back. My eyes widened, and I dove for the nearest circle. "*Rhombus!*" I shouted in relief as I skidded into it, and a gold-and-black sheet of ever-after flowed up. I didn't expect it to last long, seeing that I was using that awful, fractured ley line, but at least I had breathing space. I was safe in my bubble.

"You're like a cockroach, you know?" came a soft voice behind me.

Or not. Still sitting on the floor, I turned to see a pair of sensible black shoes in here with me. Swallowing, I followed the gray nylons up to find Brooke with her hand on a hip and a speculative look on her face. "I'm not a black witch . . . ," I whispered.

She reached for me, but I couldn't get my foot up in time, and instead of the expected grasping hand, she shifted at the last moment and fell right on me, her elbow hitting my middle. My head hit the floor, and I might have blacked out for an instant as I struggled to breathe. I tried to shove her away, but she'd filled my mouth with something that tasted like propellant.

"Turn over," she said, and arms made strong from battling waves manhandled me onto my stomach. There must have been something in that handkerchief, because I couldn't resist. My arms jerked up behind me, and I froze, tears starting from the pain. *Please don't dislocate them, please,* I thought, going passive in her grip.

With a satisfied harrumph, she slipped a ring of charmed silver around my wrist and zipped it tight. I groaned when the ever-after washed out of me. It hurt like an old ache, even if the line was nasty, and I tried to breathe through my nose. My circle fell, but I didn't think Oliver was going to hit me with his flaming ball of puking death. Not with Brooke sitting on me.

"My God," Oliver whispered over the sound of the witch retching in the corner. "Did you feel what came out of her? She could have leveled the house!"

I wheezed when Brooke got up off me, and Oliver's sensible shoes scuffed into view. "Her aura is blacker than any I've ever seen," he added scornfully, and I grunted when Brooke's foot wedged under my ribs, and she rolled me over. Three faces peered down at me, Brooke, Oliver, and the youngest, gawky guy, again conscious and holding his head. A faint sparkling sifted from the high windows, and I closed my eyes. Jax. Nick knew what had happened here and done nothing to help. *Same old Nick.*

"Oliver, get Amanda unspelled, will you?" Brooke said as she held her wrist. "And check on Wyatt while you're at it. I don't know why you use your ley-line skills. You're not good with them."

"Because you *insisted* on doing this too close to the ocean for my charms to work," he snarled.

"What does it matter? We've got her."

Interesting, I thought as I finally got that wad out of my mouth.

"Barely," Oliver said, and Brooke arched her eyebrows and nudged me in the ribs. "I didn't like this, and I still don't," he added. "We could have gotten a demon instead."

"Don't be silly, she's not a demon. She's just a witch," Brooke said. "A stupid one at that, who thinks she is in control and clearly isn't. Besides, it's not illegal to summon demons."

"It should be." Oliver was still breathing hard from the exertion, and starting to sweat.

"I think the media made her out to be more than she is." Brooke peered at me like I was a bug. "She didn't do one spell. She had the opportunity and the motive."

"It was a demon name that wizard used to summon her," Oliver protested, examining the eyes of the witch I'd knocked out before then clapping him on the back in support.

"We only have his say-so that it was a demon name," Brooke said. "He could have lied, trying to pay us off with a wooden coin painted gold."

From out of my sight, Amanda rasped between her gagging, "Oliver. Some help, please?"

Expression thoughtful, Oliver and the gawky witch went to take care of Amanda and Wyatt, leaving only Brooke. I glared at her, grunting when she nudged me with her toe.

"A witch couldn't have broken a coven circle, phone or not," she whispered, looking almost hungry. "No, you're something special, Rachel."

"I'm going to take my something special and shove it up your ass," I muttered, helpless.

Lips pressed, Brooke flipped me over. I immediately turned back, but she had taken my phone from my back pocket, and I stiffened when I heard Ivy, telling me she was going to kill me if I didn't answer her. Brooke smirked at my glare and closed the top, breaking the connection before tucking it in her pocket. The sound of chanting drifted to me, and finally Amanda stopped retching.

Brooke leaned close under the pretense of pulling me to a seated position. "Why didn't you call your demon? You know how. I can see the smut on you."

I lifted my chin. "I'm not a black witch," I said, but a sharp tug on my arm cut my argument short. "Ow! Watch it, will you?" I was sitting upright as the others came back and ringed me in a justice that went all the way back to our beginnings. No one would know. And in time, no one would care.

"Rachel Morgan," Brooke intoned, and I knew this was it. "You hereby have the choice of becoming magically neutered and rendered incapable of bearing children—or permanent imprisonment in Alcatraz."

I stared at them, appalled. "You are bullies. All of you," I said, then yelped when Wyatt shoved me over. My breath whooshed out, and I flipped the hair from my eyes, glaring at them.

"Alcatraz it is," Brooke said, pleased.

Six

The heat was on against the damp chill in the low-ceilinged room where we ate, but I still felt cold. It was noon according to the clock past the gates that separated us from the kitchen, but it was three by my internal clock, and I was hungry. The scrambled eggs in front of me were not going to pass my tongue, however. They looked good enough, but the sulfur in them would give me a migraine. It smelled funny in here, sort of a mix of dead fish and decayed redwood.

Depressed, I picked at a piece of toast, thinking the butter tasted off. *Not enough salt?* I wondered, dropping it. I almost wiped my hands on my spiffy-keen, orange jumpsuit, but stopped at the last moment. Not knowing when I'd get a new one, I licked my fingers instead. Across from me was my upstairs neighbor, a sallow-looking witch who had ignored me so far as he dipped his toast into his coffee before eating it. To my left was Mary. I'd met her earlier by way of conversation around the wall between us, and my first sight of her had been a shock; the woman was so thin she looked ill. To my right was a middle-aged guy who never spoke. Most everyone was talking. Alcatraz wasn't a big place, and it was kind of . . . homey. Maybe it was because we were on an island with no ley lines, surrounded by salt water. There simply was no escape.

Unhappy, I pushed my tray away and sat with my plastic coffee mug. I'd been here since the midnight boat brought me over with a load of canned goods, handcuffed to a pole in the middle of the boat. Since then, I'd showered in salt water in a big empty room—as if being on an island surrounded by salt water wouldn't take care of earth charms on its own—reshowered in freshwater, been poked, prodded, gossiped over, and given a new band of charmed silver with my name on it. It had been a relief to finally get to my cell, where I fell into an exhausted sleep hours before everyone else. I felt like a dog at the pound. And like a dog, I worried that my owner wouldn't come pick me up. I hoped it was Ceri who summoned me out of here, not Al. I couldn't call Al for help while I wore charmed silver, but he could summon me. I had to believe that I'd be summoned by someone, eventually.

At least I'd gotten the cremation ashes off me, I thought as Mary jostled my elbow, and I blinked when her smile showed she was missing a tooth.

"You heard about the food then?" she said, glancing at my tray, pushed to the middle.

"What do you mean?" I took a sip of coffee.

"They drug it," she said, and the guy across from us shrugged, continuing to tuck in.

I didn't swallow, my mouth full of coffee as my gaze went between them, wondering if it was truth or prison razzing. The big guy across from me seemed to be enjoying his breakfast, but Mary looked like she hadn't eaten in years.

"It is!" she said, eyes wide in her thin face. "They put in an amino acid that binds to the receptors in your brain to chemically strip you of your ability to do magic if you eat enough."

I spit the coffee out, and the guy across the table guffawed as he chewed. Feeling ill, I set the coffee aside, and Mary nodded, adding enthusiastically, "Your sentence is based on how much of your ability they want to take away. I've got thirty years left."

The witch across from me finished his eggs and eyed mine. "You'd get early parole and be out of here by spring if you'd eat," he said.

Mary cackled at that, and I glanced at the guards, busy not caring. "So how long are you in for, Rachel?" she asked, eyes on the demon scar on my wrist. She obviously knew what it was.

"Life," I whispered, and Mary cringed.

"Sorry. I guess you should eat, then. I got sixty years for killing my neighbor," she said proudly. "His damned dog kept peeing on my monkshood."

"Monkshood Mary . . . ," I said, recollection raising my eyebrows. "You're Monkshood Mary? Hey! I read about you in school!"

She beamed, extending her hand. "Hey, Charles, see? I'm still famous. Glad to make your acquaintance," she said as if having rehearsed it a thousand times, and I took her bird-light hand, feeling like it might break in my grip.

"I'm Charles," the man across from me said, and his hand engulfed mine. "That there is Ralph," he added, nodding to the silent man on my right. "He doesn't talk much. Been kinda down since the cell next to him went empty last year."

"Oh. Sorry." I glanced at him. "Someone got out, huh?"

Mary picked at her crust, skirting where the butter was. "Tried. If they catch you alive, they neuter your magic the old-fashioned way. Ralph, show Sunshine your scar."

Sunshine? I thought, not happy about the nickname, but Ralph put down his fork and pulled the hair up from his forehead. "Oh my God," I whispered, and he let his hair fall, turning back to his meal and carefully manipulating the fork . . . concentrating on it. Slowly, very slowly. They had lobotomized him.

"Tha-that's inhuman," I stammered.

Charles stoically met my horrified gaze. "We're not human."

Silence fell, and I felt cold. I had to get out of here. Like now! Why hadn't anyone summoned me home yet? Ivy said she was okay, but what if Jenks really was hurt and she'd been lying so I wouldn't worry?

I was so lost in my thoughts that I jumped when I realized someone was standing behind me. I turned, coming eye to middle with one of the biggest women I'd ever seen. She wasn't fat, she was big. Big boned, big chested, big ankles, and big hands. Her pudgy face made her eyes look small, but they glinted with intelligence.

"Hey, Mary," she said with a southern accent. It wasn't the elegant sound of a southern belle, but the ugly twang of trailer trash on the edge of the woods with a trampoline out front and stacks of *TV Guides* by the door. Her fat-lost eyes stared at me as she casually took Mary's tray, holding it over the smaller woman's head while she shoveled her breakfast into her mouth.

"Lenore, this is Rachel," Mary said, her tone shifting to a respectful fearfulness. It pegged my bully meter, and my face warmed. "Rachel has Mark's old cell," Mary finished.

Lenore's eyes narrowed. "You don't need dis, honey," she said, setting Mary's tray down and taking up mine. "Yer figure's jest fine. Let Auntie Lenore take care of yo-o-o-ou."

Just how many syllables are in "you"? I thought dryly. I wasn't going to eat it, but I wasn't going to let Auntie Lenore think she could walk over me either. Trouble was, it was kind of tight at the table, and she held the tray right over me.

I took an angry breath. Mary shook her head, scared. The posted guards weren't watching. They were careful not to, by my estimation. Fine. "Charles, make a hole," I said, and the man casually made a little hop with his hip. Three people protested as he shoved them down, but his bulk made the move fast and easy.

I ducked under the table and slid all the way to the other side, popping up beside him and stepping up onto the bench seat. Standing taller than Lenore, I jerked my tray away. Or at least I tried. The woman had a grip on it as if it was a ticket out of here.

The surrounding conversation died, and all eyes turned to us. Lenore was staring at me as we both held my tray. "You think you can take me, skinny ass?" she said, eager for a fight, and I sighed. Why hadn't Ivy summoned me out *before* I had to fight someone?

"What I think is, you'd better let go of my tray before I jam it down your shirt," I said. "Anyone ever tell you that you look like an orange in that jumpsuit? Auntie Lenore? More like Auntie Clementine." Hey, if I was going to fight this woman, I was going to do it right.

"You skinny bitch!" she shouted, and people moved. Except for the guards watching us.

"Rachel, no!" Mary said as she scrambled up. "Stop or they'll gas us!"

Not as long as the guards were in here laughing. Lenore made a fist with her free hand. The fork was in it, placed to gouge. She yanked me across the table. I let go before she could pull me into her and dropped, sitting on the table. Bracing myself, I kicked out with both feet, hoping to hit her solar plexus hard enough to wind her. It could be over in ten seconds.

My feet slammed into her. Lenore didn't move, and the shock reverberated all the way back to my spine. My jaw unclenched, and I slowly sent my eyes up to see her smiling at me. My God, the woman was built like a tank. Lenore smirked, then slammed the tray onto my head.

It hit hard, and my vision spun. "You got yerself a sparkly," she said, grabbing my wrist. Suddenly I found myself careening down the table as she walked, me sliding into everyone's trays until I fell off the end in a crash of tin and plastic.

"Ow!" I yelped as I hit, sprawled on the floor.

"Pretty sparkly," she said sarcastically, and I slipped in coffee and eggs as I tried to get up, helpless in the woman's grip. "Dey only make demon summoners wear dees," she said, wedging a thick finger between me and the charmed silver. "You summon demons?"

"No," I panted. "But I'm a liar, too."

"Then you don't need it none," she said, trying to pull it off me.

"Hey! Stop!" I yelled, but the guards only laughed. I was covered in egg and coffee, and half the table was angry with me for dragging their breakfast onto the floor. "Ow!" I shrieked as real pain stabbed through my wrist. "Let go!"

"Gimme yer bracelet," Lenore said, squeezing my hand. "Give it."

She didn't want my bracelet. She wanted to freaking break my hand.

I pulled back and gave her a side kick, but it was like kicking a tree, the woman was so big. She took it, then swung a thick fist at me. I ducked and people cheered.

"I said let go!" I shouted, throwing coffee in her face.

Lenore bellowed as her grip loosened, and I pulled away. Arms outstretched, she came at me. I ducked, scampering out from under her and slipping on eggs. I couldn't let this woman get a bear hug on me—she'd snap my spine.

Still howling, she turned to follow, moving remarkably fast. I hadn't wanted to hurt her, but I didn't have much choice anymore. Jumping onto the table, I fell into a fighting stance.

Lenore hesitated, her eyes flicking behind me. Taking a step back, she passively raised her hands, but it wasn't because of me. Too late, I turned.

Pain exploded at the back of my knees, so hard and fast that I couldn't breathe. I went down face-first. Tears blurred my vision, and I curled into the fetal position, trying to hold my knees. Someone had hit me from behind. *Oh God, I'd never walk again.*

"I's kill her! I's fucking kill her!" Lenore was screaming, and I looked past my stringy hair to see her being led away by two guards, submission holds on her with the help of a couple of sticks. Sure, big talker now that she couldn't do anything.

"Get up, Sunshine," someone said sarcastically, and I groaned when they pulled me up and dragged me between them. I couldn't straighten my legs. They hurt like hell. Apart from our table, the rest of the room was orderly. Noisy, yes, but no one was getting off their benches.

Mary held her narrow body with her skinny arms, scared. Charles wouldn't look up. But it was Ralph's expression that scared me. Terror was in his eyes, terror he couldn't express but was reliving. *Not the medical wing. God, please. Not the medical wing.*

"New girl making friends?" one of the guards said, letting go and shoving me into the wall before he jerked my arms behind me. "What is it they say about redheads?"

"The medical wing?" the other said, hesitating by a stairway going down. There was a cold draft coming up, stinking of fear and infection.

God, no. They could do it, and it would be over. My life done. I'd be like Ralph, and all the magic in the world wouldn't be able to fix me.

I gathered myself to fight again, my relief almost making me cry when the first replied, "No. She's got someone from the mainland coming over, and they want her to be able to talk."

My relief was short lived. They want me to be able to talk? I wasn't getting a lobotomy because it might inconvenience someone?

The sound of links of steel ratcheting closed around my wrists was loud. I wanted to fight, but I could hardly move, and fear hit anew when they dragged me past my cell to another part of the prison. My heart pounded, and I struggled to get up, to do something! Being hurt and cuffed wasn't nearly as terrifying as the realization that these people could do anything—cut me up like they had Ralph—and no one would think twice, much less care.

The noise from the dining hall grew fainter, and it was just me and my jailers, dragging me backward over the concrete floor past a series of close-set metal doors. They faced a solid stone wall, and beyond that, the unseen ocean. My heart pounded, and adrenaline got me to my feet when they stopped so one guard could open a cell door. It took two of them to do it, one at the cell with me, and one at a remote panel. The sound of the creaking door chilled me, and I gritted my teeth against the pain in my knees when they started to buckle with my own weight.

"Enjoy the hole," the guard said, and he shoved me past an outer metal door and a second, standard barred door into a lightless five-by-nine box. I fell, vision graying from the pain in my knees. The barred door shut before I could even pull my face up. The second door slammed behind it a moment later, cutting off the light after I saw the toilet, sink, and nothing else.

They didn't even laugh at me as their voices became faint, I was so beneath their consideration. Slowly I got my legs untangled, the motion difficult because my arms were still cuffed behind me. Feeling sick, I scooted back until I found the wall. It was metal, too, and cold. The soft sounds of my breathing became loud. Someone nearby was crying, but it wasn't me.

It would *never* be me.

Seven

The metal floor and walls were cold, but I had quit shivering hours ago, numb to it now. The backs of my knees were swollen, and I couldn't bend them. They ached, throbbing with a pain that refused to abate and that I just learned to live with. The solid outer door had remained closed, and it was close to pitch-dark. I couldn't see the walls, but I had traced their outlines to find the toilet—hard to use with my hands still cuffed—and the sink. Now I sat with my back in a corner beside the door, my legs outstretched on the cold metal floor to try to get the swelling down. Getting my cuffed hands in front of me had been torture.

I had missed lunch, by the faint scent of lasagna that had come and gone. My dinner had been salad. I hadn't eaten it, and it sat beside the interior door where the woman had left it. The vinegary dressing was probably full of magic-demoting goodness.

A scrape of nail on metal brought my heart into my throat, and I strained to see. *Rat?* I thought. I wasn't scared of them, much, but I couldn't see a damned thing. Wincing, I tried to bring my knees closer. The new scent of iron and stone tickled a memory, and hope brought me stiff. "Bis?" I whispered.

A soft thump shocked through me, and adrenaline pulsed when a pair of softly glowing eyes turned to me, hovering about a foot above the floor. "Ms. Rachel," the adolescent gargoyle whispered, his nails scraping as he came closer. "I knew I could find you!"

"What are you doing here?" I asked, relief spilling through me. I reached out to touch him, and the instant my cold fingertips made contact, the unfamiliar pattern of the shattered West Coast ley lines burst into my thoughts. I jerked back, shocked. Damn it, I really needed to touch someone, but Bis would send me into overload.

"Sorry," he said, his big supple ears drooping like a puppy's in the faint light from his eyes. His usually pricked ears were edged in white fur, as was the lionlike tuft on his thin, hairless tail. His leathery wings rustled as he settled them, and his craggy features looked young despite the crevices and pebbly gray appearance.

"How did you get here?" I whispered. "Is Ivy with you? Did she fly out?"

"It's just me and Pierce," he said proudly. "We jumped. All the way from your kitchen."

"Pierce!" I exclaimed, then winced. Any louder, and a guard might hear. "Did he escape from Al?" Oh God, I'd get blamed for that—even if I was in prison.

Bis's flat, black teeth glinted faintly. "No. After you almost died from that soul charm, the demons made him send someone to watch you. Pierce was willing, able, and cheap."

"You're kidding!" I almost hissed, but I wondered if part of the reason Al had gone along with it was because he was worried Pierce might find him sleeping one night and kill him. I'd thought those silver bands were impossible to thwart. If it had shocked me, it had shaken Al.

"Ivy is mad," Bis said, his words spilling out, sounding like falling scree. "She thinks you lied to her about how bad you were hurt. Pierce taught me how to jump here. I swam from the mainland, but it's too cold for Pierce. No one saw me. I didn't know I could ride the lines. It was cool, Ms. Rachel! First I'm in your kitchen, and then bam! San Francisco! Just that fast. The lines taste funny, here, though." He finally ran out of words, his red eyes glowing faintly.

"Pierce didn't know I was in trouble until you told him?" I insisted, not believing that Al had just let him go. And I *really* didn't like the demons sending me a babysitter. I could take care of myself. Most days. Today I could use some help though.

The small gargoyle shifted, his wings brushing my ankles to send a burst of awareness through me. "Not a clue. He's really upset. He didn't even know which line to jump to until I told him which line you came in on. That's why he showed me how to jump. Ivy said it was okay. All I had to do was listen to the ley lines. You left your aura all over the place. Following you was freakier than a boy soprano's voice changing in the middle of 'Ave Maria,' especially when the line we came out of was all broken and stuff, but it was easy! No one told *me* gargoyles could jump the lines. Even my dad doesn't know, and he's old!"

Gargoyles can jump the lines? Well, they could slide right through a protection circle, and it made Al's comment last winter about my "having my gargoyle" all the more intriguing. But why didn't gargoyles know they could? Demon censorship? Sounded about right.

"Pierce knew exactly where they had taken you when we popped out of that line," Bis said, inching closer, his glowing eyes pinched in worry. "Are you okay?"

I wasn't, but I forced a smile. "I'm much better now," I whispered. "You did good. I'm really happy to see you. Can you get back on your own?"

He shook his head, his thick canines making him look terribly fierce as he frowned. "I promised Pierce I wouldn't jump without him. He says I'm not good enough."

I smiled, thoroughly understanding how it rankled to be told you weren't good enough. In this case, though, I was all for a little adult supervision. How Pierce knew the coven would put me here sort of bothered me. True, he'd been a member of the coven of moral and ethical standards himself—before they bricked him into the ground, alive—but Alcatraz hadn't been a prison when he'd been living.

"Bis," I said, wincing when my knees bent. "Can you show me what Pierce showed you? Maybe we can get home together."

The pair of glowing eyes slowly shifted. "Not really. I don't have the words, Ms. Rachel. Pierce said people have to learn from an experienced gargoyle, not a, uh, novice. He can't jump you either. But it's okay," he rushed on when my brow furrowed. "Ivy has someone to bring you home right before the lines close to summoning in Cincinnati."

My knees throbbed, and his eyes shifted from orange to their usual dull red. Even the hard metal floor didn't feel so cold. I was going home. *Before* they lobotomized me.

Mistaking my relief for despair, Bis edged closer, almost putting a claw on my leg. "Pierce would come rescue you himself, Ms. Rachel, but the water is too cold. No one saw me swim over. It used to be an old fort, and I only needed a little crack to get in."

He was trying to cheer me up, and I nodded, not knowing what to do with my hands and aware of the cuffs for the first time in hours. Bis could slip through the smallest opening, like an octopus. It had driven Jenks crazy until one night the fun-loving teen showed him how he did it.

"I didn't know you could swim," I said softly, running a finger between me and the steel around my wrist. "The ward around the island didn't stop you?"

"It's just a modified ley line," the young gargoyle said loftily. "It can't keep me out."

"Is Ivy okay? And Jenks?" I hung on his words, starved for the memory of comfort and companionship, and I watched his eyes shift when he nodded.

"Jenks's wing is bent, but he's okay. He can still fly and stuff. They want to wait to summon you home until the sun almost rises in Cincy so the council can't summon you back again. That's what I came to tell you. Pierce is worried. He says not to eat the food."

He knew about the food? I mused, disturbed. "Nick summoned me here," I said bitterly.

"Nick?" The young gargoyle rocked back. "You're sure?"

"Yes," I answered sourly. "He walked right after, but if they throw enough money at him, he'll probably do it again." Bis had heard of Nick by way of Jenks bad-mouthing him, but obviously had never met him. "I have to talk to Al when I get home," I said, probing my knees to see how bad they were, and the dull throb turned into a stabbing pain. "I don't need Pierce babysitting me. That's what Jenks and Ivy are for."

"That's what Ivy thinks, too," Bis said softly, his eyes darting, making me think she'd said so in no uncertain words. Loud ones, probably.

I'd tried to make Al take his summoning name back before, but part of the deal was that he'd remove one of my demon marks, something he didn't want to do. I hadn't pressed the issue since Al couldn't abduct anyone if he couldn't be summoned. That the situation could be used against me had never crossed my mind. I shivered, the backs of my swollen knees pressed against the icy floor. I'd been pulled around like a toy. No wonder demons showed up pissed.

"You're cold," Bis said, as if only now realizing it. The kid could, and did, sleep in the snow.

"Mmmm-hmm." My misery was temporary. I could endure it.

"I can help," he said, and a dull red warmth blossomed in the dark, lighting my cell with a weird shadow glow as his skin turned pink. He was glowing like an overheated rock, his gray, pebbly skin taking on a luminescent sheen. Bis's big tufted ears were back like a scolded puppy's, and his pushed-in, ugly face was pinched in worry. His tail, too, was wrapped around his oversize feet to make himself as small as he could. "Bis, you are a wonder!" I said, holding my hands out until I pulled them back from the sudden heat. My shins, too, were getting warm.

The teenage gargoyle blushed, sending out a wash of heat, but then his big ears pricked and swiveled, his eyes following a second later. The sound of a buzzing alarm came faintly, followed by a key in my outer door's lock. *Shit.* Was it time for my interrogation already?

"Hide," I said, and he immediately dampened the heat and the light with it. "Don't do anything unless they try to take me to the hospital wing. They might give me a lobotomy."

"I won't let them" came his voice from the dark ceiling, and the faintest scratch of nail on metal sounded. The memory of him was a glow on the back of my eyelids, fading when the first door creaked open and harsh electric light made a long rectangle, shining on my untouched salad and my swollen knees.

I blinked, trying to move as a guard opened the inner door and stepped back. I couldn't get up the normal way because of my knees. Above me, Bis clung to the ceiling like a cat-size bat, my protector in case things went from bad to worse. My pulse hammered, and using my hands and the corner, I managed to wedge myself to my feet with my shaking arms. I would not go to the prison hospital. I'd die fighting first.

A shadow eclipsed the electric lights. The scent of roast pork slipped in, and my stomach growled. "I'm not going in there," came Brooke's voice, sour and slightly supercilious, and the light returned to the floor. *Brooke? Brooke wanted to talk to me?*

My chest hurt. It wasn't the medical people, at least. Maybe the dissension I'd seen in the coven chamber was deeper than I thought. A three A.M. meeting couldn't be sanctioned. She was here on her own.

"I'm not going in there," Brooke said, louder this time when a guard protested. "Bring her out. I'll talk to her in that excuse of a library you have."

There was a moment of muted conversation, then a masculine, "She *is* your boss's boss, you cretin! Get her out!" echoed dully.

A flashlight panned over me. "Out," someone ordered, and I shuffled into the light, feeling very . . . orange. The dried coffee on my jumpsuit looked like old blood, and I lifted my chin when Brooke looked me up and down, lingering on my swollen, cuffed wrists. The sprig of heather in her Möbius-strip pin had wilted, and I felt a pinch of worry when I noticed the same shape embroidered on all the guards' collars. Jeez, they had their own prison?

"Can you walk, Rachel?" she asked.

"It's Ms. Morgan, if you don't mind," I said, leaning against the wall. My stomach hurt and I was almost dizzy from the pain in my knees.

"The inmates aren't allowed in the library, Madam Coven Leader," one of the guards protested weakly, and she spun, giving him a nasty look.

"I'm *not* going to sit on your ugly little chairs and talk to her through plastic. The woman is cuffed. She is wearing charmed silver. She isn't going to hit me or take me hostage. She can hardly stand up, thanks to you. Rachel, this way."

"I told you, it's Ms. Morgan." Head down and my lank hair falling into my eyes, I shuffled after her. Crap, I could hardly move, and a sudden nausea made me glad I hadn't eaten. It would have been nice if someone had offered me a pain amulet, but we were surrounded by salt water. Besides, it would ruin the beating they'd given me.

The guards were not happy, but one jumped to open doors and clear the way. I looked back at my cell to see if Bis was still in there. Someone had tacked SUNSHINE over the door. Ha, ha. "What time is it?" I asked Brooke as she waited for me to catch up. I felt as if I was a hundred and sixty years old, but the hope that I'd shortly be in Ivy's black tub full of hot water kept me moving.

The woman's low heels clicked as I followed her into the main building. "A little after three," she said, sniffing. "God, it stinks like bad sushi in here."

Most of the inmates we passed were either in bed or sitting on top of their covers waiting for lights out. A whisper went out like a wave among them as they saw us. If it was after three here, then it was after six at home. Take into account the difference in latitude, and the sun was indeed about to rise in Cincy. A quiver of anticipation shot through me, and I walked a little straighter. The lines in Cincy were about to close to summoning, though if you knew how, you could still jump them no matter what time of day it was.

A quick look up assured me Bis was still with me. He was crawling on the ceiling, and I could see him only when he went over a metal bar, his skin not adapting quite fast enough. When he was older, even that wouldn't show. He was a good kid.

The whispers grew to soft voices as word traveled from block to block. Alcatraz was kind of like a one-room schoolhouse. If something happened, everyone knew it in three minutes. I walked slowly to hide my pain, forcing my shoulders back and my head high as we entered the library, enclosed with a ceiling-to-floor fence. There was an oblong coffee table with several cast-off chairs around it in a cruel mimicry of a bookstore lounge. As luck would have it, I could see my empty cell, Mary, Charles, and Ralph. Mary looked shocked, her soulful eyes wide as she sat on her bed with her blanket pulled to her chin.

"This looks . . . comfortable," Brooke said dryly as she took off her coat, hesitating briefly before gingerly draping it over the grimy chair and sitting on it.

I looked at my equally dirty chair, knowing I wouldn't be able to get out of it once I was down. The promise of a soft cushion was irresistible, though, and I almost fell trying to sit without bending my knees. The jolt was enough to bring my eyes shut for an instant, and I gasped, taking in the scent of musty fabric and discarded books left to the elements.

"How pleasant," I said so she wouldn't see Bis crawl past the windows. "What do you want, Brooke?" I said, tired. If it was three here, it was six at home, and way past my bedtime.

She shifted, steepling her fingers and eying me from behind them. "They told me you didn't eat. Good. Don't eat anything unless it comes from me."

I uncrossed my arms from around my middle. "You know about the food?"

The woman smiled, showing me perfect teeth. "Isolating that amino acid is expensive, but we've been using it for centuries. It has an excellent success rate."

I thought of Mary starving herself for another thirty years, and I unclenched my jaw.

"Not everyone thinks you should be castrated," she said as she adjusted her skirt over her ugly knees. "Magically or otherwise. I'm your friend, Rachel. You should trust me."

Oh. Yeah. That's a good idea. I looked at the ceiling, not seeing Bis, then back to her. Damn Trent back to the Turn. This was his fault. Didn't tell them, my ass.

"I alone believe that you don't need such harsh treatment," she continued. "If you can invoke demon magic, you are—"

"A tool?" I interrupted. "A weapon? Have you ever fought a demon, Brooke? You were stupid to have risked it trying to catch me. The only reason I keep surviving demons is because they want me for other things."

I shut up, not wanting to hurt my case any more than I probably just had, but Brooke was smiling her West Coast smile. "I'm trying to help you, Rachel."

"Ms. Morgan, please." I flicked a bit of dried egg off myself, almost hitting her.

"Mor-r-r-rgan," Brooke drawled, bringing my attention back. "I don't want you to become the property of a fucking elf in your efforts to survive."

Ohhh, potty mouth! I thought, smirking. "No, you'd rather see me become *your* property. The coven's secret weapon. No thanks."

The woman's tan darkened as she flushed in anger. "He can't protect you from us. Never. You think you're something special for surviving an I.S. death threat? Where do you think they get their charms from? The ones we don't keep for ourselves? We get what we want, Rachel. *Always.*"

I stifled a shiver as I recalled Vivian's charms, technically white but with devastating results, all invoked without fear of repercussion, and then Pierce, one of their own buried alive because he'd stood up to them and said that even white charms weren't enough. A fear born out of self-preservation slipped through my anger.

"Sign this," Brooke said, confident as she brought an envelope from her purse and set it on the table between us. "It gives us permission to remove your ability to reproduce and chemically take away your ability to do ley-line magic."

Somehow I managed a snort of amusement I didn't feel. "As opposed to you doing so behind prison doors and with saturated fats?"

She hesitated, and then as if having made a decision, she leaned close enough for me to smell the linen her suit was cut from, clean and light. Her eyes were bright, almost feverish, and a chill spilled through me. This didn't look good.

"I don't mind your being able to invoke demon magic," she whispered, scaring me. "I don't care that you are the beginning of demons on earth. I *do* have a problem with most of the coven unable to see past their shortsighted noses, so entrenched in old fear that they can't see what you are. They would vote against me, and the majority rules, even if the majority is blind."

My mouth went dry. "And what am I?"

"You are what we all should be!" she exclaimed, then lowered her voice as she leaned back. "The power you have? We're stunted. Half of what we could be. We can be whole, and you're the way. You are the future. I can protect you. Sign that paper, and I promise you'll come out of the anesthesia completely yourself, with your magic intact. This is a sham to get you off the coven's radar and away from Trent Kalamack."

Whoa. Schism? Try the freaking Grand Canyon. "So I'd be your personal monster, not the coven's?" I said, more than a little afraid. "I don't deal with demons."

"You do," Brooke insisted, and the soft murmur from the cells ceased. "It's on the record. You survive every time. The power you can give back to us—"

"I meant," I said, disgusted, "I won't deal with you, and I'm not signing that paper."

Brooke's expression soured. "You're being foolish. If you can't see the future, then at least look at your present. You want to go back to that hole? Fine. Or you can be moved into the warden's apartments. Low security, real food. A view." Her gaze went to the inmates watching. "Privacy. Sign the paper. You have my word you will remain as you are now."

I looked at the paper on the table between us. *Remain as I was? Cold, miserable, and a continent away from home?* "Let's just say I took a stupid pill this morning, and I sign your paper. What will I be? Soldier? Broodmare?"

The woman smiled. "Motherhood is a noble profession."

My chin went up, and I nodded. "I never said it wasn't, but anything that comes from me will be baby-snatched by demons, Brooke sweetie."

"Way ahead of you," she said, the pen she took from her purse clicking onto the table. "You will become an egg donor," the woman said, unable to hide her eager look. "The demons would never know. You could even adopt one of your own kids. I'm going to."

She wanted one of my unborn children? Parcel my progeny out to the highest bidder? "You are disgusting," I said, but all I got from her was a bemused expression. She took a breath, and I raised my cuffed hands to stop her next words. "What time is it?" I asked, and her expression became annoyed.

"Three fifteen," she said, wiry arm shifting so she could glance at her watch.

Sighing, I sank back into the rank cushions. *Almost time.* "Brooke, I'm already gone. The only reason I tried to get away from you boneheads earlier was because I wanted a couple of hours to see the sights before I headed home. Crooked Street maybe. Or Treasure Island. That sweet little bridge you're all so fond of. I can't say I like the Alcatraz tour, though. It's a little too realistic."

Brooke snorted to show her disbelief. "We are surrounded by salt water. There are no ley lines on the island. A very expensive ward keeps witches from jumping in for a rescue. Even if you could tap a line through a familiar, which I know you don't have, you wear charmed silver."

"This?" I held up my hands to show the link on my pulped wrist. It had my name on it, and a freaking serial number. "This is really pretty," I said, dropping my arm. "But, Brooke, sweetheart, you can't hold me." *Any time, Ivy.*

"I think we can." Confidence showed as she leaned back in the tatty chair.

I shook my head, smiling. "No, you can't. It's almost sunrise in Cincinnati. You know what happens when the sun rises? The lines close to summoning traffic. Oh, you can still get around with them, but a summons won't work. And you know what's going to happen just before then?" Brooke's expression was empty, but then she got it.

"You can't jump by line," she said, voice loud. "You're cut off."

I leaned forward, the beating, the humiliation, and the indignity of being locked in a metal closet all day falling from me to leave only a bitter satisfaction. "I'm not a demon," I said softly. "But I'm in their system."

A sneeze shook me, and a quiver grew in my middle. I was going home. "You should have come to talk to me," I said, wishing I could cross my knees and look smug. "I really am a nice person most times, but you just pissed me off."

I sneezed again, and a gut-cramping feeling rose, threatening worse. "I'm going home to take a hot bath and get some sleep. Tell you what," I said, gripping the arms of the chair—as if it could keep me here a moment longer—"I understand how easy it is to underestimate me. Let's start fresh. You can either instigate a war with me or come and talk. Your choice."

Eyes wide, Brooke stood, reaching across the table to grab me.

A gray blur dropped between us, hissing.

My heart beat once, hard, and I forced myself to remain seated when Bis spread his wings, tufts of fur puffed and tail switching like a cat's. One clawed foot gripped her unsigned contract, and his head was lowered, red eyes promising violence.

"Shit, it's a gargoyle!" Mary shouted, her words taken up and passed along. "Rachel has a gargoyle!"

"Security!" Brooke shouted as she stood. She was going to lose me, and she knew it.

My head spun when Bis spread his wings and hopped to my shoulder. The unfamiliar pattern of West Coast ley lines exploded in my thoughts, harsh and jagged, tasting of broken rock. Bis could feel them all the time, and when we touched, I felt them too. The young gargoyle wrapped his tail around my neck, and tears threatened. I was going home.

I wanted to stand, but I couldn't. The pull of the summons had become painful, so I made the vampire kiss-kiss gesture to Brooke as I relaxed my grip on reality and felt the lines pull me in. The smut for this, I would willingly take.

Damn, I had good friends.

Eight

There was no pain as my body dissolved into a thought and that thought was yanked across the continent. I wanted to go, and I'd already accepted the smut on my soul for the imbalance I was causing. Actually, by taking the smut on freely, the feeling of disconnection seemed to be muffled. Or perhaps if you break the rules too many times, you start to build up scar tissue. Or maybe it was because I'd slipped from the fractured West Coast lines to the solid, warm ley lines of my birthplace. It could have been simply that the memory of Bis and his tail wrapped around my neck helped to create a feeling of comfort. But whatever it was, the usual tearing apart of soul and mind almost felt good. Like stretching. Which kind of worried me.

The faint outlines of my kitchen echoed in my memory before they became real, and the woody scent of herbs and copper cleaner tickled my nose. It was more than a little relief—it would be just my luck that a third party summoned me and I ended up in someone else's circle dressed in this hideous orange outfit with *fashionable* white canvas pull-on shoes.

My will seemed to stretch forward and yank me into existence. With a jolt, everything happened at once, and my aura—which had been holding me together while I existed only as a thought in the ley lines—rose through the memory of myself to build a body. My clothes, bruises, cuffs, everything, down to the egg in my hair, would come through intact. You couldn't fool the demon archive and show up clean, rested, and in a pair of designer boots. I'd tried. The charmed silver, though, would be gone. Small favors.

I took a breath, and I suddenly had lungs. Stumbling, I stayed upright as I popped into existence between the center counter and the sink. The kitchen was dim with early sunlight, shocking since it was dark where I'd been seconds ago. Ivy and Jenks were waiting, worried and tense. Jenks was flying, and all I could see wrong with Ivy was a welt on her forehead.

Immediately the shimmer of smut-covered ever-after around me dropped. It was Ceri, then, who had summoned me. "Thank God," I said, leaning back against the center counter, my head bowed as I mumbled, "Thank you, Ceri. I owe you big." Bis wasn't here, swimming back to Pierce for the jump home, I guess.

Ivy's face was pale as she came close, taking in my tired, filthy state. "What did they do to you?" she said as she fumbled at her key chain for one of her handcuff keys. The steel rings came off, hitting the counter with a loud clatter, and I felt loved.

"Tink's little red panties, Rache," Jenks swore, pinching his nose shut as he hovered over them. "You reek like a fairy's outhouse! Ivy, get her a pain amulet, will you? And maybe one to make her not stink? Good God, how did you get so stinky? You were only gone a day!"

I smiled, glad to be home. But my expression froze when I turned to thank Ceri again. Ceri hadn't summoned me home. It was Nick.

"You putrid pile of troll crap!" I jumped for him, hands grasping. My knees gave way and I slipped, catching myself on the edge of the counter and gasping at the sudden pain. Jenks darted into the air, and Ivy reached for me, concerned.

Nick jumped to his feet. His face was tight and angry, but that was nothing next to my outrage, and I grunted when Ivy pulled me upright and I pushed her away.

"Rache, wait!" Jenks exclaimed, silver sparkles falling from him. "He's here so Jax can make peace with Matalina. He summoned you back. We couldn't find Keasley, and Trent won't let anything get through to Ceri!"

"Bull!" I pointed at Nick, standing sullenly beside the archway to the hall with his too-long hair and faded jeans. "He summoned me, then left me to fight my way out alone!"

Ivy's eyes flashed a full, dangerous black, and Jenks's wings hit an unusually high pitch.

"He did what?"

Nick backed into the hall, hands raised. A streak of pixy dust darting in turned into Jax. The renegade pixy had drawn the entire pixy clan with him, and I froze, stunned by the flitting silk and high-pitched voices as Matalina hovered over it all like a distressed angel.

"I didn't have a choice," Nick was saying over their noise. "Rachel, I owed them, thanks to you running off with the focus. I told you how to get out. And I flew back here to get you home! Will you listen to me? I'm trying to help!"

"Trying to help?" Ivy strode across the kitchen, pixies darting out of her way in swirls of color. Nick made a dash for the sanctuary, but she was faster. Like a cat after a bat, she snagged him, her hand gripping him under his throat as she threw him across the kitchen to slam into my mom's old fridge. He started to slip down, and she had him again, lifting him up and holding him there while he tried to make his lungs work. Atop the fridge, the Brimstone cookie jar wobbled and would have fallen off if not for the pixies working as a team to balance it.

"You summoned Rachel to San Francisco?" she said, showing her sharp canines. "She was driving. You could have killed us all!"

Jenks hovered beside his face, his son between his sword and the man's eye. "You were trying to help? Help yourself, maybe!"

God, I have good friends. Hurting, I staggered around the counter to the big farm table shoved against the interior wall, all but falling into my hard-backed chair and nearly knocking an express mail box onto the floor. It was from my mom, her scrawl unmistakable. I was too tired to guess what she'd sent me this time, and I gingerly felt the backs of my knees.

Nick's face was going red from a lack of circulation, and the notches in his ears gained in the rat fights stood out like bright flags. "Ivy, let him go before he files a lawsuit," I said casually. That she was slowly choking the life from him was only mildly worrisome. I'd seen her vamp out before, and this was nothing, even if she had missed slaking her hunger this weekend. If she started looking sexy and dropping innuendos, I'd be worried. This was simply anger, and she likely wouldn't tear his throat out for that.

"Why? He can't go to the I.S." Ivy leaned her face next to his, tilting her head and inhaling a line along his neck. A tingling rose through me, and Nick closed his eyes, shuddering. "He's taken himself off the grid," she whispered. "Made himself into a cookie by the side of the road. He can't complain or be jailed for his own crimes. And he wouldn't want that," she crooned. "Would you, little Nicky? Being a blood toy would be better than jail."

Okay, maybe I was wrong. Concerned, I levered myself to a stand. "Ivy—"

"Let her kill him," Jenks was saying over the sound of his kids. "We've got the graveyard right out back. Humans are like Jell-O. There's always room for one more."

"I didn't have to come here," Nick gasped, and Ivy tightened her grip until he gagged. "The coven didn't give me a choice! They yanked me across state lines and threatened to give me to the FIB. I had to tell them something. They were going to put me away!"

"Better me than you, huh?" I leaned heavily on the table, tired.

"I knew you'd escape," Nick said, spittle at the corners of his mouth. "You've got a foolproof get-out-of-jail-free card. Rachel, you took a demon's name? Why?"

My breath caught at the accusation in his rasping voice, and my anger dulled to shame. I had a demon's name. He'd used it twice to summon me. "Let him go."

Jenks spun in the air to me. "Rache . . ."

"Let him go!" I exclaimed, and Ivy took her fingers from around Nick's throat. The man fell into a tangle against the fridge, hand over his neck and coughing. Head down, he mumbled to Jax, hovering by his face, his words indistinct. The imprint of Ivy's fingers showed red and clear. Ivy turned away, shaking as she worked to bring herself down. Great. This was exactly what I needed. A jacked-up, hungry vampire and a traitorous ex-boyfriend in the same room.

Jenks wasn't happy, and with an earsplitting whistle, he chased his family out—all but a defiant Jax and a heartbroken Matalina, now perched on the fridge. Her face was riven with tears. Jax's homecoming had turned ugly.

Moving with that vampiric smoothness that gave me the willies, Ivy yanked my charm cupboard open and plucked an invoked amulet from my cache. Her eyes were still dangerously black as she strode across the kitchen and extended it. My shoulders eased as the smooth disk of redwood met my fingers. It was one of my own, and the relief from the pain was a blessing.

I'd been an earth witch long before I started dabbling in ley-line magic, and though the amulet didn't completely block the pain, it helped. Dropping the cord around my neck, I snugged the disk under the orange jumpsuit where it could touch my skin. A puff of nasty air came up and I winced. Jenks wasn't kidding. I needed a shower. "Thanks," I said, and Ivy nodded, still trying to gain control over her instincts. Me being stinky probably helped.

"I had to give them something," Nick said loudly as he pulled himself off the floor, his long pianist's—no, thief's—hands on his throat and his voice rough. "I'm sorry for summoning you to San Francisco, and I left so they wouldn't force me to do it again. I risked airport security to get here in time to summon you home, if that means anything to you."

"Yeah? You kept their money, I bet," I said bitingly, and his eyes narrowed.

"I have to eat." Shame, perhaps, made his voice harsh, but I doubted it. "Besides, I didn't think it would be you who showed up that first time. I thought it would be Al and that he would tear them and me apart. End everything."

His words hit me hard, and I looked away, sinking back down into my chair.

"You took Al's name? Rachel, why?" he asked, his voice holding an unexpected hurt. "I thought you were smarter than that. I thought you were the good one."

I couldn't look up, unable to speak. I was the good one. Wasn't I?

"Get him out of here," Jenks said loudly. "Both of them."

Jax's wings clattered, and Matalina protested, but a pop of displaced air in the hallway struck me like a slap. *Al?* I thought with a pulse of fear-based adrenaline as I looked. But it wasn't Al. It was Pierce and Bis. Duh. The sun was up.

The witch caught his balance, lurching to snag his hat as it fell off. "We're back!" Bis shouted, whirling, eyes wide as he landed beside Matalina on the fridge, making her crouch at the sudden wind. He was too big to fly in the house, and as soon as his feet touched the appliance, his wings folded and his eyes blinked shut, the teenage gargoyle going somnolent in the sudden light. As an adult, he'd be able to stay awake during the daylight hours, but as it was, he fell asleep in an instant. Probably just as well. The next few minutes were going to be ugly.

"Who the hell are you?" Nick rasped, ignored.

Sometime between my truncated lesson and now, Pierce had found a trendy pair of black pants and a maroon shirt. His new, colorfully patterned vest looked like it could be the upholstery of an antique chair, but somehow it worked. Everything fit him perfectly, right down to the gold fob running to a hidden pocket watch, and I wondered if the appearance-conscious demon had sent him like this or if Pierce had learned to dress himself.

Pierce watched me from under his wavy black bangs, trying to guess my mood as his shoes scuffed on a stray bit of salt. His eyes were fixed on mine, and I felt a ping of something, which I quickly squashed. I didn't have time for a relationship, and not with a self-oriented, black-magic-using, intelligent . . . demon killer wannabe who thought I needed babysitting.

"Rachel," Pierce said, shoes grinding on the salt as he came forward after a nod to Ivy and Jenks, and a flash of anger at Nick. His smoothly shaven face was creased with worry, and when he took my hands, I pulled away. *Had they really made Al send him to watch me?*

"Is she all together? Is she all right?" he asked Ivy, unsure at my reaction.

Ivy nodded, her eyes edging toward normal, standing with her arms across her middle as if holding back her instincts. "As much as she ever is," she said sourly.

"I'm of the mind that she's not." Pierce tried again for my hands, keeping them this time. "I've a powerful notion to fix their flint. Did they . . . Rachel, your wrists," he said, aghast as he turned them over. "They shackled you?" he asked, voice shaking in outrage.

I took a breath, but my harsh words hesitated. He'd crossed a continent to find me. Resolute, I shoved the feeling away. "Al sent you?" I asked, and he knelt to put us on eye level. "Pierce, tell me this is a joke and that Al is going to show up come sundown and drag you back."

Pierce smiled, gaze flicking to Ivy and Jenks. "Newt told the collective that Al nearly let you kill yourself, and that I kept you alive until she could save you."

"Newt?" Jenks shrilled, coming close. "You didn't say anything about Newt!"

"*You?*" I echoed, and Nick scowled. "You're the one who got me in trouble!"

Pierce, though, was still grinning. "The way she remembers it, I saved you. She made an almighty wrath, convincing them that you're too accident-prone to survive without supervision."

"I could have told them that," Jenks smart-mouthed, and Ivy waved at him to be quiet.

"Since Al can't abide here come sunup," Pierce continued, "it was either send me or give you to Newt."

"I thought you said you were the only familiar cheap enough that Al could afford," Jenks chimed in, and Pierce's lips twitched in the beginnings of a frown. Ivy, too, didn't look pleased.

"Nice," I said, yanking my hands from his. "You get yourself out of the ever-after, but I'm the one who looks like an idiot. Thanks a hell of a lot."

But instead of reacting in kind, Pierce's entire demeanor shifted to one of concern. "You're shivering," he said, glancing at Nick as if it was his fault. "A body would suspect *someone* would have drawn you a warm bath by now."

Suddenly I felt a hundred times filthier, but then my eyes widened at my sudden urge to sneeze. *Shit, not again,* I thought when it ripped through me to clear out my lungs and send a stab of pain through my knees. But it was different. There was no accompanying pull. It was just Al trying to contact me, and I looked at Pierce sourly. *Al had sent Pierce to watch me, eh? Yeah. We'd just see about that.*

"Tink's a Disney whore!" Jenks swore, darting down to the center counter and the open bookshelf under it. "Ivy, quick! Get her calling mirror out. It's Al."

"Rachel, no!" Nick exclaimed, eyes wide as he realized what was going on.

Jenks flew up, his sword bared to make Jax dart back. "Shut the hell up!" he shouted in frustration. "Open your mouth again, and I'll jam a spider's nest in your ear so they can eat that crap you have for brains! You don't know shit. *You don't know shit!*"

"Al will kill you, Rachel!" Nick insisted as Ivy silently moved to get the mirror.

"It's a little late to be afraid of Al, Nick," I muttered when Ivy slid the smooth, plate-size scrying mirror onto my lap and backed up, wiping her fingers nervously on her pants. She didn't like my magic—didn't understand it—even as she respected it. My knees hurt under the mirror's weight, even with the pain amulet. "What they didn't say was that I am his student," I said bitterly as I put my hand on the mirror in the cave of the pentagram. "I'm not saying I know what I'm doing, but I know who I can trust. And you're not on the list, so *shut up!* I want to talk to Al. See what's going on." *Get my summoning name back. I am* not *going to do this again.*

I glanced at Pierce as I said the last, seeing no fear, just a confident satisfaction. I knew I should be glad he was free of Al, but it hinged on my not being able to take care of myself. Sighing, I looked at my swollen knees and my orange jumpsuit. Maybe they were right.

"I'd be of a mind not to tell Al you were in prison," Pierce said as he leaned into the wall and crossed his arms. He was smug, and I didn't like it.

"Why?" I said, immediately wanting to do the exact opposite. "You afraid it might make you look bad?"

Pierce shifted his weight to one foot and balanced his free foot on a toe. "If you get into too much trouble, Newt might revoke your reality privileges, me here or not."

"Oh, and you'd love that, wouldn't you," Jenks exclaimed, wings humming.

I sneezed again as the cool weight of the scrying mirror sank into me. Tell Al about Alcatraz to get my name back and risk being yanked to the ever-after forever, or stay silent and risk the coven summoning me again and giving me a lobotomy. No contest. Pierce might know his magic, but I knew Al, and Al wouldn't tell Newt anything.

The onetime ghost sent his eyebrows high when I simpered at him, clearly not knowing where my thoughts lay. Feeling better, I looked at the elaborate glyph reflecting the world back to me with the rich hue of wine. The symbols I'd etched on it glittered like blood diamonds. Much as I hated to admit it, the thing was beautiful. It let me talk to demons, and I thought it was beautiful. *I am so screwed.*

Resigned, I reached out a thought and touched it to the small ley line that ran through the churchyard. I kept my attention narrow, allowing only the barest slip of energy into me, not wanting Al to get more than a hint of my emotions. The connection completed, I focused on Al, shivering when his domineering, alien presence seemed to melt into me, expanding both our awarenesses in a curious feeling of lofty enlightenment. I couldn't read his mind, and he couldn't see into mine, but focused thoughts could be exchanged. That, and emotion.

"Why is Pierce here?" I said aloud so that Ivy could hear at least half the conversation.

Not my idea, Al started, and I could almost see his white-gloved hands clench into fists. *That's why I called. That little runt of a witch is dangerous. He manipulated Newt like a damned demon suitor. It was either send him or give you to her. Which would you prefer?*

It had been mocking, and taken aback, I glanced at the ring of faces watching me. That Al wasn't happy either somehow made me feel better. "So take him back. I won't tell," I said, and Al snorted even as Pierce huffed indignantly.

Maybe if you could go one week without becoming shunned or put under a death threat you might be considered smart enough to be on your own, the demon muttered. *But no-o-o-o-o, you had to try it on your own. I told you to wait.*

"Hey! I'm not the one trying to put Krakatoa into my soul!" I said loudly, face warm.

Not Krakatoa, Krathion. And I won't take the blame for you prematurely invoking a curse when I told you to wait for me! he said, and I was silent, fuming. *I'm trying to downplay the situation,* Al thought, his emotions slowing. *In the meantime, if he teaches you one thing, one thing, Rachel, you'll be wearing his guts as hair bands. Got it?*

I glanced at Pierce, and he blinked at my sudden interest. Pierce could teach me something? "Sure . . . ," I said, starting to see the possibilities. If I could learn how to jump the lines, no one would have to watch me at all.

Rachel? Al growled, not detecting any sincerity in my thoughts.

"Got it," I reaffirmed, then took a deep breath. "Hey, along those lines, I need my original summoning name back. Like now."

From my peripheral sight, Nick blinked, almost mirroring the shocked emotion I felt from Al. *Now?* Al thought, and I felt him start to sever the connection. *You want to play in the collective when everyone is watching? Damn my dame, you do need a babysitter, Rachel. No.*

"Al, wait!" I shouted, pressing my hand harder into the glass until it felt like I'd made a soft indent in the mirror. "I just spent a day in Alcatraz after being summoned into a closed trial called by the coven of moral and ethical standards." I didn't look up, but I heard Pierce sigh because I hadn't listened to his advice. "They weren't after you, they were after me," I added.

Al laughed, and I looked past my stringy hair to Nick. He was staring at me, long face aghast. Across the kitchen, Pierce held himself still, eyes dark from behind his mop of loose curls and his hat back on his head. Jenks faced me from the counter, spilling a red dust that puddled on the floor, and Ivy stood almost in the hallway, her black eyes fully dilated.

Nice try. But no one in that pantywaist coven knows my name, Al was thinking. *And if they did, they wouldn't summon me, holier-than-thou chicken squirts. Stay out of trouble, Rachel, and this will all blow over. Two decades at the most.*

Two decades! I thought, then said, "That's what I'm saying. They didn't summon you, they summoned me! They used *your* name, knowing *I* would be the one to show up! They paid someone to summon me into a six-pointed star. I barely got out because they thought I was bound to demon law, but that's not going to work a second time. They know I can invoke demon magic, and they're going to give me a lobotomy and take my ovaries as soon as they find the next chump who knows your name!"

Who summoned you? Al said suddenly, icy calm pouring from him, and I looked at Nick, my mouth shutting. *Tell me who summoned you with my name. Tell me, itchy witch, and I'll not only see that you learn how to jump the lines, but how to survive that runt of yours.*

I closed my mind to Al and pulled my hand from the glass. The sudden disconnection jolted through me, and I started. Feeling haunted, I first looked at Ivy, then Pierce, then Jenks, who was white faced and spilling a sickly green dust. Last, I looked at Nick, standing behind that chair both angry and frightened. Jax was on his shoulder with his wings folded submissively. If Al knew Nick had summoned me, the demon would actively work to take him out—close the hole of information rather than trade our names back as we had agreed.

Ivy uncrossed her arms, glancing at Nick and then back to me. "What did he want?"

I held Nick's attention, shivering as the adrenaline washed out and the last twenty hours fell heavy on me. "Just Nick."

Nine

Water cascaded off me as I stood up in Ivy's tub, my knees throbbing from the moist heat. It was steamy in here, with the mirror fogged, and Matalina sifting yellow dust to keep her wings dry as she sat on the towel rack and knitted. Ivy's fluffy black towel was soft against my red, scraped skin, and I awkwardly tried to get the stopper undone with my toes, finally giving up and reaching for it and feeling everything protest. I'd soaked long enough to wash between my toes once and my hair twice. I'd be in there still, but I was starving.

Nick's voice was faint through the walls. Matalina's lips pressed together as she listened to the conversation, but it was too indistinct for me. I wasn't ready to deal with him or Pierce, and I was hoping to make the dash to my room unnoticed.

Nick was our unwilling guest since he could summon me at will after dark, an intolerable situation to Ivy. Jenks wanted me to give Nick to Al on the principle that he was a douche bag. I doubted Ivy would say anything if I went along with it, but I wasn't going to give Nick to Al. I wouldn't be able to live with myself. Besides, my safety would last only until the coven found someone else who knew Al's summoning name. What I needed was my own name back.

I sighed as the towel found every scrape and abrasion, my eyes falling on the ugly canvas slip-on shoes beside the toilet. I couldn't help but wonder who had my kick-butt boots, my jeans, my underwear . . , my red leather coat sticky with strawberries. Gone.

From atop the towel rack, Matalina smiled. "Oh, Rachel, you look fine," she said, and I met her gaze, thinking that I must look ghastly if that's what she thought I was sighing about. The woman appeared to be eighteen, but she and Jenks had forty-some kids, and she was nearing the end of her life span. Or so Jenks said. She looked awfully chipper for someone supposedly on her deathbed. Jax being here might have something to do with it. And I was worrying about who had my underwear?

"I'm out of the tub," I said, listening to my pulse and feeling tired as she knitted from a ball of what was probably dyed spider silk. "Why don't you go visit with Jax?"

"Because I'm angry with him for running off half trained, with a thief," she said primly.

Her expression was fierce, and I wondered if it was the thief or the half-trained part that bothered her. Guilt hit me, and I gingerly rubbed the welts on my wrists. Matalina would never forgive herself if her eldest son left again before she could find it in her heart to talk to him.

I glanced at Matalina watching but not watching me as I sat on the edge of the tub and tried to dry my feet, reminded of my first few nights in the church. It was Matalina who had kept an eye on me the night Al had almost torn my throat out. A lot had happened since then, stuff that turned enemies to allies, and allies to enemies. But Matalina was unchanged, she and her family a point of normalcy in my chaotic life. I was glad she was looking so well.

"Go talk to Jax," I said softly, and the woman sighed so loudly I could hear it.

"I will," she said. "Life is too short to carry a grudge. Especially when it's with family you thought you'd never see again." She continued to knit, smiling. "He likes you, you know."

"Jax?" I said, surprised.

"Gordian Pierce!" she exclaimed, looking up. "You can see it in his eyes."

Funny. The only thing I ever see in his eyes is trouble. Taking the towel from my hair, I went to the mirror and wiped it, wincing. I'd never get through the tangles. Never. "Pierce is a teenage crush from when I was young and stupid, and thought impulsive, dangerous men were the catch of the day, not the death traps they are."

Matalina huffed. Pixies were terribly straightforward when it came to relationships. Jih, her eldest daughter, had courted and married in less than a summer—and seemed all the happier for it. "With Jenks, I just knew," she said, a fond smile erasing her fatigue lines. "You're making this harder than it should be." I gave her a wry look as I sprayed detangler in my hair, and she added, "Does Pierce make your heart beat faster? Did Marshal? Did Nick? Did Kisten, bless his undead soul? I mean, really?"

I didn't have to think about it, and I felt like a tramp. "Yes. They all do. Did, I mean."

The pixy woman frowned. "Then you are in trouble, Rachel."

Don't I know it.

Shifting my towel higher, I minced to the door, listening for a moment before cracking it. The cooler, dry air slipped in, and I gazed first longingly at the kitchen across from the back living room, then closer, to the open door to my room. From the back of the church, I could hear Pierce and Nick "discussing" things.

Knees hurting, I made the dash, Matalina zipping ahead of me to shoo her kids out of the way. Breath held, I closed the door without a sound and leaned back against it. "Thanks," I whispered to the matronly pixy. "But I'm okay. Really. Go talk to Jax." But she only flitted to the thick cement sill of the stained-glass window and settled herself as if to watch for danger.

My shoulders slumped and I glanced at Vivian's pin, now sitting on my dresser. I'd forgotten about the coven. It would be just my luck for Vivian to take a potshot at me. I was sure she was still here, "willing to take a calculated risk."

The box from my mom was sitting on my dresser, the bottles of perfume it had displaced carefully arranged on the top of my music box to make me wonder if Ivy had moved it. My mother had been sending me things for the last couple of months as she continued to find them. Last week it had been my entire collection of Nancy Drew. Ivy had taken them off my hands, presumably to give them to the brat pack at the hospital. The way I figured it, if I had gotten along without it the last five years, I really didn't need it. *Everything* was precious to my mom, though, and I wasn't too keen on seeing what oddity she thought I couldn't live without.

Ignoring the shoe-box-size package, I shuffled through my top drawer for a pair of socks and the black lacy underwear that I hadn't worn since Marshal and I had broken up. I'd spent yesterday in prison and wanted to feel pretty, damn it. Slipping them on, I wiggled out of the towel and dropped a camisole over my damp head. Jeans next, the tight pair I hadn't been able to wear comfortably since the solstice. I hadn't eaten in twenty-four hours, and they might fit. The zipper went up with satisfying ease, and I smiled. I wouldn't recommend prison food as a way to lose weight, but if it was gone, I wasn't going to complain.

Socks in hand, I sat on my bed and slowly exhaled. Getting them on was going to be a pain. Repainting my toenails was going to be even harder. Maybe Ivy would do it for me.

Matalina's wings hummed in warning. Adrenaline surged, but she was looking at my door, not out the window. "Rachel?" Ivy called. "I made you a sandwich. Are you decent?"

There is a God, and he's good to me. My stomach rumbled, and I was suddenly ten times hungrier. I couldn't hear Nick's voice anymore, but I hadn't heard anyone leave either. Still sitting on the bed with my socks, I shouted, "Come in!"

Ivy entered with her head down and balancing a plate with two sandwiches and a bowl of cheese crackers in her hands. "I made you two," she said, her gray-silk voice carrying soft compassion as she looked up from shutting the door with a foot. "You look hungry."

I eyed the tuna sandwiches warily. "No Brimstone?"

Her placid brown eyes met mine, the barest hint of dry amusement in them. "No. But I can make you some cookies if you want."

Shaking my head, I dropped the socks and reached for the plate. I'd eaten Ivy's cookies before. Laced with medicinal-grade Brimstone, they simultaneously made me hungry and boosted my metabolism. Just what you need when recovering from blood loss, but I was bruised, not anemic. "No thanks," I said wryly. "I want to sleep tonight."

But when she sat on the end of my bed, I blinked. *She's staying?*

Matalina rose up, her dragonflylike wings unusually loud. "Ivy, if you're going to talk to Rachel for a while, I'll just pop out and see if Jenks needs anything."

Oh. I get it.

Ivy smiled a closed-lipped smile and slid the crackers onto my dresser beside the box from my mom. "He's in the kitchen with Jax."

"Thank you." Matalina left her knitting behind as she darted under the door.

I wasn't keen on everyone thinking I needed watching, but if it gave Matalina a chance to talk to Jax, then I'd deal with it. Scooting back to the headboard, I stretched my legs out and balanced the plate on my lap. "Nick still here?" I asked as I took a bite out of the first sandwich. The tang of the mayonnaise hit the sides of my tongue, and I suddenly couldn't shovel in food fast enough. "Oh, this is good," I mumbled around my full mouth. "Thank you."

"Pierce is talking to him." Her gaze was on my perfumes. She'd given most of them to me in our chemical warfare against her instincts. "He told me to leave. Said they had a gentleman matter to discuss."

"Oh really?" The sandwich was fabulous, and I forced myself to slow down.

"I think Pierce is trying to find out if you two are really over or not," Ivy said.

My eyes rolled and I swallowed. "Over? Does he need it in neon?" I said, but inside, I was cringing. Being *over* with Nick did not translate into being available for Pierce.

"You're sure you're okay?" Ivy asked, and I nodded, mouth full again.

"Until they find someone else who knows Al's summoning name," I amended, wiggling my fingers for the bowl of crackers. My thoughts shifted to Al telling me he'd finish the deal—even teach me how to jump the lines—if I told him who sold me out to the coven. Funny how things had changed when I'd brought up my ovaries. Lots of people knew Al's summoning name, and what demon summoner wouldn't trade an hour's work for amnesty? But if I gave Nick to Al, then the council was right and I was a demon, trafficking in human flesh.

Ivy passed the bowl, and grabbing a handful of crackers, I tilted my head back and dropped them in, sneaking a glance at her and wondering if she was in here trying to convince me to give Nick to the demon and be done with it. "I've always wanted to get to the West Coast," I said around my chewing, not wanting her to bring it up. "Hey, did I tell you I got a ride on a boat? I saw the bridge and everything. It's way smaller than the one in Mackinaw. There's a big chocolate factory right across from Alcatraz. Talk about cruel and unusual punishment."

Ivy wasn't listening, her eyes on that box my mother had sent. "When did that get here?" I asked as I worked a bit of cracker out from between my teeth.

Shifting position on my bed, she flushed, putting her eyes everywhere but on it. "When you were gone."

Gone, not prison. I appreciated that. Brushing crumbs from myself, I reached for the last half of my sandwich. Ivy was silent, then, "Are you going to open it?"

I smiled, my mouth full as I wiggled my fingers. She was worse than Jenks.

Ivy got to her feet with unusual quickness, and I set the last half of my sandwich back down to pull my knee up as tight as I could comfortably get it. A muffled masculine argument filtered through the wall, and we ignored it as Ivy sat close, like it was Christmas.

The box was light and kind of dusty, as if it had gone from my mom's attic, to the moving van going out west, and then right back in a mail truck to me. The last two boxes had been the same way. "I really doubt it's more Nancy Drew," I told her as I took the knife she handed me. Good grief, she'd brought a knife in for the tape.

"It might be," Ivy said. "Volume fifty-two is missing."

Oh, my God. Ivy is a closet Nancy Drew fan! Those books hadn't gone to the brat pack—they were probably under her bed! Amused, I set the knife on the dresser table and smiled at her eager expression. Her hands were carefully in her lap, anxious. I could have teased her about it, but seeing any happy emotion on her was precious. She actually sighed when I opened up the box and leaned to look in.

"It's my camp stuff!" I exclaimed, taking out my mom's handwritten note to see the accumulated bric-a-brac underneath.

"Oh look!" Ivy said brightly. "There *is* a book!"

My gaze lifted from my mom's letter, and I smirked at her as she reached for Nancy Drew, volume 52. "You opened it up already, didn't you!"

Ivy wouldn't look at me. "Don't be ridiculous. Why would I open your mail?"

"Mmmm-hmmm." HI, RACHEL, I read as she flipped through the dog-eared pages as if it were a lost book from the Bible. I FOUND THIS WHILE MOVING IN WITH DONALD. IT WAS EITHER THROW IT AWAY OR SEND IT TO YOU. MISS YOU, MOM.

Setting the letter aside, I smiled. Most of what she'd been sending me had been junk, but this . . . I gazed into the box. Okay, this was junk, too, but it was my junk.

"Look at this," I said, bringing out a lopsided clay bowl painted in garish colors. "I made this for my dad. It's a pipe holder."

Ivy looked up from the book. "If you say so."

My fingers pressed into the dents that I'd made when I was twelve. They were really small. "I think it was the only reason he had a pipe," I said, setting it back in the box. The pressed-flower album I didn't even remember, but it was my scrawl on the pages. There was a badge from the cabin I was in, dated and covered in rainbow stickers. The pair of dusty sandals on top of it were so small it was scary.

"How old were you?" Ivy asked when I held them up.

"They kicked me out when I was twelve," I said, flushing. It hadn't been fun. I'd thrown Trent into a tree with a blast of ley-line energy because he'd been teasing Jasmine. I guess they figured if I was well enough to do that, then I wasn't dying anymore and should make room for some-one who was. Trent had deserved it. I think. They had long-term memory blockers in the water and nothing was certain.

I smiled at the pair of freshwater clam shells Jasmine and I were going to make into earrings. A blue jay feather. Things that meant nothing to anyone but me.

"What is this?"

She was holding an antique-looking curved metal hook, and I reached for it as I warmed. "Uh, a hoof pick," I said, feeling the weight of it in my palm, heavy with the sensation of anxious excitement and guilt. Ivy's eye-brows rose, and I added, "They had horses, and you had to clean their hooves before you took them out. That's a hoof pick." *A really fancy hoof pick, with an inlaid wooden handle and a silver hook, of all things.*

Head cocked, Ivy leaned back and eyed me. "And your pulse just sky-rocketed why?"

Grimacing, I set the pick back in the box. "It's Trent's. At least I think it is."

"And your pulse just skyrocketed why?" she asked again.

"I stole it!" I said, feeling myself become breathless. "At least I think I did. I'm pretty sure I meant to give it back . . ." I hesitated, confused. "Crap, I don't even remember why I have it."

Ivy had a weird smile on her face. I think Nancy Drew had reminded her of her own innocence. "You stole Trent's hoof pick? What is that, some witch-camp tradition?"

"Maybe I just borrowed it and forgot to give it back," I said, guilt com-ing from nowhere. I remember shoving it in my pocket with a feeling of vindication. Trent had been there . . . and I hadn't liked him. He was snotty.

Ivy picked up the book again. "No wonder he doesn't like you. You stole his hoof pick."

Exasperated, and trying to ignore the guilt coming from a memory I didn't entirely have, I closed the box and pushed it away. "The feeling is mutual," I said, tugging on my socks. "Trent is a lying, manipulative brat, and always has been."

She handed me the Nancy Drew, exhaling slowly. "So . . . you think this entire situation with the coven is one of his scams? That Trent told them about you?"

I looked at the cover and the furtive posture of Nancy as she held a tablet engraved with ley-line glyphs, treasure hunting. *Oh, when it had looked that easy.* "I don't know," I said, miserable with confusion as I handed the book back to her to keep.

Ivy held it possessively as I looked at the closed box of memories. I wanted to be pissed at Trent about the coven, but something in my gut said no. Seeing the stuff from camp . . . things had happened there that I couldn't remember. Memory blockers were like that, clouding events but leaving emotions intact, and as the collective mementos touched on half memories, I couldn't tell if my anger at Trent was because he was a camp brat or if he was truly bad.

"I just don't know anymore," I finally said. "He is in jeopardy, too, now, and there are easier ways for him to make my life miserable."

Ivy made a soft sound and set the dog-eared Nancy Drew carefully beside her. Much as I'd like to believe he hadn't told the coven I could invoke demon magic, I was done with being stupid. It was far easier to believe this was one of his elaborate schemes. Easier, yes, but smart? Because if Trent hadn't told them, then someone else had, and I didn't have a clue as to who. Logic said he had done it, but if I was logical, I'd have made the familiar bond active between us and forced him to be nice to me. Instead I had rescued him at great cost to myself because of a freaking gut feeling. And I still didn't know why. My eyes strayed to the box, feeling as if the answer was in there somewhere.

"Why don't you use the Pandora charm and find out?"

I stared at Ivy—I'd forgotten that I even had it. "You think it's something from the camp?"

"He did say he might make you one if the memory you wanted was of camp or your dad. Well, he made you one."

"You're nuts!" I exclaimed, but she was shaking her head, smiling.

Her eyes touched on the closed box. "Whether you *remember* it or not, you and Trent go back a long way. I'd think it worth finding out if your gut feelings about him are based on something real or a childhood argument over a hoof pick. Don't you?"

Well, when she put it like that . . . From the back living room came a masculine voice raised in anger. My gaze went to my top drawer, where I had stashed Trent's charm, and I stifled a shiver. I needed to know if I could trust him, and not just with surface stuff, but *really trust him*. I needed to know why I disliked him yet would risk my life to save his worthless skin. I needed to use his Pandora charm.

My pulse quickened, and I swung my feet to the floor, wincing when my knees protested. If I was going to do this, I'd rather do it when all the pixies were spying on Nick and Pierce, arguing. "Okay, but if it kills me, it's your fault." Shuffling to my top dresser drawer, I yanked it open. *Maybe it was a memory of my dad.*

"Uh . . . ," Ivy stammered, and I glanced up to see her eyes wide in consideration.

"I'm kidding," I said. "It passed the lethal-amulet test, remember?"

"Not that. You keep it in your underwear drawer?"

I hesitated, wondering why I was embarrassed. "Well, where do you put your elven magic?" I asked, and then my fingers touched the smooth, knotty bump of the bracelet-size length of knotted horsehair. A surge of excitement went through me, and I brought the charm out.

Together Ivy and I looked at the innocuous-seeming thing. The knots were hard under my fingertips, the hair they were made from silver and black. It tingled as if the power was leaking out. Elven magic. Wild. Unpredictable. God, I hoped I wasn't making a mistake. Trent had made it, and I didn't know how good—or evil—he was. *Knowledge is power.* Frowning, I fingered the first knot. *Ignorance is bliss.*

But curiosity—even if it had killed the cat—was king, and heart pounding, I moved the box from the bed and sat down. "You won't leave?" I asked, feeling like a chicken, and Ivy shook her head. And with that reassurance, I worked the first of the three knots free.

My damp hair seemed to crinkle, and my face warmed as the elven magic rose through me, tasting of oak leaves and chill autumn air.

"You okay?"

I nodded. "The magic feels funny. Like tinfoil."

She exhaled, and the bed shifted as she stood, arms crossed over her middle. It was an unusual show of worry I totally understood. Steeling myself, I undid the second knot. My thoughts seemed to jump, and my breath quickened. To stop now would ruin the charm, and I undid the third knot, an unusual fatigue making my fingers fumble. *I hope this isn't a mistake.*

My breath came in as I looked at Ivy, and it was as if I fell into myself, like Alice down the rabbit hole. I knew I was sitting on my bed, but there were birds and the soft snuffling of horses. The twin sensations of reality and memory were eerie, but the charmed ones were becoming dominant.

"My God, Ivy. It's warm," I whispered, eyes closing as I gave myself to the dream that wasn't a dream, but a memory. I felt small, the softness of my bed becoming a hard wood floor. Fatigue crept up, familiar and hated, stealing into my bones like poison. My memories were halved, and seemingly forgetting everything I knew, I . . . remembered.

My pulse quickened to the pace of childhood, racing, and I opened my eyes to the dim light of the camp's stables.

Sniffing, I curled up tighter, bringing the cloying scent of damp straw, horse dung, and sweaty leather deep into me, trying not to cry. This sucked. This sucked big-time. Here I thought that Jasmine hated Trent, and it turned out she liked him. *Liked him!* How was I to know? She complained about him enough.

The horse stomped, and I burrowed deeper into the corner, pulling the blue blanket up and around me, hiding. I'd never seen anyone ride this monster of a horse, and he hadn't minded me slipping in. I was so mad. Jasmine and I never fought, but when I found out she'd lied to me about where she'd been, I lost it. She'd gone for a moonlight walk with little richy rich boy, leaving me alone in the bottom half of our bunk bed to listen to everyone else tell stories of their first kiss when she knew I didn't have one. She was supposed to be my friend!

I held my breath to keep from crying, my arms clasped around my knees. It was all Trent's fault, the snot. Miserable, I picked at my shoelaces, cringing when a set of boots echoed at the wide stable doors. I froze as two people went by, talking in low voices, their identities hidden by the tall walls of the box stall I was in, but I could tell it was kids, not lab techs disguised as counselors or stable hands looking for me.

The horse above me nickered. Ears pricked, he shifted to hang his head over the gate.

Crap, I thought, recognizing a voice. Stanley had been here for three days, hanging with Trent as usual. The guy had been here last year, too, managing to twist Trent's ankle in a footrace his second day. This year he'd broken Trent's hand in a canoe race. Stanley's paddle had come down right on the back of it, and snap, no more contest. Stanley didn't like to lose. And if Stanley was in the stables, then that was Trent with him.

His voice going faint, Stanley started singing "Love Song for a Vampire," changing the lyrics to something suitably rude, and my breath eased out as they went into the other wing of the stables—but the horse above me still had his ears pricked.

"Hoy, hoy, Mr. T.," came a soft voice, and the jingling of a bridle, and I froze. Trent? Trent was here? Panicking, I put a hand to my hot face and stared, seeing nothing but the top of his head. The horse blew his breath out, and Trent's voice shifted, the words slurring into a hummed pattern of crooning. It was beautiful, and I strained for more, trying to understand. It sounded like another language, and though I hated him because Jasmine liked him, I couldn't help but think it beautiful.

His tawny head flashed over the walls of the stall, giving me a glimpse of his fair skin and green eyes. He hadn't seen me, and I watched his face, empty of the scorn he usually heaped on me. Trent's eyes were full and shining, and he was smiling. His white hair was messy, and his ears showed. Trent never let his ears show, always combing his fine hair over them. He was skinny, lanky, and almost singing to the horse as he fondled his ears and fed him a treat.

Feeling my eyes on him, his gaze flicked to me.

Immediately his wonderful voice ceased. His lips pressed together, and his eyes took on a hard slant. Snorting, the horse drew back from him. "What are you doing in there?" he said, voice cracking and face going red. "Get out. You're not even supposed to be here when the stable hands are gone."

"Neither are you," I said, scrambling up and clutching the horse blanket to me as I backed to the wall. My heart pounded when he opened the gate, sliding in and latching it behind him, fumbling the first time because of his cast. I'd be willing to bet Stanley had broken Trent's hand to put him at a disadvantage for the rest of the summer. What a goober.

Trent was in new jeans and brand-new riding boots. I thought of my own nasty sneakers, and I flushed. Trent was rich. His dad owned the camp. Everyone knew it.

"They're looking for you," he said, mocking me. "You are in *so* much trouble."

The horse tossed his head, feet moving restlessly between us, and I put a hand on him to remind him not to step on me. "I can be in here if I want," I said, chin high.

Trent's white eyebrows drew together, but when the horse snorted and laid his ears back, he looked away, quieting the animal. "This is my horse," he said cockily. The cast on his hand made it hard for him to close his fingers on the horse's halter, but the animal was docile enough.

"I don't see your name on it," I said, then flushed when Trent pointed at the plaque behind me. "Oh," I said, edging away. Okay. It was his horse. Must be nice, not only having your own horse, but being rich enough to truck him up to summer camp for you.

The horse's ears flicked, and from the other wing of the stables, Stanley's voice echoed. "You need some help getting the bit in, lazy ass? Tighten that girth? Give you a leg up? Or does boy wonder think he can do it one-handed?"

Scared, I backed up. Trent was a brat, but Stanley was a bully with a mean streak.

Trent's expression soured. Glancing at me, he shouted, "I can saddle a horse with my teeth faster than you with both hands. I'll see you out there."

I swallowed hard, not caring if Trent knew I was afraid of Stanley. A feeling of gratitude pulled me from the wall. My eyes dropped to his broken hand. "Are you okay?"

Reaching up to a high shelf, Trent brought down a wood-handled hoof pick and stuck it in a back pocket. "What do you care?"

"I never said I did," I said, arms over my middle. I wanted out, but he was in the way.

Trent looked at me. "You're a crybaby. You've been crying. Your eyes are red."

I wiped the back of my hand on my face. He knew *why* I was crying, too, the brat. "So? I'm twelve. What's your excuse?"

He shifted from the gate and I bolted for it, leaving it open because he was coming out, too, his horse clopping loudly. "I thought you were in eighth grade," he said, his voice confused.

The bright square of sunlight beckoned, thirty feet away, but I lingered in the cool shadow. "I am," I said, holding my elbow and shifting awkwardly. "I skipped a couple of grades. Homeschooled. You know . . . sick and everything. I'll be thirteen next month."

Thirteen, and dumber than a stone. I could see why Jasmine liked him. He was rich, nice looking, and he had his own horse. But if you were so unsure of yourself that you let your friends hurt you, then you were stupid.

Trent didn't bother to tie his horse's halter rope to the post like we'd been told to do, and I watched him check the gelding's hooves, tucking the pick in his pocket instead of putting it away. Letting the last foot drop, Trent looked at the bridle rack, then shoved the rope dangling from his horse's halter at me.

"Hold him," he said curtly, and I dropped back a step.

"I am not your servant," I said hotly. "Tie him off yourself."

Trent's fingers twitched. "I'm not going to tie him off if you're just standing there," he said, voice soft but determined. "Hold the rope while I bridle him."

"No!" I exclaimed, arms wrapped around my middle, refusing to take the rope.

He clenched his jaw, angry I wouldn't do as he said. "I told you to hold the rope!"

Trent reached out, grabbing my wrist with his good hand and yanking it from where I'd tucked it behind my other arm. His grip was tight, and I yelped, gasping when a tingling surge of ley-line energy darted between us.

"Hey!" I shouted, jerking away, and his fingers let go.

"I wanted to know how much you could hold," he said smugly. "My dad says you're dangerous, but I've seen cats that can hold more than you."

"You little turd! You did that on purpose!" Then my eyes widened. "Holy cow! You *are* a witch!"

"No I'm not," he said quickly, as if he'd made a mistake. "I'm better than a crappy little witch like you."

My mouth dropped open, and I got mad. "What do you mean, crappy little witch! You think you're so hot? If you're not a witch, then you're nothing but a stinking little human!"

He glanced at me, almost in relief. "I'm still better than you," he said, his cheeks flushed. "Faster."

"I'm sick, you moron!"

"I bet you can't even hear that bell ringing from camp," he added.

My anger hesitated and I listened, wondering if he was just making it up.

"I bet you can't smell the bread baking either," Trent said, trusting his horse to stand there beside me as he went to get a bridle. "You are *so blind* that I bet I could sneak right into your cabin and take the ring off your finger and you'd never know."

"I don't wear a ring, Einstein," I said snottily. "And I bet I could take the pick right out of your pocket and you'd never feel it. And I bet I *can* hold more ever-after than you!" My pulse had gotten fast, and I felt out of breath. "And I'm not holding your stinking horse!" I added, going dizzy. "I wouldn't ride that nag of yours if he was the last animal on earth!"

My vision wavered, and I quit talking, content to just stand there with my knees unlocked and careful to just breathe for a moment. Crap, I did *not* want to pass out in front of Trent.

"Yeah?" Trent said, his back to me as he brushed his horse out and put a bareback pad on him. "Well, he wouldn't let you. He doesn't like witches."

"I bet he would," I muttered, feeling my heart start to slow. "He let me in his box, okay. He's not so tough, and neither are you. You're a wimp," I said, wanting to hurt him. "Why do you let Stanley beat up on you like that? All you have to do is stand up to him once and he wouldn't hurt you every year."

Trent flushed bright red, which made his hair stand out even more. Eyes fixed on his horse, he ignored me, and I knew I'd hit a sore spot. Served him right, spoiled brat. As I watched, arrogant, my hip cocked, he fumbled with the bit, needing to hold it with his other hand because of the cast. It was awkward, and the horse didn't like it, tossing his head and shifting.

Trent still hadn't said anything, and feeling bad now for the Stanley comment, I edged closer. There was no way he was going to get that bit in. "I'll get it," I offered softly, and his jaw clenched.

"I don't need your help," he said, then swore when his horse backed up, tossing his head and threatening to bolt. The bit dropped, and Trent scrambled to keep his horse from running back to his stall.

I swooped forward to pick up the bit before his horse stepped on it. "What is your problem?" I crabbed. "I know you can set a bit. Let me do it this time. Unless you want Sta-a-a-an-le-e-e-ey to help you?" I drawled his name, making it girly.

Trent had his hand on his horse's neck, and the animal calmed, standing with a pleasant posture and ears nicely pricked—looking at me and the bit. "You think you can do it?" he said caustically. "Go ahead and try. Don't come crying to me if he bites your fingers off."

I eyed Trent, half expecting him to pinch his own horse to prove I couldn't do it. I'd bridled my horse every time I went riding. This was my third year here, and though I wasn't an expert, a good horse would take a bit with no problem.

Cooing and talking to the horse to distract it, I wrangled the bit of metal between his big chomping teeth, quickly sliding the rest up and in place, but it was Trent who dipped under his horse's head to fasten the strap. He was taller than me, and I dropped back, reins dangling until Trent took them. He was fussing, making sure the mane was untangled and that the straps weren't twisted. Jeez, I *did* know how to bridle a horse.

I stood for a moment, not surprised he hadn't said thank you. Giving up, I took a step back. At least I wasn't dizzy anymore. "Jasmine is so mad at me," I said. "I didn't know she liked you. I'm sorry."

Trent turned to me, clearly surprised. My eyes warmed with threatening tears, and I turned away. Someone was calling my name, counselor by the sound of it. Great. They were going to write me up. Sighing, I started for the bright square of light.

"Do you want a ride?" Trent asked.

Wiping my eyes, I turned, shocked. My gaze went from him to the horse. There wasn't a saddle, just that bareback pad. "On him?"

His attention went out of the stables as another voice called my name, loudly, with some anger. Nodding, he grabbed a handful of mane and swung himself up like he was born to it. "If you can get up here."

There was more than a hint of challenge, and I took a step forward, looking up at him and thinking it was a long way from the ground. "You just want to knock me off," I said, mistrusting him. "Or take me out into the woods and leave me to walk in."

Not a hint of his intent was in his placid face as he leaned down and held out his hand. "You'll have to trust me."

The voices were getting louder. Maybe if Jasmine found out I'd been with him, she'd know how it felt to be ditched. It was petty, but taking a breath, I fit my hand in his. I reached up with the other, and with a lean and a tug, I found myself swung up behind him.

The horse shifted, snorting, and as Trent soothed him, I clutched Trent's waist, feeling really weird. My gasp for air brought the scent of cinnamon and green things into me, and my alarm paused at a unique sensation, a twinge of something going through me. Pride, maybe, that I was on a tall horse? The hoof pick was almost falling out of his pocket, and thinking he deserved it, I yanked it free when the horse shifted, tucking it in my own pocket instead. I'd give it back once I knew he wasn't going to dump me off on the trail. It wasn't really stealing if the only reason I took it was to prove I could, right? *Better than a crappy little witch, huh?*

"Please don't make me regret this," I whispered. Jasmine would never speak to me again if she found out, but I didn't care. His horse was fabulous!

"I won't if you don't," he said, and my grip tightened as the horse started into motion.

Whoever was shouting my name was getting closer, and the horse eagerly headed for the door. "What's his name?" I asked as we emerged blinking into the sun.

"Tulpa, but I call him Mr. T."

I looked over the empty paddock and the fenced field beyond. Two figures were coming up the dirt road, their pace quickening when they saw us. A horse and rider stood waiting where field turned into woods. Stanley. "You named your horse after a flower?" I questioned.

"Tulpa, not Tulip," Trent said. "Hold on. We have to get out of here."

"Hey!" I shouted, grip tightening when he nudged his horse into a smooth canter. But the faster we went, the easier it was, and I found myself leaning forward into Trent. My hair was pushed behind me, and I could hardly breathe. One problem. We were heading for the fence.

"Trent?" I shouted, and he kicked his horse into a faster gait. I reached behind me, making sure the pick wasn't falling out.

"I'm taking it!" he shouted. "Hold on!"

He was going to jump it? Heart pounding, I screwed my eyes shut and put my arms back around Trent. *He wanted me to fall. I knew it!* Vertigo swam up, and I felt my muscles go weak. It was too much. I knew the signs, but I held on all the tighter. Not this time. I wasn't going to pass out. Adrenaline poured into me, and the tingle of magic. Breath held, I felt a thrill down to my toes as the horse bunched beneath me. My eyes opened, and I looked.

Tulpa's feet left the earth, and he stretched forward. One with him, we leaned as well, instinct older than magic taking hold. The beating of his hooves was silenced, and the thumping of my heart was all that there was. For an instant, we flew.

Tulpa's front feet touched, and the world rushed back. The cadence of his hooves beat into me, and I shouted, letting go of Trent. It had been marvelous. Wonderful beyond belief. Exuberant, I smiled, feeling breathless and powerful all at the same time.

Trent turned, wonder in his eyes, shock almost. "You held on."

"Of course I did!" I said, grinning. "Let's go!"

He took a breath to answer me, but I never found out what he was going to say. Someone was shouting our names in fear.

Trent's horse shied, spooking. My hands clutched at Trent as the horse spun. My heels went up, and I fell backward. Trent had one hand on the reins, trying to regain control and keep his horse's head up, reaching back to me with his injured hand. His fingers couldn't grip, and I screamed, feeling myself go.

I fell as the horse leapt forward. The ground slammed into me, shocking, and I stared up at the bright blue sky, now turning a beautiful, beautiful velvet black with no stars.

"Rachel!" I heard, and someone lifted my head. My eyes wouldn't work. I knew I was seeing, but I couldn't figure out what it was.

"Rachel, breathe. Oh God. I'm sorry," Trent said. "Just breathe. Please breathe!"

And then even my ears quit working. Starved for air, I passed out.

Ten

I couldn't breathe. My lungs were starving for air, burning, but I couldn't make them expand. Stuck halfway between the memory and now, I hung, able to think, but not to do.

"Rachel!" Ivy shouted, and I felt a stinging smack across my cheek. "Wake up!"

Jenks's pixy wings clattered close, and his draft cooled my burning cheek. "Knock it off!" he exclaimed. "Hitting her isn't doing any good!"

Panic iced through me, but I couldn't move, paralyzed and running out of air.

"You let her invoke a deadly charm?" I heard Pierce say, his voice close.

"It wasn't supposed to be deadly!" Ivy snarled back. "It had already passed the lethal-amulet test. Something went wrong!"

"Kalamack crafted it? I opine that's what's wrong. He's just like his father. Sloppy."

"Look!" Jenks said. "It's still in her hands. Right there!"

My heart thudded, hurting for air; I felt shaking hands turn me over. Fingers wedged among mine, and pain shot through me. A moan I couldn't afford slipped past me.

"You're hurting her!" Nick exclaimed, completing the travesty.

"Better that than she suffocates," Ivy said. Then softer, she said, "I'm sorry, Rachel."

I clenched into myself, my head bursting in pain. Oh God. I was dying. I was going to die from a frigging elf charm. *Break my fingers. Anything!* The sharp tug on my fingers was a stab of agony, but I didn't think she broke anything as the smooth horsehair slipped from me.

Nick's voice was close and worried. "She's still not breathing."

"Tell us something we don't know, crap-for-brains!" Jenks exclaimed.

"Smack her again!" the thief said.

My hearing was going fuzzy, and the pain of the curse's imbalance was lost in the agony of suffocation. I couldn't think, but I felt the bed dip, and arms smelling of coal dust wrapped around me as my head thumped into a masculine chest. "Forgive me, mistress witch," I heard, and then a line burned through me.

I gasped, the involuntary reaction bringing a slip of air into me. It smelled like a meadow in the sun. Nausea rose and my heart gave a weak pound, but I still couldn't breathe. Somehow I managed to open my eyes. Pierce was holding me, Ivy standing helplessly, her eyes black and beautiful. "Do something!" Jenks shouted as he hovered close, and my eyes slipped shut.

"I am doing something," Pierce panted. "She took a breath."

Smooth fingers turned my chin, and I heard Ivy say, "Trent cursed her?"

"I'm going to kill him. I'm gonna kill the son of a fairy's slug," Jenks vowed.

"It's not a curse. It's a misaligned spell. I'm going to try to burn it out," Pierce said.

I jerked again as a stronger pulse of line energy lighted through me. Almost, I got a second breath, but it wasn't enough, and my heart pounded, starved for air. I wasn't going to make it. Trent had won. Son of a bitch.

"She's turning blue," Nick said, whispering. "Do something."

"Rachel!" Jenks shouted. "You stupid witch! What have you done!"

Pierce was shaking. "My God, how much line can you hold, mistress witch?"

"She can spindle it," Ivy said. "Give her everything you can handle, and then some."

It was as if light sparked through me. Pierce dove through my soul, reaching for a line through me and pulling it into himself. Gasping, my back arched and my eyes opened wide.

"You're killing her!" Jenks shouted, and I fell back into Pierce.

My arms moved, and my lungs expanded. Gulping the air so hard it hurt, I coughed.

"Catch them!" Jenks exclaimed, and my eyes flashed open as Ivy darted forward to catch Pierce and hold us both upright. His arms were still wrapped around me, and his head was beside mine. He was panting, lips parted and brow furrowed in pain. His breath came fast, and I could feel it on me, coming and going.

"I swan," he breathed. "You can hold a considerable amount of line, Rachel."

I shifted, and his eyes opened, finding mine. Something pinged through me again, painful in its exquisiteness. I recognized it, even as I tried to deny its existence. And I smiled, weak as a kitten as I rested in his arms. "Hi," I whispered so I wouldn't start coughing, concentrating on small, even breaths.

"Hi back at you," he said, the modern phrase sounding funny with his accent, and then Jenks was there, spilling a green dust and looking panicked.

"Rache, are you okay?" the pixy demanded. "Was it a curse? Trent tried to kill you?"

"Looks like it," I said, vowing to jam a curry brush down his throat the next time I saw him.

Jenks started swearing in one-word syllables. My thankful gaze went to Pierce. Damn, the man could hold a lot of energy. Maybe as much as me with a little stretching. And he was holding me. On my bed.

My expression became empty. I didn't have time for this, and it hurt too much when it was over. "Phone," I rasped, trying to untangle myself. The bed shifted as Ivy got off it, and the cooler air hit me when Pierce let go and moved to stand awkwardly beside me. "Where's my phone?" I asked, then remembered it was in San Francisco.

Nick's eyes were wide, and Jenks was spilling a red dust, but Ivy seemed to be thinking the same thing I was, and she handed me her cell. "Use mine."

"Tink's titties!" Jenks was saying, darting up and down, making me nauseous. "Rache, you're not calling him, are you?"

"Watch me." My fingers trembled as I punched in the numbers. I was so pissed. How dare he. How dare he give me a charm and try to kill me with it. Was this his backhanded way of threatening me? Do what he wanted or else? He hadn't changed at all from the brat of a boy demanding I hold his horse's head when there was a post only two feet away.

"Don't call him! He'll know it didn't work!" Jenks shouted, and I waved him back. The pixy's wings clattered noisily, but then went quiet. "You know his number by heart?"

Yes, I had Trent Kalamack's number memorized. Sort of like when you remember the name of the kid who beat you up in the third grade. Some things you don't forget.

"Quiet. I want to hear," Ivy demanded as the phone rang, and my anger tightened when Jenks landed on my shoulder. Together we listened to the line click open.

"Kalamack Industries," the woman said, but I couldn't tell if it was Sara Jane or if she'd gotten smart and run away. "How may I help you?"

A thousand smart-ass answers went through my head, but my eyes on Ivy's, I managed, "This is Rachel Morgan—"

"Yes, Ms. Morgan," she interrupted. "Mr. Kalamack has been waiting for your call."

"I'll bet," I said, but she'd already put me on hold. If there was elevator music, I was going to scream.

"Rachel!" Trent's voice came clear and clean, a hint of warmth to it that slid out of the professional into genuine pleasure.

"You son of a bastard!" I exclaimed, and Jenks snorted.

There was a slight hesitation, then, "I take it this isn't a social call?" Trent said dryly, his entire mood shifting.

How could he sit there like nothing had happened? "It didn't work, you bastard. I'm still alive, and you'd better start watching your back. I should have let you rot in the ever-after, you son of a bitch!"

"Still alive?"

I'd give him one thing. He hid his smugness well. "The Pandora charm?" I supplied to jiggle his conveniently faulty memory. "It was us riding your horse at camp. You're scum, Trent!"

"I didn't try to kill you. You fell off!" he said indignantly.

He thought I was talking about the memory? "Not the horse!" I said, suddenly unsure. "Your spell! It almost killed me. The memory ended with me lying on the ground with the breath knocked out of me, and it froze everything. I couldn't breathe when the charm ended. I could have died! If you can't have me, no one will, huh? What in hell is *wrong* with you!"

"Be reasonable, Rachel," Trent said coldly. "If I wanted you dead, I wouldn't do it with a charm I helped craft that could be traced back to me."

"I think you would!" I exclaimed. "You want me dead!"

"There are at least five people I can think of off the top of my head who want you dead."

"*Wanting* me dead is not the same as having the *resources to do it*," I reminded him.

I heard him take a breath to say something, then pause as if in sudden thought. "I have to go," he said abruptly. "You're okay? Right?" he asked, and I looked at Ivy, knowing she could hear both ends of the conversation as well as Jenks, on my shoulder.

He cared if I was all right? *And he hadn't called Lee back either when he knew I was afraid of him.* "Don't you hang up on me, Trent," I said. "Don't you do it!"

"Good, you're okay. I'll talk to you later. I have to check on something. Ah, sorry about the charm."

My breath came in fast, and I sat up. "Trent!" I shouted, but the phone went dead. "He hung up on me," I said sourly, then flipped the phone closed and handed it to Ivy.

Jenks took off from my shoulder, and a shiver coursed through me. "That sounded like real surprise to me," he said, hovering before the tight-lipped vampire.

"Me, too," she said, looking worried as she leaned back against the dresser.

"Even so, I wouldn't trust him," Pierce said. "His father was a devious sort, and I've seen nothing to convince me he's any different."

"Yeah. I know." Exhaling, I pressed my knees together so no one would see them shake. *Do I believe him, or not?* God! Why can't it be simple just once? I had invoked the charm to figure out why my gut kept telling me there was something good about this guy, and I was more confused than before. I'd give anything to know Trent's thoughts just before he'd hung up. "That was a complete waste of time," I said softly.

"I don't care if Rynn complains," Ivy said dryly. "I'm going to kill Trent. Slowly."

Pierce was nodding his agreement, but my damned intuition had me clenching my jaw in doubt. Trent had killed people before, one right in front of me. And once he had pulled out a gun and shot me with a subjugation spell, the decision made and acted on in a second. It wasn't that Trent couldn't kill me, but if he was going to do it, it would be over and done within an hour of his decision. Not like this. This smacked of cowardice. It wasn't his style.

I rubbed my wrist where he had grabbed me, feeling it as if it had just been today. He'd violated my person to see if I was as dangerous as his father had warned him—and I had thrown him into a tree the next day, proving it. He was good and bad all at the same time. God, I hated Trent. Or maybe I just hated that I didn't know if I could trust him or not.

"I opine it wasn't a curse," Pierce said as I fingered the smooth rope. "It was a spell crafted to not cleanly break. Death by something designed as innocent so as not to invoke your lethal-charm amulet. Powerful tricky. But you didn't make a die of it, and that's what matters."

My eyes went to his, and Pierce dropped his attention to the hat in his hands, his ears going a faint red. "Thanks, Pierce," I said softly. "I owe you. Big."

Jenks snorted and Ivy sighed, making motions to try to leave. Sheesh, Pierce had pulled a line through me to burn the malfunctioning charm to nothing. No wonder he was embarrassed.

His eyes met mine. "It was what any decent man would do. You owe me nothing," he said, and Jenks groaned from the overdone drama. But Pierce had probably saved my life.

Orange dust falling from him, Jenks dropped to my knee. "Well, what did you remember?" he asked, wings going full tilt. "Hope it was worth dying for."

Ivy crossed her arms over her middle to look both aggressive and pensive. "This was my fault. I convinced her to try the charm, thinking it might tell her if she didn't trust Trent because of a grade-school tiff or because he's a bastard."

"I think we can safely answer that now," Pierce muttered, but I wasn't sure, and it made me angry.

"It was just something from the Make-a-Wish Camp," I said, and Jenks buzzed his wings for more, but I wasn't talking. I was remembering all sorts of things now. Stuff like Lee being trapped in the cistern for three days shortly afterward. He was half dead when they found him, suffering badly—apparently Trent had taken my advice with an overly aggressive vengeance. And Jasmine finding flowers on her pillow every morning in contrast to the fox scat I kept finding in my shoes. I'd thought it was cabin razzing, but now I wondered if it had been Trent trying to get his hoof pick back. My stuff kept going missing that year, invariably showing up a few days later in the cabin toilet. Uncomfortable, I swung my feet to the floor, and Jenks took off. "Yes, he's a bastard all right," I said softly, not meeting anyone's eyes.

"Tink's contractual hell, you still think he's telling the truth about the coven?" Jenks exclaimed at the whisper of doubt in my voice. "He just tried to kill you!"

"I know!" I shouted, and Jenks flew backward in surprise to Ivy. "Don't you think I know that? But I can't figure him out!"

"What's to figure out?" Nick said dryly. "He's a liar. He's always been a liar, and he will always be a liar."

Frustrated, I opened up the box and took out the hoof pick, looking at it like it was a puzzle box. "Trent was that same mix of ruthless bastard and sympathetic best friend at camp that he is now. And I think I helped make him that way. Apparently I won the bet, though."

I lifted the exquisite hoof pick and handed it to Pierce, figuring he'd be interested in it. I wondered if Trent sneaking in to take my ring last year was because I had stolen his pick. Maybe he wanted it back? He *had* given me my ring back—and not in my toilet.

Nick shook his head in warning and I gave him a mirthless smile as I rubbed my aching arms. It was as if my childhood fatigue had soaked back in and wasn't leaving. I was so messed up. And what was it with Trent's pattern of taking my stuff only to give it back?

Ivy picked up the empty plate and moved to the door. "Are you sure you're okay?"

"Yeah, you were blue, Rache," Jenks chimed in.

Flexing my fingers, I felt the lack of strength. Cripes, she'd almost broken them.

Without warning, a high-pitched barrage of near-ultrasonic pixy voices rose, shrill at the front of the church. In a flash of silver dust, Jenks darted out. My eyes touched on Pierce's, and he was gone as well, his feet thumping on the oak flooring to the front of the church. Ivy was a step behind, almost shoving Nick out of the way.

Eyes wide, I stared at Nick, jumping when I felt two people tap into the ley line out back. This wasn't pixy mischief. We were being attacked!

Pierce's voice rang out from the front of the church, and then a crash of glass. Shit. He was yelling in Latin.

In a spurt of motion, I got to my feet, pushing past Nick to reach the hallway. It was empty, but a heavy thump from the sanctuary filled me with dread. "Ivy?" My knees gave a hard twinge, and my run turned into a shuffle. Breathless, I came to a halt at the end of the hall, leaning on the open frame. The bright glare of late-morning sun spilled into the empty sanctuary, stripped ages ago to walls and a wooden floor. The light over the pool table was swinging, and my heart seemed to stop when I saw Ivy flat out beside her grand piano, face turned away and hair spread.

Pixies were a dangerous cloud surrounding Vivian and Pierce, both of them standing on broken colored glass. Vivian's produce-stained coat gave her some protection from pixy steel, but blood was about her face and neck where she'd been nicked. She didn't look too happy about it. A red haze glowed around her hands, growing darker as her fingers manipulated magic and her lips moved to give it strength. I had no doubt that it would be both white—and deadly.

Pierce was grappling with her, holding her wrists with a black-and-green glow hazing out from his entire body. I had no idea what he was doing, but his face was creased with strain. The scent of ozone was heavy, and the morning air drifted in, almost too cool for the pixies.

With a cry, Vivian kicked out to shove Pierce off her. Pierce hit the floor, seizing when his magic backlashed into him. Angry, Pierce tossed his hair from his eyes and looked up at the ugly smile of anticipation coming over Vivian, widening as she finished her charm and held it, a glowing ball of who knew what.

"Hey, Strawberry Shortcake!" I shouted, pushing myself upright.

Vivian's pretty lips parted, and swearing, she shifted her aim to me.

Crap. When would I ever learn?

"No!" Pierce shouted from the floor, and I dove for the pool table, hitting the floor hard as I skidded under it. Pixies scattered as the glowing ball skipped across the felt and exploded within the arrangement of TV and chairs for interviewing potential clients. The leather couch started to melt, sending the reek of burnt flesh into the air.

"Set a circle!" Pierce shouted again. "Get yourself safe!"

Does he think I'm stupid? "Rhombus!" I exclaimed from under the table, my view of feet and legs useless. My protective circle sprang up through the slate over me, the smut-covered gold taking the hit as a second spell exploded against it and dripped evilly down the sides to pool on the floor like blood marking the rim of my circle.

And outside it, Ivy.

Fear galvanized me. I wasn't that good at ley-line magic, and all my earth charms were in the kitchen. Irate, I inched my way out from under the table, drawing heavily on the ley line when I passed through my circle and broke it. Ticked, I staggered to my feet. The line vibrated through me, and I let the energy gather in my hand.

"Rachel, stay out of this!" Pierce cried.

"Clear!" I shouted, and the pixies harrying her scattered. "You come into my house?" I yelled. "You set my pool table on fire! What in hell is *wrong* with you?" I threw the unfocused energy at Vivian. The woman ducked, then dove out of the way when Pierce sent a black-colored spell after at her in a one-two punch.

"Break my window and hurt my *friend*?" I shouted, shambling forward like a zombie.

My second ball hit her protective circle, and she went down, her fashionable high heels costing her her balance. Pierce's second spell sailed over her with a shouted *"Interrumpere,"* slamming into the front door of the church to make it crash open. The pixies dusting the fire on the pool table shrieked, and from the floor Vivian gazed at Pierce in fear.

"You go tell the coven they just made mistake number two!" I shouted at Vivian, and the woman scrabbled to reach the door, breaking her own circle and tripping over Ivy. "There'd better not be a mistake number three!" I added. "Get out of my church!"

"Animam, agere, efflare." Pierce spoke in slow, deliberate syllables, chilling me. He was wreathed in a sheet of ever-after, his entire body glowing as he summoned his magic, the black words spilling from him. He was powerful and determined, his stance firm and his hands moving confidently. The hair on my neck prickled, and a shudder rose through me. My lips parted, and even the pixies fell back. Oh my God. What was he doing?

From the floor, Vivian stared, transfixed. "Who the Turn are you?" she breathed.

Pierce smiled, his fingers stilling as a ball of black death waited in his hand. "Tell the coven that Gordian Pierce demands a powerful reckoning of their betrayal of one of their own. And if a body was smart, she'd leave while she still could."

"Get out of here!" I shouted, this time worried for Vivian's life, and she fled, clawing her way to her feet at the threshold.

"Pierce, stop! She's gone!" I shouted, seeing his blazing ball of blackness hiss through the air after her. It hit Vivian's back the instant she left the church. She shrieked as she fell down the stairs, but I didn't care what Pierce's magic had done. I was running to Ivy, hobbling to an awkward stop and falling to kneel beside her. Pain shot up my knees.

"Ivy? Ivy!" I called, picking her head up only to ease it back down. It hurt just to kneel. Pulling her head up onto my lap wasn't going to happen, and I brushed the hair from her face.

"She took a spell for me," Pierce said from the front of the church. He was poised at the door, pixies flowing in and out around him, standing with a ball of black magic in his hand and the wind shifting his dark hair as he looked out. His face was calm, and his eyes were hard.

"She stepped right in front of it and took it for me," he explained as he turned to me. "Even then, she kept coming like a caution until the harlot was obliged to use a ley-line sleep charm to down her."

"Is she okay?" I looked at Ivy, seeing her hardly breathing. "Can you break them?" I asked, scared, and he nodded.

"If I work directly upon it. The first was to slow her heart."

"That doesn't sound bad," I said, and Pierce looked up, his gaze worried under his bangs.

"Singly it isn't, but together? If I can't break them, she'll die," he said bluntly.

I felt myself go ashen. In the street, a car accelerated away. Vivian was gone.

"But they're white spells," I said, then thought about it. Alone, the charms were white, but together, the combination of low blood pressure and sleep could put her in a coma. "Pierce?" I warbled. Ivy couldn't die. I couldn't live with her if she was undead.

"Let me work," he said tightly, and I took a deep breath, feeling helpless. There was a red haze in the air that reminded me of the ever-after, and the shadow of the church's cross that once hung over the absent altar seemed to glow.

"Jenks!" I shouted, heart pounding as Pierce knelt with Ivy between us. The pixies were loud, and I wished they'd shut up. "Jenks!" I shouted again. "Get in here!" I knew I should be worried about his kids and Bis, but I couldn't leave Ivy.

Pierce's expression was empty, and I felt him draw heavily on the ley line. His hands moved in a start-and-stop motion over Ivy, as if he was unsure. There was a flash of dragonfly wings, and Jenks was back, spilling dust on Ivy in his agitation. "Sorry, Rache," he said, his sword red with blood. "I was making sure it was just the one. She waited until it was only my kids, then came in the front, bold as brass. Tink's a Disney whore, she broke the window. We'll never find a replacement for it." Excited, he looked down. "How's Ivy?"

"She took two spells. Pierce is breaking them."

"Spells? She's okay, isn't she?"

I could hardly say the words. "It's white magic, Jenks, but she might not wake up if we can't break them in time."

"Holy shit!" The pixy dropped down to dust her with the red of worry. "Pierce, I take everything back. Just make Ivy okay again. Okay? Okay!"

My gaze alternated between Ivy and Pierce, my tension growing as Pierce mumbled and a haze enveloped his hands.

"Rache!" Jenks shrilled as he dropped to her face. "Can't you just douse her in salt water? Do something!"

"It's ley-line magic, Jenks," I said, frantic as I looked at Pierce, helpless.

"The devil woman layered it," he muttered. "It's powerful tricky. Just shut-pan and let me work. She'll be fine. You're making an all-fired to-do over nothing."

Easy for him to say. My heart pounded, and Jenks and I watched Ivy breathe, each one softer than the last. The haze enveloping Pierce's hands took on a decidedly black glow, and power prickled through me. "Hurry," I whispered as his hands moved with an unconscious grace over her. I didn't care if he was a black witch if he saved Ivy.

Finally Pierce exhaled, the glow fading from his hands as the last of it fell into Ivy and he leaned back on his heels. "Is she okay?" I blurted out, and he nodded, looking haggard.

"It will take a moment to work itself through, but yes, she should wake now."

Tears warmed my eyes, and I suddenly remembered I was kneeling on the cold wooden floor, my knees the size of grapefruit and aching. Ivy was going to be okay.

"Ivy!" Jenks exclaimed, hovering by her nose and jabbing it with his foot. "Wake up!"

Ivy gasped, and I jumped as Jenks darted up, wings clattering. My hand went out, and I reached for her, jerking back when she yelped as I touched her shoulder.

"You said she was all right!" I exclaimed, horrified, and Pierce looked mystified.

"Broken," Ivy said, breath hissing when she tried to sit up. "I broke my arm when I fell."

"Ivy! You almost died!" Jenks said cheerfully. "Pierce saved you!"

Ivy glanced at him, holding her arm and pain etching her features. "Thanks, Pierce," she said dully. "Did she get away?" she asked as she took in the broken glass, smoldering couch, and burnt pool table.

Thank you, God, I thought, trying to calm myself so Ivy wouldn't know how close it had been. "Of course she did." I awkwardly took my pain amulet off and looped it over her head.

"Ow," Ivy hissed through clenched teeth as she looked at her arm and turned gray.

"Yup, that's broken," Jenks said, hovering over it and dusting heavily. "Just like the window. She broke my window, Ivy!"

"The woman didn't break the window, I did," Pierce said, looking embarrassed.

"You!" I exclaimed, and his eyes flicked to the ruination. But the glass had fallen inward. How could he have done it? Unless it had been a curse . . .

"I didn't do it a'purpose," he said, affronted. "I was aiming at the coven woman." Turning from me, Pierce leaned close to Ivy, not afraid that she was a vampire and that her eyes were going black in pain. "Ms. Tamwood," he said. "Thank you for taking the spells for me. I'm obliged to you."

"Well, if you saved my life, I'd say we're even," she said sourly. "I have to get my arm looked at," she said, her voice thready and her face pale.

I sat and twisted my knees to a more comfortable position, feeling the cool breeze coming in the shattered window and gaping door and wondering how I was going to get up. My knees were doubly in pain now that Ivy had my amulet, but I wasn't going to ask for it back. It was so unfair. The coven could kill people using white magic with no reprisal, but I use a black curse to save someone and I get shunned.

Jenks hovered between us, flying in a slow arch and spilling blue sparkles. "Ivy, I'm sorry. Crap-for-brains is gone. Jax, too."

I exhaled heavily and looked to the back of the church. *Why am I not surprised?*

"It means naught." Pierce's expression was grim. "He's a no-account scoundrel, and we're better off without. Mistress Ivy, can you stand?"

No-account scoundrel? Nick wasn't the one who'd been buried alive, I thought, disgusted with myself while eying Pierce as he helped Ivy up. God, he looked good—capable and sure of himself even as my life twisted into a more complicated knot. A pang of fear hit me, unexpected and shocking as I remembered crying for Kisten. *I can't do this.*

"Pierce, do you think you could drive if I coached you?" Ivy asked, long fingers gripping his shoulder with a white-knuckled strength.

Swallowing hard, I forced my thoughts from Kisten. Heartache echoed in me as I lurched upright, my knees protesting. "I can take you to the hospital. Where are my keys?" She needed to be checked out. Get a CT scan or something.

"Not your car," she said breathily as she gazed at the floor. "It's totaled."

"Totaled!" I cried. "When were you going to tell me?"

Jenks sifted gold dust to make a temporary sunbeam on the old oak floor. "Some time between telling you David had to drop you from his insurance and that the state is taking your driver's license. Something about a condition that causes you to vanish suddenly."

I put a hand to my middle. I couldn't take the bus for the rest of my life. This was so unfair.

"Ow, ow! Don't touch it, Pierce! You idiot!" Ivy shouted as he probed her arm. "I told you it was broken!"

Pierce pulled his hand away, glaring right back at her black-eyed stare, and I jerked when there was a scuffing of shoes on the stairs outside.

"It's Glenn," Jenks said, head cocked as he listened to his kids. "I think he just noticed the broken window and the open door 'cause he just un-snapped his pistol."

"Glenn?" I questioned, my gaze going to Ivy. "Did someone call 911?"

Ivy held her arm to her middle, looking up past her hair to the open door, shrugging.

"Hello?" the big man's voice boomed out, cautiously. "Rachel? Ivy? Everyone okay?"

Pixies flew over us in a wave, going to meet the FIB detective. I swear, the man had to have some elven blood in him the way Jenks's kids took to him. Either that, or they liked the smell of gun oil.

"Come on in, Glenn!" I called, and the light in the foyer was eclipsed.

"Ivy?" Glenn said, his gaze going first to her, standing with Pierce's support. He started for her, but his eyes were taking everything in, linger-ing on the smoldering couch and the burn ring on the pool table. I had no doubt that it had been a white spell designed to toast marshmallows, but Vivian could have set the church on fire with it.

"Rachel, what do you do? Put an ad in the paper for trouble?" Glenn asked, snapping the flap over his weapon back down as he crossed the room.

"Ha, ha. Very funny." I shifted my weight to my other foot, knees ach-ing. "Glenn, this is Pierce. Pierce, this is Glenn, my friend from the FIB."

I watched Pierce closely as Glenn came forward with his usual grace and spare motion, his right hand extended even as he slipped a supporting arm under Ivy.

"It's my arm that's broken. I can walk," she said irately, pulling away from both men.

Pierce shook Glenn's hand with a firm formality, not a hint of reserva-tion in him, even if his gaze did hesitate on his shaved head and one earring. "I'm powerfully pleased to meet you, Detective Glenn," he said, glancing at Ivy as she sat on the couch and halfheartedly hit the smoldering leather with a magazine. "You've been a friend to Rachel for a good span."

Glenn's eyebrows rose at Pierce's speech, but his smile was genuine. "Not for as long as I hope to," he said. I tried to imagine his grin with sharp canines, and couldn't.

I started hobbling to the kitchen to get another pain amulet, my grip tight on the smooth wood of the pool table. The pixies were hovering over it, heads down as they poked the burnt felt with their swords. It was totally ruined. I'd have to get it refelted. *Sorry, Kisten.*

"Ah, I came over to tell you I have an ID on the woman who attacked you," Glenn said from behind me.

"Let me guess," I said, inching along. "Vivian Smith is a member of the coven of moral and ethical standards."

"The witch broke into my church." Jenks darted about the sanctuary, counting his kids.

"Really." Glenn didn't sound surprised, and I nodded. "Didn't they already shun you?"

"Yeah. And now they want my ovaries," I said dryly. *Step-ow. Step-ow.*

Glenn looked appalled when I glanced up, and Pierce was wincing, embarrassed as he gazed at the broken glass. Pixies were darting in and out, giving Jenks fits. Matalina had the youngest, but she could do only so much.

Ivy looked ill on the pixy-dusted, smoldering couch, her arm cradled against her. "Glenn, can you take me to the emergency room? Rachel can't drive with her knees like that."

"I can so," I complained, but he was watching me inch along, shaking his head.

"Looks like you need to be admitted, too," he said. "You want to file a report?"

I grimaced. "Against the coven? Ri-i-i-ight." Accepting Glenn's help, I hobbled to the hallway. He smelled like honey and hot metal. Daryl, apparently. "I can take Ivy to the hospital," I said slowly. "My mom's Buick is an automatic. You look like you're on duty."

Jenks laughed as he got all but three of his kids out in the yard. "There's a good idea," he said as he sent the last of them to the rafters to keep watch. "The coven is trying to kill you, and you want to drive Ivy to the hospital where there are syringes and big knives."

I changed my aim from the hallway to the couch, slipping from Glenn's grip to sit beside Ivy. "I can drive," I said sourly. "I just need a new pain amulet."

"I'll get it, mistress witch," Pierce said, his feet soundless as he vanished into the hall.

"Mistress witch?" Glenn muttered, standing over Ivy as if not knowing what to do.

"He's not from around here," I said, tired. Ivy got to her feet, and I stared up at her.

"Stay here, Rachel," Ivy said as she headed for the foyer, coming out with her purse in her good hand. "Glenn can take me. I'll be gone a few hours. Can you sit tight for that long?"

She was getting bitchy. That was a good sign. "What am I supposed to do till you get back?" I said, patting the smoldering leather. "Hide in my closet? I'd rather be with you."

Jenks made a gagging sound. "This is so sweet, I think I'm going to barf fairy farts."

Glenn rocked back out of Pierce's way as he edged past him to hand me an amulet. The witch had his hat in his hand, and I wondered if he was leaving, too. My fingers touched the amulet, and a wave of relief flowed into me.

"I'll take Ivy to the emergency room," the FIB detective said as he jiggled his key. "And I don't want you to be here, Rachel, when I get back."

"Excuse me?" I stared at him from the couch.

Glenn smiled at my affronted expression. "You need to leave town," he said. "Take a vacation. Visit your mom." He hesitated, then added, "Find a hiding spot for a few days?"

My eyes opened wide as I got it, but Jenks took to the air, a vivid silver falling from him. "No fairy-ass way!" he exclaimed, his kids in the rafters going silent. "She's not leaving here."

Ivy took a defensive stance, holding her arm tight against herself. "The church is safe."

Pierce, though, was nodding, glancing at the broken shards in the sun before saying, "I'm of a mind you don't understand the danger. Glenn is right. You need to leave."

My mouth dropped open. "We don't understand the danger?" I said loudly. "Are you serious? Pierce, we can handle this. We have before." But my thoughts were on Ivy, languishing under twin white spells. Twice today a benign charm had been turned to one capable of doling out death. It was so hypocritical it made me sick.

"I'll admit your diggings are a fine defense," Pierce added when Jenks's wings clattered. "And your skills, Jenks, are a caution, but that was the coven's plumber. The best action is not to be where she expects you to be."

Confused, I asked, "The coven's what?"

"Plumber," Ivy said, looking pale as she leaned on Glenn. "You know. Stops leaks?"

Oh goodie. I'm a leak. "Look, the church has kept me safe for over a year. Jenks is here, and I'm not leaving."

Jenks landed on my shoulder, his relief obvious. Pierce, though, was scowling. "How can I keep you safe if you don't do what I say? Get your things."

Do what he says? Jenks's dust was starting to feel warm on my shoulder, and I put up a hand to keep him from flying at Pierce. "I'm not leaving," I said softly from the couch, but I was pissed. "And no one asked for your opinion. You were wrong about not telling Al about the coven, and you're wrong about this."

Pierce frowned, but my attention jerked to Glenn, who had also taken a defensive stance. "What can it hurt?" he said, and Ivy gave him a dark look. "Really, what's the big deal?"

They didn't understand. This was my place. My security. I'd made it, and to leave it felt wrong. "It doesn't feel right," I said, thinking it sounded lame, yet my gut said stay. But what the hell did my gut know? It told me there was just as much good in Trent as bad.

"Your 'doesn't feel right' will get you killed," Pierce said.

Jenks darted from me. "We can keep her safe," he said, inches from Pierce's face.

"But not from witches, and especially not from the coven." Frowning, Pierce backed up, touching everyone's gaze before returning to Jenks's. "I've been betrayed by them before. Witch magic is Rachel's greatest liability, and until she sets herself beyond it, she won't have a chance. She's not good enough."

"But you are, huh?" Jenks said snidely, hand on the hilt of his sword.

"I'm better than you, pixy."

This was getting out of hand, and I glanced at Ivy, who was watching it all with growing agitation. And what had Pierce meant by "set myself beyond it"? Did he mean until I started doing deadly black magic, like him? "Jenks, relax," I said, and he drifted back, hands on his hips and his wings clattering harshly.

"One spell, and poof," Pierce said casually, and Ivy's face creased.

"I can take a coven of witches, you fairy fart!" Jenks exclaimed. "And I can take you!"

Concerned, I looked at the broken glass on the floor, remembering Ivy lying on it. I couldn't have saved her, white magic or not. Jenks was clueless as to how close it had been. "Maybe I should go," I said softly, and Jenks spun in the air, dropping three inches.

"Tink's titties. Rache, we have this!"

I took a deep breath, my stomach knotting as I exhaled. This felt wrong.

Ivy, too, looked uneasy. "I don't think this is beyond us," she said, "but Pierce is right. A moving target is harder to hit. Rachel should go."

Jenks flipped her off, and my stomach hurt even more.

"I'll talk to Rynn Cormel," Ivy said, adjusting her purse and clearly ready to leave. "He can put us up for a few days. Sound good?"

No, it didn't sound good, but even the coven would think twice about taking on the master vampire who had run the free world during the

Turn. "Okay," I said softly, and Jenks flew an erratic path to come between Pierce and me.

"Rache, no," he pleaded. "This is wrong!"

I glanced at Ivy and Glenn, neither one looking happy. "I don't like it either."

Pierce cleared his throat, and Jenks glared at him, a burst of light seeming to push him into the air. "I'm going, too," he said. "I don't want you alone. And not with *him*! His aura is freakier than shadows during an eclipse."

"You can't," I said, remembering Pierce standing at the door watching Vivian flee, and the last parting shot that hadn't been necessary. *Animam, agere, efflare . . .* Didn't that have something to do with breathing? No wonder his aura was as dark as mine.

Jenks's dust shifted to an ugly, burnt gold. "Why the hell not?"

I looked at him, seeing the distress on his face, wishing I could do this differently. "Someone needs to stay and make sure the coven doesn't come in and grab a focusing object."

"They could hit her from a distance," Pierce said, his face so grim I wondered if he had been taken that way. "It wouldn't be legal," he said as his eyes met mine.

"But they'd do it," Ivy said softly, and Glenn frowned. I nodded, thinking of the leather jacket I'd left at the coven's circle, glad now that Oliver's charm had tainted it.

"Tink's dildo," Jenks said softly, falling until he stood on the coffee table. "Rache?"

"Glenn's right," I said, remembering that it was his idea first. "If they sent Vivian after me again, then they don't have anyone who can summon me—yet." *And if Nick goes back to them, I'll give him to Al and worry about my guilt later.* "Until then, they're reduced to snag-and-drag. If they can't find me, they can't snatch me. I'm leaving, but you're staying. I'm sorry. I need you here, Jenks." This felt wrong, but the logic was sound.

Jenks's wings hummed loudly as I stood, wavering until Pierce's fingers cupped my elbow. The Turn take it, my knees still hurt, but I could walk with the pain amulet. Maybe I could make this work for me? I had an old-lady disguise charm in the back of my cupboard.

"Ivy, call me when you know how bad it is?" I asked, and she nodded. Her hand was starting to swell, and it looked awful. Ivy's purse was in Glenn's grip, and it looked funny there. I thought of them together on a date—then squelched it.

"Soon as I clear it with Rynn, I'll let you know," she said. "Stay in a public place?"

"Not a problem." I came forward to give her a careful hug.

"This is fairy crap!" Jenks exclaimed, looking miserable as he hovered beside Glenn. "It doesn't feel right, Rache!"

"I'm right with you, Jenks," I said, then to Ivy, "You be careful." I breathed deep as I let her go, pulling the scent of vampire incense deep into me, mixing with my raspberry smell of the detangling spray and the cloying stench of the smoldering couch. I prayed that it wouldn't be the last time I saw her. This really felt wrong. "Don't tell Glenn that Nick was here," I whispered, and she sighed.

"Here, you'll need this," Ivy said, shoving a wad of cash at me, pulled from her purse, still in Glenn's possession.

I took it so she wouldn't get pissy. And then it was just Jenks and me, watching Glenn help Ivy to the door, looking right next to each other. Seeing them make their hesitant way, my heavy feeling of foreboding grew worse. The door shut behind Ivy, and the church became silent. Through the broken window came the melancholy hooting of a mourning dove.

Hand full of cash, I turned to Pierce, feeling the wrongness seep deeper into me. We were all going different ways. Not good. Forcing a smile, I started to shuffle to the kitchen. "So, Pierce. How would you like to learn how to drive?"

Eleven

My lungs seemed reluctant to rebound after I exhaled, and my breath came slowly as I sat at the small round coffeehouse table and waited for Pierce to return with a caffeine-and-sugar buzz. Jenks's tiny phone, on loan, was small in my fingers, and after making sure I hadn't missed Ivy's call, I tucked it in my bag, hesitated, then moved it to a back pocket. It was almost noon, and still no Ivy. I was worried. Jenks hadn't been happy about me leaving. Neither was I. Pierce accompanying me didn't make me feel better, especially since he was turning heads.

I was so tired. Even the picture of babies dressed up as fruit salad couldn't make me smile. Somehow we'd landed at Junior's place. Or Mark's, if I remembered properly. I'd been banned because of my shunning, but no one had given me a second look when I'd shuffled in, the heavy-magic detection amulet above the door buzzing a warning at my old-lady disguise. Mark knew me by sight, and without the charm, we would've been chased out.

Why a fruit salad? I mused, tilting my head to get my hair out of my eyes. I hadn't time to put it back in a bun, which sort of diluted the old-lady thing. But it was gray now, and I certainly acted old, walking slowly from my bruised knees. Rummaging in my bag, I took the lethal-spell and heavy-magic detection amulets from my key ring and moved them to my pocket instead in case I got summoned out at sundown.

My back was to the wall as I sat at the same table where I'd once had a conversation with a spoiled brat of a banshee and her husband the serial killer. Outside, my mom's big blue Buick shone in the bright spring sun. Yes, we should have parked it somewhere else, but to be honest, when I spotted Junior's I had all but screamed for Pierce to stop the car. He wasn't a good driver, unable to get his feet to work the brake and gas with any precision. I think I'd bruised his ego. He'd been somewhat cold since. *Sor-r-r-r-r-ry.*

I rubbed at my aching neck and smiled as I recalled his red-faced, benign cussing about jo-fired fife curs and strumpets. Gaze rising, I looked at the register where he was counting out exact change for our drinks, looking appalled by the cost. Mark was waiting impatiently, and our coffee was done and sitting at the pickup counter before the till was shut.

A sigh sifted through me, not all of it from my fatigue. Pierce looked charming in his vest, long duster, and hat, his softly waving hair almost to his shoulders. It made him look like a young Were as yet free of responsibilities. Tucking the folded receipt away, he went to get our drinks with the smooth grace of a vampire. Drinks in hand, he moved slowly, not trusting the plastic tops to keep them from spilling as he wove between the tables busy with noon customers—both breakfasting Inderlanders and lunching humans—avoiding all with the awareness of self that most witches have. It was strange watching Pierce. He was a quick study and had been among the living again long enough to pick up most things, but it was obvious he had trouble with some of the smaller stuff, like how to open a package of gum.

"Rachel," he said softly, eyes darting to mine before he placed a tall cup before me and sat at my elbow so that he could see the door as well. He looked confident but wary of the surrounding people. Furtive, maybe, as he tossed his hair from his eyes. He smelled good, too, a mix of redwood and clean hair. *And he used black magic as if it were a breath mint.*

"Thanks, Pierce." Gaze dropping, I took the lid off so I wouldn't have to taste plastic with my coffee. My eyes closed in bliss when the shot of caffeine laced with raspberry slipped down. "Oh, that's good," I breathed, eyes opening to see him smiling. "You remembered."

"Grande latte, double espresso, Italian blend, light on the froth, heavy on the cinnamon, with a shot of raspberry in it." Tilting his head, he added, "I'm not accustomed to seeing you graced with wrinkles. It takes a body a moment."

Graced with wrinkles? Can't he just say old? I shrugged, embarrassed. "If I'd been thinking, I would have grabbed a disguise for you, too."

"You'd rather I be disguised?" he asked, and when I nodded, there was a soft pressure against me, as if something was rubbing my aura. My eyes widened when a sheet of ever-after flowed over Pierce, ebbing to nothing to show Tom Bansen. Same curling brown hair, same blue eyes, same slight build, same . . . everything.

"Uh, good," I said, uneasy at the reminder that Pierce was living his life out in another man's body, dead just long enough for his soul to depart. His posture, though, was Pierce's upright stance, and the slacks and vest, which were charming on Pierce, looked really odd on Tom. "You're a dead ringer for Tom."

Pierce flushed. "I am Tom Bansen, mistress witch. The trick is to look like myself."

That gave me the willies even more, and I hid my unease behind another sip. "Call me Rachel. We belong to the same demon, I think that entitles us to some informality."

He made a noise as he found a new way to sit. "To call a woman by her given name—"

"It makes you stick out," I said, starting to get peeved.

"It's powerfully disrespectful," he muttered, shaking his hand when his coffee spilled, squeezed from the cup when he took the lid off.

My eyes were on the bright sun on the street. "It's a rougher time, Pierce." Which I thought was weird. With all the conveniences and clean simplicity we lived in, people had lost a lot of polish. Sighing, I gazed up at the ceiling, glad no one had noticed Pierce changing. Few knew that the witch named Tom Bansen had been killed by a banshee and reanimated by Al to hold Pierce's soul only moments after Tom's last heartbeat. It was black magic in the extreme, and probably why Pierce's aura was now blacker than mine—among other things.

"Has Ms. Tamwood sent word?" Pierce asked intently, a weird mix of Tom and Pierce.

Another swallow of coffee, and the caffeine started to take hold. The cup warmed my hands, and I set it down. "No. I hope everything's okay. I'm about ready to leave her a voice message. Something doesn't feel right." *Something more than you next to me instead of Jenks.*

Pierce ran a hand under his hat to get his hair out of his eyes. "I'm sorry for you having to leave your diggings, but it's not safe, Rachel. The coven—"

"Yes, I know," I said angrily. The church had always been my safe haven, and it bothered me that it was now a place of danger. It bothered me a lot.

Leaning back, Pierce crossed his arms over his chest. "A body might begin to suspect that you don't like me. I'm only trying to see you safe."

His eyes were narrowed, and I sighed. "Pierce . . . ," I started, and he looked away. *Save me from the tender male ego.* "Can you put yourself in my shoes for a minute?" I asked, unable to keep the bitterness from my voice. "Wouldn't you be the smallest bit upset if an entire society told you that you weren't able to take care of yourself? And then your babysitter told you to leave the security that you spent a year making? That it wasn't adequate?"

"You think I'm a babysitter?" he said, clearly annoyed.

"And then you realize he's right?" I continued. "And if he's right about that, then maybe the rest of them are right, too, and you aren't able to take care of yourself at all?"

His eyes flicked back to mine, and his expression eased. "I'm not your babysitter."

My shoulders slumped, and I pushed my coffee away. "I don't know if I could have handled Vivian today," I said, depressed. "She's using white magic, and she's making it deadly and totally legal. Ivy and I managed at the grocery store, but some of that was luck." I flicked my gaze up, my heart clenching at the sorrow in his eyes. "You saved my butt. Saved Ivy." Taking a deep breath, I looked at him. "I can't thank you enough for that.

I appreciate everything you did, but I don't want to be someone who needs help all the time."

I couldn't stand to look at him anymore, and my thoughts returned to the black Latin falling from him. Black magic had driven Vivian away, not me. Maybe I did need a babysitter.

Pierce resettled himself. "Al sent me to protect you," he said gruffly.

My head came up. His blue eyes were vivid as he looked at me as if he was trying to decide to say more. Past Tom's narrow face, I could see Pierce's determination, his soft confusion as he tried to fit in a world that had raced past him, and his frustration that he wasn't enough. "Is that why you stayed?" I asked. "You could have left."

"No."

My head hurt, and I looked away, but something inside me had felt the weight behind that one word. He had stayed, yes, but he used black magic with no shame, no reluctance. What was I doing here with him? This was a mistake, but what else could I do?

Chest tight, I looked over the coffeehouse noisy with conversation, only to jump when Jenks's phone rang. *Ivy,* I thought, then realized it was playing "Ave Maria." Maybe it was Matalina? When I flipped the lid, the name WARM FUZZY came up. Unsure, I tossed my hair from my face and thumbed the connection open. "Hello?"

"Hi, Rachel." Ivy's voice came clearly. "Don't tell me where you are. Are you okay?"

I blinked in surprise at Jenks's nickname for the vampire, then felt a ping of worry as I got her message that the phone might be compromised. "So far," I said, looking past Pierce to scan the tables to see ordinary people doing ordinary things. My hair started to prickle, as if we were being watched. "How's the arm?"

"Broken," she said simply. "By tomorrow, the cast will be hard enough to break heads." I went to say something, and she blurted out, "Rachel, I'm sorry. You can't go to Rynn's. I'm so angry I could rip someone's throat open."

Pierce frowned, and the feeling of a storm gathering tightened. "Why not?" I asked.

"He got a call from Brooke," she said sourly.

Slowly my shoulders fell. *Crap on toast.*

"The coven knows you have connections to him, and they asked him to turn you in."

"Nice," I whispered, and Pierce leaned closer, though I knew he had a spell to hear at any distance.

"Rynn isn't happy either," she finished tersely. "He's not going to turn you in, but if you show up on his doorstep, he can't fall back on plausible deniability. I'm sorry. They've got him by the short hairs. He can't risk the coven turning against him. He uses witch magic as much as any dead vampire. If you can take care of this without him, he'll back you, but if you show up, he has to hand you over. You want to meet somewhere?"

My hand went to my head, and I stared at the table. "No. I'm okay," I said softly. "Do you have David's number?"

"Uh," she said, hesitating.

I exhaled softly. "I'm not calling David, am I."

"He's in Wyoming," Ivy said, apologetic. "The Were muckety-mucks pulled your alpha position into doubt, and he had to go and file the paperwork in person."

I glanced at Pierce, startled to see Tom. *Never mess with a witch. Never. They fight with magic* and *red tape.* David was probably upset, seeing as it was the new moon and he'd be at his personal ebb. The coven played hardball, chipping away at my support so I had nowhere to go. "So what do I have?" I asked, my caffeine rush not enough to keep me feeling good.

"Just whoever's with you. Meet me at Sharp's digs?"

She hadn't said Pierce, which meant she didn't like him or she really thought our conversation wasn't private. Sharp's digs had to be Eden Park's Twin Lakes Bridge, and I shook my head even though she couldn't see me. "No," I said, glancing at Pierce. "I'm fine, and I need you where I can fall back on you. Okay? And tell Jenks I'm sorry."

She was silent, and my eyes fell from Pierce. I could do worse than be on the run with a black-magic practitioner on loan from a demon. *Rachel, you really can pick them.* "Um, if I don't call about three hours after sunset, will you call me?" I meant summon, and she knew it.

"How?" Ivy said, worry thick in her gray-silk voice. "I don't know how to do a summons. You want me to storm Trent's compound for Ceri or search the city for Keasley?"

"Don't do that," I said quickly. Keasley had vanished shortly after I'd found out who he was, and I didn't want to blow his cover. Going to Ceri would only give Trent the chance to wave his offer at me again, and I might be desperate enough to take it. Son-of-a-bitch elf. I didn't know any black witches who were still alive and out of jail. Except Lee, currently running Cincy's gambling cartel. I'd bet Pierce knew how to summon a demon, though.

My eyes shifted to his, and he reached for my free hand, cradling my bruised skin as if afraid to hurt me. "I won't allow them to take you again, but if they do, I'll follow you through hell. And if you should slip my grasp, I will summon you home."

Depressed, I pulled my hand from Pierce. A faint tingling seemed to slide from me, stretching between us until it broke with a snap that backlashed to warm me. I shivered even as I stared at him. It hadn't been our chis naturally balancing out. It had been something else.

"Rachel, what do you want me to do?" Ivy asked, interrupting my thoughts.

Uneasy, my thoughts went to Ralph, sitting in the Alcatraz dining hall, showing me his lobotomy scar. From there, they went to my mom, two thousand miles away, but a mere jump from San Francisco. "If I'm in trouble, call my mom, okay?" I said, jaw clenching. "Tell her Al's summoning name. Tell her to be careful because it might be Al who shows up, not me."

"Rachel."

Her voice was worried, and the coffee churned in my gut. "I know," I whispered. "This feels wrong."

Her sigh was soft. "Take it slow. Be smart."

"You, too." Unable to bring myself to say good-bye, I hung up. *Five minutes, eighteen seconds,* I thought as I looked at the tiny screen. How could my life shift so much so fast?

"It will be okay," Pierce said, and I eyed him sourly, not sharing his enthusiasm.

"I feel weird," I said as I looked at the ceiling and the turning fan. "Empty, like I'm under a spotlight. I need to get some sleep."

"It's because you've been dislodged from your diggings, your friends cut out," Pierce said. "I meant it when I said I will follow you if you're summoned. I'll follow at full chisel, should even hell's dogs be at my heels."

He wasn't helping, but when I met his gaze, my words faltered. His eyes were the same, once I got past Tom's shorter lashes. My heart pounded, and I felt a quiver in me. I went to speak, and his smooth fingers touched mine, silencing me. I remembered him silhouetted in my front door, black magic still flickering at his fingertips, and then the miserable nights I'd fallen asleep clutching my pillow, aching for Kisten. Shit. I didn't want to *do* this again. I wouldn't.

"We need to talk, Pierce," I said, and his fingers slipped away.

The chimes above the door jingled. Pierce looked toward them, and my gaze followed his when his expression went to one of surprise. My heart pounded, and I stifled the urge to run. The heavy-magic detection amulet was glaring a bright red, and a tingle came from my pocket where I'd stashed my own version. It was Vivian, pushing ahead of her a small but perfectly proportioned woman with a bright green spring hat and six-inch boots, looking eighteen fresh with snappy green eyes and a saucy step.

"Crap," I whispered, and Pierce shifted to hide behind his paper cup.

"The strumpet has a new accomplice," Pierce whispered, eyes alight with the need to act. "We should've abandoned your mother's, uh, car elsewhere."

"I don't think the car gave us away," I said, hiding behind the advertisement for ordering bunny cakes for Easter. There were too many people in here. "We need to leave."

"She won't recognize us under our charms. Maybe it's of no circumstance."

I glanced over the innocent, unaware people as Vivian limped forward, my muscles slowly tightening. "All the charms in the world won't hide us if she's got a leprechaun."

Pierce choked, and adrenaline surged as I worried that his coughing would attract their attention. "A leprechaun?" he finally managed, hat down over his face. "One of the wee folk? Walking the streets? There with her?"

I nodded, my heart sinking. Damn, the coven had deep pockets, because I'd bet every last one of Ivy's dollars sitting at the bottom of my bag that buying a wish was how Vivian found us. Even worse, I think I recognized the small woman.

Licking my lips, I grabbed my bag. "We're leaving through the kitchen," I said softly, but the soft snick of a safety going off made me freeze. Halfway to a stand, I looked up to find a dirty white cashmere coat between us and the door and Vivian smiling wickedly, one hand in her softly bulging pocket. Her hair was no longer slicked back but plain and straight, and her forehead had a new bruise. There was a rash on her neck that looked itchy. She'd been pixed.

Behind her, the leprechaun made a bunny-eared kiss-kiss at me. "There you be," she said, popping her green gum.

"Give me the bag," Vivian said tightly, her hand open but not extended for me to grab and do some damage. "Slowly."

Grimacing, I handed it to her and sank back down at the table.

"Good decision, Morgan." Vivian passed it to the leprechaun, then tossed two plastic-coated bands of charmed silver onto the table. "Make another one."

Pierce was still standing, his jaw clenched and a dangerous look in his eyes. Fear hit me—fear not for me, but for everyone else. He was way too free with the black magic. Damn it, couldn't we have had a standoff somewhere other than Junior's for once?

"Sit," Vivian said lightly, looking at Pierce. "Or I shoot her. With a bullet. Right in her gut. She'll be dead in twenty minutes. Understand?"

A faint sound of pixy wings rasped against my ear, the very familiarity of it catching my attention over the loud conversation. *Jenks?* My attention darted past Vivian to the front, and my breath caught. Nick was in the corner behind a *New York Times*. Our eyes met, and he winked. Jax was with him, waving enthusiastically and dusting an excited silver. Eyes wide, I pulled Pierce down into his chair. *What is Nick doing here?*

"Put them on," Vivian said as she stood over us, and I fingered the zip strip. I was really tired of these things. I could do something stupid and try to get it on Vivian instead of me, but I threaded my hand through the circle and ratcheted it closed. Ley lines weren't my forte, anyway. Lucky for me, my amulets still worked, and I retained the old lady look and the pain relief.

Pierce glared up at Vivian. I could feel him tensing, feel his chi beside mine glowing with ley-line power. If he put the strip on, he would be magically helpless. If he didn't, Vivian would shoot me. "Put it on," I said softly, and Pierce's eyes pinched at the corners.

"Rachel—," he almost growled.

"Listen to her, Tom," Vivian said, and my breath caught. She thought Pierce was Tom?

Pierce, too, realized the power behind the understandable mistake. His motions rough, he put the loop over his wrist and tightened it.

The tension visibly left Vivian. "Better," she said. "I'll get a bonus for bringing you in, Bansen. Where have you been the last couple of months?"

Dead, I thought, eyes on my bag as my mind went first to the money, then my splat gun, and finally the scrying mirror I'd brought so I could talk Al into giving me my summoning name back. Might be hard to explain that last one.

"I'm surprised to see you with *her*," she continued, almost cocky now that she was the only one who could tap a ley line. "Politics makes strange bedfellows, huh?"

Pierce stayed silent, knowing his speech would give him away, but the leprechaun was eying him as if she knew. Vivian assessed Pierce's silence, then glanced around the coffeehouse before pulling out the last chair and sitting down.

Behind her, the leprechaun huffed for being ignored. "How about a wee coffee?" she said, standing with my bag tantalizingly close. The charms in my splat gun's hopper wouldn't care if I couldn't tap a line or not.

"I'm not your date," Vivian said, noting where my eyes were. "Get your own coffee."

"I dunna carry cash," she said, her small features bunched up, and she gracefully clambered up onto the nearest chair with a little hop, setting my bag well out of my reach.

"You just love digging holes, don't you," Vivian said to me as she leaned back, her hand finally coming out of her pocket to scratch at the welts on her neck. "The first sign of trouble, and you go to another shunned demon summoner. Smart, Rachel. Really smart. You're lucky he didn't turn you in himself. Word is, Tom knows your summoning name, too."

Pierce's expression didn't shift as he sat like a stone across from Vivian. "It would be wise for you to walk away, witch," he said, his words slow as he chose them carefully to try to sound like everyone else. "You will be beaten soundly."

Vivian looked at him curiously, but seemed utterly unworried. "Not even a circle stops a bullet at this range," she said confidently as she tugged a slim phone from an inner pocket and flipped it open. God, the thing was as thin as a credit card. "Come quietly, or you'll be in Alcatraz for so long that you won't be able to craft a love charm by the time you get out."

My face burned at what they were doing. They had no right.

Nick was at the counter ordering and flirting with one of the clerks. He was here to help, wasn't he? The leprechaun was watching me when my eyes came back, and I dropped my gaze, resolving to not look at Nick again.

"Give me my coin," she said to Vivian, still eying me. "I need it to get paid."

I made a sour face and said, "You bought a wish to find me? I'm flattered."

"I'll give you the coin when I'm done," Vivian said, rubbing her welts.

"I want a coffee, then," she demanded.

Vivian's face darkened. "Can it wait a moment?" she snapped. "I'm on the phone."

The leprechaun sneered at her, then turned to smile at me. "I be liking your hair the other way," she said, clearly recognizing me. "Hey, isn't this the same place—"

"Yeah," I interrupted her, then shouted, "Mark, when you have a chance, can we have a tall latte over here?" Mark raised his hand in acknowledgment, and I smiled. "There's some money in the bottom of the bag. Help yourself. My treat."

Vivian stretched between the tables to snatch the bag from the leprechaun even as she continued to talk to someone in soft tones. Her eyes widened at the stash, and I wasn't surprised when both the cash and my splat gun went into her pocket. *Son of a bitch.*

The leprechaun frowned as she fingered the five Vivian had left her. "So how did the wishes go?" she asked me as we waited.

I lifted a shoulder and let it fall. "I gave two away. I'm still digging myself out of the one I used."

She snorted. "Aye, it's a good thing *you* didn't spend them all. People have been known to die from too many wishes."

"You know one of the wee folk?" Pierce said, the awe in his voice making her beam.

"I let her go for the wish I used to get out of my I.S. contract," I admitted.

Pierce stared at me, aghast. "You accepted a wish from a felon leprechaun?" he asked, making my face warm and the leprechaun frown.

"It isn't like she's an ax murderer," I said. "Besides, the I.S. wanted me to leave." *Jeez, look who was talking, Mr. Black Magic.*

Pierce lapsed into a pensive silence, and Mark came forward, handing the leprechaun her coffee and looking at me as if trying to figure out how I knew his name. She needed to use two hands to manage it, but her smile was honest enough as she took it, giving him the five and telling him to keep the change.

"Did she really use a wish to find me?" I asked her, thinking how I could use a wish right about now.

"Aye." She took a large draft of her drink as if it were cold milk, not steaming coffee. "The wish is from the West Coast, but we'll honor it. Bitch of a loss on the exchange, though." She glanced at Pierce. "Do I know you?"

His eyes wide, Pierce shook his head violently. "No."

Vivian straightened, smiling as she confidently said, "I'll see you at baggage claim," and snapped her phone closed.

"You're not getting me through security," I said. "Shunned witches can't fly."

"Then it's a good thing it's a private jet."

I sighed, and the leprechaun put her cup down with a tap. "Me coin? I do have a life. I found Rachel Morgan for you. That's all you be wishing for. You want me to help you get her to the airport, that be another wish. And you don't have one."

Eyes fixed on me and Pierce, Vivian stood, drew a coin with a hole in it from her pocket, and handed it to the leprechaun. It looked exactly like Ivy's. The small woman slid from the oversize chair and took it. "You're welcome, chump," she said loudly, then walked to the front with her coffee, smiling beautifully up at the man who held the door for her as he came in.

Nick was sitting at his table. My heart beat faster. Adrenaline washed into me like a drug, and I felt the tingle of anticipation. Pierce eyed me, waiting for direction.

"Go," Vivian said as she gestured to the door, my bag tight in her grip and faded strawberry smears marring the once-perfection of her coat. Her neck was swollen and red, and there were circles under her eyes, making her a far cry from the self-assured, posh, professional coven member I'd first seen in the grocery store. Now she was dirty, tired, and determined. Nice to know I wasn't the only one having a bad week.

"You can't hold me, Vivian," I said with deceptive calm as my foot jiggled out of sight under the table. "You just can't. Soon as I get a good nap in, I'm gone. I don't care what you do to Tom here. He's not my favorite person."

A sifting of pixy dust landed on the table, and I wiped it away. Pierce noticed, and his expression changed as his eyes slowly went from the ceiling to the front of the shop. His breathing became paced and regular. Lovely, lovely adrenaline poured into me. When it wore off, I was going to hurt, but if I was lucky, Vivian would be hurting more.

"I said, get up," Vivian repeated, her hand again in the front pocket of her coat, and together Pierce and I stood. "There's a white van in the lot. Get into it. Leave your coffee here," she added, and Pierce bumped me as he set his down.

"Do you trust him?" Pierce whispered, his breath soft against my ear.

Nick? "No. But look at my choices." I swallowed hard. "Be prepared. He's inventive."

"He is a thief," Pierce said indignantly.

"Yep. He's a slimy little thief who knows how to survive."

I stumbled when Vivian gave me a shove. "Stop talking," she muttered. "Tom, you first through the door. Then her." But true to his nature, Pierce held the door for me when we reached it, glaring stiffly at Vivian from under the brim of his hat, daring her to protest.

"Bug! In my coffee!" exploded a high-pitched, disgusted voice.

I smiled, stopping in the threshold and turning in time to see Nick trip on nothing in his rush to show the clerk his coffee. The cup went flying, hitting Vivian's face in a black wash.

"Out," Pierce hissed, pushing me, but I half-turned, wanting to stay and see the show.

People had looked up, and everyone watched in noisy, shocked concern as Vivian pawed at her face. Nick was there, patting it as he apologized, but things got worse when a shimmer of pixy dust sifted down and Vivian suddenly couldn't open her eyes.

"Ooooh, that's going to hurt," I said, stumbling as Pierce snatched my bag from where Vivian had dropped it and pushed me out the door.

I jerked to a halt at the harsh-winged clatter of an excited pixy. "There's a bus leaving," Jax said breathlessly, inches from my nose. "Don't get on it."

"Get off me!" Vivian shouted, shoving Nick. Nick flew backward into the cold shelves with their cakes and imported waters, but his foot hooked Vivian's, and they both went down.

Pierce pulled me the rest of the way out the door. The cold sunshine hit me. There was the bus, and Pierce ran for it. "Stop the carriage!" he shouted as he waved my bag and ran. "Stop the bus!" he amended, and the bus's brakes hissed as the sliding door opened. They never stopped for me. How come they stopped for him?

I looked behind me at the uproar, then to my mom's car. There was a white van across the lot, and a beat-up Impala that I'd be willing to bet was Nick's. God, my knees hurt.

"Rachel!" Pierce demanded, one foot on the bus's stairs. "On the bus!"

His eyes were wild and beautiful, and though he looked like Tom, he was Pierce. "No," I said as I stumbled to him. "We're going with Nick."

In a flash, Pierce's brow furrowed, and his eyes narrowed. "I say we're getting on the bus. Don't be difficult. Get on the bus."

I jerked out of his grip, pissed. "Don't tell me what to do!" I shouted, pulling a strand of hair out of my mouth. "I'm going with Nick!"

The driver sighed heavily. "On or off, lady."

I gave him a nasty look. "Off," I said. "Get the hell out of here."

That did it. Pierce barely got out before the man slammed the door in our faces and gunned the big engine. "This is a mistake," Pierce groused loudly as I dragged him to the nearby Dumpster. "No wonder Al agreed to send me to watch you."

"Hey," I said hotly, "I got through my first twenty-six years without you. My life may be messed up, but I *am* alive. You died, remember?" But I jerked to a stop when we nearly ran into the leprechaun, a long-stemmed pipe in her teeth as she leaned against a pollution-stunted maple and waited for her ride.

Shit. Pleading for mercy with my eyes, I shoved a self-congratulatory Pierce in front of me to slip in the small space between the Dumpster and the privacy wall. *Please, please, please.*

"Shut up," I whispered as I snatched my bag back. Crap. Could I look any more stupid?

"She's going to tell her where we are," he whispered back, his breath on my neck warm. "Damn fool woman. I told you to get on the bus."

"And I told you to shut up!" Damn fool woman, indeed. But I hadn't seen the leprechaun there when I'd pulled Pierce off the bus.

The door to the coffee shop jingled, and I heard Vivian's heels clack on the pavement. Peeved, I pushed Pierce's cautioning hand off me and went on tiptoe to peek over the top, hiding behind an empty box smelling of coffee beans. Looking haggard, Vivian ran to my car, peeked in at the empty seats, then turned to the bus just now turning the corner.

"Is she on the bus?" she shouted at the leprechaun, and I pulled my head down, pressing my forehead against the cold metal. *Not like this.*

We were so close, I could hear the leprechaun suck on the wooden stem. "I saw her friend get on the bus," she said casually, and my eyes closed in relief.

Vivian swore, and I heard her run to her van. There was a harsh revving of the engine, a short squeak of tires, and she was gone. From the coffee shop, the door jingled, and two people came out, laughing at the excitement.

Pierce and I slowly edged out from around the Dumpster. Exhaling, I took my disguise amulet off, fluffing my hair as I tucked the amulet away. I looked at the small woman, now smiling at me as she smoked. "Thank you," I said earnestly, reaching forward and shaking her hand. It felt really small in mine, but strong. "If you ever need anything. Anything at all."

"Ah, it wasn't nothing," she said, nodding to Pierce's wonder. "You look like you need a break is all." She wedged open a pocket to show a handful of bills. "You dunna owe me anything. Once a leprechaun is given money, it's hers. All she got was some dried oak leaves." She laughed then, sounding like a delighted child. I found myself smiling, not begrudging her all three thousand. Ivy had deep pockets.

My head came up fast when the door to the coffeehouse jingled and Nick stumbled out. He had a wad of environmentally conscious brown napkins against his nose and Mark at his side. The kid was apologizing profusely, shoving a bag of something at him as Nick tried to get away. He never even looked at us as he wedged Mark's hand off him and staggered to his car.

Mark gave up, standing forlornly in his apron as Nick started his car and tilted his head back against the headrest to wait. Mark went back inside, his steps slow.

"I be thinking that's your ride," the leprechaun said, indicating Nick's rusty car with her pipe.

"Only because the fool woman wouldn't get on the bus," Pierce grumbled, and I gave him a dark look. Seeing it, Pierce took a loud, slow breath, then started across the lot to Nick, his head down and his hands in the pockets of his long wool duster.

It worked, I thought, but it could easily have gone another way. Knees shaky, I started to follow Pierce, hesitating when the leprechaun tapped her pipe against the Dumpster and said, "I'm not an oracle . . ."

"But," I prompted.

She looked up at me, fingering the money I'd told her to keep. "Trust your judgment, baby witch. No one else's. You've got good instincts for someone flakier than my mum's pie crust."

Pierce waited impatiently by the open door, Nick behind the wheel. "Rachel . . ."

My judgment sucks, I thought. *She's got to be kidding.*

The leprechaun's smile faded and her fingers left the money. "I never did say thank you for letting me go. I would have lost my accreditation. I don't do that stuff anymore. Illegal, I mean." Pierce made a pained noise, and she added, "Hey, you want a wish?"

My heart seemed to stop. A dozen thoughts flashed through my mind. Jenks and Matalina living forever. Me not on the run. Ivy's soul. "No. No, thank you." I looked at Pierce beside the open door, frantically motioning for me to get in. "Thanks. But I've got to go."

"No, really. Take it!" she said, holding out a coin with a hole in it. "You could use it."

I held my breath, staring at it. Slowly I smiled. "No thank you," I said softly. "Give it to someone who needs to learn a freaking life lesson. I'm done."

The woman's red hair glinted in the sun as she laughed. "Okay," she said, tucking it away. "Watch them," she warned. "Both of them. Neither one is thinking of anyone but himself . . . yet."

I kind of figured that, and I nodded. Feeling like I was in control for the first time in years, I walked slowly to Nick's car. My knees protested as I got in and slid to the middle of the long bench seat. Pierce got in after me and shut the door. It felt too close, but I didn't care.

"Hi," I said, looking at Nick smiling at me with his bloody nose, success making his eyes almost glint. "Does this thing move?"

"You've no idea, Rachel," he said, putting an arm behind my shoulder for the moment it took to back up. Nodding, I eyed the extra levers on the dash, imagining the canisters of NOS that would fit in the huge trunk this thing had.

Pierce leaned close to my ear as we found the exit. "You should have gotten on the bus."

"Why?" I said. Maybe it was the lack of sleep, or turning the leprechaun down, or just that I loved seeing a plan fall together even if it wasn't mine, but I was in a wonderful mood, sitting between two clever, dangerous men. "I don't trust him if that's what you're worried about," I said as we pulled out into traffic. "But you have to admit this is better than being on a plane to Alcatraz. Vivian wouldn't be after me if they had someone ready to summon me back. I'm good for a while."

Pierce made a low noise of disapproval deep in his chest, settling back into the seat and adjusting his hat low over his face as we drove deeper into the Hollows. "If you say so, mistress witch."

Twelve

I jerked awake when Nick's car jiggled over some railroad tracks, snorting and wiping the corner of my mouth as I sat up. My eyes went to Jax thumping his feet against the rearview mirror, looking like his dad, and shifted back to the middle of the car. Crap, I'd fallen asleep against Pierce, but when I looked at him, I shocked myself when I saw Tom smiling at me from under his hat, eyebrows high and gaze questioning. Embarrassed, I turned my attention to the passing buildings. They were low and squat, dirty with neglect and apathy. Something told me we were still on the Cincinnati side of the river, and by the look of things, deep into human territory. It wasn't the nicest part of town, and I eyed the idle people sitting outside nasty storefronts in the thin sun.

Nick's gaze slid to me and back to the street. "Welcome back, sleeping beauty."

My pulse was slow, and I felt thickheaded. "Please tell me I wasn't snoring," I said as I pulled my old-lady coat higher around my shoulders. It was warm in here, but I felt vulnerable.

Pierce made a calculating noise, accidentally brushing my knee as he shifted. "As Jenks would say, you snore nice."

I smiled back unconvincingly. I snore nice. Not "I opine that your auditory nasal exhalations are most pleasing." He was already losing his unique speech patterns, not that I cared. I vaguely remembered hearing two male voices intertwined among my dreams in a soft, intent battle. Clearly I'd missed something. "Where are we going?" I asked, still not able to place where I was. No doubt, since I didn't get into the poorer parts of human Cincinnati much.

Nick kept his eyes firmly on the potholed streets, a soft tightness to his scarred jaw. "My place. Well, one of my places." His gaze went to his savagely marred wrist, and he looked at his small but probably expensive watch. "You'll be safe enough." Cracking a window, he murmured to Jax, "You want to get the door for us?" and the pixy flew out in a clatter of dragonfly wings. I couldn't help but notice that Jax's black shirt had a tear in it, and his shoes were scuffed. Clearly he didn't have a wife. If he wanted any kids to survive him, he'd have to start a family in the next year or so, or risk them being slaughtered by the first fairy clan to find them without a patriarch when he was gone.

Both men were silent and, uncomfortable, I scanned the shop fronts. Nick probably didn't have a problem here, but even I would think twice before walking these streets after dark. The leprechaun's words echoed in my thoughts, and I asked, "Nick, don't take this the wrong way, but why are you helping me?"

Nick's eyes searched mine before returning to the road. "It's not obvious?"

My head went back and forth. "We are done. Through. I thought I'd made that clear."

Nick stopped at a red light and rolled up his window when the car ahead of us began spewing blue smoke. "I could have let the coven take you," he said tightly.

My face burned. "Who says you didn't just save me from Vivian so you could turn me in yourself and get *all* the bounty?" I accused. "Don't give me any I-could-have-turned-you-in-so-trust-me-now crap. I could have told Glenn you were in my living room three minutes after you ran away. I don't owe you anything."

Nick's face went red, making Al's mark on his forehead stand out. "I can't fight witch spells. Besides, Pierce seems to have everything under control with his *black* magic."

Pierce stiffened. My pulse hammered, and I looked at my hands, in my lap. Nick had hung around long enough to see the curses flowing out of the church. Damn it, why was it he could make me feel ashamed for something I hadn't even done?

"So," Nick said tightly as we went through the intersection, "you know where we stand?"

Stand? We don't stand anywhere. "I don't trust you, and you don't trust me?" I guessed.

Nick's long expression was hurt. "I told you we were even."

A sarcastic noise slipped from me. "So that makes it all better?" He wanted a clean slate. *Right. After selling secrets about me to demons? Not likely.*

Scowling, Nick made a sharp left into a closed gas station that looked like a chop shop, pulling directly into one of the open bays. Seeing people inside, I looked in my bag for my disguise amulet.

"You won't need that here," Nick said, sounding insulted. "No one will squeal on you."

I hesitated before I let it drop back in my bag, not because I trusted Nick, but because I might need it later to slip out. Nick seemed mollified, but Pierce cleared his throat in an understandable warning—which ticked Nick off all the more.

Jax was hovering outside the closed window, and when Nick put his car in park, someone pulled the garage door down, cutting off the light and making me feel trapped. "Wait here," Nick said stiffly, taking the bag from the coffeehouse with him as he got out. His door slamming shut was loud, and he went to greet the man who had closed us in, doing a complicated handshake thingy. I could see Pierce memorizing it. As a ley-line witch, he probably had it down with one look.

Nick laughed, fitting in perfectly with the rough men around us, thin from Brimstone and too hard a life. Jax was on his shoulder, clearly familiar by their casual acceptance. I sat nervously and watched as Nick and the guy talked, both of them looking at the car. At us.

"I'd allow that Nick's car has a lot more levers than yours," Pierce said, eying the dash.

"Nick's car goes faster than my mother's," I said, sitting sideways so I didn't have to take my eyes off Nick. "Don't touch anything. It might go boom."

It wouldn't, but Pierce drew his hand away. "I don't trust him."

"Neither do I." Nick took a metal cutter from a nearby bench, and I fingered my zip strip, eager to get it off.

"If you're not of a mind to trust him, then why are we still here? This is vexing, sitting like a fence post."

I had to think about that for a moment, first to piece together what he was saying, and then to figure out why we hadn't left. I had nothing for Nick but bad feelings, yet here I was. "I need to sleep," I finally said, "and I don't want to do it on a bus touring Cincinnati." My gaze returned to Pierce, finding a surprising amount of tension in him. "Relax. I've known Nick for a couple of years. We did okay until it fell apart. I don't trust him, but I think he loved me in his own way once. Even if he did sell information to Al about me."

That last had been barely muttered, but Pierce had shifted to look at Nick. "The lickfinger," he said. "You're a powerful more forgiving person than me, Rachel. I would have—"

His words cut off, and I looked at him sharply. "What?" I asked, remembering his black magic—magic not only black in name but deed, too. "What would you have done, Pierce?"

He dropped his eyes at my pointed look, silent, and I turned back to Nick in a huff. The more I knew about Pierce, the more I worried. And I didn't need a babysitter.

Out the back window, I watched Nick hand the garage guy the bag from the coffeehouse and shuffle our way. Pierce squinted at Nick when he opened the door and leaned to look in. "You want those bands off?" Nick asked, holding the clippers up.

Immediately I shoved Pierce to get out, grabbing my bag in passing as I slid across and found my feet beside him. It smelled like acetylene torch and oil, and three ragged guys were watching us as I held out my wrist.

The metal was cold against my skin, and I shivered when the zip strip was clipped through. The strand parted with a little thump, and I rubbed my wrist.

"God, that feels good," I said as I reached for a ley line, realizing where we were in the process. Not far from the university. Cool. "Thanks, Nick." My chi filled, and my shoulders eased when I spindled a little bit extra in my head. It was easier now to stand confidently under the eyes of men talking in low tones and accents hard for me to follow. My knees felt better, too.

"Thank you," Pierce said stiffly, and Jax zipped down in a bow of silver dust, catching Pierce's zip strip before it hit the stained concrete, taking both of them to a high shelf. I wasn't surprised that Pierce remained looking like Tom when his band fell away. He'd probably keep his true appearance to himself for the same reason I was holding my old-lady disguise back.

Nick glanced at where Jax had left the zip strips, then turned back to us. "No problem," he said, looking skinny as he tossed the clippers to the closest bench, where they slid to a noisy stop. "You want to crash for a few hours? I've got a room across the street."

I shifted nervously, feeling cold in a garage that had never seen the sun, surrounded by concrete, tools to strip a car to nothing, and the men messing around with them—and watching me. "Sure. Thanks, Nick."

My fingers slipped into Pierce's hand as we headed for the man door, shocking the hell out of him, but I wanted Nick to know that I didn't consider his helping us as anything other than a temporary encounter. The guys watching laughed at both men's reactions, but I didn't care. If they thought I was an insecure airheaded fluff, then all the better.

Pierce's brow furrowed, and suddenly the ley-line pressure between us eased as he drew on the same line and brought himself, holding an amount of energy, nearer mine.

Nick saw Pierce's fingers intertwined with mine. Expression unchanging, he pulled open the man door fixed in the garage door. "Jax!" he shouted, and the pixy zipped back, tucking himself into the outside pocket of Nick's faded cloth coat just as the sun spilled in across our feet. "Just across the street," he said again, squinting at the bright spring sun.

Pierce and I followed. His fingers moved against mine, taking my grip more firmly, and I stifled a start when a budding sensation of warmth grew in the cup of my hand. *What in hell is he doing?* I thought, then yanked free. Pierce smiled, and I glared at him. It hadn't been a power pull, but it had been something. And I didn't like his jaunty new step either.

The building Nick was heading toward looked bigger than most. I was guessing it had once been a theater, with SALTY CHOCOLATE in faded letters where the movie titles would have been. *Dinner theater?* I wondered, changing my mind when we entered the barred door to find a wide foyer with an unlit neon sign proclaiming it was the Salty Chocolate Bar. There was another set of barred gates; beyond them were a quiet space full of tables, a dance floor with three poles, the smell of Brimstone, and a long bar. The bar had a stripper pole, too. No one was in there, but the dark light display made me remember Kisten.

"You live above a strip bar?" I said, and Nick gave me a sidelong glance, pulling a single key out from a pocket and unlocking a side door covered in thick paint the same color as the walls. It opened to a narrow stairway with faded carpet and bare walls going up what must have been three stories. I sent my gaze all the way up and winced. This was going to kill my knees.

"Upstairs, last door at the end of the hall," Nick said, gesturing for me to go, and Jax flew up first, vaulting from Nick's pocket to make a steep, glittery ascent. It looked like the two of them had been working together since Mackinaw, and I wondered if it was only the fact that Nick was a thief that made Jenks and me that much different.

The stairs creaked, and it smelled old, like coal-stoves-and-pigs-roaming-the-streets old. The occasional window through the brick wall lit the way. Pierce was behind me, and I glanced up when footsteps started down. It was a very tall woman, and I stood aside when we met somewhere in the middle. She was wearing black lace and fur, both fake. Too much blush.

"Hi, hon, love your hair," she said to me, her voice decidedly husky, then to Nick, "Hey, lovey. Where's Jax?"

"Upstairs," Nick said shortly, clearly not liking the woman, or man, I was beginning to suspect. I smiled noncommittally as she passed with her boots clunking, but before I could take another step, she made a sound of recognition.

"Tom!" she exclaimed, and Pierce threw himself against the wall when she reached for him. His expression was scared, and he grabbed his hat from his head when it started to fall.

"Hey, man!" the woman said, punching him on the shoulder to make Pierce's eyes go even wider. "Tom, Tom, the magic man. That was some serious shit you did last time you were here. Where you been? Word was you got cacked by some broad under the city. Shoulda known it was nothing but salty water under the bridge. I didn't know you knew Nicky. You going to be here tonight? I got a table for you. You just say the word, and I'll have a couple of my best girls for you, too. No charge, no cleanup fee."

No cleanup fee?

Nick watched Pierce's frightened expression. I, too, was surprised. Tom was a known face down here? Great. Just freaking great.

"You mistake me for someone else . . . ma'am," Pierce managed.

The woman looked at me and laughed. "Oh, right. Yeah. My mistake," she said. "See you around. Bye, Nicky," she said, her voice shifting higher. "You working tonight?"

Nick shook his head. "Not tonight, Annie. I'll be showing my friends the sights."

"Plenty of sights in the club," she said deviously. With a little wave, she continued down. Her shoulders were wider than Glenn's and she carried herself with much the same easy grace.

"Annie owns the building," Nick offered. "Owns the club. Takes good care of her girls."

"Takes your rent?" I guessed, and Nick nodded.

"Doesn't ask questions," he added, passing me when I didn't move fast enough for him.

I'll bet, I thought, sliding over when Pierce came up beside me.

"Law sakes' alive," the shaken man whispered as he snuck glances down at the woman, still making her boot-clunking way downstairs. "I suspicion wearing Tom's appearance isn't a powerful-good idea anymore."

His accent had gone full into the early 1800s, proof that he was shaken, and I gave him a sour look. "You got that right," I said, following his gaze to the bottom of the stairwell where the woman blew kisses to us before slipping out the side door and locking it firmly. "Why don't you put yourself back together? I like you looking like you."

Pierce glanced at the stairway. "I didn't want to be spied with two faces in the car barn."

"Garage," I corrected him, and he softly repeated the word, brow furrowed.

Nick's steps were soundless as he reached the top. A building-long hallway stretched with doors on one side, windows on the other. It looked like it had once been an open balcony looking out onto the side street, long since bricked up to give some protection from the elements.

"It's the one at the end," Nick said, seeming as eager as us to avoid any more encounters.

Someone was yelling at someone about their choice of TV and eating all the yogurt as Nick hustled down the hall, me trailing behind with my sore knees, looking out to the blah brown building across the street in the cold spring sun. I felt a tweak on my awareness, and I wasn't surprised when Pierce shuddered, and I looked to see him like himself again. Even his fingers were different. Not so thick, smaller, more dexterous.

Nick stopped at the last door, doing a double take as he saw Pierce. "That's a good one," he said as he fished out a second key. "I'd never have known it was you if you hadn't been sitting next to Rachel. Demon magic? Must have cost a lot."

Pierce shrugged, eyes on the brown building across the street. "Someone died for it. And this is the disguise, sir."

Nick hesitated with the key in the door, clearly having second thoughts.

"Thanks for letting us crash at your place," I said, not wanting to have to go back downstairs and grab a bus. "I'm amazed you found us, with me looking like an old lady."

His expression softening, Nick twisted the key and unlocked the door.

"Remember the library? When we broke in to see the restricted section? You were wearing the same thing."

I laughed, but Pierce was appalled. "You are a hoister, Rachel? Lifting books from a . . . public institution?"

My smile grew fond. "I just wanted to see them. I didn't walk off with anything." *Nick had, though.* Slowly my smile faded. That had been the night I'd met Al. He'd torn my throat out at the request of Ivy's old master vampire. I'd survived, obviously, but that was the beginning of everything that put me here, shunned and beholden to the very demon who'd tried to kill me. "I needed a look at the spell books," I finished softly.

"Then why didn't you simply ask?" Pierce asked. "Surely if you had impressed upon the librarian your plight, he would have allowed you access."

"They wouldn't have made an exception," I said sadly, knowing I was right. "People just aren't that way anymore."

Good mood thoroughly gone, I entered Nick's apartment. As I crossed the threshold into the one large room, I rubbed at the demon mark I'd gotten that night, wondering if that one decision could be responsible for the entire rest of my life. Why Pierce was scowling, I hadn't a clue. It couldn't be Nick's place. It was nice. Really nice. In-any-neighborhood nice.

It was a corner apartment with windows on two sides and a rack of plants under a skylight in the kitchen. Jax was dusting heavily among the greenery already, and the place smelled like a conservatory: green and growing. The kitchen was faded, small, and clean.

"Make yourself at home," Nick said as he dropped the single key conspicuously on the Formica kitchen table and sat down to take off his tatty sneakers.

I came farther in as Pierce shut the door, his flat black shoes making a slow turn on the low carpet. It was all one big room, with trifold screens to loosely define areas. Shelves lined the walls between the windows, each holding stuff that I'd classify as knickknacks if I hadn't known they were probably priceless. Some had spotlights. It reminded me of a museum, and I couldn't help but wonder if Nick had had this place before we broke up.

The living room was a couch before a wide-screen TV bolted to the wall, out of view from the windows thanks to the screens. Beside it in the corner—also out of sight—was a stack of expensive equipment, everything black and silver and piled as if they were worth nothing, but *nothing* was likely what he'd paid for them. The last corner between two windows had a gray slab of slate propped two feet up on cinderblocks, probably to get the underside of a circle free of pipes or lines. Beside the raised stone was a locked box. It had demon summoning all over it, and I think Pierce had come to the same conclusion, since his lips were pressed tight in disapproval.

But it's okay for you to do black magic, eh?

"This is nice," I said as I dropped my bag on the couch. The fabric was faded, and I sat gingerly on the edge and wiggled out of my coat, leaving it to slump behind me. It was warm in here, for Jax, and the windows dripped condensation.

Nick looked satisfied as he came out from the fridge with a bottled water. "Pierce, you want a beer?" he said as he threw it to me.

The water thunked into my raised hand, and I set it on the coffee table unopened, thoughts of Alcatraz's spice drifting through my head.

Pierce didn't look away from a rack of leather books, his hands behind his back as he squinted at the titles. They were regular spell books, then. Demon texts had no names. "No. I'm of the mind to remain clearheaded," he said, his voice flat.

Deciding that Nick wouldn't magic my drink, I cracked the lid and took a sip. My gaze landed on a statue of an Incan god, and I moseyed over to the ugly thing. "Is this real?"

Nick leaned against the counter with his ankles crossed. "Depends on who you ask."

Depends on who you ask, I mocked in my thoughts. Stupid ass.

Pierce's hands came out from behind him to touch a long, curved knife resting on a wooden stand before the leather-bound books. It was almost a dagger, really. "This is real," he said, turning it over and examining the detail on the engraving.

"Is it?" Carefully casual, Nick pushed himself into motion, beating me to Pierce and taking the knife from him. "I found it at an estate sale," he said as we peered at it, the lie coming so easily it was disgusting. "The woman said it belonged to a sea captain who refused to sail back to England. I thought it was pretty. Someday, I'll find out what the words on the handle mean." Setting it on a higher shelf over our heads, he put his beer on the coffee table and moved to the bedroom, defined by a large folding screen.

The words on the handle were in Latin, and though I hadn't been able to read them, I think Pierce had by his grim expression.

Tired, I turned to the big TV affixed to the wall. "I'd think you'd be worried about thieves," I said, looking at the equipment piled under it. I didn't see any security system, and though Jax was better than any detection setup known to man or witch, he wasn't here 24/7.

"Not since the first one had a heart attack in the hall, no," Nick said, and I turned to see him bring a shirt out of his dresser and drop it on the bed.

From the far corner by the kitchen, Jax piped up, "He walked right into the ward, bam! It took three days for the stink of burnt hair to go away. Annie was pissed."

Feeling ill, I sat on the couch with my back to him. That's why Jax had gone ahead of us. Bringing my focus back, I casually brought out my big-mojo amulet, glowing a very faint, almost-not-there red. Whatever safeguards Nick had, they were nasty even when uninvoked. "Got yourself a rep, eh?" I needled Nick, watching his reflection in the blank TV as Pierce tried to figure out the blinds.

Nick took his shirt off in one easy move. "Not as bad as yours."

Pierce's eyes snapped in ire, but the words never made it past his lips when he saw Nick's battered and scarred body. I'd forgotten, but Nick was covered in scars; the deep gouges never properly taken care of had mellowed to lumpy white scar tissue, crisscrossing his chest and shoulders in a bizarre pattern. Most had probably come from the rat fights where we'd met. Even more disturbing was the new demon scar with two slashes on his shoulder. Nick's gaze flicked away when he realized I'd seen it. Motions fast, he put on a lightweight T-shirt.

Peeved, I crossed my arms and sank back into the cushions to stare at the black TV. An uncomfortable silence grew, broken only by Jax's wings. In the almost-mirror of the TV, I watched Nick sit on the edge of the bed to pull a pair of stained blue overalls over his pants. I wondered if it was the same pair he'd used when he had helped me break into Trent's grounds. Maybe I was as bad as he was.

"Bathroom is behind the kitchen," Nick said as he stood and adjusted the straps about his shoulders. "I've got extra blankets under the bed if you're cold or on the off chance you're not sleeping together and one of you wants the couch."

Lips parting, I turned to give him an ugly look. Pierce's attention lifted from a rack of preindustrial buttons, his stance stiffening as he eyed Nick from under his loose black curls. "Rachel is a lady, sir, not an adventuress. If I was not obliged to abide by good manners for the turn you gave us, I'd be of a mind to settle this off the reel directly."

Nick said nothing, no emotion at all. Not watching his hands, he opened his top drawer and raked his arm across his dresser to dump everything in. Turning, he pulled something from his coat, on the bed, and dropped it in there, too, hiding what it was with his body. "Rachel isn't a lady," he said as he shut the drawer with a bang. "She's a witch, rhymes with bitch, randy and ready. Rachel, how many men have you slept with? A dozen? Two?"

"Nick!" I protested as I stood, first flustered, then alarmed when Pierce headed for him. "Pierce, don't!" I shouted as I got between them, my splayed fingers on his chest and stiff arm stopping him dead in his tracks. I felt a jump in energy between us, and he reddened, backing out of my reach with his eyes down and his jaw clenched.

"This coming from a man who lives in a house of assignation?" Pierce muttered.

Stiff, Nick crossed to the kitchen to put his shoes on again. I was about ready to smack Nick myself, but it wouldn't do anyone any good.

"What Rachel does is no one's funeral," Pierce said. "I'll allow it takes a coward to invite a woman to his diggings only to cast doubt upon her standing. Apologize at once."

Nick's foot thumped down as he slipped his second sneaker on. "I'll apologize if it's not true. Rachel? How about it?"

I couldn't say anything, staring at him with my arms over my middle. *Why is he doing this? To hurt me?* It was working, and finally Nick turned away.

"I have to go to work," he said, grabbing a torn coat from the hook beside the door. "There are eggs in the fridge, and some apples. Help yourself. I'll bring something back about six. If you leave and aren't coming back, lock the door. Jax can get me in."

My jaw clenched. He was goading me into leaving, hoping pride would rob me of a good day's sleep and a chance to shower. "Thanks, Nick," I said dryly. "I appreciate this." *Bastard.*

Pierce was stiff, and Nick's eyes flicked to him before he opened the door. A faint argument filtered in, and Jax flew out, green sparkles of discontent slipping from him. "I'm not a monster, Rachel," Nick said, hand on the door and feet in the threshold. "You loved me once."

The door shut, and I found myself shaking. "Yeah, well, we all make mistakes," I whispered. I wouldn't feel guilty. Nick had lied to me. Kept secrets from me. Still did.

Pierce cleared his throat, and I went warm, probably as red as my hair. Taking a deep breath, I turned. "Pierce," I said, wanting to explain, but he held up a hand.

"What a spit-licked son of a bitch," he said, shocking the hell out of me. Steps slow, he went to the couch and sat, his long coat falling open and his elbows on his knees. His hat he dropped on the table. For a moment, he was silent, then, "You sparked with him when you were younger?"

I didn't know if sparking meant dating or sex, but it didn't matter. Uneasy, I sat on the other end of the couch with lots of space between us. I felt like a whore, and mirroring him with my elbows on my knees, I took a drink of water and swung the bottle between my knees. I wasn't trying to impress Pierce, but who wants to be thought of as a whore?

"Yes," I said, not looking up. "A couple of years ago. I got my first demon mark because of him. I didn't know he was a thief at the time." I looked at Pierce, seeing his gaze lost in thought. "Or maybe I did and I was ignoring it. I've got a problem with bad men."

Pierce's focus sharpened, and when our eyes met, he looked away. He may as well have it all. "Nick's right, though," I admitted, watching the water swinging in my grip. "I'm not a particularly chaste woman. Compared to the women of your time, I'm probably a whore."

"You're not," Pierce protested a little too stridently, and I set the bottle down beside Nick's beer, wanting that instead. God, I was tired. And my knees were throbbing.

"I swear, and cuss," I said, giving in and taking a swig of the beer. The bitter taste tightened the back of my mouth but it was marvelously cold. "I don't take slights politely but tell people to kiss off." Ticked, I set the bottle down hard. "And I like beer."

"I opine—I think you're a woman of your world," he said from the far end of the couch. "I would have a hard time seeing you pressed and powdered, dreading a life of servitude under the name of marriage. You'd die in that mold. I like you as you are, fiery and ill tempered."

Silent, I looked at him, not knowing if he really believed it or was being polite.

My face must have given me away, because Pierce reached for me. Moving fast, I stood up, out of his reach. I went to the window to close the floor-to-ceiling blinds with fast, abrupt motions, careful to never get directly in an outsider's view. The room darkened but for the light from the skylights. Pierce never said a word.

The last blind shut, I turned, freezing when I found him right behind me. "Ah, you want the bed or the couch?" I asked, even more uncomfortable. I mean, I'd seen him look at me with abhorrence for breaking into the library. His disgust that I'd slept with Nick, slimeball and thief, had been obvious. Sure, he had started this grand adventure as a way to get out from under Al's thumb, but he knew that I was shunned, tied to demons more than my own kind. He was a demon killer—or wanted to be—and I was the student of one.

Then again, we were both dirty. His very existence hinged on Tom's untimely death and a black curse. And when the memory of him standing at my door with his hands dripping black power sifted through my mind—I shivered.

"Bed or couch?" I repeated, frightened by mistakes that I wasn't going to make this time, and when he shifted forward, I lurched out of his path, grabbing the afghan from the back of the couch. It was the same one I'd slept under in Nick's other apartment.

He exhaled, head bowed as he dropped back a step. "I'm of a mind to sit at the table," he said softly. "I don't set store by Nick's words, Rachel. A body would wonder why people think a younger time means a less randy state of mind." His lips curved up into a faint smile as he hesitated, then added, "Circumspect does not mean celibate."

My fingers gripped the afghan tighter. The scent of redwood came from him, strong and heady. I swallowed hard as he hesitated a moment longer, blue eyes nothing like Kisten's holding a hint of a question; then he moved past me, his steps silent on the carpet.

I think he just made a pass at me, I thought when he settled himself at the table. Numb, I sank back down on the couch. No way was I going to take the bed.

"I'm not happy with you making me look like a fool just so you can get away from Al for a week or two," I said, reclining with my head on the arm of the couch where I could see him. My knees protested, but it was warm under me where he had been sitting, and I could smell him there. I was so tired. I hadn't slept properly in over twenty-four hours.

"It worked, didn't it?" he grumbled, almost unheard.

"Then you don't think I need watching?" I asked, and he gave me a sideways glance.

Clearly he did, but I was too tired to be mad at him right now. His scent lingered in the cushions, the redwood blending with the whiff of electronics and burnt amber from the corner of the room. My pulse was slowing, and the ticking of four clocks became obvious. There was one on each of the four walls, and I wondered if it was part of a protection charm.

My thoughts were swirling as I tried to relax, the day's events coming back to the forefront of my mind as I finally had a chance to think about them. Until I got my summoning name back, I was vulnerable, whether I liked it or not. Uncomfortable, I wedged off my boots and tucked my feet under the afghan. Much as I wanted it otherwise, having Pierce here was a comfort. Nick might have left us only to betray us, but I doubted it. He had too much to lose by inviting Vivian or anyone else from the coven into his place. They'd clear his apartment out, then give him my old cell in Alcatraz.

"You were a member of the coven?" I asked, my thoughts jumping as sleep demanded its fair share of my day.

"Still am," he said, and I opened my eyes to see him staring at nothing as he slumped. "Once a member, always a member, until death. And I'm not dead anymore."

"They're the ones who blew your cover, aren't they," I said, thinking back to his words—no, his threat—to Vivian. "They gave you to that vampire. Why?"

He turned, straightening when he realized I was watching him. "We disagreed."

Because you do black magic? I'm so surprised. "Disagreed? They bricked you in the ground," I said, but instead of becoming angry, he chuckled, stretching his legs out under the table, looking nothing like himself as he unbuttoned his vest and relaxed.

"Yes, they did, but here I am. Go to sleep, Rachel."

I slumped farther into the couch to breathe in his scent, lingering in the cushions. "Do you think you can get them to leave me alone?" I asked, eyes closing.

"Not likely," he said, his soft voice clear over the sounds of someone's music coming through the walls. "As you say, they did brick me in the ground."

Snuggling deeper under the afghan, I yawned as I listened to a car beep in the street below. "You're just like me. Nothing but trouble," I murmured, slurring.

"My apologies?" he said, making me smile at the simple sound of it.

I wasn't thinking anymore, and I had to shut my mouth. "Good night, Pierce," I said around another yawn, unable to stop myself.

"Good night, mistress witch." But as I drifted off, I could have sworn I heard him add softly, "We should have taken the bus."

Thirteen

The scent of brewing coffee stirred me into a half-awake, half-asleep haze. I hung there, warm and content, feeling yarn under my chin. I liked warm and content, but it had been so long since I'd been such that its very presence was a warning.

Taking a deep breath, I shrugged out of my sleep, sitting up in a smooth motion and holding Nick's afghan to me. *Nick's place,* I thought as my pulse slowed and I listened to the ticking of the four clocks. The blinds were night gloomed, and the plants in the corner of the kitchen were bright under hot spotlights. I'd slept for hours. My attention went to the kitchen table, finding Pierce's coat and vest draped over the chair—but no Pierce.

Instinct turned me to find him standing before the shelf of old books in a spotlight in the otherwise dim room. Faint rhythmic thumps told me the strip club was in full swing, but it was pleasant, sort of like a giant heartbeat. The dagger that Nick had placed on the high shelf was balanced across Pierce's palms, and the greenish-black haze covering it extended up almost to his elbows. It was his aura, and he must be doing something very powerful to make it visible like that. Even so, he probably wasn't seeing it. Auras were like that. I couldn't see mine either, apart from a reflection when I made a circle or threw a chunk of ley-line energy at someone. I had no idea what he was doing, but it looked like he was using a ley line.

"I listened to you wake," Pierce said to the books, not turning. "Hearing that makes a body feel powerfully content. I mean . . . it was nice?"

The glow about his hands flickered, then renewed itself. Smiling, I put my sock-footed feet on the floor and stretched before I wedged my boots back on. The thought to phone Ivy and Jenks rose and fell. If there was a change, they'd call.

"Nice," I affirmed around a yawn. It seemed odd that here, in Nick's place, I'd be able to find the rest that comes only from feeling safe, but I did. Or had, maybe. The thief had more safeguards than a paranoid psychic with delusions of grandeur. I couldn't help but wonder what Pierce thought of me after seeing my ex. Not that I cared, but Nick was slime. Embarrassed, I eyed Pierce for any signs of distance.

Pierce looked absorbed as he stood before the books with that knife balanced across his hands and his brown shoes edging the spotlight. He had pulled his shirttails from his trousers, and a faint stubble was starting to show. It was the first time I'd ever seen him disheveled. "You look comfortable," I said, and he sighed.

"No one slicks up anymore," he breathed. "Why should I?"

It didn't sound like him at all, and rising, I went to the window, shifting the blinds to see that some of the cars had their lights on. "Trent dresses up," I said, letting the blind's slat click shut and turning. "Did you sleep at all?"

Still facing the books, Pierce rubbed his bristly chin. "Are you going to call Al?"

I nodded. I had a couple of hours before the sun would set in San Francisco. Time enough to call Al and try to convince him to make good on our deal. But what I really was, was hungry. "How come you look so rested?" I asked as I came alongside him, and the green glow about his hands went out. "You couldn't have had much sleep."

"Perhaps because I made a die of it for so many years I don't need as much."

Eying him, I carefully took the knife off his hands. The tarnished metal was warm, feeling almost like putty, but the sensation quickly faded until it was just cold silver. "This is nasty," I said as I tried to piece together the words engraved around the handle. "What does it say?" Pierce hesitated, and my eyes narrowed. "Don't expect me to believe you can't read it."

With an odd expression, the man shifted uncomfortably as I caught him thinking about lying to me. "It's a delicate matter," he finally said, and I put one hand on my hip, the other carelessly holding the knife askew. "I won't say the words," he said, gaze following the knife as I shifted it about. "I'm not skeerylike, but it's arcane, black magic. I'm not of a mind to . . . know for sure what it does. The charm is long spent."

I squinted at him, weighing his words against his body language. I mean, he knew I knew he worked black magic. Did he think I couldn't take it? Whatever *it* was? "What were you doing with it, then," I asked, waving the knife around just to irritate him, "if the spell is gone?"

Frowning, he gently grasped my wrist and took the knife. "Ley-line magic in good silver will leave a whisper of the spell after it is spent," he said, eyes on the dagger, not me. "If one is powerful delicate, applying a breath of ley-line potency into the charm can sometimes fill the channels again and bring it back to full stamina. Too much will destroy it, but if enough fills the spell before it overflows, one can make a fist of it. I've a fine enough touch, but I'm not eager to try lest I leave Nick with such an ugly thing."

Curious, I took the knife back, holding it with the right amount of respect. "You just direct a trickle of energy into it? You don't even need to know how to do the original charm?"

"That's the whole pie of it, yes." Pierce took the knife from me again and set it where Nick had left it, out of my easy reach. "It's enough to worry a man that Nick, a mere wizard, has it."

I frowned. If I wanted to look at the knife, I would. "Yeah, well, Nick has a lot of stuff he shouldn't, doesn't he?" I said, and Pierce glanced at the broken trunk. "My dad never told me that," I said to distract him. "About the imprint left on an object."

Pierce nodded. "It's not known to many, and your father was human."

I started, not having told him about that chunk of drama in my life, but then I remembered he'd been there in spirit. There probably wasn't much that had happened in the church in the past year that he didn't know about. And yet . . . he was here, standing in front of me, his shirt open to show pale skin, stubble on his face, and hair all over and tousled.

Damn it.

"Are you hungry?" Pierce asked, and I turned to the dimly lit kitchen. "Nick won't be back until long after candle lighting."

Candle lighting. I remembered that one. He meant dusk. "Famished." I flicked on the kitchen light and looked for the bathroom. "Can you hold that thought?"

Leaving Pierce to figure out what I meant, I shut the bathroom door behind me and hoped he couldn't hear as I took care of business. God, why did I even care if he might know I'd flushed the toilet, but I slumped when I caught sight of myself in the age-spotted mirror above the tiny white sink.

There were circles under my eyes, and I looked tired despite the sleep. My hair was a mess, and when I used Nick's brush, it only made it frizz out all the more. I contemplated taking my pain amulet off but decided I might need it if I was summoned out and had to fight, so I let it stay tucked under my shirt. The black camisole had been fresh this morning, and the jeans were probably good for another day. Eventually, though, I'd have to risk going home for a change of clothes and a toothbrush or spend a couple of hours at the mall.

How had I gotten here? Shunned and on the run from the coven, unable to go home for a change of undies. What scared me the most was that the coven didn't have to work within the law, or at least they felt they didn't. Maybe I should call Glenn and see if there was a warrant out for my arrest? That would be good news, because if there was, then they couldn't just pack me quietly away in a closet. Okay, so my kids being demons was a problem, but shouldn't the entire witch community have a say in whether I should be shoved in a hole or just castrated?

"Thanks, Trent," I whispered as I cleaned Nick's brush. Dropping the fistful of his and my hair into the sink, I set it alight with a word of Latin.

None of this would have happened if Trent hadn't told the council what his dad's tinkering with my mitochondria had done.

I'd been born with a common genetic "defect" that should've killed me before I was two. Thousands of witches were. The truth was that Rosewood syndrome was really an ancient elven biological-warfare device that kicked in when a witch able to invoke demon magic was born.

Turns out the elves had cursed the demons first, causing their children to be born stunted in their ability to do magic. Abandoned by demons as inferior, ancient elves called us witches and told us lies, recruiting us for what magic we retained to help them in their war. They couldn't get rid of the gene that enabled us to invoke demon magic without removing all our ability to do magic, and occasionally it recombined to full strength; hence the little genetic bomb they hooked into our DNA to kill us when the demon enzyme showed.

When Trent's dad tinkered enough, such that I could survive having the demon enzyme, he'd unknowingly fixed what his species had broken. Trent's claim that he hadn't told the coven was crap, especially when the lie that he could control and destroy me followed it.

"Rachel?" came a worried call from the door, and I looked up from the bit of ash that was left of my hair. That and a really nasty stench.

"I'm fine!" I called back. "Just getting rid of potential focusing objects."

I heard his pleased mmmm, then his steps retreated. I ran the water a long time, cleaning the basin until there was not even a hint of ash. Forcing a smile, I came out to find Pierce at the stove. "Nick said there were eggs," he said, making an odd picture of domesticity as he turned with a spatula in his hand, "but I was of the mind you'd prefer hotcakes."

A splatter of batter marked his shirt, and my smile became real. Eggs gave me migraines, but there wasn't enough of them in pancakes to matter. "Fabulous," I said as I took one of the cups of coffee waiting on the faded table. "Is this mine?" I asked, and he nodded, expertly flipping the pancake to land back in the pan.

Three pancakes were already waiting in the oven, their scent covering up the reek of burning hair. "I've never made coffee before," he said, repositioning the pancake in the pan. "Not in that fashion. But I've seen you do it enough. Is it . . . okay?"

I took a sip, grinning as I remembered his drinking my mom's too-strong coffee in an effort to impress me the night we'd met. "It's good. Thanks. You've got batter on your shirt."

Pierce looked down, dropping everything with a mild oath and dabbing at it with the damp corner of a dish towel. There was no maple syrup in the microwave, but a bottle of corn syrup was warming in a pan on the stove. The table, too, was set, so as Pierce fussed over his shirt, I went to Nick's dresser, wondering what he'd shoved in it before he left.

Another mild cuss word drifted through the apartment, and Pierce gave up on the spot. "Do you trust him?" he asked, knowing what I was thinking as I stood before Nick's dresser.

My jaw clenched, and my head started to pound. "Not where it counts."

"Then look."

Why not? I set my mug down and opened the drawer. Lying atop Nick's socks and tighty whities was my splat gun. "Hey!" I exclaimed, reaching for it only to curl my fingers under before they could touch it. "It's my splat gun," I said, face burning. He must have lifted it from Vivian in Junior's coffeehouse, but why hadn't he returned it to me?

Pierce leaned from the stove to see me. "Testing you? To see if you're trustworthy?"

Either that, or he wanted it for himself. "I guess I just got an F, then," I said, hefting my splat gun before I jammed it at the small of my back where it made an uncomfortable bump. Under the gun was a handful of ticket stubs, receipts, and handwritten notes on napkins. I peered closer, spotting a day pass to the zoo's off-hours runners' program. With a finger, I shifted a few things, not seeing a pattern to it—apart from everything being from places I frequented. "He's been watching me," I said, figuring it out. "Not lately," I added, seeing the dates, "but he has."

The oven opened, and I heard a plate scrape on the faded table. "Come and eat while it's warm," he called, sounding angry but willing to let me handle it.

Jaw clenched, I picked the bits of my life out from between his socks and dropped them on the dresser. I was taking the gun. I may as well let him know I looked at everything. Slamming the drawer shut, I stomped to the table and sat down, exhaling to get rid of my tension. The gun was uncomfortable, and I put it on the table, not caring if it looked funny next to the domesticity of plates and pancakes.

"Don't worry about it," I said as I put my napkin on my lap. I couldn't meet his eyes as I poured the corn syrup over the very brown, almost burnt, pancakes. They were kind of tough to cut with my fork, but when I took a bite . . . "Hey, these are good," I said, feeling the different texture on my tongue. "This isn't from a box."

Pierce smiled as he sat across from me. "No. The fixings were here. Nick has more than eggs and beer, though he might know naught about what to do with them. I've made a feast on less than he has in his icebox. Uh, fridge," he amended, frowning.

He saw me look at the patch of skin at his neckline, and his smile deepened, becoming almost devilish, which for some reason made me flush. I'd seen him naked in the snow at Fountain Square; why this little bit of skin was so eye catching was beyond me. God! I was *not* going to *do* this. Pierce was off-limits. End of story. Not going to happen. Blow the ship up and maroon the crew on Celibate Island.

Pulling the plate closer, I started shoveling it in, the clicks of my fork mixing with the ticking of the four clocks. I glanced at one like Cinderella, wondering if I was going to be jerked across the continent when the sun fell below the West Coast horizon. True, Nick was here—unless he'd hopped a plane back to San Francisco—but lots of people knew Al's summoning name. The council had deep pockets. Not to mention an island full of demon summoners. Dangle a get-out-of-jail-free card in Alcatraz, and I bet someone would jump at it.

My chewing slowed, and elbow on the table, I eyed Pierce past my hanging fork, worried. This wouldn't be a problem if I could line jump. "How hard is it to travel the lines?" I asked him, and he sighed. "Give me a break, okay? I'm tired of being dragged around."

"I like coming to your rescue," he said. "You're such an independent filly. It does a man good to know he's needed—upon occasion. No. Al said not to teach you."

"Oh, I thought you did what you wanted?" I said, and he chuckled, knowing I was trying to goad him into it.

Head cocked, I put down my fork and leaned back with my coffee, a silent statement that I'd not eat any more of his pancakes until he talked to me. My eyes went to the clock on the stove, and back to him. Newt had said it took a long time to learn, and apparently a gargoyle was involved. "Bis said you used him to hear the lines," I prompted.

Pierce's smile faded, and he eyed me from around the loose curls hanging in his eyes. "You're going to get me in trouble with Al," he muttered, gaze dropping.

"So? You got me in trouble with him. Teach me," I dared him.

"I can't," he said as he hid behind a sip of coffee. "Only a gargoyle can teach you how to listen to the lines, and none has the learning anymore."

Listen? That was curious. "You taught Bis in a day," I prompted.

He didn't even look up from shoving food in his mouth. "Bis is a gargoyle. If you could see ley lines in your mind, you could master it in a day as well."

Stymied, I fiddled with my fork. "Fine. I'll ask Bis the next time I see him."

Alarm made Pierce tense. "He's not skilled enough to teach you. He's a baby."

"Nice of you to notice. That didn't seem to bother you when you used him to find me."

Grimacing, Pierce set his fork down. "I know how to jump, Rachel," he said, a touch of irritation in his voice. "Bis was safe with me. A very old gargoyle taught me before she made a die of it. I think she only taught me because she knew she wouldn't last the winter. And before you go climbing any steeples, demons killed every last free gargoyle who retained the knowledge of line jumping when the elves migrated to reality."

"That's convenient," I said, and his brow furrowed.

"No, that's a fact. The only reason the gargoyle who taught me survived was because they thought she was too young to know."

He was starting to look angry, and I wedged a triangle of pancake free. They were too good to boycott. "You could *try* to teach me," I said, pitching my voice high.

Pierce glanced up and down, making a little huff of amusement. "I'll allow you're smart as a steel trap, but it's not book learning, it's learning on one's own hook that gets you there and back. And for that, you need a gargoyle. An experienced one."

Peeved, I stared at him, waiting. Pierce ate three forkfuls, each one getting a harder stab than the one before. My foot began to bob.

Making a rude noise, Pierce pushed his plate aside. "It takes a body a year of line theory to even hope—"

"So give me the basics," I interrupted. "Something to chew on. Al won't object to that. I mean, you're not teaching me anything. Just talking shop."

Taking a slow breath, Pierce brought his coffee into his hands, holding it to warm his fingers as he gathered his thoughts. "I've heard it said that a body would do well to think of time much like a stream, and we are flotsam, buoyed along," he finally said, and a surge of anticipation brought me straight up in my chair.

"Got it," I said as I stuffed another triangle in my mouth. "Next big idea," I mumbled.

Pierce's eyebrows rose. "Now you're being evil," he accused, and when I smiled and shrugged, he took a last bite from his plate. "The ever-after is said to have found its beginning when a considerable calamity struck across time, splashing a chance amount over the banks, as it were." He hesitated; then as if I wouldn't believe him, he added, "It's not really a bank, more like a straw, the insides held within it by the same fixative that holds the stars to the heavens."

I scrunched my face up, trying to put that into modern terms. "Uh, gravity?" I guessed, then added, "What makes things fall down but keeps the moon up?"

His eyes going wide, Pierce blinked at me. "To put it in a pie, yes. It's gravity, and a potency I'm constrained to call . . . sound?"

I licked corn syrup off my finger, wondering how sound had anything to do with gravity, space, or anything.

"Old sound?" Pierce tried again. "The word of God, some say."

Word of God. Old sound. I'm not getting this. "Oh!" I exclaimed, brightening. "Sound! Like the big bang that started the universe!"

"Explosions have naught to do with it," he said quizzically, but I waved my fork at him.

"Some people think the universe started with a big explosion," I said. "And everything is still moving away from it. They say space is still ringing from the bang like a big bell, but we're so small we can't hear it. Like us not being able to hear all the sounds elephants make."

He didn't look convinced. "Do tell. Students of the arcane, ah, some people believe that such drops of time that are flung near enough slip back like water drops, leaving a body with the sensation of déjà vu, but if they are large enough and are flung far enough apace, they're constrained to dry up and vanish, leaving unexplained lost civilizations."

His eyes were alight. I'd seen that look on college students debating such ridiculous stuff as how the world would be today if Napoleon hadn't stirred that misaligned spell and won Waterloo, or if the Turn had never happened and we'd gone to the moon instead. "Okay, I got that," I said, and Pierce pushed from the table to take his plate to the sink.

"Are you sure?" he asked as he worked the taps and squirted soap into the empty batter bowl. He must have seen Ivy and me do it a hundred times.

"I saw a movie about it once," I said, and he turned to me, eyebrows high.

"You are a clever woman, Rachel, but I'm not sure you comprehend the complexity," he offered over the sound of running water. But at my frown, he cautiously took my empty plate as I extended it and continued. "The ever-after is believed to have its origins in such a calamity," he said as he rolled up his sleeves to show nicely muscled arms, darker than that spot of skin at his throat. "It was orchestrated by the demons to kill the majority of the elven population during their yearly gathering. An almighty span of time was spelled from its course, landing it too far to rejoin yet being so considerable that it didn't vanish straight on, lingering enough such that the no-account makers of the curse could return full chisel to reality, leaving the elves to make a most horrible die of it."

"Demons," I said, and Pierce nodded. Demons and elves. Why did it always come back to them fighting their stupid war?

"Demons," Pierce agreed. "Upon banishing the elves, they flung themselves back to reality, their tracks scarring time and making ley lines."

"Demons made the ley lines?" I interrupted, surprised, and he nodded.

"And such was their downfall, for not only did the lines continue to funnel potency, ah, energy, into the ever-after and keep it from vanishing, as they had schemed, but it also fixed the demons to the very place they sought to escape. I'll allow the elves must have rejoiced for their continuing lives, even banished as they were, until the sun rose and the same demons who'd cursed them were flung back, trapping all together in an almighty wrathy state."

"Until the elves learned how to travel the lines and come home," I said, my eyes rising to his. "Witches learned to do it first, though." *And then demons killed all the gargoyles who knew so no one could travel the lines but them.*

Pierce turned from me to wash the plates with careful attention. "A reasonable truth when a body knows the secret of our origin," he said, reminding me that he was one of the few people to know. "Demons created the ever-after and are slung back to it when the sun rises."

"Jenks can't stay in the ever-after after sunup," I said, taking up my cup and warming my hands around it. "He popped right out. And when I was in the ever-after, it felt like the lines were running from the ever-after to reality."

Pierce set the rinsed plates in the dry sink. "Perhaps because pixies are of such a small stature. I've not the learning, uh, I don't know. The lines flow like tides. When the sun is down, ever-after flows into reality, allowing demons to visit. When the sun is up, reality flows into the ever-after, pulling them back. It's the tides that make a caution of their realm."

I thought about that, remembering the broken buildings. Standing, I started pulling drawers open to hunt for a drying towel. "So ley lines are the paths the demons took to return to reality that first time, and they flow back and forth like tides, trashing the place."

"You have it like a book!" Pierce said, clearly pleased. "The entirety of the ever-after is pulled behind us like a man hanging behind a runaway horse, fixed fast by the ley lines."

"So how do you travel them?" I asked as I dried a plate, remembering what all this history was supposed to lead up to. He hesitated, and I added, "I want to know, even if it's just theory. I won't tell Al you told me. Give me some credit, will you?"

Hands dripping suds, he squinted as if in pain, and I added, "I'm going to need something to think about in Alcatraz besides your stunning Latin syntax, okay?"

Emotion drained from his face. "You won't get there. I'll not allow it," he said, his soapy hands suddenly on my shoulders. "With Bis's help, I can find you, follow you anywhere."

My impulse to pull away vanished. As I stood there, my shoulders became damp. I searched his expression, too jaded to believe in white knights. Happy endings were never handed out. You had to fight for them, earn them with bruised hearts and sacrifices. And I just couldn't do it right now. It hurt too much when it fell apart. "Don't make me promises," I whispered, and the earnest glow in his eyes tarnished.

Head down, I ducked out from his hands, going to the table and re-capping the corn syrup as if nothing had happened, but my shoulders were cold, making it feel as if he was touching me still. I couldn't let myself like him. It was too stupid to think about.

"Look, I've traveled by ley lines a lot," I persisted, wanting to change the subject. "I can even hold myself together without help. Al hasn't had to keep my soul from going all over the continent for weeks. Can you at least tell me how gargoyles fit into it?"

His head down, Pierce returned to the sink and dumped the pan of sudsy water.

"Oh, come on!" I cajoled as I slid the corn syrup in next to the corn-flakes and shut the door hard. *Why does Nick have six bottles of corn syrup?* "I won't tell Al!"

Still Pierce said nothing as he rinsed the dishpan and put it away damp. He was frowning when he turned back, and upon seeing my arms over my chest, he held up his hands in surrender. "Holding your soul together is but a small part," he said, and I made a satisfied huff, turning to dry the silverware. "To put it all on one stick, you need to shift your aura to match a ley line."

I pulled three drawers open looking for the silverware, dropping it in when I found it. There was no order, just everything all jumbled together in an otherwise empty drawer. Ivy would have an OCD moment. "I didn't know you could do that," I said. "Shift your aura. What, like make it a different color?"

"No. Color shifts slowly with our experiences, but the sound it makes is . . . flexible."

I bumped the drawer shut with my hip, turning. "Auras make sounds?" I questioned.

"Apparently," he said sourly. "Mine never says anything that I can hear."

I smiled, relaxing at the drop in tension. "How can you change something you can't even hear?" I complained. "It's like teaching a deaf woman how to speak immaculately."

"That," Pierce said as he put the plates away, "is an almighty fine comparison. And why it takes a gargoyle to teach you. You need to know what sound your aura needs to be, and gargoyles are the only creatures that can hear auras and ley lines both."

I leaned back against the kitchen counter, wondering if this was as close to a normal life as I'd ever get: a few hours in someone else's apartment, cleaning up after breakfast and talking shop with a man who had been dead for a hundred and fifty years. *But dead no longer.*

"Bis can hear auras," I stated, and Pierce took the dishcloth from me, drawing it through my fingers. "So if I want to use the ley lines like a demon and go back and forth, all I have to do is learn how to make my aura sound right?"

He nodded. "Death on," he said, his eyes fixed to mine. "When Al totes you in a line, he first changes the sound of your aura until it's consistent with that of the nearest ley line. That draws you into it. You settle somewhere else by making your aura sound like the line you wish to be in.

A body's soul will find itself there most quick, and from there, you allow your aura to return to its normal sound to push you from the line back into reality. Demons can't hear the lines, nor can witches or elves or pixies, but with practice they can learn to shift their auras."

"And you."

He inclined his head. "And me. Because I studied on it. Most diligently. It is one of the reasons the coven branded me black, saying it's a demon art because it makes your aura smutty. But, Rachel, it's not evil. Bis is neither cursed nor smut-ridden because he can travel the lines."

"You're preaching to the choir here, Pierce," I said, watching him dry his fingers. "So, assuming I go along with this and Bis can tell me how to shift my aura, how do you do it?"

Dropping the dish towel, Pierce sat down at the table, looking excited for the first time. "Think on it like this," he said as he folded a napkin into an informal cup shape. I stayed where I was, and he looked up with an innocent expression. "Come along, Ms. Schoolmarm," he said, and I tugged out the chair opposite him and sat down.

Pierce eyed the space between us, then shook a bunch of salt into the napkin. "Be of the mind that the salt is like your aura," he said, "and the napkin is the barrier the ley line makes with all creation. The salt can't get through, agreed?" he asked, and I nodded. "But if you make the space that abides within the salt bigger, spread it out . . ."

I gasped when he dumped his cold coffee into the paper-napkin cup and coffee predictably went through the napkin and all over the table. "What are you doing?" I protested, my motion to stand halting when he reached across the table and grasped my wrist. Smiling, Pierce squished the napkin in one hand to get the last of the coffee out. Taking my finger, he traced it through the puddle and touched it to my lips, bringing the nasty taste of salty coffee to me. That's not why I shivered, though. *Stop it. Just stop it now, Rachel.*

"Just like the salt, your aura can be tuned so the gaps within it are bigger. It is still your aura, unchanged, but when the holes match up with the holes of the line, you can slip through right smart. Like magic. Each line is different. Know the line, and you can travel to it."

My lips were salty, and I felt another quiver as he held my wrist with the width of the table between us. "You've made a mess," I said, not looking from his eyes. They were blue, but not like Kisten's. Not like Kisten's at all.

"Do tell?" Pierce leaned across the table until he was inches away. His eyes were glinting. I didn't care if it was him or what he had told me that got my pulse racing. He was holding my wrist, almost pulling me closer. "Are you of a mind to try to shift your aura?" he offered. "Without Bis, you won't know what to match it to, but if I should make a die of it, my wicked witch tucked away in Alcatraz will have something to ponder."

The memory of Alcatraz was like a slap, and I jerked from him. "God, yes," I said as my hand slipped from his. "What do we do first?"

He smiled, taking a moment to swipe the coffee up with the dish towel before he held his hands out over the table, palms up. "We bring our souls to perfect balance."

My eyebrows rose. Tap a line and bring the energy in our chi to an equal state?

"My intentions are honorable," Pierce protested, but his lips twitched in amusement.

Eyes narrowing, I crossed my arms and looked at him. Balancing two people's chis was innocent enough. Sort of. It was a common event between teachers and students of the higher ley-line courses, sort of finding ground zero when learning a new charm, but it was also the same thing as a power pull, which was basically sex with your clothes on if you did it right. And I'd be willing to bet that Pierce knew how to do it right.

"If you're skeery . . . ," he taunted, leaning back and letting his hands fall below the table.

My eyes scrunched up. "This is something I really want to know," I said softly. "Please?"

His smile softened. "You are indeed a chaste woman," he said. I snorted, eying his hands, again held out, palms up. "Are you communing with the nearest ley line?" he asked.

Excitement zinged through me. Scooting the chair closer, I reached out with my thoughts and tapped the university's line, wide and slow. "Got it," I said, putting my hands atop his, palms down but space still between us.

"If you're sure," he said slowly. "I'll not have it said that I took advantage of you."

"God, Pierce!" I griped. "We're just balancing our chis. It's not like we're doing a power pull." *Not yet, anyway.* A shiver took me, and our eyes met when he noticed.

"Let's try then," he said as I stifled my smile, lifting his palms to touch mine.

My focus tightened for an instant at the connection, a knee-jerk reaction to keep my energy levels to myself, a necessity among polite society. He was still looking at me, and something in me twisted. I was in so much trouble. He was dangerous. He was quick, clever, powerful. I'd learned more from him in one night than I had with Al the past two months. But what really had me worried was that he didn't judge me by what others said, but by what he saw. And what he saw was me, not the smut or the demon pact or the shunning.

There was nothing but the soft warmth of skin between us, both of us holding tight to ourselves as if afraid. I swallowed, and on my exhale, I loosened my hold. A trickle, a whisper, a breath of power ebbed between us with the slow pace of molasses. Energy slipped coolly from me to him, equalizing. It hadn't happened in a jolting flash, telling me Pierce had an amazing amount of control. There was no titillation, or at least not much. But there could have been. There were ways, and slow was often more excruciatingly pleasurable than fast.

I stared at him, pulse hammering as our palms touched and the energy hummed between us. "I have no idea what I'm doing," I whispered, not knowing if I was talking about how to travel the lines or my life in general.

Pierce's lips twitched. "Then let me show you, mistress witch." Palms never leaving mine, he leaned forward across the table. My pulse hammered, and I thought he was going to kiss me, when he suddenly pulled back, his eyes wide and his gaze unfocused.

"What did I do?" I asked, alarmed, and then the air pressure shifted.

"Stu-u-u-udent!"

Shit. *Algaliarept.*

Fourteen

"What, by the two worlds colliding, are you doing!" Al shouted, ruddy face ugly.

Pierce flung himself back. A sheet of green-tinted ever-after rose between us, and I stood, my chair crashing to the floor.

"Al, wait!" I shouted, lurching clear when Al dove across the kitchen for Pierce, shoving the table aside. My splat gun and Pierce's hat hit the floor, victims of inertia. Al's white-gloved hand smacked into Pierce's hastily raised protection circle with an audible crunch.

"Bloody hell!" the elegantly dressed demon howled in his proper English accent and crushed green velvet as he shook his fist and danced back. "You bloody hell sewer rat. I told you no teaching her!" Looking from his hand, his anger shifted to me. "Hello, Rachel."

Pierce's face was white as he stood ramrod straight behind a shimmering sheet of green-tinted ever-after. A flair of red washed through it, and was gone. His expression was both determined and frustrated. Clearly he wasn't happy about being caught teaching me lines.

Al backed up, his head bowed over his gloved hand until a shimmer of ever-after coated it. "Maybe I should blame you," the demon muttered, goat-slitted red eyes making me shiver. "Using your feminine wiles to lead my familiar astray. If all you want is dangerous sex, I can give that to you better than he can, and I won't break your heart afterward."

Insulted, I glared, ready to argue with a demon who could snuff me as fast as I could flip a switch—but wouldn't. "He was just teaching me the theory on line jumping. More than you ever did! And I'm not too happy about you sending him to watch me. All he does is order me around, and it's not even good advice. He's part of the problem!"

Al's eyes narrowed. I had taken three steps back before I even realized it, the small of my back hitting the counter. Sure, as his student—the only one worth teaching in the last five thousand years—keeping me in good health and not bent into a pretzel was a plus, but if I went too far he might not be opposed to being known as the one who killed their chance at a rebirth of demons. Trent could make more of me, and Al knew it. Bastard.

"Pierce watching you wasn't my idea," he said smoothly, his anger an icy thread in his voice. "You'll learn line jumping when I say so." He looked at Pierce over his glasses, and I shivered. "And not from some runt with delusions of grandeur. You need a gargoyle."

My anger hesitated, thoughts spinning back to last winter when he congratulated me on "having my own gargoyle" and asking him to come share mortar cakes with Treble . . . "Treble knows how to line jump?" I asked, and Al chuckled, the noise low and satisfied.

"Of course she does. She won't be teaching you, though." Spinning on a heel he turned to give Pierce a derisive look. "You're a mess. Get out of that circle. I won't kill you today. Brew me a coffee while Rachel and I talk."

His face white, Pierce let his circle drop. Al saw the direction of my gaze, and he shook his head at me. "You look even worse, itchy witch. You simply must take more care in your personal hygiene. I'll not have it said that I'm bringing you up poorly."

"I've been a little too preoccupied to worry about what I look like," I said.

"Pish posh. Appearance is all we have sometimes. Make it a priority."

I stiffened when he stooped to pick up first my splat gun, then Pierce's hat, but he only handed me my weapon. "I smell pancakes," Al said as he jauntily smacked Pierce's hat back on the witch's head. "Did the runt make you breakfast?" Al said, leaning over the stove. "Quickest way to a woman's crotch is through her gullet, eh?" he said, leering at Pierce, who was now rinsing out the percolator. "Is it working? I'd be curious to know. I'd buy her a cake or something."

Pierce was silent, his lips pressed tight as he washed the coffeepot. I didn't know what to do with my splat gun, so I tucked it in the back of my waistband. "Al, I spent yesterday in Alcatraz," I said, trying to sound reasonable. "I want my name back. We had a deal."

Ignoring me, Al turned to the rest of the apartment, the tails of his frock coat furling. "Where are we?" he asked, flicking on lights as he passed into the living room. "Cincinnati," he said dryly, peeking through the blinds and gazing out the black windows, hands on his hips as he surveyed the street below as if he owned it. "It stinks of trains and that chili with the chocolate in it. Ooooh, books!" he exclaimed suddenly, making a beeline for the small library.

I shoved the table back where it belonged and Pierce picked up my chair, draping his coat and vest over it and taking off his hat. The man was subdued, his anger simmering. He wouldn't look at me, ticked perhaps that we'd attracted Al's attention. Watching Al coo over the books like they were puppies, I realized he'd never been here before, which begged the question of whom Nick was summoning. The raised circle in the corner wasn't for playing marbles.

"This isn't your home," Al said, pulling out a volume and laying it open across one thick hand. "Nothing smells like you." He gave me a questioning look over his round smoked glasses and snapped the book closed. Sliding it away, he reached over his head, not even looking where his hands were going as he found that ley-line knife resting out of his eyesight.

"Shiny!" the demon said, his lips parting to show his blocky teeth. "I haven't seen this since I stuck it in Amenhotep." The demon's eyes flicked to mine, his smile widening. "This is Nicholas Gregory Sparagmos's room," he said, and my breath caught. "Delightful, *just delightful*! What are you doing in Nicky's room, Rachel? Ooooh, he summoned you to the West Coast, didn't he? Did you kill him? Good for you for taking care of that little *problem*! I should give you a bunny. Where is he? Stuffed in a closet?"

Pierce shut the cupboard door hard, and I jumped. "She should have killed him, but she doesn't listen to me," he muttered, and I gave him a dark look.

"Al, why are you here if it's not to give my name back?" I asked, and the demon sighed, breathing deeply of the knife's blade.

"It's after sundown. I'm assessing whether your worry is valid." Eyes closing in bliss, Al ran his tongue up the length of the blade, a soft sound escaping him as he licked the knife clean of nothing I could see. "I'm going to rub the little wizard's head from his skinny shoulders for summoning you. I'm the only one allowed to pull you about." He put the knife away, fingers reluctantly slipping from it. "Not that I ever have . . ."

"No, you just keep crashing my life. Look—" I said, and Al grunted.

"Here it comes," the demon muttered. "Listen. Listen to this, runt. She's going to have a list." And Pierce shrugged, carefully filling the pot with fresh water.

"Hey!" I snapped, not liking either of their attitudes. "If you're not going to make good on our deal, then you need to leave. And if you leave, you might better spend some time finding a good lawyer for breach of contract! I know people, you know."

"No need to get nasty," Al said, pouting. "With this nonsense about being summoned, I felt you slipping into a line and came to check. Apparently you've exaggerated your trouble."

"Excuse me?" I stood where I was, hands on my hips. "I'm not exaggerating anything. I was in Alcatraz. I want my name back. No one knows mine but my mom, Ivy, and Jenks!"

"And me." Al ran his finger across the front of the big-screen TV, harrumphing at the dust. "You should just scare the hell out of them. Consider this your chance to practice."

"I don't need practice," I said through gritted teeth. "I need my name back. They're talking lobotomy. Sure would be a shame for your investment to end up dumber than a rock."

Coattails furling, Al strode to the pile of electronics, picking up a camera and opening the back to take the memory card and slip it into a pocket. "You are so cute when you squirm," he murmured, looking at me over his glasses and dropping the camera so it hit with a crack.

"Al—"

"I'm giving you the chance to grow," Al said as he sat on the couch, spreading his arms across the top. "I'd be a poor guardian if I fought all your battles for you. They're paltry witches. You're demon kin. What can they do to you?"

Frustrated, I held my arms out, hands in fists and palms up. "My knees are the size of grapefruits from dancing, maybe? And these shackle marks are from what?"

Al's red eyes slid past me to Pierce. "Play?" he said, his voice dripping interest. "Gordian Nathaniel Pierce's quirks are legendary. Why do you think I want the runt so badly? Size truly doesn't matter if you can do what he can."

I looked at Pierce—his softly curling hair hid his face, but his jaw was tight and his hands shook as he measured out the grounds and plugged in the percolator. Male witches' anatomy generally didn't measure up to a human's, but witch women *always* came back.

"'Course it might all be propaganda," Al said as he pulled a watch from his fob pocket. His eyes met mine, and I shivered when he rose. "Let me guess . . . ," he said as he started walking to me, each foot placed precisely. "The little wizard summoned you to the West Coast with my name knowing he would get you, then fled here to summon you out of their grasp, probably whining some poppycock bull about how he lo-o-o-oves you."

I retreated as Al advanced until my back hit the counter. "Nick is slime," I said, scared.

Al pressed close, far too close, and I held my breath, cringing. Not quite touching me, but almost, the lace at his throat shifted. "The question is," Al whispered, eying Pierce, "Nicky wouldn't know you had my name unless someone told him. Who told him, Rachel?"

"The coven." Al stank of burnt amber, and seeing me wince, he drew back, frowning. Knees shaking, I pushed from the counter.

"The coven," Al echoed, mocking me. "Yes. But who told *them*?"

I thought about Trent and dropped my eyes. "The problem isn't who told the coven your name," I said. "The problem is someone told them I can invoke demon magic. Maybe it was you trying to force me into the ever-after."

Al huffed, turning away. "Rachel, Rachel, Rachel . . . Such thoughts of paranoia. And you say you don't need a babysitter."

"I don't!"

He stood at the table, both elegant and derisive. "Then start acting like a demon, itchy witch."

"I'm not a demon," I said, glancing at the clock. Crap, it was after six. *Nick.*

"You could have fooled me." Al's white glove vanished, and he examined his hand, the thick knuckles going white as he flexed his fingers. "This entire situation is so . . . *banal*." The glove misted back into existence, and his attention landed on me. "You must do better, love, if you expect anyone to take you seriously."

"Is there a point to this?" My arms were over my chest again, and I forced them down.

"I bloody well hope so," Pierce grumbled as he set a cup beside the chugging pot.

"The point is, you could excel if you would simply exert yourself!" Al complained.

My head shifted back and forth. "I don't want to be a demon. I just want my name back so my life can go back to chaotic and weird instead of chaotic and desperate."

Al took a breath to say something, and when he held it, head cocked, my face went cold. Dragonfly wings. A slow smile spread across Al's face as he locked gazes with me.

"Jax?" I called, not seeing him but knowing the pixy was here. "I didn't call him. I didn't call him, Jax! You've got to believe me!"

In a sprinkling of falling green dust, a pixy darted into the kitchen. Jax stared at us with his mouth hanging open. His hand was over his bicep, almost hiding a new tear in his shirt.

"I didn't call him," I pleaded, and the young pixy's wings hit a new high, his mouth moving, but nothing coming out. "Jax, tell Nick not to come in!"

Jax darted to whatever pixy hole he'd come through. But it was too late, and I heard the knob turn. "Nick! No!" I shouted, running for the door.

I gasped as I ran right into Al, suddenly before me. It was like running into a tree. "Nick!" I shouted. "Don't come in! Nick! Get out!"

But with a thump of furious music from downstairs and the smell of Chinese takeout, Nick came into the shadowy apartment. Jax was a streak of silver, his voice high and unrecognizable as he panicked. "Get out!" I shouted, stumbling when Al vanished, reappearing behind Nick in the open doorway. *Oh God. Can this get any worse?*

Al shoved the door shut with one foot. "Hi, Nicky."

Yup, it can.

Nick spun, eyes wide. Dropping the takeout boxes, he scrabbled frantically for the slab circle in the corner. He didn't have a chance.

Al reached a white-gloved hand out and snagged him like an errant kitten, holding him up by the scruff of his neck and giving him a shake. "Got you, you little wizard."

Nick choked, spinning slightly with his toes just touching the floor. "Little . . . bitch," he gagged, face red and long hair brushing Al's fingers. "You little bitch. I trusted you . . ."

"Jax! No!" I exclaimed, hands high as I got between Al and the pixy. He'd get himself killed. "Take the high ground and look for an opening. You can't take a demon by the front!"

Al looked at me in question from over his glasses, but the small pixy had withdrawn in frustration, and that's all I was after.

"It's not what it looks like," I babbled to Nick. "Al, let him go. You can't snag him. He's with me." I looked at Pierce, but the man was standing in the kitchen beside the coffeepot with his arms crossed, an annoyed expression on his face.

It smelled like the demons' mall that Al had taken me to once, the burnt amber mixing with the smell of green things, takeout, and brewing coffee. Al grinned to show his thick, flat, blocky teeth, clearly pleased as he held Nick up off the floor with one white-gloved hand. "No," he said. "He owes me. Got a mark and everything. I need some help in the kitchen, and since the runt over there is babysitting you, this will have to do."

I looked at Pierce standing in the kitchen beside the gurgling coffee-pot. He wasn't doing anything! But then . . . what did I expect him to do? It was Al.

Nick's choking started to sound serious and his face went red. "Al, you're hurting him!" I exclaimed. "One mark doesn't give you the right to take him, and you know it. Let him go!"

"Make me," the demon said with a snicker, and Nick's legs started to twitch. "Let me jump you to a line, worm. It will be easier that way."

Was I going to have to force Al to hold to his agreement every bloody time? "Don't push me on this, Al," I said, pulse fast as I rocked on the balls of my feet. I could hear Jax's wings, and prayed he'd stay out of the way. "You agreed. No snagging people with me unless you have a prior claim, and you don't have one on Nick! Let him *go!*"

"I was a fool to have . . . trusted you," Nick said, gagging, hatred in his bloodshot eyes as spittle formed between his lips.

"This wasn't my idea," I barked at him. "I didn't summon him, he just showed up! Al, let him go!" I tugged the demon's arm, but nothing moved.

"Wah, wah, wahh," Al said sarcastically. "You knew what you were getting into, little Nicky. When you invite a demon into your home, you get what you get."

My face went cold. I let go of Al's arm and dropped back. Nick, claw-ing at Al's grip on his throat, sent his eyes to mine. "I'm not a demon," I said, knees wobbling.

Al pulled out a pocket watch and looked at it. "Technically, perhaps, but one can't help one's birth, can one? Ta. Must dash. Lots to do tonight."

"Rachel—" Nick choked out, fear thick on him as he struggled to find his feet and get out of Al's grip. "I'll get you for this. I promise."

"Don't be gauche," Al said before my mouth opened, all playfulness gone from his cultured voice. "You did this to yourself—summoning Rachel to the West Coast with my name? Don't deny it. I can still smell the stink of broken dreams on you." Nick's eyes squinted shut when Al pulled him close and breathed deeply of his hair. "No need to change names, now, love," the demon said. "I'd think you'd be glad to be rid of him, seeing as he put you in Alcatraz."

"We had a deal," I tried again, hearing the soft sound of Pierce pouring a cup of coffee. "If you don't let him go, I swear . . ."

Al arched his eyebrows at me, waiting. At my shoulder, Jax started humming nervously.

"You're not teaching me crap," I said, voice shaking. "And you're all but ignoring not one, but two agreements we have. What by God's little green apples are you doing for me?"

He hesitated, and I exhaled, pushing out all the tension. "Newt would love me to be her student," I said, and Al squinted at me from over his glasses. "Either you start making good or I have no reason not to accept. Hell, I'd get rid of Pierce that way. Maybe I should."

"You wouldn't," Al intoned, and Nick took a gasping breath as Al's fingers loosened.

"Why not?" I was shaking, and I crossed my arms over my chest to try to hide it. "Who's watching her?" I asked. "Anyone? She killed Minias, didn't she?"

"Rumor has it." Al loosened his fingers a touch more, and Nick's feet touched the carpet.

I felt a surge of strength. "How would all you good old boys like it if us girls got together? Huh? Wouldn't that be great? I'm sure she'll remember everything, eventually."

Al's eyes narrowed. I arched my eyebrows, wishing I could do the one-eyebrow trick, and he frowned. "You're not worth it," he muttered, and shoved Nick away.

The human went flying, hitting the door and sliding to the floor beside the spilled Chinese food. His hand was around his neck, and he was gagging, trying to get more air into himself than was possible. Jax flew to him and I slumped, feeling sick. I couldn't stomach going to Newt. But Al knew better than to call me on this bluff. If I got mad enough, I would.

"I'll see you both on Saturday," the demon said to me, gesturing for Pierce to hand him the cup of coffee. "No more parties, itchy witch."

"Looking forward to it," I said, glowering back at him. Saturday wasn't going to be fun, but at least stupid-ass Nick would be safe and sound in reality where he belonged.

Jax's wings were loud as he hovered over Nick, and the human was stumbling to his feet, using the wall for balance as he glared at me like he wanted to kill me. Al, though, was taking a sip of coffee, his eyes momentarily closing in bliss. Opening, they fixed on Nick. "Hard to imagine, my itchy witch speaking out for you. What twisted way will you find to thank her?" he mocked. "If I find you alone, I *will* take you." He shifted his gaze to Pierce, unrepentant as always. "We're going to talk, runt," he said, voice hard.

"Get out of here," Nick rasped, and in a soft haze of ever-after, Al was gone.

I took a slow breath, my knees starting to shake. "Damn it!" I shouted, startling myself as I realized what had happened. I'd saved Nick, but what about me? "Damn it to the Turn. Damn it all to hell and back!" I made a fist, but there was nothing to hit. I hadn't gotten my name back. I was just as screwed as I was when I'd been sitting in Alcatraz. "Just one break," I shouted at the ceiling. "Why can't I have just one lousy break?" Depressed, I slumped at the kitchen table. "Just one?" I asked, voice high and squeaky.

"Rachel!" Pierce shouted, and my head came up. Eyes widening, I looked up to see Nick coming at me with that knife. Gasping, I slid from the chair to under the table. Hand reaching behind me, I found my splat gun and pointed it at him.

Nick slid to a stop, holding the knife pointed backward and looking like he knew how to use it. "I trusted you," he rasped, his free hand on his throat, his blue eyes almost black in the dim light. Al's handprint was clear on his neck, and his eyes were wild.

"I just saved your ass!" I shouted from under the table, shaking. My aim, though, never shifted.

"I trusted you!" he shouted again. "I brought you into my *home*! And you summoned *him* into it. I should have let you bleed out in that library.

I should have walked away and let you die! My life has been one shit fest after another since I met you!"

Pierce was moving cautiously forward to get between us, his eyes on Nick, not the knife. His hands were utterly devoid of magic, which made me feel better. The gun I had pointed at Nick was starting to shake, but I wouldn't drop it.

"Your life has been a shit fest?" I shouted, and Pierce halted. "Don't talk to me about a shit fest! I just bluffed my way out of *you* becoming Al's latest blow-up doll!"

Someone pounded on the wall, a muffled voice demanding we shut up.

"You can get Turned for all I care!" I continued. "And for your information, I didn't summon Al! He just showed up! He does that! My life has been hell since I met you, Nick. You saddled me with a demon mark and got this started. I don't owe you anything! *Anything!*"

The last was a veritable shriek, and Nick lowered the knife. He glanced at Pierce, then me. Backing up, he set the dagger on the top shelf. Head down, he strode to the bathroom and slammed the door behind him roughly, not acknowledging what I had said. My eyes met Pierce's, and I swallowed hard when I heard Nick retching. Yeah, my stomach didn't feel all that good, either. Damn it, I was crying, too.

Jax hovered for a moment in indecision, then dropped to the floor and slid under the door.

The soft touch on my shoulder jerked me straight. Bringing the gun around, I gasped, trying to see through the tears. It was Pierce crouching beside me. "I-I . . . ," I babbled, but I couldn't let go of the gun. Nick . . . He'd wanted to kill me.

"Go away," I managed. I was crying, and I wiped the back of my hand under an eye.

"No," Pierce said gently, one knee on the faded linoleum. "I may have used your mistake to twist Newt into forcing Al to grant me leave, but I'm here, and I'm not leaving."

I looked up, numb as I wiped my eyes again. "I don't feel so good."

Pierce encircled me with his arms, and before I could protest, he pulled me out from under the table and carried me to the couch. I was trembling, and he draped the afghan over me. My blood was being drawn inward, leaving me cold. I couldn't let go of the gun. I wanted to, but I couldn't.

"I never should have come here," I said as Pierce tucked the scratchy yarn under my chin. "This was a mistake. You were right. I should have gotten on the bus."

"Just because you give a man the mitten doesn't mean you don't care for him," Pierce said, and I looked up, seeing Nick's and my words through Pierce's eyes. *A lover's spat?*

"I don't love Nick," I breathed, numb. "He's a thief, and I'm attracted to danger. That's all. The thief part I might have been able to overlook, but the lies I couldn't."

Pierce had knelt beside me to put his eyes even with mine. Damn me if his stubble didn't make him look even more appealing. His concern was almost palpable, and my heart ached for having seen that same emotion in Kisten. But he wasn't Kisten. He was different.

"You risked everything to keep him from Al," Pierce said, his strong hands adjusting the afghan, always moving, adjusting, shifting. "If that's not love, what is?"

When Pierce got it wrong, he really got it wrong. "Pierce. Listen to me," I said, feeling the gun under the afghan. "I do not love Nick. But I could not stand there and let Al take him. Not for Nick's sake, but for mine. If Al got away with snatching people once, then his word to me wouldn't mean fairy farts."

His eyebrows went up, and his hands wiped my tears away. "You have grit, Rachel Morgan."

"You shouldn't have told me anything," I said, throat tight as I felt the gun shake in my hand. "I'm sorry I ever asked. He's going to give you hell on Saturday. I'm sorry."

Pierce shook his head, his lips pressed tight. "I suspicion . . . I think Al didn't mind me telling you about the lines, or he would have broken my circle and rowed me up salt river directly. It's not worth shucks."

"He might," I said, not wanting to see Al torment him. "He knows you were teaching me. He came because . . ." I hesitated, my tears stopping. "Al said he came because he felt me start to slip into a line." My eyes rose to his. "I was doing it?" I asked. "I was tuning my aura?"

Slowly Pierce's expression went from questioning to what might have been excitement. But then I sneezed. It was followed immediately by another.

"God bless," Pierce said, but I turned back with my hand over my face, my brief joy shifting to fear. My gut twisted, and that hollow ache I had thought was from despair worsened. I reached out in panic when it felt like the world dropped out from under me, my hand gripping Pierce's shoulder. It was too soon for the sun to be down in San Francisco. *Is it Al?*

"Pierce?" I whispered, scared to death. Someone had me. "Someone has me, Pierce!" I warbled, panic icing me. "I can't stop this!"

I heard the bathroom door open, and the hum of pixy wings.

Pierce's arms went around me, and yet, I felt them become thin. "Rachel, I swan you'll be okay!" he said, struggling to make me look at him, but I was panicking. "I'll find Bis, and then I'll follow you. I promise. No one will hurt you!"

"She's being summoned?" Nick asked from the other side of the room, ignored.

To resist was stupid. The tears came down for real this time, big and heavy. "Thank you," I whispered as I held Pierce, and then my gut twisted and I had to let go as I bent double. Pierce pulled me back to him, and I breathed in his warmth. "I take it," I moaned, forehead pressed into Pierce's shoulder, my voice harsh as I tried to breathe through the pain. The imbalance demanded to be paid, or it would kill me.

As soon as I uttered the words, the pain vanished. Breath catching, I looked up to Pierce, his stubbled face inches from mine, reassurance struggling to make it past the worry in his eyes. "I'll find you," he whispered.

"Okay," I breathed, trusting him.

And then his hands slipped through me. I was gone.

Fifteen

Like water down a drain, I felt my aura collapse, pulling through me and dissolving my body as it went, shrinking everything down to the mere thought of myself. Though I didn't have a heart, I listened for it, my nonexistent breath held as I felt myself slip into the lines, trying to find something different, a new sensation, a feeling that might help me figure this out. Someone was tuning my aura—or paying someone to do it for them.

Listen like Bis, I thought, allowing a sliver of awareness to slip from the shell I had made about myself. That was a mistake.

Cold stabbed my mind, and I screamed. The agony was so intense, I missed falling into reality, my shriek exploding into existence before I did, echoing back from white walls and tile floors to sound inhuman. I took a breath to scream again, catching it back in a harsh gurgle. The gun in my hand dropped, clattering onto the white tile as I clutched at the floor. *Where am I?*

The cold in my skull dulled to an ice-cream headache the size of Alaska. "That hurt . . . ," I panted. My fingers were cramping from having tried to gouge the tile while I was on my hands and knees. I was afraid to move; it had hurt that bad. *My gun. Where's my gun?*

Panting, I looked past my hair to find a purple-and-black-tinted bubble of ever-after holding me. *Purple? I'd not seen an aura that purple in ages. Someone has an ego.*

"Is it her?" said a voice behind me, and I managed to sit, grasping my arms to get them to stop shaking. My gun was right next to me. *Thank you, God.* Brooke, in her nice business dress all starched and pressed, and her shiny red heels. Why wasn't I surprised? No Vivian, though. Maybe she got smart.

"Hi, Brooke," I said dully as I sat cross-legged and put my splat gun in my lap. I hurt too much to be scared of the two big guys in lab coats with her. Where in hell was I? The sun was still up in the West Coast. With a thought, I reached for the nearest line through the purple bubble, finding I was still in Cincinnati and at the university. My eyebrows rose. *Whatcha doing, Brooke? Working outside the coven's mandates? You bad girl, you.*

There were syringes on the cart beside the door. Looked like they were going to use human drugs instead of witch magic, understandable since earth magic wouldn't work after the salt dip I was sure was coming. Crap, there was a rolling bed with straps in here.

I've seen this aura before, I thought as I tested the bubble, curling my fingers under when they cramped and the biting tang of iron hit me. Jeez, I think the circle was made with blood.

"Drop your circle," Brooke demanded, and I followed her gaze to a corner, not recognizing the thin man pointing a shaking pistol at me. A security guard masquerading as a nurse was next to him, three muscle guys total. He was grim faced and watching the pistol, but clearly not minding it being pointed at me. My summoner was wearing a suit that looked a half size too big for him, tie askew, disheveled and scuffed, as if he'd been in a fight. Short black hair framed his small-featured face, and a new scrape on his cheekbone marred his honey-colored skin. Frightened expression. Actually, now that I was paying attention . . .

"Lee?" I blurted out, taking up my splat gun but not pointing it anywhere. He looked awful. When we'd first met, he'd been in a tux and I'd been in a borrowed dress that cost more than my car. He'd been dashing, charming, confident—and vying for the gambling cartel in Cincy. It had been a bid he'd been on his way to winning until he made the mistake of betting everything on a trip to the ever-after and pitting himself against me in a ley-line magic contest. I'd lost, and Al had taken him, the better ley-line witch, as his familiar.

The last time I'd seen Stanley Saladan, he'd been all but dead, having endured hosting Al in his head and body so the demon could run around this side of the lines for the better part of a month. Lee didn't look much better now.

Lee's eyes narrowed as I spoke, his slight Asian features angry as he held the pistol with both hands. Bullets couldn't get through the bubble—unless he dropped it. Clearly he thought I might be Al. Or not.

"No," he said in a clear Midwestern accent. "He can make himself look like her. I'm not letting him out until I hear him talk. I want to hear him talk!"

Knowing what would happen next, I checked the hopper of my splat gun and sighed.

"You are such an ignoramus," Brooke said impatiently, and gestured.

The big man in the lab coat reached for Lee, deftly smacking his arm away when Lee pointed the gun at him. Almost picking Lee up, the security guard shoved Lee into the bubble.

"Bitch!" Lee shouted, arms flailing as he hit the floor beside me, sliding clear through the bubble to collapse it. The pistol went off and ceiling tile pattered down as I scrambled to put my back to a wall, heart pounding and my gun moving. Three quick puffs, and two docs-in-a-box went down. I missed the one who had thrown Lee. He was good.

"Get her!" Brooke screamed, safe inside her little blue-tinted bubble.

Adrenaline surged, and I rolled. A sharp prick in my thigh iced through me, and I pulled a dart from it, tossing it aside. "I am not an animal!" I shouted, and plugged the last man right in the face with a sleepy-time potion. His eyes rolled up and he went down, but the damage had been done. What in hell? They didn't even use dart guns on Weres! I took a breath, holding it when the room spun. *Oh God. They'd drugged me.*

And suddenly, nothing much seemed to matter anymore. Damn, it was fast-working stuff.

My pulse slowed, and I blinked when the room tilted. "Good thing I'm on the floor," I breathed, seeing Lee across the room with his back to the wall and his gun still aimed at me. The kind with real bullets. Crap, who would he rather see dead? Al, who had enslaved him, or the person who'd tricked him into it? "I'd give anything for a dead man's float," I said, and his dark eyebrows rose. "You want a martini when we're done here?" I added, and his gun drooped.

"Rachel. Damn, girl. It *is* you. I thought they were lying. No hard feelings?" he said, glancing at Brooke screaming at the people on the floor to get up. "What the devil are you doing with Al's summoning name?"

His gun wasn't pointing at me, and I tried not to giggle in my relief. "Surviving," I said, rubbing my thigh to make it tingle where the dart had hit me, right through my jeans. "Or maybe, trying to survive. This isn't looking good right now."

He nodded, scuffing the bits of ceiling tile between us. The door was still closed. No one had come in, but they might if Brooke wouldn't shut up. "It was never anything personal, you know, between us," he said again.

Nothing personal? A spark of anger burst and fizzled as I remembered Kisten getting shot at Lee's house, and then Lee trying to sell me to Al. My leg quivered. The drug was shifting, becoming more potent. My hands opened, and my gun slid to the tile. I tried to grasp it, failing. If I hadn't been on the floor, I would have fallen. Blinking, I looked at Brooke, still fuming behind her bubble. If she stepped out, Lee might shoot her, and she knew it. But if she stayed in there, we'd simply walk out. *Neener, neener, neener . . .*

"I need . . . to know," I said, slurring. I tried to pick up my gun, but my fingers only pushed it around, and it scraped the tile sadly. "Does Al have anything on you at all? Do you owe him a cup of coffee? A stick of gum? Anything?"

Lee lifted his chin, hiding his panic at the memory of being Al's familiar. "Not anymore. The second he let go of my body, it was over. I'm no one's slave."

I managed a smile. "That's good. Good for you, Lee. You shouldn't let

Trent push you around anymore either. You want to get out of here?" Crap. My ears were humming, and I couldn't pick up my damn gun. I didn't have the luxury of holding a grudge. "I need some help, Lee. Please. I got you away from Al. Sort of."

Glancing at Brooke, Lee shook his head. "Sorry, Rachel," he stated again. "You're too dangerous. Al follows you like a puppy."

I nodded, feeling the world list. "He can't touch you when you're with me. Pr-r-romise."

He thought about that for an unreal three seconds, his attention sliding to the door and back. "I've never heard of you lying to anyone," he finally said, a glimmer of his old confidence showing. "You've got a deal."

Oh, good. I didn't think I could stay awake much longer.

"You son of a bitch!" Brooke shouted, infuriated, but Lee was crossing the room to me. "She gave you to a demon! And you're going to risk your life for her? Are you insane?"

Lee scuffed his five-hundred-dollar shoe to a halt before me. "Trent seems to think you're hard to deal with. I've never seemed to have that problem."

"Well, Trent's just a big b-badass, isn't he," I slurred.

"You leave, and you're a dead witch!" Brooke threatened from her bubble. "Dead!"

"She's stronger than you," Lee said to her, his fingers moving in a subtle ley-line charm to make my skin prickle. "And she *asked* for my help. She didn't dart me like an animal and drag me from my business meeting. Bitch." He knelt beside me, and the scent of redwood grew stronger. "Upsy daisy, Rachel. We need to find a phone. They took mine."

"She took mine, too," I whispered as he put an arm under my shoulder and lifted. Lee smelled good as I slid into him. Really good, like redwood and the sea, and I shoved my face into his chest. "You smell nice," I said, giggling, then whooped when he stood and my feet scrabbled for purchase. He'd picked up my gun, and I reached for it even as my knees wobbled.

"And you weigh more than you look," he grumbled, staggering as my balance shifted.

I could feel the energy in him tingle between us where we touched. His hands were like sparks of sensation, the curse he had prepped but not invoked hovering an inch off his skin, rubbing my aura like a power pull. Or maybe it was just the drugs.

Brooke fumed. "Don't be stupid, Saladan," she threatened, pulling out a phone and hitting a button. Though I was half out of my mind, I thought it telling that she was afraid to face him alone. She was afraid he might know black magic. How smart was it that our highest-ranking af- filiation of witches intentionally kept themselves so clean that they couldn't stand up to one black-arts spell unless they were in a group?

Lee wasn't fazed by her threats, and he took on more of my weight as he edged us around one of the downed men. "You don't get it, do you?" he said as I got my arms around his neck and lost control of my legs. Not missing a beat, Lee hoisted me up and dropped my gun into my lap. "There is *nothing* you can do that could be worse than what happened to me in the ever-after," he said, me in his arms. "So what if she might be a demon? She was born on our side of the lines. I'd like to have her as a friend. Go ahead and put me in Alcatraz. At least I'd be safe there from what's coming."

"Oh good, Lee is my friend," I slurred, then tried to swallow my spit, having to really concentrate on it. We were moving. *Isn't Pierce supposed to be here? He said he'd follow me.* The world was spinning. I couldn't focus on the door, inches from my face as Lee fumbled for the lever and used his hip to trigger it. The door cracked open, and I breathed in the scent of books and coffee-stained carpet that said university. There was no noise, and it felt damp, as if we were underground. No wonder no one had come at the gunshot. I thought we were in the basement.

Brooke confidently snapped her phone shut. "You won't get three steps out that door," she said from behind the sheet of clear-blue-tinted ever-after, afraid to come out with Lee's hands hazed by black magic even as they held me like a lover. "Filthy, dirty black-magic witch."

Lee halted in the threshold, a faint smile quirking his lips. He had a tiny scar on his eyelid, and I tried to touch it. "There's no proof that I use black magic, and my lawyers get paid more than yours," he said, then glanced at me. "What are you doing?"

"You got a cute scar," I said, and he sighed.

"You are so stoned," he said as he strode into the hallway. Lee was saving me. How screwed up was that?

A tingling went through my aura, and my eyes widened. "She's outta her circle," I said, and he turned so fast my stomach lurched. Then I shrieked when Lee let go of me. My gun hit the floor with my feet, and I leaned into him, almost falling but for the arm he kept around me.

"There," he said, lips inches from my ear as three big guys in gray literally rolled into the hallway, weapons pointed. One had a wand, the other two conventional weapons. Lee shifted his arm around my throat as if holding me captive. "I want out!" he yelled as if crazed. "My name is Stanley Saladan, and I want a car at the front with the keys in the ignition and running. Clear the halls. Or I'll fuckin' kill her!"

Brooke laughed from the doorway. "Shoot them both," she said as she filled a syringe.

I whimpered, unable to feel my feet. If it wasn't for Lee, I'd be on the floor.

"Sorry, Rachel," Lee said as he dropped me. "Cover your eyes."

Shrieking, I hit the floor. I was looking at the ugly carpet squares when a bright flash made everything white-light hot. Cries rang out, and guns popped. Nothing hit me, and I got my elbows under me and looked up. Lee was standing over me like an avenging angel in a baggy suit, hands moving as he spoke a ley-line charm. My hair began to float and I shivered. The black curse slithered over me, rubbing my aura like black silk, whispering of power. I'd felt Lee's strength before, and it had crushed me. He really *was* the better witch.

Brooke was down, one of her legs and a red shoe showing through the open door. The three men in the hall were blinking, clustered together at the center of a charred circle that ran up the walls and touched the ceiling. Doors were opening, and heads were poking out. "Leave, or you will die," Lee said, and the one with the wand bolted back the way he had come.

"No!" I shouted, but Lee threw the spell hazing his hand with dripping blackness. His magic hit the two remaining men, and they screamed, the sound clawing out of their throats as if being pulled by twisted razor wire as they collapsed into a convulsing pile. The doors down the hall shut. Someone had pulled the fire alarm, and I covered my ears.

The two men were silent, no longer moving as blood spilled from their eyes and ears. *Shit. Shit. Shit.* I was going to get blamed for this.

"You got a way out of here, right?" he asked, my hands falling as he pulled me up.

"I wish you hadn't done that," I whispered. I was going to throw up. I knew it.

"I said, do you have a way out!" Lee exclaimed, hoisting me higher and tucking his shoulder under mine. "Can you jump us out or something? You're the demon here."

"I'm not a demon," I slurred. "And I can't jump a line. Where are we?"

"University," he said shortly, lifting me back up again. "Philosophy building."

Oh, that's nice. "Gun," I reminded him, but he was irate, clearly wanting to leave it behind. That was when the pop of displaced air shocked through us.

Al, I thought in panic, but the sudden beating of wings told me it was Bis. And if Bis were here, then Pierce wasn't far behind. "Hey!" I yelped when Lee dropped me again and I fell at his feet in a pile. "Damn it, will you stop doing that!"

"Step away from the lady!" Pierce said as I pushed myself upright against the wall.

"Ow, ow, ow," I hissed, holding my elbow as it vibrated all the way to my skull. My hair flew wildly as Bis's leathery wings shifted the air.

"Rachel!" Bis shouted. "Are you okay?"

Lee looked shocked by the sight of a cat-size gargoyle coming at us. I got one good breath, and then my head hit the cinder-block wall when Bis landed on my shoulder and shock echoed through me. Stars shimmered at the edge of my sight, and suddenly every line in Cincinnati was singing in my head. *Oh God, I'm going to spew.* "Off," I whimpered, trying to get my fingers between my neck and his tail wrapped around me. "Bis, get off. Please."

Babbling apologies, the young gargoyle jumped to the carpet. I took a clean breath, but then my eyes widened. "Lee, no!" I shouted, seeing him standing between Pierce and me. His hands were dripping black, and with a shout, he flung the curse at him.

Shirttails swinging, Pierce drew a line in the air, and a sheet of green fell before him to block the blast. The forces hit in a silent, colorful concussion, and then the film was gone, having absorbed the energy and run back to the ever-after where it had come from.

"Lee, he's with me. He's with me!" I shouted, but no one was listening. "Stop fighting. Both of you!" But it was too late. His expression dark, Pierce spoke three words of Latin, shaking the air and making Lee's jaw drop.

"Sweet Jesus!" Brooke shouted from the doorway, and I saw her dart back inside.

Gun. Where's my gun? I need to shoot someone. I looked, then started crawling for it, glad my hands were working again. Lee and Pierce were going to kill each other!

There was a boom of sound, and Lee fell to one knee. He looked up, smiling, his hair falling into his eyes. I think he was enjoying this. A bubble had enveloped both of us, and under its protection, a shimmering sparkle of purple and black cascaded around us. Then the bubble was gone, and Lee was standing again. An admiring whistle came from him. "Not bad," he said, grinning. "Can you do it twice?"

"I'll allow that I'd not be wanting to make a fist with you," Pierce said. "Step from Ms. Morgan, or I'll be obliged to beat you soundly, sir."

"Stop. Stop!" I shouted from the floor, waving my gun as I found it. "Pierce, Lee's helping me. It's Brooke you need to worry about! Brooke, not Lee!"

Pierce hesitated, his fist glowing black. "The mongrel dog summoned you," he stated, blue eyes unsure.

"Brooke made him do it!" I said, and Pierce turned to Lee. Lee had his own dripping ball, and at his grin, the glow went out of Pierce's hand. "You're of a mind to help Rachel?"

"Got you, you bitch," Brooke whispered.

"Hey!" I jerked my foot as a sharp pain stabbed through my lower leg. Bis flew up in a flurry of wings. Damn it, she'd gotten me again!

Lee's face became grim. Making a decision, he flung the black goo he'd made for Pierce at Brooke. My focus blurred, but I heard her scream. It ceased with a frightening suddenness as a purple-tinged sheet covered her. She convulsed, then was still.

I didn't feel so good. Eyes crossing, I started to collapse. A warm hand caught me, and everything shifted as I slumped into Pierce. I couldn't open my eyes, but I knew it was him because I could smell coal dust and shoe polish. "I thought you were a ruffian," I heard him say, then I groaned as he stood and the world spun.

"I am," Lee said, amused, "but Rachel is the better bet this spin of the wheel. Do you have a car?"

"There are cars at the curb," he said guardedly. "Can you drive? Rachel is of a mind that I'm no good at it."

"Like a pixy drunk on h-honey," I stammered.

There was a whimper from the huddled pile by the cart, and Lee's eyes narrowed. "Next time, ask for my help!" he said loudly. "You won't get it, but at least you won't piss me off!"

Oh good. Brooke was still alive. My fingers searched blindly, finding Pierce's neck. "'Bout time you got here," I slurred, lost again in the haze of whatever drug I was on. My eyes opened, and I tried to slap his face, but it barely touched him, and I giggled. "Gun. Where's my gun? We have to take Lee with us."

"You have my apology, sir," Pierce said, his voice stiff as he hoisted me higher.

"Gun," I murmured. "I want my gun, damn it!" There was a soft breath of air, and it dropped in my lap. "Thanks, Bis," I slurred. "Toot, toot! Train leaving!"

The arms around me stiffened. "Rachel?"

"Brooke drugged her," Lee said. "I suggest the stairs." There was a slight hesitation, and then we started to move. The smell of burnt carpet intruded, then vanished.

"That was a devilishly fine ward," Pierce said, and I looked up at the ceiling as the lights passed over me, seeing Bis in flashes as he crawled along the ceiling as fast as we could walk. Smiling, I patted Pierce's stubbled cheek, amazed by how I couldn't feel his face no matter how hard I smacked it.

"I like your hat, Pierce," I said, trying to focus.

The sound of people in the hallway started to become obvious the higher we went. The fire alarm was still hooting, and the building was clearing out. I giggled as I jostled in Pierce's arms. Damn it, there was nothing funny, but I couldn't stop.

Above me, Pierce looked worriedly at Lee. "Are you sure she's all right?"

"She's absolutely fine," Lee said, and I snorted as we followed the excited students up the last stairway.

I perked up when we spilled out the small side door and into the dark. Noise hit me, and flashing lights. Three firefighters lumbered to us, faceless behind air packs and face shields.

"Downstairs!" Lee shouted. "They're four people downstairs, unconscious! Some witch knocked them all out! She's crazy!"

"Ambulance is over there," one said, pointing, and he was gone, darting through the door as another student came out. Four more guys in orange lumbered past, their breath hissing through air hoses and looking like monsters in the night. A crowd had gathered, and fending off their help, Pierce made for the lamplit street, still carrying me.

"There," he said, looking at the unattended fire marshal's car, running at the curb.

"You've got to be kidding," Lee said, looking unsure.

Pierce fumbled for the back door, and I shrieked as we fell in, me somehow ending up on Pierce's lap. His hat fell, and I managed to pick it up off the floor, putting it on my head. "You said you could drive. Let's pull foot!" Pierce said, fending me off as my mouth kept going, unable to stop singing, "Lookie, I'm Pierce," over and over again.

"Can we please go!" Pierce said, panic edging into his voice. "Rachel is not well."

"You got that right." Lee looked at the distant lights flashing blue and red in the dark, and the marshal standing with his back to us, trying to calm down some guy wearing tweed and having too many lattes in him.

"Steal the fire marshal's car," he said, yanking up the handle and getting in behind the wheel. "Why the hell not? Can't you shut her up!"

"No," Pierce said, voice mournful as we jerked into motion and I squealed in delight. "More is the pity. Drive fast."

Sixteen

I vy!" Pierce shouted, and I made *pftttt* noises at the pixies as they darted in and out of my focus as I reclined in Pierce's arms. "Some help!"

"Pierce?" I heard faintly, and then the sudden scent of vampiric incense and coffee pulled through me like a ribbon. "Oh my God, what happened?"

I couldn't keep my eyes open, and they shut when we rocked to a halt in the dim hallway. My last sight was Bis clinging to the ceiling, his eyes red and frightened. The noise grew fuzzy, but I felt myself moving until the wonderful mix of kitchen scents hit me. Pierce's voice was soothing, rumbling into me. I caught the words "Brooke" and "university" and Ivy's hiss of anger—and then I drifted off . . .

"Rachel?"

It was worried and close, and my entire side tingled from the intoxicating scent of hyped-up vampire. Poor girl probably hadn't sated her hunger since last week. My head lolled as Pierce shifted, and the hum of the fridge fought with the sound of pixy wings. There were lots of them. But no Jenks.

"I'm fine," I slurred, then giggled when my voice didn't finish the last part of it and all that came out was a messed-up, "I'm-m-m f-f-f-f."

"You're f'ed, all right," Ivy said, and my eyes opened when her cool fingers touched me.

"The coven woman dosed her with something," Pierce said, his hat gone and his hair disheveled. "And then Lee knocked her out."

"Lee?" Ivy yelled, and I remembered why my hip was sore. He'd dropped me, twice. And then hit me with a ley-line sleep charm!

"In the fireman's car!" I said, indignant, then hesitated, realizing I was still wearing Pierce's hat. "Lee spelled me to shut me up. The b-b-bastard."

Pierce winced. "A body would think it was the only way to get here without, ah, wrapping our asses around a light pole," he said, clearly repeating something Lee had said.

"Great." Ivy's voice was dry. "Remind me to drill him a new one next time I see him."

"Ah," Pierce said, and I sighed when he shifted my weight. "He's, uh, ditching the car. We couldn't have escaped without him."

"Escaped, hell," Ivy muttered. "It was probably his idea to summon you, then cozy up to Rachel with some fake story."

My breath was coming back to me, warm as it bounced off Pierce's shirt. Turning my head, I looked up at them. "Lee's okay," I said. He was terrified when he thought I was Al.

Ivy's worried face was framed against the blah white of the kitchen ceiling, bright with the fluorescent light. Frowning, I stared at the hanging rack behind her. *Why is there a dent in my little spell pot?* "I think I can sit," I said, beginning to feel better. Or at least not so stoned.

Immediately Ivy pulled out a chair. With a marked gentleness, Pierce eased me into it. Ivy was so concerned she looked like she wanted to strangle someone, and Pierce was sweet with his stubble and shirt untucked. My bruises throbbed, but with the help of the table and Pierce's support, I sat and blinked at the ceiling, waiting for everything to stop moving. I was home. *Oh, crap. I think I'm going to cry,* I thought as my vision swam.

"Rachel? Rachel!" Ivy said loudly, bringing my attention back from the pixy kids whispering up in the pot rack. Crouched before me, she made me look at her. "You said Lee. You mean Stanley Saladan? He summoned you for Brooke? Why is he helping you now?"

"You got a cast," I slurred, seeing it stark white against her black T-shirt. "Where's Jenks?" I looked at the ceiling for him, and Ivy turned my chin back to her.

"He had a bad feeling, so he went looking for you," she said. "Why did Lee help you?"

I blinked. "Because Pierce can't drive for crap." I started to list, and Ivy sat me back upright. "You have beautiful eyes, Ivy," I said, my words spilling out without thought.

She stared, a surge of vampire incense wafting through me as her eyes dilated to a sudden full black. Swallowing, she took her hands off me. "What did they hit you with?" she asked as she stood and backed away. "Will coffee help or make it worse?"

"I don't know." A soft, contented hmmm slipped from me. She looked so sweet standing there with six pixy girls in their pastel silk dresses hovering around her head. *Pixy princess. Pixy Princess Ivy with a pretty, pretty cast.*

Jaw clenched, Ivy turned to a thumping in the hall. Pixies rose up, scattering. It was Lee, looking as if he had a right to be here, but unsure as to how Ivy might feel about it. Smart man.

"You've got three seconds to explain," Ivy said, spots of red appearing on her cheeks. Not bad, considering what she'd done to Nick.

The black-haired man gave her a toothy smile and ducked his head. "Hey, hi, Ivy. No hard feelings, huh?"

"Oooh, pretty, pretty shiny eyes," I said, finding Pierce pushing me back down when I tried to get up. A tingle spread from his hand on my shoulder—the man just leaked power. His coat was on the table along with his vest and my stuff. He must have brought everything from Nick's when he came looking for Bis. What a great guy. Even my bag was there.

Ivy was wire tight. "Time's up," she intoned, starting for Lee.

Lee stepped back, hand raised. "You try getting through Hollows traffic with a stoned redhead hanging out the window shouting, 'I'm king of the world!'"

I didn't remember that, but a glance at Pierce told me it was true.

"You summoned her! Like a demon!" Ivy accused.

"She *is* a demon," he said, and Ivy's face went hard. But if I was one, then Lee was one, too. "I had to," Lee added, his voice softer. "I had a gun at my head. How many things have you done when someone held a gun to your head or said the word 'duty'? Give me a break, will you? I helped her escape."

"You locked her in a boat primed to explode!" Ivy shouted.

Lee's expression lit up in understanding. "That was over a year ago!" he complained as I gave Bis a bunny-eared kiss-kiss. He was atop the fridge doing his lurking gargoyle thing with the pixies. Some of them were getting pretty good at mimicking him, and I smiled.

"Besides, I wasn't the one who planted the bomb," Lee said. "It was Kisten." Lee's face was serious in the sudden silence. "I'm sorry about his passing. He was a good man. Come on, Ivy," he coaxed, like the successful, suave bachelor from a wealthy West Coast witch family that he was. "The boat was business. This is survival. Rachel forgave me."

I was starting to see why Trent liked this guy, even while they were business rivals. I hadn't forgiven him, but I wasn't so far out of it to make the mistake of saying so. Ivy pressed her lips together, tension dropping as she turned away. Hand reaching for the center island counter, I stood. I had to find my calling circle. I wasn't going to wait another moment to get this damned mark off my foot and my name back—my beautiful, anonymous demon name that no one but Ivy, Jenks, Al, and my mother knew. *God help me.*

Someone took my elbow, and I blinked at Pierce, keeping me upright as I stumbled the two steps from the table to the center counter. His hat was falling off my head, and I fixed it, almost falling over. "You're nigh asleep on your feet," he said. "Sit."

"Al," I said, breathing heavily when my hands smacked the top of the island counter. I'd made it. "You'd better get in a circle. I have to call Al."

Lee jerked. "This is a setup? You're giving me to Al?" he exclaimed, and I started when I felt him tap the line out back.

Ivy ducked and I yelped when Pierce flung out a hand and the ball of purple aimed at us ricocheted into the sink. The pixies scattered, shrieking. "Mr. Saladan!" Pierce shouted as I coughed at the smoke drifting out the open window. "Dash it all, calm yourself!"

"I'm not going back to that!" Lee exclaimed, determined from fear.

Ivy rose from behind the counter, her eyes black and, as Pierce would say, all wrathy. "Rachel doesn't give people to Al, *you ass*! You may deserve to be tossed into the ever-after, but that's not what she's doing! As long as you don't owe Al anything, you're safe." She hesitated, then added, "It wouldn't hurt to get in a circle, though."

Lee squinted at her, another ball of black stuff in his hand. Seeing them occupied, I dropped below the level of the counter, swearing as I slipped and fell on my butt. Moving carefully, I got to my knees and looked for my calling mirror. Al was going to pay up. I was going to make him. I was going to have one less tie to demons. It was going to be a good night.

"I've no fist with you," Pierce said, "but threaten Rachel again, and I'll give you thrice the pain you promise her."

Blinking, I stared at my spell books. My mirror wasn't there. "It's gone!" I exclaimed, then remembered it was still in my bag.

"You don't scare me," Lee said to Pierce, oblivious to my disappointment.

"Then I'm of the mind you've not been paying attention," Pierce said, making it a threat.

Above me, Bis crawled along the ceiling, almost matching the color perfectly. His ears were pinned to his head as Pierce and Lee argued. Ignored, I lurched back to the table, falling when I misjudged it, and pulling not only my bag, but all the coats down on me. I sat for a moment, figuring things out, then decided to stay there. If I was on the floor, I couldn't fall down. Slipping my mirror out, I struggled with the heavy glass. "Al?" I shouted, my mirror finally on my lap. "Get your butt over here!" I added, my hand splayed over the middle of it.

The argument suddenly stopped, and Lee edged into my sight from around the center counter. "Should she be doing this right now?" he asked, looking worried.

Ivy was suddenly beside me. "No," she said dryly, lips tight and brow furrowed as she leaned under the table and tried to take the mirror.

"Mine!" I said, yanking it back. "Let go!" I threatened, and she stood, hands on her hips and looking at me in disgust. "I want my name back. Too many people know Al's." I turned back to the mirror, seeing that there were no lines on it. It was empty. "What happened to my mirror?" I said, bewildered. Then realizing that I was looking at the back of the dumb thing, I swore and turned it over. The crystalline beauty of the contrasting wine-colored depths and the sharp diamond lines sparkled in the artificial light, and I lovingly ran my fingers over the glass. It was beautiful. Too bad it took a curse to run it.

The three of them stood over me, all watching with concern. "You're going to let her do this?" Lee asked, his brow furrowed.

"*You're* the one who drugged her," Ivy said. "Maybe one of you boys can make a circle in case she figures out which hole in her head the words come out of."

"I'm fine!" I said, squinting up at them. "I want my . . . name back," I said breathlessly, putting my back against a heavy table leg so I wouldn't fall over. "Get in a circle. All of you."

Hot damn, I felt good. That last shot Lee had given me had been the icing. "Al!" I shouted, hand splayed on the mirror, crossing lines and totally in the wrong place. "Talk to me!"

"Mayhap we should tend to our own funeral," Pierce said, opening the drawer where I keep my magnetic chalk and sketching a large circle around Ivy and Lee. "The drug will be spent soon. It's like watching a corned pixy." Finished, he stood, examined the size of the circle, then picked up my splat gun from the floor, forgotten till now.

Lee stood indignantly in the uninvoked circle. "What do you want a gun for?"

"It's a dash-it-all fine weapon," Pierce said, looking at his pants pocket and frowning. "The demon set me to watch her, so I'll be fine outside the circle, but I don't set much store on a demon's word." Pierce snatched up his coat, shrugged it on, and dropped the splat gun into one of the large front pockets.

Looking doubtful, Lee invoked his circle, and a wash of purple-tinted ever-after rose up.

"Al-l-l-l-l-l-l," I called, using my free hand to position my pinkie properly, squinting when I accidentally shifted my thumb off the right glyph. Damn it, this was hard, and I exhaled when I finally got everything in place. "Al!" I shouted, touching my awareness to the ley line out back. Power flooded into me, and I gasped. "Ooooh, that feels good!" I said, and Pierce flushed.

"Al!" I called again, glad the others were safe in a circle. "Get over here or I'm going to come over there and kick. Your. Ass." *Stupid, dumb demon,* I thought, pressing my hand into the mirror. *Trying to weasel out of our deal.* "Talk to me, Al!" I demanded. "You slimy little no-good son-of-a-bastard demon!"

My eyes widened, and my pulse jerked faster as I felt my mind expand when Al picked up. A shot of clarity struck through, showing me with a frightening sureness how stupid I was being. *Shit. What in hell am I doing?*

Good God, Rachel, can't you go five minutes . . . sweet sticky hell on a stick! the demon exclaimed, his thoughts reeling from anger to concern as he realized I was hopped up on something. *Where . . . Your church? What are you on, itchy witch?*

"I want my name back, and I want it now," I said aloud. "And take your damned mark off!

"Hey!" I yelped as Al suddenly vanished and I was thrown back into the muzzy slop of my drugged haze. Putting a hand to my stomach, I set the mirror aside and used the table to pull myself upright. I didn't feel so good anymore. "He's coming," I said. *Whoo-hoo! Here we go!*

Al popped in as if he belonged, used to my kitchen almost as much as I was to his. He frowned at Pierce, then did a double take at Ivy and Lee, safe in the protection circle. "Stanley Saladan?" the demon purred, smiling evilly, and the man's face went ashen.

"Still think I'm skeerylike?" Pierce muttered as he tucked his shirt-tails in and tried to look more presentable.

"Lee doesn't owe you anything!" I said. "Off-limits."

A trace of irritation crossed the demon's face; then he smiled as if it didn't bother him. "Rachel, my itchy witch," Al said as he tugged the lace at his cuffs. "We've talked about this. You simply must stop collecting nasty little men. How many do you really need, love?"

My knees were sore, and they were shaking. "Brooke summoned me again!" I exclaimed, pointing, then shifted my arm when I remembered where the university was. "I told you she would. She had a rolling bed with straps. I want my name back *now*!"

Al made a puff of air, but he was coming at me, and I backed up.

"They drugged me," I said, trying to smack his reaching arm away only to find myself picked up and plopped on the table, sitting on some of Ivy's papers. "In my leg," I continued as he smelled my breath and peered over his smoked glasses at me. "Shot me twice. I want my name, or I'm going to start charging you a fee every time I field something for you. And it's going to be expensive. I'm Park Place. Bud-dy."

His red, goat-slitted eyes squinted at me from over his smoked glasses. "You're more like Oriental Avenue right now, dove. What are you on?"

I pushed him away, catching Lee's awe that I was not only standing with a demon outside a circle, but that Al was treating me like an equal. *Or maybe a favorite pet*, I amended as Al caught me when I started to tilt. "I want . . ."—I panted as he held my shoulder with his white-gloved hand and kept me upright—". . . my name. Right now. This is crap! I mean it!"

Al glanced at the two people behind him, safe in a circle, then at Pierce. I wrinkled my nose at the burnt amber flowing off him, and he let me go. With a yelp, I slid from the table to land in a crumpled pile at his feet. "Ow," I muttered, seeing his cute little buckled boots. No one wears buckles anymore, and I decided to get him some real boots next winter solstice. *Some sexy guy boots. Yeah.* Fumbling, I reached to find the top of the table, and I pulled myself up.

His goat-slitted eyes narrowed and he turned to Pierce. "You're supposed to watch her."

"I am!" Pierce said, his own anger showing. "In all my born days, I've not seen a woman more prone to trouble, and your almighty refusal to settle your hash is making things plumb impossible. Give Rachel her name or I'll tell Newt I can't do this."

"Yeah," I said as I wove on my feet, trying to focus.

Al was silent, his jaw clenched as Pierce arched his eyebrows in challenge. "Come along, let's go," the demon abruptly said. "Pierce, stay here. I'll send her back before sunup."

Blinking, I stared at him. "Go? Go where?"

Al looked back to Ivy, Lee, and Pierce and sniffed. "I'm not going to twist curses in front of an audience." Al grimaced, looking pissed.

I suddenly realized that Pierce had done it. Al was going to live up to our deal. It had taken me being dragged around, drugged, and headed for a lobotomy, but I was going to get my name back. Teeth gritted in a weird smile, I looked at Ivy. *It was going to be a good day.*

"Hey!" I exclaimed, stumbling when Al pulled me to him and a puff of burnt amber rose. "Why can't we do it here?" I asked, but with a gasp, I found the air crushed from my lungs. We were gone.

Seventeen

My lungs rebounded, and I felt myself slip; then I jerked upright even before flesh had reformed to separate Al from me again. Pulse hammering, I staggered when Al let me go, narrowly avoiding a fall to the slick black stone engraved with that same pattern of intertwined icy-white-edged circles that the coven had. Wincing, I tucked my fading pain amulet back under my shirt. I leaned to snatch Pierce's hat off the floor, and my hip protested. It was probably black and blue by now.

Al had his back to me as he poked about in one of the tall cupboards, the old glass in the wooden frames making his face a blur. "Make up the fire if you're cold," he said, tossing a palm-size bag at me.

I scrambled to catch it, knowing he'd smack me if it touched the floor. The bag was squishy, probably holding coarse salt. Feeling achy, I crossed the room to set the black silk bag on the corner of the slate table standing between the smaller hearth fire cheerfully glowing and the huge—but dark—circular fire pit in the middle of the room. With a sigh, I dropped Pierce's hat on the bench surrounding the central fire. The drugs were wearing off, and, arms around myself, I weighed the trouble of starting a fire in the main pit with simply being cold for the time it would take to do the curse. *My God, he was finally going to do it.*

A soft glow blossomed in the six fixed globes when Al pulled a book from an unlocked cabinet to check on something, barely illuminating the slate table before the smaller hearth. There were two chairs at it, one at either end—the first with padded cushions and arms, the second a simple stool. It had shocked the hell out of me the first time I'd tried to sit on the stool and found myself smacked halfway across the room. I was supposed to use Ceri's comfortable chair, apparently.

My thoughts drifted back to my own kitchen and I sighed, not for missing the gleaming counters and bright lights, but for the people I'd left behind. "You know I can't start a fire to save my life," I complained as I gingerly picked out some thin sticks from the basket of kindling. It wasn't that cold, but if I was trying to light a fire, he'd stop throwing spelling equipment at me. "Don't you have some Logs-o-Fire or something?"

Al didn't even look up from his collection of knives in a locked case. "Then we'll be cold until you learn. Try not to use all the kindling. It's expensive." Seeing me stirring the ash at the center of the pit for signs of life, he crossed the room to set that ugly ceremonial knife with the writhing woman on it beside the bag.

"Can't you just turn up the heat?" I complained. His receiving room looked like a mansion, the mundane kitchen where Pierce slept was modern, and I'd never seen Al's bedroom, thank God, but here, he went rustic.

"No pipes here," he said, voice faint as he thoughtfully fingered his stash of candles.

My head bobbed. Duh. Even a hastily set circle would be secure. I glanced at the mantel where Krathion still sat next to Mr. Fish, and I shivered. How often was I going to need protection from a banshee, anyway?

Al shut a drawer hard, then set a small, thin plank of what was probably redwood out with the salt and candles. "Feeling more yourself?" he asked slyly.

Again my head nodded, and I dropped a chunk of wood in the pit to serve as a heat trap, snuggling it into the ash. "Yes," I said shortly, thinking the ash on my hands smelled better than the burnt amber that permeated the place. I was going to have to shower when I got home.

"Pity." Al turned away, scanning a shelf of metal objects and plucking one at seeming random. "I liked you drunk. You're more fun. Can I make you a cake, love?"

He was grinning evilly, and I grimaced at his ruddy face and his goat-slitted eyes. They looked almost normal in the dim light. I took a breath to tell him where he could shove his cake, but he jerked, his eyes going to the hearth and an eager light coming into them. "I knew it. Little runt!" he whispered, bolting across the room.

I stood as Pierce popped into existence before the small hearth, right into Al's grip. "Got you!" Al snarled, a white-gloved hand around his throat. Pierce's eyes widened, then he screwed them shut—right before Al shoved his head into the stone mantel. Mr. Fish splashed at the ugly thump, and Pierce grunted in pain. Pierce's hand flung into the air, and the coffee mug from Nick's apartment rolled off to shatter on the hard floor.

"Watch out for Krathion!" I shouted, seeing the bottle tip, but it rocked back, safe.

"That's for threatening me with Newt," Al said. "I *own* you. Don't forget it."

"Al! Stop!" I cried as Al shoved Pierce's head into the mantel a second time. "You're going to knock Krathion off!"

"And that's for not staying put when I told you to," the demon snarled, but Pierce couldn't possibly hear him. His eyes had rolled back and he had gone limp.

"Al!" I shouted, and he opened his hand to let Pierce slump to the hearth, out cold.

The demon turned to me, and I skidded to a halt beside the table, frightened by his seething anger. Behind him, the low fire burned. At his feet, Pierce lay, unmoving.

"What is your problem!" I asked, wanting to see if Pierce was okay, but Al's eyes were evaluating me from over his smoked glasses, and his white-gloved hands were in fists.

"The only reason you're still standing," Al said, his voice whispering an echo in the dark, high ceiling, "is because you didn't put him up to it. I will *not* be threatened by a familiar."

My mouth was dry, and I dropped my attention to Pierce for an instant before returning it to Al. "He keeps trying to protect me. Damn it, Al, I didn't ask for this."

His posture easing, Al dropped his gaze to look at Pierce. Using the toe of his shiny buckled shoe, he edged Pierce's coat away from the fire. I took a slow breath, thinking the worst might be over, but still my heart was pounding. "Maybe Newt was right," Al said blandly.

"About what?" God, he'd just knocked him out. Pierce could be bleeding inside his skull and we'd never know.

But Al didn't answer me, instead going to a cupboard and leaving Pierce crumpled where he lay. "Move him," he said, his back to me as he rummaged. "Unless you want me to do it?"

No, I didn't want Al to do it. He'd likely pick him up and throw him across the room. Knees protesting, I knelt on the hard marble floor. My jaw clenched as I turned Pierce's head to me and lifted his eyelids to make sure his pupils were dilating the way they should. He looked like he was sleeping, but there were twin lumps under his hair when I felt for them. The softly curling black was like silk on my fingertips, and I sat back on my heels and exhaled. He was probably going to be okay.

"Now, Rachel."

Giving Al a nasty look, I stood and grabbed Pierce under his shoulders. Straining, I shuffled backward, dragging him past the table and across the expanse to the fire pit. There was no way I could get him off the floor and onto the bench, so I left him there, taking a moment to arrange his arms and legs. *Where did Pierce get silk socks?*

"I can't believe you knocked him out," I said, then ducked when Al threw something at me. I spun to see a heavy copper pyramid thunk into the wall, leaving a dent.

"I told him not to come," Al said with an empty, vaguely jealous slant to his eyes. "I don't want him seeing this. Forget the fire. You won't be here long enough to get cold."

I glanced at Pierce, seeing his slow, even breaths. Mood sour, I picked up the heavy pyramid and set it on the table with an attention-getting thump. "I hate you, Al," I said, but he only started to hum as he sat on his stool with a flourish and began arranging things. "I really do," I offered again. "What if he's seriously hurt?"

Al calmly looked at me over his glasses. "Then I'll fix him *after* our chat and *before* I send him back to you. We don't want Newt saying I left you with an inferior chaperone. He'll be fine. Sit. Unless you want to keep my name?"

My heart gave a thump, and I eased into Ceri's chair, wondering if I was following in her footsteps and would spend the next millennia thinking this thing before me in lace and velvet was my world.

Seeing him busy with the bag of salt, I reached for a gold candle. Al slapped my hand, and I scowled at him.

"You watch," he said as I shoved my stinging hand under my arm. "I'll tell you when I need you, not before."

"Fine with me," I said tightly. I glanced at Pierce, but his eyes were still shut.

Still humming, Al opened the small black bag. White glove gone, he reached in and removed a handful of gray grit, tracing a foot-long Möbius strip on the slate between us. The greasy dust sifted from him as his humming took on the sound of a chant. Low and tonal, the sound struck deep in my primitive brain and made me sit straighter. It was like the chant of Asian monks, the foreign power of something else, mysterious and alien. Though nothing changed, Al looked utterly different, sitting before me with words I'd never understand coming from him.

"That's not salt," I said as the last spilled from his hand and he wiped it on a white cloth that he pulled from an inside pocket.

"I'm not going to use salt," he said, and tossed the soiled towel at me. "What do you take me for? It's cremation dust." Al's gaze went distant. "She died screaming. I was inside her at the time. God, I could feel everything. It was like I was dying with her."

What am I doing here?

Repulsed, I leaned away, my breath hissing in when Al reached over his glyph and put his hand atop mine. I pulled back, but he gripped me harder, forcing my hand to the table. His gloves were still missing, and his skin was darker than I would've thought. A tingle was spilling from him to me, and I yanked out from under him, thinking it shouldn't feel that good.

"It's power, Rachel," Al said softly, gaze fixed to mine. "Thinking that it's evil is only because of your bad upbringing. You should go with your instincts and enjoy it. Gordian Nathaniel Pierce does." His hand returned to his side of the table, and I remembered to breathe. "Give me the pyramid."

I couldn't get the frown off my face, and I stared at Al. He was waiting, confident that I'd reach across the table and hand it to him—when he was closer to it than me. The drug was completely out of my system and I felt drained. Al's gaze slid to Pierce in a silent threat, and I reached for the pyramid. To show defiance now would only hurt Pierce more.

Al's thick lips parted in a smile as my fingers pressed into the warm metal, finding purchase on the engraved figures. It was heavier than it looked, and I could feel my arm take the weight, but I hesitated as I looked at the odd writing on it that my ley-line pyramid lacked. The metal, too, wasn't friendly copper like I'd originally thought, but something denser, darker, feeling like salted iron to my fingers.

It was hard to explain, and I reluctantly set it on Al's waiting hand. His palm was crisscrossed with heavy, distinct lines where most people had only a few. I'd never seen his palm before, and he frowned when he saw me scrutinize it.

Al curled his fingers around the pyramid and placed it in the middle of the figure eight where the dust lines crossed. His chanting started up again, and I stifled a shiver. Naked fingers reaching, Al set the gray candle in the cave of the figure eight nearest me, and the gold one before him. I caught the placing words *ipse* and *alius* among his monotone mumbling.

"You're doing it wrong," I said, and Al's chanting ceased.

"I'm doing it properly—student," he said as he took up another handful of dust.

"But my aura is gold," I protested. "Why do I have the gray candle?"

"Because I say so. You're gray, Rachel. Grayer than fog, and just as dense. Besides, I'm always the gold candle."

It wasn't a reason, and I wasn't going to let him screw this up on purpose.

"Light your candle," Al said. "There are tapers in the can."

I glanced at the jar of thin strips of wood beside his hearth fire, then jerked when he snatched my wrist, forcing my palm up and dropping a handful of dust into it. It felt alive, greasy and staticky. If only to get rid of it, I sifted it around the base of the unlit gray candle saying the setting word, *ipse,* then grumbling that I should be the gold, not him.

"*Ipse,*" Al echoed, mocking me as I set my candle with the same word he used. His fingers pinched the cold wick, and when they parted, the candle was lit. Smirking, I did the same, whispering *ipse* again. The candle might be gray—which was not a good choice—but I'd set it twice with the proper word. If the spell failed to work, it wouldn't be my fault.

"Who taught you how to light candles from your thoughts?" Al said, his goat-slitted eyes on Pierce.

The man was still out cold, and I shrugged. "Ceri," I said, but my gut was tightening. This had to work. I wanted it done, and done now.

Grunting in acceptance, Al balanced a narrow shaving of redwood atop the pyramid. It was a small relief that this, at least, was unchanged. Al took off his glasses. Arms on the slate table, he leaned over the spell, now ready for the focusing objects. Expression eager, he handed me his ceremonial knife.

"Can I use the other one?" I asked, looking in distaste at the curved blade and the image of a tormented, naked woman writhing about the handle, hands and feet bound and mouth open in a scream.

"No."

I took a slow breath. *Just do it,* I thought, touching the blade to my finger.

"There is no almost when it comes to magic," Al said, and adrenaline surged when his hand clamped down over the knife and pressed it against me. I jerked, my hand suddenly warm and slick as I pulled away. Pain was a pulse behind it.

"Damn it, Al!" I shouted, staring in horror at my bloody palm, then the knife in my other hand, slick and gleaming. My grip tightened on the handle. Frightened and angry, I looked at Al, but his hand was even worse. When I'd pulled away, I'd cut him deep. Most of the blood on me was his. I think.

"I thought your blood wasn't an accurate focusing object anymore," I said, and the demon met my gaze, having been eying his palm with interest as to which lines I'd cut across.

"It wasn't—until you set it back to zero with that little stunt of yours," he said, holding his hand over his end of the balanced stick. "All together now . . ."

My heart was pounding, and my hand shook as I set the knife down. *Black magic. Just do it. Finish it.* Shivering inside, I held my bleeding hand over the stick, and with a few rubs at my finger, the blood started to drip. Al squeezed his hand until a red rivulet started down the inside of his fist. Three drops to mirror mine hit the stick, and his bloodied hand opened.

He made a pleased sound, and the scent of burnt amber rose to mix with the scent of redwood and wood smoke. Almost done. "Finish it," I said, then jerked when he leaned over the table and grabbed my wrist with his bloody, sticky fingers, yanking me half out of my chair. "What are you doing?" I demanded, scared.

"Relax," Al said, smearing our blood together on the last candle. "Count yourself lucky I don't want to share the twisting another way."

He meant sex, and I tugged my hand from Al's, only to find it recaptured and pressed against the candle again. "Try it and you'll be walking funny for a week," I said, glaring.

"One night, itchy witch, you'll come to me," was all he said. Still holding me halfway across the table with my arm outstretched, he smiled and whispered, "*Evulago.*"

My hand in his grip, I stared. My heart hammered, and the wax beneath our fingers became warm. That was the word that would start it all, the one that registered the curse and made it stick. And through my hand touching his, I felt a sensation of disconnection, as if the floor wasn't quite under me. If I closed my eyes, I wasn't sure if I would be here when I opened them, or if I'd be lost in an open, whispering space of the collective where everyone was talking and no one listened. But this time, when Al's word echoed in my head, it was as if someone paused.

Al glowered. "You've been recognized. This is exactly why I didn't want to do this."

His hand let go, and I eased away. Immediately the feeling of the open room and vertigo faded. Nervous, I picked up the white cloth he had thrown at me earlier and wiped my hand as clean as I could get it before tossing it into his hearth fire to burn. I'd not leave it around with the blood of both of us on it.

As the cloth caught, I could feel the curse winding its way through me, settling into my bones, becoming a part of me. My vision was blurry, and I realized I was seeing Al's aura, untainted and unsullied by his millennium of ever-after imbalance. Lips parted, I shifted my eyes from his to mine, also visible as we did the curse. Al's aura was a freaking gold. It was shot through with red and purple, but it was gold, same as mine. Same as Trent's.

The demon saw my shock, and he smiled. "Surprised?" he said softly, voice low and seductive. "Funny how these things work out. Doesn't mean anything though. Not really."

"Ye-e-e-eah," I drawled, gaze flicking behind him to Pierce. Either he was still out, or he was faking. Al's eyes were on mine when I turned back, and I felt cold as I recalled him tasting my aura after I did a spell to see the dead. "Can we finish this?" I said, uneasy.

Head bobbing once, Al reached out and simply spun the stick a hundred and eighty degrees. "*Omnia mutantur,*" he said firmly.

All things change, I thought, then blinked when Al shuddered. His eyes closed, and he breathed deeply, as if tasting something on the air. I'd never seen him with his eyes closed like that, and I noticed the faint lines at the corners. "I take this," he mouthed, not a sound coming from him. I remembered the imbalance hitting me when I did the curse. It had hurt like hell until I accepted it. For Al, there had been no pain—but he hadn't tried to avoid it either.

My head was hurting, and after glancing at Pierce, I breathed, "My mark?"

Al's eyes opened, landing immediately on mine. There was nothing in his expression. "It's gone," he said simply, and a thrill spun from my head to my toes.

I scooted my chair back and fumbled at my boot.

"I said it was gone," Al said indignantly.

"I believe you." Heart pounding, I wedged my boot off, and it hit the floor with a thump. Fumbling with the sock, I peeled it off like a snake-skin and twisted my foot up and around. Tears filled my eyes, spilling out and down in a warm trickle. The underside of my foot was smooth and unbroken. The raised circle with a slash through it was gone. It was gone!

Blinking furiously, I smiled. "It's gone," I said, letting my foot go. "I did it!"

"Yada yada yada," Al said sourly. "You tricked the big bad demon. Congratulations. The only way I'm going to save face is by snagging some excellent ley-line witches. Coven quality, you say?"

My exuberance died. "Al, wait," I said as I set my foot on the icy floor, feeling the cold soak up all the way to my spine. "Do you know what they will do to me if you show up and try to snag them?" I'd known this was a possibility, but at the time, it had been me or them, and me always wins when the them is a bully.

Al stood, strutting over to Pierce and looking down at him, nudging him with a toe. "Do you know how rare it is for a coven-quality witch to summon me? Raw and untutored in the art of containing a demon? They kill their own if they become skilled in the dark arts, don't they, Gordian Nathaniel Pierce?" he said to the unconscious witch. "If you can get out of their circle, Rachel, I can, too."

My face skewed up in worry as a sheet of ever-after coated him, and suddenly it looked as if I was standing above Pierce, far too sexy and slim in my working leathers, my hair wild and my lips parted. *Oh. Shit.*

"My name is Rachel Morgan," Al said, mimicking my voice perfectly. "I like black panties, action movies, and being on top."

My jaw clenched, and I wondered how much I was going to pay for getting my name back. "I'm never going to get my shunning removed if you do that," I said as I shook my sock right side out again.

"I don't give a flying damn." Looking like himself again, Al shifted his shoulders as if trying to fit back in his skin. "I don't know why you even *care* about your shunning," he said as he returned to the table and began gathering things. "I've told you you'd be welcome here. Have a name that is respected. Have I not proved we can work together? That I can honor my word?"

"Only when I force you to."

"That you're safe, protected?" he continued as if I hadn't said anything as he slid his pyramid away and shut the cupboard. "Why do you fight this, itchy witch?"

I tugged my sock back on, eyes downcast. "I'm not a demon. You said it yourself." Lee thought I was, though.

His lips curved up in a nasty smile, and he tossed the used candles into a bin. "Perception is everything, determining how others treat us. If enough people think you're a demon, you are."

Snatching up my boot, I glanced at Pierce and away. I was eager to get home, even if I was loath to leave Pierce. He wasn't my responsibility, but that didn't mean I didn't care. I was going to have to make a call. The coven still had my old cell phone. Maybe if I warned them, I wouldn't get blamed when someone ended up dead or snagged. Maybe. *Maybe not.*

"You really should stay," Al said mildly as he put the ashes back in the box he kept them locked in. "Your friends are all going to die."

"Not today they're not," I said, feeling my anger rise

Al turned to look at me. "No," he agreed. "But they will. Eventually. You won't. Not anymore. Unless you're stupid about it."

My pulse hammered, and I stared at Al. Was he kidding?

"He's going to hurt you," Al said, looking at Pierce. "I can take care of you, teach you to survive. Be there for you, even if you do hate me."

I shivered. "I don't want him," I said, and Al turned away, seeming smaller somehow.

"Mmmm." Al stood before me, running his gaze up and down and lingering on the mess my hair had become. "Do you think the coven might summon me tonight?" he asked as he took my arm and escorted me past Pierce to the elaborate glyph of the screaming face. His smile deepened, becoming pure evil. "I do."

"Al, wait," I said as I hobbled with him, one foot in a boot, one in a sock. But I knew my protests would be futile. If I warned them, I wasn't helping my case of being a white witch, seeing that I'd have to explain why Al had his name back. If I didn't warn them and Al took someone . . . Well, if he took them all, I might stay out of jail, but how could I live with myself?

"If they don't summon me," Al continued, "I suspect that they'll likely spend their resources sending assassins after you. It's a tricky moral problem, isn't it? Warn them, and they survive to kill you. Remain silent, and they die and you live. My little gray witch."

He reached to touch my face, and I swung my boot at him. Al only laughed. "Get yourself cleaned up, will you? You're a mess," he said, then gave me a shove.

I fell backward onto the screaming face etched into the marble floor, feeling my body dissolve into thought as my boot skidded across the stone floor. Before I could feel the cold of nothing, the black stone shifted to the familiar salt-laced linoleum of my kitchen. I was home.

Looking up, I found Ivy, Jenks, and Lee waiting for me. Silently they took in my blood-smeared hand and the lack of Pierce. Ivy sighed and Jenks's wings slowed and stopped. My jaw clenched, and I forced it to relax.

I was home. I'd gotten a demon mark removed. I couldn't be summoned by anyone but Al and my friends. And I didn't have the slightest idea what I was going to do.

Eighteen

enks dropped down on a column of glittering sparkles before I could get up from my hands and knees. My pain amulet was useless, the linoleum hurt my knees, and my tangled hair made a curtain between me and the world. "Rache!" he called, a gleaming sparkle darting erratically as he tried to get past my hair. "Are you okay? Where's Pierce?"

Much as I hurt, I couldn't help my smile. Melancholy and elation were a weird mix as I sat back on my heels and got my hair out of my face. I'd lost a demon mark, but Pierce was still with Al. He was being beaten because he'd helped me, and it didn't sit well.

"I'm fine," I said on an exhale, taking Ivy's hand as she extended it so she could pull me to my feet. Muscles sore and knees complaining, I got up, tossed my useless pain amulet into the sink, and looked at Lee sitting at my spot at the table with a chipped coffee cup in his short, laced fingers. Over the sink, the dark window was shining with streaks of moisture. It was raining.

Ivy let go of my hand and dropped back to put the usual space between us. "What happened to your other boot?" she asked, and a slow smile grew despite my worry for Pierce. Leaning against the sink, I painfully twisted my foot up and around to pull the sock off again.

"It's gone," I said, meaning the demon mark. "I've gotten rid of two, now. Just the one left." *The one I got thanks to Nick.*

Ivy leaned over to see, holding her hair back as she peered at my foot. Jenks flew closer, the draft from his wings a breath of chill. From the corner, Lee jerked upright in his chair. "You got a mark off?" he questioned, almost spilling his coffee. "You gave him Pierce?"

My foot hit the floor, and both Ivy and Jenks backed up. "I didn't give him Pierce. Did it look like I gave him Pierce? Huh? Did it look like I told Pierce to follow me? Did you hear words come out of my mouth saying, 'Pierce, save me!' No. He already belongs to Al. Got himself demon snagged last winter. He's on loan right now, babysitting me. He'll be back." I looked at Ivy and Jenks, frowning. "Count on it."

Lee raised a hand in protest. "Sor-r-r-ry," he said dryly. "What did you give him, then?"

Brow furrowed, I brought my other foot up and undid my remaining boot and kicked it off. Rex, Jenks's cat, went to investigate, and I crossed my arms over my middle. "I gave him his summoning name back, if you have to know. The mark I got rid of tonight was the one I originally took from Newt the day you tried to give me to Al and I had to buy my way home."

Jenks landed on Ivy's shoulder with his hands on his hips. Ivy, too, looked severe as they stared at him. Lee, though, looked just as peeved. "Who gave whom to Al?" he said darkly. "I was the one who took the long tour of hell."

"You bought your own ticket," I shot back. "Next time listen when I warn you, okay? I'm not as stupid as you'd like me to be."

Lee frowned, but then his face eased and he chuckled. "I think you're just lucky. I'm listening now, if that means anything."

Immediately, I lost my ire. Belonging to Al must have been hell. That Pierce was there now really bothered me. It would bother me more if I didn't know he'd be back babysitting me before too much longer. Unless Al accidentally killed him and I became Newt's ward. *Shit.*

"Tell you what, Lee," I said as the tension in the room eased. "How about we simply agree that you be nice to me and I be nice to you? It seemed to work today."

"He locked you in a boat and blew it up," Ivy said darkly.

"Kist planted the bomb," I said, wishing she'd quit bringing it up. My attention returning to Lee, I said, "How about it? I'm not talking about a partnership. More like a truce. You don't have to trust me, just stop pissing me off. And don't spell me again. *Ever.* Even if I am going to cause us to drive into a bus."

"You remember that?" Lee asked, and I nodded.

"Most of it." I'd be mad at Lee for knocking me out, but it was probably the only reason we made it home. King of the world . . . jeez, how embarrassing.

Lee's dark eyes became thoughtful. Jenks's wings slowed, and even Ivy seemed to relax. My eyes fixed on Lee's disheveled but staunchly upright posture, I crossed the room and held out my hand. It hung there all by itself, and I tilted my head, wondering if he was going to be stupid about this and let his pride put him in the crapper again. But then Lee's thin lips quirked, and finally a smile showed. With the sliding sound of his dirt-marked suit, Lee stood and we shook hands. There wasn't a whisper of power threatening to spill between us. His hand felt small in mine after Al's, and firm. "This is going to rot Trent's bridle," the man said as he let go.

Chuckling, I nodded. Poor Trent. Hope he choked on it. Eying Lee's coffee on the table, I turned to the coffeemaker. Jenks went to "chat" with Lee about the dangers of going back on even our informal truce, and I fumbled in the cupboard for a mug. Ivy was suddenly at my elbow, and I gave her a quick look to make sure she wasn't vamping out, then relaxed.

"Pierce?" she whispered, and my elation at getting rid of a mark *and* mending a fence with a city power evaporated.

"Al's beating him up for threatening him with Newt," I said, and she winced. "I'm sure he'll show up before long." But in what state, was the question. He should have kept his mouth shut. I was handling it. Interesting, though, that I was allowed to threaten Al and Pierce wasn't.

I bowed my head, and my hair made a curtain between me and the rest of the world as my grip tightened on the cold porcelain. This wasn't right.

Ivy's hand touched my shoulder, and she gave me a quick sideways hug. "I'm sure he'll be fine," she said, her lips inches from my ear.

I pulled out of her hold to see her smirking good-naturedly. "You're something else, vampire," I said sourly even as my neck started to tingle and she moved away, but I couldn't contain my growing feeling of excitement. My foot was clean. I had one less tie to demons. One less reason to be shunned. *One more mark to go,* I thought, looking at my wrist.

Jenks darted from Lee, satisfaction on his small features as the much larger man nodded, clearly understanding the threat that Jenks could be, even as small as he was. "Rachel," the witch asked as he set his mug down on the table, "would you mind if I used your phone? Brooke took my cell, my wallet." His face shifted, eyebrows rising. "Damn, she mugged me! I need to call my wife and tell her I'm okay. Have her send a car."

Surprised, I leaned back against the sink with my coffee mug warming my fingers. Ivy's and Jenks's expressions were as confused as mine. "You're married?" I asked for all three of us.

Lee grinned, looking like another person—a happy one. "Six weeks. Nice woman. Met her on one of my boats. She's got her own money, so I know she's not a gold digger." His head dropped, and a shocking amount of honesty shone from him when he looked up again. "I asked her to marry me for the selfish reason of making my nights easier, but I love her." He chuckled. "It's . . . weird. I never thought . . . you know."

A small sound of understanding slipped from me as I thought of Kisten. It must have been hell to be trapped in one's own skull while a demon used your body for whatever it wanted. "I'm happy for you. Congratulations."

Jenks flew to Ivy, who had slipped in behind her computer to distance herself from the touchy-feely emotional crap. Pushing myself into motion, I grabbed the cordless phone from the cradle and handed it to him. Lee took it, hesitating. "You did good, Rachel," he said, surprising me and making Ivy stop her irritating tapping. "You got rid of a demon mark without hurting anyone. The coven should leave you alone. I'd speak for you if it would help, but I'm going to be scrambling for enough favors to keep from being shunned myself."

Warmth touched my face, cooling when Jenks landed on my shoulder. "They will," he said staunchly. "Leave her alone, I mean. They can't shun you. You own too much."

"Must be nice," I said, looking at my shoulder bag on the table and remembering that Brooke had my phone, too. "Ivy, can I use your phone? I need to call Brooke so she doesn't try to summon me again."

Not missing a beat, Ivy pulled her slim phone from her back pocket and tossed it.

Lee gave me a nod in understanding, then went into the back living room with the landline for some privacy. Jenks, though, was not happy.

"You're warning her?" he said, wings clattering at my ear. "What the fairy fart for?"

I scrolled through Ivy's phone, noticing she'd been talking to Daryl a lot lately. "I don't know," I said as I found my phone number and hit dial. "It just seems fair."

"Why do you care?" Jenks needled from my shoulder. "Let Al have them. No council equals no more worries!"

He was too close to look at on my shoulder, and I grimaced. *Just what I need. My own personal shoulder devil, wearing black and smelling like the Garden of Eden.* "What if they survive?" I asked. "Who do you think is going to get blamed for the attack?"

A faint smile quirked Ivy's lips. "You sure know how to make friends, Rachel. Al is going to be ticked that you warned them."

"Al isn't trying to give me a lobotomy," I said, then turned away as the line clicked open.

"Rachel Morgan's phone," came a polite voice. "Can I take a message?"

It was Vivian, and Jenks flew backward as he laughed with the sound of tinkling bells. Both he and Ivy would be able to hear both ends of the conversation with their better hearing, and I crossed my ankles, feeling only a twinge from my knees. "Well, well, well. A coven member is playing secretary for me? I kind of like that." Vivian had to have seen that it was a known number, but "Ice" probably hadn't meant anything to her.

"Morgan!" the woman barked, followed by a muffled exclamation and a demand to pass the phone. I took a breath to say something, waiting at the distant yelp of pain.

"You're dead, demon witch. Dead!" Brooke shouted, probably having wrestled the phone from Vivian. "You signed your death warrant when you spilled coven blood. You, Saladan, and whoever that was in the hall with you—all of you are *dead!*"

"Sure. Okay," I said with more confidence than I felt. "You go ahead and bring charges against Lee. I'm sure his lawyers would love that. What was it, Brooke? Kidnapping? *Forcing* him to summon a demon? You might be able to hide me in a hole, but Lee will be missed. You want to speak with him? He's in my living room."

I could almost see her jaw clench as she said with clipped words, "I can make people disappear, Morgan. I don't care if you're *God*! You don't scare me."

Jenks was hovering a foot in front of me, and he made a motion to get on with it.

"Look, I'm not going to use up my roommate's minutes arguing with you," I said. "I only wanted to let you know that Al took his name back. If you summon me, you'll get him instead, so I'd advise against it." *And I got rid of a demon mark, la, la, la-a, la, la-a-a, la.*

"Demon scum whore. I'll give you a lobotomy myself, with a fucking ice pick!"

Ivy's eyebrows rose, and Jenks grinned. "Oooh, nice manners, babe!" he said loudly.

I sighed, wishing I'd just kept my mouth shut and let them figure it out for themselves. Lee came back in, quiet as he set the phone in the cradle and stood listening. It was embarrassing to have my baggage displayed like this, but he knew it all already.

"You're dead, Morgan!" Brooke shouted. "*Dead!*"

Faint in the background, I heard Vivian. "I'm not going after her alone again. I almost killed six people, Brooke. Innocents. You want her? You catch her."

"You had justifiable cause. There won't be any charges," Brooke said. "Relax."

"Justifiable cause?" Vivian's voice was barely audible as she shouted. "I'm not worried about charges. I'm worried about the people I hurt on that bus! She wasn't even on it!"

"Shit happens, Vivian. Grow up. You're playing with the big boys!"

I felt sick, glad now we hadn't gotten on the bus, but if we had, maybe they would have been all right. "Brooke, this has gotten out of control. How about you leave me alone and I'll leave you alone? Huh? If it doesn't work, you can kill me then."

There was silence on the other end of the line, and I shifted my weight to the other foot. Maybe that had been too much, but then she came back after a short, private conversation. "You there, demon whore?" Brooke snarled.

"Yeah, we're listening," Jenks said from my shoulder. "What do you want, flabby butt?"

Brooke made a bitter bark of laughter. "Vivian thinks you still retain your ability to be reasoned with, so here it is. You've got one chance to turn yourself in. Be at Fountain Square tomorrow at sunup, or I'm going to burn your church to the ground. Got it? And I hope you hide, because I want you dead!" she shrieked.

I went to answer, but the line was muffled as Vivian and Brooke fought for the phone. "So it's Alcatraz or be made infertile and stupid?" I said sourly, glancing at Ivy. "Nice choice." *Why am I trying so hard to stay here?* In the archway, Lee shrugged. In a burst of motion, Jenks darted out of the kitchen, leaving a sifting beam of burnt gold sparkles. From outside came a gathering whistle followed by a burst of pixy light. Looked like he was telling Matalina the news. They'd likely have pixy lines strung in five minutes flat, rain or no.

The sound of someone at the receiver pulled my attention back to the phone. "Just leave me alone, Brooke," I said. "I'm not hurting anyone." *Except myself.*

"You *are* a threat, and those are our terms," Vivian said, sounding irritated. "I suggest you take them. At least you'll be alive." There was a click, and she was gone.

Lips pressed tight, I closed the phone, unable to meet anyone's eyes.

Maybe warning them hadn't been such a good idea, but at least my conscience was clear. Crossing the room, I handed Ivy her phone, and she tucked it away. "Sorry, Rachel," she said, sounding resigned.

Forcing a smile, I turned to Lee. "How's your wife?"

"Scared," he said. "I'm going to talk to Trent. I need to be sure my kids won't be—"

His words cut off, and I finished it for him. "Demons?" I said, wincing in sympathy. "The coven doesn't know Trent's dad fixed you, do they?" I asked, realizing why Lee looked so tense in his rumpled suit. Lee shook his head, and I touched his shoulder in support. "Lee, even if they find out, you can't pass on the cure. Your kids are going to be okay. They will be carriers, but that's it. Besides, Trent won't tell the coven about you. The only reason he told them about me was to force me to come to the elf side."

"The what?" Lee asked, looking confused as well as relieved.

Ivy clicked her pen in quick succession. "Trent told the coven she could invoke demon magic to convince her to sign a lifetime contract with him."

Squinting, Lee said, "I'm not following you."

Huffing, I rolled my eyes. "Trent told the coven that he can control me since his dad helped make me, and that there's no reason to kill me if he has legal responsibility for me."

"He can't control you," Lee scoffed, and I bobbed my head.

"I know! He's doing it because he's ticked about the familiar bond we have. He says if I own him in the ever-after, then he's going to own me here." I was starting to get mad just thinking about it, and I crossed my arms over my middle and fumed.

"Sounds like Trent," Lee said, shaking his head in amusement. "You going to sign it?"

"No, she's not going to sign it," Ivy said. "We're going to get the coven to back off."

How, I didn't know right now. I was just trying to survive.

Ivy, though, was eying Lee in suspicion. "Maybe you were the one who told the coven Rachel could invoke demon magic," she said tightly. "To buy your own freedom."

"What, and have them target me next?" he said, and I nodded my agreement. Lee wouldn't tell. Not in a hundred years. Not newly married as he was. Jeez.

"You need a ride?" I asked, knowing better than to confront Trent in my current state, but hey, if there was an excuse . . .

"I've got a driver coming," he said, his hands unclenching. "You got this okay?"

I nodded. "How good are your lawyers?"

"Better than Trent's," he said, smiling. I thought it weird that Lee and Trent were still friends, even after Lee had tried to blow up Trent. But after Trent left him for three days in the camp cistern, I guess all bets were off. I guess it was no weirder than my having saved Trent when I hated him.

Jenks buzzed back in, his wings sparkling with rain. "There's a black car out front," he said, and Lee adjusted his coat as if getting ready to leave.

"That's mine," he said needlessly, his expression heavy. "Are you sure you don't want to come with me? I've got resources for this kind of thing. I can make you disappear, too, but with sunny beaches and little umbrellas in your drinks."

I considered it and dismissed it in the next heartbeat. I didn't want to hide, I just needed a place to catch my balance.

"No way!" Jenks shouted. "Rachel is not going anywhere! She left once, and see what happened? That was a bad idea. Pierce doesn't have a brain in his head. Don't listen to him, Rache. We got this."

Ivy raised her hand. "I hate the beach," she said mildly, and Lee smiled.

"Fair enough," he said, standing in the middle of our kitchen and meeting everyone's eyes with his own. "I'm out of here. Good luck."

"Same to you, Lee." I impulsively gave him a hug, whispering, "Tell Trent he can suck my toes and die, okay?"

He chuckled, rubbing my head for luck before turning and walking away. I let him get away with it, then carefully fixed my hair. There was a brief pixy hail in the sanctuary as he passed through it, then silence. The church felt almost empty. Sighing, I turned to my library under the center counter. If the coven was coming for me, it was going to be a busy night.

"You spelling tonight?" Jenks asked as I pulled a mundane spell book out and thumped it on the counter.

"You know it." Now that Lee was gone, I could get serious. My thoughts strayed to the demon texts, inches from my knees. There were things in there that would stop intruders dead in their tracks. It would be so easy. *And wrong. No, not an option.*

"I can't believe you were considering leaving again, Rache," Jenks said, indignant, his wings stilling to nothing as he landed on the rim of the spell pot I'd just gotten down. "You leave and you're dead. I don't care how far Lee's money can take you. We've been in the garden long enough to shore up the defenses, and they'll have to get through that to reach the church. How long can you stay in a bubble?"

"A bubble won't help her if they set the church on fire," Ivy said dryly.

"Maybe I could put the church in a bubble," I mused as I turned pages, thinking there had to be a way out of this. Besides going to Trent and signing his lousy paper, that is.

"Gas and electrical lines," Ivy said, always the doomsayer. "No good if it's witches coming for you. Besides, you want to hide here for how long?"

I winced while Jenks vigorously bobbed his head. "Point taken," I said. "What do you think it will be? Witches?" I forced myself to not fidget, though Ivy could probably tell I was upset just by sniffing the air.

Ivy stretched until the red stone in her belly-button ring showed from under her black T-shirt. "Well, it won't be the Weres," she said as she reached one hand for the ceiling, the one in the cast bent over her head. "And no local vamps. Rynn would bury them alive."

"Brooke said we had until sunup," Jenks said grimly, wings going full tilt and sending a silver light to fill the empty sink. "That means out-of-state assassins. That's where my pollen is. Tink's a Disney whore, Rache. Can't you go even one year without a price on your head?"

Tired, I skated my sock-footed toe around on the linoleum, staring at my book. I had until sunup to prep for who knew what. "I don't mind leaving. I'm the one they want."

Ivy smiled, a faint, amused expression, as she came closer. The width of the counter between us, she pulled out a second book and set it gently on the counter, her long fingers pale on the faded rough leather. "Leave? Just when it's getting interesting?"

My eyebrows rose when she actually opened it. Seeing her brow furrowed and her lower lip between her teeth, I wondered if she knew how provocative she looked as she tried to understand a part of me that was as foreign to her as vampire lust was to me. Probably.

Jenks landed on the open pages, hands on his hips as he looked down. "David needs a couple more days to get your paperwork," he said, eyes down. "We can keep you alive that long half asleep."

"Besides," Ivy said, looking up at me with calm brown eyes, "we don't have anything better to do tomorrow. Wednesdays are always slow."

I smiled, glad I had such good friends.

Nineteen

The wind was warm, and I could hear insect wings clattering in the tall grass as I sat beside Pierce in the vast golden field, content. Above my head, the amber seed heads of ripe wheat waved, and as I reached to tickle Pierce with a broken stalk, his eyes opened, shocking me with their deep blue depths. For an instant, Kisten gazed hotly at me, then his features melted and Pierce again took his place. The witch's loose waves were in disarray, and his hat shadowed his face. "It's almost sunrise," he said, his accent making me smile. "Time to wake."

Then his eyes shifted, going red and slitted like a goat's. His features became harder, taking on a ruddy complexion until it was Al lying before me in his crushed green velvet, one knee casually drawn up. The skies turned bloodred, and he reached out a white-gloved hand, grasping my wrist but not pulling me closer. "Come home, itchy witch."

I snorted, jerking awake.

Bolting upright, I stared at my closed window to see the fading light of sunrise against the colorful reds and blues of the stained glass. Heart pounding, I realized the clattering of insect wings in my dream had been Jenks hovering before my closed door, listening at the crack.

He had a finger to his lips, and after seeing my wide-eyed stare, he went back to the door.

Slowly my pulse eased, and I looked at my clock. Quarter after six. I'd worked most of the night, finally lying down about three hours ago to get some sleep. Throwing off the afghan, I carefully pulled my knees up to tighten the laces of my sneakers. I didn't feel so good.

"Why are you in my room?" I whispered, not knowing why I was being quiet except that Jenks had told me to be.

"It's after sunup," he said, ear to the door. "You think I'm going to leave you alone? Open season on redheads started fifteen minutes ago."

Fingers fumbling and knees protesting, I tied my shoes. Three hours of sleep wasn't nearly enough. "Where is everyone?" I asked as I rose to peek out the small stained-glass window.

"Bis is asleep, the cat's inside, Jax is on the steeple, and my kids are strategically placed in the garden with Matalina," he said shortly. "We're just waiting for God to say go. Either that, or your killers are waiting for you to walk in front of a fairy-farted window."

I backed from the window, arms around myself. *Jax is here?* "What about Nick?"

Jenks turned, hovering beside the door. "What about him?"

"You said Jax is here . . . ," I questioned.

Frowning, he muttered, "The kid either got really smart or really stupid. He came in right after you went to bed. Said he left Nick because he didn't like the way the lunker went after you with a knife. Tink's little red thong, Rachel. If I'd been there, I would've killed Nick's ratty ass. Now I don't know if I should take Jax back or send Jrixibell to see if he's spying on us."

My eyebrows rose. From the sanctuary came a loud "I don't trust you, that's why!"

It was Ivy, and she was ticked. "Who's here? Edden?"

Jenks dropped an inch in height, his wings slowing. "Pierce."

"Is he okay?" I stiffened. "How come no one woke me up?"

"Because he was fine and you were sleeping." Jenks gave up on listening and faced me with his hands on his hips in his best Peter Pan pose. "He's only been here five minutes, and already he's causing trouble. Cool your hormones, Rache."

"Your opinion of me is supposed to change my emotions for her?" Pierce's voice came, hushed but intense. "You can't assist her, vampire. Your love can only save her by limiting her. It's what you are. There's no shame but that you're using her to try to rise beyond your scope."

Great. Just freaking great. Snatching up a brush, I ran it over my hair three times before I gave up. God help him. He was stripping Ivy of the lies that kept her sane.

"Don't go out!" Jenks exclaimed as I reached for the doorknob. "They'll quit talking!"

"That's the idea," I said, jerking the door open. "Pierce?" I called, hearing Ivy hiss something. A quiver pulled through me as I felt him tap the line in the backyard. *Shit.*

"Don't do it, Ivy!" I shouted, running painfully to the sanctuary. Damn it, if she pinned him to the wall, I was going to be pissed.

Remembering what Jenks had said about windows, I skidded to a halt at the end of the hall, heart pounding. Pierce wasn't pinned to a wall, but standing beside the burnt pool table in the dusky morning light, dimmer than usual because of the boarded-up window. He still had his full-length wool duster on, and my dream rushed back. Facing Ivy, he looked wary and dangerous as he frowned, his hands in the pockets of his long coat and his hat on his head. I could almost smell the power spilling off him, rising above his pockets to spill over and eddy about his feet. He didn't look hurt at all. In fact, he looked great.

The scent of redwood battled with vamp incense to fill the church with the hint of power and sex. Breathing deeply, I took a step in. Ivy had changed into her working leathers in preparation for today's festivities, and her arm cast looked very white and new in its black sling. Her eyes were a full, intoxicating black, and she moved with a sultry pace as she circled him, eight feet back. Yup, she'd lost it. Her blood fasting was not a good idea.

She paused when she got between Pierce and me, coyly turning to me. Her expression was a sultry mix of lust and domination. "Ivy, stop it," I said when my neck started to tingle.

"He wants to take you to the ever-after," she said, fear dulling her sexual air. "Ask him."

Pierce pulled his left hand from his pocket in a gesture for me to listen, and a knot of tension eased when I saw its smooth length instead of Al's white gloves. "You must agree that though smelling almighty putrid it's safe. You'd be safe there."

I'd seen the ever-after in the daylight, and it was nasty. "Is that why you're not hurt?" I said hotly. "You got a deal going with Al? You convince me to bag reality and go hide in the ever-after, and he doesn't beat you to a pulp? I'm not a demon, and I don't belong there!"

"No." Pierce glanced at Ivy, then Jenks, before taking a step closer. "I don't think you're a demon." His left hand went back into a deep pocket, and my face got cold when he brought out the blackened, paint-peeling remains of my cherry-red splat gun. "My apologies," he said as he crossed the room and placed it in my grip. "He plum destroyed your spell pistol."

"H-how?" I stammered, then remembered that Pierce had had it when I left. Jenks whistled long and slow, and on impulse, I pulled Pierce's right hand out. The witch hissed in pain, and I turned it over to see the imprint of the splat gun's handle.

"Oh my God. Pierce. What did he do to you?" I tossed the melted gun to the burnt couch, and Pierce stiffened when Ivy approached. "Jenks, get a pain amulet," I said, and the pixy darted off. "You shot at him?" I demanded, my worry coming out as anger. "Are you crazy? I'm surprised he didn't kill you!"

Standing resolutely before me, Pierce hid his burnt hand behind his back. "I'm sure he'd rather. I didn't remain to give him the chance. My aim was poor, and he melted your spell caster after my second volley. You'd rather I remained for a beating?"

And now that the sun was up, Al couldn't follow him. *Ohhh, I bet he's pissed.*

Jenks dripped gold sparkles as he came back, and I took the amulet from him, draping it over Pierce's head and catching it briefly on the brim of his hat. Immediately Pierce's pinched expression eased, but Jenks was buzzing in alarm. "Al is going to be ma-a-a-ad," he drawled in warning. "He's gonna think Rachel gave you her gun."

Making a sound of disapproval, Ivy pushed herself into motion, her grace giving me the willies as she peeked out the front door. I glanced at the melted gun on the charred cushions and silently agreed. "I can't believe you shot at him. Come on," I said as I took Pierce's upper arm. "I've got a burn charm. It's only for stove burns, but it will help."

Pierce didn't move, and my grip slipped off him. "You're under a coven death sentence," he said, warily glancing at Ivy. "I know you're not cotton to the ever-after, but Al will take you in. The coven can't reach you there."

His language was slipping, telling me he was really upset, and I eyed him in disbelief. "I am *not* going to go crying to Al for help. I might have to put up with you, but I don't have to take your advice. You were wrong about not telling Al about the coven in the first place. You were wrong about leaving the church. And you were wrong about getting on that bus. Did you know Vivian almost killed everyone on it? I'm not leaving to hide in the ever-after!"

Pierce's brow furrowed. "Mayhap they wouldn't have died had we been there."

I frowned, having thought the same thing. *Is that his backhanded way of blaming me?*

Ivy came back in from the foyer, standing with her feet spread and senses alert, listening. Her eyes were still dark, but at least she wasn't looking like she was ready to jump anyone. Jenks joined her, the noisy clatter of his wings loud in the silence of an otherwise pixy-empty church. "We can keep Rachel alive," he said almost snottily. "We don't need your help."

Pierce crossed his arms over his chest, but I wasn't leaving, and that was it. I didn't care how much he frowned and cleared his throat. Running a hand over my sleep-snarled hair, I tried to remember how long ago it had been when I'd made a burn charm. Less than a year, certainly. But I needed a way to talk to Pierce alone. I did *not* want them hearing what was going to come out of my mouth next. "Jenks, how much feverfew do we have?"

He flew backward from me, expression cross as he saw I was clearly trying to get rid of him. "I'll go check—Rachel," he said caustically, then darted out the back.

I turned to Ivy next, waiting.

"I'll do a perimeter," she muttered. "Stay away from the windows."

Boot heels clunking in noisy protest, she left out the front, careful to make sure Rex didn't slip out with her. I caught a glimpse of the morning as the door opened to show bright sun glinting on the pavement, still wet from last night's rain. Cool and peaceful. *Well, I can change that,* I thought, turning back to Pierce.

His shoulders were stiff, his jaw clenched and his cheeks faintly red without a hint of stubble. *When had he had time to shave?* "Pierce," I said, knowing Jenks was eavesdropping. "Thank you for getting Al to . . . I mean, you didn't have to . . . I was handling it," I said plaintively, then gave up, slumping. "Thank you," I said earnestly. "Are you sure you're okay?"

Pierce's posture eased, and he lost his hard expression. "You're welcome."

"But I'm not leaving the church," I said, and his frown returned. "I tried that, and it went wrong. These are my friends, and I'm sticking with them."

My fingers lightly ran down his injured hand's arm, tugging it out to see the damage, but he wouldn't let me see. "Just how mad is Al?" I asked. Rex was rubbing against my leg asking to go out, and I picked her up. "That's why you want me to go back, isn't it? You figure if I go back looking for protection, he won't be so mad about you shooting him."

"Perish the thought," Pierce said, his eyes glinting. "It's your safety I'm thinking of."

Like I believed that. "And you think I make bad decisions," I said, carrying Rex to the kitchen as I went to get a burn charm. I knew he'd follow.

"He was savage as a meat ax," he said from behind me. "I might be beaten come sundown, but it was worth it," he muttered. "I opine that we both like what scares us most."

The kitchen was blue from the pulled curtains, peaceful. "Excuse me?"

He shrugged, his shoulders looking hunched under the duster. "I like trying to kill demons, and I think you fancy Ivy."

My fingers fondling Rex's ears hesitated. "Excuse me?" I said again, more stridently.

Pierce leaned in, surprising me when his forehead almost touched mine. "She can save you, you know," he whispered, his own fingers going out to touch Rex, between us, and I froze. "If you abandon yourself and cleave to her, fully accepting her sovereignty over you, you will be protected by the vampires to the death. They see you as their next leap."

Oh. That. I couldn't look up, and I focused on our fingers, touching among the purring cat's fur. "I wouldn't be myself," I said, wondering why he was bringing this up.

"True, you would be different. But you'd be strong. And remembered forever." He took a breath, and as his fingers left mine, I looked up. "Do you love her?"

His question shocked the hell out of me. "You are full of questions, aren't you?"

There was that same worried wrinkle above his eyes. I'd seen it before when he'd talked to me about Nick, and my pulse quickened. He wanted me to say no. "Do you?" he asked earnestly. "Don't mistake my apparent simple nature for stupidity. Vampires have existed nearly as long as we have. We aren't immune to their charms. And Ivy is charming." His jaw tightened, and I flushed. "She'd treat you well until she died, and likely thereafter as well."

I held Rex close, feeling her warmth. "Ivy and I . . . ," I started, then mentally backed up. "It's complicated," I came out with instead. "But there's nothing between us but space, now."

His eyes never left mine as he evaluated my words with what he had seen the past year. "Do you love her?" he insisted. "More than a sister's love?"

My thoughts went back to the kiss she'd given me. And the moment in the kitchen when we had tried to share something without her losing control and failed. The sensations she pulled from me were forever entwined with the vampire who had tried to bind me to him and blood-rape me. More than a sister's love. I knew what he was asking, and though I knew the answer was yes, I shook my head, thinking that what I felt meant nothing if I wasn't going to pursue it.

"I don't swing that way, Pierce," I said, voice quavering as a sudden anger took me—anger for my not being smart enough to find a way to be the person I wanted to be as well as the person Ivy needed me to be. "Thanks for the reminder."

Ticked, I turned to open my charm cupboard, the cat squirming. "I've got a burn charm in here somewhere," I said tightly as I let Rex go. "I probably have a few minutes before my assassins show."

A wave of sound shook the pots hanging over the counter, and I heard the discordant jangle of a hundred wind chimes.

Or not, I thought, eyes going to the garden window.

"Jenks?" I shouted, darting for the back door.

The bright glow of a pixy pulled me to a skidding stop in the back living room. It was Jax, and his blade was bared, already sporting a red sheen.

"Fairies," he all but spat, face twisted. "The coven sent fairies. They're attacking the garden. An entire spawn of them!"

Fairies. The word slid through my mind, chilling me. Matalina and the kids. Damn it, I was going to get everyone killed. I grasped the knob to the back door and pulled. It slipped from my grasp as Pierce pushed it shut, it having only opened inches.

"It's a lure to draw you out," he said, gaze fierce as he stood with his hand on the door.

"Then it worked." Shoving him aside, I tapped the line out back and flung the door open. Lunging, I swore as a handful of needles went thunking into the couch behind me. I dove for the bottom of the step, turning it into a roll. The soft, rain-wet earth cushioned me as I somersaulted behind the picnic table, propped up on end against the big tree for winter. I took a breath, and Pierce was suddenly crouching beside me.

"I swan, Rachel," he muttered, peeved. "You're going to be the death of me again."

Immediately I set a circle around both of us. "I thought you said you liked what scared you." There was a surge of noise from the pixies, and I peeked to see them beating the butterfly-winged fairies back, the fight rising higher as they both struggled for supremacy. The bobbing color of the fairies' wings was encroaching from over the graveyard in a highly structured pattern that went up as well as from side to side. Surrounding the stump between us were darting shapes shedding sparkles to confuse and misdirect. If one didn't know that a battle for survival was going on, it'd be breathtaking.

"Ivy?" I shouted while rubbing the dirt from my palms. Pierce took my arm and I jerked from him, only to find him take a stronger grip. "What are you doing?" I snapped.

"Hold still." His lips pressed together, and I gasped when a surge of ley-line energy spilled into me. I pulled back at the invasion, shoving him when I felt a hot pulse of pain from my arm where he was gripping me. We fell over together, but he wouldn't let go and we broke my circle. Only now did he let go, and I jerked when a new, green-tinted circle enclosed us.

"What is your problem!" I exclaimed. Great, now my knees were hurt *and* wet.

"Poison," he said as he huddled close to the old wood. "I burned it up within you."

Embarrassed, I looked down. There was a tiny hole in my shirt, the edges charred. The skin under was pink with the hint of a sunburn surrounding a nasty bruise I didn't remember getting. *Oh.* "Um, thanks," I stammered. "Sorry."

"Do tell," he said, his jaw tight and not meeting my eyes.

Peeking around the barrier, I saw a cluster of brightly colored wings rising over the protection of the shed. "Jenks! Behind you!" I exclaimed, then jerked behind the wood as three spears bounced off Pierce's bubble. Cripes, I had nothing for fairies. Nothing!

There was a high, tinkling shout, and I carefully peered around the table to see Jax's wings turn a shocking shade of yellow. As if it was a signal, a slew of pixy arrows rained down. The encroaching vanguard of purple-winged fairies went down with tattered wings. With a bloodthirsty yell, six of Jenks's younger kids dove out of my old teakettle, hidden under the shrubs, and attacked them with cold steel and vicious shouts. Three seconds later, the fairies lay dead and his children were giving one another high fives. *Holy shit. Jenks's kids were savages!*

"Rache!" Jenks barked above me, and I looked up, my expression still holding the horror. "What are you doing out here?" he asked, rising up and then down to avoid a spear.

"Taking notes," I said, nudging Pierce to take his bubble down long enough to give Jenks a place to rest. "Have you seen Ivy?" God, if she was injured somewhere . . .

The haze of green-tinted ever-after blinked out of existence, then returned. Jenks hovered before me with the scent of crushed dandelions, bringing my senses awake and filling me with the need to move. "She's practicing her moves up front," he said cryptically. Worried, I started to rise, only to be jerked back down. "She's fine!" Jenks said, laughing at my fear. "Don't go looking for her. She's vamped out." He smiled, looking devilish. "Kinda scary.

"Pierce," Jenks said, surprising me. "Rache can't do anything here. Jump her out."

"I can't jump anyone but myself," Pierce said. "Only a demon or a skilled gargoyle, which Bis is not, can carry another."

A familiar scream ripped through the air, lifting over the fairy battle cries and the breathy sounds of tattered wings struggling for lift. Jenks lifted up to the limits of Pierce's bubble, and both Pierce and I looked around the edge of the table.

"Sweet mother of Mary," Pierce whispered as Ivy vaulted over the wall between the street and the church, her curved sword in her good hand. Dodging tiny spears, she took out two fairies with ugly splats of sound. Shaking them off, she rolled to the shed, eyes wild and hair settling to hang perfectly as her back slammed up against the old wood. *Holy crap, she was like Mary Lou Retton on Brimstone!*

"Let me out, Rache!" Jenks shouted, but I wasn't the one holding the circle.

Ivy jumped into motion an instant before a barrage of arrows thunked into the shed where her middle would have been. A smattering of tiny arrows was embedded in her new cast, and she wiped them off using the sword blade. With vampiric speed and grace, she bounded back to the stump and the protection of Jenks's kids.

"Ivy!" I called, wanting her to join us—even if she was vamped out.

Across the backyard, the gate to the street was flung open, crashing into the wall with a sodden thump. Ceri was standing in the opening, the unpainted wood framing her small stature. Her hair was unbound, and the fair strands almost floated as she strode forward, anger and determination in every tiny-footed step. The woman was seven months pregnant. What in God's name was she doing here?

"*Celero dilatare!*" she shouted gleefully, and a black ball of force formed in her hands. Pink lips pulled back in a grimace, she threw it.

"Fire in the hold!" I yelled. Inking, pixies darted up, Ivy lunged to the shelter of the shed, and with a twist of her hand in a ley-line gesture, Ceri exploded her curse right within the greatest gathering of butterfly wings.

Crap on toast! I jerked behind the table with Pierce as a black-rimmed wash tinted with blue highlights colored the garden. It pulsed over Pierce's protective bubble . . . and was gone. When I looked, Ceri was standing beside the stump while the fairies struggled to regroup, scattered by what I was guessing was just a huge displacement of air. Ceri was calm and satisfied in her white dress trimmed in gold and purple. A bulge showed at her middle as she proudly showed off the life growing within her to Jenks's daughters, who took time out to feel the soft swelling through her linen dress before going down to slaughter the dazed fairies.

Lee, I thought, giving the man a silent thank-you as I rose to my feet. He must have told her what was going on and she'd left Trent's compound. She was beautiful in her anger, but I wasn't sure if it had been a curse or just a strong spell.

"Let me out, Pierce!" Jenks insisted. "Or I'm going to use your nuts for a beanbag chair!"

The bubble vanished, and Jenks darted away shedding hot sparkles.

Ivy's howl of pain iced through me. Pierce grabbed my arm, and I shoved him off and followed Jenks. The fairies were still trying to regroup. We had taken back a space, slowly widening as Jenks's kids pressed their advantage and drove them to the graveyard.

Ivy was down on one knee, holding her bicep as she leaned against the shed. I ran to her, hearing Pierce follow as he swore in words that a ten-year-old might use. We both skidded to a stop before her, Ceri right behind us. A green-tinted circle rose up and we were safe again.

"I'm fine. I'm fine!" she almost snarled, her hand coming off her bicep to show a small scratch, the edges red rimmed already and starting to go purple.

"Fine, hell, it's poison! Pierce, burn it out," I demanded, and he nodded. Eyes avoiding mine, he dropped to his knees to make his coat furl open. His hand went over the scratch, and he whispered the charm. Spell. Curse. I didn't care. Ivy jerked, her nostrils widening as a glow enveloped his hand.

"He's burning it out," I said, gripping her shoulders and forcing her to be still. "Try to relax."

"It hurts," she grunted. Her breath came with a gasp, and she held it for the count of three before it hissed out between her teeth. "Are you done yet?" she almost snarled.

Damn it, this isn't her battle, it's mine.

"You could have left," Pierce muttered as if having heard my thoughts. But if I'd left, they would have attacked anyway.

"A controlled burn?" Ceri said, voice high and interested. "You can do that?"

Pierce looked up, standing to tug his coat straight and touch his hat. "Mistress elf," he said formally, but I noticed he didn't offer his hand.

Her eyes darted behind him to the re-forming ranks of fairies. "You must be Pierce."

"I am."

My gaze jerked down when Ivy moved. "Are you okay?" I asked as she pulled herself up, sitting against the shed. Sweat ran down her brow in a rivulet to vanish under her clothes.

"That hurt," she said simply.

"You'd likely be dead if you were a witch," Pierce said grimly. "I opine being a vampire accounts for one good thing."

Ivy's eyes widened as she looked past me, and I stood and turned in one smooth motion. "Oh, crap," I said aloud as I saw the flash of flame. "Jenks!" I shouted. "They've got fire!"

The hose was less than twenty feet away, but it might as well have been across the street, trapped in this bubble like we were. Jenks rose in a burst of motion above his younger kids gathered at the teapot. He whistled, and pixies came from everywhere, standing for a final assault on their stump. After that, it would be the church. They wanted me dead, and if I continued to hide in a bubble, they'd burn everything and everyone I loved.

Ceri's eyes were positively scary with determination. Ivy slowly got to her feet, and I supported her until she found her balance. "They're swarming," Pierce said. "I've heard of this. They're like locusts. This isn't merely an assassination attempt, it's an invasion."

Jenks dropped back down before the entrance of the stump. Beside him was Matalina, her arrows slung over her back and a sword I'd never seen in her grip. To her left was her eldest daughter, Jih. To Jenks's right was Jax. Behind them gathered the rest of the children, even the youngest. Across the graveyard, the fairies grew bold, flame dancing in their hands as their wings lifted them on the morning breeze. Their pace was slow even as they shouted insults. The bows in Jenks's children's hands had taught them caution. Last night's rain would keep the graveyard and the longer grass from burning, but not Jenks's stump. I couldn't let this happen. I'd rather rot in jail.

"Let me out of the bubble," I said softly, but only Ivy heard. "I will not be responsible for Jenks and his family dying. Ceri, let me out."

"Rachel, no," Ivy said as I stepped to the edge of Ceri's bubble. "There's got to be another way!" she said loudly. "Pierce, be of some use and think of something! Don't let her give herself up. Not to those butchers. The coven will kill her! You know it!"

Desperate, I stood, helpless. Pierce searched my face, seeing my fear, my loyalty, and my decision to not risk those I loved any longer. His hand found mine and I held it. I wasn't going to let them burn Jenks's house and slaughter his children. I'd do anything. And Pierce knew it.

Giving my fingers a tight squeeze, he turned away. "Mistress elf," he said to Ceri, his voice calm and determined. "Are you skilled in casting?"

Ceri's breath came in fast. Her wild look grew more fierce. "I am," she said, standing proudly. Casting was like a net in that it took more than one person to create, but whereas a net simply contained people, a casting generally contained a havoc-producing spell. It was tricky, seldom done as it was too easy for the spell to escape.

"Do you know the spell to burn even that which has an aura?" he asked, and the muscles in my knees went slack. *God, no.*

"That's black magic," I said, pushing Pierce's hand off me. "That kills people!"

Ceri gave me a long look, her eyes still on mine when she spoke. "I do."

Frantic, I turned to Pierce, then Jenks readying his family for a final assault. "You can't burn them alive!" I shouted.

Ceri's frowned. "We have two. To cast safely from here it will take three."

"We have three," Pierce said. "One to create, one to protect, and one to define." This last was directed at me, and Pierce's eyes held the memory of a difficult decision made long ago.

"I'm *not* going to burn my garden and everyone in it!" I shouted. "Jenks is out there!"

"Anything underground will be safe," Ceri said.

"I said no!" I protested, but Ivy's eyes begged me to say yes.

"Then Jenks and his family will die," Ceri said cruelly.

I stood before her, ill with frustration. Right then, I hated her although she didn't deserve it.

Pierce drew me to him. The difference between Ceri's proud disdain and his brow furrowed in pained empathy was striking. "You are the definition," he said softly. "You can hold the strongest, widest circle. Make one to encompass the garden. I will be the safety, and I will keep the magic from acting upon us. Everything between my circle and your larger one will be subjected to a quick flash of heat."

I looked over my church, seeing it smoking and ruined in my mind's eye. Burned at my own hands? "The trees, my garden," I whispered.

Ceri turned from watching the approaching fairies, her impatience obvious and making me feel like I was stupid. "The leaves will be singed. The garden will sprout from roots. The heat won't do anything to your church but clear the spiderwebs from it. Even Bis will be untouched. Rachel, Jenks cannot last against such numbers! He and his family will be slaughtered! Why are you hesitating?"

Because it was black magic. Anything able to pass through an aura and burn a living thing was black. I'd be a black witch. I'd be everything they said I was. But to stand here in a bubble while Jenks's children were cut down and slaughtered . . .

"There is no other option, Rachel," Pierce said, and I grew frantic. From beyond the safety of Pierce's circle, I could hear Jenks shouting final instructions to his children. They wouldn't scatter but would stay to the last. Ivy begged me with her fearful eyes. I had to do it.

Without a word, I closed my eyes and set an undrawn circle wider than the one at Fountain Square. I felt it go up, encircling the church, the grounds, and a slice of the graveyard. *How many were inside it? How many would die?* I thought, pulling my hand from Pierce.

"Jenks!" I shouted, blood humming from the strength of the line. "Go to ground!"

A sharp whistle pulled my eyes open to see a flowing of pixy wings into the stump. The fairies broke ranks, chasing them faster than would seem possible. Torches made tiny flames surrounding Jenks's home. Three fairies darted through the abandoned door. Trusting me, Jenks had let them in to do battle in his own home.

"I will lead," Ceri said, taking one of my hands. Pierce took the other, gingerly since it was his burnt hand. Safe within Pierce's sheltering bubble, Ceri bound our wills together, her aura swirling, pressing against mine with the feeling of silk and the scent of sun.

A shudder rippled through me when Pierce sent his aura wider, strengthening his circle, protecting us and melting it with Ceri's aura so her magic could pass through. I couldn't have shifted my aura like that. It was beyond my skill, sophisticated magic, and Ceri smiled in devilish delight, thrilled to find another matching her ability. She looked like a fertility goddess with her bulging middle and the power leaking from her.

Beside her, Pierce was dark, masculine, strong, his thoughts here and in his past simultaneously. And I was between them, frantic. I was going to twist a black curse to save Jenks's life.

Ceri paused in her chanting, and upon feeling the weight of her stare, I swallowed hard and released the tight grip on my energies, letting them flow between us, balancing.

Pierce's breath hissed in, his fingers in mine clenching for a moment. Neither I nor Ceri said anything, but we waited until he nodded, accepting the level of power. It was a joined spell, and I could taste the three of us mixing, the bite of metal and ash, the powdery residue of sun and pollen, and the cold edge of wild, windswept water in winter. That was me—windswept water in winter. I was going to kill someone with magic. There had to be another choice!

"Stop," I whispered, and Pierce's thoughts wound into my own, holding me to the task.

"Stay the course," he said, eyes fixed on mine with an eerie intensity. "Hold."

"Everyone kills to live," Ivy whispered, vampire incense pulling through me to then vanish.

Not me, I thought, my fingers hurting where Ceri gripped them, refusing to let me go.

"*Accendere!*" she shouted victoriously, finishing the curse.

I stumbled as I jerked from them, but it was too late. Stunned, I felt the black curse tear through my brain like a heated knife, searing the knowledge into my memory. Ceri gasped, her head thrown back as the curse escaped Pierce's bubble. As if in slow motion, I followed it with a ribbon of thought, the first tendrils of silver heat darting to find the edges of the confines of my circle, widening to fill the space, crawling over the inside of the dome, snaking up the tree to crisp the leaves. The ground smoked, the wet earth steamed to show the expanding curse.

I was going to burn everything aboveground. *Everyone kills to live*, echoed in my mind.

Not me. Panicked, I threw myself from Pierce and Ceri, hitting the interior shell of Pierce's bubble and staring at them in horror. *Not me!*

"No!" I shouted, reaching out for the curse. I had seen its creation. I could call it back.

"Rachel?" Ceri called, eyes wide as she felt something shift.

Pierce stared at me. "Rachel, no!" he cried as if knowing what I was going to do.

Eyes wide, I reached for the curse, wrapped my will around it—and pulled it back.

Crap. This was really going to hurt.

With the sensation of fire, the curse rebounded into me, backlashing in my mind as if it were alive, angry to be jerked home. *Not me!* I thought as bursts of green flame lit and died outside Pierce's circle, showing where fragile wings shivered into flame. A terrible cry went up as the fairies dropped to the burning earth, and still I pulled, taking it into myself. They were dying. My head flung back and I screamed so I wouldn't go mad with the pain.

And when I had it all, when I had everything that I could bear, I pushed the curse back into the ley line. I emptied everything into it, letting go of the line with a quickness that curled me into myself, hurt. My outer circle dropped, and I took a sobbing breath in the sudden quiet.

The pain vanished from my mind, and I shook as I fell to the wet ground. *What have I become in the name of love? Of friendship?*

"Rachel!" Ivy exclaimed, but it was Pierce's arms that slipped around me, smelling of witch and power.

The imbalance hit, and I clenched anew, teeth gritting as I took it all. This was mine. The filth, the scum. All of it. And I heard Pierce sigh as I shuddered and accepted the entirety of the smut. I deserved it.

"What did you do!" Ceri shouted, angry. I could see her tiny feet as I lay in Pierce's arms, the pain now only a memory but my panic and fear growing. *What have I become?*

"Rachel! What did you do!" the elf said again, demanding my attention.

I looked up, wiping my eyes. "Is Jenks okay?" I whispered.

From the edge of the circle, Ivy said, "He's still underground. Are you okay?"

"She misaligned it!" Ceri shouted, furious as she stomped her foot. "And she did it intentionally! They're still alive! Never has anyone misaligned my work, never!"

They were alive? I looked up, not believing. My throat was raw and my muscles felt like rubber bands. The fairies were alive!

"It wasn't misaligned," Pierce said as he eased me to the ground and stood. Hands at his side, he looked irate. "She drew it back."

"Why!" Ceri shouted. "I told her Jenks would survive!"

"I have no idea," Pierce said, standing beside me as my butt got wet from the grass.

"Jenks," I whispered, and I felt Pierce let go of the line and his circle drop. The breath of a new day stained with the stink of burning shifted my hair, and I looked for the bright glitter of pixy wings. Outside Pierce's circle, paths of ash showed where the spell had started to take hold, but the garden was green. Small voices rose in pain, and my heart clenched.

Where is Jenks? My breath came in a sob when Pierce crouched before me, his unburnt hand reaching to wipe my tears away. "Rachel," he said, his hand damp when he took mine to help me rise. "We're in deeper trouble now. Best face it on your feet."

Numb, I let him draw me to a shaky stand. "Jenks!" I shouted. God, had I killed them?

Pixy wings exploded from the stump. I dropped back, relief almost making me pass out. They were okay. All of them. But as they darted over the garden, shrieks of fear rang out. My face went cold. Shit, they were killing the grounded fairies.

"Jenks! No!" I shouted. "It's done! Stop! Damn it, Jenks, stop it! Don't kill them!"

Jenks was atop his stump, having dragged a sallow-faced fairy with him. He turned to me in disgust, his sword at the helpless warrior's neck. The fairy's eyes were wide and a nasty ooze was puddling at his feet—the remains of his wings.

"Jenks . . . ," I pleaded, and with a sour look, the pixy threw his blade in the air to shift his grip. With no fanfare, he gave the leader of the swarm a vicious thunk on the head. The fairy's eyes rolled up and a ribbon of red blood leaked out.

"Damn it, Rache," Jenks said as he let the fairy drop at his feet. "Why do you make things so difficult?"

"Thank you," I whispered, kneeling to put our eyes on the same level.

"Round them up. Tie them down!" Jenks shouted, and his kids complained as he took to the air, seeming to pull me to my feet as well. Blood smeared him, and wiping his sword he said, "This is going to be trouble, Rache. You should have let me kill them."

I started backing away, my gaze darting over the garden. He was angry, motions quick as he flitted away, savage and stinking of death. His kids were cruelly driving the flightless fairies together with torments and cuts. It was survival, but it was scaring me.

My gaze touched on Ceri, the hem of her dress shaking. I'd ruined her curse—a black curse as foul as a hanging corpse. Ivy's eyes were black as she tried to regain control of her emotions, driven to the brink by the aggression around her, her grimed sword on the grass beside her. And Pierce stood watching me, a sad, tired expression in his eyes.

What am I doing? Who are these people I thought I knew, crying for death, lusting for it?

"I have to go," I whispered, backing up farther yet.

Ivy's eyes flashed even blacker, and Ceri turned, her expression hot with anger.

"Inside," I added so they wouldn't think I was leaving. "I need some water."

I headed for the porch, snatching up Rex so she wouldn't eat any of the grounded fairies.

Maybe I should have gone into the ever-after. Even Al is better than this.

Twenty

The slamming of the screen door behind me jumped through me like a spark. I had to get away. I had to go somewhere to regroup, figure out what had just happened. But as I stood in the silence, there was no peace in the living room. Ivy's couch was heady with vampire incense and memories. Leaving wet footprints, I paced into the kitchen.

My sneakers squeaked to a halt, and my heart pounded as I listened to the calls of the pixies through the window. The blue lights on the fridge's ice maker glowed, and I looked at the picture of me and Jenks standing before the bridge at Mackinaw. But the kitchen held no comfort even though my glinting spell pots and herbs made it mine. It was Ivy's, too, and the thought of her black eyes savage with the need to survive was too fresh.

Spinning, I walked past my room to the sanctuary. The hint of burnt amber coming from my bathroom and the blanket Al had given me—still waiting to be washed—seemed like a veil I had to push through, and I held my breath until I got to the wide space. As I stood at the end of the hall, the whispers of pixies at play seemed to echo from my past, the bright room a pleasant mix of all three of us and the memory of Kisten. There was no comfort here.

I was trapped by everything I cared about. I wanted to be cocooned, safe, but my security had always been the church and those in it. Right now, they were what was knotting my gut.

At a loss, I collapsed on the couch, pulling my knees to my chest and trying to find something to ease the ache. Sniffing back a tear of frustration, I thought of Al's kitchen and the hours I'd spent there in front of the smaller hearth, in the quiet with Mr. Fish and my own thoughts to keep me company. There was a peaceful security there, with the world pushed to the edges as I learned something new, gaining satisfaction and a grudging "passable" from the very demon I'd once been terrified of. I still was, but it was an old terror now, like growing up thinking you weren't going to see the next spring.

There was a scuffing at the top of the hall. Forehead on my drawn-up knees, I didn't look.

"Rachel?"

It was Pierce, and my head started to hurt. "Go away," I said. It had been his idea.

"I'm sorry," he said softly, and I lifted my head when he started to walk away.

"Wait," I blurted out, remembering the sorrow in his eyes when he had suggested the curse. He'd used it before. Maybe he knew how to justify it. "Don't go," I whispered.

Slowly he turned. Heartache showed on his pinched brow. For me? I wondered. For his part in helping me lose my innocence? The question of whether I'd use black magic to save those I loved had been answered, and I didn't know how to feel about it.

I watched Pierce's grace as he came back and sat across from me, perched on the edge of the chair with the coffee table between us. Exhaling, he put his elbows on his knees and looked at his hand, burnt and sore. I could smell the garden on him. It mixed with his redwood-witch smell, strong for just having done high magic—*black* magic.

"Is everyone okay?" I asked, guilty for thinking only of myself. "Bis? Jenks's kids?"

Pierce tossed the hair from his eyes. "Three of Jenks's kids were savaged but will mend. Jenks is death on as a strategist."

I put my feet on the floor and heaved to a stand, tired. "I should see if I can help," I said, even as I dreaded going back out there.

Pierce rose with me. "They're fine," he said, taking my fingers with his unburnt hand to give his words more strength. "It's you I'm powerful worried about."

The concern in his eyes caused my eyes to well. Damn it, I wasn't going to cry—even if I'd almost wiped out an entire clan of people. Pierce reached out, and I drew back. I needed something, but not that. I didn't deserve the comfort of another person. And not him. It would be too easy, and it might not be real.

Pierce's hand dropped, his expression becoming even more concerned as he saw my fear. "Talk to me," he said simply.

That . . . I could do, and I looked at him miserably as the band around my chest tightened. He was probably the only person who might understand. "I don't know anything anymore," I whispered. "I almost killed them. Pierce, *what am I doing*? I am exactly what they call me. A black witch. Maybe I should just go with it. Go hide in the ever-after with Al. Leave my friends . . ." The tears started to well again. Leaving was not what I wanted.

Smiling faintly, he sat down, pulling me down with his mere presence. He didn't say a thing as I sat across from him and pulled my knees to my chin, but just that he was listening without judgment was enough to make me cry. I knew Jenks had killed before to protect his family. Ceri was a bloodthirsty savage despite her elegant charm and beauty—and always had been. Ivy was Ivy. I wasn't going to pretend that Pierce wasn't capable of killing someone. It was the thought of me killing someone I couldn't handle.

"I didn't want to be like this," I said softly.

"It was a decision," he said, safe and nonconfrontational.

"A decision to kill someone," I said bitterly. "With magic." That's all the curse did. There was no pretending that it was to heat bathwater or start the grill. It was able to break through an aura to burn someone alive—black magic no matter how you looked at it.

"You saved Jenks and his family," he offered. "Would you rather they be dead?"

I pulled back, not liking what I was feeling. "There had to have been a better way," I said dryly, my gaze going past him to the burnt pool table.

"Perhaps," he said slowly. "I swan I would've killed them straight out to keep Jenks from making a die of it and you safe. I still think allowing them to live is a mistake. It remains to see if you are strong enough to see it through. And how."

"It wasn't a mistake," I said, affronted, and he sighed, burnt hand held loosely in the other as he looked down at them. Okay, maybe it was a mistake, but I'd make it again in a heartbeat. Or maybe find another way to begin with. There just wasn't an answer that I liked, and exhausted in mind and body, I said, "They're right." Pierce's eyes met mine, and I added, "Vivian. Brooke. Everyone. I'm a demon. I deserve what they're trying to do to me." I raised a hand and let it fall, staring at it on my lap and wondering if I could smell burnt amber on it. "I'm filthy."

Pierce only smiled as if I was endearing, making me want to smack him. "You're not," he said, softening my anger. "Surviving the decision of letting such ornery people live will be its own punishment. Don't look to add to it."

"I don't want to be this person," I said, frowning when I heard Ivy come in and go to her bathroom. Getting something for the scratch on her bicep, probably.

"But this is who you are."

"Only because people keep throwing this crap at me!" I said loudly. "If everyone would leave me alone, I wouldn't have to do this stuff!" Ivy's bathroom door creaked again and she moved to her room. *Can't I have one conversation without everyone listening in?*

"The council will come after you now," I said, feeling better for some reason. "They know you've been helping me."

His gaze was in the rafters. "They'd do that anyway. I was never officially shunned because I was coven and it would've been embarrassing.

Shortsighted pig farmers. That I dealt with demons in order to kill them meant nothing. What they think isn't worth a picayune."

Focus blurring, I thought about the very powerful charms, no, curses, that I'd seen him twist, and then the conversation we'd had at Nick's place. How come I couldn't not care about what the coven thought?

"Just exactly why were they so hot to kill you, anyway?" I asked. I had to know. I'd seen what he was capable of, and I had to know what he'd done.

Head bowed, Pierce looked at his hands. "My situation wasn't much of a circumstance," he said sourly. "I held trust with demons to kill them, but you can imagine that didn't mean a hooter to the coven. They were a sight more skerry of demons than they are today."

The coffee table was between us, but my skin was tingling. "That's why Al thought you'd kill me," I said. "Because you kill demons, and I'm a student of one?"

Pierce shook his head. "I wouldn't hurt you, even if you were a demon yourself."

The back door slammed behind Ivy, and I jumped, having forgotten she was in here. "Good," I said, a tad more bitter than I had intended, "because I probably am one."

But Pierce only touched his nose and smiled. "You're feeling better," he asserted.

Yeah, I was. Suddenly nervous, I stood.

"It's not what you are, but who you are," Pierce said, and when he stood as well, I started edging into the hall. "I saw you when you had just tipped the scales to womanhood, and I can tell you that you're much the same in your mind now as you were then."

"And what is that?" I asked from within the dark hallway.

Pierce was silent until he stopped right before me, his face showing an unreadable emotion. "You're firm in will, pure in intent, strong in magic. But now it's tempered with wisdom, and you're more beautiful and brilliant yet." I went to turn away, and he pulled me back. "You are shades of gray swirling, balancing needs and desires," he added, watching me. "You are good, Rachel. No matter what your choices lead you to, you will remain such."

My eyes warmed as my emotions tipped back the other way. Damn it, this was exactly what I needed, but I knew better than to trust fairy tales. "Is it harder to be good when you know too much, or is it that your mistakes make bigger messes?" I asked, miserable.

His hand fell from me. "You're moved by love. That means everything. Take it from one who's lost all and then gained more."

I dropped my head, feeling the weight in my chest start to lift. Exhaling long and slow, I realized I'd found my comfort in his words. Calm took me. Ivy and Jenks. His family. My church. Even Nick. Maybe Trent. They were all important to me. So I lived among savage people with a thin veneer of civility. Who didn't? I knew them. I loved them. I'd fight for their survival, and worry about the rest later.

"You're back," Pierce said softly. "You find your feet so fast, mistress witch. What are you going to do about the fairies?"

A faint embarrassment warmed my cheeks. "I thought we'd just let them go if they promised to leave us alone," I said as I started for the back of the church. I felt different, and I didn't know why. Maybe it was because I hadn't cried on his shoulder, but stood fast to my decisions. Accepted them. If it had been a mistake, then I'd fix it.

Pierce shook his head as he followed almost at my shoulder, and realizing I was proposing we trust a fairy to keep its word, I grimaced. "You're right. Stupid idea. Maybe I could put them in a box and ship them to Borneo."

"You can't send them anywhere," Pierce said. "They're a paltry seven-by-nine warrior without their wings. I opine, I mean, I think it's a slow, starving death they face. Living on one's own hook the way they do."

"I can't do anything right, can I?" We had reached the back living room, and I glanced at the new clock Ivy had put on the mantel, wondering if it had come from Piscary's. *An hour after sunrise, and I'm still alive. How about that?*

"It's not an issue of right or wrong," Pierce said as he reached to open the door. "I like that you create choices where none exist. I'm anxious to see how you make a fist of this, though."

"You're not going to help me, are you?" I asked, and he grinned.

"Sakes' alive, Rachel. Asking me to think is a powerful task."

My eyebrows rose, but I was in a much better mood when the sounds of the garden slipped around me. Taking a deep breath, I stepped out onto the small back porch.

The garden and graveyard beyond it weren't bad. From the vantage point atop the stairs, I could see a wide ring of burnt earth where the curse had begun to take hold at the edges, ribbons of wilting vegetation making random paths, like lightning, to it from where we had sheltered under Pierce's bubble. Imagining everything burnt made me sick. One of my neighbors was outside looking at the damage to his lawn, but he went in when he saw me. Wise choice.

Someone—Ivy, presumably—had turned the picnic table upright, and the fairies had been moved to it. They were in a circle, probably for their protection. A stash of cotton, medical tape, and antiseptic were in there with them. Two of the most able fairies were using their sharp teeth to cut the medical tape since their swords were currently being sported by Jenks's children. I'd always wondered where his kids got fairy steel. Now I knew.

The pixies hovering above them were not being nice. Pierce was right. This was bad. I couldn't ask Jenks to let them stay in the garden under his protection. He'd never forgive me, and it would probably kill the fairies. Death by pride.

Ivy looked up from dabbing an antibiotic cream on her arm as I schlumped down the stairs. Rising, she came over with a bandage, glancing back once at the fairies when Jenks's kids started shouting a vulgar song at them. "You okay?" she asked as she handed me the bandage and I pulled the tape off, fixing it in place over the tiny scratch and surrounding bruise.

"Not really." I crumpled up the tape and shoved it in a pocket. Behind me, Pierce eased over to the table, sitting down and forcing the pixies back with his presence. "How about you?"

She shrugged, and our attention went to Ceri, her back to us and her dress charmingly tied up around her knees as she knelt in the grass and helped three of Jenks's youngest kids prop up a bush that had gotten caught in the vanguard heat trails.

"Sorry for running off like that," I said. "Is Ceri still mad at me?"

Her eyes came back to me, a wide rim of brown around them in the sun. Nodding, she said, "Jenks caught a scout on his way to send word to the coven that the attack failed. Chased him down the block. We've got a small space before they send something else, I imagine, unless they're watching us."

I hope not, I thought, wondering if Vivian had seen it all. "Where's the scout?"

"Funny you should ask." She started back to the table, not answering my question.

Pierce looked up from a conversation with the fairy that Jenks had almost killed in front of me. I wondered what the fairy was saying—his thoughts I'd almost permanently silenced. Not ready to talk to him, I looked to Ceri. Pulling my shoulders up, I reluctantly went to her. The pixies with her scattered at her soft word, and I sighed.

"Don't talk to me," she said curtly as she tended the shrub. "I'm angry with you."

Her hands were busy with the plant, and I knelt beside her, my knees getting damp again. "I'm sorry," I said, thinking it was weird to apologize for not killing someone. "I couldn't do it."

Ceri pressed new dirt around the shrub. Her fair hair swung, but her motions were losing their sharpness. I handed her a twig to prop up a stem, and she snatched it. "Lee told me what the coven was doing," she said unexpectedly. "He said you'd be under siege, so I came to help. I left Trent to do it. Left Quen." She looked up, and I blinked to see tears in her eyes.

"Trent won't let you come back," I said, surprised. Damn it, she had left her secure home and excellent care for her unborn baby to help me, and I'd thrown her help in the dirt.

"I can," she said, her gaze on the dirt under her nails. "But I won't. I failed."

Huh?

Ceri took a deep breath and stood, still graceful despite her pregnancy. "Why do you think I was staying at Trent's estates?" she asked as I stood.

"To be closer to Quen?" I guessed. "Trent's gardens? His hot tub?"

Making a rude noise, she undid the ties, dropping the hem of her dress. "I was spying," she said wryly. "I was trying to keep you safe. It was what I was trained for." Her voice grew airy, almost sarcastic. "Educated by my mother to be married off to a rival family to spy on them and make sure treachery wasn't planned against us. Al used me as such, letting others borrow me on occasion. I was good at it." Her eyes flicked to mine. "At least I thought I was. When I finally find something worth spying for, I fail. I had no idea Trent was tangling you up. Not a hint beforehand, and none even after it happened."

"I'm sorry. I should have tried harder to reach you," I said, and she shook her head.

"You can't get through. Security has been tight since he decided to announce his candidacy for mayor this Friday, but it makes no difference. I failed."

Her head dropped, and I gave her shoulder a squeeze. "Don't worry about it. Trent's a tricky bastard. I'd be willing to bet he didn't tell Quen, even. How were you to know?"

"Oh, they all knew," she said bitterly. "Anything Trent knows, both Quen and Jonathan know. It's like a bloody men's club. Worse than the demons. Rachel, I can't go back."

Was it fear or shame? I couldn't tell. "Trent wouldn't hurt you," I said quickly. "Quen wouldn't let him."

"No," she agreed so confidently that I believed her. "Trent wouldn't hurt me, even if Quen wasn't there." Her gaze went to her swelling middle, and she made a rude face. "But I should have known that you were in trouble. If Trent would let pixies in his gardens, I'd have a hundred eyes and maybe be of some help, but I've nothing. I'm useless."

She sounded forlorn. Reaching out, I gave her a hug. The hint of ozone clinging to her mixed with something wild that might be her child growing within her. "You aren't useless. Ceri, don't be so hard on yourself. Trent is good at this."

The clatter of pixy wings pushed us apart, and Jax darted between us, Jenks's oldest son shedding orange sparkles of discontent. "Ms. Morgan, what do you want to do with the wingless wonders? They're starting to stink."

My brow furrowed as I turned to the picnic table. Giving Ceri a touch on her shoulder, I followed Jax back to Ivy and Pierce . . . and the fairies. Tired from a lack of sleep and the spent adrenaline, I sat beside Pierce. Before us on the old wood under a green-tinted sheet of ever-after were the survivors. Sixteen. That was it. The rest had "accidentally" died at some point between me destroying their wings and now. The scent of hot chitin and burning hair smelled faintly like a lobster boil, and it made me ill.

I could tell the leader from the rest by the bandage around his head where Jenks had struck him. He looked proud, his long pale face stiff with anger. All his teeth were sharp, more savage than a vampire's, and they showed when he talked. His eyes were black and too big for his face. Fairies were a savage race, and without the softening of the wings, they looked like pale grim reapers in their flowing white, almost ragged clothes made from spider silk. All of them without exception had white hair, the men keeping it as long as the few women I could see. The women had smaller teeth and were somewhat shorter, but otherwise, they looked the same.

The leader was staring at us, standing proudly even though he was clearly unbalanced by his missing wings. None of them had shoes, and the belts hanging tight around their waists were empty of their swords and bows. The last of the burnable weapons was going on the fire now, and I watched a young fairy snarl and throw an ichor-soaked wad of cotton at the barrier as presumably her weapons went on the blaze.

Jax hovered beside me, his hands on his hips, looking a lot like his father. "You should have let us kill them," he said, worrying me.

The leader lifted his chin. "You did that when you gave my sword to a pixy brat," he said, his words having a soft lisp and almost lyrical pacing.

Jax rose up, shouting, "You're an animal! Destroying everything in a garden when a little care and precision enriches it. We have to fight you or you'd destroy everything! You leave barren lots and weeds! Locusts. That's what you are. Bugs!"

The fairy looked up, hatred in his black eyes. "I'm not talking to you, maggot."

Pierce waved his hand to get rid of Jax's heavy dusting, and the pixy darted up and down, wings clattering. "Are you the leader?" I asked, not surprised when the fairy nodded.

"I'm not above anyone," he said, "but I made the decision to be here, and others followed. I'm Sidereal."

"Sidereal," I echoed. "I'm Rachel," I said, "but you probably already knew that."

"The name of a lesser soon fades." Sidereal corrected his slow tilt forward, a blush of anger coming over him at his own ineptness in maintaining his balance without his wings.

"I wish you hadn't attacked us," I muttered.

Sidereal began walking in a careful, slow circle. His balance was better when he was moving. "It was a good gamble. If we won, we would survive until the fall migration. If we failed, we wouldn't care." He stopped his pacing, hand against the barrier between us. "Keeping us alive won't give you a bargaining chip with the coven. We're tools to be discarded."

My eyes widened. It had never occurred to me to use them as hostages. "You aren't tools," I said, nervously picking at the table. "And you're not hostages either. I broke the spell because there has to be another way. You're still alive. When there is life, there are choices."

Sidereal turned, almost falling as he overcorrected his balance. "We are the walking dead," he said, huge eyes dark with anger. "Our wings won't grow back. My people are flightless. We can't migrate, and we can't fight. We were going to gain the land we needed or die in glory. Now we have nothing. Less than if we'd kept to our faded land and died as paupers. You've given us a very hard death, demon spawn."

Pierce smacked the table to make everyone jump. "Don't call her that," he threatened, and Sidereal gave him a sour look.

"I was the walking dead once," I said, and Ivy snorted. "I am right now, actually. But I try."

Sidereal turned away. The stumps of his wings were covered, but pale ichor had discolored the gauze. My gut twisted. Pierce was right. Without their wings, they couldn't compete. Death, though hard, would have been a blessing. A blessing I took from them. *Think, Rachel.* "Maybe there's a charm to mend your wings?" I offered.

Head tilted, Sidereal turned. "We still have no land."

"Then maybe you can stay here."

"Filth!" Jax shouted, wings a harsh clatter and sword pointing. "Never. Never!"

Ivy frowned, and Pierce looked worried. "There's got to be a way to fix this," I said.

Sidereal strode forward, having to catch his balance with a hand against the inside of the bubble. "You'd make us live under the protection of pixies?" he snarled, showing his fangs. "You'd make slaves of us?"

"They are backstabbing sneaks!" Jax exclaimed, drawing the attention of the pixies at the fire. "We'll kill them before letting them into our garden!"

"What's the big deal?" I said tightly. "You don't even eat the same things. It's just a matter of agreeing to abide by the rules of courtesy. And it's not your decision, it's your dad's." Sitting straighter, I looked for Jenks. "Jenks?" I called, tired of Jax's adolescent intolerance. It wouldn't be easy to get pixies and fairies to coexist, but they were going to try.

"They will destroy everything!" Jax exclaimed, red faced as hot glitter sifted from him. "You're an ignorant lunker!"

Ceri was smiling with an I-told-you-so expression, her arms crossed to show off her middle, and I frowned. "Jenks!" I shouted, listening for his wings and hearing nothing. My gaze slid to Ivy, alarm trickling through me. "When was the last time you saw Jenks?"

"When he told me of the scout," she said, rising fast.

"Jenks!" I shouted, and even Ceri dropped her arms and looked into the trees.

For five long seconds, we listened for his wings while fear wound tighter through me. Motions rough, I got up from the picnic table, hitting it hard enough to make my leg hurt. Ceri's hushed "Go find your father" to Jenks's kids made my chest tighten.

"If you killed him, I will squish you myself," I threatened Sidereal, and he bared his teeth and hissed at me like a cat.

"Looking forward to it."

Jax was a flash of pixy dust, and he was gone, having flung himself forty feet straight up to do a rough visual.

"Where are you, Jenks?" I muttered, seeing the darting sparkles of his kids making patterns in the bright sun as they searched. There'd be no reason for him to leave unless . . .

My face went cold, and I looked at Ivy. "Matalina," I said breathlessly, and Ivy's face paled. I hadn't seen her since their last stand.

Shit.

Twenty-one

I'll check the church," Ivy said, then took the steps two at a time. She was gone even before the door slammed shut. The fairies watched in satisfaction as the entire feeling in the garden turned to fear. But it wasn't until I saw Rex that my panic almost swallowed me.

The small orange cat was oblivious to the darting shapes, her ears pricked and her movements sure as she paced across the mown grass, let out when Ivy went in. With a little jump, she gained the small stone wall that separated the garden from the graveyard. Focus intent, she vanished into the taller grass.

"Pierce?" I said, glancing from where she'd disappeared. "Watch the fairies, will you?"

Nodding, he stood, face sad and head bowed.

I followed Rex through the wet grass, moving as if in a dream. My tension eased when we passed the ring of burnt ground, and I felt even better when I found Rex sitting at the edge of a small, familiar plot, her tail curled around her feet as she sat in the sun and cleaned a paw.

I knew this grave. The pixies frequently played around it despite—or maybe because—the site being snarled with the thorns of a rose gone wild. The marker itself was decorated with the statue of a childlike angel not much bigger than Rex, the chubby features somehow not destroyed by time. It was a child's grave, and innocence seemed to linger yet.

Creeping forward, I exhaled in relief when I heard Jenks. Until I realized he was singing. Tears filled my eyes and I swallowed a lump when from behind the tombstone came a mournful, stop-and-go duet with heartrending gaps. Only one voice was raised.

Dreading what I might find, I moved forward until I could see the base of the tombstone. Jenks was on the ground, his wings still and drooping as he held Matalina, cradling her, keeping her from touching the earth. Ringing them in the pressed grass were four dead fairies, their wings tattered but unburnt. Jenks's sword was in the nearest, the fairy still holding the blade as it punctured his middle. Arrows littered the ground, and the scent of broken green was strong.

He looked up at me, his voice cracking and his wings lifting slightly. Moisture shined his cheeks, turning to dust as it dried. "Rachel is here, Mattie," he said, turning back to her, and hope jumped. She was alive?

Jenks brushed her hair from her eyes, and the pixy woman took a pain-racked breath. "She can take you back to the stump in three seconds flat. And she can turn you big. Just for an hour. You can do that. Please, Mattie. No more arguments. You'll live then. The spell takes all the pain away. Makes you brand new. Please don't leave me." He was begging now, and I felt tears prick. "I can't be alone for the next twenty years."

It confirmed something I'd been suspecting for the last few months as Jenks grew faster, while Matalina declined. The curse he'd taken last summer had reset his biological clock. Excited, I dropped to my knees beside them. I'd gotten my twenty years back that my childhood illness had stolen, but what caught my breath was that Jenks wasn't going to die. Matalina either.

"Matalina," I said, bending close and making my words soft. "Ceri is here. She can make you well." *They'd live forever, both of them. It was going to be okay. It was going to be okay!* Finally something was going to be okay!

I held out my hand to take her, but Matalina's soft "no" iced through me. *No?* What did she mean, no?

"Rachel, do this for me," Matalina said as Jenks tried to hush her, but a sharp gleam came into her eyes and she put a small, beautiful, and deathly white hand to his mouth. Jenks kissed it, going silent as tears fell on it and he wiped his dust from her. "This is my decision," the woman said, her fervent gaze fixed to mine. "I only ask that you keep Jenks alive through it."

My tears started, and I swallowed hard, grief rising from hope, seeming all the harder for the brief respite. *No? Why?*

"Mattie," Jenks protested, and her bird-bright eyes fixed on his. She was seeing around corners. *Damn it. Not again!*

"I don't want to start over, Jenks. I'm tired. But I'm proud of you, my visionary." Her hand shook as she touched his cheek, leaving a smear of blood. "For you to see the endings of what you've started is right, but I don't want to live beyond my children. I'm a mother first. You're a force, Jenks, and I thank my luck for having bound myself to you."

"You can be a force, too, Mattie," he began, his voice breaking when she shushed him. There was an ugly stain of red seeping from under her, and I knew she had only moments. Still, she smiled, giving him her love to the end.

"No," she said firmly. "I want you to stay when I go. Break tradition again, my love, and burn me alone in the home we built. I don't want you with me. You aren't done. You see too far ahead. You need to make the world in your thoughts a real one that our children can fly in."

"Take the charm, Mattie," Jenks said roughly, "and we'll see the future together."

"I'd rather hear it from you," she whispered, and my throat tightened as the tears slipped down. "I want to watch your eyes light up when you tell me. I'll wait for you under the bluebells. I'll be there always."

"Mattie?" Jenks cried, pulling her closer as he sensed her slipping away. "I don't want to be without you. I need you!"

Matalina's eyes opened wide, but I wasn't sure she was seeing him anymore. "Not as much as you . . . think," she said carefully. "Look what you've done. I'm going to die happy. All my children will survive. What mother can say that on her last breath? Thank you, Jenks. Sing to me? I'm so tired." Her eyes closed as she struggled to take a last breath, not to continue her life, but to breathe her last words. "I love you."

"Please, Mattie!" Jenks cried, desperate. "We can do this together. We can do anything together! Please . . ."

But she was gone, and he was alone though he held his wife, rocking her as he cried.

Twenty-two

I could do nothing, helpless as I looked down on them. *Jenks* . . . My tears hit the ground beside him, and I struggled to do something—anything—but I was useless. I was too *damn big.* "Jenks?" I whispered, my hands corralling him.

He blinked, the green of his eyes going deep into me. "She's not here . . . ," he warbled, as if in shock.

I was too big. I couldn't hug him. I couldn't tell him it was okay by holding him until he found himself. "Ivy!" I shouted, then dropped to my elbows, trying to get closer. Matalina's face was streaked with blood and a silver dust, making her look like a weary angel. "Jenks, I'm sorry," I whispered, my throat too tight for more. *God, I'm so sorry.*

His eyes were wide, and the tears still spilled from him, turning to glittering sparkles as they dried. A smear of blood was on his cheek where Matalina had touched him last. "She went to guard the back door," he said as if dazed. "They must have been holding back," he said, and my chest clenched. "I should have sung her to sleep. She was so tired, and she wanted me to sing." Bewildered, he looked at me, his wings unmoving. "I'm alone," he said as if in wonder. "I promised to stay with her forever. And here I am. Alone. And she's gone."

"You're not alone. Jenks, please," I said, unable to stop the tears from slipping down. Somewhere I'd heard pixies died of heartache when their spouses died. "It's going to be okay. You've got Ivy and me. We're here. We need you. Matalina told you to stay with us."

The clatter of pixy wings came just before Ivy's footfalls. Rex hunched furtively. In a swirl of blood-stained silk, the entire clan dropped to the ground as a great keening rose. Unable to take it, the cat ran away. Ivy stood above us, and as I looked up, her eyes spilled over with tears. I could say nothing, my heart aching for his pain. *Matalina.*

"Oh, Jenks," Ivy breathed as she dropped to kneel. "I'm sorry."

He had turned back to his wife, trying to smile as he brushed her face and arranged her hair. "She's here, but I'm alone," he said as if trying to figure it out. "I don't understand."

The keening lifted and rose, and Ivy's jaw tightened. "You're not alone, pixy. Don't you dare go somewhere to die!"

Face riven, he stared blankly at her. "I am alone," he said simply. Getting up, he found Jax standing miserably, holding Jih as she cried into his shoulder. "Jax, the garden is yours," he said, and the younger pixy jerked. "Keep Rachel alive if you have an ounce of respect for your mother," he finished bitterly. And as Ivy and I stared, Jenks took Matalina and walked into a shadow that hid the back tunnel to their home.

A wailing grew, turning into harmony with no words, heartrending in its beauty. The pixies joined together, rising up with wings turned blue from sadness, the tears sifting from them to make them glow. All but Jax, his feet riveted to the wet earth.

"No! I don't want the garden!" he shouted at the small opening. "I don't want your dreams, old man! I have my own!"

I turned to Ivy, scared. "What does he mean, the garden is Jax's?"

Jax rose up, and I sat back on my heels to keep him in sight. "I'm to find a wife and keep the land," he said. Wings clattering, he flew to the empty tunnel but didn't enter. "I don't want it! You can't make me do this!" he raged into the darkness. "This isn't what's supposed to happen!"

"This is Jenks's land," I said, scared. "He's my backup, not you."

Ivy was crying, the tears slipping down her pale face with a slow misery. "He's gone to ground with her," she said. "He's not going to come out. Ever."

Fear pulled me straight. "What do you mean, ever?"

"He's going to kill himself to stay with her."

"Jenks!" I shouted in a panic, dropping down to put my face beside the hole and seeing for the first time the small black stones that lined the walls to hold back the earth and make the opening look like a shadow. "Jenks, I need you!" I shouted. "Come back!"

There was no answer, and I turned to Jax, shaking inside. "Go in and get him."

Jax bowed his head, his arms over his middle. "I can't," he said, turning away.

He can't, I thought, confused. Heart racing, I stood. The morning was just as beautiful, the trees just as green and the soft sounds of the city coming faintly as humans headed to work. But now it was different. Broken. There had to be a way to fix this. I wouldn't accept this end. Not by a long shot.

As if in a dream, I started back to the church, my shoes getting wet from yesterday's rain.

"Ceri?" I called, jerking to a halt when Pierce stepped from behind his own tombstone.

"Jenks?" he asked, eyes hopeful but his stance weary.

My mouth opened to tell him, and grief hit me, shocking my breath away. "Matalina," I choked out. I couldn't say the words. If I did, I would start to cry again and never stop. It was so awful.

Pierce took my arm to pull me close in comfort, and it didn't matter how brave I wanted to be as my next breath came out in a sob. "She's gone," I managed. "Jenks is going to kill himself to stay with her. I have to get small." Eyes wet, I looked up as Pierce pushed the hair from my eyes. "Do you know the curse for that?" I asked.

"No," he said, gently, the pain in his eyes echoing a loss from his past.

"That's okay," I said, head hurting as I struggled to stop my tears.

"Ceri probably does." Disentangling myself from him, I started back across the graveyard, skin tingling as I passed through the ley line. I could hear Pierce behind me talking with Ivy. Desperation kept me moving forward, and finally I reached the knee-high wall separating the graveyard from the garden—the dead from the living. Miserable, I stepped over it, wondering if the spirits of the dead could watch us by crossing a barrier just that easily. Thoughts of my dad made the tears prick again, and I wiped my eyes with the back of my hand. "Ceri?"

It was obvious by the way she stood with her hands clasped before her middle that she knew what had happened. High above the garden, I could hear Jenks's children filling the world with their grief. Tears glistened in her eyes, and she held out her hands to pull me into a hug when I came close. "You'll miss him dearly," she said, smelling of cinnamon and earth.

Hands going to her shoulders, I pushed us apart. "I need your help," I said, heart breaking. "I need to get small. I have to save Jenks."

With my peripheral sight, I saw Sidereal turn, shushing the fairy woman he was talking to. Ceri's eyes widened, and dropping back a step she asked, "Why?"

Desperation turned to frustration. "Why? He won't come out, and I have to tell him it's going to be okay," I said. "Shrink me down so I can fit in his stump. Can you do it?"

Pierce's voice rose over the distance, telling me that either he was using his magic to listen in, or Ivy was relaying the conversation. "Make me small as well!" he shouted, voice softening as he got closer. "I'm going with her."

I watched Pierce and Ivy step over the wall. *From grave to garden in one movement.* When I turned back, Ceri's eyes were a deep green with tears, but her face was resolute. "Rachel," she said, taking my hand and holding it. "I understand this is hard. For you especially, having lost so many already, but who are you doing this for?"

Doubt hit me, followed quickly by resolve. "What do you mean, who am I doing this for?" I said, imagining his heartache, alone in his stump with Matalina and thinking his life was over. "Jenks kept me alive for two years through two death threats, a crazy banshee, and at least two serial killers. It's about time I return the favor! And if I can't, then I can sit by his bed and hold his hand as he dies, 'cause I've had plenty of practice doing that, too!"

Crap, I was crying again, but Ceri shook her head, eyes downcast. "I understand your frustration, but he's lost, Rachel," she said. "I'm sorry." Her gaze shifted behind me to Ivy and Pierce. "There will be no others like them," she whispered.

"He's not dead yet!" I shouted in sudden anger, born of helplessness. "Matalina wanted him to live on, and you've already got him in the ground, you cold, unfeeling bitch!"

"Rachel!" Ivy exclaimed, and immediately I relented.

"Ceri, I'm sorry," I said with a bad grace. "I didn't mean that. But Jenks is alone." My eyes started to fill again, and I wiped a hand over them. "He shouldn't be."

"I understand," she said stiffly. "It's the grief speaking. You do realize, none of this would have happened if you had killed the fairies."

My jaw clenched, and I turned away. I suppose I deserved it after calling her a bitch. Depressed, I sat, slumped, at the picnic table, as far from the fairies as I could get. This was so wrong. Jenks thought he was alone, and unless I could get in there, he would be. Damn it, he couldn't die. He couldn't! And not alone.

Pierce put a hand on my shoulder, but I didn't look up. My heart was breaking, and I held my breath until my head started to hurt. *Why? Why hadn't I just killed them?* But what kind of monster would I be if I could choose who lived and who died?

Ivy stood with her arms crossed over her middle, her cast awkward and her eyes red. "Ceri, she's right. Whether we can convince Jenks to live or not, one of us should be there with him. His wife just died. Don't let him grieve alone."

"I never said I wouldn't do it," Ceri said tartly, and my head came up. "I just think it's time for Rachel to grow up. Face the facts. Pixies die young. That's why you befriend a family, not an individual."

I spun where I sat to look at her, aghast even as my chest hurt from trying not to cry. "You *are* a coldhearted bitch. You think it's time for me to grow up?" I said as I stood. "Accept everything that happens to me as fact? Jenks is not a *life lesson* to help me grow up. He's my friend, and he's hurting!"

I wasn't thinking clearly, but I didn't care. Jenks thought his life was over, and I couldn't get to him.

"He's a pixy, Rachel," Ceri said, eyes flicking over Ivy, probably calculating the odds that her next words might send the vamp after her. "This is what they do."

Emotions jumbled and numb, I looked over the garden for something, anything, seeing the fairies at the edge of their prison, listening. Jenks had let them live. Something no other pixy had ever done.

"Yeah," I said bluntly, not ready to let him go just yet. "Jenks is a pixy. And pixies die of heartache when their spouses die. But Jenks is more than a pixy. He went into partnership with Ivy and me; no other pixy has done that. He owns property. Has a credit card. Minutes left on his phone. He's probably going to live another twenty years because I reset his biological clock by accident last summer. He showed mercy and let those who attacked his garden live. What happened with Matalina is tragic. It's my fault she's dead. I can't sit here and just let him die as well. I can't."

"People die, Rachel," Ceri said, her cheeks flushing.

"Not if I can help it," I snapped. "And not of a broken heart. If you could, I'd be dead already." I turned away, frustrated. "Please. At least let me be there so he doesn't die alone."

Ivy's breath caught. "I want to go, too," she said suddenly, and I turned to her, shocked. She would take a curse?

"Me as well," Pierce offered.

Ceri's lips pressed as she saw our united front. "Fine," she finally said, and the sudden relief almost collapsed my knees. "I don't agree with this," she added. "You are all only going to hurt Jenks. Pierce, you're familiar with twisting curses. I'll need help to make three quick enough to do some good. You can help."

Pierce's expression was a mix of relief and heartache. "Of course," he said, gesturing for Ceri to accompany him inside. But the elf would have none of his courtesy, and with her head high, she stalked up the stairs and into the house with a loud bang of the screen door.

Ivy exhaled long and slow. Pierce seemed to relax as well, and he touched my arm and smiled. "It's a curse," he said, startling me when he leaned in and gave me a chaste kiss on the cheek, leaving me with the scent of redwood swirling in my brain. His steps confident, he rose up the stairs as well, closing the door behind him without a sound. A moment later, the kitchen window slammed shut, feminine fingers on the sill.

The hint was obvious. Stay out.

Shaking, I sat back down. With a sigh, Ivy slipped in to sit across from me. We exchanged a long look, both of us knowing that Ceri and Pierce had the easy part. It was going to be up to us to find a way to convince Jenks that life was worth living when his reason for living was gone. Deciding what to do with the fairies could wait.

Twenty-three

It was almost noon, and I was still sitting at the picnic table, my upper body slumped against the damp wood and my head down, staring at Jenks's stump. I'd be dead if Brooke knew the fairy attack had failed and decided to come after me twice in one morning, but I didn't care. I was waiting for a sign of life from Jenks's stump, and I wasn't going inside and possibly miss it. Ivy had gone in to find out how much longer it would be, but that had been, like, five minutes ago.

The spring breeze shifted a curl into my eyes, and I brushed it away, staring, still staring, at the stump as my hip ached from hitting the floor too many times, my arm hurt where the fairy dart had found me, and my fingernails stank of burnt amber. At the end of the table, the fairies were moving around, recovering from their wounds and learning how to walk without their wings, still waiting to learn their fate. The garden was almost silent. Not a bird or insect, not a clatter of wing or pixy wail of mourning. It was eerie, and I sat up, feeling my back crack. "Where is everyone?" I whispered, not expecting an answer.

"Scattered," a fairy said, and I looked at Sidereal standing at the edge of the bubble. "When parents die, the young scatter. They die, or find mates and probably die. None return."

"Jenks isn't dead," I said quickly, feeling the hurt to the bone, and he grinned to show me his sharp teeth. Stifling a shudder, I looked back to the stump. *Jenks's kids were going to leave?* "Why leave?" I asked. "The garden isn't going anywhere."

Sidereal shrugged, his wicked grin turning to a grimace of pain when the skin on his back pulled. "It prevents inbreeding. They're only animals. We drift on the currents far above, listening for funeral songs like wolves listen for the ailing elk. The mourning pixies abandon their garden, and new ones won't move in until all evidence of habitation is gone. That's what we do. Wipe the slate clean. And they call us animals."

I was sure they scattered from heartache, not to prevent inbreeding, but I said nothing.

"There isn't even a fight unless another fairy clan claims it, too." Sidereal reached over his shoulder with disjointed arms to fix his clothing, rubbing the stumps of his wings. "That the pixy told his eldest to maintain the garden was unusual. Disgusting, when you think about it."

"It's not disgusting," I said, insulted. "Jenks told Jax to maintain the garden because he thinks I need pixy backup." But Jax was gone again, abandoning his father's dreams to follow his own. It was hard to find fault with him, though.

Sidereal was silent for a moment. "Your magic can make you as small as this?" he said doubtfully, looking down at his white, robelike clothes.

It hurt to talk about Jenks, but I said, "Yes. I made Jenks big once."

The fairy made a dry hiss I was starting to identify as disbelief. "He wouldn't be able to fly that size. The weight would be too much."

"He didn't have wings." I looked at the porch, then back to Jenks's stump. "He didn't need them when he was that big." I was struck by a sudden thought, and my eyes flicked to Sidereal. I could make them big, then small again to give them their wings back.

Then what? I thought. Pat them on the head and tell them to be good? If I gave them their wings back, they'd have a renewed life as well, with no promise that they wouldn't turn around and murder me in my sleep. They had already tried to kill me with that dart. Ivy, too. No, I wasn't going to make them big even for a second.

Sidereal's lips were pulled back in a long-toothed grimace, and his expression was cross. I wondered if he'd had the same thought when he turned away, hissing. "*Schhhhsssss.* The coven is right. You're a black witch. Cursing yourself to save a pixy."

"The coven is a bunch of jealous hacks," I said, not believing it but enjoying hearing the words come out of my mouth. "What's the point of being able to do all this if you don't do anything to help your friends? I'm not hurting anyone but myself by getting small. His wife just died, and he needs someone to hold him. And how can you call them animals when they pine to death when the other one dies?" *Oh God. Jenks, we need you. Don't follow Matalina just yet. She wanted you to live.*

"Your kindness hurts, witch," Sidereal said bitterly, stretching a hand behind him to hold a new pain. "It hurt my people when you saved us from death, and it will hurt the pixy. You are truly a demon."

My face warmed, and I barked, "Who asked you?" I wasn't hurting Jenks, was I? Should I just let him die with Matalina? Was I being selfish? Maybe . . . maybe a pixy loved so deeply that to continue on would be hell?

Sidereal's black eyes squinted at me as my face went cold, but the creak of the back door turned me around. Adrenaline pulsed as Pierce came out. Ivy was behind him, and then Ceri. Anxious, I stood and wiped my hands off on my jeans. "Where's the other one?" I asked, seeing only two potion vials in Pierce's hand. Ivy winced, and I got it. "You aren't going?"

Ivy took a vial from Pierce and handed it to me. "I saw what went into it," she said as she gave me a hug. My eyes closed and I felt the tears prick again. There was worry for me in her touch. "I can't do this," she whispered, sounding ashamed. "You can."

Why wasn't I surprised? "Am I making a mistake?" I asked her, miserable about Matalina, but wanting to keep Jenks alive.

Ivy shook her head. Seeing it, Ceri cleared her throat for my attention. "The curses need to be invoked," she said, and I took the finger stick she was extending.

Invoked with demon blood since they were curses. Numb, I snapped the top off the finger stick with my thumb and pricked it in one smooth motion, practice making it easy. The wind ruffled my hair as I massaged the digit, three drops plopping first into my vial, then Pierce's. The scent of redwood blossomed, but my face went cold in the slight breeze when I thought I smelled a hint of burnt amber. No one else seemed to notice it.

Damn it, how much more proof do I need?

Shaking, I looked at Pierce. His expression was empty, and he downed it with no hesitation. "It tastes like the fall," he said as he ran his tongue around the inside of his mouth.

"Dried leaves," I whispered, remembering Jenks saying the same thing. The fairies at the end of the table were all watching, and I wondered, if I freed them would they go back to the coven and tell them everything they had witnessed? Did I even care?

Gathering my courage, I raised the vial . . . then paused. "Clothes," I blurted out. "I can't walk into Jenks's house naked."

"Jih is bringing them," Ceri said patiently. "For you and Pierce both."

Satisfied, I downed the vial, waiting for Jenks's snide comment about naked witches in his Garden of Eden, but of course it never came. My heart clenched. The dusty taste of the potion seemed to dry my mouth, and I swallowed, tongue running over my teeth to try to get it off. "That's awful," I said as I made a face and tapped a line. All that was left were the magic words. "What's the word to turn back?" I asked.

Ceri shrugged. "The same to invoke it."

I thought back to the size charm for Jenks last summer. *"Non sum qualis eram?"*

The woman's eyes widened, and I had one gasp of air before it was shoved out of me.

Just that fast, it took hold. There was no pain, but I could feel the rush of the ley line spill into me, vibrating every cell until I felt overly full. A sheet of smut-tainted ever-after enveloped me, making my hearing muzzy, but there was a clicking like a trillion abacuses as my cells prepared to shift, turning things on, turning other things off. Then the flow of energy hesitated.

I got another breath in before it was shoved out again. I felt as if I was being squeezed like a tube of toothpaste. Energy flowed out of me as I shrank. My eyes quit working, and I panicked. There was the shattering of something: a hard crack followed by the tinkling of shards. I thought it might be my soul.

With a final pulse echoing in from the line, the curse played itself out. My ears popped and everything sounded off. I opened my eyes to find I was in a black-sheened world of cotton smelling like soap. My shirt. I'd done it. I felt behind me, exhaling when I found no wings.

"I take the smut," I said as I felt the first ping of returning sensation from the ever-after. The rising wave of pain crested, then broke about me to lap a new film of black imbalance over me. I tasted it as I grabbed a fold of shirt and tried to cover myself, thinking the new coating had almost a metallic tang to it. My legs were hairy, as in I-can't-find-my-razor hairy. I wasn't going to look at my armpits, knowing what I'd find. I suddenly realized I'd reset my biological clock yet again. No wonder demons lived forever.

"Nice," I whispered, looking up as I heard the hum of pixy wings and a shaft of light pierced in. It was Jih, looking like an angel as she clambered into my shirt, a haze of blue sparkles about her. A green dress with gold and silver lace was over her arm. Under it was a set of green trousers and a shirt—for Pierce, I was sure. The young pixy woman pushed aside a fold of cloth and stood. She looked to be ten inches shorter than me if we had been human size. Her face was streaked with glitter from her dried tears, and she looked miserable. I knew she was a full adult with a husband and a garden of her own, but she looked ten to me, and my heart went out to her. I wasn't the only one grieving.

"Ms. Rachel," she said, holding out the dress. Her voice sounded exactly the same, which I thought odd. Mine did, too.

"Thanks, Jih," I said, quickly taking the dress and accepting her help putting it on. It crossed over itself in the back and tied in the front to allow for wings. The fabric itself was soft and so light I hardly knew I had it on, making me feel naked anyway. Silver and gold lace decorated it, and apart from my embarrassingly hairy lower legs showing, it fit perfectly. "This is beautiful," I murmured, and Jih managed a sad smile, meeting my eyes for the first time.

"Thank you," she said softly. "I made it last year. It was the first time I'd ever tried making that pattern of lace. It took me all week to convince my mother—"

Her words stopped, and my heart just about broke when she covered her face and started to cry. "Oh, Jih," I said, immediately stumbling over the inside of my shirt to get to her. "I'm so sorry." I gave the young wife a hug and she sobbed all the harder. "We are all going to miss her, but you probably most of all. You knew her your entire life."

Pulling back, she nodded as she wiped her eyes with a small cloth pulled from behind the bandage on her arm. She'd fought beside her parents, another pixy tradition broken.

"D-do you think you can get my papa to live?" she stammered, her eyes bright with unshed glitter as she looked up at me, hope in them for the first time.

"Do you think I should?" I asked, wondering if me messing with pixy culture was the right thing to do. It seemed every time I tried to change things for the better, I messed them up.

Jih's tears slowed. "I don't know," she said wistfully. "I never thought about having just a mother or a father. They were always one thing."

She looked up as both the sky and the light were eclipsed. "Excuse me," she said, gathering up Pierce's clothes and darting away. My hair flew everywhere from her backwind, and alarm filled me as my footing became unstable when Ivy carefully pressed the shirt down, exposing me to the world. Pierce hadn't shifted yet, and he blinked at me in bemusement. I wondered if I looked like a woman from his time, making me feel even more awkward.

"Rachel?" Ivy's voice boomed out, and I cowered, hands over my ears.

"Not so loud!" I shouted, and she drew back, uncertainty in her big, fat face. How she looked enormous and the sun and clouds looked the same was beyond me.

"I can't hear her," Ivy said to Ceri. "She just squeaks."

"Well, I can hear you!" I shouted. Feeling exposed, I awkwardly climbed over my shirt to the ground. My feet were bare, and the earth was squishy. Sure, the dress made me feel like a princess, but it was a pain in the ass. I sure hoped there weren't any rats round. I'd be doing the classic stupid-girl fall if I had to run.

"I couldn't duplicate the pixy magic that amplifies voices," Ceri said, and I jumped when Ivy put her face right next to mine.

"Wow, Rachel," she whispered, sending her orange-juice-scented breath all over me. "You look like a Bite-Me-Betty doll in a prom dress."

Slumping, I sighed. I couldn't help but wonder if this feeling of being small was why Jenks was so bad tempered. I was never going to get in his face again. Damn it, I had to get in there. He was alone, grieving for his wife.

A series of clicks drew my attention up, and I blanched at the row of savage faces staring down at me from the top of the picnic table. Holy crap. And I thought they were scary when they were six inches tall. Now they were downright terrifying. Sidereal had his arms crossed, his expression unreadable as a bandaged woman stood on tiptoe and spoke in his ear, her white hair all glittery and her legs showing. She dropped back down to her heels, touching her hair as she looked at mine, making me self-conscious about my red hair color.

Above me, Pierce took a breath as I felt him tap a line, but he jerked when Ivy grabbed his arm with a white-knuckled strength. "Keep her safe," she threatened.

"Ivy!" I shouted, or squeaked, rather, and Ivy's brow furrowed. Jih flitted a nervous arc between him and Ceri, Pierce's clothes still in her arms.

"No, I'll allow that's fair," Pierce said, his gaze flicking to me and then back to Ivy's grip on him. "I'm by no means the biggest toad in the puddle when it comes to magic, but Rachel will be safe. See that you do your part in keeping the garden safe." He touched her hand, and she jerked away at the pulse of green-tinted ever-after. "The coven will assume failure shortly, and I don't want to be burned alive from a fireball shot from a passing carriage." Frowning, he took a step back as Ivy rubbed her hand. "*Non sum qualis eram.*"

A film of black ever-after coated him. His eyes widened, and then he was gone, his clothes collapsing in a pile. My hair shifted as they hit the ground beside me, and my pulse hammered. He had taken the smut on himself. I knew without asking. I owed him, but he was probably not going to see it that way.

Jih hovered over Pierce's old clothes, calling out before she dropped his new ones from about a foot up. The young woman was flustered when she flew back to me, her hands going out to my hair almost before she landed. "Let me fix it," she said. "Quick, before he gets here."

"It's fine, Jih," I complained, but she tsk-tsked me, slapping my reaching hands when they got too close to her work.

"It's awful," she pronounced, making me feel like a Neanderthal next to her lithe grace. "But it won't be if you would be quiet and let me do this."

Chafing at the wait, I held still while Ceri and Ivy peered down at Pierce's clothes and waited for him to emerge. Jih quickly braided my hair into a complicated knot that would at least keep it from getting into my face with all the wind from pixy wings and shrinking men. "Now you look better," the pixy said, her grief abating slightly in the task of caring for another.

"Thank you," I whispered, feeling like a princess as she stood beside me while Pierce made his way to us, testing his hand and marveling that the burn was gone. His beard was back, and he looked like an older version of one of Jenks's kids, the one with dark hair, dressed in the traditional tight trousers and gardening jacket. The jacket was loose since it tied in the back as well as the front, and he couldn't manage it alone. It was the same fabric as my dress, but clearly masculine. His feet were bare, and they looked kind of thin. He even had a hat, perched rakishly on his head.

"Rachel," he said as soon as he was close enough, his worry obvious. "Are you well?"

"I'm fine," I said, wishing we could just get moving, then frowned at Ivy and Ceri who were whispering about how cute we looked. "I thought you might sound like Mickey Mouse," I said as he came to a halt beside me.

"Who?" he asked, rubbing his new beard.

"Never mind," I said, gesturing for him to turn around so I could lace his jacket up.

His neck went stiff, but he turned to show me the undone laces. Jih made an embarrassed sound as I tightened them, and I wondered if I was breaking a pixy rule by lacing up an unmarried man's shirt. Rolling my eyes at her fluster, I tugged the last one tight and tied it off. "There you go," I said, and Jih's wings blurred to invisibility to make a silver dusting.

The light was suddenly eclipsed, and I jumped, startled when Ceri bent down to us.

"Jumpy little thing, isn't she?" Jih said, and Pierce smiled slightly, startled as well.

Ceri patiently waited until we were all looking at her. "Jih will escort you to the stump and give you a good dusting," she said, looking at us in turn. "I hope you know what you're doing." She stood, and skirts shifting, she walked to the stairs and went inside, the door slamming behind her in rebuke. I looked at Pierce, doubt rising. I wanted this, Ivy wanted this, but more important, Matalina had wanted this.

"After you, madam pixy," Pierce said, and Jih darted off, gone in an instant.

"Jih!" Ivy shouted, and Pierce and I cowered. "Sorry," she whispered as Jih returned.

"I wasn't going to leave them," she said, hands on her hips as she hovered over us. "I was just making sure it was safe for ground travel."

"Where's Rex?" I asked, fear stabbing through me.

"Inside." Jih moved forward and then back. "This way. Mind the glass."

Glass? I thought, cold, miserable, and worried about Jenks.

Ivy sat at the table beside the fairies, clearly going to stay out here when I was in the wilds. Giving her a wave she couldn't see, I followed Jih. Pierce had one of the fairy swords on his hip, and as the grass closed in, I asked him, "You know how to use that?"

"Absolutely not," he said, "but isn't it a caution? Dash-it-all fine Arkansas toothpick."

My eyebrows rose. "Oka-a-a-ay."

We soon found the glass—the remnants of my potion vial, I guess—and we wove through the thick shards carefully, following Jih's gold-dusted path. Every birdcall made my heart race. Every gust of wind in the leaves brought my eyes up, scanning. The grass we walked through had been cut, but it came up to my waist, growing in clumps. A skittering jerked me to a stop.

"Holy crap!" I exclaimed, and Pierce brandished his sword at a hard-plated bug the comparative size of an armadillo. Its antenna waved at us, and I froze, wondering if I could kick it or if it would chew my foot off.

Jih, who was flying a nice safe four inches off the ground, looked down. "It's a roly-poly bug," she explained, her tone saying I was a baby.

"I've never seen one the size of my head before," I muttered.

She dropped lower to give it a kick and it vanished. "It's safer when you can fly," she said lightly. "I was grounded an entire month when I snapped the main vein in my right lower wing. I hated it. Never went outside the entire time."

No wonder nothing fazed Jenks. Just walking around took guts.

Jih stopped short, her face pale as her wings dusted a melancholy blue. I pushed past her, halting when I found we were at Jenks's stump. The grass ended, giving way to a flat sheet of earth that I remember spanning only a foot or so, but now looked enormous. It was littered with the remnants of battle. The fire where the fairies' weapons had been burned was almost out. The air was clean, but memory put the scent of blood and burnt hair drifting through the clearing. It was quiet. Empty.

Pierce edged even with me, and together we looked at the understated entrance to Jenks's home. It was almost invisible, cut to look like a part of the stump itself. "It's round," he said softly. "I've not seen a round door before."

"Maybe it's for the wings?" I guessed, glancing up at Jih. "Thank you, Jih. Do you want to come in with us?"

Jih's feet touched the earth beside me, head bowed to hide her tears. "I'll not go any farther," she said, her voice a whisper. "My husband thinks it was wrong for me to have even joined the battle, seeing as it's not truly my garden anymore. But I didn't see any harm if I 'visited' my sisters while he was at home making sure no one took our own land."

"You are your father's daughter as much as your mother's," I said, touching her arm and making her look up. "Always bending the rules."

She smiled forlornly, causing her to look beautiful, dashed the glitter from her face, and looked at her first home with a faint smile. "I think I'd like my papa back if he was happy."

I nodded, feeling for the first time that I might be doing some good. "I'll try."

She rose up with a soft hum, shifting a dust of sparkles over us. Pierce sneezed, and I held my breath. "Now you'll smell right," she said, and with no more, she flew away. The sound of her wings faded remarkably fast.

Pierce smacked his clothes to get the dust off. "Don't you want to smell right?" I asked him, and he raised his eyebrows.

"It's a right smart amount she put down," he said. "Why do we have to smell anyway?"

I didn't know. I really didn't care. Melancholy, I looked out over the distance, feeling the breeze, tasting it almost. It was too quiet for my garden, so long holding the singing or giggling of pixies by sun or starlight. They were either gone or hiding. Pierce gave a small start as I slipped my fingers into his. So I needed his moral support. Eyes forward, I stepped out, feet silent in the manicured dirt as I crossed the opening and watched the door get bigger. My pace didn't falter until I reached it.

My knees went wobbly as I stared at it. Jenks was behind it, mourning his wife. Of all the demons I'd faced, of all the wicked witches, wild Weres, and evil elves, this was the most daunting thing I'd ever done. Jenks's life was on the line. I couldn't fail.

"Should we knock?" Pierce asked as we looked at it.

"Absolutely." Gathering my courage, I knocked, knowing by the flat sound that it wouldn't carry into the stump any distance. Pierce cleared his throat and pulled himself straight, as if we were calling on neighbors, and after a moment, he glanced at me.

"Can you tap a line?" he asked, his blue eyes showing a hint of trepidation. "I'm a mite skerry to try. I'm of a mind it might explode in me, being so small."

"I've been connected since we did the spell. It's okay."

"Oh." He hesitated, and I felt a tingle between us. "I think we should just go in," he said, his eyes on the wooden door.

Nodding, I pushed the door open.

Twenty-four

Jenks's front door opened to a black tunnel slightly larger than the door itself. We had to step down to enter, and the unusually deep drop jarred all the way up my spine. It was dark but for the light coming in behind us, and there was no echo. The air smelled of ginger, and my clenched jaw eased. There was a tweak on my awareness, and a soft glow grew at Pierce's feet. It was that mundane ley-line light charm he knew, and I gingerly picked it up, able to handle the globe where Pierce couldn't. If he tried, his aura would probably break the charm. The ball of ever-after was cool to the touch, and slippery, as if it was going to ooze right through my fingers.

Pierce took his hat off and shut the door behind us. Wonder crossed him, and I followed his gaze to the ceiling and walls. Pixy dust coated everything, catching the light and throwing it back to make it brighter yet. Grooves had been carved to collect the pixy dust, and they glowed the brightest to show fantastic patterns of swirls and spirals. It was singularly beautiful, and I wondered that it had all been made in less than two years. Jenks's family was amazing.

"Jenks?" I called softly, remembering we hadn't been invited in.

Pierce's hand landed on my shoulder, heavy with warning. "Wait."

I turned in protest, only to watch as a green-tinted bubble of ever-after snapped into existence around us. "Holy crap!" I shouted, pressing into him when a wasp as big as my entire upper body landed on the circle, stinger probing the bubble for a way in. "What in hell is that!"

Pierce put an arm around me so I wouldn't hit his circle. "That's a rip-roaring fine guard dog, that's what that is," he said, and the scent of redwood hit me hard. "I don't think we would smell right even if we swam in pixy dust," Pierce muttered, and I silently agreed, thinking Pierce smelled fine just the way he was.

I wasn't afraid of wasps, but the thing was the size of a goose, crawling over the bubble with its wings at an angry tilt. "I'm going to fry it on the count of three," I said, thinking that enough raw ever-after energy ought to stun it at least. Why I didn't balk at killing a wasp was simple—wasps weren't intelligent. "One, two, three!"

The bubble dropped, and I pulled on the line, throwing a ball of smutty gold at the insect. Fear gave it more force than usual, and my eyes widened as the energy swarmed over it and the wasp curled up and fell at our feet. Pierce grunted his approval, and I breathed a sigh of relief seeing it on the floor where Pierce could simply stab it . . . and then it exploded.

Shrieking, I ducked as hot splatters hit the walls to make an ugly sound. An awful stench rolled over us, and I straightened, horrified. Pierce's ball of light rolled until it found the wall and stopped. Embarrassed, I turned to Pierce only to laugh. He was standing ramrod straight with splatters of wasp on his beard and chest.

"Pierce, I'm so sorry!" I said, reaching to wipe it away, his lips pressed tight.

"You have no control," he said stiffly, clearly peeved. "None at all."

Sobering, I looked for something to clean it off him, having to settle for the hem of my beautiful borrowed dress. Gathering it up, I wiped his face, jumping when Pierce flung his hand out behind me. Twin flairs of light burst into existence, the shadows shifting as the light fell. Turning, I saw two more wasps curled up on the floor, one moving until Pierce pushed past me and stabbed its head with his "Arkansas toothpick." Bug goo squished out, and I cringed.

I watched the ceiling as I went to pick up his light. "Do you think there are more?"

Pierce came close. His eyes held concern as he looked me over, using his thumb to wipe a stray bit of goo off my cheekbone. "I've heard that wasp larvae were raised as sentries," he said, "but I never thought I'd see it up close and personal like. I suggest we move deeper."

"Yeah, but do you think there are more?" I insisted.

Pierce said nothing as he put a hand on my shoulder and guided me past the fallen insects. He wasn't worried, but I kept looking over my shoulder as we went down the gentle incline. The glow from the walls grew brighter, and I wasn't surprised when the confines of the hall opened up to a large open space the size of say, the sanctuary at the basilica.

"Well if that doesn't cap the climax," Pierce breathed, and I held his light high when it doubled in intensity. Even then, the glow barely touched the distant walls. It looked like we were half underground, half in the stump, with black stones the size of my hand embedded in the earth to hold it back. At the center of the room was the glow of a banked fire. Under our bare feet was the feeling of plastic, and I looked to find it was poker chips, arranged in a pleasant pattern of colors. "Jenks?" I whispered, hearing only my voice echo back.

"I'll tend the fire. See if you can find a door," Pierce said, and I gingerly headed toward the wall, Pierce's light held high. Slowly the light from the fire grew as Pierce built it up using wood from a rabbit Pez dispenser.

Evidence of tasks dropped and left undone were everywhere—life interrupted. Bits and pieces of stuff belonging to both Ivy and me were among the organized clutter, surprising me at first, then irritating me. In one corner was a small calculator I thought I had lost, the slate and chalk arrangement beside it making me think it was an impromptu schoolroom. The ticking was the watch I'd misplaced last year, the band being used for who knew what since it was being held up now with a bit of lace I recognized as being from Ivy's black panties. Not that I paid attention to that sort of thing, but I did fold clothes occasionally.

Closer to the fire, the poker-chip floor was covered with a soft gray fur.

Mouse, I decided by its softness under my bare feet. A barrette that I'd lost behind my dresser and never bothered to retrieve was being used to hold a magnetic calendar with WERE INSURANCE on it. Postage stamps decorated the walls at odd heights. Some of them had frames built of garden materials. Pictures, I decided, seeing that most of them were of outside shots.

I paused when I got to a huge glittering figure eight on the wall. Reaching up, I touched the bottom loop to decide it was made of fish scales. Maybe they were from the wishing fish Jenks and his family had accidentally eaten. It looked important, stretching up almost four times as tall as I stood. As I watched, a dot of sun shining down from a hidden upper window slowly slid onto the scales to make them glitter brilliantly.

"Noon," Pierce said from the fire pit, and I looked to my borrowed watch, seeing it said 12:35, not noon. But then I realized that it wasn't our noon, but the real noon of when the sun reached its apex. The figure eight was a clock to show seasons, not hours. It was something a pixy would have to be very sure of so as not to get caught unaware by the cold. "Cool," I said breathlessly, following the shaft of light up to a small patch of sunshine high above our heads.

"Do you see a door?" Pierce asked, satisfied with the state of the fire and joining me.

"I think they're all up there," I said, pointing to shafts opening up about two pixy lengths over my head. Pierce sighed, and I looked around for something to stand on. There was an arrangement of cushions and chairs in a lowered pit, which was no help. But between it and the now-cheerful fire was a long table made of popsicle sticks, stained red and dovetailed together to make it longer. Maybe we could prop it up against the wall, like a ramp.

I was just about to suggest it when a scuffing from the ceiling jerked our attention upward. *Wasps?* I thought in fear.

"Jenks?" Pierce called out, and I tensed when a harsh clatter of wings came and went.

"Who's here? Jax, is that you?" said a slurred voice from the high patch of sun. "'Bout time you showed up. I gotta tell you about the water rights with the clan next t-t-to ours."

"It's me, Jenks!" I called out, thinking it was one of the dumbest things I'd said in a while, but I was so relieved to know he was alive I didn't care.

"Rache?" The shadow between us and the light staggered, then fell backward. There was a crash followed by a weak "Ow."

I looked at Pierce, then the upper patch of light. "There's a room up there," I said. Another brilliant observation. "How are we going to get up there?"

"Stairs," Pierce said, pointing, and I realized that there was indeed a thin excuse for a stair, without so much as a hint of a banister, snaking upward in a wide spiral running along the outside wall of the main room.

"Who, by Tink's little red thong, put the floor up here?" drifted down.

Oh God. He was drunk. I gathered up my skirts and dropped Pierce's light into them, anxious about what I might find. The higher I went, the brighter it got. The air, too, felt different. Moister. I wondered why there were stairs at all, seeing that pixies could fly.

Finally I reached the top, blinking in the strong sun. Jenks was flat on his back beside a fallen wire-and-cushion chair. Dropping my skirts and Pierce's light, I went to him.

Pierce came up behind me in a soft padding of bare feet. "I swan, this is the most beautiful room I've ever seen," he said as I knelt beside Jenks.

The bottoms of six glass pop bottles were wedged into the earth wall to let the sun in, but the ceiling was actually the stump. The long, curving room was moist, and the soothing sound of water dripping came from somewhere. Moss grew on the floor with tiny white flowers growing from it. Even the benches under the windows were covered in green, making soft hummocks. A small table made from a big button and plastic-coated paper clips stood before an empty fireplace that looked like the bottom of a throat-lozenge box. The chairs were of wire and cushions, and I recognized them as looking almost exactly like the tables and chairs from the island resort at Mackinac Island. The top of a saltshaker was in a corner half full of dirt, and infant seedlings grew close to the windows. Manicured grass rose tall at the back to hide the wall.

No wonder Jenks is here, I thought as I pulled on his arm to get him up. Matalina's grace was everywhere.

Jenks finally focused on me as I got him upright, his wings bent behind him as he sat on the floor. Not a glimmer of glitter was on him anywhere, and he was still stained from the battle. "The Turn take it, Rache," he said, pushing my hands off him as he sat propped against a hummock. His wing was caught under him, and he shifted a tall vial of honey to his other hand to reach back to free it with a tug. "Can't you just let me die in peace? Matalina died in peace."

Pierce sighed. "He's corned!" the witch said, and I looked at him, annoyed.

"Of course he's drunk," I said sharply, trying to get the vial of honey away from Jenks. "He just lost his wife." Oh God. Matalina was really gone, and my heart ached for Jenks.

Jenks wouldn't let go of the vial, and I gave up. With a huff, he tilted it up, and a slow avalanche of honey fell into him. "I'd have to be drunk to imagine you're in my s-stump," he stammered after swallowing. "Wearing Jih's dress. And a little furry man with you." Squinting, he looked closer. "Pierce! Son of Tink. What are you doing in my nightmare?"

Wings humming, Jenks started to collapse.

"Look out, Rachel!" Pierce exclaimed, lunging forward to catch him about an instant too late. With a whoosh of air, he landed on me, pinning me to the floor.

"Holy crap, Jenks," I said as I wiggled out from between the two men and tripped on Jih's dress as I found my feet. "You're heavy."

"Watch the wings!" Jenks slurred. "Fairy farts, I don't feel so good."

Shaken, I watched Pierce help him to a bench and drape a rough-silk blanket over his shoulders. Crouching, the witch forced the pixy to look at him. "How long have you been like this, old man?" he asked.

Jenks's bloodshot green eyes focused from under his curly, smoke-stained bangs. "Forever." He raised his glass in salute and drank some more. I didn't like seeing him like this, but being drunk was probably why he was still alive. With a surge of recognition, I realized his pointy-bottomed glass as a solstice lightbulb with the wires removed.

Concern and empathy were heavy on Pierce as he stood and looked down at Jenks. "Time to sober up, pixy buck. Rachel wants to talk to you."

"I'm not a buck, I'm a schmuck," Jenks slurred. "Mattie. Oh, my Mattie." His head bowed, and a faint dust slipped from his eyes. "She's dead, Rache," he said, and my heart broke again. "She's dead, and I'm not," he lamented as I knelt and gave him a hug, my own tears starting. "That's not right," he slurred. "I should be dead, too. I'm dead inside."

"You're not," I said, holding him tight. *It was worth it. All the smut was worth it.* "She wanted you to live. Jenks, please. I know you love her, but she wanted you to live."

"I've got nothing." Red-rimmed eyes met mine when he leaned back. "You don't understand. Everything I did, I did for her. Everything." His head drooped, and he was silent. His fingers opened, and the vial of honey hit the floor. Pierce plucked it up before the honey could spill, and set it aside. Just that fast, Jenks was asleep.

"Do you want to take him out now?" Pierce said. "Ceri twisted a curse to turn him big so you could keep an eye on him."

Jenks took a slow breath, his honey-stupor sleep giving him a respite. Slowly I stood and looked down at him. "No. He'd never forgive me. Let's let him sleep it off."

"Mattie," Jenks mumbled. "Don't leave me. Please . . ."

I eased Jenks down onto the moss-covered bench, chest heavy as I went to the table before the fire and sat where Matalina must have sat a thousand times before. I put an elbow on the table and dropped my head into my hand. Saying nothing, Pierce crouched at the fire.

I felt awful. Jenks would be awake again in five minutes, tops. This time he'd be sober. "Am I making a mistake?" I whispered.

Pierce looked up, his gaze on the fire poker as he tried to figure out what it was. I couldn't place the thin piece of hard plastic either, but I was sure I'd seen it before. "I don't know," he said simply. "It's a sin to end one's life, but judging Jenks by human or witch morality isn't fair."

"He loved her so much," I said. "But he's got his entire life. He might learn to love again. Maybe pixies marry for life because their lives are too short for second chances."

Pierce rocked to the toes of his feet, still crouched before the fire. "Ask him what he wants." His blue eyes flicked to Jenks, now snoring. "When he's sober," he added.

I looked at the slant of the sun, wondering how this day would end. "Am I being selfish?"

Not answering, Pierce went to the miniature carved statues of insects on the mantel. "These are beautiful," he murmured. Even wearing a pixy buck's trousers, long-sleeved shirt, gardening jacket, and hat, he didn't look anything like a pixy. Not only was his hair not right, but he was too muscular. Feeling my eyes on him, he turned, his expression making my heart jump.

"Where do you suppose Matalina is?" I asked softly.

From behind us came Jenks's dead-sounding voice. "She's in our bedroom, pretending to be asleep."

Warmth flooded my face, and I spun to see Jenks's eyes open, watching us. "I'm sorry," I said, realizing he was sober already. "I didn't know you were awake. Jenks, are you okay?" Yes, it was dumb, but I didn't know what else to say.

Jenks sat up, elbows on his knees and his head bowed as he held it. "My head hurts," he said softly. "You shouldn't have taken smut to help me. I'm already dead. My heart knows it, but my body won't listen."

Feeling awkward in my borrowed dress, I went to sit beside him. The sun was warm on my back as it came in through a circle of thick glass, but I felt cold inside. "What's another layer of smut?" I said, believing it. "Jenks, I'm sorry if it sounds trite, but it's going to be okay. It just takes time. Hundreds of people in Cincinnati lose the person they love every day. I survived losing Kisten. I—"

"Shut the hell up!" he shouted, and I drew my hand back. "It's not going to be okay. You don't understand. Everything I was *ended with her*. I loved her."

My face warmed, and I couldn't stop myself. "I don't understand?" I said, my fear that he was going to die coming out as anger. "I don't understand?" I stood, heart pounding. "How dare you tell me I don't understand!"

Pierce's eyes were wide. He clearly thought yelling at Jenks wasn't the best way to convince him to live, but I wasn't going to let Jenks fall into the poor-me syndrome and die.

"You saw me suffer after Kisten died," I said, and his dust-wet, red-rimmed eyes went wide. "You yourself told me I was going to be okay and that I'd love someone again. I lost my dad when I was ten. I watched him die like you watched Matalina. I held his hand and promised him I'd be okay. My mother told me it was going to be all right, and one day it was. Don't sit there and tell me that because you've got wings and cry sparkles your pain is more than mine. It hurts. It hurts like hell. And it's going to be okay! Don't you dare give up because it's hard," I said, vision swimming. "Don't you dare, Jenks."

Tears falling, I turned away. "I need you too much," I added, shaking Pierce's hand off my shoulder. Damn it, I hadn't wanted to cry in front of him—in front of either of them.

"I'm sorry," I said miserably. "I can't tell you how sorry I am about Matalina. You were beautiful together." I was still staring at the wall, seeing it swim. Taking a deep breath, I wiped my eyes. "Matalina is gone, but you're not. She wanted you to live, and I need you. It's selfish, but I do. You've done too much to give up and not see how it ends. You said last year that you were angry because you were going to die and Ivy and I were going to continue on." I turned, and the grief in his eyes made a flash of guilt rise in me. "Life's a bitch, Jenks. But if you don't live out what's given to you, what's the point?"

"I didn't know it was going to hurt this much," Jenks said, eyes going almost panicked. "She told me to live, but there's no reason to. She was why I did everything!"

He was only eighteen. How could I help him find a way to understand?

Pierce's voice eased into the moss-smelling air as if it belonged, shocking me. "Living on is not betraying her," he said, standing alone by the empty fireplace at the far end of the room.

"It is!" Jenks stood, catching his balance with a hum of wings. "How can I feel anything when she is not here with me? She said to live, but why? It doesn't mean anything!"

With the patience of hard-won wisdom, Pierce raised his eyes. "It will."

"How do you know?" Jenks said bitterly. "You've never done anything, dead in the ground for a hundred years."

Face placid, Pierce said, "I have loved. I have lost everything because death came early. I've seen it from your view. I've lived it from Matalina's. She wants you to live. To love. To be happy. That's what she wants. I can promise you that."

"You . . . ," Jenks started vehemently, then hesitated. "You have," he whispered.

Pierce set the figure of a mantis back on the mantel. "I loved a woman with all my soul. And I left her though I strove not to. She lived on, found love, married, had children who are old today, but I saw her face in their pictures, and I smiled."

I sniffed, thinking my coming here was a travesty. I was trying to help Jenks live when Pierce had lived more than both of us put together. Not in years, but in experience.

Seeming to start to understand, Jenks collapsed back onto the hummock of moss. "When does it stop hurting?" he asked, hand around his middle.

I lifted a shoulder and let it fall. All of us were damaged, but it made us stronger, maybe. Maybe it just made us more fragile.

"The mind numbs," Pierce said. "The memories blur. Others take their place. A long time. Maybe never."

"I will *never* forget Matalina," Jenks vowed. "No matter how long I live."

"But you will live." Pierce faced us squarely. "Others need you. You know it. Otherwise, why tell Jax to take the land? That's not pixy tradition. It's against everything you know. Why do that if you don't feel a responsibility for something else?"

Jenks blinked fast as he thought about that, and Pierce stood beside me. "You've reached past your limits, pixy," he said. "Now you have to live up to your ideas. You have to *live* up to them."

A light silver dust was sifting from Jenks as he silently cried. "I'll never hear her again," he said softly. "I'll never know her thoughts on a sunset or her opinion of a seed. How will I know if it will grow? She was always right. Always." Misery in his face, he looked up. Relief spilled into me. He wanted to live. He just didn't know how.

Pierce handed him his glass of honey. "You'll know. Come with me on the first full moon of spring. We will tour the cemeteries. I need to find my sweetheart. I need to put flowers on her grave and thank her for going on without me."

My chest seemed heavy, and my throat was tight. I couldn't help but wonder, though, if Pierce had been measuring me against his eighteenth-century love. That was something I could never be. I didn't know if I even wanted to be with a man who wanted a woman like that.

"I will," Jenks said seriously, not drinking the honey. "And you will sing with me about Matalina."

Hope mixed with melancholy, and I crossed the room to give him a hug. "Are you ready to go?" I asked him. Matalina wanted him to burn their home.

Jenks's eyes flicked down to the glass in his hand. "Not yet."

I took the solstice light out of his hand. "I missed you, Jenks," I said, giving him a hug and shocking myself when I found wings back there. "Just for that breath of time I thought you were gone. Don't do that to me again."

He took a breath, then another. It came ragged, full of his emotion. "I miss her so much," he said, and suddenly he was holding me tight as he cried angry sobs into my hair. "I miss her so damn much."

So I held him, my own tears falling anew as we gave comfort to each other. It had been worth it. All the blackness on my soul was worth this. And no one would convince me that this was damning. It couldn't be.

Twenty-five

There was a hollow place in my middle that wasn't from not having eaten all day. The sun was nearing the horizon, and the leaves that hadn't been burned were stark against the blue and pink of sunset. Almost like an oil, the scent of ash coated me. The heat from Jenks's stump burning was a gentle warmth this close to the ground instead of the expected inferno.

To one side of me, Pierce stood, his hands clasped before him with a white-knuckled strength, his expression pained from a memory he wouldn't share. Sunset would be here soon, and he'd ignored all my suggestions to leave. He claimed Al would leave him alone as long as he was "protecting" me. I didn't need protecting. Okay, maybe I did.

One of Jenks's returning children had given Pierce a heavier coat, garden stained and looking like it hadn't been washed since last fall. It went all the way to the ground, and Pierce looked odd with his dirty bare feet peeping out from under it.

Jenks was a tortured presence at my other side as his home burned with Matalina inside it. Tears glittered into dust as they fell from him, a pure silver that gave him an unreal glow, almost as if he were a ghost. Each breath was pained, rising from deep within him, hurting.

His children were in the garden, silent. All but Jax had returned, their grief tempered with the unknown. Never had a pixy tried to live past his or her spouse, and though happy they were together, there was no understanding of what came next—joyful that their father was alive, yet mourning their mother. They were confused, not understanding how they could be both.

The flames took on rims of blue and green as the rooms laden with pixy dust caught, a funnel of heat making the flame swirl into a spire, as if reaching for the heavens. Jenks's fingers brushed mine and took them. Fire cleansed, but nothing could stop the heartache.

"Tears could not be equal, if I wept diamonds from the skies," Jenks whispered, empty and bereft. "My word silent, though I should howl. Muffled by death, my wings can't lift me high enough to find you. I feel you within. Unaware of my pain. Not knowing why I mourn."

He lifted his eyes to mine, a glimmer of tears showing. "And why I breathe alone."

I shifted my bare feet, cold on the earth. I wasn't a poet. I had no words. Tears blurred my sight as we stood and watched his life burn.

Today had been harder than anything I'd ever endured, watching Jenks's children come home, one by one, each not knowing why they were drawn back or how to react. I could imagine what usually happened to the lonely souls that were cast into the world, hurting and alone. Watching them realize that they had one another to share their grief with was both painful and a joy. Jenks was the binding force, the gravity that had brought them back. Even the fairies, now released from their prison to find food, were subdued.

"I'm sorry, Jenks," I whispered when the flames grew higher, warming my face but for the tear tracks. "I want you to stay in the desk."

Taking a deep breath, his wings shifted, then stilled, lying like gossamer on his back. Saying nothing, he pulled his hand from mine and looked up at the faint noise the fairies were making as they hunted for spiders in the chill evening. Apparently their wings were why they destroyed a garden in their efforts to reach food, and they were amazed by their new dexterity, relishing being able to duck into small places. Better yet, they weren't damaging the garden.

"No thank you," Jenks said, his voice low as he watched the trees. "I couldn't live in the stump anyway." His faint smile was because of parental pride. "The kids will be fine. They have huts all over the garden. I'll just sleep in my office."

I couldn't bear thinking of him setting up residence in the flowerpot he'd turned into an office at the edge of the property. I was itching to push him into taking the potion that Ceri had made to turn small things big, but I daren't mention it yet. I shivered, and Jenks turned from the fire, his shoulders slumping. "You should get big again. It's too cold out here for you."

"I'm fine," I said, clearly not.

At Jenks's pointed look, Pierce took his coat off and draped it over me. I would have protested, but it was warm and smelled like him and the garden both. A puff of redwood rose as I tugged it close, and Jenks eyed the witch, the first glint of anything other than grief in his eyes.

"You're smaller than I thought you'd be my size," he said dryly, attention going to his home as a weird keening rose. The flames had eaten through the ceiling, and the wind was being sucked in through the tunnels, feeding the fire. It sounded like the wood itself was moaning, and it gave me the creeps. "Maybe I should hit you now for when you make Rachel cry."

"I'm not going to make her cry," Pierce said indignantly.

Jenks's wings lifted slightly, turning red from the increased circulation and heat. "Sure you will. All her boyfriends do. Why would you be any different?"

"Because I am," he offered.

"Pierce is not my boyfriend." Frowning, I shifted from foot to foot and glanced at Ivy, a good six feet back from the stump as it burned. Her jaw was set and her feet were spread wide, hands on her hips and just about daring the coven to bother us. To anyone else, it'd look like she and Ceri were doing some garden burning, oblivious to the funeral and the fairies scattered in the garden like, well, fairies.

"Maybe you should go, Pierce," I said to the sky. "It's almost sundown. You think getting away from Al is hard now, I imagine it's impossible when you're only four inches tall."

Pierce glowered at me. "In all my born days, I've not seen a witch as skeerylike as you about being demon snagged. Al won't bother me. I'm watching you. He can't touch me, or Newt will have his—uh. Never mind," he stammered, face reddening.

Grimacing, I turned back to the flames. I thought it odd that fire looked the same no matter what size I was. A hiss of fabric whispered behind me, and I spun to the silken thread coiling on the ground. It was Sidereal, and as he snaked down it, Jenks spit on the ground.

Slightly more subtle, Pierce sidled closer to me. "I don't like them," the witch said, eying the much larger fairy. Pierce and I were pixy size, which put the fairies two inches taller than us. Or like two feet, in pixy terms.

"Yeah, me neither," I said, remembering that poison dart Pierce had burned from me. But when Jenks loosened his sword, I felt a moment of worry. "Easy, Jenks," I murmured, not wanting a repeat of this morning. "Let's hear what he has to say."

Sidereal found his feet, his expression pained as he shifted his shoulders and adjusted his raggedy, spiderweblike attire. He looked like he was smelling something rank, his lips curled back to show his vampirelike teeth. Honestly, with their pale complexions, long faces, and those teeth designed to eat insects, they were some of the scariest Inderlanders I'd ever met.

"I'd thank you for letting us out of your prison, but it would show weakness," the fairy said, lisping around his long teeth.

"I'd apologize for burning your wings, but it would do the same," I said, wishing Jenks would back off a little, but I could understand. They'd killed his wife.

"You . . . I should have slit your throat!" Jenks shouted, his wings a blur as he rose a breath from the ground. "You killed my Matalina!"

The fairy bared his teeth again, and I felt a moment of panic. "Jenks, it's *my* fault Matalina is dead," I said. "I'm the reason they attacked. I'm sorry! If I could do it again . . ." I closed my eyes in a long blink and tried not to cry. Damn it, it was all my fault.

Immediately Jenks's face went ashen. "That's not what I meant."

"But it's true," I said, not knowing what I could have done differently— except kill them. "They never would have attacked if it hadn't been for me."

Pierce edged closer to Jenks, eying the tension between Sidereal and the pixy. "Jenks," he said cautiously. "Can I speak to you alone for a moment?"

Jenks frowned, clearly knowing that Pierce was trying to separate them. His angular features were tight and his fingers moved to rest on the hilt of his sword. Sidereal started to hiss, and I pleaded with Jenks with my eyes. *No more. Please, no more. Not today.*

Abruptly Jenks spun, stiffly walking away with his head down. Pierce draped an arm over his shoulders and went with him, his head close as he talked. Uneasy, I turned back to Sidereal, surprised again by how tall he was. Imagine a seven-foot, skinny vampire in white ragged robes and with two rows of sharp teeth, and you might have it.

Sidereal was watching Jenks's home burn, confusion on his face. "I never would have guessed he'd burn his house. Perhaps pixies can be civilized after all."

Anger tickled deep in me. Jenks wasn't burning his house, he was burning his past.

I cleared my throat, and Sidereal looked at me, his dark eyes reflecting the fire and turning red, like a demon's, but with round pupils. "Are we to be let go?" Sidereal asked when our eyes met. "Is it a slow death you give us? To die of starvation or the cold of winter?" His attention slid to Jenks and Pierce. It was likely they were listening in thanks to Pierce's eavesdropping spell.

"Mmmm," I said, giving Pierce a look to make him cringe. "Do you want to sit down?"

Sidereal sighed. "It must be bad," he said. "I never ask anyone to sit unless it is bad."

A faint smile quirked my lips, and I moved to a pixy-size bench. Nearby was a loom and a vat where Matalina had soaked spider nests for the silk. It made me heartsick. The bench was too small for Sidereal, and after looking at it and indicating that he'd rather stand, I sat, bringing one cold foot up onto the bench to try to warm it. The soles of my feet were black, but I didn't care; there was no demon mark on them.

"How are you feeling?" I asked, and a flash of pain crossed Sidereal as he winced. I belatedly realized he had tried to shift his wings, a fairy's version of a shrug.

"Better now that my middle is full and I can pee without people watching," he said dryly.

I nodded, my memory of Alcatraz surfacing for a moment. "If you were able to live in a secure space with room to grow, could you stay as you are?" I asked, and Sidereal stiffened.

"I won't ask my people to exist at the mercy of pixies. You can make us whole. You owe us—"

"Nothing," I interrupted calmly, setting one foot down to bring up the other. "I was defending my garden. You attacked, and I spared your life. I don't owe you anything but what my conscience demands, and you'll be happy with what I give you."

He hissed at me with those long teeth, and I lowered my voice before Jenks stormed over and cut his tongue out. "I want to ask a favor," I said softly.

Sidereal's hiss cut off, and his silver eyebrows rose. "A favor? Of your vanquished?"

My insides quivered. God, I hoped he'd go for it. I really needed to make something good come out of this. "What do you think about her?" I said, pointing with my chin to Ceri, now standing next to Ivy and talking to three of Jenks's kids.

Sidereal's expression became guarded. "She twisted the curse that made you small."

I nodded. "She was also a third of the spell that would have killed you. She's mad at me because I stopped it. What do you think about that?"

"I'd be angry, too, if a trusted warrior stayed my hand," he said cautiously. I could understand his dilemma. Ceri had tried to kill him, but she also had the skill to make them whole, and he knew it. "I've heard it said that elves were once valiant savages," he added.

"She's my friend," I said, pulling my first foot up again to sit cross-legged, the pain in my knees utterly gone. "She's taken it upon herself to live among my enemies as a spy. She wants to go back, but she needs eyes with her. I want you to go with her. All of you."

Sidereal looked at Ceri, then me. "Why would I help her?" he said, anger in his lisp.

"I brought you to this, not her." Sidereal ran his hand forward from his chin outward, and guessing that was fairy for "say your piece," I took a breath. "She lives in Kalamack's gardens."

His silver eyebrows rose again. He was interested, and I felt a stirring of hope. "There are no birds, no pixies, nothing," I said, and Sidereal glanced up into the tree, clearly wanting to share this with someone. "You could live there unnoticed, spying for her. For my benefit."

Sidereal's wicked grin made me shiver. "That might be acceptable to my people," he lisped. "I want to leave someone here, though."

Oh, really? Curious, I held my filthy foot, trying to warm it. "Why?"

The fairy's shoulders slowly rose and fell as he tried a human shrug. "To better kill you if you plan treachery."

I smiled, liking his honesty, and after a shocked moment, he smiled back. It was a fair answer. Behind him, Ceri was teaching Jenks's kids a song of loss to help them deal with their grief. The four-part harmony was enough to break your heart.

"I won't be able to get Jenks to go for it, so pick someone who can hide well," I said, and he hissed. I looked at him in alarm until I realized he was laughing. "Talk to your people," I said as I stood and a whiff of pixy and witch came up from the coat. My hand came out, and he stared at it. "I have to get big," I explained. "This is likely the last time I'll see you my size. Big people clasp hands when they meet and part in goodwill."

His hand came up, and we touched. "In goodwill," he said, brow pinched.

Sidereal's fingers were too big around mine, and curiously rough. I felt like I was shaking hands with my dad. "And trust," I said and our hands parted.

The fairy smiled, making me shiver. Stepping back, he tangled his foot in the silken line, but then he paused. "When my people part, they say gentle updrafts."

"Gentle updrafts, Sidereal," I said softly. "I wish this hadn't happened, but maybe some good can come of it."

Long face quirking in a terrifying smile, he glanced up into the tree. "Who's to say why the Goddess chooses." He plucked the silken strand, and with the signal, he was hoisted up.

I didn't watch him go, instead turning to find Jenks. I was confident they'd go for it. All I'd have to do then was roll with the consequences of inviting dewinged, fanged fairies into Trent's backyard. God, they were savage looking. Served him right.

"Jenks?" I called, wanting to say good-bye.

Strands from my tattered braid flew everywhere when Jenks landed beside me. Clearly he'd been watching. His face was sallow, but anger still colored it.

"I don't like them creeping around the garden like spiders," he said, his feet still not touching the ground as he looked into the trees. His face turned to me, and the anger shifted, almost to panic, when he saw my expression. "You're leaving."

My heart gave a thump. "I'm just going to get big. I'm still here."

The winds of his emotions shifted, and his feet touched the ground. His eyes began to glitter, and he wiped them, disgusted with himself. "Tink's titties, I can't stop leaking dust." He took a breath and exhaled. Me getting big was going to be hard. I wished he'd come with me.

Heartache hit me again, and I gave him another hug, surprising him. His arms went around me, and I felt him hesitate when he didn't find wings at my back. The silken whisper of his brushed my fingers, and when he went to go away, I tightened my grip to linger a moment more. "I would have twisted a thousand curses to be with you today," I whispered.

Slumping, Jenks let his forehead thump into me. "It hurts," he whispered, his hands falling to his sides. "All the time. Even when I try."

Tears warmed my eyes, and I pulled back so I could look at him. "It will stop one day," I said as I gave his shoulders a squeeze. "Even without your trying, and then you'll feel guilty. After that, you'll wake up one morning, remember her, and smile."

He nodded, gaze directed down. God, it hurt to see him with such heartache.

"Are you sure you don't want to become big with me?" I asked again, and my hands fell from him as he wiped his eyes, shaking the glittering sparkles from himself.

"I don't like being your size," he admitted. "Nothing smells right. And my kids need me."

His kids needed him, I thought, feeling the fingers of relief steal into my soul. He felt needed. It was a start. Damn it, Matalina was really gone. "Come with me to the church?" I asked rather weepily. "Just to the door. Those pill bugs scare me."

Saying nothing, Jenks stilled his wings and dropped to the ground. Side by side, we started through the shoulder-high grass to the looming presence of the church. The steeple stood out black and strong against the pale blue of the sunset sky, and I wondered how Bis would take it when he woke up. Must be a bitch to be out of it so deeply.

"I don't know how you do this," I said as we detoured around a rock that was probably only the size of my thumb.

Jenks's wings shrugged. "It's easier when you can fly. They'll have a hard time of it."

He was talking about the fairies. "Feeling sorry for them?" I asked.

"Tink's panties, no!" he protested, but it was wispy and drained. Jenks turned at a thumping of feet, and I wasn't surprised to see Pierce jogging to catch up with us.

"You're of a mind to untwist the curse?" he asked, face shadowed in the dusk and the fire behind him. His features were indistinct, and I shivered again. It was so cold.

Pierce was on one side of me, Jenks on the other, and it was the safest I'd felt in a long time, though a snake could eat me. "I have to talk to Ceri about the fairies. I asked them to live with her," I said, and Pierce started, a happy grunt coming from him.

"That's an all-fired good scheme," he said, and Jenks looked over my head at him.

"Of course it's a good plan. Rache doesn't come up with stupid plans. She's always got an out. You just think she doesn't know what she's doing."

I wish. I held the coat tighter, my feet numb with cold. I'd been thinking all day about how I might get the coven off my back. They seemed to think that Trent could control me, so if I could control Trent, I might have a chance. Not through the familiar bond, but good old-fashioned manipulation. The Pandora charm had reminded me of an old tradition, one I needed to start again.

"Fairies in his garden," Jenks said, clearly liking the thought. "And wingless ones at that? Trent is going to be more unhappy than a skunk in a troll's garden."

Seeing him nearly smile, something went to my heart and twisted. God, I hoped he found a new love. But where? In a few years, he'd be the oldest pixy to ever live. He wasn't going to find anyone with the emotional experience he now had. He'd need that. Deserved it.

We reached the steps, and I looked up. It was only four steps, but they looked huge. Turning, I found Ivy watching. Ma-a-a-an, I did not want to be carried in like a baby.

Jenks's arm slipped around from behind me, and I gasped when my toes lifted and I was airborne. In three seconds flat, my bare feet were stumbling on the faded wood of the stoop.

"Holy crap! How about some warning?" I exclaimed, but I turned in his arms, not letting him go. This might be my last chance. "I'm sorry, Jenks," I said, giving him another hug. "Take what time you need. Ivy and I can finish this coven thing. I've got an idea."

He gave me a squeeze, then space appeared between us. "Just tell me where to fly, Rache. That's what I'm here for. I'll be ready."

Ivy was waiting at the bottom of the stairs, her hand on her hip. She could just stand there for a few moments more. Pierce, too. "This is hard," I said, sniffing.

"I'm not going anywhere," he said, his roving eyes returning.

"You're going to be all right?"

Jenks looked across the garden to the sound of his children. "I think so. I've never done anything like this before."

I touched his arm, trying to smile. "You're good at doing new things."

Finally he looked at me, and the full force of his heartache hit me. My smile faltered, and tears threatened. "I . . . I'd better get Pierce," he said, and in a clattering of wings, he was gone.

Blinking hard, I looked at the fastened cat door. *Where's Rex?*

The stairs shook, and I stumbled when Ivy clomped up them. "You changing?" she asked quietly, but before I could answer, she opened the screen and interior door both.

An exuberant howl pulled my attention up to see Jenks flying past with Pierce dangling.

"That's something you don't see every day," Ivy muttered as they vanished into the hall and presumably to my bathroom where Ivy had put his clothes.

My kitchen looked awe inspiring from my new vantage point, and Ivy stayed behind me as I hugged the wall to my room. "I've got this!" I shouted, and she looked at me.

"I lost track of Rex," she said, not hearing me, but my waving hands were clear enough.

"Oh." Suitably subdued, I waited by the nicked floor molding while she pushed my door open and did a quick look for felines. "Uh, she's under the bed!" I exclaimed when a pair of yellow eyes looked at me from beside the laptop Ivy had given me last summer.

Ivy didn't hear, her head in my closet, and panic iced through me when the cat stood and started pacing forward. "*Non sum qualis eram!*" I shouted.

The breath in me turned inside out, and I reached for something, anything. Dizziness roared in, and I was already mumbling, "I take the smut, I take it," before even the hint of it could lay me out. Unlike an earth charm that changed a person, a demon curse didn't hurt—unless you refused the smut. My vision swam in a nauseating swirl, and I took another breath, my lungs starved for air as they formed, empty and slack.

"You okay?" Ivy asked, close and worried.

Blinking, I found she was holding my arm to keep me upright. Rex was at my feet, tail twitching in confusion. And I was stark naked, as hairy as an orangutan. "Oh, for God's sake," I muttered as I snatched my pillow and covered myself. *Eaten by a cat. Wouldn't the coven love that?*

Ivy grinned, her eyes black because of the emotions I was kicking out. "Welcome back," she said wryly, letting me go and sauntering out my door. I heard a thump and a sigh as she leaned her head back against the wall in the hall next to my door, and when I went to shut the door—which she'd left open—Ivy put a long hand in the way. "I want to talk to you," she said from the hall.

I hesitated, then tossed my pillow back on my bed before I yanked my top drawer open and pulled out a bright red pair of undies. Yeah. Red would be good today. Rex jumped up on my bed, chirping for attention, but I couldn't bring myself to touch her yet. A soft bong from the belfry told me the sun was down. Bis had taken to tapping it when he woke. My thoughts drifted to having gotten my own summoning name back, and I smiled. I could lounge around in my robe, or shower, or even shave, maybe, without worrying about being jerked out. Slowly my smile faded. *I was not feeling bad for Al. No freaking way.*

"Can I come in yet?" Ivy asked from the hall.

I pulled a camisole over my head, red to match my underwear. "I'm not dressed."

The click of my door closing pulled me around. "I said I'm not dressed!" I exclaimed, seeing Ivy with her back to it, her eyes a nice steady brown, but her expression grim.

"I, ah, looked Pierce up on the Internet," she said, and my anger shifted to worry.

Oh. Avoiding her, I dug around in my top drawer for a pair of ankle socks. My feet, once cold and dirty, were clean. My scars were gone again. Apart from the hair thing, demon curses were better than a shower. I glanced at my snarled hair in the mirror over my dresser. *Almost.* The neurotoxins from my vampire bite were still there, and the tweaking to my mitochondria, too. My ears, too, needed piercing. Again.

"How bad is it?" I asked, yanking open a lower drawer and pulling out my TAKATA STAFF shirt. I figured she would look him up, and I wasn't sure I wanted to hear this. I was starting to like Pierce, which meant he was bad news.

"Bad enough."

The shirt scraped my nose as I pulled it on, and feeling a little less exposed, I went to my closet for a pair of jeans. Ivy was sitting on my bed with Rex, her long fingers between the smiling cat's ears. "He told me he's a former coven member," I said, shoving first one leg, then another into the fresh cotton and zipping it up. *Much better.*

"Once a member, always a member," Ivy murmured when I turned around with my socks and sat on the end of my bed.

"Even when they kill you for knowing black magic." Sure, you could kill a busload of people by perverting a white spell, but they'd shun you for doing a harmless black one. Damn hypocrites. Twisting my foot up, I marveled at the pristine smoothness of its underside. "Pierce told me they blew his cover because they didn't like him summoning demons, but he was doing it to kill them."

"That's what I found," she said slowly, "but there's more."

There was always more. "He knows about the demon thing," I said, seeing her eyes downcast and clearly reluctant to say anything. "He's not going to hurt me."

But my confidence trickled away at her expression. "Ask him about Eleison."

I bent to reach my running shoes, under my bed. They'd cost me a fortune, but were the most comfortable pair of shoes I had since Alcatraz had one pair of my boots and my other was split between here and the ever-after. I had to talk to Al, tell him the gun wasn't my idea. *What an ass, shooting at Al.* "Is Eleison his girlfriend?" I asked. Dead girlfriends, I could handle.

Looking ill, Ivy shook her head. "It was an eighteenth-century southern town."

Was? Oh. My eyes went to the wall as if I could see through it to where Jenks was with Pierce. My breath tight, I asked, "What did he do?"

Ivy let Rex drop to the floor, and the cat waited impatiently under the doorknob. "He used black magic to vaporize it while trying to kill a demon."

"Mmmm." *Good thing I didn't like the guy.* "Are you sure it was him?"

Ivy nodded. "Four hundred innocents. Dead."

My fingers tying my shoes were slow. "I guess putting four hundred people in the ground might explain why he was in purgatory."

I looked up when Ivy shifted closer. "Rachel, I don't care if you sleep with the guy, but do it fast and get it over with. He's going to get you killed. He won't mean to, but he will. People die around him."

People die around me, too. Depressed, I let my foot hit the rug. "I'll be careful." Eyes rising, I found hers pinched in an inner pain. "I'll be careful, okay?"

She stood up as I did, her smile thin. "Okay."

I'll ask him about it. Get the whole story, I thought, feeling refreshed in my clean clothes and the entire night spreading out before me. *I'm in control and not upset. I can work with this.*

"Do we have anything to eat?" I asked, thinking about the now-useless sleepy-time charms I'd made last night. "I've got spelling to do tonight." *Maybe find one that lowered your blood pressure.* "I have an idea of how to get Trent *and* the coven off my back."

Ivy gave me a look before opening my door. "The coven isn't going to give up on you."

"I have to try," I said as I followed her down the dark hallway. Pierce was talking to Jenks behind my closed bathroom door, and my chest tightened. *Good thing I didn't like him.*

"I'll talk to Rynn," Ivy said, her voice wispy as she entered the kitchen and thunked the light on with her elbow. "Maybe he'll help now. Sending fairies to burn our church isn't right."

"My idea doesn't involve Rynn Cormel," I drawled as I headed for the fridge. Coming out with a carton of cottage cheese, I caught the spoon that Ivy threw me. "Do you have David's cell number? I need him to bird-dog some legal stuff for me."

Ivy smiled. "Way ahead of you," she said as she went to her computer.

I shoveled a huge spoonful of cottage cheese into my mouth, eyes closing in bliss at the soft bite. God, I was hungry.

But my eyes flew open at a soft tremble from under my feet. Ivy's eyebrows rose, and then a rumble rolled over the church like distant thunder. From the belfry, the bell bonged, and a shiver cascaded through me. The big mojo amulet on my bag flashed red, then went quiet. Holy crap. Someone had just rung the bells.

The bathroom door crashed open, and from the back of the church, I heard Ceri's steps as she came in from the garden. Jenks flew in, his dust carrying a hint of gray, but his wings were bright red in excitement. "It wasn't me!" I said as the pixy landed on the center island counter.

"That was an explosion!" Jenks said.

Ceri slid in with her hand to her hair to keep the fair strands from floating. "It was a magical explosion!" she said breathlessly. "Someone just rang the bells!"

Pierce came in behind her, and my heart clenched. He had shaved and was back in his usual dark pants and vest, his eyes wide and his hair tousled. He looked entirely in control, and yet . . . like he belonged in my chaotic life. *Eleison*, echoed in my thoughts. *Four hundred people.*

Looking away, I downed more cottage cheese, not knowing when I'd get another chance to eat. "I think it was Brooke," I said as I dug my spoon in. It was after sunset. She'd tried to summon me. Stupid woman. But I could make it work for me—twice over.

Pierce edged past Ceri to stand beside me. I eyed him, then put my attention on my lunch. "She summoned Al," he said flatly. "The fool." Pushing from the counter, I ate one more spoonful and put the lid back on. Ivy's eyes were on me as I opened my charm cupboard and pulled out a pain amulet. *Yeah. I'll need this.*

"What are you doing?" Ivy asked.

Not turning, I pondered whether I could do this without my splat gun, deciding I'd have to. "Al is on this side of the lines. Brooke summoned him," I said.

"Rachel!" Ceri said brightly. "You don't have to worry about the coven coming for you anymore. Isn't that wonderful?"

I turned, an invoked pain amulet dangling. "Brooke summoned him, not the coven, and since everyone knows Al is my demon, I'm going to get blamed for it." I hated saying that, but it was true. This sucked. But I was going to make it work for me, damn it. Don't reject, rejoice? *God help me, I'm in trouble.*

One by one, they reacted as they figured it out. In a flash of dust, Jenks was on my shoulder, ready to go. Telling him he couldn't come wasn't going to be fun. There was only one person joining me. One person I was sure would be okay.

"Bis?" I called, and Jenks's wings hummed as the lumpy shadow above the fridge lost the yellow of the walls and became the young gargoyle. He was really getting good at this. Ivy started, and even Pierce seemed surprised, but I'd known he was somewhere close. I could feel the lines better when he was around.

Ceri's expression was worried as Bis crawled down the fridge like a bat and made the hopping flight to the counter beside me.

"What are you doing?" Ivy said, her pupils dilating.

"Trying to save Brooke's ass," I said shortly, then turned to Bis and wiped my fingers off on the dish towel. "Think you can jump me there? Can you follow Al's aura signature?"

The gargoyle nodded, but I didn't hear what he said as everyone protested at once.

"Have you been sniffing fairy farts?" Jenks shouted.

"You can't jump. You don't know how," Pierce said.

"You're going to get yourself killed!" Ivy said, more angry than afraid. "Al's going to think you gave Pierce that gun, and you want to parade in, telling him he can't have Brooke?"

"Yup." I put my elbows on the counter to have my head even with Bis's. "I might be able to create some goodwill between me and the coven if I'm not too late. They can't help Brooke—they probably don't even know she's in trouble."

Ceri was standing at the back of the kitchen, her uncertainty clear. "I'm coming with you," Pierce stated, coming around the center counter to join me.

"You're going to help me save Brooke?" I said. "From Al? After you tried to shoot him? I don't think so. You're staying here. I don't need you when I'm with Al."

Pierce went to protest, and I raised a pain amulet. "Unless you want to take your beating like a man?" I said, and he dropped back. *I'm no one's ward to be babysat.*

"You can't jump," Pierce warned me. "Bis can, but not with you!"

"What can it hurt to try?" I said confidently, and Bis shivered his wings, clearly eager. "Al himself said I was slipping into a line, and I didn't have a gargoyle helping. It's just a local jump. It's not like I'm trying to shift realities."

"Rachel . . . ," he growled, but I wasn't listening. Ivy wasn't happy, and Ceri looked just as worried. I had to get out of here or they were going to sit on me.

"Glad we got that settled," I said brightly. "Bis, we're out of here."

Jenks rose, horrified as Bis took to the air. "Rache! Pierce says you're not ready—"

But I didn't want to wait. I didn't *have* to. I had been snatched, jailed, drugged, and treated as less than a person. I doubted very much I could save Brooke, but the attempt might be enough to get the rest of the coven to listen to me. Besides, I did have to talk to Al.

Bis landed on my shoulder, his light weight barely recognizable. His tail wrapped around my neck, and his wings cupped behind my head, unexpectedly funneling the shouts of protest. I reeled—every line in Cincinnati was singing, and through Bis, I could hear them.

"We can do this," I said, reaching out and touching a thought to the nearby ley line. If I could shift my aura to match the tone of it, I'd be inside it, even though I stood in my church's kitchen. I could feel the line outside myself, warmer than I was, tasting of chlorophyll, sour like dandelion sap. My entire soul vibrated, and I let the line pour through me, trying to match its resonance. Warmth, taste, sound, they all blended, and with a gasp, I felt the line take me.

Bis's tail tightened, and I felt him do that curious step-the-mind-sideways twist that Al always did when he pulled me to the ever-after. *Yes!* I thought exuberantly as I mimicked it and felt my bubble snap into place around me as my body dissolved.

And we were gone.

TWenty-six

Listen, I thought, feeling the ley line within me, tasting it. I was everywhere, in every line on the continent. Or at least I had the potential for it. Bis's presence was with me. His mental texture slipped through my protective bubble, bringing with him the discordant sensation of another line. It was as if I could see, taste, hear, the lingering aura that Al had left behind on it, shifting the sound a little deeper, the taste a little more bitter. It was the weirdest thing I'd ever felt. Bis brought the taste of the new line in with him. Otherwise, I'd never be able to sense it past my own bubble. And now that I knew what it sounded like, I could find it.

Confident from success, I reached a thought past my bubble to pick out the line he'd used from the myriad lines crisscrossing the Cincinnati mindscape.

That was a mistake.

Shock vibrated through me—and then the pain hit.

I had no breath, but I screamed. Fire poured through my veins to illuminate my soul—the entire line filled me, unfiltered. My mind rebelled, and my thoughts went white. *Tulpa!* I screamed, but there was too much. I couldn't spindle creation, and my neurons burned.

Al! I begged in my thoughts, but he couldn't hear me. I'd done something wrong. My memory was charring, flaking from me in sheets of thought.

I had to get out before I burned to nothing. There had to be a way. I had . . . to listen . . . through the pain. Where was Al?

Somehow I found him. Somehow I found Al's sarcastic thoughts, bitter and old. Tired, angry, bored. Alone.

Whimpering, I shifted what was left of my aura, modifying it to match the line he had used, and with a last gasp, I shoved myself into it. With the feeling of spiderwebs made of ice, and fog made of fire, I tore my way back into reality.

My face hit a dirty flat carpet, and I dropped my pain amulet.

"Oh. Shit." I breathed, arms shaking as I tried to push myself up, failing. *That's okay. It's nice just to lie here.*

"Rachel!" I heard Bis cry. Al snarled something, then bellowed in pain. And then Bis was with me. "Rachel, I'm sorry. I didn't mean to leave you. I'm sorry! I'm so sorry!"

"It's okay," I said, hoping he didn't touch me. I'd freaking pass out. My eyes were shut, and slowly my mind was rebuilding itself. A savage smile curled my lips up. I had done it. Damn it, I had jumped the lines!

"Brooke, there's two of them!" I heard Vivian exclaim, but I couldn't move yet.

"Only one of them is Rachel," Brooke snapped.

"Which one?"

Bis hissed, and I heard a scraping of claws. A sharp sound of a smack, and a feminine hand grabbed my wrist. "Ow!" I yelped as Al, looking exactly like me, jerked me up.

"I'd say the one not in charge," Brooke said, sounding smug.

My breath came fast, and I scanned the dirty, rectangular room as I found my balance: wood floor with a glowing pentagram laid down with salt, cement-stone walls, low ceilings, really small windows, and a broken table shoved against the big archway leading to a balcony barely big enough to stand on. I could hear water running over rocks somewhere in the dusk. Bis was slumped against the far wall by the stairs, shaking off Al's blow. Brooke and Vivian were standing before us, Vivian looking like she wished she were somewhere—anywhere—else, the skin around her neck red and blistered from being pixed, her clothes a mess, and her heels scuffed. She'd been taking a beating the last couple of days, and it showed.

Al had already gotten out of Brooke's circle by all appearances. No wonder, seeing that he looked like me in black leather and a TAKATA STAFF T-shirt. *How had he known what shirt I was going to wear? And where am I?* I thought, still confused.

It looked like a bad Hollywood set lit by candles, smelling of spilled wax, dirt, burnt amber, and mold. It was the last one that did it. "Holy crap, are we at Loveland Castle?" I asked, and Al gave me a shake, swinging my attention back to him. Or me, maybe. Damn, he'd even done the eyes this time, and it was like looking in a mirror.

"What the Turn are you doing, jumping with an untrained gargoyle?" he said as he held me up by one shoulder. "You could have killed yourself!"

I couldn't focus well yet, and my stomach lurched. "Well, maybe you should teach me how, then." My bile rose, and I forced it down. I was not going to barf on Al. Not in front of Brooke. Maybe later. *Where's my pain amulet?*

"I told you this was a bad idea," Vivian said. "Now there's two of them."

Oh God, my head hurt. Al let me go, and I staggered, only to fall down again in the middle of that big pentagram. He was wearing my boots, or at least replicas of the one I'd left in the ever-after. It was the only difference between us. Fingers stretching, I reached for my amulet, sighing when my fingers snagged it and the pain in my head dulled.

"You didn't do it right, itchy witch," Al said, then flung out a hand when Brooke threw a ball of something at us. "Bitch," he said absently as a black sheet of ever-after sprang up around us. He'd set a circle. Al had set a protection circle. I'd only seen him do that once, maybe twice, before. "Look what you made me do," the demon snarled. "I hope you're satisfied. I had to set a circle. I've not set a circle this side of the lines since Piscary tried to get me to kill you. Proud of yourself?"

His syntax sounded funny coming from my face. "Not especially," I said, then yelped when he yanked me to my feet. From the rafters, Bis hissed.

The pop of a spell hitting the black-sheened protection circle thumped through me. It was followed by several more as Vivian and Brooke tried to break through with their lethal white charms. I tried to see a glimmer of Al's gold aura, seeing only black. Nothing remained.

"Let her go!" Bis exclaimed, ignored as he dropped through Al's circle.

"I ought to throttle you," Al snarled, red hair twin to my own swinging into his face. It sort of put a new spin on the phrase killing yourself. "And your little gargoyle, too," he added, making Bis dart back out of the circle when the wood at his feet started to smolder.

Oh yeah, my fuzzy brain thought. *Pierce and the gun.*

"I didn't know," I gasped. "I forgot Pierce had my splat gun. Damn it, Al, I was stoned out of my mind! Why am I always trying to prove myself to you? How about a little trust?"

Al loosened his hold. It was like looking in a mirror, but I doubt I ever had that angry a snarl before. His attention jerked past me as I felt a drop in the ley line. They were trying to reset their summoning circle to trap us. Grimacing, Al muttered a word of Latin.

Vivian yelped, leaping to the side when Al's circle dropped, broken by his magic tearing through it. A new, nasty ooze dripped from the wall behind her.

"Pierce is a jerk," I said, feeling the ice pick in my head start to dissolve. "You were right. I'm wrong. His shooting at you wasn't my idea. You know he's trying to kill you. What did you expect?"

Al's eyes went from green to their usual red, goat-slitted ugliness. "I'm right and you're admitting it?" he said, his tone lightening. His hand opened, and I fell, yelping. The scent of musty carpet puffed up, and I looked around the sunset-gloomed air. *Loveland Castle?*

I got up and looked at Brooke, taking in her bloodied lip, wild hair, white face, and grim determination. It seemed like we were at a stalemate. "Loveland Castle?" I questioned her. "You've *got* to be kidding me."

"You are on thin ice, student," Al interrupted, his accent perfect, proper highbrow English coming from my body.

Brushing myself off, I sidled next to him. "Good thing I know how to skate. You mind not looking like me?" I knew I should be scared, but hell, I'd jumped a line to be here.

Al smirked at my sour attitude, and a sheet of ever-after coated him. He gained bulk, height, and a ruddy complexion. "Being you got me out very quickly," he said, again himself as he tugged his lace straight. "It's amazing how your pretty face opens doors."

"I bet."

Another drop in the line brought both Al's and my attention up, and we were trapped as Brooke's circle rose again. "I have you!" Brooke exclaimed. "You're mine! I did it!"

Sighing, I shook my head in disbelief as Al grumbled. This was not my day.

Bis dropped through the circle holding us, his red eyes whirling and the white tuft of fur on the end of his tail bristling. Wings beating to make my hair fly, he landed on my shoulder. Cincinnati's lines exploded in my mind, and my knees buckled as I reached for Al.

The gargoyle hissed as Al pulled me up. "Make a circle around your thoughts," he muttered so only Bis and I could hear. "You look like a drunk like that."

It wasn't hard, and immediately the humming between my ears stopped, and I stood under my own power. "Thank you," I whispered, trying to get a finger between Bis's tail and my neck. The kid was scared to death. He had abandoned me in the lines after I'd fried myself. It wasn't his fault, but I'd be surprised if he left me now even if I told him to go.

Brooke was almost hopping in delight, but Vivian looked ill. "Brooke," the youngest coven member said, "there are two of them in there."

"I know!" she said in delight. "We circled them both!"

"*You* circled them," Vivian said. "Not me. This is against the coven. One of them is a demon."

"The hell with it!" Brooke said, her delight tarnishing. "They're all shortsighted hacks."

"I didn't agree to this!" Vivian protested, backing up. "You summoned a *demon*, not Rachel Morgan! Did you stop to think about what that makes you?"

Brooke's eyes narrowed and she stiffened. "I have *control* of this *situation*," she said stiltedly. "I'm not a demon summoner. I just want the one to kill the other is all."

Whoops.

Bis's wings shifted as I turned to Al. The demon's eyebrows were high as he eyed me over his round smoked glasses. "Perhaps you should do something, Rachel?" he suggested.

"Demon!" Brooke exclaimed as I touched her circle to find it humming a warning at me. "I demand that you kill Rachel Morgan."

I spun to face Al, my back hitting the bubble until I jerked away at its burning. *Kill me?*

Bis spread his wings, claws pinching my shoulder. "You're not touching her," he hissed.

Al, though, wasn't moving. He gave me a glance, then put a hand behind his back to look elegant in his crushed green velvet and shiny buckled shoes. His visible hand became a fist in its white glove, and his lip curled in disgust. "Who?" he said disdainfully; then he muttered to me, "Best hurry, itchy witch. I can stall for only so long."

My breath exploded from me. He didn't want to do it, but he would.

"That demon in there with you, dolt!" Brooke shouted, pointing.

Holy crap, I had to get out of here!

"First," Al said dryly, "my name isn't dolt. And second, I'm the only demon here."

Brooke fumed. Vivian's expression was puzzled. "I demand you kill Rachel Morgan this instant!" Brooke stated.

Al reached into a pocket, pulling out a small tin. "There are thirty-five Rachel Morgans on this continent alone," he said, opening it. The scent of Brimstone hit me, and I sneezed. "Which one would you prefer? The one in Sacramento or the one in New Mexico? You can't mean the newborn in Kalamazoo . . ." He sneezed as well, snapping the lid to the tin and tucking it away. "A coven member sending a demon to kill a newborn? And people say I'm a sadist."

I was frantic, almost not hearing Bis when he leaned forward and whispered in my ear, "Can't you circle Al?"

My scanning of the floor for a weakness ceased. *Circle Al?* I looked up to see Al smiling at me. I had promised not to, but I think he'd overlook it in this case.

"That one!" Brooke shouted, pointing. "That witch right there!"

Al turned to me as if seeing me for the first time. "That's not a witch."

I had nothing to make a circle with. It was a good thing Brooke didn't know my third name. Maybe this was why the tradition of having three started. Giving up on finding anything useful, I awkwardly ran my finger across the dusty carpet, crab-walking around Al. He could have moved and avoided it easily, but he didn't.

"Just kill her!" Brooke screamed, and I invoked the circle.

I exhaled heavily as the smut-coated sheet of gold-tinted ever-after rose up, loosely imprisoning Al. It was like tying a stallion with string, but Al rumbled appreciatively.

"Took you long enough," he sniffed, poking at it only to draw back when it almost fell.

Shaking, I turned to Brooke, totally pissed and smiling. The woman was staring, clearly recognizing that something had shifted, but not making the connection. She was a white witch. She had no clue that she'd just lost control of him. Vivian, though, was backing up, her face whiter than her coat used to be.

"Algaliarept, kill the woman standing beside you," Brooke said, and Al blew her a kiss.

"Too late, Brooke. I circled him. He's my demon," I said, hearing more than my words were saying. Al was my demon. I admitted it. It was time to live it. It was the only way I was going to survive being me.

"No!" Brooke exclaimed, her face becoming livid. "I circled you. I circled both of you! Rachel, I demand you do what I say and release that demon!"

"That doesn't work on me," I said smugly as Al chuckled. "I'm not a demon. We've been over this." I wasn't a demon, but Al didn't think I was a witch either.

"I've had enough," Al said, reaching out to push through my paltry circle.

"Wait," I said, and he hesitated. "I have an idea."

"This had better be good," he warned me, eying me over his smoked glasses.

"Break my circle, and you're still stuck here with me. But if I banish you . . ."

Al smiled, his thick blocky teeth showing full and white. "Itchy witch, I misjudged you."

"Demon," I said firmly, "I demand that you depart from here and go directly to wherever your little demon heart desires."

Al's smile widened. My hair shifted from the displaced air, and he was gone. I was alone in Brooke's circle. I was betting I wouldn't be alone for long. *Please come back, Al.*

"Rachel! I demand you do what I say," Brooke shouted, beginning to look frazzled in her begrimed business suit.

"You can suck my toes, Brooke." Bis's tail tightened, but I smiled sweetly, hand on my hip. *Al, I summon you. Al, I summon you. Al! Get your ass over here!*

Oh God. What if he didn't show? Had I just given myself to the coven?

Vivian stiffened, eyes wide. I felt a drop in the nearest ley line, and we all turned. "Hello, Brooke Sondra Stanton," Al said, and I sagged in relief. He'd come back.

"*Abire!*" Brooke shouted, dropping her circle around me to throw all she had at Al.

"Grab some air, Bis!" I shouted, lunging out of the circle to roll and rise to a stand. Bis was in the rafters, and hands in fists, I jabbed a side kick into Vivian, even as she held up her hands in surrender. I had no pity for her. She was here—she was going to get smacked.

Vivian fell, stumbling back into the narrow stairwell. She only went a couple of feet down the deathly narrow spiral staircase, but it'd keep her busy for a few minutes.

I turned to Al, then spun back around as the hair on the back of my neck prickled. *"Rhombus!"* I shouted, cowering as an iridescent ball of ever-after hit it, thrown from Vivian. She hadn't gone as far as I had expected and was crawling up the stairs.

"You're pretty good," I said, then did a low front kick, smacking Vivian's chin and sending her head snapping back. Eyes rolling up, she collapsed on the stair.

Brooke's ugly cry turned me around. "No!" I shouted, lunging past the broken table only to skid to a horrified stop. Al had her on the floor; he was sitting on her hips and pinning her wrists to the dirty wood. She was helpless. Even without the witch/demon discrepancy, she didn't have a chance. I stared at her wide eyes as she panted in fear, only now realizing what she'd done.

"Al, please," I asked. Behind me, I heard a scuff of feet, and I held a hand back in warning. "I'm trying to help her!" I shouted, and Vivian halted. Thank God.

Al wasn't amused. "Tell me you're joking," he said, standing and dragging Brooke up by the neck. "That little understanding we have doesn't cover people who summon me." Grinning to show his flat teeth, he lightly thunked Brooke's head into the wall. "Let me jump you," he said. "I don't have a lot of time to waste today."

"Go . . . to hell," she said, trying to spit on him only to have it drip down her own chin.

"That's what I'm trying to do," he intoned. "Be a good girl. It won't hurt if you don't resist. You're already sold, love. You should leave demon summoning to the professionals."

A chill went through me as I remembered him calling me love. My hand out to Vivian in warning to stay put, I edged closer to Al, feeling like a human trying to take a lion's kill. "Al, I need your help. That's why I'm here, not because of Brooke. I need your help *right now.* I don't have time for you to mess around with some lame-ass witch."

"Lame-ass witch?" Al looked at me over his glasses. "This here is coven quality, grade-A witch ass." He hesitated, and Brooke took a clean breath as his fingers eased. "You want my help, you say?"

"Demon spawn!" Brooke rasped.

Al's fingers tightened, and he shoved her head against the stone wall again with a thunk. "You say that like it's an insult," he murmured as she whimpered. Leaning toward her, he whispered something in her ear that made her eyes close in horror.

Vivian was inching closer, and I impatiently gestured for her to give me just one more minute. "Al, do this for me, okay? Can't you just take someone I *don't* know for once? I'm going to get blamed for this."

Al leaned back from licking Brooke's neck, tightening his grip on her until she started to claw at his hands around her throat. "You don't belong here, Rachel. You belong with the demons in the ever-after."

"Yeah, okay," I admitted, and Vivian gasped. "I might belong with demons, but I belong here, too, as a member of society, not an outcast on the run, and this isn't helping." Moving closer, I put a hand on his arm. Brooke's breath rasped, sounding pained. "I need your help. Please. I know how I can fix this, and I need to borrow a demon locator charm from you. I don't have time to make a witch charm that I can't invoke anyway."

Al turned to me. He let Brooke breathe, and she took a gulp of air, her hands scrabbling at his grip on her neck. Behind me, Vivian's foot scraped as she moved a step closer. Bis landed between us, and I felt better at his warning hiss. I didn't dare turn to look.

"You'd rather use a demon curse? One I made?" Al asked, and I nodded, my face warm.

Brooke rasped, "Filthy demon sexpot."

"Sexpot!" I exclaimed, affronted. "I have never had sex with Al!"

Al sighed. "More's the pity," he said, eying me. "You'd really enjoy yourself."

I took a step back, wiping my hand on my jeans. "Not happening."

Brooke suddenly screamed, and I winced, knowing Al was done messing around. "You, though," he said as he flooded her with ever-after, "couldn't survive sex with me, Brooke Sondra Stanton. I'd burn you out like dandelion fluff."

Vivian was threatening to test Bis's resolve, and I grabbed Brooke's arm, taking the ever-after coursing through her into myself and leaving her untouched. It was a lot, and I winced as she sagged, gasping for air with little whimpers. Al frowned at me from under pinched brows, redoubling the force running through her.

Again she screamed, falling into sobs when I took it as well. "I like it here," I said, dizzy from the energy, but handling it. "I need your help. Are you going to help me or not?"

Knowing I was the one keeping her from pain, Brooke brought her gaze up, shocking me with her hatred instead of gratitude. Al saw it, and jerked her from me, but he'd stopped flooding her with force, and she only grunted from being yanked about.

"You want me to help you?" he sneered, but he was listening. "For gratis?" Attention going to Brooke, he said, "Let me jump you. Rachel can't save you. You're *mine*."

I glanced at Bis, wondering how much longer his hissing and stalking back and forth was going to keep Vivian at bay. "What is a favor owed without a mark worth to you?" I asked. "One based on trust."

At the last word, Al sighed. His goat-slitted eyes narrowed, and he looked at Brooke, growling. "This one is mine. I need to make a living, or you're going to be stirring your spells on the surface in the shade of a sun shelter."

I shifted to stand next to Brooke so he could see both of us. "I need to find Nick. Like now. Yes or no?"

I could smell Brooke's sweat, almost taste her fear on the air, her anger that I was so sure of my station I could argue with a demon threatening her with a lifetime of degradation. This, too, I wanted the coven to see.

"You need to find Nickie, eh?" he asked, and I nodded. "Are you hungry, itchy witch?" the demon said suddenly, a curious lilt to his voice. "I'm feeling a bit peckish myself."

Thunking Brooke's head hard into the wall, he tucked her under his arm and put his free hand on my shoulder.

I stared up at Al, an unreasonable fear coming from nowhere. *Not the lines!* I thought, frightened of being hurt again, but the enfolding warmth of a line soaked into me, and Loveland Castle vanished.

Twenty-seven

I was holding my breath, afraid it was going to hurt, and it seemed as if I could feel a sandpaper-like sensation across my mind despite the thick bubble I'd made around my thoughts. My lungs re-formed, and I breathed, feeling them expand as they filled again for the first time. Throat tight and eyes clamped shut, I stood braced, as if I was going to be smacked, hands in fists and tense. A heavy weight was on my shoulder: Al's hand. I could smell burnt amber and feel the lack of an echo. It was warm, too.

"Hell's bells, where are we?" Bis whispered, and I realized it wasn't Al's hand on my shoulder but Bis, his tail wrapped around my neck and the faint scent of iron lifting from him.

I cracked an eyelid, finding only rich browns, golds, and reds in a low-ceilinged room, no Al. I was standing on a raised circular area, my running shoes on thick carpet. The lighting was dim, a small puddle of light glowing on the arrangement of two tall chairs and a couch bracketing a coffee table before a stone fireplace. It was built into the curving wall, and a thick layer of coals radiated heat. "Opulent" would be the word. There wasn't a circle in sight, making me think this was a spot of privacy where you would never need one.

"I've never been here," I told Bis as I looked behind us into a lowered, large circular room filled with books. Lots and lots of books. My shoulders eased, and I reached to touch Bis's clawed feet, wishing he wouldn't pinch so hard. "You okay?"

Someone breathed behind me, and I spun. The snap of Bis's wings brushed my ears as he found his balance. It was Al, and he ignored me as he stood before the fireplace and took off his green velvet coat and draped it over a nearby wing-back chair. Heart pounding, I dropped my hand from Bis, watching Al's considerable muscle moving under the thin white silk.

"This is my library," he said, his voice preoccupied as he shifted his shoulders in the new freedom. "I recently got it back." He turned his head and smiled. "Isn't it pleasant?"

I didn't like his mood, both satisfied and evil. "Where's Brooke?" I asked, wedging a finger between my neck and Bis's tail.

Al took off his glasses and set them on the long table. His gloves landed beside them. "I told you," he said, squeezing the bridge of his nose with his thumb and index finger. "I got my library back. Nothing is free, itchy witch, especially in the ever-after."

Crap, he'd sold Brooke. In the time it took for me to catch my breath and turn around, he had sold her. I was going to get blamed for this. "I thought you had to wait until sunset to sell someone," I said, and he eyed me.

"Private sale. Prearranged." Seeing me on edge, he smiled, worrying me more.

"You snagging Brooke is not going to help my situation," I said, watching him move to the fireplace and crouch before it.

"It's helped mine." Al dropped a piece of wood onto the flame, making sparks fly. A lick of flame rose, and the wood caught. "This is what I do, Rachel. You need to worry about yourself, love. I want my conservatory next, and living things are *always* more expensive."

My face blanched when he stood and turned. If he was calling me *love*, I was still in trouble. Brooke could wait. "I didn't give Pierce my gun," I said, moving to put one of those tall wing-back chairs between us. "It's not my fault you didn't search him. I forgot he had it."

Looking totally different without his coat, glasses, and gloves, Al rummaged in a basket beside the hearth. "Make yourself at home. You and your gargoyle, Bis. Would you like something to eat?" His eyes met mine and I stifled a shiver. "I'll make cake."

I didn't trust this at all. His show of congeniality was more disturbing than if he were howling at me. But if I sat down, I might be able to get Bis off my shoulder.

Watching him, I went to sit. I didn't want to get smacked by sitting in his chair, but they both looked alike. The fireplace was to my right, and the dim library spilling out and down to my left. "You okay, Bis?" I said, hoping he'd move, but the kid was terrified and only nodded.

"No cake?" Al murmured with forced idleness—scaring the crap out of me. I'd gone to him for help, but now . . .

"I can't *say* how pleased I am that you're accepting your place," he said as he filled a kettle from a pitcher and set it over the fire. Coming close, he seated himself on the adjacent couch facing the fire, his knee almost touching mine and his burnt amber scent pinching my nose. "First a new vanity curse to hide your bite, and now asking for a curse when an earth charm exists. Bravo."

I put a hand to my neck, glad that he couldn't see my hairy legs.

"Don't hide it," he said, ignoring Bis's hissing as he took my hand and pulled it to him. "Your skin is beautiful. None of those lowbrow vampire marks anymore. You're worth more than vampire teeth, itchy witch."

Worry tightened my gut even as I nudged Bis to be quiet or get off my shoulder. "I can't invoke a locator charm made from earth magic," I said, remembering last winter when I'd stirred a batch to find a banshee, only to learn that my blood wouldn't invoke it. Marshal had done it. Seemed the more complex the magic, the more the subtle difference in my blood mattered.

"Neither can I," Al admitted lightly. "Welcome to the club."

"I'm not a witch," I admitted, scooting into the cushions to get some space between us.

"You're not really a demon either." Al's eyebrows rose.

Forcing my jaw to unclench, I blurted out, "I didn't give Pierce my gun. He took it when I was hopped up on that drug. I thought he had it to keep you from taking Lee or Ivy."

"Which is why you're here, itchy witch, and not screaming in my bedroom."

Fear came out as anger. "Knock it off, will you? That doesn't work anymore."

I had time for a breath, nothing more. Al was on me, pushing me into my chair, his face inches from mine, his arm under my chin. Bis fell back, wings flailing as he left my shoulder.

"I need to work harder at it, then," the demon said, his words clipped.

I could feel my pulse lifting my skin to touch him. His heavy weight pressed into me, and my breathless reflection was in his red, goat-slitted eyes. "Get off," I panted.

Bis hissed, and I saw a flash of reaching claws.

"You need to learn your place, 'goyle," Al said, and I jerked when his eye twitched and Bis thumped to the carpet, unseen but wheezing in what had to be shock and pain.

"Hey!" I shouted, squirming to get out from under Al.

The demon leaned into me harder, and my breath whooshed out. "And you need to develop some manners. Or is it respect?"

A part of my brain realized he wasn't using magic, and I struggled to move. My hand got free, and he shifted to grab my wrist, bringing it to his nose as he breathed deeply. Sensation spilled down, and I realized he had the wrist that carried his mark. *Damn.*

Behind me, Bis mewled, "It's gone. It's gone. I can't hear them."

Double damn, I was in trouble, and I tried to see Bis, failing.

"That runt of yours tried to drop me with *your* charms, Rachel."

My eyes flicked back to Al's.

"Lie to me," he coached. "Tell me you had nothing to do with it or you will fund my mansion. I don't care if your brats will be demons or not."

"What are you doing to him!" I exclaimed as Bis mewed. "Bis, go home!" I added, knowing a circle couldn't hold him.

"I can't," the kid panted. "I can't feel the lines. Rachel, I can't see them!"

Holy crap, what had Al done?

Al pressed my wrist against my chest, his fingers against me. "Pierce could have *killed* me. Me, who has survived . . . everything!"

Teeth clenched, I grunted, "Let Bis go."

"I'd be more concerned about yourself, itchy witch. Bis is simply existing without contact with a ley line. It hurts the mind. Deprivation." He eased up a little, and I got a good breath of air. "The sooner I'm happy, the sooner I'll stop blocking his contact. Is killing you going to make me happy, Rachel?"

Burnt amber coated me, and I could feel myself start to sweat. "Pierce took my gun," I said again, hoping he believed me this time. "I didn't know he had it when he followed me. I forgot, I mean. I really did. Go ahead, search my thoughts. I'm telling the truth. Why would I want Pierce to kill you?"

Shock flickered in the back of his goat-slitted eyes. He let go of my wrist and pushed himself to a stand. It was too fast for me to get in a parting shot. Shaking, I straightened in my chair. Bis's whimpering took on a shade of relief, and I looked for him, finding him curled into a ball beside my chair. My hand dropped to touch him, and he clenched into himself. "Bis, go home," I said, and he looked up, his ears pinned to his skull, making his eyes look even bigger.

"Not again," he said, tail uncurling from his feet as he shook. "I won't run away again."

We both jumped when Al looked at the ceiling and bellowed, "Treble!"

His gargoyle? I thought, excitement mixing with my fear and spent adrenaline to make me feel ill. Was he going to teach me now so I didn't try again and kill myself? It would almost be worth the pain of pushing myself out of that line.

Bis shivered, and Al put his glasses on and turned to the lit fireplace as a gargoyle three times Bis's size scraped from the flue, wings spreading submissively as she hopped to the hearth.

Treble had black tufts on her ears, long and flowing, where Bis had white. The lion tuft on the end was black, too, and her entire tail looked shorter in proportion than Bis's. Stubby horns like an antelope's were between her ears, and when her golden eyes landed on Bis, she hissed, wings spreading aggressively and black teeth bared.

"Manners, Treble," Al said lightly as he rummaged in a chest to bring out a tin and a coffee press. "Bis is a guest."

Bis hugged my leg, and I extended my hand, helping him up to sit on the arm of my chair, putting him even with the larger gargoyle. His ears were pinned, and his red eyes wild as he shook, his tail wrapped around my wrist like he was holding my hand.

Al's posture was again his completely proper British nobleman, and I wondered if I'd been seeing him as himself earlier—which just made me wonder all the more. The tin opened, and the smell of burned coffee drifted out. Al's back to us, he measured a portion of the grounds and tapped them into a dry coffee press.

"Bis, this is Treble," he said, and the large gargoyle hissed all the louder. "When you're older, she's going to teach you how to properly jump the lines. Until then, you stay *out*."

"Why not now?" I asked, feeling betrayed and disappointed.

"Teach him? Never, never!" Treble protested, tail whipping almost into the fire. Her voice had that same deep resonance that Bis's did, but was more musical. Glaring at Bis, she spread her wings and hissed, her long, forked tongue raised aggressively.

The air seemed to crack, and my mouth dropped open when ever-after cascaded over Al to turn him clawed, winged, and blacker than sin. Treble cowered, abasing herself and going utterly white. I pressed back into the chair with Bis, horrified.

Like Dante's demon, Al stood over her, wearing nothing and his well-endowed privates not so private anymore. The hint of hard muscle I'd seen under his shirt was like sheets of obsidian, throwing back the fire-light in gleams of red. He blinked, his red, goat-slitted monstrosities chilling me. Was this what he really looked like, or was it simply what scared Treble the most? On my wrist, Bis shivered, stinking like cold iron.

"You refuse?" Al hissed, his new forked tail shifting like it had a mind of its own, curling about to tuck under Treble's chin and lift it. "Why do you think I let you live this long?"

"Oh God, no," Treble whispered, her wings spread so the tips came to a point past her bowed head. "If I teach the young buck, you'll kill me!" she added, squirming to get out from under him, her skin a pale white. "Like you did my mother and brothers!"

"Kill you?" Al said, his voice like gravel and his tail whipping back around himself. "No. I want you to teach Bis so he can teach *her*. Look at them. Tell me I lie."

I shrank back even deeper into the burnt-amber-smelling cushions as Treble sent her golden eyes over me. They flicked to Bis, and her lips pulled back from her pushed-in face, and she smiled wickedly. "Fortunate, fortunate witch," she said slyly. "But teach him? Why? The little gravel pit has no finesse, he's tearing holes every time he jumps." She turned her gaze on Bis, her skin darkening. "Don't think we can't hear what you're doing, stumbling into lines, breaking songs and rhythms, making everyone else step to your stumbles!"

Bis lowered his ears, and I put a hand on his shoulder. God, Al looked scary. Hung like a horse. No way was he getting anywhere near me.

"That's why you're going to teach him . . . Treble," Al said, his voice precise and so low that it was almost hard to hear. "We can't have a repeat of this evening." Looking like the devil, he turned his goat-slitted eyes to Bis in recrimination, and Bis's breath caught.

"Don't worry, Bis," I said, putting a hand on his clawed foot. "You can't know how to do it right unless someone shows you properly," I said pointedly. Clearly Pierce hadn't.

His gaze fixed on Al, Bis crawled up to my shoulder and wrapped his tail around my neck. Treble gave him a yellow-eyed stare, and I almost choked when his grip tightened.

"The lines are still ringing from his latest jump," Treble said caustically. "He's thicker than a rock. And too young. Can't even stay awake when the sun is up. I wouldn't teach that pebble if he was the last living 'goyle in either plane," she said disdainfully, then glanced at Al. "Unless I was told to."

"Well, I'm telling you," Al said, his features melting into his familiar vision of himself in lace, clothed once more. "You weren't any older when I stole you from your mother."

My shoulders dropped, and I exhaled, surprised that the crushed green velvet and lace that had once terrified me had become not only familiar but welcome. And yet, if I squinted, there was a hint of that black monstrosity in the curve of his shoulders, the depth of his chest.

Treble crouched, her skin darkening. "Right before you killed her. Bastard."

Treble's words were harsh, but her tone was bland, like a response in a play that has run too long. Al wasn't really listening either as he took the steaming kettle from the fire and poured the boiling water over the grounds. Even Bis had relaxed his death grip on my throat.

"So you'll teach him?" Al asked, the hidden threat obvious.

"I'll teach him. I'll teach him for *her*." Laughing at the pair of us, Treble did a little half hop toward the table. I could smell coffee, and my head started to hurt. "If anyone can teach him, I can. I know the taste of all lines on this continent," the gargoyle said in pride, her claws going silent on the carpet. "Even the shattered badlands where the great wars were fought."

Bis was listening intently, but Al wasn't, his thick fingers pressing the plunger on the coffee press to make swirls of denser brew rise and fall, unvoiced thoughts making him grim. Still silent, he poured two cups of coffee into twin, tiny white cups he took out of the cabinet. His mood was guarded, but it seemed he'd forgiven Treble as he placed a cup and saucer before me, then slid the soggy coffee press to Treble. "I think we should have Dali look at you, Rachel. Just to be sure you're not damaged after sliding into reality like that."

Dali? My fingers reaching for the cup drew back. "I'm fine. It just hurt is all."

Bis twitched his tail. "I'm sorry, Rachel."

Grimacing, I touched his flank. "Neither of us knew what we were doing. Don't worry about it." *But we'd done it.*

"Still . . ." Al exhaled as he sat in the chair across from me. His shirt was open, showing a sliver of smooth flesh. "Pushing through a line is like scraping your bike on the pavement."

Treble had a thick claw delicately in the coffee press as she plucked out a tablespoon of the wet grounds and ate it. "I'll say. She made one hell of a ley line, dragging her sorry existence a full twenty feet as the earth turned under her until she got out."

I made a what?

Al choked, setting his coffee down and dabbing at his lips. "Treble, leave."

She glared at Bis. "And you left her there!" she berated him, making his ears droop even more. "Ignorant pebble. Stay out of the lines until you're taught, or I'll stone you myself!"

Bis was trembling, unable to look up, and I had my hand atop his back. *I'd made a ley line? No freaking way!* "You need to lighten up," I said, and she hissed, her tail lashing as she started jamming coffee grounds into her mouth as if she'd never see them again.

"Rachel, don't threaten the gargoyle; they bite," Al said, his furrowed brow giving me the impression the gargoyle had let slip something Al hadn't wanted me to know. "Treble, leave."

"Well, she did!" Treble protested, grounds spilling from her mouth.

Al's skin tone went black, and I swear, a hint of horns appeared. He was halfway between himself and that vision of a demon god. *"Leave."*

Sullen, the gargoyle hopped to the fireplace, hanging by the mantel with her wings wide to block the heat. Folding them, she scuttled up the flue, making bits of mortar fall into the fire. Bis's claws relaxed, and I yelped when they dug into me again when Al said, "You as well, Bis. Let me jump you home. No need to make any more holes, yes? I want to talk to Rachel."

"Uh," I stammered, trying to get Bis's claws out of me as my thoughts flashed back to the vision of Al naked before the fireplace as a black-skinned devil.

Al smiled at Bis, playing the good cop as his skin lightened again to its usual color. The demon appeared relaxed, resting easy in his chair in a soft white shirt and with a tiny cup of coffee. "You should tell Ivy and Jenks that Rachel is okay. I'm sure they're worried."

Since when was Al concerned about Ivy and Jenks? Bis shook his head, but scary visions of a naked big Al aside, I wanted him out of here so I could hear about the ley line I'd made. *No. Way.* "Go on, Bis," I said, unwinding his tail from me. "If I'm not back by sunrise, have Ivy summon me home."

Al grunted, a ripple on his cup giving away his surprise. Clearly he'd forgotten about that. 'Course, he could summon me back. He'd had *my* name for almost six months.

Bis eyed me with big, sorrowful red eyes. "I'm sorry," he said for the umpteenth time, and after nodding to Al, he vanished with a soft whisper of collapsing air.

A sigh slipped from Al, and he pinched the bridge of his nose again. I figured it was an act to lull me into a relaxed state, but he'd pinned me to my chair not five minutes ago and I wasn't buying it.

"You're lucky, you know," he said as I sipped my coffee only to spit it back out. My God, it was awful. The taste of burnt amber made it rancid.

"I'm like a freaking rabbit's foot on fire," I said dryly, setting the cup down.

He looked at the cup, then me. "Very few demons can survive getting out of a line when they've not been taught."

"Really?" My stomach rumbled, but I wasn't going to drink the "coffee." "Who else can do it?" *Please don't say Newt . . .*

His eyes almost appeared normal in the dim light as he stared at nothing, his white shirt with lace at the cuffs and collar making him look like a tired British lord at the end of the day. "Just the handful of demons still in existence."

Oh? Pierce had said demons had flung themselves back to reality after stranding the elves, accidentally scribing the ley lines and stabilizing the ever-after. Which meant that Al had been there. Survived it. And the gargoyles who then taught them how to do it without hurting themselves were either killed or enslaved. Nice.

"I'm not a demon," I said. "And I'm not going to use Bis like a familiar either. It's wrong!"

Cup perched in his fingers, untasted, he said, "Rachel, if you would be patient and listen to me, you wouldn't have to make the same mistakes we all did."

Crap, he was starting to sound like my dad. Another man who, the more I knew, the more I didn't know. Leaning back, I crossed my knees. "Which line did you make?"

Al's eyes squinted. For a moment he just stared; then he set his cup down and rose in a rustle of fabric. *Fine. Don't tell me.* "Treble doesn't like you," I prodded. "You trust her?" What I really wanted to know was if that black monstrosity was really him.

"Absolutely." Al unwrapped a cloth-covered basket and brought out half a loaf of bread.

I snorted, earning a dry look, and then I asked, "How come Bis has to teach me? He's a good kid and all, but wouldn't it be easier if Treble did it?" He was stalling, trying to keep me ignorant, and I wasn't going to let him.

"Treble?" Al carefully cut perfectly equal slices off the loaf, one by one. "She can't get through your aura like Bis can."

"Bis can get through yours. What's the difference?" I almost accused him.

"Bis is young." Al turned with six slices of bread in his hand. "He'll be able to cross any circle until he bonds himself to an aura. He seems to like you, but even so, you'd better be careful or you'll lose him to Pierce. And there you'll be, forced to steal another baby from the basilica and having to wait another fifty years to learn how to jump the lines."

"Whoa, whoa, whoa. What's this 'bond' thing?" I asked, worried. *Gargoyles to witches, as pixies are to elves?* "Bis is not my gargoyle," I protested, and Al chuckled as he pierced each slice of bread on a set of long forks.

"I wasn't too keen on Treble either," he said. "Still am not. But once a gargoyle takes to you, it's not as if you have much say. It's in their makeup, you see. Engineered in."

They had *made* them. Demons had *made* gargoyles, creating the ability to hear the lines and the need for them to bond so they wouldn't run off and teach us poor witches and elves. No wonder free gargoyles hung out on churches. Oh, this wasn't good. Bis and I needed to talk.

"Done and done," Al said with a tone of finality as he propped the six slices of bread on their toasting forks against the heat. "I believe you didn't help Pierce, Rachel Mariana Morgan. Tell me your plan to get the coven off your ass and Nicholas Sparagmos into my kitchen."

Apparently we were done talking about gargoyles, but at least I knew he believed me. My sigh of relief was loud, but then I tensed. "I never said Nick in your kitchen was part of the deal—," I started, but my words cut off when he turned, a big-ass knife in his hand.

"Rachel, we've been over this. This is what I do," he said, crumbs of white cheese falling from the knife. "Find a way for your lofty, unrealistic ideals to deal with it."

"But I'm the one who gets blamed!" I exclaimed, frustrated. I *knew* Vivian was going to ask me to rescue Brooke or get caught trying to do it herself. Then I'd get blamed for that, too.

"So stay here with me." He was slicing more cheese, his broad back to me as he worked. I could almost imagine sharp-edged, shiny wings. "I'm touched that you came to my rescue. And with nothing but a pain amulet. You are either truly overconfident or truly stupid."

"I didn't rescue you," I said quickly.

The fire snapped as he wiped his fingers on a white towel, casual and totally out of character. There was enough cheese for two, and I eyed it hungrily. "Looks to me like you did," he said. "It has been untold ages since I worked with anyone like that. I'd quite forgotten. It does give one a thrill, not knowing what might happen."

My held breath slipped out, and I frowned. "Okay, maybe I did," I admitted, "but I did it because I need you to find Nick, fast. Can you give me a locator curse?" I asked. Crap, this was risky. Asking Al for help was easy, like a wish, and you always paid for those in the ass.

Al tested the toasted bread between a finger and a thumb. "Rush, rush, rush. You have no need for haste anymore. Tell me your ideas while we eat. There's always time for coffee."

I grimaced at my cup, and he put the fork back, clearly not happy with the brownness of the bread. I didn't say anything, and he finally rose, standing so the flames warmed him. "It's been a bitch since Pierce left to watch you. I've had to do my own cooking. I hope you don't mind cheese sandwiches. It's all I know how to make."

With the toast done on one side, I thought, eying it as my stomach rumbled again, and I sat up to hide the sound. Elbows on my knees, I hung my head, going over my plan and trying to decide how much to tell him. It was Trent's idea, thanks to his Pandora charm. "I need to be charged with a crime," I started.

Al laughed as he shoved his hands in his pockets and rocked on his heels. "I can think of a few. Let's start with uncommon stupidity for jumping the lines untrained."

My head came up, and I frowned. "I managed it, though, didn't I? I'm serious. The press is always watching me, so I may as well use that to my advantage. I need to be caught at some crime that is both spectacular and relatively harmless, something that people will fall in love with, maybe see as noble. Nick is the perfect choice."

"Noble," Al said, taking up two of the forks. "Like a new modern-day Robin Hood."

Yeee-haaaa. "If the press is paparazzing me, the coven can't tuck me away in Alcatraz."

Al layered a slice of cheese between two pieces of toast and set it on a black plate that hadn't been there a moment ago. "Ahhh . . . ," he said as he quickly made three sandwiches, divvying them up between two plates. "If they give you a trial, what you are comes out, and where all witches have their beginnings. Or they leave you alone and pray you don't cross them. Or they try to kill you without the press knowing. Double jeopardy?"

I nodded, eying the two sandwiches on that second plate. "It's worth the risk. Either they let me go when I promise to be good . . ."

"Or they kill you."

The cheese smelled all melty as Al slid the plate with one sandwich in front of me beside the nasty coffee. I looked at it. *Al made me dinner?* "That's why it has to be spectacular," I said. "I want Trent involved. He started it. He's going to have to call them off. He doesn't want me dead. He wants me to work for him." I thought of that paper he wanted me to sign, wondering whether I'd do it now if given the chance.

Al sat at the far end of the long table, pulling his plate closer and picking his first sandwich up with a napkin that appeared from nowhere. "I've never agreed with this long leash you're giving your familiar. See what he's done? In a mere six months? Bring him in. I can whip him into shape in half that time. Give him back to you as a present. I'll put a bow on him and everything." Al quit waving his toasted sandwich and took a bite.

"Trent is not my familiar." I leaned over the plate and picked up my sandwich with my bare fingers, wondering why Al didn't want to touch his. "I don't need one, okay? This entire mess is because of him thinking I might use him as a familiar."

Elbow on his knee, Al leaned forward, chewing. "So I gathered."

I watched him for a moment, then looked at the sandwich. It smelled wonderful. "Thank you," I said, then took a bite. *Oh God, it tasted wonderful.*

Al seemed pleased when I followed my first bite with another. "Why do you want Nick?" he asked. "Not that I'm agreeing to help you . . . yet."

I looked for a napkin, hesitating when one misted into existence under my fingers. "I know him," I said, dabbing my lips. This was really weird. Dinner with Al? Kind of like tea in the Sahara. "He's a thief, and a damn good one. Mmmm, this is tasty." *Flattery is always good.*

The demon's smile widened. "Trading him in for space would get a fine room for you."

My chewing slowed. " 'Scuse me?"

"Your pet rat. I can get you a good price for Nicky. Trade him for a very nice starter room connected to my space. Unless you really like sleeping in the workroom? Let's bend that request you made of no snag-and-drags of people with you. I pop in on the excuse of checking on you, then trade him in for a space of your very own. What do you owe him anyway? He told me secrets about you. Good ones. Things that only a lover would know. How do you think I got Brooke to let me out?"

I sucked my teeth to get the cheese out of them. Interesting. Twice now he'd asked me to stay, first in his rooms and now in my own. I set the crust down, and Al eyed it. "I'm asking Nick for his help, not his soul. I don't belong here. I like the sun."

"So do I, itchy witch, but here I am."

He leaned back, and I fingered the crust, thinking about living your life underground.

"Be honest, dove," he coaxed, an ankle dropping onto a raised knee. "You don't have it in you to make your sewer rat do what you want. You're not nearly pissed enough at the world."

"I'm going to ask," I countered. "Persuasively."

"He hates you," Al said, his tone returning to his usual pomp and extravagance.

A smile lifted the corners of my mouth as I thought of Treble. "He'll help me. He won't be able to resist. The guy has an ego the size of Montana."

"Well, if you're going to stroke his ego," Al grumbled. "Honestly, this preoccupation you have with nasty little men is going to get you killed."

I eyed the second, untouched sandwich on Al's plate. "That's why I've got you, Al, to keep me alive." I licked my fingers. "Are you going to eat that?"

Motions slow, he carefully slid his plate to me, the china scraping loudly on the wood. This was kind of nice, and I looked around as I filled my stomach, enjoying the crisp bread and the cheese. I couldn't place what kind it was, and frankly, I didn't want to know. "Thank you," I said, lifting the sandwich so he knew what I was talking about. "I like your library."

Al had pushed himself into the corner of his massive chair, scowling, though I think he was secretly pleased that I liked his cooking. "Don't become comfortable in it. I'm not granting you any private peek into my existence. The workroom is messy is all."

I swallowed, washing it down with a gulp of that awful coffee. Memories of my dad's fairy tales lifted through me, but the caution there had been don't eat food with the sidhe or elves, not demons, and I'd already had breakfast with Trent. "Pierce made a mess, eh?"

"Mmmm," was his only answer, but his eyes held amusement when they met mine. "You should have seen his face. I'll beat him soundly when you finally come home for good, no question about it. Maybe I'll let you help. Sell him, and you could buy your own address."

Third offer, a place of my own. Better and better. "Al, don't start," I said with a sigh, and he laughed. The sound shocked through me, and he quickly sobered when I stared at him. "So . . . are you going to help me?" I asked.

His eyes shifted everywhere, and I felt like I was on trial. "Perhaps," he drawled. "I want to know why the change of heart. You told the coven you're not a witch. You asked for my help right in front of them. You told them that you shunned *them*."

My eyebrows rose. *I shunned them?* I'd never thought of it that way. It sort of put me in a position of power. *Pride goeth before the fall, Rachel.* "I'm tired," I said, and Al made another hum of sound. "I'm tired of fighting. I'm tired of trying to be who I think I should be. It's not working. Don't get me wrong," I added when Al's expression shifted. "I'm not stupid. Just because I'm asking for your help doesn't mean I like you."

A black haze of ever-after covered him, and suddenly it was Pierce sitting before me, his slight build making his silk shirt loose and almost falling open. His smile was devious, and something twisted in me. "Are you of a mind to like me now?" he said, hitting the man's accent perfectly, and my heart pounded.

"Stop it," I said, but I knew I'd given myself away. "I don't trust Pierce either."

I felt a tweak on my awareness as he returned to his usual self. "Good," he intoned, warming our coffee with a gesture. "You just might survive to make history, my itchy witch. It's better hot. Go on, try it."

Yada yada yada. I was done eating, and I wiped my fingers. "You going to help me?"

"You want my help just because?" Al said dramatically. "For the hell of it?"

"Jeez, Al," I complained. "It's only a finding curse."

"And the jump to go with it," he added.

"Look. Forget it," I said, then stood to make him blink up at me. "Thanks for dinner. Just send me home. I can do this myself." Nick couldn't be too far. I'd ask around. I could find him. Or Ivy could. "I just have to scare him into it. How hard can it be?"

"You!" It was a bark of amusement, and I frowned at Al. "Yes, do this yourself. You start using demon magic intentionally, and you're going to screw up more than Marie Antoinette on her wedding night. I'll scare him for you."

I paused in my first thought of saying no. Had that been a back-assed yes? I met his gaze, breath held, but he was holding up a thick hand.

"A bet might make this go down my greedy soul easier," he said, and I felt a drop of ice slide down my spine. "I'll find Nick. Even jump you there if you bring me along for shits and giggles. But if you can't get the coven off your back and your shunning removed, you forget all this nonsense and move in with me. Here."

Oh. I paused, then sighed. Double jeopardy. But if I couldn't do this, then the coven would have my head on a platter. Or maybe my brain scrambled and my ovaries in the fridge. "Deal," I finally said, my heart jumping when he clapped his hands once in delight. "But Nick is not snatched, and I get to play bad cop. I never get to play the bad cop."

Al laughed. "You don't have it in you, itchy witch."

Simpering, I felt a stirring of anticipation. "Try me."

He looked at me, hesitated, then smiled. "I can't cross uninvited, but you can," Al said, standing and grabbing his coat from the back of the chair. "We need something from my kitchen. Won't take but a moment."

Oh God. What am I doing? I thought, but Al's thoughts had enfolded mine, and we jumped.

Twenty-eight

I opened my eyes as I felt myself become solid again, or at least I thought I did. It smelled like wood smoke, burnt amber, and ozone, all characteristic of Al's kitchen. There was a soft scrape of my foot on stone when I moved it, but it was pitch-black, the echo of two people's breathing coming back with an unfamiliar, acidic scent.

"Al?" I ventured, his harrumph beside me coming as small comfort.

"A moment," he said elegantly, and I jumped when there was a sliding crash. "Mother pus bucket!" the demon swore, and I wished I could instantly set a light with my thoughts like Pierce. But the spell I knew was a curse, and took me forever and a handful of stuff to do it.

Al, though, could do it, and a small globe of gray light blossomed four feet away to show the demon holding his shin and the shattered remains of the slate table that had been in front of the hearth. What it was doing over here was the question.

Seeing my raised eyebrows, Al brushed himself off and tugged his frock coat straight. I went to say something, then hesitated, staring slackjawed at the chaos the once orderly room was in. Al's light wasn't bright, but the damage was obvious. One cabinet was a burnt ruin, the books covered with a brown slime. Scorch marks went all the way to the ceiling.

Firewood littered the floor among the shattered remains of the slate table. The tapestry of shadowy shapes I swore moved when I wasn't looking was slumped in a corner, exposing the wall it had once hidden. The stone was twisted, as if something had melted the wall trying to get in or out, but I'd bet the damage was old and not from Pierce.

A huge chunk of rock was missing from the circular fire pit, and I searched the mess until I found it against Al's largest, now-dented spell pot. Above it, the candle chandelier was dark, the candles having melted into splattered puddles that had completely ruined the dark cushions running atop the stone bench about the central fireplace.

"Pierce did this?" I breathed as Al tried to yank open a drawer, the tight wood not giving an inch.

"*Adaperire!*" he shouted, and my hands jumped to my zipper, yanking it back up again as every door, cupboard, and box suddenly opened.

"Your boyfriend is a pain in the ass," he said, looking embarrassed as he plucked three black candles from the drawer.

"He's not my boyfriend." I gingerly touched the goo on the books to find that, like Jenks's dust, it came away cleanly, rolling into a ball and falling to the floor. Where the goo was, the fire hadn't burned. Clearly Al had used it to protect his precious spell library.

Al looked at the empty mantel where the candlestick holders used to be, his expression going tighter yet. "Rachel, be a dear and see if you can find the sconces? I believe they're at the tapestry. That's where he was when I threw them at him."

I couldn't help my smile as I crossed the room. No wonder Al had been ticked.

"There's *nothing* funny about destroying my kitchen," the demon said as I used my foot to feel the crumpled tapestry and look for the metal candle holders. I didn't want to touch the oily fabric that had been hiding a melted wall.

Finally I found one of the holders, and using a chunk of burnt firewood, I levered the tapestry up, shuddering when the colors shifted to hide underneath. I wasn't going to reach under there, so I flipped it over.

"Got 'em," I said, breathing easier as I picked my way back across the broken room. Al had placed our chairs back where they belonged, an expanse between them to show where the table ought to go. He had already started a fire in the small hearth, and he tossed the table's legs into the larger, central hearth, adding torn cushions and whatever else he didn't want before muttering in Latin and exploding it into flame.

The light from the two fires was brightening the room to where his dim globe was inconsequential. Without direction, I set the black candles in the holders and lit them myself. I felt kind of bad about the mess, and I swooped about, finding ley-line equipment and trying to put things back to rights. The clatter of Al doing the same seemed loud. It might sound funny, but I'd spent a lot of time here, and seeing the mess Pierce had created made me feel . . . violated.

Al noticed what I was doing, and with another sheepish look, he touched his dimly lit globe and the light went out.

"Why didn't—," I started.

"I just make a brighter light?" he said, head down as he fingered his five-sided pyramid. Eyes meeting mine, he held my gaze. "It's glowing brighter than the sun," he said. "That's all the light that can get through the smut."

I couldn't hold his gaze, and I turned away. "Sorry," I whispered. "I didn't know."

"No worries, lovey," he murmured, his gloves showing the black of ash as he set the pyramid away. "It's a small thing."

"I meant about Pierce trashing the kitchen," I said, not wanting him to think I cared.

His eyebrows were raised. "As did I." Spinning to make his coattails furl, he crossed the cleared floor to an intact cabinet. "We will find Nicholas Gregory Sparagmos most easily by way of his demon mark," he said as he opened the cabinet, reaching into the back of the clutter for a folded bit of paper. "And for that, I need this."

He turned, handing it to me triumphantly. It was a page from a spell book, the charm handwritten and smelling old. There were spots of black on it, and with a start I realized that they weren't drops of ink, but blood. Nick's blood. My thoughts zinged back to his demon mark, and I looked at Al. "This is from the basement library," I said, and he smiled with his flat, blocky teeth. "From the night you tore my throat out, then sold us a trip to the church to save my life."

"Two demon marks in one night, yes. Clever, clever little witch for you to guess! Capital good instincts!" he said, just about bursting. "What bit of bloodied thing do you have of Trenton to find him? Nothing?" he almost drawled. "What a shame. You should rectify that. Give him a bloody nose next time you see him, and save the hanky."

I sighed, wondering what bit of bloodied thing in that cabinet was mine. There had to be about fifty things in there, all from people halfway belonging to Al.

"Now, we have to do this a little backward," Al was saying, pulling me to that ugly face he used as a landing pad and having to kick the tapestry out of the way. My face went cold, and I looked to the other side of the room. *I knew it had been over there.*

"Wait. Wasn't that over there?" I said, hesitating, but Al yanked me forward, pulling me to stand right next to him.

"Probably," he said, kicking backward at it again. "I can't pop into reality uninvited unless I'm checking on you. I'll get you there, and you summon me. Immediately." His eyes narrowed, and I shoved his tightening grip off my arm. "It's that trust thing you've been whining about," he growled. "I *trust* you to bring me along."

"And I trust you not to throttle him," I said, and he made a pained face.

"Abso-o-olute-e-e-ly," he said, so slowly I doubted him. "Tap a line, Rachel."

Doubt or not, I tapped the line, feeling the curious ache of using a line this side of reality. My eyes widened when the bit of paper flamed up in Al's white-gloved hands. "You can only do this once?" I asked, amazed as he breathed in the smoke, eyes closing in bliss, but my shock redoubled when I realized the paper wasn't being burned.

"It's not real flame," Al said, then gave me a shove. "Go!"

"Hey!" I shouted in protest, but my lungs compressed and the line took me. With an almost absurd quickness, I popped back into existence in a dark, low-ceilinged room. It was stuffy, with the light coming from a bank of electronic equipment. I could smell stinky socks and what seemed like too much occupation. The walls were painted cinder block, and there was the tang of mold. Flat brown carpet lay over what felt like cement. Metal and wood racks made aisles from floor to ceiling, all holding wooden crates wired shut.

Oh. My. God. Am I in Nick's mother's basement? But then I decided that it was more like one of those bio shelters they made during the Turn with filtered air and bottled water.

"Al, I summon you," I mouthed, and with that tiny bit of invitation, I felt his heavy presence mist into existence beside me. He made a low growl of sound, pleasure and satisfaction. It went right to my middle and burned. I knew what he was feeling, and I cursed myself. It was the thrill of not knowing if he could trust me.

"Are you sure this is the place?" I breathed, feeling small with Al beside me.

Al raised his hand, a steady finger pointing out a rumpled shape sleeping on an old military cot. "Go get him, itchy witch," he breathed in my ear, and the burning sensation in me redoubled. "Let me see you make your first kill."

I knew he was speaking metaphorically, but I couldn't help being reminded of Jenks's wildlife programs of a lioness wounding prey to let her cubs practice bringing it down. My jaw clenched and I shoved the thought away. Nick had lied and tried to scam me in what would have put me in jail after I saved his ass from militant Weres. I didn't owe him anything, not even my respect. It wasn't as if I was going to snatch him.

I crept forward, my sneakers silent on the musty carpet. Nick was snoring. I stopped when he took a deep breath, a frown line showing as his eyes opened, not moving as he stared at the ceiling. "Shit," he breathed, and I realized the reek of burnt amber had given us away.

Pushing myself into motion, I jumped for him, landing on his bed and pinning him there. It would have been a simple matter to throw me off, but he didn't, staring up at me in shock, his brown eyes wide. "Hi, Nic-k," I said, hitting the *k* hard. "How's it hanging, buddy?"

Hidden by the covers, I felt his hands move, guessing that he was an-gling for something. "You," he said, his eyes darting behind me to Al.

"Me," I drawled, shifting my weight to stop his motion to his pillow. "That's Al, and you, of course, are the rat." I leaned in, inches from his face. "Isn't this nice, all of us here together? Do me a favor. Don't get up. Just sit there and listen, and maybe I can convince Al not to steal every-thing in your little rat hole here."

"You bitch!" Nick spat. "You did it again! You brought a demon into my home!"

My face twisted. "Yeah, but this time, I did it on purpose."

I could hear Al humming "Tiptoe Through the Tulips," punctuated by little mmms of discovery as he unearthed who knew what from the crates behind me. I'd seen Nick's apartment. What he had here in his last-ditch hidey-hole was probably priceless.

"How did you find me?" he said, anger creasing his brow.

I pushed his hair back to run a finger over the scar Al had given him. "How do you think? He knows when you are sleeping, he knows when you're awake."

From the corner, Al shifted his tune. "So be good, or I'll rip your fucking head off."

Nick sat up, shoving me back to a stand. In his hands was an amulet. Al hissed, but I was way ahead of him, snatching up the clock and swing-ing it by the cord into Nick's fist.

Swearing, Nick dropped the amulet and I kicked it away. "Don't touch it, Al!" I warned when the demon went for it, and Al stopped, looking at me indignantly, until a demon-size bubble rose from it. If he'd been any-where nearer, he would've been caught.

"I knew it was a trap, itchy witch," the demon said, but then a flash of white exploded against the inside of the circle. I felt the bubble go down, leaving a white disk of ash where the carpet had burned away. "But I didn't know it was a lethal one," he continued, and I fought the urge to smack the sniveling human. Nick had wanted me in it, not Al.

Nick bolted, and instinct kicked in. Lunging, I grabbed him around the waist, letting go before we hit the floor, then rolled into a stand and smacked a front kick in his middle. His breath whooshed out, and he clutched his stomach. Swell, he was in his underwear. I hated arguing with men in their underwear. "Get up!" I shouted, hoping there was no one upstairs.

"Ohhh, nice one, little grasshopper," Al said as he rummaged through a crate.

Ignoring Al, I yanked Nick to his feet and shoved him back on the bed, where he hunched over his knees, feet on the floor. "Poor Nicky," I said as he struggled for air. "Can't make a bubble 'cause I'll just shove you into it. Can't tap a line 'cause we're better than you. And your pixy is gone. Don't you even wonder where he is? Or did you send him to spy on us?"

Nick looked up, ears red and having gotten in only one good breath. "What do you want?" he wheezed. "You want something, bitch, or you wouldn't be here." Hunched over, he glared at Al. "Don't touch that!"

From the edge of my sight, I watched Al raise a multiple-pipe instrument to his lips. It looked old, and with his fingers bare of his usual gloves, he played a few notes, then carelessly tossed it back into the crate. Nick cringed, and I brought his attention back to me with a shove that pushed him into the wall.

"I want you," I said, answering his question. "Or more specifically, I want your nasty, devious, light-fingered skills. Wanna job?"

Nick looked up—I hadn't hit him that hard—and smiling, as if I'd just given him the upper hand, he pointed to his pants on the chair. Wary, I checked the pockets before throwing them at him. "Right," he said as he shoved one foot, then the other, in. "Why would I help you?"

Behind me, I heard Al sigh dramatically. "I told you, itchy witch. Let me. Violence works so-o-o much faster."

My eye twitched at the sound of Nick's zipper. "Oh, he'll do it," I said, tension winding tighter. "He won't be able to resist."

Eyebrows raised, as if asking for permission, Nick clicked on the small bedside lamp sitting on a milk crate. His scars became visible, reminders of our beginnings. "I'm not doing a job for you," he said as he roughly pulled a white T-shirt on to hide them. "I don't care that you have your demon on a leash."

Al growled, and I hoped he'd keep playing the good cop. Maybe I needed to get rougher.

"Al leashed? Right," I said, standing with my hip cocked. "The only reason you're not on the auction block buying me a set of rooms in the ever-after is because I don't want you."

Nick hesitated, eying me as he shoved his arms into the sleeves of a plaid shirt. Long fingers moving dexterously, he stood before me in the low-ceilinged room and did up the lowest four buttons. "You admit you're a demon," he said bitingly.

My face burned, and I stayed silent.

"What do you want?" Nick yanked a pair of white socks from a pile and sat on his bed.

Al was rummaging again, and ignoring his muttered prediction of doom, I said, "I want you to help me steal something."

Nick, true to form, sucked on his teeth and eyed me. "What?"

He didn't mean "what" as in "excuse me." He meant what did I want him to steal, and a quiver rose and fell. I almost had him.

Nick waited for me to answer, and when I didn't, he pointed to his boots, out of his reach. "Fair enough," he said. "What's in it for me?"

Smiling, I felt his laces, sensing the charmed silver in them. Nice. "Nothing," I said as I yanked the laces free and tossed him the first boot. "You get nothing. Not a damn thing."

His second boot landed next to the first, untouched. Sitting on the low cot, Nick put his elbows on his knees and looked up at me from around his shaggy hair. An almost-hidden disappointment was in him for my having found his means of possible escape, and I could nearly see him reassessing the situation. "Remove my mark, and I'll think about it," he grumbled.

Al came forward, and as I handed him the laces, he intoned, "It's my mark, not hers."

"So she owes you a mark instead of me," Nick said. His tight face turned to me. "I bet you could get rid of it overnight, Rachel. Or don't you charge for your services?"

I hardly felt Al's hand on my arm as I shoved it off. Feeling like Ivy, I sauntered to him, confident, in control, and pissed to the ends of the earth. *Did he just call me a slut? Again?* "I'm not taking your lousy little mark," I said, close enough to do some damage if I tried. "I'm still trying to get rid of the one you foisted on me."

Knowing he'd gotten to me, Nick smiled. "We have nothing to talk about. Get out."

This wasn't going well. Maybe Al was right and I didn't have it in me to be the bad cop.

Al was gleefully rubbing his hands together, and my promise to abandon reality if I couldn't do this came crashing down on me. "I told you!" he crowed. "What color do you want your walls painted, Rachel? Snag him now and be done with it."

Nick's face got ugly, and I held up a hand. "You owe me, Nick."

Grabbing an unlaced boot, he shoved his foot into it, hard. "I don't owe you anything."

"How do you figure that?" I shot back, hand on my hip.

He wedged his foot in the other boot. "The focus?" he mocked.

"You sent it to me!" I said loudly.

"I thought you were dead!" he shouted back.

"And you never bothered to check!" I said. "Not my problem!"

Al chuckled as he tried on tribal masks, and I frowned, not liking him watch us argue.

"I had to get it back," Nick said sullenly. "I'd already promised it to the coven."

"And you gave them me instead," I said bitterly. "I was in Alcatraz, Nick. They want to give me a lobotomy. They lace the food with compounds that block your ability to do magic. I don't owe you shit."

He stood, and seeing a hint of remorse, I crossed my arms over my chest. If he was going for the door, he'd find himself on the floor again. "Maybe lying to me is acceptable to you," I said. "And maybe selling information to demons about me is not a problem. And maybe I was a naive sucker of a girl who deserved everything she got." My voice was rising, but I couldn't help it. "But if that's what I was to you, then that's what I was. My mistake for thinking I was something else."

I sounded like a hurt girlfriend, and I hated it. I thought I'd let this go, but apparently not.

"I've learned one thing through this crapfest, Nick," I said, forcing myself to be calm. "People treat you like they see you, not who you really are. Let's say you're right. Let's say I'm the bad guy here, and you're the poor abused human. Is that who you want to be? The helpless human? 'Cause that's not how I saw you. And if I'm the big bad witch who is unreasonable and mean, then that's how I'm going to act."

A year of bottled-up frustration surfaced, and his eyes widened as I came at him.

He raised a hand to block my punch, and I shifted my grip, levering his own arm under his chin as I shoved him back into the wall. Yelping, he froze when I used my free hand to find his nuts. That fast, it was over, and Al was laughing.

"Still think you don't owe me anything?" I shouted, inches from his face, and giving a little squeeze. Okay, maybe I could do bad cop.

"Ow," he said, not moving apart from his chest as he breathed fast. "Let go, Rachel."

"Why?" I said. "You don't use 'em!"

"I'm not helping you," Nick said breathily. "You can go screw a demon for all I care."

From behind me Al chuckled. "No offense, but this is a lot more entertaining."

Having made my point, I let go and backed up out of his reach. I was shaking inside, but I wasn't ready to give up yet. Not by a long shot. "You're not the man I thought you were," I said. "Thief extraordinaire? Right. Fine. I'll go talk to Rose. I should have gone to her anyway. Come on, Al. Nick doesn't have the guts for it."

"Rose?" Al said, confused as he looked at me from around an open crate.

"Yeah, the gal at the place with the thing?" Turning my back on Nick, I went to the middle of the room and stood as if waiting for Al to join me so we could pop out. In a bad temper that wasn't faked, I scoffed, "You don't think you're the only thief I've run into, do you? The Turn diamond?

Or England's lodestone? Who do you think lifted them?" I was making this up as I went along, but the diamond was legendary, as was the lodestone.

Catching my drift, Al sidled closer to me. "You are a versatile itchy witch," he cooed, and I wiggled my fingers to get his lips away from my ear.

Nick, though, had paused. "No one's lifted them," he said, doubt on his face. "They're right where they belong, under enough security to kill a cockroach."

I smiled brightly. "I'm sure you're right. Al? We've got only a few hours."

"Quite right!" he said brightly, and I slipped my arm in his, dropping one foot behind the other to pose with him. God, Nick was easier to manipulate than my brother.

My heart pounded as I felt the line take us, and I had a moment of panic. This didn't count. If Al took me out of here before I could finish the deal, it didn't count!

"Wait!" Nick's voice came thinly, and I heard Al swear, but we misted back into existence to see Nick standing there with his long, sensitive hand outstretched in doubt. A surge of adrenaline and sexual excitement pulsed in me. *Shit, I'm not getting turned on over this?*

Al must have sensed it, because he leaned closer, his hand curving around my side, then withdrawing lightly across my back to make me quiver. "Sweet mother of chaos," he breathed. "Rachel, you are indeed one of us. Have your time in the sun. You're worth the extra wait."

Licking my lips, I stood, unable to move. The blood pounded low in my groin, and I clenched my teeth. Damn it, I was not getting turned on by besting Nick in a game of bluff!

Am I?

"What's the take?" Nick asked warily, eying me so closely that I had to wonder if he knew what was going through my mind.

Swallowing, I pulled from Al. "I want to steal something from Trent." *Something more than his hoof pick this time.*

Al dropped back, humming happily about this little witch of mine.

Nick looked me up and down. "Lab, office, or living quarters?"

Damn it, I think I've got him! There'd be the obligatory pissing contest, but he'd do it. "Thief's choice, just not his living quarters."

Nick grabbed a couple of twist ties from the trash and laced a boot closed. "Why not his rooms?"

I shrugged, shifting farther from both men. "I promised I wouldn't."

"Can I take a person?" Nick asked, and I recoiled.

"No. A thing. I don't care what it is. I figured you'd know better than me what Trent has in his basement that he's not sharing with the world. It has to be something embarrassing and sensational. Something he wants back, bad, but doesn't want to admit having."

Nick looked up from tying his second boot with a twist tie. "Blackmail? He gets the coven off your case or you go public with it?" His head shook. "He'll just kill you."

"Which is why I'm giving it back before he has the chance," I said. I didn't think Trent would kill me. If I died, even disgraced and shunned, his biolabs would hit the front page.

Nick looked at me in disbelief. "You want me to steal just so you can give it back?"

"That's my itchy witch for you," Al said with a sigh. "Nicholas Gregory Sparagmos, I will take your mark back for everything in this room."

"Only if I'm not included on the list," he shot back, and Al scrunched his features up in disappointment.

"Damn."

"It's a prank, Nick," I said, bringing the conversation back to me. "You know, for fun? Trent is going to announce his candidacy for city mayor on Friday. The press will be there. I'm going to give it back then."

His expression brightening, Nick bobbed his head. "He'll press charges."

My breath puffed out of me. "Only if I'm really lucky," I muttered.

Nick looked at me, read my tells, and knew I wasn't lying. I needed him, and that alone was enough. Not because he liked me or wanted to help, but because when it was done, I was going to owe him, and he'd never let me forget it.

Still balancing on a no, he eyed me. "I don't see what you're getting here," he said.

Smiling, I sauntered forward, moving slowly as I put my arms around his neck and leaned in. "That's because you're a thief, Nicky," I whispered, lips next to his ear. Pulling back, I gave him a kiss. It was dead. There was nothing there. No hatred, no anger, no love. Nothing. I didn't care. He was a means to an end. Nothing more.

Our lips parted, and I waited. I could see in his expression that he knew it was done. And somehow that moved our relationship to a completely unexpected level. *Business.*

"I know exactly what you need," he said, and I smiled.

Twenty-nine

I took a deep breath, pulling the garden-damp air deep into me and feeling as if the golden haze of afternoon pooled inside me, all yellow and swirly. There was a hint of chill in the air this early in the spring, and the tang of Jenks's stump, still burning, reminded me of fall. It might burn for months, the roots smoldering underground as it slowly erased Jenks's heartache. Even so, it felt good to be home and in the garden.

There was only the faint hissing of cars to remind me that I was in the suburbs of Cincinnati; all else was quiet. Jenks's family was in mourning, and the garden seemed empty. In my hand was a handful of hickory twigs, still green and sporting new leaves. I'd used the last of the bark scrapings this morning making up a new batch of pain amulets. I wasn't sure exactly what I was going to need for tonight's escapade, but pain amulets were a good bet. Especially if I didn't have a splat gun— thanks to Pierce.

Motions slow and provocative, I went up the worn back-porch steps, daring the coven to take a potshot at me, but it was probable that Vivian was at the coven, relating how I'd given Brooke to a demon. They had to have heard about the fairies by now, too. Ceri had taken the survivors with her when she'd left in the same cab I'd pulled up in this morning with Nick. All but one fairy, apparently, which I had yet to see and Jenks didn't know about.

My hand on the screen door, I looked over my shoulder at the garden, remembering how dangerous it had been when I was four inches tall. Fairies and pixies were the Arnolds of the Inderland world as far as I was concerned. Suddenly uneasy, I looked to the invisible ley line, feeling like someone was watching. My eyes rose to see Bis sleeping on the steeple. Creeped out, I darted inside as if the monster under the bed had taken up residence under my porch.

The screen door smacked behind me, making me jump, and I kicked my running sneakers off, leaving chunks of dirt that Ivy would eventually yell at me about. I shut the main door by leaning back against the thick wood, and my gaze fell on the tiny arrows still in Ivy's couch. Had it been only yesterday?

Ivy and Nick's soft bickering in the kitchen was soothing. They'd been at it since downloading and printing out the blueprints of Trent's outbuildings from the city's public files. Ivy insisted that she'd gone through a secure server and that the download would be undetected, but I was sure we were on someone's list now.

Twigs in hand, I went into the kitchen, my peace growing as I found them reasonably calm at Ivy's big table, construction blueprints between them. Nick and Ivy had been modifying them, changing what was on file at the city to match what had actually happened at the construction site. The taped-together pages covered the table, and most of Ivy's stuff had been stacked on the floor to make more room.

Only Pierce looked up as I entered, standing at the fridge with a glass and playing with the water dispenser. At the table, the argument over some small placement of a camera continued. Ivy was edging into a vampy state, her eyes dark and motions quick, but she wasn't sultry, which was her big tell for losing it. Her black mood wasn't bothering Nick, and he was strenuously arguing a point, erasing her marks and penciling in his own. The white flash of her new cast had been covered with a black stretchy fabric that might have been a sock with the toe cut off. I had no doubts that being in a cast wasn't going to slow her down at all.

Standing on the paper, Jenks watched. I was surprised he was here, but the garden was probably too painful. His classic Peter Pan pose had slumped into a depressed hunch with his arms over his middle, and his wings were against his back. Jax, back again and sitting on Nick's shoulder, didn't look much better.

Jenks looked up when I dropped my twigs on the center counter, a flash of guilt crossing him in that he hadn't gotten them for me. I smiled, and a black dust sifted down. Reaching for the last dirty spell pot, I dunked it in the warm sudsy water.

"What about the security at that level?" Ivy said, tapping the paper. "You know they have more than cameras down there. Spell detectors, too."

"Tink's titties, Ivy," Jenks complained, his wings perking up. "That's what I'm for! Uh, we're for," he amended, looking at his son when Jax scraped his wings.

"The pixies have this," Nick said dryly as he tossed his pencil down and leaned back, scowling. "You've really got a problem with trust, vampire."

Ivy's eyes narrowed, and my neck tingled. "I trust the pixies. You, I don't."

I gave the spell pot a quick rinse in my saltwater vat, then ran it under the cold tap. The copper needed a good polishing, but not today. Pierce silently took it from me before I could set it to dry, yanking the dish towel from the rack and making good with it. I gave him a quick smile. He'd been a big help today, and I'd gained a deeper respect for his skills. It was a lot like when I worked with Al, but Pierce wasn't as quick to play teacher—which I appreciated.

Behind me on the center counter were three disguise potions. Okay, they were curses, but the twisting of them had been exactly like a standard disguise potion, except instead of ingredient X to give Y result, I had used a focusing object from the person I wanted to look like. For any other witch, the result would be a potion that would do nothing, but if I tapped a line and said the magic word, my blood—my demon-enzyme blood—would make it work.

By all appearances, Ivy, Jenks, and Nick had forgotten we had to get out again, too, so while they fussed and fumed about how to get in, I'd made up the curses to escape under fire. Soon as we were discovered—and we would be discovered—the codes to the locked doors would change, so I picked three people who wouldn't need any freaking codes. Even with Ivy planning this, something would go wrong. As Al always said, the demon's in the details.

The first potion in the tiny vial had been sensitized from a page of one of my newer ley-line textbooks, written by Dr. Anders. The second had a chunk of Ceri's smashed teacup, and the third, a strand of hair from the Pandora charm that Trent sent me. The rope had been made from his horse's tail, and it was probably the best focusing object of the lot. Getting Ivy to take hers wasn't going to be fun.

That there were only three curses hadn't escaped Pierce's notice. He wasn't coming. We had too many people running this job to begin with, and someone needed to stay home and watch Jenks's kids. And he *was* a babysitter.

Pierce hung the dry spell pot up over the center counter, and Ivy stood, a hint of sexual dominance in her as she went to the fridge. "Trent's compound isn't one of your pantywaist museums," she said as she yanked open the door. "You've never been in there. He has redundant systems on his redundant systems. Quen's been studying pixies for at least six months. He's got something for them by now."

I crouched at the center counter to put my books away, not feeling at all guilty that most of them were demon texts. Quen probably had something for doppelgänger charms now, too, since I'd shown him my skill last Halloween, but what was on the counter now weren't charms, but curses. *Na-na. Na-na. Na-a-a-a, na.*

Nick cleared his throat, and I could almost feel the tension spike, but it was Jenks who took offense. "You telling me I can't do this?" he said with a shadow of expected indignation.

Orange juice in hand, Ivy softened as she nudged the fridge shut. "No. I'm saying I want a plan for when it goes wrong. This is Trent. I know you're good." She looked at Jax and exhaled softly. "But you don't get second chances with Kalamack." Leaning back against the counter, she drank right from the container, her cast making it awkward. "Right, Rachel?"

I stood from putting my spell books away, not happy about the reminder of my stint as a mink in Trent's office. I shrugged, and Nick said, "Just because your plans are inherently flawed doesn't mean mine won't work."

"Flawed?" Ivy's fingers tightened until I thought the container would cave.

"Guys!" I said, setting three caps by the open vials. Demon magic. I was going to pay for this in spades, but if I was going to use black magic to save my friends, then I was going to use it to save my own ass. "Can we find a plan you both like? It's almost dark."

Nick made an innocent face, then focused on the blueprints. Pierce was a shadow, silently putting things away exactly where they were supposed to go. It was eerie, and I didn't know if it was because he'd been in the church for over a year before gaining a body, or if he was a quick study from having watched me get everything out. I appreciated the help, though.

Ankles crossed, Ivy kept her distance, allowing herself the space she needed to calm down. "I want a second plan if something goes wrong," she said softly. "Rachel can't use offensive magic or she'll end up in worse trouble than she is now. I don't even like the target. A painting? Sounds to me like you're funding your own retirement island—Nick."

Nick flipped through the blueprints, shifting only the corners. "If I take something from Trent's cache, it won't be a cheap, poorly done canvas," he muttered.

"Then why are we stealing it?" Jenks flew up when Nick flipped to the page he wanted.

Ivy was silent, and Nick stuck a pencil between his teeth. "Ask Rachel," he said. "She wanted something embarrassing but not priceless. That's exactly what it is." The pencil came out, and he looked at me, turning slightly in his chair. "It was painted in the fifteenth century by a nobody, and Ivy, before you go off on a nut, the reason we're targeting it is because the subject looks like Trent but is actually a savage prince in the mountains of Carpathia."

Jenks landed on my shoulder as I put my new pain amulets away. His wings were a depressed blue, cold when they brushed me. "If it were me, I'd burn it," he said.

"I think he's proud of it," Nick said. "Lets him think he comes from evil kings." Looking up, he shook his head as if I was making a mistake. "Rachel, he's just going to put you in jail—if you're lucky. Prison does not equal safety from the coven *or* him."

Don't I know it. Confident, I shut the cupboard door with a thump. "Trent won't press charges. It's a game, Nick. Like for fun? We've been stealing things from each other and giving them back since before you hot-wired your first car." *Oh God, what if I was wrong?*

Jenks's wings hummed to life, sending the scent of burning leaves over me. "Like when he took your ring and mailed it back! I still don't know how he did that."

"Or me stealing his hoof pick," I said, feeling a flash of guilt quickly followed by a surge of anxiety. "It's the same thing, and as long as I give it back . . ." He wouldn't press charges, but it would get his attention, and that's what I wanted.

Ivy poured the last of the juice into a glass and rinsed out the container. "All this aside, I've never heard of it," she muttered suspiciously.

"It's been in his basement." Nick turned back to the blueprints. "Passed down."

Pierce and I exchanged knowing looks. *But you've heard of it?* I questioned silently. "Sounds like you've had your eye on it for a while," I said, brushing the used bits of herbs off the counter and into my hand.

Nick gave me a familiar smile that used only half his face. "I have. It's worth a fortune."

Glass in hand, Ivy was the picture of tense belligerence. "You just said it was worthless."

"It *is* worthless, but public image is worth a lot more than money to Trent," Nick said.

Pierce leaned forward, breathing into my ear, "I don't set much store by his story."

I stifled a shiver at his breath on my skin and Jenks's warning wing draft on my other side. Unfortunately I agreed with him, and after muttering to Jenks that I had this, I turned to dampen a washcloth. My back to Nick, I asked, "So . . . if it's been in Trent's basement for generations, how did you find out about it?"

Nick was silent. I turned, jaw tightening as he looked at me innocently. Far too innocently. His eyes dropped, and my pulse quickened as Jenks pointedly cleared his throat. "It's amazing what you hear when you ask the right questions," Nick finally muttered, rattling the papers. "Will you get out from behind me, Ivy? You're giving me the creeps."

My expression wry, I exchanged a look with Ivy as I ran the cloth over the center counter. Moving slowly, she shifted to stand in front of him, setting her glass down right on the sum he was figuring in the margin. "If you even think about crossing us . . . ," she threatened, and Jax spilled a frightened green dust.

Using two fingers and a thumb, Nick moved her glass, letting it drop the last quarter-inch, hitting with a thunk that almost spilled it. "You can have the painting," he said, tossing his hair from his eyes as he looked up. "That's not what I'm after."

Pulse fast, I stood with the center counter between us, the damp cloth in my hand. "What *are* you after?" I asked, and Jenks hummed his wings in agreement.

Nick's eyes were placidly blue as he looked at me. "A clean slate."

Pierce grimaced, but I only laughed as Jenks darted from my shoulder, his dust shifting to silver. "Dream on, rat boy," he barked. "You think we've been eating fairy farts for breakfast?"

Ivy sat before her computer. She was scowling, making me feel even more uneasy. Shaking the towel over the sink, I draped it over the spigot and turned. I knew Nick. Pierce might believe Nick was doing this to get back in my good graces, but once we were in Trent's compound, Nick was going to add a little to his own personal agenda and steal something that was going to move this stunt from teenage double-dog dare you to grand larceny. I knew it. Jenks knew it. Ivy knew it. And if we knew it, we could plan accordingly. *Stupid ass of an ex-boyfriend.*

I had to get Trent and the coven together and threaten them both with going public with their dirty laundry unless they backed off. Trent wouldn't agree to a meeting unless I had a door prize, one sensational enough to get his attention, and innocent enough that he wouldn't try to kill me.

"I can get you your canvas," Nick said, his voice even. "All you have to do is get me into the main compound. The rest is easy."

That's all, eh? I found a finger stick in the silverware drawer and broke the safety seal with a sharp snap, slamming the drawer shut. "I can get you in," I said, poking my finger and massaging blood to the tip to invoke the demon doppelgänger curses. "I have. I can do it again."

Nick sighed. "I'm not talking sneaking into the public areas with a landscaping truck. I'm talking high-tech security in the basement labs."

Ivy snorted, and I made a moot face at him. "I'm not playing tiddledy-winks in the ever-after, Nick. I can get us in." *And out.*

"It's getting out that I'm worried about," Pierce muttered.

I shrugged, counting three red drops as they plunked into the first vial. Like a wash, the scent of burnt amber oozed over the top. *Crap!* I thought, capping the vial before anyone other than Pierce noticed. Ivy would freak. But at least I knew I'd done it right.

"When have I ever not gotten out?" I said, perhaps a little too pride-fully. Sure, I always got out, and it cost me every single time.

Nick wouldn't look up from his blueprints. "There's a first time for everything."

"You got that right," Jenks said, his hum by my ear prompting me to move my hair out of his way. "I never thought I'd see your ass in our kitchen again. Least not outside a *jar*."

I couldn't help my smile as he landed, smelling of green things. "You doing okay?" I asked when Ivy went to argue with Nick about how fast a pixy had to fly to evade detection.

"I'm fine," he said, the draft he was making dying. "My stomach hurts, is all."

His stomach hurt. God, his wife wasn't gone even a day, and he was try-ing to work, trying to escape the pain in the garden, maybe. My heart seemed to darken as I quickly finished invoking the other two potions, capping them and setting them aside. It didn't seem right to be doing this when Matalina's ashes weren't even cold yet, but Jenks seemed eager for anything to distract himself. I wouldn't be doing this *at all* except that Trent was going to announce his candidacy for mayor tomorrow at Fountain Square. It was the perfect opportunity to return what we stole amid a media circus.

Jenks was frowning at the three vials, his gaze going to Ivy and Pierce as if wondering which one of them was going to be left behind.

"I don't like this," Jenks said softly from my shoulder as I fanned the faint burnt amber smell away. "Nick isn't getting anything out of this. Not even notoriety."

"I don't trust him either," I said, loud enough so everyone could hear. "That's why Ivy is going with us. She's going to babysit him."

Ivy smiled, tipping her glass in salute, but Nick sputtered. Pierce's expression became dark, a protest forming. Nick, though, was faster.

"Ivy is *not* coming," he said hotly. "It will increase the risk of getting caught by eighty percent."

Ivy bristled. "I won't be the one to get us caught, you infected blood clot."

"You're not going into the belly of Kalamack's fortress without me," Pierce said. "His father was a traitorous, untrustworthy worm and Trent is the same."

"She's coming," I said to Nick. "Make it work, genius." And then to Pierce, "Tell me something I don't know. You're just worried Al is going to be pissed, and Al is pissed at you already. You're staying. You reach too fast for the black magic, and though that has saved both Ivy and me, using it now will land me in an Inderland jail, or worse, in the ever-after."

"I opine I know how to keep my magic to myself!" Pierce said indignantly.

Striding across the kitchen, I put myself right in his face, making Jenks dart away when I put my hands on my hips and leaned in. "No," I said firmly. "I've put up with you for three days. Watched you for three *very long* days!" I said, then dropped my voice again. "You have saved my life. You have saved Ivy's. I owe you everything. But you keep *overreacting*! Tell me I'm wrong, Pierce, that you *like* using black magic? Tell me that."

"I do not overreact," he said, suddenly unsure.

"You do," I insisted, "you overreacted when you broke the church window, and you overreacted when you almost fried Lee in the university's philosophy building. But the reason you're not coming is because you have bad ideas, Pierce, and you act too fast on them."

Ivy was wide eyed, and even Nick had sat back, pencil almost falling out of his mouth.

"Do tell." Pierce's lips were tight, and his brow was furrowed.

"You said to keep quiet to Al about Alcatraz, but the coven wanting my ovaries had a lot to do with convincing him to give me my name back. You nearly dragged me onto that bus that Vivian crashed into a bridge. And what's with shooting at Al with my gun with my charms in the hopper? What if you had killed him? Who do you think the demons would blame for the death of one of their own? You, the familiar? Or me, the one whose gun was smoking? Now I'm down a splat gun until I can find someone who doesn't know I'm shunned and will sell me a new one! I can't trust you in a pinch, and because of that, you're watching Jenks's kids. Got it?"

"I can fix the window and I'll get you a new gun," he said, and I made my hands into fists, frustrated. He'd saved my life and I owed him, but half my problems this week were because of him.

"The gun isn't the problem," I said. "You keep telling me what to do. You don't ask. You don't suggest. You tell. And I don't like it. I have people to help me who I trust won't overreact and make things so out of control that it takes black magic to fix. You aren't coming."

I was out of breath, and I stopped, waiting for his reaction. By the frown on his face, it wasn't going to be nice. "You don't want me to help," he said, voice tight.

"No," I said, then added more gently, "Not today."

Pierce clenched his jaw, and without another word, he turned and strode from the kitchen. Jenks's eyes were wide, and I exhaled when I heard the back door slam. Shaking inside, I turned to Nick. "Did you have something to say about Ivy coming?"

Nick glanced at Ivy, his eyes dropping to her cast, then rising to me.

"No, but her being there is going to increase the time to cross the main floor by at least three seconds. I don't know if the camera sweep can handle that. If you get caught, it's not my fault."

Jenks darted up, then down. "I'll worry about the cameras, rat boy. You worry about not tripping over your big fat wizard feet."

I took a deep breath to get rid of the adrenaline. Telling Pierce off had been something I'd been wanting to do all day, and now that it was done, I felt guilty. Glad I'd done it, regardless, I followed Jenks to the table to study the papers. I couldn't make heads or tails out of what they had scribbled. "Why can't we go downstairs from a low-security office, work through the underbelly in the lab where security will be light, then come up on the other side?" I asked, then tucked my hair behind my ear when it fell forward.

Both Ivy and Nick looked at me like I'd just said we should take a train to the moon. "You mean, like in the air ducts?" Nick finally offered.

"Yes," I said, wondering why Jax was smirking. "We can all go mink or something."

Ivy looked at Nick, and I swear . . . I saw them bond.

"No," Nick said, white faced.

"I'm not going to turn into a rodent," Ivy said, her voice low and throaty.

"A mink is not a rodent," I snapped. "God! Everyone but Trent knows that."

Taking the pencil from behind her ear, Ivy circled a camera and drew a cone around its scanned area. "I'm not turning into anything," she said, glancing at the potions on the counter.

This might make our getaway more complicated. "You're afraid!" I accused, putting a hand on my hip. "Both of you. I know how to do this! I'm not going to leave you that way! You just have to think the word to break the curse."

Nick cleared his throat, and I got more ticked yet. It would be so easy if they weren't afraid. Maybe I should just do this by myself, just Jenks and me.

Ivy looked up, her gaze distant. "There's a delivery truck at the door," she said, and the doorbell rang. "If you don't hurry, they'll take it back to the depot."

Unfortunately she was right, and I spun away, almost running in my sock feet down the hall, shouting that I was coming. They wouldn't leave packages since I'd been shunned.

Behind me, I could hear Jenks saying, "Tink's panties, Ivy. She's right. If you got small, it would be a snap. You're both chicken shit. Rachel doesn't mind. She looks good small."

"I'm not going to turn into anything," Ivy growled, followed shortly by Nick's fervent agreement.

I ran through the church as the hefty revving of a diesel truck shook the windows—apart from the one Pierce broke that was covered with plywood. Flinging the door open, I shouted and waved, snatching up my lethal amulet from my bag by the door as I ran down the steps in my sock feet. Looking almost disappointed, the guy in brown got out, coming to meet me with a package.

"Thank you," I said as he handed it to me, and I half expected him to ask for some ID. He was a witch. I could tell from his disdainful look. My amulet was a healthy green, and snatching the small package from him, I turned and went back into my church. What did I care what some guy in brown shorts thought? Even if he wore the uniform very well. Damn, where did they go to hire these guys? The gym?

The church felt empty when I came back in, absent of pixies after the long winter. Feet silent, I padded to my abandoned desk, turning at the last moment to sit in one of the leather chairs around the coffee table. The return address was from a shipping place downtown, and tearing open the gummy label, I shook the hard plastic of my phone out onto the table.

"Oh," I said, drawing my hand back as it spun and settled. Eyebrows raised, I cautiously looked inside the package for a note, not finding one. The coven had returned my phone? I eyed my lethal-spell amulet again, still not wanting to touch it. Hell, I'd seen Vivian almost kill Ivy with two white charms. I wasn't about to take anything at face value.

"Hey! The coven sent me my phone!" I shouted, waiting for someone to come look. But no one did. "Jenks!" I shouted, scowling, and the hum of pixy wings sounded loud over Nick's argument from the kitchen.

"What?" the pixy complained. "We're kind of in the middle of something."

I looked up at him, hovering five feet above the floor, his hands on his hips and spilling a lavender dust. "The coven sent my phone back to me. Is it bugged?"

He flew a sweeping arc over it and back to his original position. "Yeah. Can I get it later? They've almost agreed on something."

My mouth opened to protest, but he was already gone, yelling at Nick to shut the hell up and that Ivy was right before he even reached the kitchen.

Slumping into the soft leather, I got brave and thumbed the phone open. It was on and charged . . . and I had a message.

Curious, I hit the button and listened to the prerecorded preamble. But when a high-pitched, familiar voice came through the earpiece, I sat up, heart pounding. Vivian.

"Rachel Morgan," Vivian said formally, and I pressed the phone to my ear to catch every nuance. "As of last night, and the . . . incident at Loveland Castle, we are reassessing the threat you represent. I told them that Brooke was trying to circumvent coven mandates and had summoned a demon after you warned her not to, and that you tried to stop him from taking her, but they think I'm *lying*."

Her last words sounded accusing, and I sat on the edge of the couch. "We know you used a curse to kill the fairy clan. I'll be honest with you. A reassessment is not necessarily a good thing, but you'll be given a chance to come in peacefully before we take action again. If you force this from a quiet acquisition to a public one, we'll bring your family into it."

Son of a bitch. I stiffened as I thought of my mother in Portland.

"I don't even know why I'm telling you this," she said, "except maybe to thank you for trying. With Brooke, I mean. I may be a lot of things, but a liar isn't among them, and I wanted you to know that I'm not behind that accusation. Brooke did it to herself."

The message clicked off, and I scrambled to save it, exhaling when I hit the right button. Snapping the phone closed, I slumped back to stare at the empty rafters with not a speck of dust or cobweb on them. Frustrated, I tossed the phone to the table for Jenks to debug later. I'm glad she believed me, but what good was it going to do?

Sighing, I levered myself up and headed back to the kitchen to finish up the plans. I wasn't keen on testing Trent's security, but I didn't have much of a choice. I had to get my shunning removed. To do that, I had to survive the coven. They weren't going to back down unless I got Trent to vouch for me without signing that lame-ass paper of his. Which meant blackmail at the worst, and uneasy truce at the best. I was hoping for the truce, but after that Pandora charm had gone deadly, I didn't have a problem with the blackmail.

Getting into Trent's fortress was going to be the easy part. Getting out would be the kicker. But having Ivy and Jenks with me would make this as easy as falling off a log.

Right into the pit of snakes.

Thirty

I'd never been to Trent's primary stables, just his foaling stables a stone's throw away. But the rough-cut boards and smell of hay still felt familiar after the Pandora charm, even if the memory had almost killed me. It made stealing from Trent really easy on my conscience. Stupid elf. I waited in the glow of the security light, feeling exposed with my back pressed against the vertical boards. There was no moon, but there was nowhere to hide either, and I listened to a sitcom come down from an open window on the second floor. Breeding racehorses, Trent forced an early April foaling, so the staff on hand here would be correspondingly small.

Ivy was a shadow at the corner of the building. Jenks, Jax, and Nick were at the window beside me, more of a door, really, where they tossed the hay in. It was locked, of course, with sensor pads. The pixies were trying to find the right amount of electricity to keep the circuit closed even when it was open. They'd been at it long enough to make me nervous. It never took Jenks this long. The entire job was being run like it was a damn committee, and I hated it.

"Are we there yet?" I whispered, and Jax's wings spilled a silver dust. Sighing, I leaned back and fingered my belt pack, holding a couple of pain amulets, the three potion vials—and Trent's dad's hoof pick. I was hoping that if I gave it back, Trent would realize that it was a game and not kill me outright. Even if Pierce hadn't melted my splat gun, I wouldn't have brought it. If I got caught, it wasn't going to be with a potentially lethal weapon on my person. Using my splat gun without the backing of a warrant would put me in jail faster than Bis could hit Pierce's tombstone with a wad of spit, game or no. Any charm I used would leave a trace that the I.S. could track right back to me. I was going in almost naked, and not happy about it.

It was almost three, right when pixies and elves were about to wake up and witches about ready to crash. Crashing sounded good. I was tired. Evading Vivian this afternoon had been harder than I'd thought it would be. We'd finally resorted to jumping stores in the mall until we all went out different delivery entrances to take the bus to one of Ivy's friends. His car had gotten us to the interstate, and from there, we'd walked in across the pastures where they couldn't use motion detectors because of the horses. Everyone had an Achilles' heel, and apparently Trent's was his horses.

"Got it," Jenks said, making a quick circle around me before darting off to get Ivy. Nick gave me a toothy smile as he carefully opened the wooden door, hesitating to allow Jax to oil the hinges with pixy dust when they squeaked. A horse nickered at the new draft, and we froze, listening as the muted conversation from upstairs continued and the laugh track exploded. The pixies vanished inside, and Nick leapt easily to the sill, disappearing soundlessly.

Alone with Ivy, I exhaled in worry. I didn't like how many people it was taking to do this, but I wasn't going to miss out, and Ivy wouldn't let Nick and me do this alone.

Her hair in a black scrunchy, Ivy vaulted easily through the black window. Her hand without the cast came out, and I took it, using it to find my way inside.

I felt like a thief as I landed, my dew-wet running shoes quiet on the swept concrete. The fragrant hay made towers around us, and the soft, inset lighting of the stables was enough to see by. Jax was gone or not moving, but Jenks came close, landing on my shoulder to whisper, "We've got the alarms disabled and the cameras on a loop. Ivy's going to take care of the two guys and the vet upstairs. Hang tight."

I nodded as I took the cloth that Ivy had used to wipe her shoes. Calm and confident, she headed into the aisle and to the heavily polished stairway to the living quarters. There were inlaid lights on each step, and it looked far too fine to be in a stable. Arm swinging, Ivy looked more like she was crossing a bar to get a drink than going to knock out three men without raising an alarm. But having Jenks with her meant it wasn't going to be an issue.

A horse blew at us, and after handing Nick the cloth to wipe down the floor where we'd come in, I went to calm the animal, finding he was free in a nice-size box stall. The horse wouldn't come to me, but at least his ears pricked.

For no reason I could see, the hair on the back of my neck rose, and the horse's ears went back. "How you doing?" Nick whispered, right freaking behind me.

I tried not to jump, but I figured he knew he'd startled me by his smile when I turned. "I have done this before. Nic-k," I said tightly.

He went to say something, but our attention went to the ceiling at a soft thump. I tensed, relaxing when Jenks flew downstairs, dusting a soft gold. "Remind me never to piss off Ivy," he said as he hovered before me. "She dropped them faster than a slug takes a crap."

Ivy sauntered downstairs, her silhouette confident and slim as she tugged her sleeves down and pocketed something in her belt pack. "We've got ten minutes," she said sounding loud as she broke the hush. "They'll wake up in fifteen minutes thinking they fell asleep. Which they did." She patted her belt pouch and smiled, her fangs making me shiver. "I could have made it longer, but they check in with security every half hour."

Nick was eying her belt. "What is it?"

"It's mine," she said, shooing Jax away before the smaller pixy could get a good sniff.

Nervousness seeped up through me as if rising like fog from the earth. Whatever it was, it had been illegal. We were sliding into this criminal thing far too easily. Did it matter if our motives were good if the means were bad? Or was the real question, did I want to go to Alcatraz and get my ovaries taken out and wind up lobotomized? This was survival against illegal action, and Trent was at the root of it. Guilt could take a long walk in a short shadow.

"Okay. Spread out," I said. "We've got ten minutes to find the door to the tunnel."

Immediately Jenks took off, his wings a slow, depressed hum. Jax was hot in the other direction. It was obvious that Jax was trying to impress his dad with his backup abilities. Jenks didn't seem to care, still hurting about Matalina. I hadn't even wanted him to come, but he needed to be needed right now, not alone in a church.

Ivy started for the front of the stables, and Nick followed Jax to the back. I poked about after Jenks, checking out the opposite row of stalls. Somewhere in here was a passage under the road and back to the main compound. It wasn't on any of the plans, but if you brought up the public record of who got paid during the construction of the stables, it was obvious that there was one here. You don't write a check for the materials and equipment to make a tunnel just for grins. I only hoped it didn't go right to Trent's private quarters.

The lights were low as we searched, and the horses were getting nervous. Nick wasn't comfortable with the big animals, and Ivy was like having a panther among the herd. Me, they ignored as I tapped the walls for an echo and looked for unexplained worn spots on the floor.

"What's the time, Jenks?" I asked as I rapped my knuckle against the wall holding a dozen different saddles.

"Five minutes, twenty-six seconds," he said, skimming the floor where it met the wall.

"I've got it!" shrilled a high-pitched voice, and the horse across the way snorted, her ears objecting to Jax's exuberant call as much as mine. "I think I've got it!"

Jenks was gone in a burst of dust. Breath held as I walked through it, I followed his sparkles to the end of the stables. Ivy came even with me, smelling of vampire incense. She was enjoying this. It had been a while since we'd done anything together, and I'd missed seeing her happy.

"Good going, Jax," Jenks was saying as the pixy hovered in a double-size box stall, making the black horse in it toss his nose at the dust sifting down. "How did you find it?"

"There's a draft," he said, dropping down to show his dust being pulled under the straw. "See? There's a trapdoor right here."

The horse swung his head to try to bite him like a fly, and Jax darted out of the way, glowing a bright red as he landed on Nick's shoulder. The man was standing in the dead center of the aisle, uncomfortable. "Nice," I said, eying the horse, who now had his ears back, evil as he swung and tossed his head, daring us to come in.

"Girls like horses," Nick said, arms crossed. "One of you can get him out."

Ivy frowned. "Oh, for God's sake," she muttered, reaching for the gate.

"No!" I shouted, seeing the not-so-subtle equine signs.

The horse lunged forward, but Ivy was quicker, pulling her hand back an instant before the horse got his teeth on her. He stomped, tossing his head with his ears back. "Little sucker," she said, clearly shaken as she dropped back to where Nick stood.

Jenks smirked and flitted into the stall, not a hint of dust showing as he avoided the horse's bite and vanished under the floorboards. An instant later, a soft electric glow leaked up through the cracks. He'd found the lights.

"Did he get you?" I said, taking Ivy's hand, but apart from a bad mood, she looked okay.

A silver dust sifted over our fingers, and I let go when Jenks rejoined us. "It's a passage, all right," he said as Ivy shook her head. "It runs under the road. This is it."

Nick crossed his arms. "With hell horse guarding it? Ivy, will your drugs work on it?"

She shook her head. "I don't have enough. He's got to weigh over a thousand pounds."

"Hit him over the head with your cast," Jenks said. "Use what you got."

Ivy just looked at him, and I sighed, standing outside easy bite range. "I'm *not* going to be stopped by a freaking horse!" I said.

The horse's ears flicked forward, and his nose toss took on a less aggressive slant. My breath caught, and Jenks landed on my shoulder. "Did you see that?" he said, and Ivy chuckled.

"Rachel, I think he likes you."

"No way," I said, but the monster's ears flicked forward again, followed by a happy step toward us. My lips twisted, and I gazed at Ivy, mystified.

Jenks laughed. It was the first time I'd heard it since Matalina died, and something eased in me. "Well, I know you're not a virgin to soothe a savage beast," he said, and I swatted at him, missing him by a mile. "Go pet the horse, Rachel."

Nick scuffed his feet. "We're running out of time here . . ."

"Go pet the horse," I grumbled. "Do you people know the bite pressure of those teeth?" Wiping my hand on my black slacks, I reached out, jerking when the horse hung his head over the wall and head-butted me.

"I'll be damned," Nick swore, and Jenks laughed again.

"I don't get this," I said, as shocked as Ivy appeared, her black eyes wide and wondering. My hands went up to touch him, and I looked for a halter to put on him so I could lead him out. But when my gaze fell on the nameplate, my jaw dropped. "Tulpa?" I said, and the horse blew at me, seeming to be disappointed that I didn't have a snack for him.

"Ivy, this is the horse I fell off," I said, seeing that she was allowed to touch the gate now. "It was like thirteen years ago. Horses don't live that long and look this good." My focus went blurry as I pieced it together. "You're Trent's familiar, aren't you, old boy," I said as I slipped inside the stall as if I belonged. Tulpa wouldn't hurt me.

"Tick tock, Rache," Jenks said, and I cooed at the huge animal, not caring what Nick or Ivy thought as I ran my hands appreciatively over his black coat, glistening with the first hints of silver. God, the muscles on him. "Come on in," I said as I shoved his shoulder, and the horse obediently shifted to the wall of the big stall. "Back. Back up," I said, my hand on his neck giving a soft pressure, and I smiled when the horse took two more steps off the trapdoor. At least Trent's horse liked me. I should write him a letter and tell him. It would make his day.

Ivy came in, and Jenks, eying the blowing horse as she found the lever and swung the small trapdoor open. Clearly the horse was used to it, making only a snuff at the artificial light at his feet. His head dropped as if searching for a familiar face coming up and perhaps an apple. Ivy started down the metal stairs, her vamp reflexes making it easy one-handed, but Nick was still in the hallway.

Jenks put his hands on his hips and hovered. "What's wrong, crap-for-brains?"

Her head even with the floor, Ivy hesitated. "You don't have to come."

Grimacing, he eyed me and the horse. His hand on the gate prompted a sudden shifting from Tulpa, but I pushed him back. Horses were great. Once they accepted your dominance, there was no question. They sort of seemed to like it.

"Just get down the stairs, Nick," I said, and he slipped inside, almost skating down the metal framework in his haste. Jax was with him, and it was with an odd reluctance that I left Tulpa, giving him a pat before taking the stairs and unwedging the rod that had propped it open.

"Thanks, Tulpa," I said wistfully as the door shut, inches from my head. The last sight I saw was a floppy pair of lips with bristly whiskers snuffling at the narrowing crack. I turned and went downstairs, sighing at the thumps of his hooves overhead. I'd forgotten how much I liked horses.

Jenks was waiting for me, his hands on his hips as he hovered in his black thief outfit, looking better even if his grief was just out of sight in the back of his eyes. "You really get off on the big dumb animals, don't you," he said.

"Shut up, Jenks," I muttered, pushing past Nick and starting down the long, unremarkable hallway slanting downward. I couldn't help but wonder if I had picked out of my forgotten memory the word "Tulpa" as my word to spindle energy in my head. Probably.

"Cameras?" I asked as I came even with Ivy. The walls were white and I could feel the faint brush of air vents. I still thought using the ductwork would have been easier.

"No," Jenks said, wings a soft hum, then amended, "Well, just one where the elevator is. We've got a half-mile hike."

I nodded, feeling the strain of matching Ivy's vampire-quick pace. Nick gave up and began to jog, which made Ivy smirk. We looked out of place among the white halls and taupe carpeting, all of us in black but Jax: Ivy and me in leather, Jenks in his silk body suit, and Nick in a faded T-shirt and dark jeans. God, couldn't the man have dressed up a little for the occasion?

The end of the hallway was almost unrecognizable until we were on it. "Dad?" Jax questioned, and I jerked to a halt when Jenks flew in front of us.

"Yeah," the pixy said as he flushed. "Give Jax and me a minute to get the doors open without triggering something. 'Kay?"

The two pixies darted around the corner, gone. Fidgeting, I adjusted my belt pack, feeling the tiny ampoules of potion through the fabric. What if I ran into Ceri looking like her? This was so illegal it wasn't funny. Illegal, but in no stretch of the imagination deadly.

The whisper of pixy wings gave me bare warning as Jenks flew back around the corner. "We're good to go. Ivy, can you get the elevator doors open?"

Nick pushed forward around me. It's always the token dumb human who gets it first in the movies. I followed to find the hall dead-ended with the familiar silver doors of an elevator. Nick was trying to wedge the dead doors apart. Muttering "damn testosterone," Ivy strode forward, and with their joint efforts, the doors slid open to show an empty shaft. Jax hovered by my ear as we all looked up, and then down.

"Down, right?" I asked, thinking that if we had had more than a day to plan this, we could have swiped an entry card or something. No one said anything, but Jenks dropped into the darkness. Nick, too, swung into the shaft, easily grabbing the service ladder. I looked up, wondering how often they used this thing. "Down," I whispered, wishing it had been up. That half-mile hike had probably put us across the road and under Trent's business complex. I hoped.

Ivy was next, trying to stick closer to Nick now that we were actually behind the walls. The metal was cold in my hands, and it felt too small as I descended.

Jenks's pixy wings clattered as he landed on my shoulder. "Hold up," he said, and I hooked an arm in the ladder and glanced down. "Nick is trying to get the door open by himself."

"Get the hell out of the way!" filtered up as Ivy pushed past him on the ladder, despite the cast. Smirking, I was slowly descending a few more rungs when a soft artificial light blossomed in the shaft. I reached for the edge and found Ivy. She extended an arm to help me in, but I still almost fell into the carpeted hallway.

Catching myself, I looked back into the elevator shaft. "Never thought I'd ever do that," I muttered, then frowned when Nick left a smeared glove print where he'd pushed the silver doors closed. Idiot.

Jax was busy with the hall camera, and if I hadn't known we were several stories underground, I'd swear we were in an upper interior hallway with the usual flat beige-and-white carpet, wooden doors, and frosted windows that looked into the offices, all of it combining to give the illusion of an upstairs office.

Jenks hovered to inspect the clean door while Ivy finished putting her tiny spray bottle of cleaner in her belt pack. "We need to move in stages," the pixy said. "The cameras down here won't stay tripped unless you're right there babysitting them, so we're going to leapfrog it. Jax will hold one camera as I scout to the next, and so on. There will be some time where you'll show, but it can't be helped. Shouldn't be too many people watching. It's between shifts."

"Got it," I said around a long exhale, then eyed the nearby camera. The only evidence of Jax was a silver dusting slipping from it, almost unseen in the bright light. I had a fleeting thought that I hoped I could trust Jax; then I berated myself.

"Give me a sec," Jenks said. "Jax will tell you when I've got the next camera."

I didn't even have time to nod before Jenks took off, skimming just below the ceiling and around the corner. Almost immediately I heard a faint, almost ultrasonic wing scrape, and I winced when Jax shouted for us to move.

"Let's go," Ivy said, breaking into a jog. Nick was quick to join me, and we loped down the empty corridors, the pixies trading off their positions as each one found the next camera.

I was starting to think that we just might be lost down here and that the pixies were leading us in circles when Jenks doubled back. A spike of fear dropped through me at the glitter of orange dust. "Back!" he said, waving his arms. "Someone's coming!"

Nick turned to run, but it was too far away to hope to get around the last corner. I grabbed his arm to keep him from moving as Ivy kicked the handle of the nearest office door. It popped open, and I shoved him in. Ivy was close behind, and I crouched, holding the door shut with an ear pressed to the crack.

"Stay put," I heard Jenks whisper, knowing he was talking to Jax, who couldn't possibly hear him. "Just stay put, son."

The scent of vampire twined around me like a vine, and I stiffened. I glanced up to see Ivy standing right over me, tense and listening to the approaching steps. It sounded like two people, and I hoped the frame wasn't visibly damaged. Feeling my attention on her, Ivy looked down and smiled, sharp pointy canines catching the light. *Just when I forget what she is . . .*

The voices of the two people chatting grew stronger. "It's two lab guys," Jenks said. "You want their cards? They might help in getting out."

I had an image of two geeky guys tied up and shoved into a closet, scared and noisy. "No," I said, standing up and backing away from the door. "Not worth the risk."

His wings clattered in indignation. "It's not a risk."

Ivy had her ear to the door, her cast held tight to her middle. "Shut up. Both of you."

Brow furrowed, I held my breath as they passed. Ivy slowly stood. Her hand went to the door; then she froze at a sudden shout.

"Shit," I whispered, adrenaline spiking at the sudden thumping of running feet. We'd been spotted.

Ivy tensed, suddenly four feet deeper into the room and ready to hit whatever came through the door, but the feet continued on without a pause. Relief slumped my shoulders when someone shouted they'd hold the elevator.

Coming forward, Ivy cracked the door, and Jenks slipped out. She counted to ten and then pushed the door entirely open. "Let's go," she said, face grim. "We just spent all our luck."

My knees were shaking at the near miss. They still didn't know we were here. I hoped.

Nick was sober as he came into the brighter light, and after a quick look behind us, we continued forward. We found Jenks hovering at a juncture, and my heart sank. We were lost.

"That way," Ivy said, pointing to the right, but Nick shook his head and pointed left.

"No," he said, looking determined. "You're right that magnetic resonances are capable of hiding the opening to the vault, but the vault isn't where the resonances are being generated. The vault is where the line is being pulled out of its channel."

Nick pointed the other way, and I sighed. God, not again. We'd already decided this.

A dangerous glint came into her already black eyes, Ivy said, "Fine, you go that way, I'm going the other. To the vault."

"We are not separating," I said, thinking Nick would rat us out.

"Trent won't put his vault next to a magnetic resonator where people work every day," Nick said irately. "The resonator is warping the nearby ley line, and where the line dips, that's where the vault will be, not the resonator itself. Watch, I'll prove it."

He turned to me, surprising me when he said, "Rachel? We're too deep for a line, right?" I nodded, and he added, "Reach for one." My eyebrows went up, and he said, "Just do it!"

"All right, all right," I muttered, relaxing just enough to do it. We were too deep for me to reach a ley line. Three stories at least. But my breath caught when I felt the faintest glimmer of strength not that far ahead and to the left. "I don't get it!" I whispered, telling Jenks with my head toss to get the camera's looping on the left corridor, and he buzzed off. "We're too deep."

"You've got to be kidding me," Ivy grumped, but when Jenks's ultrasonic wing scrape made my eyeballs hurt, I started forward.

"It's just devious enough to be true," I said dryly. They couldn't hear the pixy signals. Lucky them.

Nick all but sauntered beside me, and Jax joined us after we turned the corner. "It's Trent's magnetic-imaging system," Nick said. "Trent is going to use magic as well as technology to keep his vault closed. And for that, he'll need the ley line, unexpectedly pulled downward by a very powerful magnet, something no one would think twice about in a facility such as this."

He was right, but how had he known such a thing was possible?

"I'm telling you Trent won't use magic to close his vault," Ivy grumped. "He doesn't like magic."

But his security expert loved magic. And his dad had, too.

The hallway dead-ended at an encouragingly formidable set of double doors. The line had to be behind them, though; they were the only doors in the entire hall. The carpet was pristine, no coffee stains or scrapes. The air, too, felt stale. Jenks was at the camera in the corner, and when Jax took his place, the more experienced pixy dropped down to hover with us as we faced the oak doors. Reaching past Nick, I tapped it with a knuckle. Thick.

"Well, wonder boy," Ivy said sourly, "let's see what's behind door number three."

"It'll be there," Nick said indignantly as he slid a wired card into the card reader and proceeded to play Mr. Accountant on the attached device.

I shook my head, brow furrowed. Dropping back to where Jenks hovered, I fidgeted. Beyond the door were untold riches—my ticket to getting Trent, the coven, and Al off my case. Was I a thief if I was going to give it back? Did I care?

"Are you sure those cameras aren't recording?" I asked. Down at the end of the hallway, Jax huffed, and I tossed a strand of hair out of my eyes. "I feel like I'm being watched."

"This would be *easier* if it was *quiet*," Nick said, and Ivy frowned. Nick took his fingers from the keypad and cracked his knuckles. A slip of pixy dust dropped down to lubricate the electrons as much as for luck, and Nick hit the big green button.

The red light on the pad went out, and the green one lit. There was a faint buzzing, and Nick grabbed the card out of the reader with jaunty swiftness and turned the handle. My gut clenched, but the twin doors opened silently. "QED," he said, gesturing for me to go first.

Ivy caught my shoulder. "In my family, that means quite easily dead. I'll go first." Giving Nick a mistrusting once-over, she went into the dark room. Fluorescent lights flicked on at her presence. It worried me, but it was unlikely they'd monitor the lights when there were other ways to detect people.

"It can't be this easy," I said as I followed her with Nick tight on my heels. Jax was with him, and Jenks slipped in an instant before the doors shut.

"Maybe because it isn't," Ivy said, and I stared at the blank walls of the large room.

"Where's the vault?" I asked, then turned to Nick. "Where's the freaking vault!"

"Right in front of you," he said, and I spun, in a really bad mood. "Rachel, where's the ley line?" he added, and frustrated, I hesitated.

"Uh, right here," I said, eyes going wide. "You don't think the way into the vault is . . . through the ever-after?" I asked, and Nick smiled deviously. "But you can't do that!"

It was a beautiful thought if it could be done, though. The perfect door. If the magnets were unpowered, the line wouldn't even come close and the door wouldn't even exist. Closing my eyes, I reached for the ley line, shocked when I found it, bent and running through the wall just as he'd said it might. A quiver went through me. Trent's dad had gone into the ever-after with my dad and come out, not bought a trip from someone. He could shift from reality to the ever-after and back using a ley line. And so could Trent, apparently. He must *really* not want me to know he could if he had risked everything last summer buying our way in and out of the ever-after.

Nick's smile was wide when I opened my eyes, and he pushed himself from the wall. "So where's the door?"

Heart pounding, I scanned the empty room. "Right in front of us. Let me pull up my second sight and see what's going on." Damn it, Nick knew witches couldn't do this. *But he thought I could?*

It was weird, how the magnets had pulled the line deep into the earth. Weird, and really clever. But even that thought vanished when I brought my second sight up to find that instead of the expected rock and rubble of being underground, we were in an open space, with tall ceilings and flat floors, colorful banners, and the phantom sound of eighties music done instrumentally.

"Holy. Crap," I gasped, shocked when I recognized it. It was the demons' mall. Al had taken me here once when he was out of powered rock from Pompeii. My hand went to my throat as I saw the demons and familiars going about their business. I'd be unseen unless they used their own second sight. I was like a ghost, not really in the ever-after but just looking at it. I turned to the wall, blinking. It was gone, a coffeehouse catering to demons and familiars alike in its place.

"Whoa. Dudes," I said. "Ivy, you're not going to believe this. It's a mall." It was times like this that made me glad demons couldn't pop over to reality whenever they felt like it but had to be summoned. Nothing could stop them from looking, though.

Nick grunted, and I turned from the juxtaposed views of the wall and coffeehouse to see him, seemingly standing in the mall, oblivious to demons going past. Nick's aura was a lot darker than the last time I'd seen him. Jax, on his shoulder, was a spot of rainbows. "Can you get in?" Nick asked.

Feeling ill and disoriented from holding two visions of reality, I blinked, deciding that his black smut was a lot thicker. The mark that Al had given him was like a black hole, sucking in all the light around it, twin to the new one on his shoulder. Seeing him waiting for an answer, I nodded. "Probably." Witches couldn't shift realities by standing in a ley line, but I wasn't a witch. *Shit.*

Nick bobbed his head. "There should be a panel on the other side. Just hit open. You've probably got thirty seconds to get me in so I can enter the code to disable the alarm."

"Alarm?" Ivy said, probably thinking that's why I looked sick. "You didn't say anything about that before."

He turned to her. "And you thought the vault was being hidden in a magnetic resonator. Roll with it, vamp. Or can't you function without a plan to blow your nose?"

"Uh, Rache?" Jenks interrupted, looking worried. Rainbows spilled from him, his aura falling like pixy dust. He knew what it might mean if I could do this, and I hoped he'd keep quiet about it.

"Just . . . let me see," I said, then faced the blank wall, shaking out my hands and trying to find a sense of calm. This wasn't like trying to jump from one line to another. I simply wanted to slip into the ever-after through a ley line. Just go into the ever-after, walk three paces, then get out of the line. Right into a demon coffeehouse. Great. And hope that when I reappear in reality, I'm in an open room and not buried in dirt. If Trent could do it, maybe I could. I'd never be trapped in the ever-after again, either, provided I could find a ley line.

"Rachel," Nick said, bending close. "There is a room behind the wall. Why have a lock on an empty room? I trust you. You can do this."

I eyed him and his smutty aura, and he took his hand off me. How come he knew I was different? This didn't smell good at all.

But closing my eyes, I strengthened my second sight. Once more, the red-tinted burnt amber smell enfolded me. The ley line ran right through the wall. Best to take two steps maybe.

"Rachel?"

"I'm fine, Ivy," I said, my voice harsher than I had intended. "Jenks, don't even think about it." *Just do it,* I thought, and then I stepped into the line and let it take me.

The smell hit me, jerking my eyes open. Noise jangled, a hundred conversations, arguments, loud gossip. Shit, I'd done it. I didn't know if I should be happy or depressed. It sounded like Takata being piped in. It was hot, and sweat threatened to break out. Pushing my hair back, I took a shallow breath. I was what I was. The door to the coffeehouse was ahead of me, THE COFFEE VAULT painted on it in big silver letters. *You've got to be kidding.* It was too obvious to ignore. Grasping the handle, I pushed open the door and went in.

Two demons looked up, the laughter of their joke still showing on their faces. Dressed in leisure suits I wouldn't be caught dead in, they looked me up and down, assessing how high I was in the familiar hierarchy. I felt naked without Al, and I gave them a bunny-eared kiss-kiss. "Hey, hi," I said, feeling stupid. "Just passing through." Damn it, I shouldn't be able to do this.

The better dressed of the two eyed me. "Who the hell do you belong to?"

Ambivalent, I let the door shut behind me. There was a room mirroring this one in reality. I could sense it, like an unheard echo. "I'm Al's student. Nice to meetcha."

The second demon smacked the first on the shoulder. "See, I told you she was alive."

Alive? I thought, wondering what the gossip had been. "Toodles," I said, blowing him a sarcastic kiss and stepping from the line and back into reality.

The noise cut off with a suddenness that almost hurt. The air was cooler. Dark. Black. In the corner, a shadow moved. Shit, something was in here! *Not a demon,* I told myself, panicking. They couldn't just slip into reality like that. Not like I could. *This is good, right?*

Heart pounding, I backed up into the wall I'd just walked through. Not taking my eyes off the moving shadow, I fumbled, finding the light switch. Light flickered into existence, and I sighed. It had been me. The movement had only been me, my shadow reflecting off the ornate mirror propped against the wall.

Slowly my pulse eased. Before me, large racks held old clocks, locked metal boxes with faded index cards, and slatted crates. One side of the room held a huge chest freezer. Actually the entire room looked a lot like Nick's basement in a much higher tax bracket. If I was lucky, there wasn't a camera. I thought of the demons at their table, able to see me with their own second sight but unable to cross over, and I shivered. The Coffee Vault, indeed. At least I'd never be trapped in the ever-after again.

Spinning to the wall behind me, I found the thin lines of a door and the expected keypad. "Come on in, guys," I whispered, and hit the green button.

There was the hum of machinery, and I backed up. The two panels slid apart like the doors in a science-fiction movie to show Ivy, Nick, and Jenks, hovering with brow furrowed. "Rache?" Jenks questioned.

"We'll talk about it later," I said, and Ivy bumped Nick when he bent to pick up his stuff. Scowling, he caught himself and followed her in, immediately plugging his card into the panel.

"Cameras?" Ivy asked, scanning the room, and when negative wing chirps came from both Jenks and Jax, she went to the canvas display. "So this is Trent's basement," Ivy said as she started leafing through the hanging canvases, arranged like posters in a pagelike display. Nick made a satisfied grunt and pulled the card from the reader.

"We're good," he said, his gaze fixing on the picture Ivy had turned to. "That's it," he said, eyes eager as Ivy paused at a really small painting. It was hardly a foot by a foot, showing a dark background of snowy mountains and a castle, the foreground taken up by a satisfied-looking young man in a red robe and funny hat, fur around his collar and three downy feathers in his lapel. That the man looked like Trent was almost anticlimactic.

"That's it?" Jenks said, landing on my shoulder as we eyed it. "It's not very big."

"Kinda ugly, too," I said, getting a funny feeling about this. I didn't want to say this was too easy, seeing as I'd used a door neither a witch nor a demon could open, but everything was going too well.

Nick was spreading a black silk cloth on the coffin-size freezer. "It's not the size, Jenks, it's how you use it," he said, smirking. "It doesn't need to be big if it looks like Trent."

Well, it did look like Trent. Jenks wasn't laughing, his hands on his hips as he moved out of the way while Ivy took the picture to Nick. "It stinks. Almost as bad as you, Rache," he accused.

"I smell?" I said, flushing.

Holding the canvas at the unpainted corners, Ivy frowned at him. "You were in the ever-after," she said, one shoulder lifting in a shrug, and I took a step back from them, feeling unclean. Great, I hadn't even noticed.

Oblivious, Nick carefully took the picture from Ivy, making a production out of rolling it up in the black cloth to put into the mailing tube he'd been carrying across his back like a sword. I couldn't help but sourly wonder if it was stamped and addressed to his latest girlfriend.

While the two of them discussed who was going to carry it, I unzipped my belt pack and brought out the hoof pick. I'd leave it here where Trent would be sure to find it. If he didn't make the connection that he was going to get the painting back, I might be in trouble.

Jenks joined me, and together we looked at the beautiful inlaid wood one last time before I set it on an open display case, bright with mirrors and lights. "I should have done this a long time ago," I said softly, wondering if I'd ever get my entire memory back. But who really remembered anything about being twelve?

"Oh my God," Jenks said, eying the statue next to it. It wasn't any bigger than he was, but I felt myself warm as I looked more closely. It was two men and a woman, buck naked, doing the nasty. At the same time. One in front, one in back. She looked like she was enjoying herself, though, ample breasts heaving and back arched, which kind of made it hard for the guy in back, but by his expression, he didn't care. They had pointy ears, the woman sporting a cute pageboy haircut and the men having hair past their shoulders, wild and feral.

"What is it?" I said, wanting to pick it up but feeling it might leave me sullied.

"Tink's dildo, you're asking me?" he said with a snort, but he didn't elaborate. Not even one rude gesture or comment. The unusual restraint was clear evidence of his depressed state.

"Ivy?" I called. This was too good not to share, timetable or not. "You gotta see this."

She came closer, Nick trailing behind as he capped the top of the tube the picture was now stashed in. "Whoa," she said, nose wrinkling. "Elf porn?"

"It's my ticket out of this life," Nick said, and Ivy grabbed his wrist when he reached for it.

"Hey!" I said as he twisted out of her grip, frowning at her. "We're not here to steal a statue. Didn't you learn anything from last time, Nick?"

Expression angry, he picked it up, the small statue fitting neatly in his palm. "I'm not walking out of here without something to show for it. And don't tell me you didn't expect me to help myself. That's the only reason I agreed to this, and you know it." His blue eyes were mocking, daring me to say anything. Just once, I wished I could be wrong.

Pissed, I barked, "Put it back!"

Jenks rose from the shelf, and Jax chimed out, "Uh, Nick? An alarm just went off."

Thirty-one

Ivy's eyes went a deeper black. "You son of a bitch."

"Put it back!" I shouted. "Put it back now!"

Nick shoved it into a jeans pocket, where it made a small bulge. "Doesn't make a difference. Let's go."

"You idiot!" I exclaimed. "It *does* make a difference. I'm not here to take anything I can't return!"

He smiled from the keypad, using only half his face. "You won't get caught. Promise."

Promise? What in hell is that supposed to mean?

With a satisfied smirk, he dropped his card into the reader, hit two buttons, and the doors slid open to show the first empty room.

Ivy was a blur of motion, picking him up and throwing him to slam against the closed twin wooden doors to the hall. The gadget swung from the reader, and I lunged for it before the wires snapped. Almost cross-eyed, Nick gasped for air as Ivy pinned him, her cast under his chin. The hidden door started to close, and after yanking the card free, I slipped through. I had time for one glance at the hoof pick, and then the door shut. Jenks was a blur beside me, and Jax was already with Nick, screaming at Ivy to let him go.

"Ivy, we might need him to get out!" I exclaimed, dropping his equipment by the closed hall door. "I've got a spell to make him look like Trent. Don't give him a bruise you can see!"

Scowling, she thought for three seconds, an eternity for her. "We're not using those."

I touched my belt pack, my heart pounding. "Yes, we are."

Shoving him into the doors, she dropped him. "You know I don't like your magic."

The faint honking of a claxon was obvious, and my pulse was fast. It felt good, and I rocked to the toes of my feet as Nick rubbed his neck, his cocky mood now sullen as he gathered his equipment. God, I was not going to get excited about this. But it had been ages since I'd done anything even remotely resembling a run, and I was riding the high already.

"I'm carrying the picture," I said, snatching it from Nick and draping the tube over my back. "Everyone, take what I give you and swallow it. Ivy, I mean it. Don't give me any crap."

The room went silent but for pixy wings as I pulled out a vial, gave a sniff, and imagining the faint scent of tea mixing with the reek of burnt amber, I downed it. All eyes watched me as I made a face. "Tastes like lemon pop," I lied, shoving the vial away and bringing the next out.

"I'm not drinking that," Ivy predictably said, but this one smelled like horse under the burnt amber stench, and I handed it to Nick.

"Nothing happened," he said, and I made a face at him like he was being stupid.

"I've not invoked it yet." *Dummy.*

"Who takes the smut?" he asked as his fingers encircled the tiny vial, and Jenks bristled.

"I do, now drink it!" I said, handing Ivy the last one. "I'll invoke them together. You uninvoke it by saying the invocation word again, so don't say it until you mean it. Got it?"

Ivy hesitated, and Jenks got in her face. "Do it, you chicken-shit vamp!" he yelled, and she did.

My breath exploded out of me, and I touched the line, strengthening my grip on it. The thing was right next to me, and the hair on my arms was standing on end. Maybe the demons were watching, getting a good laugh.

I put my hands on Ivy's and Nick's shoulders, and said, "*Quid me fiet!*" What am I becoming? Yeah. It fit. It was a freaking demon curse. I'd made it, and I was using it.

Ivy jerked, and I held on to her, not letting her break my gaze as the magic cascaded over us together. Her eyes widened as she felt herself change, her own face going longer and thin, aging a decade or two, and her hair silvering. Her clothes, too, changed, becoming what I remembered from the last time I'd seen Dr. Anders. Dark slacks, white shirt, and a lab coat—no hint of a cast. Demon magic. You've got to love it. It was only a glamour, though, not her real body. Under my fingers, I could feel the hardened plaster.

"You're Ceri!" she said, and feeling the magic soak in, I let go of her and dropped back.

"I take it," I whispered, accepting the smut for all of them, and I stifled a shudder as I felt it lap over me, settling in like a blanket, smothering. I'd never be free of it.

Ivy turned to Nick. "You look like Trent," she said. "My God, Rachel. How long have you been able to do this?"

I followed her gaze to where Jax was flitting like mad over Nick, who indeed looked like Trent, dressed in his usual suit and tie. It was demon magic at its best, but it was only an illusion. "Not long. It won't hold up to touch. I mean, you aren't really dressed in a lab coat, and your arm is still broken. It's all an illusion that goes no deeper than your aura. Cheaper that way. Let's get out of here."

My brief high was gone, and I felt sick. I'd made the curse, taken the curse, made my friends take the curse, and then invoked it. Bad tempered, I reached for the door.

"You're not pregnant," Jenks said, and my mouth fell open. I knew I'd forgotten something!

"Shove your belt pack under your shirt," Ivy suggested, and as Jax slipped out the crack in the door to get the camera, I swung it around and did what she said. It was too big for seven months, but it was better than nothing. The picture, draped across my back, showed, and Nick had his card reader. I stank like burnt amber, too. Dead. We were so dead.

"Let's go," I said, and Nick opened the door.

Jax took the first camera. Jenks buzzed on ahead, his ultrasonic hail hurting my ears as we got to the corner. Jax was a blur, racing over our heads to leapfrog ahead.

The sight of two security people jogging down the hallway spiked my adrenaline. "Here we go, boys and girls," I said, glancing at Ivy and trying to remember if Dr. Anders had eyes that dark or if Ivy's curse wasn't covering all of her.

"Sir! Ma'am!" the one said, coming to a breathless halt, his hand on his holstered weapon. "What are you doing down here?"

I tensed. If Nick was going to betray us, it would be now. Ivy kept her mouth shut, knowing she wouldn't sound like Dr. Anders, and I jumped when Nick took my arm as if in support. "Someone got into the vault," Nick said, lifting his card gadget. "With this. I think they're headed for the upper floors." The two men stared at him. "Well, go get them!" he added, and they turned to run the way they had come, shoes clacking as they radioed ahead.

Swallowing, I looked down at the fake bulge at my middle. "That was close," I said, knees shaking as we started forward again.

"If we're not out of here in two minutes, we're caught," Ivy muttered. "How fast can a woman seven months pregnant run?"

"This one can run pretty damn fast," I said, and we jogged to the elevators, waving a worried encouragement to the occasional face that peeped out from an office or lab, wanting to know what was going on. Soon as Quen showed up, it would be over. God, what I would give for my splat gun. Good thing I didn't have it.

The sight of the elevator sent a surge of excitement through me. Almost there. If we could just get inside the workings, we'd be all but home free. Feeling like actors in a sci-fi film, we slid to a stop. As Jax kept the camera on a loop, Nick and Ivy both reached to wedge the doors apart, Ivy using her hand not in a cast.

"Come on. Come on!" I encouraged, but then the little ding of an approaching car iced through me, and the doors slid open. Six security guys were in it. All of them were looking at us in surprise. *Not my day. So not my day.*

"That way," Nick said, doing a credible imitation of Trent on a bad day. "They gained the vault. Check every room from here to there. Now!"

"Mr. Kalamack," one said as the others jumped to obey. "Allow me to escort you to the upper floors. I understand your interest in the vaults, and you, too, ma'am," he added, looking nervous as he shot me a glance, "but Quen would have me on grocery detail if anything happened to either of you."

I breathed easier when Ivy subtly shifted out of an attack position. Down the hall, I could hear doors opening and shouts of a negative nature. Jaw tight, I silently walked into the elevator. Riding would be easier, but frankly, I didn't think it would be stopping on our floor. We'd have to get out another way, not through the stables.

As I stood pensively next to the security officer who had accompanied me in, I motioned with my eyes for Nick and Ivy to join me. *See you up top, Jenks,* I thought, wishing him luck. I knew he and Jax would make it okay, but my gut still tightened. How were we going to ditch these guys without knocking them out and giving it away that we were the ones they were after?

"I want an office-by-office search," Nick said as he joined me, and Ivy gave him a nudge to keep his mouth shut.

The officer seemed to be waiting for something, and Nick started patting his pockets as if for a key card. "Allow me," the man finally said, running his card and hitting the R button.

R? I thought. R for residence? Not good.

My stomach churned as the lift rose. Silence grew heavy, and I started to sweat as I noticed the officer looking at my slightly too-large middle, then the card and wire thing still in Nick's grip. *Oh God. I smelled.*

"Thank you . . . Marvin, for accompanying us," Nick said, bringing the man's attention back to him.

Ivy stood stock-still in the corner, eyes down as she filled the car with the spicy scent of vampire. Damn, damn, damn! Stinky vampire, stinky witch, and stinky sneakers. Okay, they looked like dress shoes, but Nick's boots smelled like leather soaked in salt water and left for a year in the back of a closet. This guy had to be on some major allergy medicine to not notice the stink of burnt amber. And how were we going to get out of the residence wing? If we didn't run into Trent, we'd run into someone who'd just seen him. Maybe we should have hit the man, but then we'd have to run out of here over the pastures. This way, we might get a car.

Looking at the array of buttons, I leaned into Nick. "I don't feel well," I whispered, trying to make my voice wispy. "Trenton, I need some, ah, feverfew."

Ivy stiffened, and Nick turned to me.

"Feverfew?" he echoed as the doors opened to the familiar low-ceilinged, brown-and-gold opulence of Trent's bar, his living room and wide windows looking out onto the landscaped pool spread out before us. Into the lion's den. This was not going well, but I lurched out, at least knowing where we were. Ivy came with me, and Nick. And the security guy, of course. Damn it.

"I saw some from the car the other day as we drove into Cincinnati," I said, babbling. "Please, I need it now." I put a hand to the belt pack to shift it to the middle as I walked, making a beeline for the kitchens and the garage beyond. "It's for the baby."

"The baby!" Nick exclaimed, his pale eyebrows raised, taking my elbow as he paced beside me. "You there," he said to the faltering officer. "Call ahead for a car!"

Jeez, he was doing it wrong. Trent never demanded anything, unless it was for someone to kill me. Hunching close, Nick curved an arm around my waist, looking like he was leading as he followed my subtle motions, telling him which way to go. My face scrunched up in an ugly mask, and I would have slugged him if I could have gotten away with it. He was being too strong with the staff, thinking power and money meant you had to be a hard-ass.

Ivy stood beside us, blocking us from view from the main room. It was unlikely anyone would notice us under the bar's low ceiling, but the security officer had paused to talk to someone. I caught, "I thought he was in his office," and I moved faster.

Voices were echoing down from the unseen open walkways two stories above us. They were growing tense, and I silently prayed I wouldn't hear Trent's. "Just keep moving," Ivy said, her hand on my back, and I shivered. The twin doors to the kitchen were a relief, the empty stainless-steel counters even more so. Just fifteen more feet, and we'd be in the garage. I'd be willing to bet Nick could hotwire a car if it didn't have the keys in it.

I'm going to steal another one of Trent's cars. What is wrong with me? But really, compared to what was strapped to my back, I didn't think he'd care about the car.

"Sir?" a voice queried behind us, and Nick reached for the big door to the garage. It didn't move. *Damn, damn, damn!*

"Shit," he said as he tugged, his worry looking wrong on Trent's face.

"It's locked?" I hissed, and Ivy's hand left me as she tried the door.

"Sir!" the voice came again, closer, and I stiffened. "Let me get that for you. We went into lockdown. That's why your card isn't working. I've got a car coming up right now."

I turned, and his face mirrored my relief. "You're a blessing," I whispered, holding my fake middle. Ivy and Nick went one way, and I went the other, allowing the security guard to run his card in the almost invisible card reader. Nothing happened. The little light stayed red, and looking nervous, he ran it again.

This time, it turned green with a friendly little beep, and Ivy pushed the door open. The scent of cold, dark garage and the sound of a running engine slipped in, cool around my ankles. "You need to get that card looked at," Nick said, lurching after us as Ivy strode to the driver's door and yanked it open.

I held my middle and ran forward, not waiting for anyone to open the door for me. I dove in, yanking Nick after me when I thought he was moving too slowly. God, he was taking this Trent thing too seriously. He slid in with a show of irritation, and I leaned past him to grab the door and slam it shut.

"Get out, or I'm going to break your arm," Ivy said, discussing things with the driver. "Ceri needs feverfew, and as her doctor, I'm going to see she gets it." Too stunned to move, the driver stared until Ivy reached in, plucked him out, and tossed him to land ungracefully at the curb. The watching security officer ran to help him up, only now starting to look unsure.

"*Before* the sun goes nova?" I said, and two streaks of silver zipped into the car.

"Go, go, go!" Jenks shrilled, darting from the front to the back of the car like he was on steroids. "Communication is down, but they know what they're doing, and it will be up in three minutes! You gotta get through the gate by then!"

The security guy was fumbling with his radio, and Ivy hit the gas, maneuvering the big car in a tight circle to head for the faint patch of lighter dark that was the exit. Jax landed on Nick's shoulder, the winded pixy breathing hard and his wings drooping. Keeping up with his dad was harder than it looked. We were going to do this, and I started to laugh, taking the canvas off my back and laying it across my knees so I wouldn't squish it.

"We're not out yet," Ivy said as Nick braced himself to keep from hitting the roof when we bounced out of the underground garage and into the dark. "We have the gate to get through."

"Piece of cake," I said, remembering the flimsy gate I'd busted through the last time.

"Rachel, that was fantastic!" Nick was saying, his image blurring as the car's jostling made his aura shift. "The stuff you could do. My God, you went right through that wall!"

Sobering, I pushed back to a corner. "Yeah," I said, looking at the bump in his pocket, and his expression looked wondering at my less-than-enthusiastic response. "The stuff I can do. Is that all you see? How to use magic to steal stuff? I'm doing this to save my life. And I'm giving the picture back." My eyes went to his pocket. "I'm not a thief."

The car grew quiet. Nick's pensive features made him look even less like Trent. Jax was on his knee, the pixy with his head between his knees as he tried to get his sugar levels back where they belonged until his dad threw a ball of something at him and he ate it.

"We've got people in the road," Ivy said. "And a big gate. What do you want to do?"

Shifting to the middle, I looked. The front gatehouse was all lit up with big lights to look like day. There was a new, much more substantial gate, and a big sign warning cars to stop to avoid tire damage. Swell. Trent had gotten a new gate. I should have guessed. "Um, stop?" I said, heart pounding as I shoved my belt pack in place.

Coming to a slow halt, Ivy rolled down the window. Nick sat quietly beside me, thinking, which was worrisome all by itself. Jenks and Jax had hidden themselves, but I knew Jenks, at least, could react in an instant. Jax was still recovering. Maybe he, at least, had learned something. The guard on duty, flanked by two more officers, came forward, each taking a door. The tension wound tighter.

"Dr. Anders?" the approaching man asked in surprise, the usual clipboard absent.

"We're going for a drive," she said imperially, sounding a lot like the distasteful woman. "Ceridwen needs a plant to stop her labor."

"I'm not in labor!" I said, earning a quick glance. Jenks buzzed a hidden warning, and I pushed myself back into the shadows.

"I need to see some identification, Dr. Anders."

Nick leaned forward. "Do you know who I am?" he asked.

The officer's eyes grew predatory. "No, sir, but seeing as I just talked to you and you were in your office, I know who you aren't."

Shit.

The click of safeties sparked through me, and I sank back into the cushions. Had I really believed I could do this? "Job's over," I breathed, seeing weapons pointed at the car. Twenty feet from us, the comforting black of the night beckoned. Twenty feet. It might as well have been the moon. We'd tried. I didn't want to give up, but I didn't want us dead either. There had to be a way, but if I brought Al into this, he'd say he'd won the bet, and it would be over.

"Out of the car, please," the man was saying, backing up to give us room, and my breath came faster. "Fingers laced above your heads. Now!"

We couldn't get through the gate. Not in the car. But maybe we could make a run for it if we got over it. Sweet, sweet adrenaline pounded into me, and my head started to hurt.

"Rache?" Jenks whispered. He, at least, would be safe.

Nick reached for the handle. "Get yourself out, Rachel," he said. "I'll take care of this."

"What are you doing?" I said, bewildered. "They know it isn't you!"

"Something I should have done a long time ago," he said, and I blinked when he leaned over to give me a chaste kiss. "Do what you need to do. I'll make a distraction so you can get away."

"What?" Ivy barked, and from outside, the security officer demanded we get out.

"I'll be fine," Nick said, opening his door. "I always am."

Stunned, I did nothing as someone opened my door and I was yanked out to the tune of Ivy fighting. A band of silver was slipped over my wrist, and I still did nothing. I felt a wash of ever-after flow out of me, but the curse was demonic, and I still looked like Ceri. Small favors.

"Rachel?" Jenks said, hovering before me.

People were shouting—mostly Ivy—and someone shoved me to the ground. My arms went out instinctively, and I caught myself. Staring at the shiny shoes to my right, something ignited in me. It was not going to end like this. I tensed, playing passive, hearing Ivy resisting.

"Rachel!" Jenks cried again. "What do you want me to do?"

There were only two people watching me, the rest occupied with Ivy. "Tell Ivy to give them hell and meet me on the road," I said, and he darted away trailing silver dust.

Face scraping on the pavement, I looked the other way. Nick was on the ground, men screaming at him. I mouthed the words "Thank you," and he smiled. His attention went up, and I followed his gaze to Jax, looking like a silver mote high above it all. As I watched, the pixy dropped something.

"Ivy!" I shouted, clenching my eyes shut. "Down!"

I heard her drop, and the grunt of someone falling on her.

A boom of sound ripped through the night, shaking the ground I pressed into. My ears went numb, and I looked up, my hearing muffled. The two men watching me had collapsed to the pavement, out cold. Dust hung in the air, and what movement there was, was scattered.

I got up, awkward and clumsy. Ivy was pushing men off her, knocking them senseless as they tried to figure out what had happened. "Let's go!" I shouted, not hearing myself. People were starting to get up. We had seconds.

Staggering, I reached her. "Let's go!" I shouted again, almost getting hit when she didn't recognize me right off. Then I shrieked when she grabbed me and threw me over the gate.

I screamed, landing hard on the road. "Son of a bitch!" I said, only to be jerked to my feet by Ivy, her cast not slowing her down at all. "Are you trying to kill me?"

Her eyes were black, and without a backward glance, she started hauling ass, dragging me until I found my pace at her side. Damn it, the painting was still in the car. But we were out and running. Memories of being chased by Trent and his hounds slammed into me, and I ran faster. The pavement seemed to rise up to hit my feet, every strike felt clear through my thin-soled running shoes. We couldn't make it back to Cincy, but the alternative was not pretty. I prayed Jenks was okay. My hearing was coming back. I could hear a claxon honking behind us, and someone was shouting to get the gate open, but I'd bet the circuitry was dead. I felt a surge of hope and started to angle into the woods, but Ivy grabbed my arm, stopping us.

"Car," she panted, and I looked up into the glow of approaching headlights.

"You want me to lie down in the road, or should you?" I said, only half kidding, freezing when the car swerved to the right, spinning in a wobbly, terrifying half circle around us. I could have cried when I saw Pierce in the front seat, covered in pixies. He was saving my ass again. Even so, I swear, if he did any black magic, I would give him to Newt myself.

"Get in!" he shouted, the squeal of pixies and their darting shapes adding to the mess.

I opened the front door, shoving Pierce to the passenger side only to have Ivy shove me to the middle of the long front seat of my mom's Buick. "How did you know we were in trouble?"

"You're always in trouble, Rachel," he said, fixing his hat firmly back on his head.

"You'd think she wasn't glad to see you," Ivy said, pushing the accelerator down even before her door was shut.

Pierce only grinned as he leaned me upright. "No magic, Rachel. I promise. I opine I can make a fist of saving you without any at all."

Jenks dove in the open window as we tore down the road, all of his kids shrilling in excitement. My hands went over my ears, and I cowered. "Jenks!" the hyped-up vamp shouted as she waved her hand in front of her face. "Get your brats under control! I can't see!"

A sharp whistle reverberated through the moving car, and I gasped. Crap, we were headed for a tree! "Look out!" I screamed, and Ivy jerked us back on the road.

"Holy shit!" Jenks shrilled. "Watch where you're going, Ivy! My kids are in here!"

"Really? I hadn't noticed!" she said, rolling the window up with one hand as she awkwardly drove with the one in a cast.

My elation shifted to dread. "Nick," I said, turning to look behind us at the fading glow of Trent's guardhouse. "We have to go back!"

"Are you nuts!" Jenks shouted.

"*Quid me fiet*," I said, touching Ivy's shoulder, and I shivered as our curses untwisted and we became ourselves again. "We have to go back for Nick," I said as Ivy turned off the lights and we drove in the dark. God, I hoped her night vision was better than mine. "He sacrificed himself to save us. You heard him!"

Pierce was silent in the corner, but Ivy wasn't saying anything either. The car jostled into the night, never slowing. "We are not going back for Nick," Ivy finally said.

"How can you?" I admonished, looking back at the black road. "He sacrificed himself so we could get out. Damn it, we left Jax, too. We wouldn't have gotten out without them!"

"I think you wouldn't have gotten caught without them either," Pierce said sourly.

"I don't believe this!" I shouted. "You're ditching him! After what he did?"

Jenks landed on the dash, glowing brightly. All his kids were in the back, adding to the noise. "Turn it on, Ivy," he said grimly, and I hesitated in my feeling of frustration.

"Turn what on?" I asked, and Ivy twisted, unbuckling her belt pack and tossing it to me.

"Just hit the button," she said, eyes glued to the black night. No one was following us, but I wasn't surprised. They had Nick, and all they had to do was radio ahead.

Feeling sick, I found a small recorder in her stuff. "This?" I asked, holding it up, and Jenks flew to me, kicking a small recessed button. The device warmed in my hand, and a soft squeal came from it, almost unheard, hitting the bones in my ears, not my eardrum. "What is it?" I asked, and Jenks's wings sifted a gold sparkle and all his kids complained.

"The bug we put on crap-for-brains."

My eyebrows rose, and Jenks wrapped his arms around a dial, turning it until the static cleared. I heard the sound of flesh hitting flesh, and Jenks hovered backward, expression angry. Clearly Nick wasn't wearing his demon-born disguise anymore either. I didn't think they'd smack him if he still looked like Trent.

"Enjoying yourself?" I heard Nick say, almost laughing. He had been tortured for days by fanatic Weres. Being slapped by Trent's security officer wasn't going to scare him. My heart gave a thump. We had to go back. Maybe not this instant, but soon.

"Leave off," came a high voice, followed by Nick's raw cough. "Mr. Kalamack's here."

I held the device tightly, staring at it when the unmistakable creak of a door opening came from it. "Leave us," Trent's cool, confident, and ticked voice said softly. I shook my head at Nick's ever trying to duplicate it.

"Sir?"

"He's cuffed," Trent said, voice harsh. "I want to speak with him before Quen arrives."

"Sir." It was respectful this time, fearful. We couldn't just leave Nick, and my fingers tightened as I heard the door close and the soft creak of plastic as Trent sat down.

"What happened?" Trent said, his voice low. "You weren't supposed to get caught. Rachel was."

My lips parted, and I think my heart skipped a beat. God bless it. Nick had screwed me over again! The slimy little rat fink! Jenks's wings lowered in pitch, and he landed on my hand. I hated the sympathy in his eyes. No wonder Nick had known I could get through that elf door. Trent had told him.

From the black plastic in my hand came the jingle of cuffs. "Think you could get these off me?" Nick said, the slimeball.

"Quen is in the vault," Trent said, his beautiful voice icy. "The inventory isn't complete, but more than that canvas is missing. I gave you the code so I could catch Rachel with a fake picture, not let you steal a sensitive artifact."

Trent knew I could jump realities on my own, and hadn't bothered to tell me. My entire body warmed as I started to shake.

"The statue?" Nick said, the cuffs jingling again. "That's why I stayed behind. Let myself get caught. The witch took it along, with the canvas. I lifted it from her before she ran. You won't believe what she wanted to do with it."

He's blaming me for his theft?

"Ran off?" Trent said, and I heard Nick grunt in pain. "Your bug of a pixy dropped a magic-generated pinch on my gatehouse. Thirty-six seconds it took to reboot. Do you know what can happen in thirty-six seconds? Just whose side are you on, Sparagmos?"

"Mine," he rasped, taking a new breath. "But I know who's running Cincinnati. Don't get your wick out of whack. She may have taken it, but I swiped it back."

There was a creak of plastic, and I couldn't breathe. Nick was blaming me for his theft, the lie falling from him like a baby's giggle.

"I figured you'd want it," Nick was saying, and my eyes warmed as Jenks's pixy dust sifted onto my fingers, trembling as I held the radio. "So she escaped. So what? You'll get her, and now you still have your statue. I look like a self-sacrificing hero in her eyes—she gets a worthless picture."

It was worthless. The painting was worthless. Just like Nick. Angry and hurt, I wiped a hand under my eye. It had all been faked, even down to the kiss and his self-sacrificing drivel.

"Where is it?" Trent's voice was intent, and I took a breath, holding it.

"In my pocket," Nick said smugly, and I heard the thunk of someone hitting the floor, followed by Nick cursing softly and the rasping sound of him trying to get up off tile.

"This is a saltshaker," Trent said, and the scuffling sound redoubled, making it hard to hear Nick, but one thing was abundantly clear. He was not happy.

"No!" Nick exclaimed. "She did it again! The bitch! She did it to me again!"

In a turmoil of betrayal and frustration, I looked up at Ivy—smug, satisfied Ivy with her eyes black and her fangs showing in a savage grin.

Jenks flew to her, and the two exchanged a high five, Ivy using a single digit so as not to send him flying backward. Pierce breathed a heavy sigh of relief. "Got you, you sewer rat," Jenks said, spilling a clear pixy dust to light Ivy's belt pack. Inside was the statue.

I took a breath, then another, trying to figure it out. "She didn't take anything but the painting, did she," Trent said, pissed. "You took it, and when you couldn't get through the gate, you came up with this cock-and-bull story about picking it from her."

Nick grunted in pain, and I heard something scrape on the tile.

"How?" I whispered, and Ivy glanced at me, her eyebrows raised and her smile wide. "When? You never touched it!"

"I lifted it when we were trying to get into the kitchen. Rachel, I don't trust him. Anything he took was going to be more valuable than a picture so new that the canvas could roll up that easily."

I frowned, thinking I must look really stupid.

"Especially one that still stank of oil," Jenks added, doubling my shame.

"He lied," I said, feeling depressed. "He lied to me. I'm so stupid."

From the little receiver came a high voice, shouting, "This isn't my fault!"

Trent's voice made me shiver. "Make yourself comfortable, Sparagmos. I won't be crossed like this. Morgan, at least, has values."

He thought I had values? My focus blurred and I thought about the Pandora charm. Had it been an accident? Maybe Trent just wasn't that good at magic.

The sound of a distant door opening was heralded by the sudden office noise and Quen saying, "It's gone, Sa'han. This was left in its place."

"My father's hoof pick . . . ," Trent said, his shock obvious.

"I don't understand," Quen said. "You lost that—"

"Morgan has the statue," Trent said, interrupting him. "Sparagmos took it, intending to keep it, and somehow Morgan got it. I don't know how the pick fits into it."

My eyes closed, and I prayed he'd figure it out before he sent Quen to kill me.

"This is going to be a problem," Quen said softly, and then louder, with some authority, "What is Rachel going to do with it, Sparagmos?"

"Give it back to you—ow!" Nick barked, then went silent.

There was a moment of silence, and then I shivered when Trent said, "Give him to Jonathan. He likes this kind of thing."

"Hey!" Nick said, and I heard him being dragged away. "I thought I had it! You've got to believe me!"

"Oh, I believe you," Trent said, distance between them now. "I also know you were going to sell it if you managed to get out of here alive. I doubt Rachel picked your pocket. It was probably Ivy. She's got a good friend there."

I glanced at Ivy, who wouldn't look at me, eyes fixed on the dark night. "I've got two good friends," I whispered, and Jenks's wings clattered.

I didn't want to hear any more. Nick . . . Well, what had I expected? At least now I could write him off. I mean, I had, but now there were no lingering doubts that he was only doing what he had to in order to survive. He'd lied about my stealing the statue. But as I looked at the erotic thing in the faint light, I decided that nothing had changed. Nick might have been working both sides to get us in there, but I was the one who walked through the wall. It wasn't all fake. We could still do the sting, and the pornographic statue would be a better attention getter than a doctored picture. Trent seemed desperate to get it back. And I started to smile.

"Sir," Quen said as the office chatter grew loud again. "He's bugged."

"Shut the door!" Trent said, and the sound of steps rang out and then the thump of a door.

"Shit," Nick exclaimed. "Rachel, this isn't what it looks like!" he cried, but it was far too late to lie to me again.

There was a tussle, and a loud scraping. From a distance now, I heard Nick take a rasping breath and his soft swearing. "I think this is exactly what it looks like," Trent said, his voice very clear. "Rachel, if you're listening, think about who you're playing with. Return that statue or I will kill you. Not your mother, not your friends. *You.*"

There was a crunch, and the high-pitched, bone-vibrating sound exploded into existence. From the back, the pixies all squealed, and Jenks stomped on the off button, his hands over his ears and his wings flat against his back.

"Return it is exactly what I intend to do, Mr. Kalamack," I whispered, dropping the radio in Ivy's bag and hefting the statue instead. It wasn't very big, but it was heavy.

Ivy slowed and took a quick right into a pull-off, and I put a hand to the dash. "We're at the river," she said, and I felt a sliver of fear. *Why are we stopping?*

"Whoa, whoa, whoa," I said as she put it in park. "We are *not* going to abandon my mother's car and run out of here, Ivy."

Dogs. Trent had dogs. I'd stolen something from him before, and he'd ridden after me. The moon was new. It was the Hunt. But no one was listening. And as I sat, terrified, Ivy got out, quickly followed by Pierce on my other side.

"I'm not getting out of this car!" I shouted, my grip tightening on the statue. "Ivy, he's got dogs! I'm not going to be torn apart by a damn hound!"

Pierce leaned in, taking my hand to draw me into the night, where I stood and listened to the wind, searching for the singing of dogs in the rustling leaves. *Not good. So not good.*

Grit scraped under Ivy's heel as she slammed her door shut and turned to the distant glow of the city. "What are we doing?" she asked as she put her belt pack back on.

"We're getting in the car and driving out of here!"

Ivy shook her head. "The road is blocked already. Are we finishing this job or not?" she prompted, and I calmed myself, looking down at the ugly statue in my hand.

The thought of the dogs made me shiver in the cool night, but even so, there was a sliver of strength growing in me. I would forever have the refuge of the ever-after, especially now. All I had to do was find a line. And better yet, I knew my gut instinct about Nick had been right. It had only been my heart that had gotten in the way. I didn't have to feel guilty about hating him. And that . . . felt kind of good.

"Rache? We doing this?" Jenks asked as his kids chased the bats over the river.

I smiled up at him, pocketing the statue in my belt pack and zipping it up. "Yes," I said, and both he and Ivy relaxed. "We got what we needed," I said, following it up with a quick "True, it didn't go off like I had intended, but we got something better, I think. I say we forget about crap-for-brains and just run the job as planned. If Nick talks, then so much the better."

"Yes!" Jenks shouted, a burst of light coming from him.

Still listening for dogs, I turned to Ivy. "Can you take care of getting the paperwork from David to claim FIB jurisdiction?" I asked. "I know I was going to, but I can't go back into the city until we're ready to give the statue back."

"Got it," she said as she turned to the distant glow of Cincy. "Where are you going?"

I exhaled, knowing they weren't going to like this. "The ever-after,"

I said softly, and Jenks darted to me, getting in my face and half blinding me.

"No!" he shouted, and his kids paused in their play before going back to tormenting a bat they'd caught. "Rache, no!"

"Where else can I go?" I said, dropping back a step to see them ringing me in the faint light reflecting off the river. "Not the church. Not anywhere in Cincinnati. Trent is going to be hot to find me. I'm surprised the dogs aren't baying already." I shivered as I remembered the sound. "They'll be following my scent, not yours. You should be fine."

Looking calm, Pierce cleared his throat. "I know of a place this side of the lines."

Ivy gave him the once-over, her hip cocked. "You know of a place. Why didn't you mention this before?"

"Because it was abundantly clear that you didn't want my help," he said dryly, hands clasped behind his back and coat shifting in the wind off the water.

"You're not going to take Rachel alone to *your place*," Jenks threatened.

I shifted nervously, thinking that standing on a riverbank with dogs coming for me wasn't the best time to be eating crow, but I would. "Pierce, you're my freaking hero for driving out here and saving my ass, but this is Trent we're talking about. The ever-after is the only place I'll be safe. If I run, his dogs will find me." I stifled a shiver, but he saw, and I crossed my arms over my chest, pretending to be cold. I hated Trent's dogs. I really did.

Pierce raised his hand in disagreement even as he pulled a pair of heavy-duty clippers from a back pocket and cut the zip strip off me. "I'm not an innocent in evading dogs," he said, eyes meeting mine from under his loose curls. "I know a spot nigh close to here. An almighty safe place this side of the lines." His eyes went to me, black in the solid darkness of a night with no moon. "There will be no black magic. You have my word."

No black magic. Again I shivered as I remembered the awful sound of animals singing for my blood. We had left Trent's woods, but he'd ride for me anyway. He was probably saddling Tulpa right now, cleaning his hooves with his daddy's hoof pick.

Pierce took my hands. Ivy cleared her throat and Jenks clattered his wings. "I can offer you nothing but a hole in the ground," he said. "But it is a hole never found by dogs or men with rifles. It was used to hide men and women on their way to freedom and is deeply spelled for safety." He looked over the river as if looking into the past. "I used to be a conductor on the underground railroad, or did that not find its way into Ivy's computer?" he said dryly.

I bit my lip, and Jenks's sour look eased. "It's better than the ever-after and Al," he said to Ivy, and the vampire grimaced.

Go with Pierce? Alone? Was he kidding? Ivy clearly wasn't happy with this either, but she finally nodded. "I'd rather have you on this side of the lines," she said sourly.

Pierce frowned at her mistrust as Jenks dusted a bright silver. Standing beside the river, the witch seemed to change. His mood darkened, and his gaze lingered on the moving water as if testing it. Hands in the pockets of his coat, he asked me, "Can you swim?"

Suddenly the ever-after was looking a whole lot better. "You want me to get *in* the water?" I asked. "It's freezing!"

Ivy's steps were loud on the gravel as she came up to us, but any hope that she was going to side with me died when she took my elbow and started walking to the river. "Rachel, Pierce is right this time," she said, and I made a noise of disbelief. "Trent owns Cincinnati. It's a death trap. The ever-after is just as bad. Go with Pierce."

"Ivy!" I protested. My feet splashed into the water, and I jerked out. "It's cold!" I said, pulling out of their reach and staring at the fast-moving water.

"Don't be a girl, Rache," Jenks said, hovering over the water and jerking up three more feet when something jumped at him.

"Look!" I said, pointing and backing out completely. "There are fish in there!"

Pierce ducked his head, muttering, "I think she's afraid."

I huffed, but Jenks came to my rescue. "She doesn't need to be. I'm going with her."

Ivy's eyes, black and glinting in the starlight, widened. "You are not leaving me alone with your kids and that gargoyle."

"I can't bring my kids with me!" he protested. "Come on, Ivy, give me a break!"

I jerked when Pierce pulled me off balance and into the water a step. "Hey!" I shouted, hearing it echo on the flat water. "I said I'm not getting in the water! I almost died the last time." Memories of ice and Trent surfaced, and I wrapped my arms around my middle. *I had saved him, and he had saved me. What was wrong with us?*

Ivy spun to me. "Shut up. Go with Pierce. Jenks will go with you so we know where you are, then he'll come back and tell me. I've got the kids." She glanced at Jenks. "Okay?"

"Okay," the pixy said, and I wondered if he'd really leave me. Except that if he didn't, she'd never know where I was.

"I'll get everything set up for Fountain Square," she was saying. "At least we didn't tell Nick everything about that! You keep the statue in case Trent follows me. I'm going to Rynn's, but better safe than sorry. Get in the water, Rachel. They can track you to here, but the water will kill the scent. I imagine you'll go down about a mile before you can make it across."

"Depends on how well she swims," Pierce said, his feet already in the water, and I shivered.

"Guys, this isn't a good idea," I said as the cold seeped into me, but no one was listening.

"Jenks will come back when I've got everything set and bring you anything small you might need." Ivy was starting to babble, and she shut her mouth, her eyes frightened. She didn't want to leave me, and I gave her a hug just to shut her up.

"Thank you," I said, breathing her in, and her arms went around me tentatively. "Thank you for helping me today." I put her at arm's length and smiled, feeling my eyes warm with unshed tears. "I don't deserve people like you and Jenks."

"Aww, I'm going to barf fairy farts," Jenks said, but he landed on her shoulder, shedding a bright sifting of pixy dust.

She dropped back, our hands parting. "Then I'm gone," she said, walking backward a hesitant step. "You're going to be okay? Be smart."

She was talking about Pierce, and I nodded, feeling him behind me in the water.

"God, Ivy, just go!" Jenks shouted, and she turned and started jogging, a passel of pixies lighting her way. She could probably outrun any dog. She'd be fine. *Right?*

I felt the statue through the thin fabric of my belt pack, worried about her. Ivy thought Pierce's hole was going to be safer than Rynn Cormel's stronghold. Or maybe she just didn't want to dangle such a priceless piece of blackmail in front of the master vampire. "See you tomorrow!" I shouted, and got a backward wave.

"Can we go now?" Jenks said snidely, his gold dust turning yellow when it hit the water, looking like sun sparkles in the middle of the night.

"We can go now." I slipped as I edged back into the river, caught by Pierce until I jerked away. Yes, I was grateful for him saving me yet again. But I'd been burned too many times by strong, capable men with a past. A pang of something lit through me as I saw him in the water beside me, the current eddying about his ankles and the starlight lighting his face to show his grim mood.

"You've got a place on the river, huh?" I asked, and he nodded, not smiling at all.

"Take off your shoes," he said as he shoved his hat into a back pocket. "Drop them somewhere in the river."

Standing at the edge, I slipped them off. "Will it help throw them off the trail?"

Pierce turned to me, already calf deep. The light sort of seemed to slide off him, blurring his features, and I shivered. "The weight of them will pull you down. Your clothes should be fine, seeing as you're not in skirts. I can't tell you how many women I lost at the end in the name of modesty. Do what I say when I say, and don't stop or you'll die. Understand?"

Turning his back, he waded into the water.

Jenks landed on my shoulder. "Talk about a hard-ass."

"Yeah, and he's telling me what to do again." Shaking, I yanked the other shoe off and threw them both back at my mom's car. Slowly I turned to follow Pierce, wincing as ice-cold muck squished into my socks.

Fine, I'd do what he said, when he said. *For now.*

Thirty-two

My head was above water. Barely. There wasn't ice on the river, but there might as well have been. I was so cold, I wasn't sure my legs were moving. Numb, I forced myself to keep kicking. Jenks was my guide, and his dust lit the way. If not for that, I was sure I would've gotten lost trying to cross this dumb, stupid, cold river. What a good idea, swim the Ohio River. We couldn't steal a boat or anything. No-o-o-o-o, we had to swim it.

"Almost there, Rache," Jenks said as he darted back from the soft splash of Pierce confidently moving forward. His wings were a worried green. "Get your witch ass moving!"

"Go to hell," I gasped. My lips were inches from going under, and I got a mouthful of river. It went into my lungs, and I panicked.

"Rache!" Jenks shouted as I stopped swimming and tried to breathe. The current took me, and I floundered. Jenks's shouts became muffled, turning into a black swirl of bubbles. Coughing, I clawed my way to the surface.

"Pierce!" Jenks shrilled, and I went down again.

My arms were leaden. A blessed warmth was stealing into me, and I listened to the rumble of the water. Numb, I drifted, letting the bubbles slip out. At least the water had gotten warm. The last time I'd fallen asleep in the Ohio River, it had been warm then, too.

A sharp pain in my scalp jerked through me, and I gasped as the cold air hit my face.

"Rachel!" a high-pitched glow was screaming, but I couldn't move to smack it away.

I was still in the water, but stars were playing hide-and-seek among the black leaves overhead. One of them kept moving. It was swearing, too, spilling a glow all over my face. Confused, I felt the ground scrape under my back. Water flowed over my legs, but someone was whispering, covering me up with something heavy and wet.

"I'm not of a mind to understand," the voice was saying. "It's not that cold, and she's a considerably skilled woman. Fit as any."

"She's sensitive to the cold, you ass," the star was saying, dipping close, and the slits of my eyes closed again. "You're going to kill her! Look, she's blue. She's freaking blue again!"

"She'll be fine," the low voice said, and something cold shifted my head and breath touched my cheek. "Stop acting like an old woman. I've seen worse. Rachel? Open your eyes!"

Like I could? My head lolled as I felt myself rise. "Sensitive to the cold," he whispered irately. "How's a body supposed to know? She looks as healthy as a plow horse."

Plow horse, I thought, hazy, my weight shifting.

"She's going to be okay," he said again, but this time, I could hear worry.

"Why, because you think you love her?"

It was my star again, my lucky star, and it was hovering above me to shine a light on the man's face. His features were dripping, creased in worry, and his black hair was plastered to his face. "I shouldn't," he said to the star, and the star's glow dimmed.

"But you do. You're going to kill her. You're going to break her heart and then she'll get sloppy and die."

The world jolted as Pierce stumbled, and I lost track of everything. My existence became a confused motion of stops and starts. Once I felt the hardness of ground under me and smelled earth, and then nothing until I realized I wasn't moving anymore, and I woke up.

It was quiet. It had been for a while, I realized, feeling a pleasant warmth flowing through me. That was wrong. I'd been suffering from hypothermia. I should be shivering, and I wasn't. There was the strong scent of river, wet leather, and . . . redwood. My eyes opened.

I was lying on my side on a dirt floor with a dirt wall rising before me within arm's reach, going only four feet before turning into a dirt ceiling. A small globe of green-tinted light rested in a wooden lanternlike affair in the corner at my feet. It looked old and dusty. There was a scratchy wool blanket over me—and a masculine arm.

Shit.

My pulse quickened, but I didn't move. Pierce spooning behind me would explain why my backside was so warm. I'd not felt the comforting heat of a real body next to me since Marshal, and I missed it. Careful to not move my head, I looked at his arm, seeing it through his thin white shirt. It was a nice arm, settled perfectly at my waist so it wasn't squishing me. His soft breathing told me he was still asleep. Why he was spooned up against me was obvious. The cold of the river had nearly brought me down, and there was no other way to warm me. This must be his hole in the ground. I hadn't thought it would be a real hole. *Safe?*

I didn't move, wanting to pretend that I had a right to enjoy the sensation of having another person this close, the comfort of just being together, the trust. I was deliciously warm, almost as if I was in a ley line, and I couldn't help my sigh.

"For land's sake!" Pierce exclaimed, pulling up and away from me. "You're awake!"

The warmth cut off, and I felt the energies in my body jump, feeling the lack of what *had* been a ley line running through me. There was a scrabbling of noise, and my back went cold as Pierce's light flashed an alarmed brightness. I sat up, grabbing the blanket and skittering to the other side of the small underground room to stare at Pierce in the green light.

That *had* been a line! Had he been pulling a line through me? While I was unconscious? Not a power pull since my chi was empty, but something else? Who did he think he was?

Pierce sat with his head a foot below the ceiling, his back to the opposite wall, one leg bent on the earth, the other propped up. He was fully clothed, but wearing almost nothing—his coat and clothes were hanging on pegs hammered into the wall with a puddle of mud under them. A white shirt and matching trousers covered almost all of his skin, but I could see the outline of his body well enough.

"I'm sorry," he said, his expression alarmed and his eyes wide. "I didn't take advantage of you. Rachel, you were cold. I was trying to warm you up. It wasn't a power pull."

"You were pulling a *line* through me!" I said, angry. "I was freaking unconscious! What in hell is *wrong* with you!" Sure, I'd been dying of cold, but I didn't even know what he'd been doing. It sounded close to what a witch did with a familiar.

Pierce looked at the ceiling. Now that the light was brighter, I could see it was of wood so old that roots were coming through it. "It wasn't a power pull. Lower your voice."

"I will not!" I shouted, starting to shiver. "I'm not your freaking familiar! Pull a line through me again, and I'm going to . . . sue you!"

His lips tightened, and he frowned. When he shifted as if to come closer, I flung out a hand in warning and he rocked back. "You have a right to be in a fine pucker, but I'd sooner die than impugn your honor. I didn't pull a line through you, I simply included you in my communion with one. I'd never seen anyone in all my born days as cold as you, and it was to warm you. It was a mistake to take you into the water. I didn't know you were susceptible to cold. And lower your voice. There are dogs in the woods."

At his last words, my attention slammed to the ceiling. Fear plinked through me, stealing my breath as the memory of Trent's hounds tracking me hit a deep chord and resonated. *Dogs.* There were dogs in the woods. The same ones who had tasted my scent. The same who had run me through Trent's beautiful, silent, and deadly woods.

In a heartbeat, the memory hit me of being unable to breathe because my lungs hurt so badly, my legs leaden and scratched, the water I'd splashed through making me slow, and the mud mixing with my tears as my breath rasped. I had *never* been hunted like that, chased by an animal who single-mindedly thirsted for my death, eager to tear my flesh and take joy in burying its nose in my warm insides. And now I was in a hole in the ground, helpless.

My God. I had to get out of here!

"Rachel, you're all right," Pierce whispered, inching awkwardly across the dirt floor to me, his heels in the air and toes shuffling. "Please, you're safe. Be still. There's a hole for air, and enough to breathe. The walls are firm."

Images of being pulled from the ground and ripped apart mixed with the reality of having been chased before. "I have to go." I lifted a hand and felt the ceiling, bits of it falling on me. *I had to run!*

"Rachel, be still!"

Frantic, I stood, crouching, putting my back and shoulders against the ceiling to push. I had run before. I had run and survived. I had to run now!

Pierce shifted forward, and I grunted, head thunking the wall when he was suddenly on top of me. "Let me go!" I shouted in panic. He didn't understand. He didn't know! I tried to shove him away, but he caught my hand. His grip was tight, and I went to kick him.

Wise to it, he dodged, pinning me to the wall with his weight. My air huffed out, and I wiggled, trapped. "Let me go!" I said, and he covered my mouth with a hand smelling of dirt.

"Shut pan," he hissed, his body covering mine. "I know you're scared, but you're safe from all creation. They'll be gone like greased lightning if you would just be still! Couldn't you have stayed asleep but a hooter more?"

A horn sounded, faint. Panic jerked my eyes to the ceiling. They were above us? Right now? Again the horn came. And dogs. Baying for my blood.

Fear hit hard, and I struggled. He pulled me into him, his arms wrapped around my body, his legs around my waist, and his hand over my mouth as I fought. I was crying, damn it, but he didn't understand. Dogs never gave up; they never quit. They sang for your blood as you ran, heart pounding and lungs burning, until they clawed you down and tore you apart and your screams mixed with their snarls for your blood. I had to get out of this hole. *I had to run!*

"Go to sleep, baby, Mama will sing. Of blue butterflies, and dragonfly wings," Pierce sang in a whisper, his lips by my ear, and his hand clamped over my mouth, hurting me. I fought, and he squeezed me harder.

"Moonlight and sunbeams, raiments so fine. Silver and gold, for baby of mine."

He was rocking me, his hand hurting, and his arms too tight. My sobbing breath came in through my nose, and I began to shake. He wouldn't let me go. I couldn't run. I was going to die. I was going to die right here, and it would be *his fault!*

"Sing with me, Rachel," he whispered, eyes on the ceiling. "Go to sleep, baby. Sister will tell, of wolves and of lambs, and demons who fell."

I didn't know the words, but the tune plucked a faint memory. Sing. Why do they always sing lullabies? Stupid asses.

A thumping cadence came right overhead, and my eyes shot to the ceiling. Terror filled me, and I whimpered behind Pierce's hand, pressing into him.

Pierce's singing cut off. "Sweet mother of Jesus, protect us," he whispered.

My heart pounded so hard I thought it would kill me outright. A dog bayed, muffled but clearly right over us. I jerked, Pierce's grip tightening even more. I started to shake, my eyes clamped shut as I remembered the crashing of branches and the sound when the horses and dogs grew close as I had tried to escape. I couldn't outrun them, but the horror of being torn apart alive had pushed me through the brambles and across swales of thorns. I trembled in Pierce's arms. We should have run. Tears leaked out. I couldn't breathe. Oh God, we should have run.

A horn blew more distantly, and the dogs answered. My eyes flashed open at the soft patter of dirt falling on my face in time with the thumping of horses' hooves. And with a rapid cadence . . . they were gone.

My gasping breath came in around his fingers, wet with my tears. Pierce's arms wrapped around me eased. He didn't let go, shaking himself as his fingers fell from my mouth and I took a clean breath of air, almost a sob.

"I opine that was as near to death as I'll get afore I make a die of it again," he said softly.

They were gone? I sat there, not believing it. I shouldn't be here. There had been dogs, dogs tracking me. I had survived?

Breath fast, I looked at the wall, not understanding as reason started to trickle back. Pierce's head thunked into the dirt wall as he looked up. He was warm behind me, smelling of sweat, dirt, redwood. Masculine. They were gone. "Let me go," I whispered.

Pierce loosened his grip. In a smooth motion, he slipped out from behind me, taking his warmth and comfort to the other side of the hole. The light in the corner dimmed.

Cold and sick at heart, I fingered the abandoned blanket closer and draped it around me, shaking as I looked back at my panic. God, I'd completely lost it. What in hell was wrong with me? And yet I was still shaking. "Thank you," I said, looking at my trembling hands, covered in dirt and stinking of the river. "I don't know what got into me. It was . . ."

His eyes meeting mine were dark with pity. "You've been run by dogs before?"

I nodded, looking at the ceiling and pulling my knees to my chin. My leather pants were damp and icky. Freezing. His thin clothes were dark with moisture where he'd held me.

"I can tell," he said, frowning as he remembered his past. "It's always the ones who have been run before that give me the most trouble." Smiling faintly, he returned his attention to me. "I'm sorry if I hurt you. It wasn't my intent."

My gaze dropped, embarrassed, as I remembered my terror. "No . . ."

"Oh, Rachel," he said softly, and I looked up at the compassion in his voice. "I don't set much store by what happens in a hole in the ground. It's of no circumstance. None at all. There was one time, I swan, it took three of us to keep him down and quiet. When elves ride, they magic fear into their prey. And Kalamack's spawn has hunted you before."

Instead of making me feel better, I felt even more stupid. It hadn't affected him. Expression sour, I peeled my socks off my feet and checked between my cold toes to make sure I hadn't picked up any leeches. "I flaked out. Sorry." I remembered his warmth behind me, and his voice, calm and frightened all at the same time, begging me to be quiet as he sang about silver and gold. "You've done that before. Kept a person quiet."

He nodded, not looking up. His brow was furrowed.

"Does it always work?"

He shook his head, and I shivered. I had a right to be afraid, then.

"You're cold," he said, seeing me with my arms wrapped around my shins. It was the cold, sure, but it was the spent adrenaline, too. There had been nothing but fear in it. No high, no euphoria. God, I was stupid. Or maybe I was starting to get smart.

I looked over the small room, gaze lingering on the fieldstone wall. "Where are we?"

"A short stretch from the river."

My belt pack was in the corner, and I eyed it. I was cold, hungry, and in a hole in the ground, but at least I had my elven porn, damn it. "Jenks?"

Pierce settled himself, gaze on the ceiling. "On his way to Ivy," he said. "He was determined not to mosey off until satisfied you were sound, but after you pinked up, he left."

Wiping my hand under my nose, I found a more comfortable position. There wasn't much room here. It was bigger than say . . . two coffins, and about four feet tall.

Pierce's bare feet shifted as he found a new way to sit. "We're likely to be some time. I'm of a mind sharing that blanket might make it nicer."

My attention jerked to his, suspicion rising high. "You can have it." I pulled it from around my shoulders and tossed it to him. It landed between us to somehow look dangerous.

Pierce leaned forward, his expression cross as he dragged it to himself and watched me shiver. "I won't say you're a cold woman, Rachel, because you're not. But you're . . . a sight too wary of those whose aim is but to give you comfort. Grit your teeth if you must, but I'm coming over and we're sharing this blanket."

"Hey!" I said loudly, then froze, looking at the ceiling, fear spiking through me. "You stay right there," I whispered, hand outstretched in warning. "I said you could have the blanket."

He hesitated, crouched awkwardly because of the low ceiling. His black hair was in disarray, and his white underthings covered everything and hid nothing.

"What are you going to do?" he asked. "Hurt me because I want to share a blanket? I won't impugn your honor. You're an ornery woman if you won't allow a man even that."

He moved forward again, and I pressed into the wall, feeling its cold through my thin chemise as he came on. "I said stop!" The pitch of my voice halted him, and he hesitated, a foot back. Heart pounding, I whispered, "I might. I've hurt people before. It's what I do. Demon kin. I'm demon kin, and tonight proves it."

"Aye, you might." Pierce's eyes narrowed. "I'll chance it."

I didn't have time to react as he shifted to sit right next to me, pushing my arm away when I went to shove him back, slipping the blanket around us and drawing it close.

"You son of a bitch," I said, and he caught my wrist as I went to shove him, tucking it under his arm so he could pull the blanket closer over my shoulder. "Leave off!"

"A body is just trying to get warm!" he said, irritated. "Hold still."

He moved to block another smack—and both my hands were caught. "You've been giving your trust to the wrong people. Nohow can you fix it," Pierce said, and I quit, surprised. "What do I have to do to win your trust? Damnation, woman, I just saved you three times, and the sun isn't even up yet."

Panting, I stared at him through my lank strands of hair. "I trust Jenks and Ivy."

His eyes were inches from mine. "You trust on the surface, but no deeper. You don't know how. For a clever woman, you took the short end of the stick when it comes to men."

I shoved my shoulder into him, seeing as he had my wrists in one of his hands. "Get off! I don't want to play this game, Pierce."

I tapped a line—ready to risk Trent's feeling it—and Pierce's grip on my wrists tightened. "Game," he said, voice angry. "It's an all-fired serious game, and we're going to settle it off the reel. I don't set much store by the lies you tell yourself to protect your heart. Tell me a truth, and I'll let go of you. Use that line upon me instead, and I'll smack your head into the wall."

Yeah, he probably would. "This is stupid, Pierce," I said, heart pounding. "Let me go."

"Aye, stupid," he muttered. "Tell me a truth, and I'll let go." I wiggled, and his grip tightened. "You can't think of one dash-it-all truth?"

"You scare me," I blurted out, and he exhaled. The furrow over his brow eased, and he loosened his grip on my wrist.

"Why?" he said, but he didn't sound surprised as he gazed at me, a new stubble on his face and his expression unforgiving.

I thought of his sorry state, stinking of river water and prickly, then the time I'd seen him standing in my church, clean and dressed impeccably, with a hat. *Who wears a hat anymore?* "Because I'm attracted to you," I whispered. "And every man—or woman, for that matter—I'm attracted to is dangerous. They betray me or end up dead or . . . hurt me somehow."

My heart pounded as he thought about that. "That's half a truth," he said, and let go of one of my wrists.

I rubbed my wrist, trying to erase his touch. "I'm afraid that anyone who can look past my shunning and smut is a bad person and not to be trusted. Like you."

Emotion crossed his face, too fast for me to read. "There's the other half," he said, letting go of the other wrist and settling himself more comfortably beside me, our shoulders touching. "One that I deem hogwash, but if you believe it, I'll allow it."

Feeling less penned in, I shifted my half of the blanket up around my shoulders. "I want to know what you did for the coven to kill you," I said, then hesitated. "Why you're still helping me when you know I'm demon kin. You kill demons. Or try to, anyway."

He stared at the rock wall across from us. "You don't know how to play this game. Those are wants, not truths."

My wrists were fine, not even red in the dim light as I rubbed them, and I could feel his warmth on one side of me, though space was between us. This was okay. We could share a blanket. I guess. "How about playing *my* game, then," I said. "The more you talk, the longer I'll sit here under your blanket."

He smiled at that, but it faded fast, and he stared at the stones and into his past with his hands laced over his shins.

"Did they kill you because of Eleison?" I asked, pulse fast. *Please don't let it be bad.*

"Eleison wasn't why, but it was the beginning of my end," he said, voice soft in the glow of his magic-made light. "You know I destroyed it? Every last living soul?" he asked, his expression haunted, and when I nodded, his gaze became distant again. "They forgave me for that. What came afterward . . ."

The blanket slipped from my shoulder when he shifted to find a more comfortable position, and I tugged it back up, sending his scent over me along with the blanket. "Eleison was a small town, rife with foul magic," he said softly. "I was a minor coven member, young. Newly taken to my vow. I was the plumber, as Ivy would say, out among the people settling issues, fixing things so that the secret of our species might not be espied. I was sent to Eleison to evaluate and bring back word, but when I found a black coven with a demon and three girls in their circle . . . I swan, their fear was a powerful thing. It would have been a sin to Moses had I not done something. The circle broke when I made my presence known, and the demon made his escape. I expected to make a die of it, but he didn't kill me. Not right off the reel."

His voice faltered, and I felt a surge of pity, imagining it.

"Every last person perished before the sun rose, each more foully than the last," he breathed. "The demon murdered the three girls by a most horrible means, thinking that they meant something to me. Witches of skill were taken to the ever-after, and warlocks and children of no account . . . slaughtered like chickens and left askew with their limbs tangled."

I had to say something. "You tried to stop the demon," I offered.

"Of course I did. But the demon set no great store by my efforts, and my skills saved only myself. Not even a child could I spare." His gaze became angry. "A coven member, helpless. I was a dash-it-all coven member, and I was helpless. It was my dang-blamed innocence of the way things are, ignoring the truth of it. I opine you're wiser than me, having followed your heart from the beginning and being open with your choices, not hiding them behind lies even if it made your path harder."

God help me, he thought my acceptance of black magic was a good thing? Hadn't he been watching this past year?

He hung his head, saying, "The coven hid the massacre as a sickness, and knowing they wouldn't cotton to it, I began studying on it in private. How can you fight a winning battle with something you don't even know the limits of? When by chance a twist of black magic saved my life and hurt no one, I went to the coven with my thoughts. They said they would consider it and sent me to find a rogue master vampire while they discussed it at length."

My shivering had stopped, and I stared at the same nothing he was. "Christopher," I said, remembering the vampire we'd tagged on my nineteenth winter solstice. *Was I attracted to Pierce because he believed what I wanted to think was the truth? That demon magic wasn't bad unless you made another pay the cost? Were we both delusional?*

He nodded. "They betrayed me, giving him warning that I was coming and the knowledge to implicate me as a witch and the wisdom to make me helpless, bound with silver my own mentor had charmed. There was no one decision that landed me in your graveyard, but I'll allow it started with Eleison."

The coven had buried him *alive*. In my backyard. In a hole like the one we were in now. *And I'm flaking out about dogs?* "I'm so sorry."

He smiled sadly at me, and I noticed his stubble was coming in red, though his hair was black. "I'm not," he said. "If I hadn't paused my life in purgatory, I'd not be here to see the wonder of planes, computers, and orange juice. Or you."

I drew back, suddenly conscious of my nasty hair and river-water-soaked clothes. His presence beside me grew obvious, and the moist warmth between us rose up, carrying our mingling scents. "Are you cold?" he asked softly.

Shit, shit, shit. I knew what was happening, but I didn't want to stop it. Be smart, Ivy had said. Was this smart? "No," I whispered, pulse racing. I was not falling for him. I wasn't! But a small voice inside me said I might have, and what was left was only justification and trying to find a way to live with the coming heartache when it ended.

I'd asked for the truth, and he'd told me. He knew who I was. Had for a long time. And he was sitting beside me, having dragged me out of the river and kept me from being torn apart by dogs despite what I was. Who I might become.

Slowly, I shifted my weight to lean into him. My heart pounded at the simple motion that was anything but. I felt his warmth mingle with mine as the curious sensation of hesitant trust and tension swirled, sparking even more desire. Damn me back to the Turn, but I wanted this. Bad track record, obvious warnings, and roommates aside, I wanted to see where this might go. More important, I was strong enough to see where it might end, and it would end. Smart decision? Probably not, but it was being made with my eyes open.

He was a black-arts witch who made no apologies. He didn't care what the coven thought, and even more telling, he had the ability and the strength to stand up to them, thumb his nose, and still be who he wanted to be. That was what I wanted, too.

He leaned toward me, and I stiffened at the thrill of wanted emotion spilling down my side where we touched. Feeling it, he hesitated. "I truly scare you?" he asked, inches away.

"Yes." I took a breath, poised on something new as I gazed at him, remembering him wrapped around me as I tried to bolt, holding me—protecting me from myself.

He paused, eyes fixed to mine. "I'm of a mind that you're lying now."

I shifted, lips parted as I looked at him. "You do scare me. You're a dangerous, threatening witch, and me associating with you isn't going to help me get unshunned. You use black magic too quickly, you tell me what to do as if you're in charge, you're way too cocky with Al, and people around you die." *But they die around me, too.*

The blanket fell from my shoulder, and nodding his agreement of my assessment, he leaned to pull it back up around me. My eyes flashed to his when he didn't slump back, but instead hesitated, his lips inches from mine. Waiting. "So?" he asked, the modern phrase sounding odd from him.

People die around me, too. Not caring about tomorrow, I lifted my chin to meet him.

Warmth spilled through my body, and my grip tightened. His lips were warm against me, with just enough demand in them to ignite my own passion. A small noise slipped from me, and my eyes closed. I shifted closer, wanting this.

Our lips parted, and I met his eyes, wondering what I'd find. My worry vanished at the hot desire mirrored in his. I wasn't going to think anymore. Trying to plan my life wasn't working, and this felt good. In my gut, in my heart. I didn't care if it didn't last.

Rising, I put my knees on either side of him to sit on his lap, my head almost touching the ceiling. His smile didn't last long, or at least I didn't see it because I leaned in and kissed him.

Pierce's hand went behind my head, holding me firm. A tingle of ley-line energy threatened between us, and my breath came fast. Oh God. I'd forgotten about that, and my hands twined behind his back as his hand at my spine made a fist and his lips stopped moving against mine. "Don't stop, Pierce," I said, breathless, and he gazed at me, blue eyes serious.

"You know what we're doing and where this might go?" he asked as if I were a child.

I bent forward to whisper in his ear. "Yes." My breath turned to nibbles, and I felt him grow hard under me. Oh God, this could be so good if I let it happen.

His hand moved again along my back, but it was slow and devoid of intent. "My pride won't take being one of your mistakes," he said softly.

He's worried I'm going to leave him? I hesitated. Pulling back, I searched his gaze as the heat he had instilled in me lingered. "It's only a mistake if one of us makes it so," I said. "I'm not asking anything of you. I have today and tomorrow—I can't look further than that. You know my past. You know I can't make promises."

Pierce took my hands from behind his neck and solemnly held them between us. "You've given up on love."

Shaking my head I lifted our entwined hands and kissed his knuckles. "No. But it hurts too much when you want it to last and it can't. I'm sorry, Pierce. I can't give any more than this."

"Rachel . . ."

I stopped his words with a shake of my head. "I'm not giving up on love, but I'm not going to cry anymore when it's over." *Liar, liar, pants on fire.*

Distressed, he said, "I'm not going to leave you."

A shiver went through me, and though we sat poised on a new beginning, I looked at our past and what he had done: taken another man's body to be alive, learned black magic and used it openly, tried to kill Al. He had great power, was as black as me, and he thought he loved me? He hardly knew me. "Pierce, you will."

"But staying with you is what I wish to do," he said earnestly, his hand brushing my skin.

A slow smile curved over my face, and I leaned down over him. "No," I said. "Wishes are lies. Tell me you're going to leave. Tell me you're not going to stay. Tell me that it's only for a while so I can enjoy today," I whispered in his ear, as if saying it louder would break me. "And when you go, don't think me cold when I don't cry. I can't cry anymore, Pierce. It hurts too much."

He pulled me closer, and I shifted to lay beside him, his arms twined around me. "I cannot stay," he lied for me, eyes averted. "I'm only going to be here for a time, then leave you." His gaze met mine. "And I will cry when I go, because I could love you forever."

My eyes were wet, and he brushed my hair from my face, wiping the tears from me as I heard in his voice that he didn't believe anything he had said but the last bit. I searched his gaze, emotionally spent, though nothing had happened. His eyes closed and he leaned in. His mouth met mine, and he delved deep, his tongue finding mine in a way I'd never imagined from him.

I will cry when I go echoed in my thoughts, and I tightened my hold on him. *Because I could love you forever.*

It was what I was down to. It was all I could accept, all I could give.

So I gave myself to the now, to the only thing I had. I moved suggestively against him, and his hand found my hip, the other sliding upward to cup a breast. Oh God, he was leaving tingles everywhere, his fingertips raising gooseflesh as he created a ley-line imbalance between us. "Pierce," I said breathlessly as he pulled me closer and gently kissed my neck.

He was touching me, running his hands on my back, but he wasn't moving forward with what I really wanted to do. "Pierce!" I said more urgently as he found my breasts again.

"What," he said, clearly preoccupied, but if he didn't do more, I was going to scream.

I licked my lips, shuddering and having to take his hands in mine so I could think. "How long has it been for you?"

The darkness of his eyes made me shiver. "So long I'd likely kill you if I'm not careful."

My smile grew wicked. "You wouldn't believe how uncomfortable these pants are."

A work-roughened hand slid down the soft skin of my side, lingering at the waistband. "I opine mine are a mite tight right now," he admitted. He curved an arm around me, and I made a little gasp of a giggle when he spun us around, landing me under him. The blanket was sort of under me, and with a surprising pop, the light went out.

"Pierce?"

Alarmed, I went to sit up, rising right into him. His hands caught my face and he kissed me as he knelt over me. It was as awkward as all hell, and I fell back down under him. My hands went to the ties of his pants, but before I could do more, he was pulling my shirt over my head and I had to let go.

Making a soft moan of sound, I tried again, only to have him pull back out of my reach as he fumbled with my side zipper. My pants were still wet from the river, and he had to pull them off inside out. He was swearing mildly, making me smile when he came back, and I reached up, running a hand over his shoulder, enjoying the way the fabric bunched when I moved to his front and found him taut beneath the thin fabric of his trousers.

I undid the tie and his pants were loose about his hips. My hand dipped inside to find him, and his breathing grew rough. Anticipation was a silver thread of adrenaline through me, and I pulled him down on top of me.

"How are you with ley lines?" I whispered, wanting to be sure he knew what was what.

"I swan, I won't hurt you, Rachel," he breathed. "But you told me not to."

I thought back to waking up with the warmth of a ley line running through me. "I lied," I said, running my hand over him just to enjoy the feel of him.

Making a satisfied sound, he eased to the blanket under me, and I turned to face him. Stretching out my awareness, I touched a ley line and filled my chi, jumping when his free hand slipped low across my back. From his fingers, threads of ley line spilled to melt into me, flowing up and through me to where his lips played with the skin under my ear.

It was like he was a ley line, alive and given a body and a will. I gasped, pulling back from his lips in surprise. This wasn't a power pull, which was finite energy from one's chi. No, this untold power was spilling into me, through me, like I was part of a line itself. Done slow and gentle, it was the most erotic thing I'd ever felt.

My hands on him tightened, and he ended his kiss. The flow of warmth from his fingers ceased, though his hand's motion did not, sliding down to trace my outlines. "What . . . ," I said, blinking, "was that? It wasn't a power pull."

There was the faintest glow in the corner from his light, and in it, I could see his outline beside me, smiling devilishly. "I told you once before that it's me including you in communing with a line," he said. "It only works when I'm touching you in two places."

He leaned forward, and as he kissed me, his hand rising slowly across my lower back spilled energy into me and then out again where our feet touched. My breath came fast, and I followed it as it seeped through me, rising upward to make my lips tingle. I pulled back, licking them, remembering the feel of the line in me.

"This is a demon thing, isn't it," I said, heart pounding.

I saw his outline nod. "You want me to stop?"

In answer, I reached down to find him. His breath came out, and curving an arm under me, he shifted me underneath him. My pulse hammered as I looked up at his indistinct outline. I reached up and sent my hand down him when he bent his head and found my breast.

My eyes closed, and my hands jumped to his hair, twining in his loose curls. Pierce's foot hooked under mine, and I gasped when the line he was connected to flashed through me, running from his mouth down my body and to my foot. *Oh God.* If he had been inside me . . .

I made a little moan, shivering at the thought. Seeming to know my mind, he broke his hold on me, making little hop kisses up to my neck, each time sending a tiny surge of ley line through me. We were already moving together, and my hands on him tightened when he entered me, slowly, as if he might hurt me. The tenderness was more arousing than if he'd been aggressive, and I groaned from the anticipation. God, he was perfect, able to move deep without discomfort, his breath fast upon me in desire.

Just this much was exquisite, and it would have been more than enough, but I knew there was more. My hands slipped around his neck to tangle my fingers in his hair. His head nudged mine, and his lips found my neck, lightly biting. And then, without warning, he bore down, spilling the line already running through him back into me.

I gasped, arching my back as the heat dove through me to my groin. Our rhythm hesitated as I hung there, almost climaxing at the sudden sensation. His lips fastened tighter upon my neck, and the energy between us ebbed. Oh God, he smelled good.

Panting, I opened my eyes. "Rachel?" he asked as if wondering if I was okay.

"Mmmm-hmmm." My hands, which had fallen back to clutch at the blanket, found his lower back again. I rose into him, claiming his mouth. Our motions grew faster, and I felt the heat between us shift, become demanding. Again, he touched the line, and I gasped as the heat burned hotter than before as it ran through me.

"Don't stop, don't stop," I panted as he hesitated, my chi roiling with energies.

"Rachel, I can't wait," he breathed, the hint of desperation igniting me.

"Not yet," I moaned.

Hesitating deep in me to prolong it, his lips found my breast, and as he pulled on me, I felt him touch the line again. The glittering heat pounded in waves from his mouth to my groin.

And suddenly, I couldn't wait either. "Oh God. Pierce!" I said, eyes wide and unseeing as I felt my aura melt to match the resonance of the line. Like an exquisite ping of eternity, I became one with the line he was drawing on.

The energy that had been flowing from Pierce to me suddenly flashed in reverse. Pierce gasped. His head came up, eyes wide in shock. Scrambling, I reached after the energy, pulling it back as the first hints of it dove through him.

What in hell had I done?

Whatever it was, it was our undoing. Pierce's breath hissed in. With a groan, he climaxed, his hands clenching on me. My body reacted, and wave after wave cascaded through me as I did the same, adrenaline igniting my being.

For a moment we hung in bliss, unaware of anything other than the perfect sensation of the line and our souls in perfect alignment with it. And then it was over, and I took a breath.

With a soft sigh, he dropped gently on me, and I opened my eyes, staring at nothing. God, that had felt good.

"I've never before . . . had anyone . . . learn how to commune with a line . . . while under me," he said, starting to chuckle. "Rachel, you're a quick study." He hesitated. "Could you, ah, be of a mind to let me go?"

I could hear him smiling from his tone, and I blinked. Commune with a line? When I'd been eighteen, I thought communing with a line meant tapping into it, but now I was wondering if it really meant matching your aura to a line in order to jump into it or . . . whatever that was we'd been doing to each other. "Sorry," I said, dropping my hands from his shoulders.

"No, I meant a little lower."

I flushed red. "I'm working on that," I said, embarrassed, but it was kind of nice doing the nasty with a witch, where I didn't have to explain myself. Biology was grand. Male witches were not as well endowed as humans, and to make up for it, we girls had a couple of extra muscles that didn't let go right away. I didn't have control over it, actually, and the saying was that the better the sex, the longer it took. Right now, it seemed like it might be a while.

A faint glow showed in the lantern, and Pierce rolled us to our sides to get his weight off me. Stretching, he reached for a fold of blanket, giving me flashes of his anatomy until we were covered. Propping his head up on an elbow, he tucked a strand of hair behind my ear. "I'm in no hurry to mosey off," he said, but he was hiding a wince.

"Oh God!" I said, thoroughly embarrassed now. My body was betraying me. "Pierce, I'm sorry. It's been a few years since I've been with a witch, and I think the hormones are overcompensating." This was utterly mortifying.

He leaned in and gave me a kiss on the forehead. "I'm not of a mind to complain. I should have taught you how to shift your aura sooner. I swan, I lost it when you traced a line through me. I didn't know it made a body feel so all-overish."

All-overish? I blinked when the light went out and he gathered himself to me. "What time do you think it is?" I asked.

"It's dark," was his answer. "Go to sleep."

Our legs were intertwined, and I could feel things loosening up. I didn't think this was quite what Ivy had in mind when she said to be smart. Or maybe it was. Sighing, I tucked my head under his chin and listened to his heartbeat. His arm was over me, and I was warm. I was warm inside and outside. Everything. This was a damn fine hole in the ground.

"Thank you, Pierce," I whispered, and I felt my hair shift when he chuckled.

"I opine you'll feel different when your business partners fill your head with gum-flapping nonsense."

He sounded irate, and I pulled back, trying to see him and failing. "When have what they said ever changed my mind about someone I liked?" He made a soft mmmm of sound, and my fingers drifted down to his chest. "I meant thank you for understanding that this isn't forever."

He gathered me closer, my arms folding between us. "Nothing is forever unless you make it so," he breathed. "I don't want to be alone. I need you, Rachel. And for now, you need me. I pray that I'm not parted from you until you don't need me anymore."

I went up on an elbow again, looking at him. "What do you mean, until I don't need you anymore? You think I'm going to throw you away like an old sock?"

Smiling, he pulled me back down. "You're going to live forever, mistress witch. I want to see you happy while I'm here on earth. Leave it at that."

Eyes wide open, I settled back against him, shifting my back to him now that I'd let go of him and I could. His arm was warm around me, and we spooned, the line that we'd been connected to washed through us again, a gentle flow to warm us both. It was how I'd woken up, but now, everything was different.

Live forever—Newt had said the same thing, and Al. Were they serious?

Thirty-three

The cadence of Pierce's breath shifted, and I woke. Eyes flashing open, I searched the dim confines of the hole. It was silent, a soft glow of natural light showing where the ventilation hole was and that the sun was up. Pierce's stubble, too, said it was tomorrow. I was still lying beside him, his arm over me protectively and one of my legs atop the blanket. It had gotten warm. Pierce was awake and listening, and when he made a soft *sh-h-h-h* of sound, adrenaline shocked through me.

"Morning," he whispered, eyes on the ceiling. "Someone's in the woods."

My breath came fast. Stiffening, I stared at the ceiling, remembering my panic last night and trying to relax. "Trent?" I whispered back, and he shook his head, not moving.

"No dogs or horses. I think it's . . ."

The hum of dragonfly wings grew from a muffled hesitancy to a full clatter, and Jenks dropped in from the far corner of the ceiling, shedding glittering sparkles to double the light. "Rache! Glad you're . . . Tink loves a duck!" he said, wings clattering. "It stinks of sex in here. God, woman. I leave you alone for one night, and you're humping the ghost."

I sighed, and Pierce finished sourly, ". . . it's a pixy."

"Jenks, show some class," I said as Pierce sat up.

The pixy flew over the confines of the hole in three seconds flat as he took inventory. "You know me, Rache. I ain't never been to get no schoolin'. I don't have class."

Pierce got to his knees to reach for his clothes. He was still naked, as was I, and seeing him, Jenks shot to the ceiling, gold sparkles falling from him to make a puddle of light. "Oh! God! Naked witch!" Then he hesitated, his altitude slipping. "Hey, dude, I'm sorry about that."

He was laughing, and I frowned, seeing where Jenks was looking.

Pierce snatched his underthings, sitting on the corner of the blanket as he put them on. "He's just tired, little man. He had a busy night."

This was *so* not how I envisioned my day starting. Wincing, I sat up, blanket held tight to me. I was a mess. "Jenks, in this case, it's truly what you can do that matters."

Jenks was waving his hands at me, hovering backward. "Oh God! Shut up!"

"Then you shut up," I said, eying my clothes, abandoned in the corner. I didn't want to put my leather pants back on, but I didn't want to walk out of here in a blanket either. Stretching, I reached for a sock, feeling its stiffness before dropping it. No way.

Pierce looked at Jenks with a dark expression and, rubbing his thicker stubble, said, "Can we get out of this hole, master pixy?"

Clearly in a good mood, Jenks dropped to alight on the peg holding Pierce's still soggy coat. "Yeah, the woods are clear. Ivy's in lockdown at Cormel's—"

"What?" Suddenly I was a lot more awake.

"She's fine," he soothed, his glow dimming as his wings quit moving. "The coven's on the scout for you, and Rynn won't let her out for her own safety. She is so pissed."

"I can imagine." I glanced at the ceiling as Pierce, now wearing at least his thin shirt and trousers, grabbed his hat and crab-walked to the far end. Good thing I kept the elven porn. I'd never get it back from Rynn Cormel and not get caught. How we were going to run the end of this without Ivy might be tricky. Plans were going to have to change.

With a sifting of earth, Pierce slipped the locking bar out of the trap-door and opened the hatch, carefully shifting it to the side to keep the moss from being damaged. Sun and noise spilled in, shocking after so long a silent existence. Birds were singing, and a flickering sun made shadows on the earth floor. I had to get out. The fresh air only highlighted how nasty it was down here.

Pierce stood up through the opening, eclipsing the light until he levered himself out and the sun beamed in again, unimpeded.

"Don't worry about it, Rache," Jenks said as I gathered myself to move. "There's something about a hole in the ground that just turns a person into an animal. Every time I got Mattie alone in one of the back tunnels—" He hesitated, then smiled, his head down and his wings still. "Tink's titties, I miss her."

I could only smile sadly with him, but I wished I could give him a hug. I was surprised he was talking about her already. Maybe the pixy psyche was like that, live hard and fast.

Jenks darted out and away as I wrapped myself in the blanket and shuffled to the opening. Standing creakily, I blinked in the sun, relishing the fresh air and being upright. Pierce was under a huge oak, hands on his hips and doing some kind of nineteenth-century exercise that looked stiff and about as effective as toast, though seeing him doing them in his underthings had a certain appeal. The chatter of the unseen river was obvious. Jenks was a hum of noise beside me, and gazing at Pierce, I whispered, "Don't drive him away. He's a nice guy."

"Yeah, yeah, yeah." Jenks perched on a fern, looking like he belonged, his bright red bandanna catching the sun. "Did he make sparkles sift from you before or after he told you his lies?"

"Sparkles sift from you" was nicer than "porked you," or "boinked you," or "had crazy monkey sex," and I smiled. "After. Not that it's any of your business." Jenks's wings dropped, and I added, "I know he uses black magic. So do I. I like him even if he's a pain in the ass, and he makes me feel less evil, okay? I'm not going to be stupid. I know it's not forever." My thoughts flashed to Kisten, and I sobered.

The pixy didn't say anything, just looked sad as Pierce approached, looking rejuvenated and a little less rumpled. He extended a hand to me, and with his help, I scrambled out. My bare feet touched the moss, and it was as if I was reborn, new again with hope.

"Thank you," I whispered, meaning about six dozen things. *Thank you for last night, for thinking I'm worth sacrificing for, for holding me when the dogs came, for giving me hope, for not leaving . . .*

His hand fell from mine. "You're welcome. You're a sight in the morning sun, Rachel."

I put a hand to my hair, knowing it was matted and that I stank of river and dirt. "I must look awful."

"You're grand," he affirmed, blue eyes delighted. "The sun is in your hair, and it's all over in a most comely fashion."

"Yeah," Jenks said, interrupting. "Rachel looks good after she gets boinked. It's the only time she relaxes."

Ignoring him, I shivered as the leaves shifted in a gust. It looked about nine. We didn't have much time, and I was almost naked in the woods, miles from Cincinnati and no transportation back. "Jenks, do you know if Trent filed a police report?" I asked, anxious to find out what had happened while I'd been . . . preoccupied.

Jenks's grin eased my worry. "Nope. He doesn't want anyone to know he lost it, which puts you in twice the danger since Trent is going to take care of you *himself.* There's a message on the church phone to call him, which I think is funny. He's increased his security by the looks of it. You'll never get close enough to him without a disguise."

A disguise that I didn't have time to make and couldn't buy because I was shunned. "Good," I said, very relieved. Maybe the hoof pick had been enough to get him to trust me to give it back. If Trent had filed a report, then there was no chance this was going to work.

His wings dusting an odd shiny purple, Jenks hovered before me. Angular features creased, he said, "I don't know. How are we going to do this? Ivy's out of the picture and you're in the middle of the woods in a blanket. Bis is asleep, and I can carry only so much."

Smiling, I looked at Pierce—who was grinning. "Pierce can jump the lines."

Jenks's wings stopped for a second, and he quickly caught himself. "Not without Bis," he shot back, "and he's asleep."

Pierce took my fingers carefully, as if he wasn't sure where we stood. Something in me jumped, and I squeezed his fingers. I wasn't embarrassed about last night, but I wasn't an idiot to think that this was going to be easy. Eventually he was going back to Al—unless I remained just stupid enough to require a babysitter. Maybe we could do this . . .

"He can't jump without Bis," Jenks insisted.

"Thank you for not leaving me last night," I said, my thoughts returning to my terror.

"Never, Rachel," he said, a new, soft expression on his face. "Besides, Al would have skinned me like a cat."

Jenks darted up between us, his hand on his sword hilt and his wings clattering. "What the fairy farts is going on? You'd better start talking, or I'm going to pix someone!"

I dropped back, putting space between us. "Pierce can jump lines without Bis," I told Jenks. "He needed Bis only when he didn't know what line the coven summoned me through."

The pitch of Jenks's wings shifted. "Oooo," he said. "You can jump to the church."

Pierce was nodding, running his hand over his hair, stiff and untidy from the river. "What do you want me to bring back?"

"Ivy's tub," I said dryly, feeling gross. "A bucket of water? Soap? Paper towels? New jeans, a shirt, shoes and socks."

"Underwear," Jenks interrupted. "I'll show you where she hides her sexy ones. How about a contraception charm. You got any of those in your cupboard, Rache?"

My expression blanked. *Shit. I've got to get to a convenience store.* My gaze went to Pierce, who was three shades lighter. Good. The feeling was mutual.

"Uh, no," I stammered, trying to remember how long I had before I was going to ovulate. Twenty-four hours? Crap, I didn't have time for this.

"I'll stop at an apothecary," Pierce said, clearly worried.

"A gas station would have it," Jenks offered.

I stiffened. "I'm not going to trust a gas station charm!" I protested, and Jenks hovered backward, laughing. "Pierce, I know they have them at the grocery store three streets down."

His blue eyes were relieved when they met mine. "The one where you get your emergency ice cream?"

My lips parted that he knew, but then he would if he'd been lurking at the church for a year as a ghost. "Yes," I said slowly, wondering what he thought about Marshal. God, I must look like a whore. First Nick, then Kisten, followed by Marshal, and now him, all in the span of two years.

"I'll pick one up," he said firmly, not a hint of recrimination in his body language.

"Thanks."

"Okay," Jenks said snarkily, hands on his hips. "Now that we got the baby thing taken care of, how are you going to get close enough to give Trent his statue back without him or the coven taking a potshot at you? Rynn Cormel isn't going to help. That's why I flew all the way out here. Trent knows something is up. He's got more security going into place than when the last presidential hopeful came through trying for the vamp vote."

I turned to the unseen river, assessing what we had. "Is David back yet?" I asked, looking for a tree. There had been a deep hole in the ground in the hidey-hole that neither of us had used, and a tree would be a big improvement.

Jenks's wings hummed. "No, but he is on the way."

My head was bobbing. I had to get Trent and the coven together at the same time or this wouldn't work. The FIB was going to be my neutral ground. "We can work with this," I said as I spun around to them and pulled my blanket back where it belonged before it could slip any farther. Ivy was out, Glenn was in, David was on the way . . . and Pierce was here to help. I was sure his protective instincts had been ratcheted up because of last night, and I hoped it wasn't going to cause more problems than he might solve. But as I listened to the wind in the trees and felt the warmth of the sun on my feet, all of the fatigue and terror of last night shifted to the background of my existence. If I worked this right, the next few hours might bring a return of my honor, vindication in my beliefs . . . and freedom.

"Jenks," I said, feeling the wind find its way under the blanket. "Did Ceri leave that charm to go small that she made for Ivy?"

I glanced at Pierce as Jenks darted up and down in the sun like a yo-yo. "No way!" he shrilled. "Rache, you going small again?"

Tugging the blanket tighter, I nodded. "Yup. Just to get close, and then I'll untwist it. It's a demon curse, so it won't trigger any charm detectors. Pierce can carry us in looking like Tom Bansen. The guy was in the I.S. Jenks, you can fly me up the rest of the way to Trent, and then pow! I give Trent his statue."

"Pow, you'll be naked!" Jenks exclaimed, sifting a bright gold dust. "On camera, in front of a couple thousand people."

It wasn't the thousands of people I was worried about—it was Trent, and I winced at Pierce's aghast expression. "It will be all over the news across the country," I said, feeling uncomfortable under his stare. "I'll probably make the late show. And because of it, the coven won't be able to kill me and hide me in a hole." I looked down at my dirty, cold feet, showing from under the blanket. "At least not for a week and they find something else to sensationalize," I finished softly.

God, my mother would be mortified, but then maybe not. She *had* grown up in the sixties. She'd probably call her friends.

Pierce still hadn't said anything, and I felt a quiver of worry. I had too many exes, and now I was going to go naked in front of local TV, sure to be syndicated around the country. But if I was naked, they probably wouldn't shoot me. "You okay with this?" I asked Pierce, hating that my voice went up.

The rims of Pierce's ears were red, and he flicked his gaze to me and away. "Remind me to tell you about my aunt Sara someday," he said, the words deep in his throat.

My eyebrows went up, and Pierce exhaled, seeming to settle himself. "It sounds like an almighty good scheme. And when you are naked in front of all creation, how will you give Kalamack the statue?"

"I thought you could throw it to me?" I said hesitantly, and Pierce laughed.

Thirty-four

I didn't like being small. And I was just small, I wasn't a pixy. Unlike Jenks, I didn't have a quick escape if Pierce stumbled other than to grab a silky fold of his vest and hope he didn't squish me when he fell down. If being small in the garden was bad, being small in the streets of Cincy was terrifying. Everything was loud, big, and heavy. I honestly didn't know how Jenks survived. About the only pleasant thing to have come out of this so far was that I was clean—really clean—again. I didn't even care that I was hairy once more.

Jenks had stayed with me while Pierce jumped back to the church for the size-down curse and something small for me to wear to go with it, and I glanced down at the exquisite light green silk that fluttered about my bare feet in the draft of our motion. I was guessing it belonged to one of Jenks's daughters, and I held a hand to the low neckline as I began to feel seasick at Pierce's quick pace. I didn't have a scrap of red on, and it worried me.

Jenks was quiet as he stood beside me on Pierce's shoulder. He wasn't wearing any red either, dressed for work in his usual skintight black silk and thin-soled high boots. If we entered another pixy's territory without red on, we'd be accused of poaching and might find ourselves attacked. His wings were a depressed blue even as they hummed to maintain his balance, but he stood ready to grab me and fly if anything should happen.

The heat of the city felt good, and I shivered when Pierce hit the shade of a tall building. He was getting nervous, and the smell of the witch overpowered the stink of the city. I breathed him in, liking the redwood scent and the bite of shoe polish. He'd taken the time for a hasty shower at the church before borrowing Ivy's sister's car and coming out to find me, and the smell of soap mingled with the silk scent of his heavily patterned vest. Looking at him, you'd never know he had a chunk of elf porn in his pocket as he gave everyone we passed a nod.

And yet, he was nervous, feeling his pocket for the statue yet again as we slowed at a crosswalk and waited for the light to change. I could see a slice of the square a block up, and anticipation made me shiver. "I'm of a mind we might be able to walk right up," he said softly.

"Not likely," I said, the only reason Pierce could hear me was because I was right next to his ear.

"You go straight here," Jenks said, his voice magnified by "pixy magic" and attracting the attention of the woman next to us. She gave a start until she saw Jenks and me, and then she was charmed, scaring me and putting Jenks in a foul mood if his comment about her perfume and a fairy's hind end was any indication.

Edging away from her thick finger poking toward us, Pierce adjusted his hat and muttered, "I know how to get to the square. The dash-it-all thing is right in front of us."

Impatient, I held my breath against the gas fumes and fidgeted. Jenks could fly me across the street, but I didn't want to leave Pierce and the statue behind. Trent's voice was being piped out over the sound system and a live video was being displayed on the news screen they'd put up the last time they revamped the square.

Son-of-a-bitch elf, I thought, remembering the Pandora charm and his claim that he hadn't tried to kill me. Add to that the fact that he and Nick had been in cahoots to nab me, and I had no problem embarrassing Trent in front of national TV cameras with an erotic statue. Unless Nick had gone to Trent after I hired him? Sort of a last-minute effort to stick me with more trouble? I just didn't know enough.

Impatient, I got to my feet, and Pierce winced when I grabbed his ear for support. But my nervousness shifted to fear when my gaze found a pair of uniforms standing across the street—waiting for us. Damn. I had hoped to get closer before we were IDed.

"Uh, Jenks?" I said, pointing, and the pixy's wings lifted, taking on a more normal hue.

"I see them," Pierce said, having heard my tiny voice. "I'll cross Main instead and come up on the other side of the street."

With a last awkward look at the cooing woman, Pierce sidestepped away and crossed Main, almost jogging to make the light. I clutched his ear, my dress flying up as Jenks took my shoulder to keep me from falling.

It had begun. Steady and sure, the adrenaline seeped in, bringing me alive.

"Good going, Sherlock," Jenks's dry voice said tightly as we reached the curb and Pierce slowed. "They're watching you now because you changed your mind."

"They were watching us before, Jenks. No big diff," I said. "Pierce, you want to shift your look?"

He nodded, and I shivered as a wave of ever-after cascaded over him when he stepped off the curb to cross Government. No one noticed, or at least no one commented on it in the throng of people trying to get to the square. Pierce now looked like Tom Bansen, which might get us stopped, or it might get us through, seeing that the dead witch had also been a corrupt I.S. cop. In either case, if the two officers on the corner had been watching for Pierce, they'd be looking for the wrong man.

We were almost there, but when I looked back, they were following us on the other side of the street. "It didn't work!" I shouted, and Pierce winced.

"I see them," he said, not looking. "I opine things will get rough from here. Rachel, watch yourself. I'll get you as close as I can."

"No black magic!" I exclaimed, and he sighed.

Jostled, we reached the corner of Fifth and Main, stymied by the light again. The square was right in front of us, and Trent's speech was in full swing. The cops shadowing us were clearly from the I.S., and I scanned the area for FIB agents, not seeing any. The I.S. flunkies were watching, waiting to see what we were going to do. One was on the radio. The net was being thrown. I had to stay smaller than the holes they were leaving. Pixy small.

The skin around Pierce's eyes crinkled as he glanced at the waiting I.S. officers. "Jenks, we're going to be here a moment. Why don't you see what they're talking about? Make yourself useful, little man?"

Snarling something lost in the roar of a bus, Jenks darted over the organized chaos. I felt naked without him, and I held Pierce's ear more tightly. "News vans, news vans," I murmured, feeling better when I spotted them. I hated news vans, but they were going to save my butt today. The coven could be anywhere. If they didn't show, I was screwed.

My attention went to Trent, at the podium. Quen was behind him, and I felt a jump of worry. The man was better than me at just about everything. "I have enjoyed serving you in the capacity of councilman," Trent was saying, "and could be happy for years more, but I see the corruption, I hear your frustration, and I want to do more. It is my responsibility to do more!"

The crowd liked that, and I jumped when Jenks landed next to me with a clatter of wings. "I don't know how, but they know it's you, Rache."

Nick maybe? I thought, but I didn't say it aloud.

"We've got two I.S. agents ahead of us, four behind, and the two on the right," Jenks continued. "Trent has his staff on the stage, but it's mixed up with I.S. people. I say we get our asses up there, and trust wonder ghost here to join us when he can."

Pierce tried to look at us, failing. "I can get you across the street."

He looked almost eager for a fight, and I became even more nervous. Damn it, if Pierce messed this up I was going to be pissed! "No black magic!" I demanded, and his jaw clenched. "I mean it! The coven is out there. No black magic! If you can't do it the way I want, I'm not going to let you help me!"

"*Let* me help you?" he muttered, clearly upset. "I opine you wouldn't know help if it smacked you in the face. Stubborn, bullheaded, wild fey thing of a woman."

I frowned, teeth clenched. Clearly we had a few things to work out. But the crossing light had switched. I wobbled when Pierce took a step, and Jenks's wings hummed, ready to snatch me if I fell. The pavement threw up a wave of heat, buoying Jenks up like a balloon, and he finally took to the air to maintain his balance. Ahead of us waited two more cops. Vamps by the looks of it.

"Steady, Rache," Jenks said. "I'll be with you the entire time."

"Don't you patronize me, too," I said, heart beating fast. How did he survive being so small?

From the stage, Trent was saying, "My family has lived on this land for three generations. In that time, Cincinnati has grown to magnificence, but today she falters. We need to cull the programs that don't work and foster the ones that do, throw out political agendas and instead give the power back to the people so that Cincinnati may regain her greatness! My record speaks for me, and *I will speak for you*!"

Head down, Pierce angled to get away from the cops, but it wasn't going to happen.

"Hey, you with the hat!"

"I'll get to the stage, Rachel. Don't worry," Pierce whispered, and I shrieked as Jenks snatched me around the waist and darted off. Pierce went the other way, gone in an instant.

"Get the pixy!" rang out, but Jenks and I were across the street and in the square, flying through a forest of polyester slacks.

"Up! Go up!" I shrilled, terrified he was going to run into something, but Jenks laughed.

"They can't hit us down here," he said, and I shrieked, my legs swinging when he darted suddenly to the right. I caught a whiff of ozone. There was an ugly splat, and a woman screamed in pain. Great, they were using spells.

"Son of a Tink," Jenks muttered. I never even saw what it was—Jenks was already three people deeper into the crowd. He went low, wings clattering as the shade of lunkers cooled us. I hung from Jenks's arms, help-less, wide eyed, and feeling like I was on a roller coaster with no brakes. "Hold on!" he shouted as he jerked to a stop.

My head swung forward, then back, hitting his middle. The momentum of my legs pulled us forward, and I squinted at the sudden silver dust as Jenks back-winged us through it.

A haze of brown-tinted ever-after hissed in front of us. It hit the legs of a man. He turned. Shock registered, first at us, and then his legs, now encased in the brown goo. He shrieked, making everyone around him look. Horror filled him, and he tried to push it off, but it clung to his hands and crept up his arms. In seconds he was on the ground, unconscious in a widening circle of fear.

"Oh, that's nasty!" Jenks exclaimed, and I lost my breath as he shot straight up, my ears popping. For an instant, the entire Fountain Square spread before us, a mass of noise and movement, and then he dropped.

"Je-e-e-enks!" I shrieked, terrified. I flopped like a rag doll, but we were almost there.

The pop of radio chatter was a blur as we headed for the stage. "Where in hell is the sticky silk!" someone shouted. Another voice demanded, "Get Kalamack out of here! She's got something in her arms!"

They thought I was Jenks? Were they blind?

News crew lines lay across the gray granite, and the whine of electronics hurt my ears as we dipped and swooped. Adrenaline surged as we found the stage. People in suits fell back at Jenks's darting form, as if he was a deadly bumblebee, and I found Trent at the podium. Two I.S. cops were with him: a vamp and a witch. I pointed to the plywood stage, and Jenks dove for it.

I stumbled as my feet found purchase. Jenks's grip slipped from me, and I looked up to see Quen trying to hustle Trent away. Trent's eyes met mine, and he stopped dead in his tracks, wanting his statue back, no doubt.

"Morgan?" he whispered, his voice finding me over the noise. His eyes narrowed, and Jenks flew up to protect me. There was a hiss of propellant, and he darted away, one wing tangled in sticky silk.

"*Non sum qualis eram!*" I shouted as brown shoes circled me, making the stage shake.

The world seemed to collapse into me. Sound sucked inward, taking the heat of the sun and the rising damp from the plywood under my bare feet. I felt the curse take hold, and the clicking of a thousand abacuses grew as I was reduced to a thought and rebuilt from the idea of myself stored in the demon database.

I pay this cost, I thought in the perfect silence of nothing. No heartbeat, no pixy wings. Nothing. The smut from the curse coated me in a soothing layer of black, and I shuddered.

I felt the magic rise from the singular point of existence that I was, rushing through me, and I expanded. My aura rang as it adjusted, and suddenly . . . I was back.

Noise hit me, and I sucked in air. Jenks had gotten me here, but he was paying the price for it, sitting on a news crew antenna trying to get the sticky silk off.

"She was a pixy! You see that? She was a pixy! That's Rachel Morgan! Get a picture!"

"Oh my God," a feminine voice exclaimed as the crowd reacted. "She's naked! Where did she come from? Are you getting this, Frank?"

Frank, the cameraman, was indeed getting this, and I looked for Pierce, almost panicking when I didn't see him. I was absolutely naked and in front of rolling video cameras. I didn't want to think about the Internet in two hours' time. God, my mother . . .

Trent stared, his one look down and up making me flush. "What the devil are you doing, Rachel?" he said as I snatched his speech from the podium and tried to cover myself.

"Rachel!" I heard, and my head swung around. It was Pierce, three I.S. cops elbowing and tossing people out of their way to get to him. "Catch!"

He threw the statue over six rows of people. It glittered in the sun even as the I.S. agents fell on him. Fear and surprise rang out when Pierce vanished from right under them and they landed on nothing. My hand went up, and with a solid thump, the erotic statue hit my palm. Everyone was looking at the I.S. cops on the ground, not me. Everyone but Trent. He'd seen the statue, and he shoved the pulling hands off him, his want showing, full and hungry.

I eyed Trent, flushed with embarrassment and premature victory. *Try to scare me into signing that lame-ass paper, huh?* "I'm trying to return your statue, dumb ass," I said to him over the noise. "Come talk to me in jail if you want it back." Then louder, I wailed, "I can't do this! I'm not a thief. I'm a good girl! I don't care if the coven gives me a lobotomy, I'm not a thief. Take your freaky statue back, Mr. Kalamack!"

I threw the elf porn at him like a girl, feeling a shiver go through me as it left my aura. He caught it, and someone grabbed me from behind. A coat fell over my shoulders, hitting just under my butt. "I made a mistake!" I shouted as I struggled to keep facing the assembled people. "I'm not a bad witch!"

Trent gripped the statue, frozen, wonder on his face.

"Get a shot of that," the newswoman said, then smacked Frank. "Not her, the statue!"

At my feet, Frank panned to the left, and my hands were wrenched behind me, making the coat flop open. "Hey!" I shouted, going down on my stomach. Flat on the stage, I was at the same level as the news crews. I tossed my hair out of my eyes and looked at Trent. He'd slipped the statue into his suit jacket's pocket, but Quen—wise-to-the-world Quen—was pulling it back out and tucking it in his own.

"Watch it!" I shouted, trying to breathe as there was the cool feel of a zip strip around both my wrists and the ever-after flowed out of me. I was yanked to my feet, stumbling. *Where in hell is Glenn?* "I'm a good witch!" I shouted over the uproar. "The coven made me do it! But I had to give it back to Trent. I'm a good witch. I am! I'm just scared! The coven is trying to kill me!"

It was going too fast. The coven wasn't here yet! Rough hands were tugging me to the steps, and I hooked my foot behind the man's ankle and sent him down. I fell on him, my elbow somehow managing to hit his solar plexus. His grip on me fell away, and I got to my feet, struggling with the next guy. Where in *hell* was Glenn?

"Get back!" his voice thundered, and I almost cried. "Get off the woman! Can't you see she doesn't have any weapons?"

"She hardly has any clothes," a man at the front of the crowd said, but I didn't care when Glenn's muscular, bald, big-black-man's presence shoved his way to me. One hidden punch, and the I.S. guy holding me went down, gently eased to the stage floor by Glenn.

"About time you showed," I said as he zipped my coat closed. "I think that guy felt me up."

"You okay?" his voice rumbled, and I searched his eyes.

"Just tell me you've got David's paperwork for an FIB arrest."

His grin was like sunshine, and I felt this just might work.

"Ms. Morgan! Ms. Morgan!" the newscaster was shouting, holding her mike up over her head. "You claim the coven told you to steal Mr. Kalamack's statue?"

I couldn't answer that without outright lying. "Take me in!" I begged as Glenn pushed our way to the steps, and I tripped, falling right in front of her. "Please," I begged to the camera, stalling, so Vivian could show up. "I'm a good witch! They made me do it! It was my only way out!" Which they did. Sort of. In a roundabout way.

"Corruption in the coven. I'm going to get an Emmy for this," the woman said, then turned to Trent as Glenn hoisted me out of her reach. "Mr. Kalamack! Sir! Is that your statue?"

Trent was behind three big guys, but he wasn't leaving. "I've no idea what is going on."

The FIB had taken the stage, and with his hand around my elbow, Glenn hesitated. "Sir, if that's not yours, we need it as evidence."

Trent's face went white. Slowly Quen brought the statue back into the sun, and cameras whirred and snapped as it changed hands. Trent's look at me was murderously calm. If this didn't work, I was going to be so-o-o-o dead.

"It's his," I babbled for the cameras. "I stole it out of his vault yesterday. The coven shunned me. I had no choice!" *Where in hell is Vivian?*

"Will someone read that woman her rights and get her to shut up?" Trent said, but the cameras were on me.

"The coven told you to steal it?" one of the reporters asked.

Glenn's grip on me tightened, and I followed his gaze to where the crowd was parting. Black suits and power ties. It was the coven, but it wasn't Vivian, it was Oliver!

"That woman is mine!" Oliver shouted even before he found the steps, his face red as he strode forward, amulets swinging and Möbius cuff links shining in the sun. "I claim jurisdiction. She is a black witch, shunned, and I won't have her spreading lies of corruption in the coven!"

I pressed back into Glenn, the air cold on my knees. It was about to get tricky.

"Sir!" the reporter was saying, her mike aimed at Oliver as he found the stairs. "Did you tell Morgan to steal the statue from Mr. Kalamack to get her shunning removed?"

The man stopped on the stairs, looking aghast. "Of course not!"

She looked at her ring, and I realized the thing was an amulet, glowing a steady green. It was a truth charm. Shit. I had to work fast. Good thing I hadn't lied.

"I tried to keep the demon from taking Brooke," I babbled. "Friday. At sunset. You heard the explosion. All of Cincinnati did! Oliver, you have to believe me. She summoned a demon. I told her not to, but she did. I tried to save her, and she told him to *kill* me!"

The newscaster's amulet stayed green, and the woman's eyes grew bright. Corruption in the coven indeed.

Trent pushed forward. "Get her out of here," he hissed to Oliver.

"I'm trying," Oliver said, his fingers encircling my arm.

"No!" I said, shrinking back, my fear real. "I want due process!" Anywhere other than an FIB cell, and I was dead or lobotomized. And Trent smiled, the bastard. *I hope you choke on it, elf boy.*

The newscaster held her mike higher, flushed. "Mr. Coven Leader, has a member of the coven been demon-napped in conjunction with Morgan's assassination attempt?"

Oliver hesitated. It was his downfall. Guilty or not, he looked it.

Smooth as silk, Trent stepped forward. "I'm sure the coven leader will give you a statement in due time." Turning his back to the crowd, he hissed, "Will you get her out of here?"

Oliver tugged on me, and I pressed into Glenn. "I didn't want to do it!" I shrieked. "I didn't want to break into Trent's vault. I don't care if I go to jail, but don't let the coven take me. They put me in Alcatraz with no trial. They sent fairies to burn my church. And they summoned a demon to kill me!"

And of course the newswoman's amulet stayed a nice, beautiful green. Eyes bright, she stood on tiptoe, her mike above her head. "Sir! Is there any connection between Ms. Morgan's claims of an attack and the 911 call to the Hollows at 1597 Oakstaff yesterday morning?"

Innocent as a lamb, the man stammered, "I wasn't aware of an explosion."

Her ring glowed red. Trent's head bowed and he started distancing himself. I felt a glimmer of hope. Oliver had lied, and the reporter knew it.

"Sir, is it coven policy to take contracts out on shunned witches?" she insisted as if sensing blood. "Did you tell Morgan to steal for you to escape such a punishment?"

"Uh . . ." He hesitated, then shouted, "I'm taking custody. She is a black-arts witch! Look, I have the paperwork."

Crap. I'd forgotten that the coven loved red tape as much as David. "Glenn," I said, my fear very real, "don't let them take me. Please!"

But he could do nothing as a wheezing, red-faced Oliver handed him a paper. Damn it, I was not going to die from paperwork. "Ah, Rachel . . . ," Glenn said, his face becoming concerned as he looked up from it. "We might have a problem here."

"Glenn," I breathed, knees going weak. "They'll kill me! Don't let them take me!"

Oliver made a satisfied huff. This was not happening. This was *not happening*!

As if in a dream, I heard Glenn promise he'd get me back, but it wouldn't matter. In five minutes, I'd be in a van, hopped up on drugs. An hour after that, I'd be on a surgery table.

Someone took my elbow and tugged me to the steps. "No!" I shouted, and the crowd responded. In a panic, I yanked out of Oliver's grip. Three more men grabbed me. I struggled, but sheer body mass overcame me, and I hit the floor, awkward with my hands bound behind me with that damned charmed silver. Tears started from the impact, and my breath huffed out when one of them landed on me.

"Rache!" Jenks shrilled, inches from my face and almost under someone's shoes. "Pierce says he's sorry! He can't allow the coven to take you!"

My heart sank. It was over. Pierce was going to do something. It was going to be powerful, wonderful, and completely cook my ass and label me black for sure. "I'm sorry, too," I whispered, hearing Glenn shouting about due process, stalling. "I really thought this would work." Oh God. I was going to have to spend the rest of my life in the ever-after. Damn it! Damn it back to the Turn.

Jenks flashed me a grin, shocking me. "No, you idiot. He's going to magic your zip strip off. He's sorry because it's going to burn."

He's going to what? I was yanked up, the flash of Jenks darting away was almost lost amid the shouting crowd and the reporters demanding statements. My shoulder hurt, and I spit the hair out of my mouth. I inhaled sharply as my wrists flashed into flame.

Over? I thought, gritting my teeth in a savage smile as the men flashed papers at each other and argued over who was to have me. *It wasn't over yet.*

Glenn was blocking the stairs, his compact bulk not backing down from a black-eyed living vamp insisting he get out of the way. I had the fleeting thought that his time with Ivy was serving him well. Behind my back, hidden by the overly long sleeves of my borrowed coat, my wrists burned where the metal touched me. Taking a breath, I pulled. And damn me back to the two worlds colliding if the charmed silver didn't give.

My heart leapt as the silver parted with a soft ping. The two I.S. officers at my shoulders were oblivious as the ever-after flooded in from the university ley line. My head snapped up, and I took a huge breath, palming the still-warm metal. Trent saw my expression, and somehow he knew. He touched Quen's arm, leaning to whisper in his ear. Quen's eyes flicked to mine, and I swear if he didn't smile, even as he started pulling Trent away, jumping to the pavers and almost yanking him down.

You'd better run, I thought dryly. Right to the FIB building to wait for me. Glenn had the statue, and I knew Trent would come for it. No one watched their retreat, the ring of reporters trying to get quotes from the much louder drama Oliver was making. All, that is, but the one reporter watching Quen drag Trent through the crowd, her eyebrows raised in speculation.

Over the noise and swirling motion, I found Pierce, standing alone and apart in the sun at the edge of the square, his feet spread wide and his hat pulled low to put his face in shadow. Looking at me from under its brim, he smiled, and it was as if everything else melted away.

"Thank you," I whispered, feeling my heart pound. He could have saved me with black magic. He could have blown in with spells flashing and outrage as his sword—but he didn't. He trusted me to save myself—the way I wanted to.

"That woman is a black witch!" Oliver shouted, red-faced as he waved his paper in front of me. "She is coming with me!"

I could have reached out and smacked him, but instead I clasped my hands behind my back, preserving the illusion that I was bound. My gaze went over the crowd, over the strung lines and amplifiers to the fountain, silent and still but still holding water. I needed a focusing object; my spit would be enough.

"Jenks!" I shouted, and the one reporter at the front met my eyes. "Go to ground!"

I flung out a hand, the ever-after in me a ripple of warmth down my arm and to my fingers. "*Consimilis calefacio!*" I shouted, willing the energy to flow. It was a charm to warm water, utterly innocuous and unable to work on living things with an aura. The fountain, though . . .

With the force of the university ley line behind the simple spell, the water in the fountain erupted in a thunderous boom of sound. All heads turned, but it wasn't just the noise that I wanted, and shouts rang out when the water turned to harmless steam. In an instant, the square was lost in fog.

Fear rose, and the officers moved to hold me. They didn't know I was free, though, and with a few well-placed knees and elbows, they went down. I didn't want to escape. I wanted my FIB cell. Smiling, I reached out for Oliver.

"You . . . h-how?" the older man stammered as I grabbed his shirt and yanked him to me.

"Look, Oliver," I said, just the two of us lost in the fog for a few seconds more. "Either you let me go and come see me at the FIB, or the next thing I vaporize will be your blood. Got it?"

His mouth opened and closed. "You *are* a demon!" he said, and I saw fear flicker. "That's a black curse!"

Crap, scaring him this much wasn't what I wanted. If he was scared, then he'd fight me. "I'm a demon only if you call me one," I said as I eased my hold. "If you call me a witch, then I'm a witch, and a witch doesn't know the curse to boil blood." I eyed him, letting his front go and rocking back. "Wouldn't me being a witch make everything a hundred times easier?"

His fear shifted to anger as the wind rose, scattering the mist. We were alone no more, and I rocked back.

The crowd was frightened, the people on the outskirts making a hasty retreat. Pierce, too, was no longer there when I looked. Here at the stage, however, no one had moved. There was a slight stir at the two downed officers, but I was standing passively, hands behind my back. The reporter knew, though, watching me with a knowing glint.

"Mr. Coven Leader!" she shouted, loud over the surrounding calls. "Is Ms. Morgan going with you, or to the FIB for due process as she clearly requested?"

The crowd hushed somewhat as Oliver clenched his jaw and tugged his clothes straight. He glanced at my arms, held behind my back, and I wondered which had scared him more, that I might know a curse to boil his blood, or that I got out of a pair of charmed handcuffs.

"It won't ever be said that the coven wrongfully denied an accused witch due process," he said sullenly. "I will accompany her to the FIB to be sure that she doesn't escape, but she may officially enter the FIB's custody."

Someone in the crowd actually cheered, and relief took the strength from my knees. I would have fallen if Glenn hadn't caught my arm, and, as the crowd became noisy, he escorted me down the stairs to a waiting FIB car, Oliver lagging behind. Everyday people wanting to know about the fog pressed close, and Glenn had to force his way through. I felt small beside him, and damn it if a tear didn't well up. I'd done it. No, *we'd* done it.

Head high, I placed each bare foot precisely, looking neither to the right or left as I crossed Fountain Square. I might be wearing nothing but an I.S. coat and six weeks' worth of hair on my legs, but this was my city, and I'd go to my cell with pride.

The clatter of pixy wings was almost unheard over the din and requests for answers from the press. "Way to go, Rache!" Jenks said as he joined us, flying a good two feet over my head. "Pierce says you did good. He's going to go watch my kids so I can come with you. He says you'll be okay now. You smoked them, Rache!"

"Good," I whispered. "That's good." The tear brimmed and fell, but there was only one, easily wiped away with my shoulder as Glenn opened my door and I got in, carefully so as to not let the coat ride up and show my ass. Jenks slipped in at the last moment, and the crowd became even louder as my door shut.

"Damn, Rachel," Glenn said as he got in the front and put on the lights. "When did you get your cuffs off? I didn't know you could do that."

"I can't," I whispered, not knowing what I felt anymore as I gazed through the tinted glass at the people crowding the car. I was shaky, watching them protest as I sat in peace. "Think they'll come talk to me?" This could still crash down and leave me with nothing.

Glenn chuckled, making his siren whoop twice before pulling out. "Oh yeah. They'll be there. Count on it."

Thirty-five

The scent of subgum rose from the softly steaming takeout box, filling the gray interrogation room at the FIB with the scent of steamed pea pods, sautéed mushrooms, and broccoli. My chopsticks were not the usual splintery pulpwood, but a nice set of olive wood. Apparently Glenn was a regular at whatever Asian eatery he'd placed the order. More than a regular, I'd imagine. The sticks were beautiful.

I wrangled a water chestnut into my mouth, jamming the sticks to stand straight up as I reached for the fortune cookie. I was never one to wait. The snap of the cookie breaking was familiar, and I smiled as I read, KEEP YOUR FRIENDS CLOSE, YOUR ENEMIES CLOSER.

Eating the entire cookie at one go, I pushed back from the scarred table, crossed my ankles, and gazed at the dirty ceiling as I chewed. I was dressed now in a pair of jeans and a short-sleeved top, patterned too brightly for my liking. Flip-flops kept my toes from the tile, and I was sporting brand-new blah underwear from the lockup downstairs. None of what I was wearing was mine, but it was clean and better than an orange jumpsuit. I didn't ask what had happened to the people who used to own these clothes. Someone had *my* red leather jacket.

I reached for the box of takeout and I rubbed my last demon mark, sore where Pierce's charm had burned me. My eyes drifted to Trent's statue, and I reached for it. Cripes, the thing was graphic. No wonder he hid it underground.

The knock at the door startled me, and I dropped it. Scrambling, I stood it upright. It was Jenks and Glenn, and I wiped my hands on my borrowed jeans as I saw the stack of paperwork in the FIB officer's hand. "Hi, Rache," the pixy said, doing a quick circuit and landing on the tips of my chopsticks, poking out of the takeout box, to enjoy the rising heat. "Trent's here. And the coven guy. Glenn's got your papers to sign first, though."

"Thanks, Jenks. Are you sure your wings are okay?"

Making a face, he sent them humming so fast that the dust from him rose high in a pixy-made draft. "Yeah, they're fine. Bastard I.S."

Glenn was smiling when he slapped the papers down on the table. "David is *still* stuck on the tarmac," he said as he handed me a pen, "but he had his brother fax everything here."

Nodding in understanding, I flipped to the first flag and signed with my first name, middle initial, and last name. "This is for the trial, yes?" I asked as I found the next flag.

"According to David," Glenn affirmed as I finished. "I won't file it unless you say so or go missing for more than three days." He glanced at Jenks, then me. "Rachel," he said, seeming to lose some of his professional polish, "I'm required by law to inform you that your proposed actions are both risky and prone to landing you in prison, permanently incarcerated if not worse—"

"It's all she's got, Glenn," Jenks said, rising up on a silver column of dust.

Hand raised, Glenn smiled. "Personally, I think it will work," he finished, and the pixy relaxed. "I don't know Oliver well enough to give an accurate estimation of what he might do, but if what you say is true, I think he'll go for it."

"He'll go for it," I said, worried. "Can I keep the paperwork here? Visual aids help."

Glenn nodded. "You signed two originals," he said as he took half the stack and tucked it under his arm. "If you're ready, I'll send them in." His gaze dropped to my dinner as I picked it up. "Good?" he asked.

"Delicious," I said, reaching for it. "Thanks, Glenn. For everything."

The man smiled wickedly. "Any time, Rachel. Have fun."

He left the door open, and I could hear Trent's beautiful voice in the hall. He was talking with Jonathan, and Jenks's wings clattered as my blood pressure rose. I hated the man. "Jenks," I said on impulse as I dug into my dinner. "You go, too."

"What?" Peeved, Jenks confronted me. "Why can't I stay?"

"If you're in here, Trent might want a witness, too. I don't want Jonathan with him."

The pixy turned in midair, hands on his hips. "I could do a little dusting," he said, and my lips curved up in a smile. Jonathan wouldn't know what hit him.

"You do that," I said, then drew back as Trent pushed the door open. Oliver was behind him, all bluster and huff. The two men gave Jenks a cautious look as the pixy laughed, darting out over their heads singing "London Bridge Is Falling Down."

Watching me, Trent shut the door with the tip of his shoe, and the silence of a sort-of-soundproof room soaked into me. "Please, sit down," I said to the two men, gesturing with my chopsticks. "I'm glad you agreed to see me. Do you want anything? Coffee? Subgum?"

Sitting on the green, thinly padded metal chair, Trent clasped his hands and rested them on his crossed knees. His face lacked all emotion, waiting. "No thank you." His eyes shifted from the paperwork to the statue, and I smiled. *Thanks, Nick, even if you are a bastard.* God! I couldn't believe he went behind my back to work a deal with Trent. On second thought, I could. And what was it with Trent not telling me he thought I might be able to do that elf trick of shifting realities using ley lines?

Oliver stood, his arms crossed. "You are a black witch," he started, his words harsh.

Going back to my subgum, I said mildly, "And the coven of moral and ethical standards is corrupt, having a demon-summoning black-arts practitioner among their number. You sure you don't want a coffee?"

"We do not!" the man exclaimed.

"Wrong!" Taking a breath, I jammed the sticks in the takeout box, thinking they looked too aggressive pointing at him like that. "Brooke tried to make a deal with me to put one of my demon children in her cradle and me off the lobotomy table intact and in her private army."

Oliver's round face looked horrified.

Trent unclasped his hands and tugged his sleeves. "Can we skip this part? I have an appointment in half an hour with the press."

His hand fumbling for the back of a chair, Oliver sat. I didn't think he'd known that. Good. Maybe he would listen to me. "Sure," I said slowly, answering Trent's question. "We can come back to it if we need to. Let me tell you what I want." *I'm going to make a deal with two men who tried to kill me. Was I stupid or really smart? Sidereal didn't have a problem with it.*

Oliver scoffed. "You're in jail. You're in no position to be asking anything."

Trent hid a smile, and I picked through my dinner to find a water chestnut. "I'm in jail because I choose to be. You don't think that performance in Fountain Square was anything other than to get the media's attention and you in front of me, do you? It's safe here, and the food's better than at Alcatraz." I looked up, allowing a sliver of my irritation to show. "Ever try it, Ollie? It's got this really tasty spice in the saturated fats."

Oliver frowned, and Trent interrupted with a brusque "Listen to the woman, or this will take all day. She'll make it quick, and then you can spout off all you want."

Expression cross, the witch leaned back in his chair, and I eyed Trent, thoughts of his Pandora charm and the deal with Nick making me tense. His words about me being honorable had been a surprise, and I'd swear he hadn't known about the bug before then. But lying was one of his skill sets. Bringing my conflicted gaze from Trent, I pointed my chopsticks at Oliver. "I want my shunning removed and the threats to my person stopped."

He huffed, tugging his sleeves, making his cuff links twinkle. "That action requires a full quorum, which we won't have until the next public meeting and we reestablish our number."

Public meeting . . . the witches' conference? Nice stall. "Give me some-thing," I said, "or my next conversation will be with the press and it will come out that not only does a schism exist in the coven, but that some of you are corrupt and summon demons."

"We're not corrupt!" Oliver exclaimed, making Trent wince. "No one will believe you!"

My eyebrows rose. "Talk to Brooke lately?"

Oliver's bluster evaporated. Honestly, they needed to pick these people more carefully. He might be a crackerjack witch, but he was telegraphing his entire thought process, and my estimation of the coven dropped more.

"I didn't know what she was doing," Oliver said slowly. "And Vivian, as a minor coven member, had her hands somewhat tied. Brooke has been officially shunned, stripped of rank."

I dug into my subgum, saying, "Good thing she's in the ever-after, or you'd brick her in the ground alive, huh? Who'd ever think being a de-mon's lackey would be a good thing?"

Looking up, I caught Oliver's shocked look. "We will deny every-thing," he said, and Trent sighed loudly. "The words of a shunned witch are unheard!"

"How about the words of a coven member?" I asked. "I have a re-corded conversation of Vivian telling me you *did* know of the attacks, that you were reassessing my case, and that action might be taken against my family if I didn't submit to chemically neutering my ability to have chil-dren and work magic. It's on my phone, Ollie. I think she's pissed you called her a liar."

The man looked aghast, and Trent cleared his throat, clearly uncom-fortable with the man's ineptness. I was kind of embarrassed, too, and I picked past the broccoli to find a squash slice. *This was what our yearly dues bought?*

"This is how it works," I said, trying not to sound irate. "I give you something, you give me something. We all go home happy." Seeing him silent, I added, "This is what is *going* to happen. If you don't rescind my shunning and agree to stop trying to kill me, I'm going to demand a fair trial of my peers, thanks to this pile of paperwork here. And the press running with the idea that the coven is corrupt means I'll get it. TV coverage, radio, everything."

Oliver was eying my papers, and I rested my hand on them protectively. "Even if you do manage to refute my claim that the coven is corrupt, the truth will come out that our history is based on ancient elf propaganda and our beginnings are rooted as stunted demons, the result of an elf curse. Ought to do wonders for our public image, both witches and elves." I glanced at Trent. "Not that anyone thinks *they're* still around, but hey, there it is. I'll probably end up in jail, but any time I want, I just talk to my demon teacher, and I'm out of there, leaving you to deal with the fallout."

"You wouldn't!" Oliver said, appalled. "It would mean genocide!"

"She would," Trent muttered, clearly not pleased I'd brought the elves into it.

"I will," I said, putting my dinner aside. "Thanks to you gentlemen, I've got nothing to lose. You put me in this place, and I'm going for broke. If I'm going to be persecuted solely on the basis of being a stepping-stone between witches and demons, then I'm taking you down with me." I glanced at Trent. His public persona was cracking, and he looked pissed. "And if you don't go along with it, Mr. Kalamack, I'll tell them how I got that way."

His focus on me sharpened. "My father saved your life," he said bitterly.

"Which doesn't give you the right to run it." Tired, I fingered the fortune cookie's advice. I didn't want to bring this up in front of Oliver, but why not? "Trent, I'd appreciate it if you would drop your attempts at trying to make me your property, okay? If you've got a problem you want help with, come talk to me. If you give me five minutes' notice, I'll even make sure the pixies are in the garden."

Trent uncrossed his legs, the rasping silk loud in the hush. "I didn't tell the coven, but I'll be damned if I don't capitalize on it. I am *not* anyone's familiar."

"Trent . . . ," I almost whined. "I'm not going to make good on that. Will you let it go?"

Brow furrowed, he leaned forward, flicking a glance at Oliver. "Listen this time. You *claimed* me. I don't care if you never enforce it. There is a mark on my shoulder. It matches yours. Get it annulled."

My hand crept up and touched it, hidden under someone else's shirt. Slowly my face became empty of emotion. He was right. The truth of the matter was, I'd been enjoying the little bit of power I had over him—like Al had over me. "You're right," I said, hating to admit it. "But I've been mad at you for a long time." I put my hand on the table and met his gaze. His green eyes were intent, fixed on me with frustration, irritation . . . but nowhere did I see the hatred in him that I had when he hammered my head into a tombstone and tried to choke the life out of me. Maybe it was time to stop taking enjoyment from making him angry and . . . grow up.

"Trent, I need to know," I said, gaze fixed on his. "The Pandora charm you gave me was modified to not break cleanly, and I almost suffocated. Is that what you intended?"

Trent frowned, and his gaze flicked to the hallway, where Jonathan waited. "No," he said, looking exceptionally pissed. "I apologize, and I'm taking care of it."

Feeling oddly satisfied, I leaned back in my chair. *Jonathan. Son of a bitch.* "Thanks," I said, believing him. I'd find out about the ley-line door later when Oliver wasn't around. I took a breath, gaze flicking to Oliver and back. "I'll ask Al how to break a familiar bond. If there's a way without hurting either of us, I'll do it. But you need to stop trying to make me your slave in all but name, okay? And maybe stop telling people I can invoke demon magic? Can you do that? Give me my life back?"

Head shaking, Trent leaned forward. "I never told anyone, Rachel. It wasn't me."

Oliver snickered. "It was Nick Sparagmos, children."

My heart seemed to stop. I stared at Trent, reading his own surprise and anger. I couldn't remember how to breathe, and I forced my lungs to work. Nick? Nick had told them?

My thoughts jerked back to the circle in his apartment and the two strikes on the demon mark on his shoulder. Undoubtedly that was how he found out. God! Nick must have thought I was a fool when I asked for his help to steal from Trent. And Trent had looked even more stupid, trying to do an end run with Nick to catch me. Nick had played both of us off against each other, not once, but twice.

"You're both idiots," Oliver said, as if delighting in the fact that we were so dumb. "Two people so intent on getting the best of each other that you can be manipulated into anything."

Damn it, he was right. My eyes closed in a long blink, and I loosened my clenched jaw, trying hard not to show my growing anger. Maybe I'll have to make another excursion into Trent's compound tonight and find Nick.

"Nick is gone," Trent said, voice hard as he answered my unspoken thought. "He slipped my guards yesterday before I . . . went for my evening ride."

Before he rode for me, I thought, shivering as the anger Trent felt for Nick landed on me.

"I never—I didn't know," Trent almost whispered, clearly upset as his fingers twitched. Stilling his hands, he flicked his gaze to the statue at my elbow. "I'll give you until the witch conference to resolve the issue of the mark between us," he said suddenly. "If my mark isn't gone by then, this starts up again."

I swallowed my own anger at Nick for later. "Fair enough," I said, feeling stupid and mad at myself.

Trent's gaze dropped to the table. "Can I have my statue?"

My breath came in fast. "Oh! Yes," I said, having forgotten about it. Using two fingers, I pushed it across the table. Trent took it, shoving it into a pocket, the tips of his ears reddening.

Settling back, I laced my hands and set them atop the table and looked at Oliver, my anger at Nick still making my features tight and pissed. The coven leader was smug, and it irritated me. "I don't have a statue for you, but I've got a pocketful of silence," I said. "How about it? I drop my claim of corruption in the coven, and you drop me completely. Shunning. Death threats. Everything." *God, if I ever get Nick alone, I swear I'm going to give him to Al before whatever demon he's been summoning takes him.*

Oliver snickered, thinking that my being stupid gave him the advantage. "Don't think so. You're a black witch." Chin high, he crossed his arms over his chest. "I'd rather kill you."

I couldn't stop my sigh. Trent shifted, clearly wanting to end this so he could start looking for Nick, maybe.

"Oliver," Trent said, and my eyebrows rose in surprise. "What do you hope to gain here? It's not good business anymore."

He turned to Trent, indignation thick on him. "Good business?" he blustered. "I'm trying to keep the world from knowing witches come from demons, and you're worried about your *career* being ruined by a pornographic statue. Why do you even have that?"

"It's an object of ancient art, and it was in my vault, not my bedroom," Trent said dryly. "If you're so concerned about your secret, perhaps you should give Ms. Morgan what she wants? Being in favor with someone who can go into the ever-after with impunity might be good."

Do tell? I thought in amazement, using one of Pierce's favorites. Maybe he's more ticked at Nick than I thought.

"Blackmail!" Oliver stated, pushing back from the table and standing up.

Trent was searching his pockets. "Business. Morgan has a commodity. Silence." Finding a pen, he looked up. "You're going to have to buy it from her or kill her. Take it from someone who's tried, even if she is dead, the truth will come out and she'll bring you down from the grave."

He's helping me convince Oliver? Are frogs coming from the sun in spaceships, too?

Unable to sit still any longer, I said, "I'm not a bad person, Ollie. I have a cat and a fish, and I don't kick stray dogs." *I do burn the wings from fairies, but damn it, they attacked me first.* "I don't want the world to know that I'm a stepping-stone to demons or that our beliefs are based on ancient elf propaganda. But I don't want to live in Alcatraz or the ever-after either. I just want to make a living doing what I do best."

The coven leader turned from the curtained one-way mirror, shaking his head. "Destroying society? I've seen what you've done to the Weres and the elves."

Trent, who was clearly looking for something to write on, silently gestured at the little slip from the fortune cookie, and I pushed it to him. "I prefer calling it restructuring," I said. "I don't hear them complaining, but what I meant was, I want to operate my runner business and rescue familiars out of trees. It's you guys coming at me that makes me do all this weird stuff that gets you in a tizzy."

Clicking his pen closed, Trent tucked it away. "Oliver, she's a little backward in her methods, but her heart is in the right place. You saw what she did at the square. She could have killed you, but she didn't. Let this go. I'll watch her until she gains some finesse."

I turned to Trent. "Excuse me?"

Once more the suave, confident city son, Trent smiled. "If you want to play with the big boys, you'll need a chaperone. I could've spared you a bloody nose on the playground at least."

He was talking metaphorically, but I still didn't like it. "No," I said, looking at the folded strip of paper in his hand, then back at him. "You're not my frigging mentor. I've already got a demon for a teacher in the everafter. I don't need another one here. I just want to be left alone."

A strangled cough came from Oliver, and I turned. "You got a problem?" I snapped.

His head was going back and forth as he stood before us. "A demon teacher," he said softly. "It's just . . . you're so casual about it."

"Casual keeps me sane. If I think about it too hard, I'll go nuts." I set my palm on the table, fingers spread. "Are we doing this, or does Jenks come in here and things get ugly?"

Oliver's expression was unsure. He eyed Trent, who made a "we're waiting" gesture. The witch shifted his feet, and I held my breath as he reluctantly sat back down. "How?" he stated, not looking up from his hands resting on the table. "You've already implicated us, saying that we're corrupt. The press isn't going to forget that."

My heart pounded and my stomach seemed to unknot. It was all I could do to not jump up and scream, "Yes!" I had them. At least I think I had them. "Got it covered," I said.

From across the table, Trent exhaled, tired. "Why am I not surprised?"

I glanced at him, then turned my good mood on Oliver. "We're going to tell the press that this was a double-blind test of Trent's security system."

Trent cleared his throat, and my attention shifted to him. "Knowing witches were the biggest security threat, you went to the coven and asked them to send a witch to try to break into your vault and steal a fake statue. If your witch failed, he'd know he was secure, but if your witch succeeded, Trent would give the coven . . . a million dollars."

The last bit was a sudden inspiration on my part as I tried to find a way to get Oliver interested. As expected, the man's eyebrows rose, whereas Trent just frowned at Oliver's greed. A million dollars was nothing to Trent.

"You, being smart," I said to Oliver, fluffing his ego, "knew that black witches were the bigger threat. Going all out, you decided to drum up a false charge and get me shunned in order to encourage me to use the strongest means available to see if I could break in. Black magic. And now that I've proved I can, you can rescind the shunning."

Both men were silent. A pang of worry lifted through me. Maybe I'd misjudged Oliver's greed. "Uh, maybe the reward was two million," I added, and Trent blinked.

Beside him, Oliver said, "You want us to lie for you."

I had a brief memory of asking Minias the same thing, and I shoved it away. "Yeah," I said with forced casualness. "But it's not hurting anyone's reputation, property, or business. It's a big, freaking white lie, the same one we've been telling ourselves for the last five thousand years. Is that okay with you, or do you tell your wife she looks fat in her favorite dress, too?"

The man made a soft noise of negation, but Trent's nod was even more positive. "What about Brooke?" Oliver asked, and my mood was tarnished.

Eyes down, I said, "I can't get her back. She was sold three seconds after hitting the ever-after. I'm sorry. I really did try, but she did summon him."

"I can't do this!" Oliver said, unable to let it go, and Trent seemed to collapse in on himself in exasperation. "I can't allow it! Reverse her shunning? Let her run around capable of twisting curses and setting demons loose on the world? It's insane!"

"Oliver!" I shouted, seeing Jenks's wings silhouetted against the thick glass in the door. He was hearing all of this, I was sure. "I'm not a black witch. I just twist curses instead of stirring spells. There are a hundred mundane ways to kill a person, and you *don't* put people in jail just because they *could* do a crime." He was listening, and I gestured, pleading, "You're going to have to trust me. But if you think I'm bad now, just keep this crap up. I don't have to stay here. If you make me leave, you can bet I'll be back, and I'll still be pissed."

Oliver leaned over the table, not cowed at all. "We can find you anywhere."

"Yeah, but you can't *follow* me everywhere," I said, and a flicker of doubt crossed his mind.

"Find a way to work the deal, Oliver," Trent said. "You're letting pride get in your way. She keeps her word. I doubt that Ms. Morgan will have children anyway. If she does, they will be kidnapped by demons. Not your problem anymore."

It was sad but true. Watching Oliver, I held my breath and scooted to the back of my chair, waiting as thoughts flitted across his face. I thought he was almost going to say yes, but what came out of his mouth was a flat "I can't."

Trent sighed, and Oliver turned to him. "I can't!" he said louder. "I am one of six, and I'm not going to sit here and tell you I can grant you a pardon when I can't. You're going to have to stand before the coven and beg for leniency."

"What?" I yelped, sitting up fast.

"On your knees," he said, finding his courage as mine evaporated. "Even if I go out and give the press that cock-and-bull story, the coven will know the truth, and the fact remains that you performed black magic and you consort with demons."

"That's not fair!" I said, infuriated.

"If you want your shunning removed, that's what you're going to have to do. You don't think we can simply let you admit you did black magic, then let you walk because we say it was a test? No. You're going to have to beg for our pardon."

I inhaled deeply to let him have it, then hesitated. Slowly my breath slipped out. "Fine," I said sullenly. "I'll come to the next witches' meeting, but I'm not going to get on my knees. I'll say I'm sorry, and you can wave your wand and say I'm really a good witch. Shunning rescinded. Okay? But until then, you back off or these papers get filed."

Oliver smiled in a not-nice way, and I wondered if they would kill me between now and then. "Double-blind study?" he said and I quivered. "Will they really go for that?"

The air shook in my lungs. "Oh, yeah. The news loves making me look like a fool."

I jerked as Trent stood up, his chair loud against the tile. His hand was out, extended to me. Slowly I stood and took it. His hand was cool, fitting nicely in mine with the perfect amount of pressure. "Congratulations, Ms. Morgan," he said, his voice rising and falling like water, not a hint of anything but honest pleasure. "Come and see me before the annual meeting. I'd like to talk to you when you have a moment."

There was a strip of paper in my hand when he pulled away, and I palmed it. "I'd like that, Mr. Kalamack." Maybe he had some idea of where Nick had gone.

Oliver had stood as well, but his hands were behind his back. "You're really going to go out there and say it was all a test of your security system?"

"That's exactly what I'm going to do, Oliver. And if you were smart, you'd back off and give her everything she wants." Smiling cockily, Trent inclined his head to me. "Good evening, Ms. Morgan."

My lips curved up, but inside I was shaking. *I'd done it.* Holy crap on toast. I wish they'd hurry up and leave. I was going to pass out. Trent opened the door, and the sounds of the FIB spilled in to replace him.

"See you around, Trent," I whispered, falling back in my chair. My attention dropped to the little slip of paper. "See you tonight . . . ," I murmured, reading, TONIGHT. STABLES. WEAR YOUR BOOTS.

Jenks buzzed in, and I crumpled it.

Thirty-six

The slamming of my mom's car door was loud, echoing in the moist, sunset-gloomed air from the distant forest. My gaze lifted across the pastures, and I pulled my jacket tighter around my shoulders. The dogs on the hill were silent, and I shivered when I realized they weren't in their kennel.

Okay, I didn't have a valid driver's license anymore, but no one had stopped me, and I wasn't about to ask Ivy to drive me out here to Trent's stables. It had been hard enough slipping out of the church without Jenks knowing. Trent's note hadn't said to come alone, but the fact that he'd written it down, not said it where Jenks could hear, was telling.

Arms swinging, I walked silently across the sawdust parking lot to the stables. Ivy would say I was a fool for coming out here. Jenks would have a fit. Pierce . . . I smiled as I fingered the contraception amulet around my neck in case shifting twice in quick succession hadn't prevented pregnancy. Pierce would have wanted to come with me, and he had a grudge against the man. I was trying to see Trent as an adult, and for some reason, it was easier now that I remembered him as a kid.

Hoping I wasn't being more of an idiot than Ivy would say I was, I pushed open the stable's door. The scent of clean hay and oiled leather spilled out, and my shoulders relaxed. I couldn't help but wonder what Trent wanted. Band together to get Nick, maybe?

"Hello?" I called, seeing the stables dim but for the usual security lights.

"Back here," Trent's voice rose softly, and my gaze shifted to midway down the long stables where a lanternlike flashlight hung in the aisle.

We're alone? I could tell just from his voice that we were. Unsure, I stepped inside and shut the door. The air in here was warm, a sharp contrast to the cool, damp air rising into fog in the pastures. My boots clunked as I walked past the empty stalls, and I felt a flush of embarrassment when I found Trent in with Tulpa over the trapdoor to his tunnel. He was brushing the horse down, and Tulpa shuffled forward, hanging his head over the side and shoving me. "Hey, big guy," I said, rubbing his neck in self-defense, almost.

Trent straightened, watching me. His eyes were dark in the dim light, and he looked really, really good in his English riding outfit, the trousers tucked in his boots and a cap on his fair hair. "He likes you," he said, watching Tulpa nose me.

"He always has." Smiling, I stepped out of the horse's reach.

Trent took the horse's bridle, and seeing him angle to the gate, I opened it up. "Got your boots on, I see," he said cryptically, and I looked at them, seeing their newness.

"That's what you said." Why was I out here? Did he want to go for a ride? Take me out to the woods and shoot me? *Oh God. Where are the dogs?*

Trent tied Tulpa to a post beside a rack of saddles. "You probably don't know how to ride English, do you?" he asked, and when I didn't answer, he turned to find me in the middle of the aisle, my face cold.

"We've got western," he said, and I backed up a step.

"I'm not going riding with you," I said, unwrapping my arms so I could move.

"Why?" he asked lightly. "I know you're not afraid of horses."

"I'm not going riding with you!" I shouted, and Tulpa tossed his head. "Your dogs are out of their kennel!" Oh God. I had to get out of here.

I spun, striding away.

"Rachel."

"Nice try, Trent," I said, feeling for my keys.

"Rachel."

He touched me, and I turned, finding him three feet back, his hands raised in placation. Damn, he was fast. "I'm not going to let you get me on a horse so you can lure me into the woods and hunt me like an animal!" I shouted, not caring if I sounded scared. I was.

"No," he said, voice calm. "That's not what this is about."

Shaking, I forced my arms from around myself. "What is it then?"

Trent sighed, shifting his weight to one foot. "It's the new moon," he said. "You're late. Ceri and Quen are already out there. I was waiting for you."

I tossed my hair, my stomach clenching. "For what?"

"To ride, of course."

I exhaled, shaking. "What makes you think I want to ride down a fox and watch dogs tear it apart? I've been on the other end of this game, Trent, and it's—"

"It's not a fox," Trent said grimly, crossing the aisle and getting out a second, brown horse with a beautiful black mane and tail. "I thought you might want to take part. Seeing as, well . . ." He hesitated, the horse snuffling behind him. "I will not be crossed, Rachel. I want to count you as . . . well, not a friend, exactly. Maybe a business associate. And a hunt is one way to cement ties."

"What are you hunting?" I asked, scared for an entirely different reason. "Trent? Answer me."

Trent led the brown horse past me, her hooves clopping on the old wood. "It's not a what, it's a who."

Oh. My. God. "Nick?" I said, eyes wide.

Jerking, Trent seemed to reassess his thoughts. "No. He vanished right out of a very secure cell. Jumped a line is our best guess." He looked at me questioningly. "I take it you didn't pull him out?"

I shook my head, arms around myself as I thought that through. "How long have you known I can shift realities with a ley line?" I asked.

Trent grimaced, appearing embarrassed. "I've been trying to get into my father's vault since he died, Rachel," he said, the rims of his ears going red. "I didn't even know I could do it until Nick suggested you could."

Oh, that was damn peachy keen, and I couldn't help but wonder who Nick had been taking to. Minias? Newt? Both of them knew my history. Dali? God, I hoped not.

My head turned and a shudder passed through me as I heard a distant horn. Heart pounding, I paced to where Trent was calmly saddling the brown mare with a western saddle. "Who is out there?" I asked, and when his jaw clenched, I breathed, "Jonathan."

The man gave me a sideways look, fingers never stilling as he cinched the girth. Still not answering me, Trent handed me the reins, then untied his horse and led it to the second, much larger door that opened up onto the paddock. I stood there, thinking. "Tell me that's not Jonathan," I called after him.

"I'm telling you it's not Jonathan!" he shouted back, then stopped in the doorway. "If you don't want to ride the Hunt, we can go over the pastures, but it's a new moon, and I'm getting on a horse."

I remembered his anger in the FIB interrogation room when he told me Jonathan had used Trent's work to try to kill me. I didn't believe him. Slowly I tightened my grip. My feet moved, and the horse—I didn't even know her name—followed me with eager steps. But when I reached the opening, I paused.

Trent sat bareback atop Tulpa, looking like he belonged there. The sun had gone down behind him, making the still-bright sky pink and blue. Fog was rising from the damp hills, and I breathed it in, feeling the cool all the way to the bottom of my lungs. According to my dad, to ride with elves meant abandoning your life, to possibly become lost forever. The faint baying of the hounds pricked the horses' ears, and Tulpa stomped impatiently. A shiver went through me.

"Why are you doing this?" I asked, scared.

Trent pulled Tulpa back, the move easy and full of grace. He was different on horseback, wild, dangerous. I thought of his demon mark tied to me, just under his shirt. A thread of anticipation pulled through me. I wanted to ride.

"Some of it was Lee," he said. "He told me what happened, what you did, how you handled yourself afterward. Some of it was that damned hoof pick, believe it or not."

I couldn't help the smile quirking the corners of my mouth.

"But most of it," Trent added, "is because of my father."

My smile faded as I remembered the Pandora charm.

"My father was friends with your father," he said, head bowing for an instant. "He trusted him with his life. They fought to find a way to bring the war between the elves and the demons to an end. I think that's why my father chose you to live. Fixed you."

I took a step forward. "And."

"And you did that. Or at least gave us the way to make ourselves whole again. It's just like my father, the bastard, to use the same tool that saved us to save the demons."

"You think I like having been your dad's science fair project?" I said, and the horse beside me nickered at my anger.

"No," Trent said. "But you can't simply pretend that you're like everyone else."

I wasn't liking this at all. "So we're good?"

He laughed, his face growing darker, harder to read as the night took over. "No. If my familiar mark isn't gone by the end of the witches' meeting, I will kill you to nullify it. I hope it doesn't come to that."

Yada yada yada. But I couldn't read him while he was on Tulpa, and it made me nervous. "You still haven't answered me about why you asked me to ride with you."

Tulpa pranced, impatient, and Trent soothed him, whispering in a language I couldn't understand. "My father saw you as a way to save both elves and demons," he said when the horse was still again. "Why don't you want to run Jonathan into the ground, ride after him with hounds at his heels, see his terror, know that he fully understands the folly of betraying those who trusted him?"

I shifted the reins in my fingers as the horse dropped her head, snuffling for something to eat. "Pity, I suppose. Having been on the other side . . . I can't do that to anyone, even Jonathan." *Nick, maybe.*

Trent was nodding. "Get on the horse. The Hunt awaits."

Looking up the tall expanse, I shook my head. "Why?"

He sighed. "You want to live in your church, going about your life as if you're like everyone else."

"So?"

"You aren't. And because of that, someday you're probably going to find yourself in a position where your choices will have an impact far beyond what you see right now. And when that happens, I want you to remember what it's like to ride through the woods on horseback under a night sky with no moon and *nothing* stronger than you are. I want you to know so you will fight for it. So that my children will know of it. You have to keep the demons where they are, Rachel. No one else can do it. You won't fight for us unless you know. Let me show you what you're fighting for."

He was entirely dark now, a shadow on a moving wisp of wind, eager to be away.

My heart was heavy. I didn't want to believe him. I wanted to be like everyone else. I'd worked *hard* to be like everyone else. I'd gotten the coven to rescind my shunning, even if it was only temporary until the official meeting in June. My name was cleared. I'd failed Brooke, but I'd found Pierce and the chance for what might pass as a normal relationship for me. I even had the joy of knowing that Jenks was going to survive. I had my life back. But someday it was all going to end and I wouldn't be able to rebuild my walls of pretend. I should play while I could. And tonight . . . I felt good.

Taking a deep breath, I gathered myself and swung up into the saddle. The horse under me shifted until I pulled the reins in, demanding obedience. I started this morning crawling out of a hole in the ground, and now I was riding with elves.

"Race you to that tree over there," I said, and with a wild yell, I thumped my heels into my horse . . . and we were gone.